COLIN OAKES

CADISTON –
A NEW BEGINNING

novum 🔳 pro

This book is also
available as
e-book.

www.novum-publishing.co.uk

© 2023 novum publishing

ISBN 978-3-99107-680-3
Editing: Nicola Grün
Cover photo:
Andreiuc88 | Dreamstime.com
Cover design, layout & typesetting:
novum publishing

www.novum-publishing.co.uk

Climate neutral
Print product
ClimatePartner.com/16547-2201-1002

Contents

Preface

The Mandaten family are making the final arrangements for their big annual event which is to take place at the weekend. They have all been summoned to the Manor to discuss certain aspects of the continuance of the Mandaten family dynasty. One and a half hours after the last member of the family had driven through the gates, they were all sitting in silence around the dinner table.

Mandaten Manor had been the family seat since the Norman conquest back in 1066 when the Baron Louis François Mandaten arrived in England with William. Generations later, the head of the family, Lord Lionel Mandaten, is seriously ill and has been told that he has just a few months of life remaining and, knowing this, the time is short to announce his successor. There are fourteen family members present at the table and there is an uneasy air as they eye each other with suspicion, knowing that the time will soon be here to lay their father to rest. Though ill, he still sits at the head of the table with his wife, Florence, sitting at the other end facing him. At the table sit the two daughtwers and three sons with their respective wives and husbands. The Mandatens have two girls and one set of boy twins and a younger brother.There is also the adopted son who they have a disliking for and his wife.The four grandchildren are due to arrive on Thursday 25th.

The household comprises three housemaids; two footmen, and a very old butler, Mister Bradinham. In the kitchen are two cooks, accompanied by three helpers, all overseen by the housekeeper who is the butler's wife. The stables and livestock are controlled by the Livestock manager, whose wife, is the head cook, he is assisted by their sons. Running the farm and living in the Manor farmhouse is the arable farm manager. His wife is the second of the cooks, he is assisted by their three sons. They have one daughter, who also works in the kitchen. These families have all worked faithfully through the generations for the Mandatens and at eighty-five, the old butler has been the longest-serving current employee and has been with them for sixty-four of his eighty-five years. Alongside him, and always close at hand, is his faithful wife. The rest of the staff range from five to thirty years respectively.

The three sons eagerly await to hear who will become the next Lord Mandaten, all of which have a plan to achieve this and ensure it is they who will inherit the Manor, its land, and the amassed fortune, with evil eyes they watch each other all were wondering who would be the one to be crowned the next Lord Mandaten and after that to inherit everything, it would take time and patience was not one of their strongpoints.

Chapter One

The Family Dinner

The gates to Mandaten Manor stood wide open, waiting for the arrival of the family who had been summoned to arrive early by their father, Lord Louie Mandaten. The livestock managers son, Jeremiah, had reluctantly left the stables and waited patiently at the gates for the family members to arrive before he could close and secure them.

The first car to arrive was that of the twins: Malcolm, accompanied by his wife, Greta, and his brother Grant, accompanied by his wife, Bonnie. There was no mistaking the friction between them as Jerimiah could hear the arguing even as the car sped past him. "No change there then, always arguing and getting at each other it is no wonder that they do not kill each other, they have everything where there are so many people that have so little and they are never satisfied. The best one is their adopted brother, Chadrick. He is so different from the other three, now there is a real gent." Whispered Jeremiah. Thirty minutes behind them, in separate vehicles, came the two daughters: Lizabeth with her husband Tomas in their Rolls Royce, followed by Sammie with her husband Walter in their Jaguar. It was all they could do to greet Jeremiah with a wave.

"And hello to you as well, (Jeremiah mouthed and almost put his fingers up but thought better of it, they were now well past and well out of earshot so his voice was raised.) snobs! That is what you lot are, not a bit like your parents – now there is a real Lady and Gentleman. One more to arrive in my reckoning. Hope they get here soon because I want to get back to my mare, she is due to foal at any time now and I want to be there when that happens." Jeremiah heard the vehicle coming down the private road long before he saw it and was surprised when a taxi drove slowly through the gates he was quick to step in front of the vehicle, it immediately pulled up. The instant that he saw who its passengers were, he was quick to apologise, "Sorry Master Chadrick, Miss Demmie, I did not realise that it would be you in a taxi. Hello ma'am it is good to see you both again." "You too, Jeremiah, are the others here?"

"Master Kevin and his wife have been here three days, everyone else has arrived in the last hour and a half, you are the last, sir." "Drop the sir please, Jeremiah, and the master, I have said it before, just call me Chadrick or even Chad. The others may but I do not want any formality or standing on ceremony and neither does my wife, do you Demmie?" She did not reply but gave a long stare of indignation at this statement. It was noticed by Jerimiah but missed by Chadrick. "Now a personal question for you, how is Star doing? Has she foaled yet?" "Any time now, sir, sorry Chad." "Then my friend, we will get out of this taxi and walk from here so that the gates can be closed and locked, then you can get back to her." "But it's a tidy step up to the Manor."

"Not a problem my friend, (Chad was quickly out of the taxi and handing over the fare to the driver, Demmie relucktantly followed him.) anyhow, a good walk will do us both good and give us a chance to stretch our legs after all the sitting to get here." Demmie threw a look of disagreement but Chad was out of the taxi with their cases from the boot, the driver was paid so she had no choice. "Now then without argument, you get away to your mare my friend and we will close the gates for you". "But I –" "No, but Jeremiah, get on that horse and be away with you and let us know when the foal is born".

"God bless you both and thank you Chad, you are a real gent." In seconds Jeremiah had mounted his waiting horse and was galloping away. The taxi reversed and with the gates closed and secured, Chad and Demmie began their long walk up to the Manor.

"Glad we decided to travel light and only have one small suitcase each." Said Chad "I bet that your brothers and sisters have a lot more luggage than this and even if they did not, they would not make this long walk." Demmie said grudgingly then added. "Ten pounds bet on the luggage." "Cannot do that my

dear because what is mine is yours and what is yours is mine."
Replied Demmie slyly, "True, and that is one of the reasons that
I love you, we share everything equally. You are not a bit like
my sisters or brothers, they are filled with greed and out for all
they want and can get and now that father is seriously ill, they
will be even more at each other with their bickering and wanting to cut everyone's throat as they continue with their fighting
to gain the title of Lord in fact, I am surprised that they haven't
killed each other this far as they each stand in the others way."

"They are welcome to all this wealth and grandeur Chad, we
may not be rich but we are comfortable and I am quite happy
with our simple way of missing, thank you." He smiled and although he said nothing, he sensed an air of falseness in her statement. "You do not want me to be the Lord of the Manor then?"

"You Chad?" She shook her head and laughed quite loudly, "Most definitely not you, well the very thought." He sensed
something truthful in her reply but did not challenge it. "Well
anyhow, I don't think that there is any chance of that, besides,
the title usually goes to the eldest son and that is Malcolm by
four minutes and fifteen seconds over his twin Grant according
to what has been said." Remarked Chad, "And Grant should be
the one to have it all."

"Grant hmm, tell me Demmie, why do you say Grant"? She
answered without a seconds hesitation. "No reason other than
otherwise it will go to Malcolm and not to Kevin." He thought
her answer was extremely strange so he asked again, "Why do
you say Grant should be the one?" This time she hesitated before
replying, "No reason, just a name slip I guess," "Well, you can
be sure that he will want it over the other two and I can guess
that they each have a plan to gain the title so there will be a lot
of rivalry and animosity between them. Even the two sisters will
want a bite of the cherry because they all want to have the title
and all that goes with it, it is just a simple matter of who father
thinks will be the best suited for the role." "Will they physically
fight each other for the role?" "You can bet on it and knowing
them it could turn particulary violent."

"You do not count yourself in the running then and do not come into the equation?" "I am not of Mandaten blood so that counts me out straight away and either sister would only stand to inherit if there were no male heirs to bare the title. They are both filled with greed and I feel very sorry for Tomas and Walter, it is just as well that they did have fortunes of their own thanks to Father, although they are sinking and in the current climate, they will need to appraise their businesses." "Not like us then?"

"Not like us, having too much causes problems and I can well do without them, what do you say?" "Well, let me think, with all that wealth I would wear designer clothes and there would be no more work or having to do the washing, cooking or any house-work at all, I would have staff at my beck and call … Umm, now that would be really lovely, oh how I want that." He glanced at her, a bit surprised at her answer and again felt that it carried a note of truth, and then she produced a forced half-smiled. "Only kidding, it would all be far too much to handle anyway, we are fine as we are." "We sure are but for a minute there I thought you were being serious." He looked ahead just as her face changed into a full smile. He noticed that she was beginning to tire so he tried to give some encouragement. "Well, there she is, Demmie, there stands the good old homestead Mandaten Manor. She looks very impressive and you will not need to walk much further as we are almost there."

They must have been observed walking up the long drive be-cause waiting at the front door were both footmen and as they ap-proached, Alfred disappeared. "It is good to see you both again. Come right in, now let me take your cases and show you to your room." "Good to see you, Jonas." Walking up the long staircase, they continued to chat, "The Sir Lowel Mandaten suite?" "Just so, it is ready for you and as we observed you walking up the long drive, we timed it to let Katrine know so she will have a hot bath already run for you, she will be your maid for your stay. Dinner will be served at seven-thirty sharp and as you know his Lordship does not like to be kept waiting." "Thank you for re-minding me, Jonas, Father was always a stickler for punctuality,

I guess that comes from his days in the army." Arriving at the Lowel suite, they were greeted by Alfred. "Welcome home Chad, Demmie, everything is ready for you, this is your room key although I have never known the doors to be locked and we hope you both enjoy your stay." "Thank you and I can safely say that it will not be as enjoyable as three months ago with Father being taken so suddenly ill."

"Very true Chad and it did come on extremely suddenly, one day he was absolutely fine and even went for a long ride on Thundist, then in the evening started to feel unwell. The next day he was rushed off to hospital but if I may speak out of turn?" "Just between us then."

"He has had a good life, although tough at times and my grandfather served in his regiment during the great war and was sadly lost at Pashendale, the were both young but went anyhow and your father has reached his ninety-seventh year and it seems to me that he will just go on and not roll over and die, definitely a tough old cuss if you will excuse the saying." "Just between us, you are perfectly right, Alfred, and I for one wish that life would allow it to be so and he could go on forever." "You are a good man, Chad, not a bit like your three brothers and we would all be more than happy to serve under you if it were you who was our next Lord." "Thank you for that Alfred but not possible as I am not a Mandaten by birth. I have a hard job to understand their way of thinking, maybe because I am from a different stable but that is the greed in them." "As far as we are concerned and that is all of us that work here, you are a pure true blood Mandaten." "Thank you for that, Jonas, and the time is ticking so now we had better get a move on." "Us too, Chad, so we will leave you now as we have to finish preparing the dinner table." They both turned and left.

Demmie shook her head as though in despair, "Goodness gracious, you amaze me how you talk to the staff the hired help and allow them to talk to you, surely there should be some sense of decorum between you and them. From the moment that we came through the gates and you spoke to Jeremiah, you told him no formality or standing on ceremony and I felt that it makes you just like them. To my mind, to an outsider nothing more than just one of the employed personnel, it may be alright for you but for me, I do not like that. I guess in your mind it does not really matter what anyone thinks. You told him not to call you master or sir so do you not think that you should be a little bit better than that and rise up a bit more so that they know that you are above them to ensure that they know their lowly station?" He sensed a touch of anger and snobbery in her voice and that was something he had not experienced before. "Not at all Demmie and I am surprised that you should say such a thing because like them is just what I am my darling woman, I have no visions of grandeur and I have never and will never consider myself any better than they are. Lord Mandaten, as you know, adopted me minutes after my birth and he is the only father that I have ever known and his wife the only mother, and that in my book makes me no better than any of the members of staff that are employed here or, come to that, those that we employ. They are all working for a living just as we are, the only difference is that we run our own business and they work for us and my mother and father." He shook his head in total disbelief at what she had said. "Hmm, of course, you are right Chad, it just seems so strange to hear you speak to them on the same level, your brothers or sisters would not accept it and, I dare say, neither would their respective wives or husbands."

"True, they would not but I am not them. Besides, there is one who seems much different in their way of thinking and that is Malcolm's young second wife, Greta. She is a very nice person and appreciates everything that she has but as for the rest of them, they always want more and think it is beneath them to treat the staff with respect. Plus, they have always been a bit above themselves. I, for one, will always treat everyone as a human being on the same playing field and not as they do – like a doormat to wipe their feet on. Our staff works hard for us and I always promised that as we made money through their endeavors, they, in turn, would make more through their wage packets and I have stuck to that." "And if you had not paid them so much we would have a lot more". "I told them they would do well and better as the business grew and that is my agreement with them and will not be changed". She now sensed his anger so changed her direction. "That is why all the staff in our business and here at Mandaten like you because you treat them all with respect and they return it to you." "You have to earn respect Demmie, it is not something that is just given. My father told me that a long while ago and that is why his soldiers liked him, and all the staff here like him and mother equally and that is why they have remained faithful to them for so many years. He has been a strict disciplinarian but because they have always been fair with all the staff they both have their respect." "I know that it cannot be and will never happen but that fairness, I can see, would continue with you as the next Lord and in charge of the estate and all that is connected and goes along with it. But don't you think you would be too soft on them and that they would take advantage of that? Now, your Brother Grant, on the other hand, is much stronger than the other two and he –" He could not understand her attitude and did not wish to discuss it further so he raised his hand to stop the conversation from progressing further. "Grant again, enough said on that subject and as I have already said I am not my brothers, plus, I am not a Mandaten so I do not come into the selection at all. Now we have less than an hour to get ready for dinner so into the bath with you before it gets cold." She looked at him then with a scowl and attempted a curtsy and said sarcastically, "Yes my lord and master." He tapped her across the bottom.

"Lord and master indeed, not me cheeky."

She mumbled under her breath, "Too right you are not." Right on time, the family had bathed and dressed, ready for their evening meal and observing protocol, took up their respective position at the dinner table, and were standing by their chairs, waiting for their parents to arrive. At precisely seven twenty-seven p.m. they walked in and immediately took up their seats, the footmen instantly slid the chair into place for them to sit. With a wave of the father's hand, the family followed suit and the instant they were all seated, the first course arrived and was served.

"Have you remembered our daughter-in-law Bonnie's nut allergy Bradinham"?

"We have, my Lady, and as before, cook Flora has prepared all her meal with the greatest of care." "Thank you, Bradinham." After grace was said, the meal began and there was complete silence while they consumed the first course as the rule of the house was 'no talking whilst eating'. The moment that the cutlery was laid down, Malcolm broke the silence. "I find this all a waste of good money but why did you need to call us to be here today, Father? As you know, we are all busy finalising our own section of the arrangement for the weekend's show, plus we normally arrive on a Thursday with the children, not the Monday so would that not have been soon enough?" "What gives you the right to question why Malcolm?" "As the eldest son and in line to be the next Lord, I would say that gives me the perfect right, Father." "You presume much, Malcolm. Now that aside, I have asked you all to be here early because, as you are aware, I have been informed that my remaining days are limited and while I live, I must choose and nominate my successor to be the next Lord of the Manor. My will is already written bequeathing to those that I desire the things specifically for them to have. But the matter of who steps into my shoes is a totally separate issue and it is for that reason I have brought you together early so that I can have the time to make my decision."

"Fair enough, Father, but as the eldest son, surely there should be no question at all as to who it should be and an easy decision to make as it is I that should automatically be the next Lord. And while I am on the subject, isn't this all very grand, and do you not think that as costs are rising, this type of formal family gathering is a bit too costly and well outdated?" "You grow very bold, Malcolm, but while I still rule at Mandaten, it shall be so." He glanced at the three sons, Malcolm and Grant and then Kevin. "You can be sure that I am fully aware of all your thoughts and I made a special point of knowing yours just because you are the eldest son and I do not like or agree with any of them." "My thoughts, Father? But how could you possibly know them? Surely you are not some kind of mind reader?" He then chucklad, his father smiled at him. "I have my ways and they are for me to know. I know that you would sell the Manor to the National Trust to be kept for prosperity and take up residence in the Manor farm house, which would turn our farm manager, Jacob, and his family out and I can assure you that is not going to happen. We have given a good number of local people work and have gained their loyalty and it is my desire that this continues and you, Malcolm, would break up what has taken us years to build so I will hear no more of it." "B-but I —"

"Silence!" He said in a raised voice. "I said that I will hear no more of it."

Kevin smiled and took his chance to speak. "Do as Father says big brother. I, for one, have no desire to see what has taken years to build broken in the stroke of a pen."

"Well, no big surprise there, little brother Kevin, of course, you would not want to break anything up, you may be the youngest but let us face it, you would like to be the Lord and master of all this just as they both would," Grant replied, directing his comment at Kevin and his two sisters. Demmie almost rose from her seat but instead sat bolt upright before speaking.

"I agree with you, Grant, and I do not think I know that you would not see it broken up, what is ours shall always be ours if you were at the helm," Demmie stated with a smile. All eyes were on Demmie now, all surprised at her comment. Demmie knew that she had spoken out of turn and turned sheepishly away trying to avoid their stares.

"Strange for you to join in, Demmie, as it does not concern you in the slightest. Now, it does concern you three boys and quite honestly, all you brothers make me sick the way that you all squabble, admit it you all want the title. So do not make it any more difficult for father than it already is please," said Chad angrily. "Even our darling sisters, who look so demure, have a problem, the three of us are in their way." Grant said with a

17

provocative grin. "True, Grant, so that makes all of us want to rule." Kevin said. "Not all of us, Kevin, you three brothers can fight it out amongst yourselves with pistols, swords or with whatever you chose. I have no desire to be at the helm so leave me out of the equation." Chadrick said looking extremely annoyed. "You are a little creep, Chadrick, anyhow you are not really one of us true blood Mandaten's and not to be considered in the running at all." Said Malcolm. "That is very true, you are only adopted so your thoughts do not count. Plus, as Malcolm said you are not a Mandaten so you are in no position to be a Lord. In fact, I do not know why you are even here." Lizabeth spat. "Well said, Lizabeth, and so say all of us, so that is clear enough, Chadrick, you may as well toddle away as you are not wanted or needed here and never have been." Grant then made the movement of walking with his fingers.At this remark, Lord Mandaten snapped. "Enough of that kind of talk, Grant! Malcolm, Lizabeth, all of you, Chadrick has always been much more than a good son to us and a very good brother to you all. You have a very short memory and you forget easily that if it were not for him, even though he was years younger when it happened, then you would not be here today Grant, for you would have surely drowned in the lake if he had not risked his own life to save yours."

"True enough, Father, and I am not allowed to forget it and that act sticks in my throat. He has been thanked for it many times and I have been reminded on more occasions than I care to remember but we do not live in the past, Father, and need to move forward if we are to survive in the future." Grant said with a sour look on his face."You have all done very well with what the Manor Estate has given you and that is only because it has been well run and we have indeed moved with the times and the changing situation." He glanced around his family with steely eyes. "I can smell the greed in all of you as it spills out like an overflowing cup. I can also sense your jealousy and dislike of each other, even though you are brothers and sisters, your falseness and lies are like n overflowing cup. There are only two amongst you that have none of those traits and that makes my task extremely difficult.

Now all be silent and eat." Lord Mandaten said and focused on his plate. "And we can all guess who one of them is." Grant said bitterly. "I said silence Grant and –." Lord Mandaten then began to choke and without hesitation, Chadrick was the first to react and be at his side. He spoke calmly. "Take it easy Father, it is not worth upsetting yourself over, they are only words and they do me absolutely no harm." Lord Mandaten calmed and patted him on the hand. "Thank you, son, you are a good boy and I will be alright now." He returned to his seat under the evil constant stare of Malcolm, Grant, and Kevin, there were also long stares of hatred from Lizabeth and Sammie. Their father's angry, long, and ice-cold glance was more than adequate to reign them in and once again silence reigned supreme but whilst they ate the building hostile atmosphere between them could be cut with a blunt knife.

With the main course finished and the cutlery laid still, the signal was given and instantly the table was being cleared. "May I be excused please, Father, as I need the restroom?" "At last some respect and not from one of my own children,you are excused Demmie." "If she is to be excused, may we be also father?" Lord Mandaten gritted his teeth as he could sense the animosity in Lizabeth's voice, "Lizabeth, Greta, you are also both excused." "Thank you father." Replied Lizabeth. The three girls rose from the table and made their way silently from the room. In the hall, they saw the trolley filled with their desserts and noted the one that was separated from the others with Bonnie's name clearly marked on it. "They all look very nice." Remarked Greta but Lizabeth and Demmie appeared to pay little attention although observing all that the trolly contained. Alfred and Jonas were busy removing the used main course dinnerware and, although they noticed them, paid little or no attention to the three girls as they walked past. The three met again in the hall and, without a word passing between them, re-entered and took up their seats in the dining room. "The ladies are returned, Bradinham, so serve the desert." Bonnie's was the first to be served to ensure that there could be no possibility of it being mistaken or contaminated. "Bonnie, I must say that your dessert looks rather delicious, cook has excelled herself for you." said Demmie. "So do all of yours. Look delicious." Replied Bonnie. "Enough chat, I will have silence at the table." "Please accept our apologies, Father." Said Bonnie shyly. With a nod of his head, there was silence again.

The only sound to be heard was Bradinham as he breathed erratically, the only other sound was the occasional chink of a spoon as it connected with the dessert dish. They were all enjoying the dessert and when they had finished, the spoon was laid down. "That was —" Greta never finished her sentence because suddenly Bonnie started to choke and convulse and moments later, collapsed, falling heavily from her chair. Demmie cried out, "Bonnie, what is it? what is wrong?" There was no response. "Quick, call for an ambulance, she is struggling to breathe and her heart rate is very rapid or even low —. Oh I don't know but it is not right!", cried Sadie. "Look at the raised rash, what could be wrong with her?" "If Kansas was here now, then he would know." Lizabeth wailed. "But he is not here, is he? And will not be until Thursday, will he Lizabeth?" Grant's snapped. "No need for that, Grant, Lizabeth is only trying to help." Snapped her husband, Tomas. "I am not clued up on medical conditions but knowing Bonnie and her condition, plus, I have seen this once before,as one of my staff has the same condition, it looks as though she is suffering a reaction to something that she has eaten, get the Epipen she has in her handbag we need to try that." Chad administed the pen but it appeared to have little or no effect, "Dam", said Chadrick looking very concerned."But how can that be, Chadrick? Everything was prepared with great care and she has not had a problem before as Cook is very particular when preparing Bonnie's meals." Said Lady Mandaten.

"Well, she has eaten something now, Mother." snapped Grant, who was by her side trying his best to keep her breathing. Demmie moved forward to be right at his side and with her hand resting on his shoulder she whispered in his ear, "It will be alright, Grant." "For goodness sake, move back all of you and give her room to breathe." Shouted Greta as she ushered the family away from her, they all wanted to be by her side but were helpless as none of them had a clue what to do and could do nothing to help her. Greta began to cry and held her hand. "I wish that I knew what to do, oh! my dear sweet Bonnie." But all that could be done was to wait for the ambulance to arrive.

A call had gone to Herbert the livestock manager who had sent one of his sons to open the gates and within eight minutes the medical team was in attendance. "This is very serious, Rob, she is suffering a severe anaphylaxis reaction and is in a deep anaphylactic shock, almost a coma. Her airway is terribly restricted and almost closed. She needs an emergency tracheotomy, try the Epinephrine and hopefully that will help." "Trying to establish a tracheotomy that but this is not good, not good at all. I feel that she needs to be somewhere with someone who is much better equipped than we are to carry out the required procedure quickly if she is to be saved. We will keep feeding her oxygen and get her to the hospital as quickly as possible. Make the call ahead so that everything will be in place for our arrival. Now let us be away." In a matter of a few minutes, the ambulance was on its way and speeding down the road with the siren blasting out and the blue lights flashing, following in its wake was Grant. Demmie sat beside him, calling out as she ran to his car, "He should not be going alone." And before Chadrick could answer, she was in the passenger seat and they were speeding away. "Kevin, Lizabeth, Sammie, with me, the rest wait here for news, they will not want us all there, especially if not blood family." Malcolm said with urgency staring directly at Chadrick.

Malcolm had his car fired up and hardly before the doors were closed and the safety belts fastened, he had the car in gear and was chasing after Grant and the ambulance. The ambulance crew fought hard to keep Bonnie breathing and stabilised whilst in transit and their efforts were being rewarded but she needed urgent care if her life was to be saved. Arriving at the hospital, there was no delay and when the ambulance pulled into the parking bay, two porters were already opening the rear doors before the vehicle had come to a complete halt. As they wheeled her in, the consultant called out, "Ok team, let's hustle and do our best to save this young lady's life."

"This is Bonnie Mandaten, she is suffering a severe allergic reaction and has been unconscious for at least twelve minutes. We tried to bring her around without success and on the way here, she suffered a cardiac arrest, we managed to resuscitate but she is very unstable we tried to do an emergency tracheotomy to open her airway but were unsuccessful and her airway is virtually closed, we also administered Epinephrine but it appeared to have little effect." Said Dave the paramedic. "Ok team, let's get those drugs running and –." Before the consultant had finished speaking, at that moment Bonnie's body arched, held for a few seconds, then collapsed "Cardiac Arrest." Said the sister in charge. "Stand clear, paddles ready!" shouted the consultant with his medical team of doctors and nurse's in close attendance. Her body jumped as the charge ran through her. "Nothing." Cried the emergency sister. "All clear, paddles ready!" said the consultant as he prepared to deliver another shock, Again her body jumped. "Nothing, she is gone." Said the nurse as she felt for a pulse. "Once more please team, clear paddles ready." Said the consultant and delivered another shock to her body. Again Bonnie's body jumped as the charge passed through her chest but there was no response, the emergency sister felt for a pulse, then shook her head. "We are too late, she is gone." She said reluctantly. "I think that we will need to have a post-mortem to see what has happened to this young woman and confirm the cause of death but by the appearance of the swelling and the rash on her body, it was very severe Anaphylaxis. I will do the unenviable task of breaking it to her husband."said the consultant. Grant, with Demmie at his side, was the first to arrive and they were in the family waiting room when the rest of the family turned up. "Any news Grant?" "Not yet, Lizabeth, they would not let us in with her and we got ushered into here so don't know a thing yet, only that they are fighting for her." Grant replied. At that moment, the door opened. "I am Mister Manier, the emergency consultant, and have been treating Bonnie Mandaten. Which of you gentlemen would be her husband?" "That would be me, tell me what is going on, and do not fob me off with any of the medical jargon, just give it to me straight, is she alive or dead." Grant said sternly. "And are these people with you?" "They are, so you can speak freely in front of them, is Bonnie going to be alright?" Grant urged. Before answering, the consultant hesitated for a moment, shaking his head. "I hate this part of my job." He said quietly. "It is my solemn and sad duty to inform you that your wife sadly passed away precisely ten minutes after her arrival, we tried desperately to carry out an emergency procedure called a tracheotomy to open her airway." He shook his head "It is unfortunate as she had another massive cardiac arrest and regrettably we were unable to save her. We did everything that we possibly could to save your wife, Mister Mandaten, but sadly her condition was beyond serious. Because of the way that your wife died we will need to carry out a post-mortem just to be certain of the cause of death, we must do that for the record. We will also need to inform the police, merely a formality, you understand because of the suddenness." "Is that really necessary when you already know the cause of death?" Grant sounded dismayed. "It is, sir, I am deeply sorry that we failed in our attempt to save her and you have my deepest sympathy." Said the consultant. "Thank you, can I see her?" Grant's voice shook. "Give us a few moments, then a nurse will come to fetch you." The consultant turned and walked away. "Bonnie's gone, I can hardly believe it, we were eating dinner only half an hour ago, and now this. Grant, you must be devastated at this." Said Lizabeth and started to cry. "I don't know why you are crying, the tears are all false. Besides, you did not really like her anyhow." She stopped crying instantly. "You ask how I feel, well, I don't know how I feel, Lizabeth, just numb is how I feel at this moment. Time is nine p.m., you can all go back to the Manor now. Demmie will wait with me and she can drive me back." Grant said sharply. Kevin hesitated before speaking, "Should it not be one of us family staying with you?" "Maybe Kevin but I would like it to be Demmie, she will have a calming effect on me." Grant looked at the sad faces staring at him then continued. "A family member may be a bit stressful." "Alright, Grant, if that is your wish, I will not argue the point, not the time or place. Come on then the rest of you, we will be getting back to inform the others." Said Malcolm in an authoritarian voice. In silence, they left the waiting room, and as the car made its way home from the hospital, not a word was spoken, they had sped there but the return drive was much slower. As the car pulled up near the Manor, Malcolm seemed to growl. "Someone will pay for this and heads will roll, her allergy was well known to every single person employed so it is quite apparent that sufficient care could not possibly have been taken in the kitchen." "I think that Father will have something to say on that score, brother." Kevin said. "Well not without our input, Kevin, this is a case of just plain carelessness by either of those cooks and look at the outcome – a death." Malcolm said irritably. Lizabeth swallowed hard then spoke, "True, but even so we cannot go jumping to conclusions can we Malcolm." "Clear enough to me, Lizabeth." They left the car and went into the Manor. Waiting back at the Manor, the rest of the family were eagerly waiting for news and when they heard the car pull up at around nine twenty p.m., they could hardly contain themselves and began to ask questions even before the returning family members were through the front door. "What happened?" said Chadrick. "Is she alright?" cried Greta. "The news, one of you for goodness sake tell us the news!" said Chadrick as he looked at the returning family. "I see that Grant and Demmie are not with you, why is that and what is the outcome? Is poor Bonnie going to be alright?" "She stayed with Grant, Chad." "Stayed, but why Sammie?" Chad sounded confused. Sammie replied. "To drive him home, of course, as that was what he wanted." Said Kevin.

"Well, all of that is immaterial so If you are quite done move away from the door so that we can come in, the sad news is that Bonnie did not make it. There is no easy way to explain or to say it but straight to the point and that is simple, truth is, she is dead. Grant is waiting to see the body and requested that your wife stays with him, said she would have a calming effect, where-as we, as blood-family, may be stressful." Again, Malcolm had to get a dig at Chadrick's adoption and continued, "He said that was what he wanted so due to the situation we did not argue the point." "But surely one of you should have done that even so?" Chadrick said. "That is what Kevin said but Grant insisted on Demmie staying and, quite honestly, under the circumstances, we were not going to argue." Replied Malcolm. Chadrick looked sad and wiped a tear from his eye before replying, "Understandably, he must be devastated."

"Lizabeth asked him that and he replied that he was just numb." "He did seem remarkably calm, though." Said Sammie. "Probably because the truth of Bonnie dying so horribly has not hit him yet." Replied Lizabeth. "Give it time, Sammie, and when it does, we must all be there to support him." Said Kevin.

"And we as a family most certainly will." Replied Malcolm looking at Chad as he spoke. "Of course, that goes without say-ing, after all, he is our brother." Replied Sammie.

"Better go tell ma and pa the sad news, we will leave that to you, Malcolm, as you are the oldest." Said Kevin. "Thought you might, you all go through to the lounge and I will get some coffee sorted, then find them." Kevin gave a salute, "Yes sir", then turned and walked away. They all headed in one direc-tion while Malcolm went in the other. They entered the lounge in silence and were surprised to see that their parents were al-ready there. They looked at each one individually as they en-tered. "No Malcolm? And I see no Grant or Demmie, where are they?" asked Lady Mandaten. "Grant and Demmie are still at the hospital and —" Just at that moment the door swung open and Malcolm walked in. "I was about to say he is ordering some coffee and looking for you but no need as he is here now." Said Sammie, wiping her eyes. "So, tell us, my boy, what is the news on Bonnie?" Their mother asked.

"No easy way to say it, Mother, Father, Bonnie is dead and that is the truth of the matter. They fought as hard as they could and did all that was possible to save her life and, regrettably, they were not successful, therefore someone will pay for it." Malcolm announced. "Do not presume, Malcolm, because while I live, I am still the head of this family and it is I that will make that decision once we know all the facts. Until then, we support Grant, got it?"

"Got it, Father." There was a knock at the door and upon its opening, in walked Mister Bradinham the old butler, followed by Alfred the senior footman, with a tray containing the jugs. They were closely followed by the junior footman Jonas who had the cups and when each person had received a cup of coffee, the old butler asked, "Is there any news about Miss Bonnie, sir?"

"Not that it is any concern of yours as it is a family matter and you are just our butler but for your information – she is dead." Snapped Malcolm in reply. Even at his age, he was close to tears. Bradinham, with his two footmen, turned and left. "There was absolutely no need to speak to him in that way, you are such a pig and after all, he was only showing concern." Chadrick said with a tone of disgust."None of this concerns you or them, it is a family matter, so save your sympathy, Chadrick – oh, I forgot you are one of them and not one of us, definitely not a true blood Mandaten." Sneered Malcolm.

"Bradinham has been with us since before you were born and he has become a part of our family and has grown with us." Lord Mandaten glared at his son and continued,"Your bullish attitude is helping me to make up my mind, Malcolm. To step into my shoes and be the next Lord, you must also have compassion, be caring, understanding, and have some gentleness and that is something that you most definitely lack. Now, we will wait for Grant to return and that shouldn't be too long. You were back promptly at twenty minutes past nine, therefore, allowing for the necessary to be done, maybe he will be here at ten-thirty. Then he can tell us more on the cause of death."

"And that is what we all want to know." Said their mother. "No more to be said on the subject just now, my dear, and until Grant is home, we shall keep a silent vigil with our thoughts of dear sweet Bonnie." He glanced at them all as he spoke, they all obeyed the words of their father sitting in silence sipping their coffee. It was almost one in the morning before Grant arrived back and was ushered straight into the lounge with Demmie following close behind him.

"I am surprised to see you all still up." Grant stated.

"Could not possibly go to bed before we knew what the outcome was and the cause of – well, only one word can be used, death." Said Lizabeth. "Before another word, a cup of coffee and a brandy, Grant?" Demmie asked.

"That would be good, thank you, Demmie." "While I am at the coffee pot, is there anyone else who would like another cup?" Demmie looked at everyone. Cups were passed and once filled, she handed them out, leaving Chadrick's to the very last. "Now, however painful the result, please son, tell us."

"From the initial examination father, mother, and the analysis, Bonnie died of a massive heart attack, cadiac arrest they call it and it may have been brought on by a severe case of shock due to her nut allergy. They said that they had dealt with cases before and had never seen such a severe reaction with a dose of epinephrine failing to work and it will be necessary to carry out a full post-mortem." "When will they do that son?" "Tomorrow, and there is something else." Grant continued. "What else could there be son?" asked his mother. "Try the police, because of the suddenness, it will be the police mortuary technician that carries it out and as they were informed of her sudden death, questions will be asked. They said that we can expect a visit from them in a couple of days, once they have the post-mortem results." Grant explained."Did they tell you that? And why involve the police? Surely it was just a case of an accident or not paying enough attention in the food preparation." "That is just what we said when we saw her lying there, Sammie, but they told us that it is a requirement and protocol for them to be informed of a sudden death, so there you have it. That is all there is to say so I do not have any desire to talk about it any further tonight or any other night. I am off to my bed, so goodnight all." Grant took hold of Demmie's hand. "Thanks for tonight." Then he winked. "The night is not over yet Grant." She whispered in reply. He smiled, then turned and left them listening to his slow footsteps as he climbed the stairs. "Should someone go up with him?" Greta looked concerned."Best to leave him to deal with it in his own way, Greta." Malcolm said still watching the place Grant had exited. "Yes, but it is so sad."

"He needs to get used to being alone Greta and you are probably right, it is sad. Plus, he knows that we family are all here if he needs us." Replied Lizabeth looking at Chadrick as she spoke. "Like I said, best to leave him to deal with it in his own way."Malcolm said. "Yes, you are right son."

"That is no surprise mother as Malcolm is always right." Replied Lizabeth sarcastically after which they fell silent. Slowly and silently, the lounge door swung open and a footman entered. "Alfred, glad you are still up, I need you to go and get a message to Herbert, tell him to have the black stallion Thundist saddled and ready for me by six a.m. sharp." Malcolm demanded.

"I do not wish to question, sir, but at that early hour there will still be a lot of fog or mist about and he does not react kindly to that so for your safety, would it not be better to make it a bit later?" Alfred asked carefully. "How dare you question me?!" Malcolm snapped. "If I had my riding crop, I would beat you for that insolence. Just do it if you want to keep your job and know what is good for you." Said Malcolm angrily. "I meant no offense sir, it shall be so." Not wishing to antagonise him further, Alfred removed the used crockery and left the room. He knew it would be no good to phone and that the only way, at this late hour, that Herbert would know of master Malcolm's request, was to make his way to his cottage and wake him now. Chadrick stood silent so nothing was said until Alfred had left the room. "Again, your bullish belittling behavior strikes with precision. There was no need for you to speak to Alfred in that manner, he was only looking out for you and to say you would have beaten him is an outrage." "Nothing to do with you adopted boy, you can let them speak to you how you like but as for me, they will show respect." Replied Malcolm smugly. "You have to earn respect, Malcolm, it is not a god-given right, irrespective of who you are or your position in life." Chadrick said tiredly. "I am not going to banter words with you, Chad, and you will find that out when I am the next Lord and master of Mandaten, so take heed and be warned." Malcolm looked the other way. "If Malcolm, if." Malcolm gazed in the direction of the voice and watched as a chair turned. When it was stationary, a figure rose and there stood their father. "Sorry Father, I thought that you had retired to bed." Malcolm said quickly. He raised an eyebrow. "Apparently so but as you can see, I have not, I have heard enough so I am about to do so."

"Then I bid you a good night and rest well, Father." Malcolm said. Lord Mandaten glared and just hummed, "Hmm." They watched their father leave before any further conversation took place. "Put your foot in it that time, big brother." Kevin teased. "Shut up, Kevin." Malcolm spat back. "Temper, temper. Now then, your ride, where will you head big brother?" Kevin asked.

"Up around the lake and across the meadow, then through the woods, follow the lane, then past the old Manor ruins and Devil's Dyke and back across Rudslip Meadow, down by the stream." Malcolm declared. "You would not get me up there by the Devil's Dyke." Lizabeth's eyes turned big. "Nothing up there for you to be afraid of, Lizabeth." "Nothing you say, the old Manor ruins and Devil's Dyke? Nothing there to be afraid of? Not in my book, you know that they are haunted by the Lady Mary Lowell Mandaten as she drowned in that dyke back in the late seventeenth century." Lizabeth's eyes darted as she spoke. "Haunted, Lizabeth, that was just a tale told to us when we were young to stop us from going anywhere near them. So that is my route."

"Well, Malcolm, you may not believe in the ghostly reappearance of Lady Mary, but I do and so should you. The atmosphere and weather conditions are just perfect for her to appear and you do know that she has been seen recently." Said Sammie. "And when was the last sighting sister dear?"

"Now let me think, after several years absence, she reappeared about three, four, maybe five years ago, and since then, she has been seen every two to three months. You ask when the last sighting was, well, that would be three months ago around the time of the last family visit." Informed Tomas.

"Well Tomas, I am taking a loaded gun to bag a deer, if possible, so if she shows up, then I will shoot her and then she will have died twice." Malcolm mocked. "You may joke but strange things have happened up there since she has reappeared." Remarked Lizabeth. "All staged and done to scare us away from that area when we were very young and impressionable." Malcolm rolled his eyes. "I do not think so, things have happened, the latest being the migrant workers." Said Chadrick as he began to feel very sleepy. "Who cares about them you may but not me, we are now grownups and that is all behind us, and, well, I am going and that is that." "Well as you say Malcolm, that is that then, no more we can do for now and I am suddenly feeling rather dizzy and sleepy, I feel so tired my eyes are beginning to blur, so bed it is, enjoy your ride Malcolm, you coming Demmie"? Chad's words were now becoming slightly slurred. "Lead on, Chad, it has been a very traumatic and a trying time and although I am tired ..." She sighed and continued, "I still do not think that there will be much sleep for me on this night." "Goodnight all and try to sleep." Grant said as he left. They listened to his slow footsteps and as the conversation was over they began to follow him. "Night both," was the reply, they turned and wached Grant's slow pace up the stairs. One by one, the family left the lounge and retired to their rooms, leaving Malcolm sipping his brandy. "I am going up."

"Ok, Greta, I will just have a brandy, then I will join you."

As Greta passed the Lowell suite, Demmie called to her. "I did not like to hear Malcolm raise his voice, Alfred was only looking out for him and his attitude will get him disliked by them all." She said. "I did not like it either but that is how he is and has been all the time. I do not see him changing his attitude and it is too late for him to change anyhow, as they already have a disliking for him. These are all good people who work here but he was only angry because Alfred tried to ... Well, it does not matter." Greta sighed. "But you do look very upset." Demmie rested a hand on her arm. "It does no good, he is very stubborn and will still go on his early morning ride on Thundist. I am worried because it is far too early, plus, the fog will be hanging there and that is when Lady Mary Lowell walks. Alfred knew this and tried to help but he insisted on it being six a.m. and Thundist is a very powerful animal." Greta sounded concerned. "He is an excellent rider and has ridden in, and won, several competitions over the years, not to mention the Gold medal at the Olympic Games. He will be absolutely fine, what could possibly happen to him as he is such an expert rider. I am sure that there will be no cause for alarm." Demmie soothed. "You are right, I guess that I am worrying over nothing, Demmie, especially after poor Bonnie." "Yes, a very tragic thing to have happened but Grant seems to be taking it very well. I don't think the reality has hit him yet." "Maybe Demmie, but I know that things were not all rosy with them, Bonnie confided in me and said that she thought he was having an affair but, well, it does not matter now if he was or wasn't as she is gone." "An affair you say, did she have any idea who it might be?" "She had some suspicions and was going to tell me later tonight but she is dead now and it is too late." "Who are you talking to out there?" Chad asked and again his words were slurred. "Greta, she is a bit worried about Malcolm, he is still going on his early morning six a.m. ride." Demmie called into the room.

"He will be fine, Greta, and if he should see the Lady Mary then he will just say hello and ride on. He is a better horseman than the rest of us put together, now, I am feeling really tired and my head is spinning, I am fighting to keep my eyes open, we all need to get some sleep for I feel that it will be an early start for all of us tommorow, so good night, Greta." "Night Chad, night Demmie." Greta turned and walked toward her room. Demmie was about to close the bedroom door when she heard Malcolm's heavy footsteps and kept it open just wide enough to watch him as he walked past. "Well now, you think that you will be the next Lord, I think not Malcolm Grant has a plan." She whispered. "Are you coming to bed or staying up all night by the door?" Chad slurred. She silently closed it and walked over to him. "What did you two have to talk about anyhow?" "Bonnie confided in her and thought that Grant was having an affair but that does not matter anymore as poor Bonnie is gone." She said. "Very sadly, yes, but an affair, Bonnie could give him everything he needed so I see no reason for that. She was a little bit snobby at times maybe but if he was, then he is a fool, now enough chat, let us get to bed, I have had it." "Dammit!" She said. "Problem?" "Yes, the zip has got caught up somehow." "Come here and let me try." Chad's head was ringing and with his eyes blurring, he began to examine the zip. "I cannot see straight but your dress is torn, that is why the zip is caught, it's caught in the tear and what is more, there is a nasty stain on it right near your bottom on it too, torn and stained." "Stain? Ah yes, it must have been at the hospital, I do remember scraping on a trolley that had some sort of liquid on it." Said Demmie.

"That must be it then, well the dress is ruined so I guess it's for the bin."

"In that case, just rip it off." With his eyes blurred he fumbled, then, as he took a firm hold and pulled hard, the material tore easily and in seconds it was placed in the wastebasket. His eyes were blurring even more now as he fought against his needed sleep. In the haze, he could still see that she stood there completely naked. "No bra? And I thought that you were wearing undies, especially at Father's dinner table?" "I was wearing some but remember I had to be excused." "I do. He said sleepily. "Well, I was trying desperately to hold on but unfortunately before I got to the restroom. I had begun to wet myself and in light of the situation, I threw them in the bin."

"That explains that then, but what about your – Oh, my head, no matter now, let us get some sleep." "I'll just have a quick shower, although a nice soak in the bath would be nice but whatever, I will be quick and be right with you."

"Ok, if I am asleep when you come to bed, don't bother to wake me." She smiled, "You most certainly will be asleep, I have seen to that and I most certainly will not wake you." He had not heard her remarks as they were almost in a whisper She turned and entered the bathroom closing the door silently behind her. His eyes were unusually heavy with the eyelids appearing to be lead weights and he could not understand why. He had been fighting to stay awake after his second cup of coffee and with a constant buzzing in his head, the instant that his head was resting on his pillow and all was quiet, he succumbed and was immediately lost in a very unusual deep sleep.

Malcolm had taken his time but was now in the bedroom looking at his wife. "What is it Greta, got something on your mind woman?" "I am not at all happy with you going on that ride, especially up there by the Devil's Dyke. There have been many accidents up there, the last one was just three months ago around the time of our last visit." She tried to plead."Anything else, woman?" "Yes, I did not like how you spoke to Alfred the footman, he was only looking out —" He then snapped at her. "For goodness sake! Hush up, Greta. I will speak to the hired help how I please and put them in their place if they step out of line just as I see fit. Now, for goodness sake, stop all your worrying and get to bed, I will be fine." "You had better be, Malcolm, I would be lost without you." "That is right, Greta, for once you are absolutely right on that score. You most certainly would be lost without me, I am glad that you realise it at last. Now, hush up and go to sleep, I have an early start this morning." No more was said and with their clothes discarded, they climbed into bed.

On this night, a few would toss and turn as they tried to piece together the events that led up to the untimely death of Bonnie: at least those who cared for her would.

The old Manor had finished with its creaking and groaning as it settled for the night but in the silence, although no one could be seen, the sound of mysterious footsteps would have been heard for any that remained awake.

Chapter Two

An Early Morning Ride

Five fifteen on Tuesday morning and there was not a sound to be heard as Malcolm slid silently from his bed and, without hesitation, he was quickly dressed in his riding gear. He threw a quick glance toward his wife who still slept. "That's it, my dear, no need for you to worry your little head, you sleep on, give it sufficient time and my plan will come into fruition and all will work out just fine. And then I will be declared the next Lord. I have a plan to achieve this and have planted a seed to begin the process, I will soon be putting it into full action. I don't know why, but for some reason that adopted interloper Chadrick has always been the top dog with father, at least that is how it has always appeared to be. He will never be the Lord of the Manor, of that you can be sure. I will see to that, as I already said, I have my plan set to deal with him and anyone else that gets in my way. Then they will be of no further problem. As for Grant and Kevin, well, after this ride, it will be put into action and that will make certain that none of them become the next Lord. Father does not know it yet but when I am Lord, the bastard son and interloper will be cut off completely and out of my life. As for the others …" He smiled to himself. "Well, wait and see. Now, enough of that for the time being as I am away for my ride and will see you after breakfast, you look so sweet lying there with your brests all bare I could … Well, enough of those thoughts for the moment now I am off for my ride".

He wasted no time and, walking briskly, was at the stables by five forty-five a.m. Herbert the livestock manager was already there and had bridled and saddled the big powerful black stallion for him. "Good morning, Master Malcolm, and a very foggy morning it is, especially around the lake. Far be it from me to instruct you but you will need to take great care and as you already know, Thundist does not like the fog, never has. He knows that things can hide in it and that is why your father only rode him in full clear daylight. If you intend to ride up past the old Manor ruins and Devil's Dyke, be very wary as the conditions are perfect for the Lady Mary to walk. It may well be a myth to some people who just laugh but strange things always seem to happen up there. We were there yesterday morning and it was very eerie in the mist, we all thought that we saw a figure disappear into the old Manor ruins. The ground is very hard in places but soft in others, need a good rain to regulate it. For some reason, Master Malcolm, Thundist is very restless and agitated this morning, unusually so and that worries me. It is as though he has been disturbed by something in the night, probably the fog so he will be quite a handful." "Herbert, quit your twittering." He said snidely "And if you have quite finished twittering then I will get going. You got it right, I do not need you to tell me how to ride or what my father did, or the conditions, I am an expert and have gold medals to prove it and I am quite aware of the ground and the fog and that makes it all the better because the deer herd will not hear or see me as I approach so I may just bag me one of them." "Hence the reason for the gun." Observed Herbert. "Well I would not carry an empty gun case, now would I, stupid man." Herbert bit back his anger. "Indeed not, sir, now what time will I expect you to be back, Master Malcolm?" "I will not hurry so around ten should do, now out of my way, man, I have already wasted quite sufficient time and want to be going instead of listening to you twittering." Herbert stepped aside but maintained his hold on the bridle, he watched as Malcolm swung onto the horse's back and the moment there was weight upon it, he began to lightly buck.

"Steady on there, calm down, damn you, Thundist! Why are you still holding on Herbert? Release his bridle, man, I have him." "He is your horse, Master Malcolm." Herbert said, releasing the bridle. "You have got that right Herbert, he is mine, along with everything else at Mandaten, now come on, big fellow, let's have a good run." With a tap on the horse's flanks, the black stallion reared again and Herbert had to move quickly to avoid its flailing hooves. The instant that all four feet were on the ground again, and after a loud shout, and with Malcolm's whip across Thundist's flanks, "Come on, damn you", followed with another dig in his flanks, Thundist was sent speeding forward and raced away. Herbert remained, watching, as he galloped away, making a ghostly figure as he finally disappeared into the swirling fog. Well out of earshot, he began to mumble to himself. "Dam that man, he is so arrogant and may consider himself to be an expert horseman and that may be the truth but he has absolutely no idea how to treat the animal properly and Thundist unseats him then it will be his own fault. He thinks, like most of the family, that they are here just to serve, just as they think we all are but one day, the animals and us will turn on them and then they will regret that they did not show them or us any respect. One thing is certain, the three brothers, him, Kevin, and especially Grant the one called his twin, not that he is anything like him, are certainly nothing like their lovely father Now there is a real gent. Now, on the other hand, take young Chadrick, he is a different kettle of fish altogether. He is a gentleman through and through and to be honest, he is more like Lord Mandaten than his own three blood sons. Kind and considerate, and, although over us just like his father he is, like one of us. That is why they have our respect. Now, as for the two sisters, I feel sorry for their husbands as they are both very bitchy, greedy and now their bussiness's are in difficulty they … Ah well, moaning about it will get nothing done so come on, Herbert, get you to work". "Talking to yourself father?" "Sometimes helps, Jeremiah, sometimes helps son." "I know just what you mean pops. Just saw that Malcolm ride away, he is a nasty piece of work to be sure and he has such a nice pretty young wife." "That he has, Jeremiah now Greta and Chad would make a nice couple as Lord and Lady Mandaten, ah well, they married the wrong person and Chad is not a Mandaten by blood, more is the pity."

"I just hope that Malcolm treats Greta better than he did his first wife, us and the animals. Heaven help us all if he gets to be the new Lord of the Manor, and as for the rest of them —" Herbert raised his finger to his lips. "Be careful what you say, son, you may think no one is there to hear but remember walls have ears. It's alright to think things but not to say them out loud." Just then, they heard footsteps and turned to see Malcolm's wife, Greta, walking toward them. "Good morning, Herbert, Jeremiah. I heard you two talking and knew the voices were not his masters voice, and I guess that it is safe to say that I have missed trying to stop him and he has gone?" "That he has, Miss Greta, just a few moments ago. He is a fine horseman and will be fine so no need for you to worry." "Did he say when to expect him back? And by the way, you have no need to worry about what I just overheard you both say. And just between us, I agree with you. I cannot complain as he treats me well enough most of the time but ... Well, he needs to put some of that care into how he treats others. I know that he is my husband and I should not say this to you as he would be extremely angry if he knew but he could learn a lot from Chadrick." "Now there is a real gent, he treats us all with respect, Miss Greta, and he is so gentle with all the horses and other animals around the estate and they know it and love him. When he and his wife arrived yesterday, one of the first things that he wanted to know was how Jeremiah's mare Star was and he was the only one of the family to ask. He is a fine fellow, if I may be so bold to say miss." Said Herbert. "I wanted Malcolm to stop but him and Grant were in the middle of a ragging argument, as usual, and he was driving the car like a mad man and almost crashed twice. I have seen them at each other's throats on many an occasions, but this time it was almost violent, this one was something else. I should not be saying all this to you, should I? But ..." She paused for a moment. "It is said now, so that is done. Back to Chad, he certainly is and, maybe I again should not say it, but maybe I married the wrong brother. Uhm, forget that I just said that, both of you, please." She blushed. "I suddenly went deaf, did you say something, Miss Greta?" They both smiled. "Yes, I asked how is the mare?" From the swirling mist, another figure appeared, "You have not answered Greta's question Jeremiah, I guess that means I will ask the same again, how is that mare of yours doing?" "Morning Chad, this stable is beginning to get busy, wonder who will turn up next. As for the mare, she had her foal, a colt, early this morning, hence we are all about extra early and Thundist was unsettled so we put it down to a nervous expectant father but then well –." "Can we see him?" "Would you like to see the new foal Miss Greta?" "I would love to, Jeremiah, if you please." "Then follow me and I will take you to see him."

They followed him into the next stable block and were led into a stall where mother and foal were stabled. "What a beautiful looking foal, just look how his coat shines, it seems to sparkle in the early morning light, just like a bright diamond." "Then, Greta, sorry, excuse me for my error, Miss Greta, he shall be named Diamond. We have Jade, Ruby, and Pearl. His mother is Star, his father is Thundist so why not a Diamond as well." Jeremiah said with a smile.

"Why not, indeed, with all these jewels you have a rich stable and another thing, if it were up to me, it would be fine for you to call me Greta. My husband would never allow it, however, when he is not about, it will be fine."

"Thank you for that, it shall be so." While they were chatting, they had not noticed that Chad had entered the stall and, without any objections from Star Chad stroked the newborn foal. The mare walked up to him and affectionately nudged him for attention and he was not slow to reciprocate. "Alright, Star, you will get some attention as well." He spoke softly to her and she rested her head upon his shoulder. "As if I would leave you out, there you are now, you are a clever girl to give birth to such a fine son, isn't he a beauty." He continued to run his hand down her nose and the mare gave a few low whinnies as if she understood him. Greta stood watching and at first smiled, then had tears in her eyes. "What is it, Greta, what has upset you?" Asked Chad. "It is just that seeing you there and how you have an understanding with the horse, my husband has never had that, in fact, he would not lower himself to even enter the stable block at all he said it is the place for the staff and not him." "Do not upset yourself Greta, there will come a time when he has to enter, there will be no option." "Help to make it soon Chad, please." She said quietly wiping a tear. "Do anything for you Greta, so I will do my best for you, that is all I can do." Their eyes met and he smiled in such a loving way that Greta blushed. "Thank you, Chad, I can ask no more of you, so that is good enough for me, now we had better be getting back to the Manor as the time is almost eight." "You are right and for a moment there, I forgot why I was out so early, when I woke up, Demmie was not beside me so I thought that she may be out for an early morning walk. Although, thinking about it, that would not be like her as she goes out more in the evening. I just threw some clothes on and came out to look for her. I don't suppose that any of you have seen her this morning?" "Sorry, Chad, have not seen hide nor hair." "No problem Herbert, she can't be that far away." Said Chad. "Let us get back to the Manor and check if she is there and if not, then we will start a search for her." "Seems a bit drastic, Greta, to search for her as if she is a missing person." They all chuckled. "Joking aside, Chad, if you do not find her back at the Manor, let us know and we will help to look for her on the grounds." "That we will Pops". "Thanks, Herbert, Jeremiah." He glanced at his watch. "Good grief, it is past eight already, how time flies when you are having fun. Come on, Greta, we had better get our skates on, breakfast is sharp at eight-thirty." "If I had my running shoes on,I would give you a race but not in these shoes." Greta smirked. "Running shoes, why didn't I think of that? Probably because my head still feels fuzzy. I had the weirdest feeling after my second cup of coffee last night. Maybe she has gone out for an early morning run. She has been doing a lot of that just recently, as well as the evenings, although mainly evenings. Disappears for hours at a time, leaving me to do all the work. Said she is training for the London Marathon next year." Chad said. "That is some race if I am not mistaken." Said Greta. "That it is but now we have our own race, we will just walk briskly, so long you two, and say hi to Jason." "Will do, he is moving the sheep from the Rudslip meadow onto the lower river meadow, better grazing there." Replied Herbert. With their hands raised in a wave, they walked away. The instant that they were well out of earshot, Jeremiah turned to his father. "You know something, pops, those two would make a lovely couple Lord and Lady Mandaten ... Ah well, sadly they are both married to someone else so that can never be." "You are right in what you say, Son, they would make a fine couple, you know something, sometimes, strange things can happen." "Never did really like Chad's wife. She seems so false to me and I bet a liar also, there is just something that seems sinister about her and I do not trust her. Come to it, don't like Malcolm much either, if at all, shame it is that they married the wrong person as they like each other and maybe deep down love each other a lot. A great shame, anyhow, breakfast Pops?" "Too right, Jeremiah, Mother has left it all prepared for us so just need to cook it." "Race you to the cottage pops." Jeremiah said with a wink. "You will need to give this old man a head start then, Son." "Not that old pops, anyhow how far?" "Oh! Just up to the front door." Herbert was already running as he finished speaking. Arriving at the cottage, they saw Jason coming through the paddock and shouted to him, "Come on, Son, eggs and bacon are calling." "Sounds good to me, Pops, now what time do you expect Master Malcolm back?" "From what I think his route will be and if he stops to bag a deer, I would say as he said, around ten." "Plenty of time then."

"Plenty." "Better be at the stable by nine-thirty just to be on the safe side pops." "Just to be on the safe side, Jason."

Back in the Manor, Chad and Greta made their way quickly to their rooms, they had just fifteen minutes to get down to the breakfast room and be ready in time for breakfast at eight--thirty. Chad went straight into the bathroom to freshen up and was surprised to find his wife still asleep, lying in the bathtub. He turned the hot tap off and shook her gently to wake her. "Oh! I must have dropped off in the bath." She said.

"And you had left the hot water tap running at a trickle." Chad said angrily.

"That was just to keep the hot water topped up, sorry." "Not as sorry as you would have been if it had overflowed onto the floor and not gone down the overflow pipe or if it had got unbearably hot." "Are you angry with me?" She asked. "Angry with you? Definitely at the waste of so much water. Cold is bad enough but hot, yes, most definitely angry, at you for falling asleep in the bath. No, not at all. I should have come in here first, before rushing out to look for you. I would have found you sooner. Never mind, found you now. Went to the stables and saw the new foal. Greta was there, worried about Malcolm going on his early ride alone. Now then, if we do not hurry, we will be late for breakfast and Father is a stickler for punctuality. We have just ten minutes to get down to the breakfast room." "Better get out of this tub then and get a move on." Chad picked up the bath towel ready to dry her back, she refused to allow him to dry her naked front. It was touch and go but they just made it with a few seconds to spare. The family were all there and just before eight-thirty, their parents arrived. "Good morning Father, good morning Mother." Lizabeth said. "Not a good one, me thinks, Lizabeth, especially not after yesterday's happening," Lord Mandaten said. "True Father, Bonnie will be greatly missed." "Grant not down yet?" Asked Lady Mandaten. "Not yet, Mother." They stood by the breakfast counter deciding what to have and a further ten minutes had passed when Grant walked into the room just as their mother spoke, "I am not surprised Grant is down late he probably had little if any sleep last night without Bonnie beside him and dora the dog is no substitute." "Dora was in our room mother" said Chad. "I am here now, Mother. I apologise for being ten minutes late down." "Under the circumstances, Son, it is to be expected. We will all miss your Bonnie greatly, she was a lovely girl."said his father. "You look very tired, Grant, how did you sleep?" asked his mother. He glanced at Demmie, "Hardly at all and when I did, badly, Mother, thank you. Cudling a pillow is not a substitute nor a dog, I do not wish to discuss it or talk about it anymore." "All right, Son, just as you like, now have some breakfast before it gets cold." He gave a slight nod of his head and made his way to the hot service table. He pondered there for a while, then helped himself to his breakfast meal. "Strange that Malcolm is not present either, Father." Said Grant smiling. "Not so strange son, he is out on his early morning ride, he always did like to do at least one thing to defy me from the moment that he found out that he could crawl. He will learn his mistake, maybe the hard way. Now be silent and eat your breakfast." When they had all finished, the bell was rung and a few minutes passed before the old butler and a footman entered. "Ah now, Bradinham, we will be holding our own little investigation to try and discover what went wrong to cause Miss Bonnie's death so tragically. I will question each member of staff in the long room, starting with cook Flora." "Very good, my Lord, I will send her to you." Said Bradinham. "Do you want all of us blood family to be there, Father, to ask any questions?" "All Lizabeth without exception." In silence, the family made their way down the hall to the long room while the breakfast room was being cleared and once there, waited for the first member of the staff to be questioned. "A bad business this, Mister Bradinham." "Indeed, Jonas, a bad business, indeed, now, you must hurry with the clearing while I fetch cook Flora for the master." The old butler walked slowly as he led Flora into the long room to be faced by the Mandaten family. "Come in, Flora, and sit here." Chad said. "Thank you, Master Chadrick." "Just Chad will do, now, there is nothing for you to worry about, nothing at all. Father just wants to ask some questions, alright?" Chad tried to reassure her. "Alright, Chad, and I will answer them truthfully." "I know that and never doubted it for a minute Flora." Chad smiled. "Now then, Flora my dear, firstly, before I start, as Chadrick has already said there is nothing to be alarmed about. Secondly, I want you to be completely relaxed so only when you are ready will I begin." Said Lord Mandaten. "I am ready, thank you, my Lord." She said. "All we want to know is exactly what went wrong with Miss Bonnie's meal." She had tears in her eyes as she spoke. "My Lord, Lady, Master Grant, I have racked my brain to try and see if I could have made an error in the preparation and the more that I question myself, the clearer it all becomes. Miss Bonnie's complete meal was prepared with the utmost care and kept completely separated from all other foods in its preparation and storage, if anything, we were all being over-cautious. I just cannot understand how anything that she was allergic to could get into her meal and how such a tragic thing could have happened. Especially when we have been cooking for her over the past five years, since she and Master Grant were married. I am so sorry, Master Grant, but if I felt for one minute that it was in any way my fault, then I would gladly own up. It is such a tragedy and should not have happened." "Well it did so there, it is done and cannot be undone," grunted Grant. "Thank you, my dear, now send in Bernice." Said Lord Mandaten. Flora bowed and left the room. "You know why you are here." Lord Mandaten said calmly to Bernice. "I do, my Lord, my Lady, Master Grant, but I cannot see how I can shed any light on the matter or how such a terrible thing could have happened. Flora was very particular and would not allow anyone else, not even myself, to prepare any of Miss Bonnie's meals. In fact, we were not allowed anywhere near her in the preparation or storage of any ingredients that she would use. No one went anywhere near any of it until it left the kitchen and was served by Alfred and Jonas. In fact, Flora kept it all safely locked away." Bernice said. "Thank you, now send in Ruth, Zoe, and Amanda your kitchen helpers." "All together, sir?" "All together, please Bernice." She left the long room. "I do not wish to question your motive, Father, but all three kitchen maids together?" Asked Grant. "Yes Grant, this incident is quite a mystery and I do not think for one minute that any of them had a thing to do with Bonnie's food being tampered with, for want of a better way to put it. But if we question them all together, then we may be able to find something out. Any little piece of evidence will help to solve the why and how, so let us see if we can find it." Lord Mandaten explained. "Or not find anything, as the case may be." Remarked Demmie with a smile. "Indeed Demmie, indeed." Answered Lord Mandaten. They had only a few minutes to wait until a gentle knock was heard, the door was instantly opened to allow the three kitchen maids to enter. Chad was there to guide them into the room, "Please sit, Father wants to talk to you about what – Well, you know what about, Father?" "So, what have you to say on the subject?" Lord Mandaten asked. "I can shed absolutely no light on the tragedy, sir, I had nothing to do with any of the preparation, none of us did. Cook Flora did it all and if we got too close, we would be ushered away."

"Thank you, Amanda, and is that the same for you all?"

"It is, sir, when it was prepared, it was locked away but cook Flora did give us a taste of Miss Bonnie's desert when it was all finished and there was absolutely no taste of nut at all." Said Amanda.

"Fruit – yes, cream – yes, but no nut, sir. In fact, cook made us remove everything from the kitchen to the cupboard that might have the smallest hint of nut in it." Added Zoe. "Even the nut oil, used for cooking, was removed, sir, and as Miss Bonnie had eaten her starter and main course and then collapsed after eating her desert, we assumed that it must be something to do with that. We are at a loss, sir, and we cannot understand how that could be."

"One should never assume but, in that, you are right. That is all, now back to your duties." Lord Mandaten spoke calmly. "If I may just speak out of turn, my Lord." Asked Rose, with a wave of his hand, she continued. "I would just like to say to you all that we are deeply distressed over what has taken place and we all would like to know how this dreadful thing happened. I do not know why but we all have a feeling of guilt, even though we had absolutely nothing to do with it. Master Grant, our deepest sympathy." They rose from their seats and left. "Well, that is all the kitchen staff and we are no closer than we were before speaking to them." Kevin said."Maybe, Kevin, or, on the other hand, maybe not." Lord Mandaten said. "Well, I cannot see any progress and you are talking in a riddle father." "Then you have not been listening properly Kevin, just one little thing, one or a few little words, can make all the difference but for now I will keep it to myself." Lord Mandatens eyes scanned all their faces and he made a mental note of their expressions. "Now, who else could be involved, the butler and the footmen, we will speak to them next." "Yes father", said Sammie as she pulled the bell cord that was instantly responded to. "You call for me, my Lord?" "Yes Bradinham, can you shed any light on the incident at dinner last night?" Lord Mandaten asked. "I wish that I could, my Lord, it is a complete mystery to me. I only know that cook was very cautious and meticulous, as were all the kitchen staff. Mrs. Bradinham had them under her watchful eye and Alfred and Jonas were under my gaze for most of the time from the moment the meal started right up to the tragedy. The desserts were on the trolley, ready to be served, and were only briefly out of sight while the table was cleared and there was no other person present anywhere near them, sir, apart from when Miss Demmie, Lizabeth and Greta walked past the trolley to the restroom."

"And the housemaids were not on duty?" Asked Grant. "They were not, Master Grant." "That will be all for now, thank you, Bradinham." He turned and left. "Well, that was not much help and a complete waste of time. Someone is covering up for someone else, that is obvious to me. All I can say is maybe the informing of the police and their involvement will shed more light on it and find a proper solution. No offense meant, Father." Said Grant.

Lord Mandaten smiled. "And none taken on this occasion. Grant, for once in your life, you seem to care and as for what you said, not much help, well, maybe, just maybe." "It is now nine-forty, I expect that the post-mortem is well underway and once that is done and they have the results, they will inform the police who will deal with the case. Then we will get a visit from them. Until then, I guess that we just wait." "Thought that it was the police forensic lab doing it." Said Sammie. "Just so." Lord Mandaten replied. "Now we wait and twiddle our thumbs then father?" Lizabeth asked. "Just so, Lizabeth, just so." "We have not questioned the two footmen Father," "Bradinham has answered for them Grant he was watching them all the time". "Okay, guess that will have to do." He replied. Demmie walked calmly over to where Grant stood and placed her arm around him giving a gentle affectionate squeeze. "You could be right, Lizabeth, but we will be by your side, Grant, while we just wait and twiddle our thumbs. It must be awful for you but one thing you must remember, I am, I mean, we are here for you. You will have my – our full love and support, you know that." "I know that I have your love for all time and that is appreciated, now let us get off the subject. I fancy a walk in the gardens, who wants to come with me?" "Might as well all go, at least it will kill a little time, oops, sorry Grant, bad word to use, should have said use up a little time." Said Kevin. "Look all of you, what has happened to my Bonnie is tragic and I did not want anything like that to happen to her but, well, it happened and cannot be undone so I do not want you walking around on eggshells picking and choosing every word that you speak. I can handle it and although it may be difficult at times, we must carry on as normal. That is what Bonnie would have wanted and that is what I want. We can do nothing for the dead and life is for living so let us get on with living. We can do nothing for the dead except remember them but the living, now, that is different altogether, we can give and receive love and look after the ones that we love." Demmie glanced at him with affection when he mentioned the word love, she was dismayed because he was looking away from her. "But your love has just sadly passed away Grant." "Time, Lizabeth, time and I will have and declare my new love to you all and that again is what Bonnie would want for me." Demmi looked at him with affection in her eyes, to her dismay, he did not return the look. "I am much too young to be alone, therefore, after a suitable grieving period, I will declare my love for another and as for now, we will carry on as normal." This time he did glance at her and she assumed that the comment to declare his new love was meant for her, which brought a smile to her face which Greta noticed. Seeing the look raised her suspicions about an affair.

"You all heard the man." Said Kevin. "Now who is up for that walk?" "A change of footwear and we will be away." They all disappeared and quickly returned, then they set out to walk around the gardens. Before he left, Chad approached his father who would not be making the walk due to his health. "A quiet word, Father?" He asked. "Speak freely, Son." "What you said about the one little thing that you would keep to yourself, well, I think there may have been more than one." Said Chad. "I also picked up on more things, just small things, in the spoken word and in a glance, one was by your wife, the other by Grant, but I will still keep them to myself just for now until we know more about what happened and you must also, agreed?" "Agreed, Father." Just then, a voice called from the open door that led into the garden.

"Come on, Chad, we are waiting for you." "Sorry, Greta, just wanted a quiet word with Father but I can say nothing more than that just for now." "Well, whatever it was is between you two, now are we off for that walk?" "A fine morning, Kevin now that the mist has cleared, so let's go." The walk was slow with a little idle chat taking place as they studied the fine array of late summer and early autumn flowers and shrubs that adorned the garden. From the flower and shrub beds, they made their way to the herb garden and every step of the way was filled with the fine variety of the many different aromas.

"Bonnie loved the aromatic smell of the herbs but –" There was a tear in Greta's eye. "She will never smell them again, she –" At that point, tears ran down her face. Chad placed a comforting arm around her shoulder and passed her his clean handkerchief. "It is sad, Greta, and easy to say but try not to distress yourself, we all have some wonderful memories of her and that will keep her alive in our hearts." Back at the stable cottage, Herbert and his two sons had finished their breakfast. "Only eight-fifty but had better get back to the stable just in case Master Malcolm gets back sooner than expected."

"Well, I am away as I have got to get the Heath Meadow ploughed today as I told Jacob that I would do it for him." Said Jeremaih as he left the table. "Catch you later, Jeremiah, as we look after all the animals, not just the horses and stables, I am off to the cattle shed. As you know, we have two sick cows,

Dandelion and Buttercup, and the vet will be here soon. He said eleven a.m. so I want to check on them before then." Good thinking Jason", Jeremiah replied. "On your way then, Jason, I can do what needs to be done in the stables and need to be there for Malcolms return, so see you at … Well, my sons, whenever." Said Herbert."Whenever Pops." Jeremiah turned and hurried away. Herbert watched his sons until they were both out of sight.

"Good lads, the pair of you. Now then, as for you, Malcolm, I guess that I will wait for your return." He had other jobs to be carried out at the stables so made his way quickly there and was very surprised when an agitated Thundist greeted him. He was unusually edgy and acted very nervous. Herbert also noticed that the reins appeared to be broken and hung loosely down. He was also aware that one side was longer than the other.

"Whoa there, Thundist, calm down boy, steady now, you know me. Steady big fellow, easy, now, easy." Slowly but surely the horse reacted to his calming voice and after a few minutes, his wild eyes had become clear and he became settled. "Now then Thundist my friend what has put the frighteners into you, my boy? Is it that beast, Malcolm, did you get your ownback on him and throw him off, I would not blame you if you had? Come to it, you were looking wild-eyed before you left but you should have calmed. Now something else has really spooked you. Best get you settled in your stall and give you a good rub down, just look how you are sweating. That Malcolm must have ridden you ridiculously hard just for the sake of it, he has got absolutely no idea how to treat you. Champion rider he may be but … No good going on about it. Steady boy, come on now and I will get you cooled." While he was caring for the big black stallion, he continued to speak softly to him and as he rubbed him down, the horse became reassured and after a time, became completely calm. Almost an hour had passed before he was satisfied with the condition of the big, black stallion who now had a glossy shinning coat. "Saddle will need a good clean but the rein, now, that is strange. Thought it had broken but now that I look closer at it, not so sure. Best I hang on to that, might be of interest, just in case. Right, that is you settled, big fellow. That's my boy, you tuck into your hay while I go and have words with that Malcolm. Even if it costs me my job, he will get a large piece of my mind leaving you like that. He has absolutely no idea how you should be treated and cared for, the lazy, uncaring so and so. Well, you are calm and settled now, it is me who is all stirred up so here I go to the Manor to give him a piece of my mind, must stop all this talking to myself." Thundist whinnied as though he understood Herbert's words. He was fired up and ready, then, with a final pat on the big stallion's neck, he stormed out of the stable ready, to tear Malcolm of a strip. He forgot all about protocol as he was fuming and wanted to see Malcolm face to face before he had a chance to calm down and would then regret not saying all that needed to be said. He had almost run to the Manor and entered by the side staff door and without waiting, he had stormed straight through into the hallway and marched into the lounge, only to be greeted by Lady Mandaten. "My goodness, Herbert, whatever is the meaning of this intrusion? You look absolutely furious, now, tell me at once my good man what perplexis you so." Asked Lady Mandaten.

"I must apologise for the intrusion, my Lady, and realise that it is not my place or protocol and that I should not be in here especially not in the lounge. But it is with the utmost urgency that I must speak with Master Malcolm. I thought that he might be in here but as I can see, apparently not. Again, I beg your forgiveness for my unusual intrusion but if you had seen the state that he has just left Thundist in, you too would be furious and so would his Lordship. I have just spent the past hour or more calming and tending to him. He was in a right old state, I can honestly say that, in all my years with you, I have never seen him like that. I beg your indulgence, my Lady, and even if it costs me my position, I would like to give Master Malcolm a right good telling off and a piece of my mind. I am absolutely fuming and although it may be out of order and not my place to tell him off, or within the bounds of correctness, but it needs to be done and quickly." Herbert said in haste. "And it shall be, Herbert, you can be assured of that the moment that he gets back." Said Lady Mandaten. "But it is strange that you say he is not back, even though the horse is. I have no wish to alarm you, my Lady, and that is why I thought he had returned to the Manor." "That then raises the major question, Herbert, if Thundist is in the stable and Malcolm is not here, then where is he?" With a worried frown, Lady Mandaten thought carefully for a moment then, pulled the bell cord. The clock ticked slowly, tick-tock and appeared to be extremely loud while they waited, and a few moments elapsed before the old butler walked in. "You rang for me, my Lady?" "Yes, Bradinham, has Master Malcolm returned from his ride yet?" She asked. "I have not seen him personally, as I have been otherwise engaged, but I will go and enquire if any other member of the staff has and then I shall return to you immediately." He turned and left the room. "Shall I wait here, my Lady, or return to the stables?" Asked Herbert.

"Wait here, Herbert, if the stallion is back and he is not then –"

"Let us not think that thought until we know for certain, my Lady, I am sure there will be some simple explanation it is Malcolm we are talking about."

"Probably, and the instant that he walks through that door, you have my full permission to rant at him." Said Lady Mandaten. "And that goes for me also, Herbert." Said Lord Mandaten. "Ah, you are awake, my dear, you heard Herbert then?" "I heard most of it and be assured that your position is quite safe, Malcolm needs a darn good talking to, leaving an animal in a state of stress. You do what you have to my good man and to hell with protocol." Said Lord Mandaten then he coughed lightly. "So you rip right into him, Herbert, rip into him just as much and as hard as you like. You have my full permission and after you have finished with him, then he will get a tongue lashing from me and on this occasion, Herbert, to hell with protocol,what do you say my dear?" "Absolutelly agreed," replied Lady Mandaten."As you say, my Lord, my Lady it shall be done". Herbert nodded. Fifteen minutes had passed before Bradinham returned. "I am sorry it took so long but I actioned a search of the whole Manor and Master Malcolm is nowhere to be found on the premises. Not one member of staff has seen him since last evening. I just do not know where else to look or where he can be." "Thank you, Bradinham." Said Lord Mandaten. "My Lord, my Lady, shall I show Herbert out?" "No, thank you, he has some work to do." The old butler turned and left. "He took Thundist out at five-fifty a.m. and it is now a minute to noon, we need to start looking, my Lord."

"That is a long time and it is over six hours now, my dear, I do fear the worst scenario." Lady Mandaten said concerned. "What worst scenario, Mother? What is wrong and what is Herbert doing here in the lounge? He should not be and looking for what?" "Not for you to question, Lizabeth, but as for the worst, it is your brother, Malcolm, he appears to be missing. His horse has returned to the stable and Herbert has spent more than an hour caring for him as he was in a state and wanted him settled before tearing a strip, with our full permission, off your brother. Now that is where there is the problem and the worst scenario is that no one has seen him." Explained Lord Mandaten. "What is that, Father? Malcolm is missing but the horse is back in the stable?" Said a frightened Greta. "It would appear so, my dear, but let us not panic or think the worst just yet. Herbert, I will leave it to you, get all the farm workers and your boys from whatever they are doing and go find my son." Said Lord Mandaten. "It shall be done, my Lord, with all haste."

Herbert was almost in a run when he left the lounge and was in a run down the hall. Once outside, he got messages to everyone telling them to drop everything that they were doing and meet him at the stables post haste. He did not tell them why, only that there was a real emergency and they were all required to play their part. The call had gone out and tractors, quad bikes, and a Land Rover turned up at the stables and all had arrived just fifteen minutes after the first call went out.

"What's the emergency then, Herbert, and why are all these horses saddled? What emergency could need all of us?" enquired Jacob the arable farm manager. "All of you listen it is

Master Malcolm he is missing. He went out early this morning, it is now almost past one p.m. and he has not been seen, so we all need to start a search for him. Jacob, you and your sons ride from here along the stream and the low meadow, making your way up to Rudslip, then the old Manor ruins, and the Devil's Dyke. We will take the other route around the lake, across the open meadow, and through the woods. Then we will all meet up at the Dyke and let's hope that one of us finds him quickly and he is still alive." Instructed Herbert. "Not to speak out of turn but he wouldn't be missed." Said one of Jacob's sons. "Hush up with that kind of talk, Freddie, our job is to find him as quickly as possible. Now mount up, spread out, and let's ride." The search had to be meticulous as every part of the route had to be inspected. There were many places where a person could fall from a horse and be hidden from view so the horses that they rode walked slowly forward and the search had begun. With Jacob and his sons out of earshot, Herbert turned to Jeremiah. "It pains me to say this, Son, I have a very bad feeling about this, I think it best to bring a taupe with us just in case we find what we would rather not."

"It is two fifteen already, Mother, surely they should have found him by now?" Whailed Greta. "I know it is hard for you, my dear, they will soon be back and his period of being missing will be explained." Lady Mandaten said calmly. "I know that the waiting is much harder for you than for us, Greta, as Mother just said, I am sure that they will soon return and then all the worrying will have been for nothing. You see, he will walk in with a smile on his face and some silly explanation." Demmie said brightly.

"I am not so sure, Demmie, he went at almost six a.m. and that is eight and a quarter hours ago. I cannot help but fear the worst especially where he was going to ride." "Courage, Greta, whatever has happened to him has happened, it may have struck him just as suddenly and unexpectedly as it did my Bonnie and, well, unexplainable things do happen." Grant said with a smile. "I know, Grant, forgive me, it was a selfish thought, especially after your sudden loss." Greta spoke quietly. "Hush now, Greta, no one blames you for worrying. It is extremely sad how Grant's Bonnie died but this is a bit different." Said Demmie.

"How is it different, Demmie?"

"Bonnie was in here and Malcolm is out there, but not the time to ask questions or have explanations, Kevin." Answered Sammie bluntly. "We will just wait then, wait until they bring us some news. From my reasoning they have been searching for over two hours so who knows what Malcolm's route was?" "We all did Lizabeth". Said Sammie. "He was going around the lake, through the woods, and past the old Manor ruins, then the Devil's Dyke and back via Rudslip and the stream." Said Grant bowldly. "That is a good long ride, Greta, and takes all of three or four hours unless you punish your mount and run it to an inch of its life." Said Lizabeth. "Herbert said that Thundist was in a bad state and –." Said Sammie. "Oh! Please, no more talk, I cannot stand it." Demmie placed a comforting arm around her shoulder, then with a glance toward Grant she whispered. "It will be alright, Greta, everything is in hand and will turn out just fine, you see it will all work out for the best, now, sip some brandy, it may help to calm you."

Three hours had already passed since the search began and back at the Manor, there was a great deal of uneasiness, and even though not said aloud, they were all thinking the worst scenario. "Three hours and still no sign of the search party or of Malcolm."

"Patience, my dear Greta, patience." Said Lord Mandaten calmly.

Out on the search, a radio crackled to life and they were in contact with each other. "Herbert, you hearing me?" "Go ahead, Jacob." "We have made a slow advance, as you requested, and searched thoroughly but so far we have seen nothing. We are now passing over Rudslip and still not a sign of him but there are plenty signs of a frightened horse. Looks like he was really scared from the deep impressions." "Got that, we are now through the woods and can see the old Manor ruins, we are about to cross the driveway and ride the old Manor road, nothing unusual so far just normal hoof prints this way. I guess he got to here without incident and whatever happened did so past the old Manor."

"That would be somewhere near the dreaded and haunted Devil's Dyke."

"Just what we are all thinking, be there in about fifteen minutes Jacob."

"About twenty for us Herbert, see you there, out." On they rode and the closer that Herbert and his sons got to the Dyke, the larger the hump grew in the track ahead of them, the hump grew larger the closer they came to it and they all had their eye fixed on the same point. "My God, I think that is him, ride, boys, ride!" With a gentle tap, the horses galloped forward, coming to a sliding halt when they reached the spot where the body lay. They looked down on the lifeless form and could see a dark patch on the ground where his head rested. They all recognised it as blood. "It's him alright and I think he is dead. Stay back, boys, we do not want to disturb the area more than necessary." "Had we best make a call for an ambulance pops?" "That we should, Jacob, then get to the main gate and show them the way here on the old road. I think it would be for the best if we call the police as well. Now go and we will stay here with Master Malcolm. Not that there is anything we can do for him." Said Herbert. The call was quickly made and with the ambulance and police on their way, Jason waved and rode away to open and wait by the main gates for the arrival of the police and medical assistance.

Herbert approached the body carefully, taking great care not to make a disturbance of the area. He stood and gazed down at the still form, shaking his head and took a deep breath, held it for a few seconds, then slowly exhaled. He knew instantly that it was Malcolm and that he was dead. Jacob and his sons had arrived now and with instructions, they kept their distance but observed exactly what was going on. "Pass the taupe, Jeremiah, and let me get him covered." Herbert said. "How do you think it happened, pops?" "From what I see and from the first impression, the horse must have thrown him off, maybe back there, he was dragged and must have hit his head on that bloodied piece of old masonry." "Looks like a piece of the old Manor ruins but ..." He paused while he studied the terrain. "If it is from the ruin, it fell a mighty long way pops." Observed Jeremiah. "Could have bounced, I suppose, and if you study those tracks, it looks like he did fall back there and was dragged. Hmm, It looks very strange to me Jeremiah." Jeremiah looked harder at the tracks, then gave his thought. "You could be right, pops, very strange. There is an indentation here and a dark stain that could be blood then the drag marks originate from it. I am no detective but when you know horses, as we do, the tracks just do not look right. Just a guess is that he fell off here, got dragged when Thundist bolted and cracked his head open on the piece of fallen masonry. At least, that is how it looks but it does not add up pops." "Looks that way, Son, you can tell a lot from the tracks, and, as you said, when you know horses, as we do, it does not add up. but it looks that way. He must have tried to keep a tight hold on the reins because it looked like they had broken but I am not so sure. He has still got a piece in his hand, a tragic accident by all accounts but, then again, I am not an expert. Nothing more we can do for him so now we will wait for the ambulance and the police. A good detective may have another theory as to what happened." "Wonder if the ghostly Lady Mary had a hand in it?" "Don't even think on those lines, Jerimiah. Jacob, my friend, it is a nasty job that I now ask of you but will you return to the Manor and break the bad news to the family? Just say that we have found Master Malcolm and are waiting for assistance to arrive. Go back the way that you came because we do not want to disturb the scene of this tragic accident any more than is completely necessary. Try to keep clear of the prints you saw." "Will do Herbert, Come on, boys, the family must be beside themselves with worry so the sooner we tell them, the better. Not a nice thing to do but it has to be done." With a wave, they were on their way back to the Manor.

"Now they are gone, Pops, what do you really think happened up here? Accident or something else?" Jeremiah asked. "I can't be sure, Son, but the fall and being dragged seem mighty strange, the hoof prints don't add up and I saw how he handled Thundist before riding off. Plus, Master Malcolm must have had a real tight grip on the reins right up to the time that he struck his head and the reins broke. I have the broken reins at the stable and it appears … Well, I can't be sure so no matter. If only that piece of masonry wasn't there, then he may well have survived the fall, even with being dragged but doesn't matter what we think happened. There is nothing we can do now but wait for the ambulance." Said Herbert.

"Do you think that the police will turn up as well to investigate pops? It may well have been a tragic riding accident, even though we both have our doubts. Do they have to be here to confirm that is what it was?" "Who knows, Son, but at least we have called for them, we will know the answer to that when the ambulance arrives and if they are with them." "Shouldn't be long now, should take about twelve minutes to get here from the station and ten have already gone by. If the police are involved, let us hope that they send a good detective." "I second that thought, Son." Herbert said concerned.

"Well there is one thing, if this Dyke is haunted by the Lady Mary, then she will have company so now they can haunt it together." "Over the years she has had plenty of company with the incidents that have happened in this area. Strange though, until about three, maybe four, years ago, although there were the old stories, she had been very quiet." "Must have been taking a holiday." "Not a thing to joke about, Jeremiah." "Sorry, Pops, you are right, I was just thinking, first poor Miss Bonnie, now Master Malcolm. You know what they say, never a second without a third." "I hope not, Son, two deaths so close together is hard enough to handle so please, not three. That would be unbearable for the family." "His Lordship is on borrowed time, so to speak, so maybe he is to be the third." "At least his passing is expected so although it will be a sad day when it does happen, it will be a little bit more bearable for the family." "True enough, Pops, now I think I can hear the ambulance."

They both listened and sure enough, they could hear the siren as it sped along the open road. "Not long to wait now, Son." "How long will we need to wait once they get here before we can return to the stables pops?"

"I would think that once we have handed Master Malcolm's body over to them and they are on their way back to the hospital, we can go. The family will have been told by now so we can go straight back to the stables. Then, once the horses are settled, go to the Manor so that we can pass on all our condolences."

"Good thought, pops." They could now clearly hear the engine as the ambulance made its way steadily up the old uneven roadway.

"If I am not mistaken, Jeremiah, sounds like two vehicles." "It does, pops, I can see the ambulance, and tucked in just behind it is the police car."

"They will probably have to ask us some questions but that is only to be expected." "We have nothing to hide so no worries about that is there pops."

"None at all and that, Son, is a fact." Jeremiah stood with his stare fixed on the taupe that covered Malcolm and upon his face was a look of anguish.

"Something troubling you, Jeremiah?" "Just Wondering, Pops, could it be happening all over again?" "You mean the strange incidents that have befallen the family for decades?" Herbert asked Jeremiah. "Exactly, Pops, the last incident to befall the family was three or four years ago with Lord Mandaten's only remaining brother's family being wiped out." "I remember that, Son, all too vividly and that was closed as a tragic motoring accident, although there was some doubt. Lord Mandaten suspected foul play but that was all pushed aside by that police sergeant, what was his name?" "Can't think of it just now but it will come to me, Pops." "Yes, Lord Mandaten did not like him as he put his suspicion down to his sadness, stress, and depreciation after the closure of what they called a tragic accident." "Can you remember who investigated it pops?" "Cannot call it to mind just now, Son, but it will come to me but right now I can hear the ambulance getting very close." "Well, I, for one, hope it is not reoccurring again as there are so few members of the family left." "As do I, Son. I most certainly hope not, that ordeal with the Lord's brother cut the family up something terrible." "Just wondered as we have just lost Miss Bonnie and now Master Malcolm." "Just coincidence I would think, Bonnie was in the Manor and from what we hear, it was a very tragic thing, all due to her ... Now, what was it they said it was called? Anlaxtive?"

Jeremiah smiled. "You mean anaphylaxis, Pops." "That's it, anaphylaxis. I see no connection with these two deaths, however, I am not a detective. A real detective may look at it differently and we will get one now and will find out if he is good or bad. As I said, Miss Bonnie was in the Manor and, well, Master Malcolm is up here at the Devil's Dyke, there surely cannot be a connection, or can there? I see no connection between them Jeremiah." "Even so, there could be some doubt in a good detective's mind and he may want to investigate both the deaths closer. I don't know about Miss Bonnie but, well, I am very suspicious about Master Malcolm. As we said, the signs just do not look right and if it was not an accident then −" (Jeremiahs eyes widended.) "I hope it's not brushed under the carpet, Pops." "Me too, Son, me too." "Now I wonder who the police have sent to look at this incident pops." "As long as it is someone who will discover the truth, Son, and not just push it under the table as they did with the car incident four years ago." "It sounds to me like you are not at all convinced that this was an accident pops." "I am no detective, Son. You saw the same as I did, the signs just don't look right."

"I am with you on that, Pops. As you say, let us hope for the sake of the family that they have sent someone who is a good detective and who will uncover the truth."

Chapter Three

Cadiston's First Suspicions

Jason was now in plain sight and riding at a steady trot just in front of the ambulance that was following close behind him and clearly visible behind that was a police car.

"Ambulance is almost here, Pops, and looks like we do have the police." "Thought that we might. Well, that's not a problem and to my mind is a good thing, if he or she knows horses they may well see what we can clearly see, but I don't know time will tell Son, the signs just do not fit, I have my doubts and maybe our detective will see what we see son hopefully."

"Likewise pops so let us hope that they have sent a detective that will not just skim over the surface and search out the truth and not just fob it off. The sooner this matter is sorted, the better it will be for the family, especially after the tragic death of Miss Bonnie yesterday." Herbert raised his hand and the ambulance drew to a steady halt, the side door was open and the medic, who was wasting no time, was out of his seat before it had come to a complete stop. "I see that you have covered the body, will you tell me why?" asked the medic. "Thought it was the best thing to do, the dyke flies have already been on him and I would not be a bit surprised if the darned rats from the Dyke have had a go as well they like dead meat." "Not very pleasant for you to find then?" "Not at all but better us than his poor wife." Jason had dismounted and stood beside the ambulance, watching as the police car also came to a halt. Leaving the driver in the car, they watched as two plain close policemen were walking briskly toward them. The first was an older man with a rather stocky build, while the other was a younger man who was smart, good looking, and well-built. The older of the two spoke rather abruptly first. "I am Sergeant Standish and that (pointing,) is training detective Constable Cadiston. Now, what do we have here, and has the area been disturbed a lot since the incident?" "Name is Herbert, Sergeant, me and my son have kept the area as clean, I believe is your expression, as possible so in answer to your question, no, it hasn't." "Good man." Said the Sergeant. "Just one small query for you, a trainee detective, should he be looking or doing anything here?" Asked Herbert. The sergeant smiled, "He is in the final stages of his training and this is to be his first proper case. No need for concern as it will be conducted under my precise supervision. He is young and quite keen to do well but he will be fine, and I will ensure that he arrives at the correct conclusion. Now from what I see here, this is nothing more than a tragic riding accident. Now, enough idle chat as we do not want to be here all day, which I am sure you do not either so we must get on." He turned from Herbert with a wry smile on his face. "Doc, can you wait before you inspect the body? I would like to take a closer look at the scene to assess what might actually has happened here."

"Not a problem Cadiston, as I fear that there is nothing that I can do for the poor fellow anyhow so, please, be my guest." "Well, there you are, Cadiston. Your very own first case so you are in the driving seat. Not a thing for me to do but observe. It is all up to you so take charge and let's see what you can do for real and not in the classroom. Now is your chance, go do your stuff." He sensed sarcasm in the sergeant's voice but as he had a cool head on his shoulder's, he was not about to challenge him and chose to ignore it. "Thank you, and that is what I fully intend to do." His first task was to carefully inspect the scene of the incident. With his notebook in hand, he began his investigation. He noted the first indentation in the ground and the dark stain, he then inspected the drag marks that led from it up to where the body lay. Every single detail was being written meticulously down. When not writing he was taking photographs of the scene gathering all his evidence. With a tape measure, he made notes of every footstep, especially their depth and then the surrounding area. As the minutes turned to an hour, Herbert asked, "Don't want to rush things, Sergeant, but why is he taking so long?"

"Patience, Herbert, I told you he is new to this and this is his very first case in the field, so to speak, and is inexperienced.

He may be just a little bit over-particular with his investigation because, as anyone can see, this was nothing more than a tragic riding accident and that will be what he finally comes up with under my guidence." Said the sergeant. "So, if I understand you correctly, his final decision will depend on you?" Herbert asked. "It most certainly will, I have to let him look as though he is doing the detecting but don't worry, if he takes much longer with his looking then I will step in and hurry him up, alright?" "Ok, Sergeant, we will just wait quietly over there." Herbert took a step back. "Good man."

Returning to stand with his son, he watched, and could see that this young detective was no fool. "I like this young detective but not the sergeant, there is something familiar about him and I feel that I should know him." Said Herbert to his son Jeremiah. "I agree, that sergeant would have taken one look and that would be case closed but not this young detective. He is being very thorough." Cadiston could sense his sergeant's agitation and knew that he wanted a quick closure, just as he had on the many other cases that he had attended with him. That was not going to be his way and even at this early stage, he had noted many discrepancies. It may be his very own first case to solve but he was determined not to rush and risk missing that vital clue if he was going to expose what had taken place on this day and not as it had been made to look. His mind was working overtime and the question entered his thoughts as he investigated: Was this a clumsy attempt to cover murder or was it really an accident? His thought and suspicion was murder. He knew that he had to look at every possible scenario and from his initial inspection of the incident site and the position of the body, his suspicions were immediately aroused. He looked very carefully at every aspect three times before he finished with his examination of the terrain. Thereafter he turned his attention to the body of the deceased. He noted where he had first fallen and the heavy blood stain on the ground. He was suspicious about how the body had been dragged and the small piece of rein that was grasped firmly in his hand.

"Doc, I would like that piece of the rein when you can remove it." Said Cadiston. "I will make sure that you get it." "Thanks, Doc." He also noted the angle of the blow to his head, which he compared to the piece of fallen masonry. He was thinking hard, shaking his head, and had a puzzled look on his face while he stood for a moment by the body. He then re-measured the spread of the blood stain that had covered the ground where the first indentation was, which signified that was where he had fallen and bled the heaviest. Then he moved to where the body lay and noted that the bleed was not as heavy. Again, he knelt beside the body for several minutes with his thoughts before he spoke a single word. Nothing was going to be missed and everything had been meticulously documented. Now on his feet, he still pondered over his evidence, tapping his pen on his notebook as he thought before he spoke. He had noticed that the hoof prints appeared strange for such an incident and this was noted and documented with pen and photograph. "The body is yours to examine, Doc, don't forget the piece of rein. Otherwise, I have all that I need." He then turned to his sergeant. "It all looks a bit strange to me, Serge." "Strange, you say, clear cut to me so just what do you mean by strange?" "Well, if you firstly look at the position of the body and if you look at the drag marks and the blood stains, you will note that there are more there ..." He pointed to the indentation which one could clearly see was the site of his fall. "than where the body is lying now and that tells me that his head was struck there and not where he is laying. I will take a sample from them both for analysis." "Samples, there is no need for that, this is just as I had expected, your inexperience is causing a problem. I told the superintendent it was far too soon to put you in the field. Anyone with an ounce of sense would see that this is just a tragic riding accident and dragging it out will only cause additional grief to the family." He said angrily.

"Not so, Sergeant, the first instinct is to think this is an accident but when you look deeper into the evidence that presents itself here, there are sufficient discrepancies to demolish that theory. I can see that this is not just a simple case, Sergeant, so, like it or not, I have my suspicions that it is not an accident. I will now have a word with the two men that found him." Cadiston said. "Wasting time, that is what you are doing. This case should already be closed but the Super said this is to be your case so do what you think is necessary. You will soon learn not to read too much into an incident such as this but go ahead and do as you think fit. But be quick about it as we have already spent far too much time on this simple case." Said the sergeant.

"I think not serge and completely disagree with you this case is far from simple". He walked purposely over to where the men stood and could determine by their facial expressions and body language that they were both very distraught.

"I am Detective Constable Cadiston and you are?" He asked.

"Herbert the livestock manager, Detective, and this is my son, Jeremiah."

"Any more children, Herbert?" Asked Cadiston. "A son, Jason." He pointed. "That is him over there near the ambulance. My wife, Flora, is the head cook at the Manor." "Thank you for that. Now, tell me what you can about this incident." "I had Thundist saddled, ready for Master Malcolm by quarter to six and that is when he arrived at the stables. I tried to advise him not to ride as the horse doesn't like the fog and there was still quite a bit about. He was also very agitated, not just by the fog but by something else. It was as though someone had deliberately upset him. Well, that is my thought, and he just would not settle. Anyhow, he would not listen to me and rode off. I watched him until he had disappeared into the fog. Then, as I was about to get on with my work, his wife turned up, maybe only two or three minutes after he had gone." Hebert explained. "And her name is?" "Greta. Anyhow, I told her that he had just left and as we talked, Chadrick turned up." He continued. "And who is he?" Asked Cadiston. "Lord and Lady Mandaten's adopted son."

"Adopted son? Now, that is interesting, please, carry on." "Well, we chatteed ... Ah, something I forgot, Jeremiah had arrived at the stables just before Greta. Well, we all chatted, then went to see the new foal. By then it was almost eight a.m. so

Chadrick and Greta rushed off and we made our way home for breakfast. On the way there, Jason returned. He had been moving the sheep flock from Rudslip to the river meadow – better grazing there."

"Then you went home and had your breakfast. So when did you know that Master Malcolm was not coming back?" Asked Cadiston.

"That was not until around eleven maybe eleven-thirty. I do not keep track of time unless there is a real need." "Understandable, please continue."Said Cadiston. "Well, I went back to the stables at around nine and Thundist was already there." "Thundist is the horse that he rode?" "That is so, now where was I? Ah yes, now, I was mighty angry because of the state that the horse was in and it took quite a while to calm him and clean him up. Thinking that Master Malcolm had returned and just left him there in that state it made my blood boil and my anger towards him rose. I decided there and then that after Thundist was calmed, cleaned, fed, and back in his stall, I would give that Malcolm a piece of my mind and to hell with the consequences. I stormed off up to the Manor to give him a piece of my mind. I don't mind admitting that I was furious and was very fired up. I was ready to take him on, completely prepared to meet him head-on with all guns blazing, err, that is just an expression." "Don't worry, Herbert, I do know that. Now, continue, and I must say at this point you are giving a very detailed and precise account of everything and it is all written down. That will be a great help in reaching my conclusion. Now, continue from where you stormed into the Manor." "Well, I forgot all about protocol and went straight into the lounge and found Lady Mandaten there. After I had explained everything and there was no sign of Master Malcolm, a search was started. I called everyone in, including all those on the farm, and we searched his route and ended up here, at the reputedly haunted Devil's Dyke, and that is all I can tell you. We found him lying there and called for the ambulance then waited with him while Jacob and his sons went to inform the family back at the Manor that we had found him." Herberts voice trailed off.

"Very concise, Herbert, and is it haunted?" Cadiston wanted to know. "Who knows but over the years there have been several unexplained incidents up here. But it had been very quiet until it started up again about three or four years ago. The last incident was here three months ago when a farm hand was found drowned in the Dyke."

"And what was the verdict on that?" Cadiston asked. "Accidental death." Said Herbert. "Can you remember his name?" "Santos, Pedro Santos, a migrant worker and a very good one. Talking of poor Pedro has just jogged my memory. Now, if I remember it correctly, I believe that your Sergeant Standish over there investigated it. And Jeremiah, you asked who investigated Lord Mandaten's brother's family deaths, well, it has come back to me and he is over there, Sergeant Standish. Did not like him then and do not like him now." Grumbled Herbert. "Now that is an interesting fact and very helpful as I can check his file – just to verify what the verdict was on both cases." "Tragic accidents he recorded." Said Herbert. "Thank you for that, Herbert. Now then, anything to add, Jeremiah?" "Nope, before breakfast, I had finished the early milking and was putting the herd back out to the west meadow. Then, after breakfast, as promised, I went to plough the heath meadow as I told Jacob that I would do that one for him. I was there until Father called me back." Answered Jeremiah. "One more thing, do you know which way Malcolm would have ridden?" "From the stables, he headed toward the lake and once around that, he would cross an open piece of land past where they are preparing for the show. Then through the woods, up past the old Manor ruins and Devil's Dyke, then across Rudslip and back along the stream. Why do you need to know what his route was? I can see no importance in knowing that piece of information." "Thank you, very good evidence Herbert, now, that is for me to know. I will have a word with Jason now." He walked calmly toward the ambulance, glancing at the medics that were examining Malcolm's body. He also made a mental note of Jason's body language. He had written down every detail that had been said in his own fashion and knew that he would read it all again as his investigation into the untimely death of Malcolm continued. This was his first case and he wanted to get it right but he had noticed Standish's impatience and how he wanted to stop him from collecting what he deemed vital evidence. He felt as though Standish was trying to silence him and stop him from investigating properly but he wanted to ensure that he reached the correct conclusion for the family, and for himself, and not just settle for Standish's suggestions. "Hello, Jason." "Detective." Jason nodded. "Please, call me Cadiston, everyone else does." "Ok, Cadiston, how can I help?" "Just tell me what you know of the incident and include your movements." "When I got up, which would have been around four a.m., I went straight out with my two sheep dogs to move the flock from Rudslip to the stream meadow. Took around four hours to round them all up and drive them on, which went very smoothly. I got back and met Jeremiah with Father, and we all went home and had breakfast. That was around eight-thirty. After that, Jeremiah went to plough the heath meadow, Father returned to the stables to wait for Malcolm, and I went to the cowshed. We have two sick milk cows and the vet was coming at eleven. Jeremiah had checked on them earlier this morning and I wanted to check them out again and have everything ready for the vet when he arrived." "Vets name please, Jason?" Cadiston wanted to know. "John Harring. And while he was there seeing to the cows, I got a call from Father to drop everything and get to the stables as everyone was needed. So, I left the vet with the cows and that is what I did. We started the search and the rest you know, we found him."

"You moved the flock from Rudslip. Now, Malcolm would have ridden across that meadow on his return if he had not fallen. He set out at around five-fifty so how long would it have been before he reached there?" "If he rode hard and straight on, without taking a stop, then he would have got there in about two-and-a-half, maybe three, hours." "So that would put him at Devil's Dyke in about two hours, correct me if I am wrong." "Sounds about right." Said Jason. "Hmm, and you would have been on Rudslip." "Hang on there, what are you trying to do?"

Jason asked defensively. "Just get to the truth and the facts."
"Well, I had nothing to do with his demise – although there are
plenty who hated him."

"Hated him enough to kill?" Asked Cadiston. "Hang on there,
I wouldn't go as far as to say that. I know that I sure as hell didn't
kill him. Anyhow, it must have been a terrible riding accident.
No one could get here and back to the Manor, stables, our cottage, or the farmhouse in such a short time not unless they were
a trained distance runner. If you are going where I think you are
going with this investigation, it had to be planned well ahead.
Maybe they had a cycle close by. Timing is all wrong for me as I
was back at the stable cottage and having breakfast by eight-thirty. That's all I know so may not be of much help to you." "You
would be surprised just what helps in a case, even the smallest
word or detail is important. Well, thank you, Jason, you can join
your brother and father now." Jason sighed with relief and leading his horse walked steadily back to his waiting kin. "What did
he ask you, son? You seemed to get a bit perturbed?" "I did but
it is alright, he was just getting the timing right – but had me
going for a moment." Said Jason.

"Thank you, gentlemen, you can all get back to the Manor
and your duties. You have all been very helpful and if you think of
anything else that may be relevant, do not hesitate to call me. Just
ask for Cadiston and they will know where to find me. Thanks
again, gents. Herbert, one more thing before you leave, there is
a piece of rein in Mister Mandaten's hand. What I need to know
is do you have the rest of it from the horse in question? Have
you still got it?" "That I have and detective, thought it strange
that it should have broken or maybe it did not … The break is
far too clean so maybe it was cut. But you will know better on
that score, with your forensics, lab, and the like. Would you like
it as evidence?" "Maybe as evidence, Herbert, but, yes, I would
like to have it so hang onto it and it will be picked up before we
leave the Manor. Now this area will be cordoned off to secure it
for further investigation and that means it will be out of bounds
for quite a while." "Understood."was the only word that Herbert

said. They all mounted up and hesitated as they watched the crew place the body of Malcolm into a body bag, then onto a stretcher, before it went into the ambulance. "What about the taupe, Pops?" Asked Jeremiah.

"Leave it, Son, we will dump it as we don't want a reminder of what it was used for." "Pick it up later then, when the police have completed their investigation and the area is cleared." Said Cadiston. Herbert just nodded. The ambulance doors were closed and with the crew on board, it prepared to leave. With nothing more for them to do, they rode slowly back to the stables.

"Doc, a moment?" "Yes, what is it now, Cadiston?" "Can you give an approximate time of death?" "Flies had been on the body and rats had had a chew, difficult, but I would say between six and eight a.m. The post-mortem will give a more defining time. Oh, nearly forgot, here is the rein you wanted."

"Thanks." Cadiston stood looking over the incident site while the doctor walked over to where Standish stood, observing his every move. "What do you think then, Doc?" Asked Standish. "From my initial examination, he cracked his skull with force on that piece of masonry, most definitely rendering him unconscious, and then he just bled to death but the post-mortem that Charles will carry out will give the chance to examine the body much more thoroughly. In my opinion, this is a tragic riding accident but then I am not a detective." "Thanks, Doc, my opinion as well but he is still completing his training and this is his first case so being new to the job, maybe he is a little bit too enthusiastic. He is complicating things as he thinks something is wrong and this may be more than an accident. I will just play along with him for the time being but we both know the answer, now don't we?" They both cast him a sly glance and smiled. He was totally aware of their attitude toward him and he did not care. This was his first case and his suspicions had been raised, making him determined that he would see his investigation through to the right conclusion, irrespective of what Standish thought or said. "What now then, young Cadiston, gathered all your evidence?" "Maybe Serge, but I think that we should keep this area closed off and get the forensics team up here to thoroughly check it over." Standish shook his head. "Not at all necessary, you have gathered all the relevant information and it would be a total waste of time and resources for the forensics. They have enough to do. Clear cut case, in my book, nothing more than a tragic riding accident."

"I am not so sure about that, there are some things that just do not fit right for it to be just a simple, tragic riding accident. The horse tracks, the blood stains the indentaion the position of the piece of masonary, just for starters. I feel very strongly that a full investigation will be needed. There are the two clearly visible blood stains and the si —"

"Hush up now, none of that is needed. You will only lead the family down the wrong path. This is clearly a clean case of a tragic and unfortunate riding accident and nothing more."

"I am sorry but on the other hand I am not sorry and, as this is my case, I totally disagree. If you looked at the evidence as I have done, then you would see that all the evidence that presents itself points to much more than just a simple tragic riding accident. Now, maybe a visit to the family. They should be told officially of what is going on and that there will be a post-mortem on Malcolm's body and an ongoing investigation." Cadiston said firmly. "Post-mortem will show you that I am right, Cadiston, and you are wrong and are reading too much into the incident. You should be guided by me back to the car now and the Manor it is." The car was moved to allow the ambulance to turn around and then they followed it down the old roadway until they reached the gates. The ambulance went one way to return to the forensics mortuary, while they turned the other way and drove slowly toward the Manor to inform the family officially. "I know that it is just a tragic riding accident. That is very clear to see from my many years of experience but tell me Cadiston, what are your findings?" Sergeant Standish had a stifled grin on his face. "Difficult one, Serge, and not a bit as straightforward as you think. I have looked very closely at the scene and from what I have observed, most things do not fall into place. As I have already said the hoof prints blood stains and other aspects just do not fit into it being a simple riding accident. I cannot help feeling that we are missing something. There are quite a few discrepancies in the way things are, those small footprints, for example. I would like to have a plaster cast made of them and get the forensics up here."

"Nonsense lad, no need for all that palaver, as I already said, clear cut, a tragic riding accident. This is a straightforward case, Cadiston, a tragic riding accident and nothing more. I thought that you would see it quite clearly as anyone with an ounce of knowledge would see that was the case. Oh! I am not saying that you have none but to be fair, I am the one with the experience and I do think that you are going a bit over the top with this. I understand that this is your first case under my supervision and guess that it is because of this that you are overthinking it but never mind, I will straighten it out in my end report. Now we have arrived at the Manor and it will be best for the family if you let me do all the talking. The family will be upset enough at the sad loss of a son and brother. I do not want to add to their grief with you asking any silly or awkward questions and that being the case, I will do all the talking and you will remain silent and listen got it?" "Got it, Serge." The door chime played its tune and the door opened. "How can I help you, sir?" "And you are?" Asked the sergeant. "Alfred, I am a footman, and you are?" "I will ask the questions, I am Detective Sergeant Standish, this is trainee Detective Constable Cadiston, we would like a word with the family." "Who is it at the door, Alfred?" Called Bradinham. "It is the police, Mister Bradinham, they would like to speak to the family." "Very well, show them into the long room while I inform the family." "This way, if you please gentlemen." They followed Alfred down a corridor and into the designated room. "Please be seated while you wait for the family to arrive, it may take a little while as they may not all be together so may I fetch you some tea or coffee?" Asked Alfred. "Coffee would be much appreciated, thank you." He quickly disappeared but his footsteps could be clearly heard as he walked along the hallway to reach the kitchen at the far end. "Lovely room this,

Cadiston, magnificent old house as well." Said the Sergeant. "This is a Manor, Serge, get it right. This is a Manor and it has been in the Mandaten family since the Norman conquest in 1066. The original old Manor, that is where we have just been, burnt down in, let me think, around 1648 and by all accounts, if we had been around in those times, then we would be looking for an arsonist and murderer as two members of the Mandaten family died in the fire and the Lady Mary was drowned in the Dyke. The building work had already started on this magnificent Manor that we now have the pleasure to be standing in and has been added to over the years. During the English Civil War in 1642 to 1651, the family members were royalists but when they found that the Parliamentary Forces or the roundheads, as they were better known, were winning, the day Lord Francis Louis Lowell Mandaten cleverly changed sides, they became inform-ers on other royalist families – thereby saving the family and all its wealth." Cadiston said. "I don't know where you got all that information or where it originated from and we are not here for a history lesson on the family, thank you, Cadiston." The ser-geant said annoyed. "School history lessons and research of the area in which I work. Just pays to know about the family that is being investigated." Answered Cadiston. "No family investiga-tion is needed, a tragic accident is all it was so get that into your head. Now, remember keep quiet. I will do all the talking and you will listen, got it?" "Got it, Serge, but there may be some-thing that I would like to know as it is my case." "Shut up now, I think I hear them coming." Said the sergeant. "Not them, Serge, only one person's footsteps, and my guess would be that our coffee is about to arrive." He was correct in his assumption and sure enough, the door opened and in walked Alfred, carry-ing a tray with two cups and a pot of coffee.

"There you are, gentlemen, the family have been informed and will be with you presently."

"Thank you for that, Alfred, just before you go, a quick ques-tion." Said Cadiston. "Yes, sir." "Where were you at approxi-mately seven to eight a.m. this morning?" "At that time, sir, I would be preparing the breakfast room with Jonas, is there anything else?" Standish sent Cadiston a stern look.

"No, nothing for the moment, thank you, maybe later." Before Cadiston had poured his coffee, Alfred had left the room, leaving him standing silent observing his footsteps as they slowly faded away. "I told you, I will do the talking and you will listen." Standish said angrily. "True, but to ask a simple question is not out of place, now is it, Serge?" He paused for a moment and listened. "Now, that is the family coming. At a guess, I would say twelve, one has to be wheeled and I would say that is the Master of the Manor, Lord Mandaten, himself." Cadiston observed. "Well, remember my words, I will do the talking and you will listen." The sergeant repeated. Cadiston just shrugged his shoulders. They stood silent as the family entered and when they were all seated, Standish began. "I am Detective Sergeant Standish and that is training Detective Constable Cadiston." "My memory may be failing but I feel that I should know who you are, Sergeant Standish, not young Cadiston but not a problem, it will come to me. Now, what brings you here?" Asked Lord Mandaten. "A tragic event and a very sad day for you, sir. In fact, for all the family, my Lord, but firstly, allow me to say that you all have our condolences and deepest sympathy over the sad loss of Master Malcolm. We have carried out our investigation and are certain that this was nothing more than a very tragic riding incident." Lord Mandaten could see the look of disgust on Cadiston's face at this statement. Then Standish continued. "Now, there will be a need for a post-mortem to secure the time and cause of death but from the initial investigation, your son fell from his horse, was dragged, and struck his head on a piece of fallen masonry, fracturing his skull. Sadly, because there was no immediate attention, he bled to death. That is all I need to say at this time, unless you have any questions for me.""So, let me get this straight, you are informing us that our son, Malcolm, was officially declared dead at the scene of the incident and the case is virtually closed without further investigation. Your manner is extremely cold Standish and is it not rather quick to have the case virtually closed already, just as was that of my brother and his family four years ago?" Lord Mandaten asked. "Just so, sir, but that one was totally different. That was a road traffic accident. Now, this one that we have here is simply a tragic riding accident." "Maybe." Said Cadiston to Standish's distaste. Standish glared at him and mouthed the words "shut up" to Cadiston. "It is nothing more. Now, if there are no further questions for us –." "I have a few that I would like to ask." Cadiston said.

"Hush up, Cadiston, there is nothing more to ask and you were told to just listen." Snapped Standish but Lord Mandaten had taken an instant liking to this smart young man and could see the potential in him. "Let him ask his questions, Sergeant, if it will help to achive the truth." "Thank you, Lord Mandaten, all I would like to know, to be able to build a full picture, is where everyone was between the hours of six and eight a.m. this morning." Cadiston said cooly. "One by one, tell the officer where you were and if there is nothing else that he needs to ask, you may leave." In tears, the first stepped forward. "I will speak first, I am Malcolm's wife, Greta, and at that time I was at the stables." Cadiston spoke softly "Thank you, Mrs. Mandaten, I am deeply sorrow for your loss and I can inform you that fact has already been established. I am sorry that I needed to ask as I appreciate just how stressful this will be for you. My condolences on your loss and, as I said, your whereabouts have been confirmed already." "My husband and I were dressing for breakfast. Oh, I am Lizabeth and my husband is Tomas. It can be confirmed by Charlotte, who entered our room at around eight a.m. to strip our bed." "Thank you." Cadiston nodded. "I am Sammie and my husband Walter. He stands over there. (She pointed at him then continued.) Like my sister, we were getting dressed for breakfast and we met on the stairs going down to the breakfast room together." "Kevin Mandaten. My wife and I left our room at around seven-fifty and had a short walk before entering the breakfast room. Jonas can confirm that as he unlocked the door for us." "Thank you, and that just leaves you, sir." "Chadrick, and at that time I was also at the stables and met Greta there. We spoke to Herbert and his son, Jeremiah, then went to see the new foal and got back in the Manor about eight-ten. We had to rush as there was not much time to get to the breakfast room for eight-thirty." "Thank you, sir, and that also has been confirmed." Cadiston added.

"I do not need to ask you, Lord and Lady Mandaten." "Nonsense man, everyone must disclose where they were. Our whereabouts can be confirmed by our butler. He brought us an early morning cup of tea to our bedroom at precisely seven-forty a.m." Said Lord Mandaten. "Thank you for that, my Lord, is there anyone else whose whereabouts I should like to know, apart from your staff?" "Me, I am Demmie, the wife of Chadrick and although I do not like to admit it openly, I fell asleep in the bath last night and was awoken by my husband at eight-fifteen." "That is true, when I finally woke and got out of bed, I discovered that she was not beside me in our bed so I dressed quickly and went to look for her and that is when I met Greta. On my return and upon entering the bathroom, there she was in the bath, still asleep."

"I am the last, Grant Mandaten, and it was my wife, Bonnie, that passed away yesterday. We are waiting for the post-mortem result and a visit from you lot but on all accounts, it was her nut allergy and someone's carelessness, a slip-up, or however it is put, that caused it. Now my brother Malcolm is dead, he thought he knew everything about riding but apparently not. My guess would be that he must have gotten overconfident and has been very careless and now he has paid the price." Cadiston noted his blasé attitude but now Demmie began to cry. "Now we have two tragic deaths in the family, it is so unfair. There is so much to do with our busy weekend coming up and Christmas is so near, it is just too much for us to bare so can we go now?" Cadiston noticed that there was a distinct falseness in her voice and that her tears were not real. He also noticed how she kept looking toward Grant.

"I am sorry for your sad losses, yes please, do leave and thank you all for your indulgence and the moment that we have any further details, we will inform you, thank you again for your time." Cadiston said.

The bell cord was pulled as the family left, leaving their parents in the long room with the two police officers. "Are there any more questions for us? Now let me see detective … Cadiston isn't it?" asked Lord Mandaten. "It is, my Lord, just a formality question, sir. Would all the staff be about their duties at that time?" "Just so, Jonas, is it not?" "It is, my Lord." "Well, it pays to be thorough, however uncomfortable or awkward, the situation and this was certainly that. You may be young and inexperienced as a detective and I say this with all honesty, you handled it extremely well, young man." The tone in his voice now changed. "And as for you, Sergeant, I guess that you need to monitor him being your junior trainee constable, but I did not like the way in which you tried to silence him. In an investigation of any sort, to arrive at the whole truth, everything relevant, or even what seems nonrelevant, must be uncovered. So there you have it, Sergeant. Cadiston my boy, I see a good detective in you."

"Thank you for your kind words, my Lord." "You have the makings of a fine police detective in that you show determination and consideration. I wish that I had been fortunate enough to have someone like you in my regiment. Now, do your investigation, my boy. You do what you must, however distasteful it may be. Now then, that name Standish – Standish – I know who you are, Standish, your name sounds very familiar and it will come to me but no matter, now I will bid you a good day." Said Lord Mandaten.

"This way, gentlemen, please, I will show you out." Jonas led them to the door and with a solid clunk, it was closed behind them.

The police car was driven slowly up the long drive and sitting in it was a very long-faced, aging, and disgruntled Sergeant Standish and a much younger, smiling Cadiston. Standish's voice carried an angry tone which was very noticeable when he spoke. "I told you that I would do all the talking and you would just listen, you deliberately disobeyed me Cadiston and that is black mark against you, and what is more you made me look like a fool in front of his Lordship." The driver looked at them in his mirror and smiled. "And you can wipe that smirk off your face and just drive, PC Foulshen." Cadiston answered but his voice was calm "Not how I see it, Serge, they possibly think that it was all part of the investigation – good cop, bad cop routine maybe and if there was something amiss, then they know that we will surely find it." Standish was far from calm and his anger remained. "Something amiss my foot Cadiston, get it through your thick stubborn head, it was purely and utterly a very tragic riding accident, just as everything else was." "Well then, I guess that we will just have to differ on the subject, won't we? I may be inexperienced compared to you but something in the back of my mind tells me – call it a sixth sense if you like – but it tells me that there was more to this death than meets the eye, just as the visual evidence shows. And what did you mean by 'everything else was'?" He made a mental note of this statement and would remember it. "No matter, it is unimportant, now then, Cadiston, you are starting to really annoy me greatly. I will tell you this only once and if you want to stay on the force and become a detective, you had better heed to my words. Drop your foolishness and silly suspicions, and do not try to override me just accept that it was nothing more than a tragic riding accident and let that be an end to it." "I was told in training school to look at all the evidence that presents itself, to search for the hidden evidence that has not presented itself, and when satisfied that there is no more to be found, sift through it all again before you reach your conclusion. The tutor also said that sometimes there is so much evidence that is hidden, that you need to rely on gut instinct sometimes if you want to find it and solve a case." "That is all very well and good in a tutorial but not in this instance as it does not apply. There is no case to solve or find answers to here, it was just a terrible riding accident and that is what will be in my written report. Now, we will speak no more of it, got it?" Cadiston remained silent but his mind was still very active. "You did not answer me, Cadiston, I said have you got it?" He threw a glance toward the sergeant. "Got it, but even though you are the pro and I am the novice, I have my suspicions and still think no I know that you are wrong."

Back at the station, they were called immediately to see the Superintendent. "Sad business, Standish, two deaths at Mandaten in two days." "That it is, sir, but after careful investigating, my decision and conclusion is that this was a terrible and tragic riding accident, isn't that right, Cadiston?" He shrugged his shoulders. "So you say, it was supposed to be my case." The Superintendent looked at him. "Explain yourself, Constable Cadiston, just what do you mean by that remark?" "I am sorry, sir, but my opinion is very different from Sergeant Standish, I am fully aware that he has years of experience under his belt and that I am the new kid on the block, so to speak, but I can still have an opinion." "That you can, Cadiston, there is no law against that. So what is your opinion, now tell me?" the Superintendent asked. "It just did not all fit, sir. For example, the position of the body in relation to the piece of masonry and how the skull was struck. Another example, the ground that was blood-soaked, there was a much larger pool in the place where he fell and a much lighter one where he finally lay. That tells me that he was struck there. Another thing, after falling from his horse, the body had allegedly been dragged but the drag line was smooth and dead straight and that is just for starters, sir. My suspicions mean that I have serious doubts and in line with my training, I feel that further and deeper investigation is required. For example, we should have our forensics check over the area. We were told by –." "I know exactly what you were told in your training, Cadiston, but this is the real world that you are in now and not a school or college. This is a real situation, not a fake one, and although I appreciate your thinking on this occasion, I am with Sergeant Standish. After the result of the post-mortem, which will determine the time and cause of death, that is the end of the case. Now, you have a good teacher in Standish so listen to him and let him lead you. Now, that is all on the subject, dismissed." They turned and left the superintendent's office. "Finally got it, college boy? It can teach you the basics but in the real world, as you will find out, things are completely different." "You can say that again, not allowed to have an opinion and want to investigate a case deeper to discover the truth. Well, I am off to the canteen for a bit of late lunch." "I will write up the report on this case so no need to trouble yourself over that. A terrible riding accident is what it will read."

In disgust, Cadiston turned and walked away. Sitting in the canteen, he pondered over Malcolm's death and was only disturbed when Mac sat opposite him. "What's up, Cadders, my friend, what's with the long face? You look like you lost ten pounds and only found ten pence. Come on now, spill."

"Can't Mac, just not satisfied with the outcome of our case but the super says it's done so there you have it." "You are with Standish, aren't you?" "That's my sergeant, more is the pity." "Why say that? He is a good one by all accounts, at least, that is what some say. He is not well-liked but he has a lot of arrests under his belt and many closed cases so wish he was my serge. You want to make the most of his experience. He retires in a couple of months so not much time for you to learn all you can from him, that's my advice." "Not so sure I want to learn anything from him, I do not like his methods for a quick case closure without a proper and full investigation so on that score, enough said, Mac. There is something about him that I −." Just at that moment, his phone rang. "Well, never mind that but thanks for the advice. Now, better take this, it is the forensic mortuary. Cadiston here." "We have the post-mortem results on Bonnie Mandaten so thought we would call you first as you are now out of school and in the field. If you would like to come over and collect them from us as I think you will find some interesting facts and it makes for an interesting read." Said the voice on the phone. "Shouldn't you have rung Standish first as he is the training sergeant?" Cadiston asked.

"Probably, but we have had dealings with him before and he just ignored our findings he always thought that he knew better than us who are trained to carry out our procedures so, as far as we are concerned −, shall we say we tried but couldn't get hold of him? What a shame, so we called you as his protégée." "Understood, I will leave now so I'll be there in twenty minutes depending on traffic." Cadiston said into the phone. "We will be here, bye."

He forgot about his sandwich and coffee and was out of his chair and in his car in a matter of minutes. The engine was fired up and he was on his way. His drive to the mortuary was unhindered and as he had said, he was there within the twenty minutes. On his arrival, he wasted no time and was almost in a run to get to the examination room.

"Charles, Samantha, what have you got for me?" Cadiston asked upon arrival. "We have Bonnie Mandaten's post-mortem result and I can tell you that it makes for an interesting read. I guess that maybe we should have persevered and tried to contact Standish but felt that even with this evidence, he would still shelve it. Just between us, personally, I don't like the man and I am not alone in that sentiment and know for certain that there is no love lost between you two either. He just wants to close cases far too quickly and without proper investigation. He annoys us immensely as he thinks that he knows better than us when it comes to the examination of a body. He wants his reasoning and not ours as the resulting verdict. So my friend, with that in mind, we decided to bypass him and pass it on to you." Said Charles making it perfectly clear that he had a disliking for Standish.

"Mac just told me there are some that praise him." Cadiston said carefully. "Must have spoken to the wrong people." Charales replied. "You can join the hate-Standish-club along with several others then, me included. Now, the report please Charles." Holding out his hand, Cadiston took the folder from his wife Samantha who was also a forensic pathologist working with Charles and with the report in his hands he immediately began reading.

"Good grief, I am glad that you bypassed him. What in heavens name? This is something else. She suffered from anaphlaxis and, if I am reading this report properly, then it was no accident. You believe that she had an induced anaphylactic shock because of the quatity of peanut you found in her tissue samples, which put her into a state of total unconsciousness, and the level of nut that you found in her system is one of the highest that you have ever seen. Her airway was almost completely closed and although they attempted to do a tracheotomy, they failed, and that means she would have struggled to breathe. She suffered a series of heart attacks, cardiac arrests and it was a major heart attack cardiac arrest that took her life. Not a natural death by a cardiac arrest, heart attack, you believe that it was brought on by her anaphylaxis. So, although she died of natural causes, my suspicion tells me that there is a strong possibility that it was forced upon her, hmm, now all I need to do is to prove it by finding the concrete evidence to back up your post-mortem."

"A very strong possibility, Cadders, in your hand. You have our full report and findings and they do not lie." "Indeed, most definitely not, Charles, and I have just read this final part, which throws a completely new light on her death. To my mind, her death is filled with suspicion but to find out that she was also two months pregnant adds to my suspicions. This is not a straightforward case of natural causes but raises suspicion for murder. In fact, we are looking at two deaths – a mother and her unborn child. Now, two questions come to my mind, who would benefit from her death? And just who would go to such lengths to get her out of the way? When I have found the answer to one question, they will both be answered together. To my mind, this has been made to look like a natural death but there is a definite flaw in there and needs further investigation. I think that there is something much more sinister at work here and I need to find out just what that is. Somehow, someone induced this unnatural quantity of peanut into her system, knowing of her allergy, and it had to be completely tasteless and odorless." He thought for a moment. "Someone had to produce it and that says, without a shadow of doubt, murder to me and so an investigation is called for and the killer is someone at the Mandaten Manor."

"Our thoughts exactly, Ashton, Standish would want to just close the case quickly, labelled as death by natural causes, cardic arrest as diagnosed by the post-mortem and forget about the abnormal amount of peanut in her tissue samples but we both, like you, think not."

"Thanks for calling me, Charles, see you at home later, Samantha." He shuffled a bit by the door. "For goodness' sake, Ashton give your wife a kiss so that she can get on with her work." Charles said rolling his eyes. "I Shouldn't, not whilst on duty but if you insist." He smiled. "I will do so, Charles." He kissed his wife, then turned toward the door. "One thing before I go, you have had the body of Malcolm Mandaten brought in. It's an alleged riding accident but I have different ideas on his death so, will you check the body over very carefully? But keep it between us. Look at every little mark on the body, especially where he struck his head. I have been told to drop it and forget about my suspicions as the case will be closed as a tragic riding accident. I cannot do that. It is Standish who wants to call it a tragic riding accident but from what I have seen and observed at the scene, I am not so sure. Standish is writing the report as we speak so I don't know how to ask this." Cadiston said. "Straight out is the best way but I can guess what you want. Correct me if I am wrong, two reports, one for you to take home and one for the file, right?" "Right, I know that it is a risky thing to do and I should not ask but can it be done quietly because if there is foul play, which I strongly suspect, I would not want to alert the perpetrator of it." He shook his head. "Now that I have Bonnie's result, it makes me even more suspicious about Malcolm's death and the evidence makes me sure that both these deaths, correction, all three of these deaths, were definitely not tragic accidents but made to look that way and were, in fact, planned murders. Well, that is my thought and my suspicion." "If Malcolm Mandaten's report shows what you suspect, then they will be our thoughts also but being sure is one thing and proving it is another. A post-mortem result, although it can be used as evidence on its own, is no good. There must be just cause and other concrete evidence at hand to back it up if it is to be deemed worthy and to bring a case to court." Charles explained.

"Then I must find it and I know that it is out there somewhere waiting for me. I can almost hear it calling come and find me Cadders. Bonnie and her unborn child will be a difficult one to find any evidence showing how it was manipulated and to prove that their deaths were not from natural causes, but were very cleverly made to look like them. There is no disguising it and I know that I have a mammoth task facing me and that is a fact." "So, Ashton Cadiston, if I have this right, then you intend to pursue your course of action and try to prove that it was murder, even though the chief has told you to drop it?" "Well, this one he has not seen yet but when I go through it with him and explain its findings, he must see that it needs investigating. Anyhow, Charles, I have got to, for my own peace of mind. If there is a murderer out there, then I need to catch him or her. Three deaths in the same family within two days of each other, very strange. Miss Bonnie and her child on Monday and Master Malcolm on Tuesday. I hope there is not another one on Wednesday. Just had a thought, they have the Black Powder Gun Show this weekend, 27th and 28th, and that is an ideal time for a staged accident. Ah well, I had best get on. I have already taken up too much of your time so best be getting back with this post-mortem report on Bonnie and her unborn child. I reckon I will be told not to take it any further and to that, I will vigorously protest. Two tragic accidents, I do not think so, my friend, I smell a rat – a great big fat dirty stinking and ugly rat. In other words, I smell murder."

"Well, good luck with that. Now, as for Malcolm, we will let you have our findings on him as soon as possible." "Thanks, Charles." He turned and walked slowly back to his car with his mind racing, trying to think where any sort of clue or evidence, however small, could be hidden. He knew that he must find something tangible to prove the need for him to open a full investigation into the death of Bonnie Mandaten and her unborn child. He knew that if there were such items, then he had to find them quickly and that had to be before the actual perpetrator or perpetrators of the crime could destroy them. "Ah well, best get back to the station and speak to the chief about these findings. I know that Standish has years of experience but I feel certain that he is wrong about Malcolm. As I have said with other cases of his that I have been on to observe but he never listened to my opinion and I was always silenced by him. But that is the past, enough is enough, so not anymore. I must speak out even if it costs me my career and, from what I have seen and heard, Standish is not all that he seems. There is something about him that reads a bit crooked and as he is coming up to his retirement soon, he wants to leave a closed book behind him –." He paused his thought briefly. "Unless, there is another underlying reason not to have a full investigation into the Mandaten deaths and if there is, then it is up to me to find it. Ok, back to the station." The engine roared into life and he was on his way.

"Your husband is a very determined young man, Samantha, and I have no doubt that he will make an excellent detective but I think that he may be taking a mighty big gamble. Plus, the risk is high and he could be skating on thin ice. He may have been top of the class and, as I said, I know that he will make an excellent detective but if it should be found out that he has ignored and gone against orders from the chief and carried on with his own investigation, he will be for the high jump. Just had another thought, if it comes out that we supplied two copies of this post-mortem and assisted him in that endeavour, then we are in trouble also." "But have you thought, Charles, what if he is right and all these Mandaten deaths are not accidents but a cover-up for murder?" "I certainly hope that he is right, for all our sakes. It will not be very good for the Mandatens to have two, no, correction, three family members murdered. At least the truth must be better than a crime covered up with a lie and a killer allowed to walk free and to possibly kill again." "Well I would most certainly want to know the truth and when Ashton gets a bee in his bonnet, then he is determined to see it through and that is why he has been top of the class – through his sheer determination and not accepting things on face value. When they had a mock case to solve and he had that feeling, others gave up on it and walked away but not Ashton, he would not let it go, when he was proven right that was the bonus." Samantha said proudly.

"I hope you are right, Samantha, or rather that he is right, it is terrible for the family to have its family members murdered but it must be better to know that and to bring the guilty culprit to trial and justice than to have it brushed under the carpet. Now we have wasted enough time so let's get Malcolm's body out and get the post-mortem done. Then we will see what we can find to substantiate your husband's theory. If your husband is right with his suspicions, who knows what we will discover on the body to answer the question: tragic riding accident or an attempt to cover up three cold-blooded murders? Probably not get it all done today but late finish me thinks, Samantha."

"Not a problem, Charles, he has often finished late so fully understands when I am late. I know that he is very – or should I say extremely – keen to have this report and I strongly feel that it will confirm his suspicions."

"Confident of that then, Samantha?" "Absolutely, Charles, and I have confidence in my husband's abilities." "You know something Samantha, so have I so let's get it done for him." Cadiston's first suspicions had been aroused during his inspection of the Devil's Dyke – the site of Malcolm Mandaten's death. He was not satisfied with it being an accident, and the report that he now held only served to add to his suspicions that there was more to the deaths than natural causes or tragic accidents. He knew that the report had to go to his superintendent but before taking it to him, he read it through carefully again. The more that he read it, the more convinced he was and his suspicion grew that this was not just a simple case of someone lapsing into carelessness. He already had his suspicion about Malcolm's death and now with this report, his suspicions rose even higher about him and that this was, in fact, a clever cover-up to the double murder of Bonnie and her unborn child – making it three murders Bonnie's post-mortem disclosed that she was carrying a little girl and that brought a tear to Cadistons eys and made him even more determined to find his evidence and their murderer, and somehow Standish was involved. To prove that this was indeed the case, he needed solid evidence and, better still, visual evidence. Something that he knew all too well was that the post-mortem results on their own and his suspicions would not be evidence enough to bring a case to court. He knew that it would raise questions but where and how would he find the evidence to back up the post-mortem and his suspicions about Bonnie and her unborn child? He was determined to try and get the case opened so that he could investigate it properly and knew that his training sergeant would try to silence him and close the case without any form of investigation. Although he felt strongly that his suspicions of foul play in both these cases were well-grounded and that he would pursue them, he also knew that if it turned out that he had been proven wrong and they were nothing more than tragic accidents, at least he had taken the required steps and found the truth and therefore his conscience would be clear.

On his drive back to the station, he pondered on his suspicions about the incident involving the death of Malcolm Mandaten. He could see clearly that the signs denoted that this could not have been a simple accident, there were far too many discrepancies. The deep indentation and the amount of blood that had soaked into the ground where he first fell, followed by the straight line as he was being dragged, culminating in his head striking the piece of fallen masonry. Although the piece of masonry was heavily bloodstained, there was a lack of blood around where it lay. He had inspected the ground around both sites very carefully and had noted that there was no sign of it being struck with force as it was lying on the surface with no indentation in the ground. If they were to believe this myth, then it should be and would have been pushed into the ground. The more he pondered, the stronger his suspicions grew to enforce the theory that this was most definitely not a simple riding accident but a preplanned murder. Lying on the seat beside him was the post-mortem report carried out on Bonnie Mandaten which he had read carefully and again made him suspicions. As he thought about the day's events, he wondered how he could override Standish. He knew full well that he would do everything that he could to silence him and stop any form of investigation to search out the truth and in doing so, would mark them both up as tragic accidents and close both the cases without an investigation. Perhaps if he could speak to his superintendent first and make him listen by presenting the information to him without Standish being present to silence him, he could get his suspicions of foul play across, and both the cases would then be investigated fully. At least, that was his theory and he knew that he could only try. He had made up his mind. As soon as he was back in the station, he would bypass Standish and go straight to his superintendent's office.

Chapter Four

The Black Powder Gun Show

At the station he saw Standish sitting at his desk but detoured unseen around him and made his way straight to the superintendent's office. "Bonnie Mandaten's post-mortem result sir." "Thank you, Cadiston, and I take it that you have already read it and formed your own opinion?" "As to that, I have, sir, and I will say that it makes for an interesting read." "I thought that you would have done so and now it is my turn to read it and form my opinion. I will take a look and see what it throws up." He stood silent while the chief read the report and when he had finished, he thought for a moment, then looked up at him before speaking. "Straight forward then, Cadiston, death by natural causes cardiac arrest possibly brought on by Anaphylaxis. A tragic mishap and this last part is especially very sad that she was also pregnant." He thought for a moment while he stared at Cadiston, studying his facial expression. He was testing him and smiled as he raised his eyebrows before speaking. "Unless you have other ideas on the subject?" "I most certainly do, sir, and the more that I read the report, the more convinced I became that this was not accidental but a cover-up for murder – a double murder, in fact. It was cleverly thought out and executed using Bonnie's allergy and her condition to hide, or attempt to hide, murder, sir. Two murders in fact." "Murder you say? Isn't that is a bit heavy?" "Not in my book. Just think about it, Chief, do you not think it a bit strange that there have been two sudden deaths in the same family in just two days, three deaths in fact, sir. Bonnie Mandaten and her unborn child on Monday 22nd, then Malcolm Mandaten on Tuesday 23rd. Today I dare say that his post-mortem will show up discrepancies as well which will serve to confirm my own suspicions. I made a detailed study of the incident site and there were far too many discrepancies for it to be a simple accident. I do not wish to speak out of turn, sir, but I know that Sergeant Standish will try to silence me and declare it a tragic riding accident. If I am to become a detective sir, I must be allowed to have my opinion and my suspicions and, in all honesty, sir, they should be acted upon as it was my case to investigate sir." The chief raised an eyebrow again. "Hmm, so you think that there is more to these cases than just mere accidents? First Bonnie Mandaten and child and you have suspicions about the death of Malcolm Mandaten —" He paused for a moment. "Hmm, now that is interesting because according to Sergeant Standish, there was absolutely nothing suspicious about it. He laid the case out for me in some detail and ensured me that it was not a bit suspicious in his book and that you were putting far too much dramatisation into the incident as it was to be your first case in the field." "He made no attempt to look at the crime scene sir so has no true judgement at all sir".

"My first case, yes sir, that much is true but overdramatising? Definitely not and the evidence at the scene shows that there is just cause for further investigation. If Standish cannot see that then he is looking with his eyes closed, sir, correction he did not look." "Strong words, Cadiston, you are very young and enthusiastic but in time you will learn that these things do happen on occasion and although sad when they do, it is just one of those unfortunate things about accidents. Sad yes but tragic accidents as Standish has said. Close the file now and we will hear no more of it, here take it to him." He was angry at being silenced and wanted to put his case forward so pressed hard. "I mean no disrespect to you but for goodness sake, sir, surely what is in Bonnie's post-mortem report about the extremely high quantity of nut solution found in her blood and tissue samples is sufficient to throw some suspicion in the way that she and her unborn child died. Certainly enough to carry out a full investigation just to be sure that the correct conclusion has been achieved sir."

"I admire your zeal, Cadiston, but I have already spoken to your sergeant about your progress and he has told me and assured me that you could be a bit over anxious to get your first real case solved. He has also assured me that in the case of Malcolm's death, it was nothing more than a tragic riding accident and Bonnie is a case of natural causes. He may have a point in that you were, mainly because it is your first case, maybe a bit overzealous in trying to prove yourself away from the clasroom. Now, I have no more to say so take it to him and he will write up the report. So, Cadiston, now the case is officially closed, how do you feel?"

"How do I feel? Sir, the truth is that I feel very let down. I have accompanied Standish on a number of his cases and, quite honestly, I do not trust his methods one bit. The evidence on these two deaths show that there is definitely a case to be investigated but he wants to silence me and stop an investigation but ... Well, I will say no more, sir." His superintendent looked hard at him. "Hmm, I will pretend that I did not hear your last comment, you can go and do some real police work now or you will find yourself back on the beat, got it?" "Got it, sir." Feeling a bit dejected but also feeling that there was something hidden in the chief's words, he returned to the office.

"Ah there you are at last, Cadiston. I've just been to see the chief. Judging by your expression, you got nowhere? I expected as much as I spoke with him earlier. That must be Bonnie Mandaten's post-mortem result that you hold. I expect that you have already read it and formed your opinion on the subject? But that is for me to assess now. When my report is written, I will go to the family and tell them the findings myself. You will not need to be with me as you may throw a spanner in the works with one of your totally unfounded suspicions or asking questions that have no place or bearing. It is ok, I have spoken with the chief again." He had a smirk on his face as he spoke. "So I know your thoughts on the subject but will say no more." His face carried a sinister smirk. "You can go now and leave me to write the report to close another case successfully." "I suppose that you will want to do that and, close both cases even though there is conflicting evidence in both cases and without a proper investigation." Standish had a scowl on his face as he spoke. "Be very careful, Cadiston, you are not fully qualified yet and a word from me can end it all for you." He made a gesture of cupping his hands. "I have you there, right in my hands, and I have the power to make or break you so do not forget it." His scowl had changed into a wry grin and he felt pleased with himself. His words had not gone unheard and as Cadiston walked away from him, a door was heard to close. He had remained calm and without saying another word, he returned to his desk. With his elbows resting on it and his head cradled in his hands, he felt that he wanted to scream but remained silent. In his heart, he was not at all happy and in his mind, his thoughts were creating a riot. He remained calm and was determined that he would not be beaten. "What is it all for?" He whispered. "Was it like this for you, Grandfather? And your father before you in the early days of the peelers? Maybe I should not have followed you and gone with Father into the antiques trade." He sat quietly with his thoughts, then from nowhere it was as though a voice spoke to him. "Don't give up, son, you have come this far and must overcome this hurdle. Just persevere and it will come right." He looked up expecting to see someone there but there was no one. He shook his head and whispered. "Alright, Grandfather, the keyword has got to be persevere."

"Father, as we have had two tragic accidents in two days and have lost Malcolm and Bonnie, will the show still be on for the weekend?" "Most certainly it will, Sammie, a lot of time and money has already been spent on the arrangements and a lot of work put in. People are already arriving to set up for their part to play to make it a successful show again this year. At this late date, it is impossible to cancel it. We have already sold well over sixty thousand tickets in advanced bookings and that number will increase on the sales at the gate. So, we cannot possibly cancel it must go on." "It will be very hard for Greta and Grant." Sammie said. "How would you feel about having a plaque written in memory of Bonnie and Malcolm, to which the show will be dedicated?" "That will be a nice thing to do, Father, I think that Greta and Grant would approve. Now, I had better go and get on with my side of the organisation." "That's my girl, we all have to do our bit and that will ensure that it all goes well." "It always has so far, Father, and we have run a show for many years now and everyone enjoys the variety of activities that are put on throughout the day. We have an extra attraction this year with the wild west shootout, that will be fun."

"Everyone or, at least, almost everyone loves the old west with the cowboys and shootouts. Kevin's Black Powder Gun Show, as we have called it this year, will top the thrill." "I will get on then, Father." Sammie turned and left the room.

"Excuse me, my Lord, but there is a policeman to see you and Master Grant, said his name is Sergeant Standish." Said the old butler Bradinham.

"Standish again, I do not like that man. Standish … I feel that I should know that name, if only I could jog my memory." He thought for a moment before continuing. "Ah yes, now I remember him, he was here about three months ago when that poor chap, Pedro Santos, was found in the Devil's Dyke."

"The very same, my Lord." "That young Cadiston was not with him on that occasion and now my memory is returning, that is not the only time that he has come into our lives." Said Lord Mandaten. "Indeed, it is not, my Lord, it was he that investigated your brother's family incident four years ago." "Well remembered, Bradinham. I simply detest the man but if that is who they have sent, best go and show him in and then go find my son." "Right away, my Lord." Bradinham left and five minutes later, he brought Standish into the study. "Sergeant Standish, my Lord." "Come in, Sergeant, I cannot lie and say that you are welcome. I see that there is no young Cadiston with you today?" Said Lord Mandaten. "Not today, sir, no need to bring him along. I just have to inform you and your son of the findings and confirm the cause of death of your son's wife, Bonnie Mandaten." Standish said sternly. "And what was that, Sergeant?" Asked a rough voice from behind him. He turned to see who had spoken and saw that it was Grant. "Natural causes, sir. A massive heart attack or cardiac arrest claimed your wife, sir, possibly brought on by her Anaphylaxis." Confirmed Standish. "And definitely no foul play is suspected?" Asked Grant. "Foul play, good gracious me, sir, whatever gave you that idea? There is none, it was as expected – a tragic accident due to her allergy and may I take this opportunity to offer you our condolences." "Thank you, Sergeant, if there is nothing else, you may leave." Said Lord Mandaten. "There is just one more thing, sir, one thing they found in the post-mortem that I must mention, Master Grant … Did you know that your wife was two months pregnant with a little girl?" Grant stared at Standish before speaking.

"Pregnant? I did not know, she had not told me. Well, that has no bearing or consequence now that they are both gone so it does not matter in the slightest." "I guess not, sir, your wife's body will be released after 9 a.m. on Wednesday the 24th. Now is there anything else that you would like to know or that we can help you with?" Asked the Standish. "Not a thing unless you can tell me why it happened." "Sorry, sir, I cannot. It was a very tragic incident and must have been devastating for you." His reply came with a shrug of his shoulders with a devil-may-care attitude. "I will survive it and get on with my life." "Indeed sir, now if that is all, then I will take my leave of you." "Bye, then." Grant turned and left him standing there at a bit of a loss. "Forgive my son's manors but I believe under the circumstances, it's understandable." Lord Mandaten said. "Nothing to forgive, my Lord, I see that there is a lot of activity going on in the grounds." "Preparations for the Black Powder Gun Show this weekend." "Of course, I should have remembered as I have tickets for Saturday, I almost forgot. I will take my leave of you then if there is nothing further." Standish said. "Nothing at all." The bell cord was rung and minutes later Bradinham had shown the Sergeant out.

Back at the station, Standish met up with Cadiston and with a wry smile on his lips, approached him.

"Ah, Cadiston, I have just been to the Manor and confirmed the cause of death of Bonnie Mandaten. As I said, all quite natural. Sad thing for them was that she was two months pregnant." "Did her husband say anything when you informed him of that?" Asked Cadiston. "First asked if foul play was suspected and after

92

I told him that his wife was pregnant, which surprised him, he just said he had no idea and it bears no consequences now that they are both gone so it doesn't matter in the slightest." Standish said. "Anything else?"

"Questions, well, nothing much, just when I said it must be devastating for him to lose a wife and a child, he just replied that he would survive and get on with his life." "That is a rather cold and callous attitude, don't you think? Surely that must give cause to suspect that something was not as straight forward as you think?" "There you go again, Cadiston, you have been told to drop all this and let your suspicions rest. There is nothing at all suspicious in those remarks so don't you go getting any ideas. It is just his emotion talking. Now, that is an end to it. Don't want to say I told you so but told you so."

"Whatever you say, Standish, whatever you say but with the way in which her death occurred and with Bonnie being pregnant, that sheds a new light on her death." "New light my foot. Now, let it go, Cadiston, I will not tell you again. It is terrible, yes, but a tragic death from natural causes cadiac arrest for Bonnie and a tragic riding accident for Malcolm. Now, that is an end to it so let it go. My end report is done and submitted to the chief so there you have it, two cases are closed and will be filed. Well, that's me done. Two more cases with a conclusion that are now a closed book for me so I am off home. No more duties until Monday, 29th next week, a good thing this slow breakdown to my retirement." He glanced at his calendar. "That just leaves me nineteen more days to take me up to the last of my work, then relax and enjoy my retirement. Next week, four days to work, brings it to 2nd October, then Friday till Tuesday 7th, off, and finish on Sunday 12th. After that, you can do as you like but only with my input and on the understanding that it will only come about if I ..." He emphasised the I and pointed to his chest. "decide to pass you as fit for being a detective. What do you say to that then, Cadiston? The Mandaten cases and files are closed and both deaths are of natural causes and in time, you will learn when and how to distinguish the difference." "A post-mortem is there for a reason and is a valuable tool." Said Cadiston. "I do not need any post-mortem to tell me anything, now that is me done so I am off home." "Night then, have a good break." Cadiston thought ★Out of my hair for a few days good★.

"Good break, that I will, taking my two grandsons to see a bit of the old wild west on Saturday at Mandaten Manor." "Going to The Black Powder Gun Show then?" "Exactly, I am taking the grandchildren and it will be a real treat for them – the two boys anyway. Now, no more chat, I am out of here." He turned and walked quickly away.

Cadiston sat at his desk and opened his note book, turning it to the page that he had started for Bonnie Mandaten, and wrote a new entry. He had read the post-mortem report and known that she was two months pregnant but with Grant's comments, they had added to his suspicions that the two deaths were not an accident. With the book closed, he then fired up his computer and the instant it was loaded his fingers began to click on the keys, "Now let me see, Mandaten Manor Black Powder Gun Show. There you are, tickets available in advance, twenty pounds per adult or purchase on the day for twenty-six pounds. Half price for children seven to fourteen and free entry for children under the age of seven. Last day for online ticket purchase Tuesday 23rd. That is today." He whispered, then read on. Booking office closes at eight p.m. He glanced at his watch and whispered.

"Just got time to make a booking. Now, next thing."

Click here to purchase now, it read.

"Done that." He mumbled.

Number of tickets: two.

"Done that."

Payment method, it read. "By visa card, done that."

He entered the long sixteen-digit number, the security code, and the expiry date.

"Done that."

Enter the name as it is shown on the card, he read. "Done that."

Now he waited in silence. Checking the card details, he clicked to finalise the purchase.

"Done that."

He entered the address to which the tickets were to be sent amd confirmed.

"Done that."

The screen read: Congratulations your purchase is approved. A big THANK YOU from all the Mandaten family for your purchase, ENJOY THE DAY.

"Now that was easy, perhaps if they know we are there, no accidents will happen. Hopefully."

"Hey, bad habit talking to yourself Cadders."

"Not as long as you don't answer yourself, Mac."

"I saw Standish leave, got some days off hasn't he?"

"Yes, thank goodness. He is a real thorn in my side."

"Heard him talking earlier so can understand why, not getting on very well with my sergeant either but if I fail, there is still the beat. Night then."

"Night, Mac. Good grief, it's almost eight. Just got those tickets ordered in time. Better be getting off myself. Samantha will be home and wonder where I am." "Doing it again, Cadders." Remarked Mac as he left the office.

"Suppose you never do it, then?" He shouted back. He was just able to hear Mac's voice trailing away. "Sometimes, Cadders, sometimes." Then he laughed.

"How are you getting along with the final arrangements and organization Chadrick?" Lord Mandaten asked. "Everything is well on schedule, as usual, Father, the marquees are all up and by tomorrow evening, the wild west arena will be completed. Also, Thursday will see the arrival of your grandchildren and we will see the stage coach arrive and the seating for the falconry and the arena area cordoned off and completed. The birds arrive on Friday and as everything has gone exactly to plan, except for losing Bonnie and Malcolm …" He paused briefly. "Friday will see total finalization with everything complete from A to Z. Everyone has worked extremely hard and one last inspection on Friday evening will see everything from arenas to zipwire checked, checked again and, for good measure, checked a third time. We have gone the extra mile this year, Father, and have several different activities, all timed and scheduled with a little bit of leeway inBetween, just in case of an overrun. Kevin is cleaning and checking every single gun yet again in his preparation and is getting all the black powder weapons ready." "Cleaning again, you said?" "Yes, he has cleaned every weapon from the wheellock to the flintlock, from the percussion cap to the bullet and cartridge three times. Every weapon to be used has been methodically and thoroughly checked by the gunsmith and each piece has been passed fit to use." "Good, you are all doing very well and have taken all the burden from me, now, I think it is time for our dinner." Said Lord Mandaten.

Wednesday had come and gone and the activities to get the grounds ready were in full swing. The whole family was busy checking and rechecking the gang of men that were building stands and marking out the designated areas for the various side shows. The main attraction that the majority would want to see would be the use of the black powder firearms. A large area had been set aside for this as every safety precaution had to be taken if they were going to avoid any kind of accident taking place. The loads were measured carefully so that the full range potential would not be met and as an added precaution, the area behind the targets was completely cordoned off.

There was great excitement amongst the family. Even though they had all the hard work of organising everything, they each enjoyed the days just as much as the spectators and visitors did. Alongside the main attractions taking place in the Black Powder Gun Show, certain older parts of the Manor would also be open for the public to view. These were the parts that dated back to the early sixteen hundreds when the building work on the Manor that stands today began. The family no longer had cause to use this older section of the Manor but as it was a grade one listed building, the family had always maintained it just as it was when the Manor was being rebuilt in the mid to late seventeenth century, after the old one was burnt down, to comply with the law. Lord Mandaten, with his wife by his side, would also talk about the family history from its origins up to the present day and show a chart of the family tree; if it became too much for him, then she was on hand to take over. Most of the people that came to look at the old part of the Manor would have an interest in this type of thing. There are not many people that can trace their family tree back to the invasion of William the Conqueror and the battle of Hastings or for others, it was called the Norman Conquest of 1066. The day had gone well with everything completed that needed to be done. Grant was the only family member who had been absent because he had decided to follow the mortuary transport back to the funeral home with Bonnie's body, even though he was not bothered in the slightest and was just there for the pretense of caring about his wife.

"Leave it all to us, sir, we will do our very best to return her beauty. I see that you have brought some home clothes for her to wear." "Yes, this is, or was her best dress and shoes, she also draped this shawl around her shoulders, I guess wearing a jewel is not allowed." Grant said. "If there are to be viewings to say farewell, we can place it in position but before the final committal, it will be removed."

"I do not see why as she will be placed in the family vault on the grounds of Mandaten Manor with all the others. Over the centuries, they were placed there wearing their jewellery so there must be a small fortune in the family crypt. *Hmm, now there is a thought★*," he whispered "Then maybe an exception, sir, leave everything with us and rest assured that we will do everything." "I leave her in your care and capable hands then." He had false tears in his eyes. "Call me when we can view my Bonnie." He said.

"We will, sir, we will." He turned and left with a smile on his face and headed back to the Manor. "That poor man, to lose such a young and beautiful wife must be devastating." Said Fred Gunter the undertakers clerk. His false facade had given the impression that he was a very caring and loving husband. Before her death, Bonnie had confided in Greta, who had taken an interest, and Lizabeth, who had none, that she suspected him of having an affair and how he treated her. But now, sadly, she had been silenced and would not be able to tell or confront anyone.

Thursday was upon them and the assembling and inspecting continued, the archery targets were set up and the various bows checked. They had examples of the English longbow that had served them so well in many conflicts. They had crossbows and bows from the American Indians, from India, from Japan as used by the Samurai, and a variety of bows from every country around the world. The arena was set for the horse displays and arenas for dogs, sheep, pigs and cattle, and a special area for a variety of different and rare breeds of cattle, pigs, sheep, goats and a special area for the children to hold and touch animals such as rabbits, guinea pigs, hamsters and pygmy goats. There were various craft stalls, food stalls, and a large play area for young children. There was even an area set aside as a baby crèche. This area would also have trained child minders and a nurse in attendance at all times to allow the parents to see and participate in some of the activities that small children could not. They could do this, knowing that their children were entertained, safe, well and being professionally well cared for.

Thursday evening was upon them and the family retired to the manor for their evening meal and were glad to be joined by their own children they were James, Lowell, Jennifer and Kansas. While they had nothing to do with the organization, they were to participate in the many events of the day. Friday, 26th September, the final day before the gates would be open to the public, went exactly as planned. Only when the very last item had been checked, checked again, and ticked off, did they breathe a sigh of relief.

With nothing more to be done they all returned to the manor, "That's it, everything is done then, well done family, and now we are ready. Early start in the morning and that denotes that an early night is called for, me thinks." Stated Lord Mandaten. They watched as their parents were driven back to the Manor in their carriage before starting to make their own way back. "These will be a demanding and tiring but enjoyable two days."

Said a tired Kevin. "They most certainly will be, Kevin, and if all goes according to plan, a very profitable one." Added Sammie. "Extremely", added Tomas. "It certainly will, Tomas." Replied Lizabeth. "All has gone well and according to plan so far. In fact, better than expected, me thinks, so indeed, it will be a great weekend." Said Kevin. "Well, I don't know about the rest of you but I am going to make my way back to the Manor for a shower before dinner." Chad looked across to where his wife stood. "Are you coming Demmie?" "Not yet but will be in a few minutes, you get going, Chad, I have just got to look at something that I forgot to check, just to make sure it is alright, then I'll be with you." "Ok Demmie." Chad said. "We are all done so we will walk back with you." Said Greta. Demmie disappeared into a marquee and as the others began their walk back to the Manor, Grant stopped suddenly. "Blast!" He said loudly. "What is it, Grant?" asked Sammie.

"Forgot my blasted radio and it will need to be charged up to be ready for tomorrow. You all go on and I will catch up." He replied and walked briskly away. The rest of the family continued their walk back. Every few paces, Chadrick turned to look behind them. "What are you looking for, Chad?"

"Just wondered what is taking Demmie so long, Greta." She whispered back to him. "Grant still missing as well." "Exactly Greta." "Makes me wonder about those two, Bonnie was about to tell us something on Monday but now she cannot." Said Greta with tears in her eyes. "Hmm." Chad replied with his own thoughts running rampant.

They continued their walk and thirty minutes later, with the Manor in clear view, they heard the roar of a quad bike engine. Turning, they saw that riding it was Grant with Demmie at his rear. "All right for some." "Forgot that this bike was up there. Got the radio, then noticed that your wife was checking something out in the beer tent so I waited to give her a lift. No more room for passengers though, hold tight Demmie." He then chuckled. "See all you at the dinner table." And with that, they roared away. Chad and Greta could not help but notice the way

Demmie was tightly holding on to him. "Phew, that is not right, not right at all, the way she is holding onto him. She never held on to me like that." Greta looked sympathetically at Chad, and even though still in pain from the loss of her husband, she tried to comfort him and as their hands brushed she almost held his but refrained. "Probably nothing to it, Chad." "Maybe, Greta, but of late … Well, I don't know, what do you think Bonnie wanted to tell you?" "Can't talk now but I will tell you later." He smiled and winked at her in understanding. Back at the Manor, they made their way to their rooms and were glad to shed their dirty work clothes and take a shower or bath to be ready for the evening dinner. In their room, Chadrick could hear his wife in the shower. He wanted to confront her as he had not liked the intimate way that she had been holding onto Grant. He wanted to tell her so while it was fresh in his mind. He saw her clothes strewn about the floor and began to tidy them up when he noticed that there was the smell of aftershave on her top and it was not his. "Now that I know is Grant's aftershave. I wonder –." He carefully checked the rest of her clothes and found other stains and marks that he could not easily explain. He vaguely remembered seeing such stains on her clothes before. His memory was very hazy as it was on the Monday after Grant and Demmie had returned from the hospital late, and after his second cup of coffee given him by Demmie, it was then he had suddenly been unusually tired. He also remembered that she had been talking to Greta and had said that Bonnie confided in her and thought that Grant was having an affair and would be able to say who it was that evening. That was on Monday the 23rd but before she could tell who it was, Bonnie had died. He recalled seeing strange glances across the table from Bonnie aimed at Demmie and began to mull past events over in his head, allowing his mind to wander. He whispered to himself. "I wonder, could Bonnie have been correct in her assumption that he was having an affair? Could it be – is it with my wife? We had only been married a few months when she started going on her long runs and extra use of the gymnasium. Then there were the times that she went away for long weekends, allegedly for a marathon, leaving me to run the business on my own. Strange thing is, I saw no news of one. She went with him to the hospital and they did not return until well past midnight, almost one a.m., in fact. Then there was her torn dress and the stain on it and no bra or undies in fact naked without the torn dress on. I don't want to think them capable but maybe I had better keep a close eye on them both and watch for the intimate signs. It is most definitely his aftershave and if I challenge it, she will probably say it must have been when she was on the quad bike but there have been other events and other smells that make me suspicious. After all that she said on the way here, that she did not want me to be the next Lord and said that Grant should have it –. Has she been filling me with lies since we met just to be near him? Better stop whispering to myself, I think she is out of the shower."

"I heard you talking, who was with you?" She asked stepping out of the bathroom. Wrapped tightly in a large bath towel. "Not a soul my dear, just mulling over some events of the past weeks and speaking my thoughts out loud." "Ok, I am finished in the bathroom so in you go, it is all yours." "Time is pressing so I will be quick." He closed the door behind him. While he was in the shower and feeling bodily relaxed in the hot water, his mind was continuing to work overtime. "Bonnie is dead and that makes Grant free, his first wife died, or rather was murdered, and now his second wife is dead. He is free again but Demmie is not and that puts me in the way. I wonder, would he kill his first wife to be with Bonnie and then kill her and then me, to be with mine? But what about Malcolm? He was not in their way. Hang on though, of course, he stood in Grant's way to get the title. I can see the reasoning for killing Bonnie, a bit extreme but that is to free Grant, and then kill me to free Demmie. He needed Malcolm to leave the way clear for him so was that their plan? Is that why she said that Grant should be the next Lord? Maybe. Hmm – plenty to think about. But then Kevin, although younger than Grant, might be in the way, have they also thought of that? No, a stupid thought, they would not go that far and to those length – Commit multiple murders, just to be together and gain the title or –" He paused? "Would they? Malcolm was the eldest and in line to be the next Lord ... Could they have? Would they have? Best to keep that thought to myself and watch my back." He paused again. "Maybe I could talk to Greta, I will see." He quickly finished his shower and returned to the bedroom, where his wife was already dressed and standing near the door with it slightly open. He was not sure but thought he heard the words "All is going better than planned." The door was closed very quickly as he entered the room.

"Someone there, Demmie?" "I thought there was but when I opened it, nobody was. It must just be the creaky old floorboards talking in this lovely old Manor. Now, we need to hurry, it is already seven-twenty and dinner will be prompt at seven-thirty." "I am ready so let's go down." They entered the dining room and saw that everyone else was already there and now with the grandchildren present, their table number should have increased by four. Instead, it had only increased by two as Bonnie and Malcolm were no longer with them. At precisely seven twenty-eight, their parents arrived and, as before, the instant that they were all sitting the meal service began. The meal was eaten in silence but inbetween each course, a few words were spoken.

"An excellent day, Father, all is set and ready." Said a smiling Lizabeth. "We have a few additional activities this year." Added Sammie. "I have made sure that all the smaller children are well catered for this year, Mother." "An excellent idea of yours there, Sadie." "Thank you mother but –." She wiped a tear from her eye. "The idea was not mine, it was Bonnie's and I have merely gone along with her plan, here is the sketch that she had made. (Sadie passed the paper to her mother.) I have made it in her memory, I had a sign put up and have called it 'Bonnie's Children's Play Area and Nursery'. I do not think anyone was aware that she was expecting her first child so –," again, she wiped a tear away. "We have, in effect, lost two members of our family with her death." "Pregnant? Bonnie was pregnant you kept that one quiet, Grant? Or didn't you know?" said Lady Mandaten in surprise.

"Not until that police sergeant, what was his name? Standish, that's it. He told Father and me when he came to confirm the cause of her death mother sorry did not give it another thought", Demmie and Grant were staring at each other while he spoke. "Grant, you poor thing, to lose Bonnie was bad enough but a baby as well, you —." Greta started to speak but was silenced. "Enough talk of that, Greta!" Grant snapped. "They are both dead and my life goes on so there is an end to it. Father likes complete silence at the table, now shut up and eat." "No need to speak to Greta in that tone, Grant, she was only showing concern which is more than you do." Chad had spoken softly but Grant's reply was very bullish. "Who asked you to pipe up, Chadrick? So you can keep your nose out of it unless you want it bloodied, she is not your wife and it has absolutely nothing to do with you." Chad remained calm in his response and although he would have good cause, his voice was not raised but remained soft. "Irrespective of that, Grant, I make do without bad manners as there is no need for them. You forget yourself and the fact that Greta is still grieving after losing Malcolm only a few days ago as you would be losing Bonnie and your unborn child, that is if you really cared." "You should keep out of it, you are nothing but a meddling interloper, I have had it with you. In the old days, I would slap your face and swords would be drawn." "Anytime you are ready, Grant, I will be glad to oblige." Their father had heard enough and spoke angrily. "Silence! I will have no more of that talk at this table and I should have thought that you had leaned your lesson by now Grant challenging Chadrick as he has bested you on every occasion." He glanced around the table at the glum faces. "Now, all of you remain silent until we have finished our meal." "Yes Father, you are right, sorry." Grant just received an ice cold glance.The remainder of the meal was carried out in complete silence and at its end, the family retired into the lounge to enjoy their coffee and brandy. "Do not stay up late, any of you, early to bed for all and that is an order. We have a very big day tomorrow." "Good night, Father, Mother, sleep well." Lizabeth just received a nod. Greta followed them up to her room with the grandchildren bringing up the rear, the next sound after their footprints was the solid clunk of doors being closed. The air was hostile between the siblings of the family and the atmosphere could be cut with a blunt knife. The silence remained but the icy stares that passed between them were not for the faint-hearted. With an angry tone in his voice, Grant spoke. "I am for an early night. I am sick and tired of that invader to our family interfering, for some reason he has always shone in our father's eyes but very soon now, his light will be extinguished for ever then he will get his final comeuppance and be gone for good." Kevin's reply was calm. "Do I sense a bit of jealously, Brother?" "Shut up, Kevin, I know that there is no love lost for him from you either." "True enough, Brother, but it is better to bide one's time and only strike when your victory is assured." "Is that what you intend to do then, Kevin?" He smiled. "Maybe, Brother, maybe." He smiled again. "And as Father said, he has bested you in every confrontation so, Brother, you will just have to wait and see what is planned, won't you?" "Well, things are going to be very different around here when – Well, nevermind the when." He then grunted and headed up to his room. "What was all that about, Kevin?" "Nothing at all, Lizabeth, just Grant being Grant. He has never liked Chadrick. Not from the moment that he was brought into the family home as a small baby and even less after a much younger Chad rescued him from the lake. He has also bested him in the fights that Grant has started with him over the years. Plus, he has made something of his life, unlike Grant who, if I speak the truth, is a total waster. It is clear for all to see that he has a great big streak of jealousy and a real hatred running through him and no good can come of that." "That is very true and what about you, Kevin? Do you share the same feelings as your brother?" He smiled at his sister. "I decline to give an answer to that question, Lizabeth it is far to incriminating." "In that case, I will take it as a yes. Well, out of you four boys, even though he was adopted, I must say that he always did seem to be the apple of daddy's eye or maybe the blue-eyed boy, whichever you prefer. I must say that he always appeared to be more like

Father than the rest of you and maybe he was that because he was never any trouble or bother to our parents unlike you three always were." "What you just said, Lizabeth, there is also something about him, not strange but … Well, maybe strange and that is that he really does seem to be more like our father than Grant ever was. Come to that, Grant has never really seemed like a twin to Malcolm. He is so different in every aspect." "I think that we have all noticed that, Sammie, but talking of Chad, do you mean that he was or rather is a goody, goody two shoes?" "Maybe not quite that but, yes, something like that." "Yes, for sure something like that. I guess all us boys have a streak of jealousy and hatred for him. You two girls are not to be denied that either, now are you? But no matter, I think that Grant has it all in hand."

"I don't have a clue what you are whispering and chatting about in the corner but Father left his instructions. It is getting late and I feel that we should all be heading up to bed. The children and our parents have retired for the night so I think that we should all follow suit and have an early night. We have a long weekend ahead of us and there will be little sleep between the closure of the Saturday and Sunday's show. Father and Mother went straight up after dinner so did Grant and the children and I think we should follow their example so bed everyone." "You are not the Lord of the Manor or the master of the house and never will be Chadrick so do not presume to order us." "Nothing of the sort, Kevin, I was merely reiterating Father's words." "He is not your father so get that straight." Kevin then let out a loud grunt and left the room. He was followed by the rest of the family without saying a word but brushing past Chad as though trying to brush him away, with them all gone it left Chad in the lounge alone. "Well, good night all. Now, that just leaves me." He turned to head upstairs when he heard his name being called and was surprised when his parents re-entered the lounge. "Mother, Father, I thought that you had gone to bed." "We nearly did, son, but made a detour when we heard all the bickering, we decided to eavesdrop and were listening to all the conversations taking place from the other room. Now that they have all

left, we came back in to have a word before you retire, my boy."
"What is it you need to talk about, Father?" "I have given this
matter a great deal of thought and deliberation and have talked
it over with your mother and well, I know what you have said
but there is only one person in this family that we would truly
trust with the Mandaten Estate. That one person that we trust,
Chadrick, is you. We need to hand the helm over to the person
that will maintain the estate and keep all these good people in
employment for the foreseeable future. Someone that will not
fritter everything that has taken years to build and the only person that meets that criteria, is you. You have been much more
a son to us than our own three blood sons have ever been and
it has not gone unnoticed. Malcolm was overzealous but sadly is gone and Grant is so different from him, it is as though – I
cannot put a finger on it but he does not seem like a Mandaten
and to look at him, he has none of the family traits. Kevin, now,
Kevin I cannot understand at all but you, my boy, you are like a
true son should be and the strange thing is that even though you
are not of our blood, you do have the family looks so that is my
decision. So, it is said and there you have it, Son, it is our joint
decision and is settled. You, Chadrick, shall be the next Lord
Mandaten." "Thank you for your confidence in me and to me,
you are and always will be my true mother and father but surely the title should be kept within the bloodline and that is Kevin
or Grant and not me. I am not of your bloodline." "To us, you
are our true son and much more a Mandaten than our own three
sons have ever been, especially Grant. After this event weekend,
I shall be giving my announcement and there you have it. Now,
to bed with you and keep it to yourself." Said Lord Mandaten.
In deep surprise at this revelation, Chad made his way upstairs
but unbeknown to them all someone hid in the shadows and other ears had listened to what should have been their private conversation. As he closed his bedroom door, he heard the familiar
creak of the floor boards but when he looked out to see who it
was, there was no one to be seen but the boards still creaked as
though someone was walking on them.

"Now that is strange, strange indeed. The boards creak and footsteps are heard but there is no one to be seen. Strange but there must be a simple explanation." He closed the door and began to undress. "Everyone else has come up so what took you so long?" Demmie asked. "Father needed a word."

"Father? I thought he had already come up?" "As did I but not so." "What did Father want you for?" "Nothing much, why do you ask?" She hesitated slightly before giving her reply and when she finally answered, he sensed a difference in her voice. "Oh! No particular reason but you can tell me now anyhow." He eyed her with suspicion. "Just checking on something for the weekend show, that's all." "It was nothing much then? I thought it may be to do with who is to be the next Lord." He sensed that she was digging for information on that subject and wondered why. "The next Lord, now why on earth do you think that he would ask me anything about that? I am not even of the family bloodline, now am I?" "No, you are most certainly not so nothing of much importance then?" "Nope." "Big weekend for all of us and if all goes to plan, it will work out just fine." Moments later, they were in bed.

"Night, then." She said. "Night, sleep well." Turning over, he settled but silently he was asking why his wife was so insistent in knowing what his father had wanted him for. The Manor was now silent, apart from the usual settlement sounds as the old timbers settled like them to rest.

For the past few days, Cadiston had lingered and did not appreciate being idle when in his mind he should be carrying out a full investigation into the two suspicious and unexplained deaths. He glanced at Standish and his anger began to rise but he remained calm while he examined the best way to tackle his situation tactfully. His sergeant may just write these deaths off as that was his style but it was not Cadiston's and he was very determined that if he could prove that murder had been committed, then he would not allow these deaths go unpunished.

After all the work involved in the preparations for the show, the first big day, Saturday 27th September, was here at last and all the members of the household were awake bright and early. There were no idle hands and they were all involved in making their final checks before the gates could be opened to the public. In the kitchen, the staff had been at work even earlier and were busy baking meat and fruit pies, cakes, sausage rolls, fresh bread, and a host of other items that would be for sale on their market stall alongside the variety of produce from the estate garden. A variety of fruit and vegetables had already been selected and arranged, along with flour from their own mill and a variety of plants. All they needed now was the customers. Greta had made her way to the main gate, accompanied by her son, Lowell, and her daughter, Jennifer, to check on the tickets and take the payment from those that had not booked beforehand. Once settled, the gates were opened. The instant that all the other family members had taken up their respective places, from archery to the zipwire, the horn was sounded and the flow of visitors began to pass through the gates. Everything had been carefully signposted so that the people could locate the activity or side show that they wanted to see or partake in easily and within a few minutes of the gates being open, the whole place was a hive of activity. Thousands of guides and maps had been printed so that everyone who attended would receive a copy, free of charge on entry. Things could not be going better and there were no disruptions as the steady flow of traffic was directed to the controlled parking area with ease. Jacob's sons Freddie and Charles acted as parking attendants.

The warmth of the September sun greeted them all on this first day of the show. There was a great deal of excitement and the day had begun well. As the numbers of visitors swelled the seating for each event, as had been expected, it was filled to its capacity. A contingency plan was in operation to allow those that could not see the first display of their choice, to be issued with a ticket with priority seating in the next one that was scheduled. The day had run smoothly and at the end of the day, most of the visitors had seen and done all that they wanted to on the first day of the Black Powder Gun Show. These visitors left extremely happy and satisfied with the organisation and value for money and did not hesitate to express their pleasure. Only a small number of them had failed to achieve this because there was so much to see and do. Once again, this had been expected so those that wanted tickets for Sunday's show paid a reduced rate and were given priority tickets for the side shows that they had missed. This was to give them the opportunity to see and do what they had no time for on Saturday. With the final car driving away, the gates were closed and locked. With a sigh of relief, Greta and her family climbed aboard their pony-pulled trap and began their long drive back to the Manor. "Mother, pull up a minute, I cannot be sure but isn't that uncle Grant over there?" "Where, Lowell?" Greta asked."I am sure that was him I saw near the black powder marquee." "I cannot imagine why. It is closed up and Kevin and James are already heading back to the Manor. I can see them walking in front of us."

"I see them too, Mother, so shall I go check or shall we just wait for him?"

"No need, Jennifer, if it is him, then he can make his own way back."

Back at the Manor, as there was to be no cooked evening meal, the family had gathered in the breakfast lounge where a buffet of snack items had been left ready for them. There was plenty of talk and the room buzzed and vibrated with all their chatter of the day's events. "Well done all of you, it has been a brilliant first day, my children. Absolutely brilliant."

"Thank you, Father, and I must say it has been most enjoyable." Said Lizabeth joyfully. "We had several inquiries about the date for next year's show so I gave them our advanced booking leaflet. They said it had been so brilliant again this year, even if the show was the same next year, they would still want to come. They wanted to make sure of the dates so that they could arrange their holiday days well in advance." Said Greta with nods of agreement from her son and daughter Lowell and Jennifer. "I think it is quite safe to say that everyone had a fantastic day." Said Chadrick. "Some of the parents wanted to know how much they would need to pay to leave a child in the supervised play area or the infant care center and could hardly believe it when I told them it is a free service to enable them to do their own thing." Said a smiling Sadie. "We had only one injury all day and that was when Jacob got a small slither of wood in his finger from one of the wooded crates." Added Sammie. "A great, successful day all round. Well done, family, and when tomorrow is over then all of our staff must be congratulated also for their hard work and contributions to its success.". Said Lord Mandaten with a smile. "And they will be, Father. If I may, I suggest a little extra in their pay packet." Chad said. Grant and Kevin, along with their two sisters, aimed angry ice-cold glares at him but Grant was the first to speak. "You must be joking, Chadrick, tell me that you are joking. We pay them a darn good wage for their work and that should be sufficient. Besides, it has nothing to do with you as you are not real family."

There was a short silence while the thunder grew, then it was their father that retaliated. In a very strong and dominant voice, they felt the lash of his harsh tongue. "Again, I need to tell you that I will not tolerate any of that kind of talk. I saw the ice-cold stare that you gave our son Chadrick and can tell you that you are all on thin ice with me. I can tell you now that if, at this very moment, I had to make my choice between the two of you boys and Chadrick to be the next Lord, then I would pick Chadrick without question. I have said it before and will say it again, he has been more of a son to us than the pair of you put together and that is a fact so I will hear no more of this petty bickering and jealousy. Now, that said, back to the subject, I think it is a wonderful gesture of goodwill toward the staff and you do not have to like it, any of you, but I agree with Chadrick. I will leave him to think of a suitable sum." "Thank you, Father, on your behalf, it shall be done."

"I wish that you would stop calling our father your father as he is not yours. You were nothing but an unwanted baby and a basted child until adopted, you are not of our blood and not a Mandaten so –."

"Enough, Grant!" Snapped their father. "Sometimes I wonder if you are of our blood as you are totally different in every way to your brothers. I would not want to do it but I have the power to strike you from my will, leaving you not a thing, absolutely nothing –." He coughed and gasped for air. He slowly composed himself and steadily recovered. "Best you keep that in mind before you next speak. Chadrick is as good a son as any parents could wish for and has been in our family since his birth thirty years ago so it is high time that you accepted it. He has been in this family from only a few hours old and we are glad that he was as he replaced the son that sadly died at birth and he helped us to get over the pain of that sad loss. He has had nothing more than the rest of you and has been given the same opportunities as you all have had and has never been in any of your shadows. He has made the most of his life, taking the opportunities as they were presented and worked hard to achieve something – unlike some that I could mention who have relied on the estate to make a living. Now, that is enough I will hear no more of that kind of talk and I am sick and tired of telling you." He signaled to Alfred who turned his wheel chair and pushed him away. Grant turned and walked away in anger and could be heard mumbling incoherently. "He is not a son of Mandaten not as I am and no brother of mine. Malcolm is gone and that means I am next in line and that means that I will be the next Lord and master, no one will stand in my way. When I am, or even before, he will be gone for good, never more to darken the door with his shadow and that will be the very second after Father is dead and that will be very soon. His comeuppance is planned and will be implemented when the time is right. Now, as for Kevin, he could be a bit of a problem although I can deal with him accordingly. As for Lizabeth and Sammie, not a problem at all, they will be dealt with in time accordingly. Now that I am the eldest son, it stands to reason that I will be the Lord of the Manor, the title will be mine, then my family shall have it all and not a thing, absolutely nothing, will stop me. Bonnie is gone so that means me and my new lady shall rule unhindered."

"Incoherent mumblings from Grant, I guess that he is not a happy bunny."

"Hush, Tomas, he will learn soon enough." "Rightly so, Lizabeth, rightly so." Under his breath, he added." "As will they all even you." Grant returned when he had finished with his mumbling and after pouring a large whisky, sat in the corner just staring with hatred at Chad. His eyes were filled with evil, showing their deep hatred for him.

They had all eaten their fill of food from the variety of food stalls throughout the day and it had been agreed in advance there was to be no cooked dinner. It was a good thing everyone had agreed to this for the hour was late when the last vehicle had left and the kitchen staff had already retired to bed as they were all tired after their four a.m. start. They would be up and working long before the family on Sunday morning, preparing more freshly baked products to sell at the market stall.

"You lot can all do as you please, as for me, I am for my bed. The young ones have already gone up so good night all and see you in a few hours. You coming, Demmie?" Chad made his way to exit the room.

"Not yet, just finishing my drink." Said Demmie. He did not reply to her and just glanced in her direction. "Chad is right, I am for my bed also, I will walk up with you, if that is alright?" "Absolutely fine, Greta." Chad said. The rest of the family followed, leaving Grant and Demmie alone in the lounge. As they walked toward the stairs, they heard the unmistakable chink of glasses and assumed that that had poured another drink.

"Greta, can I have a quiet word with you?" Chad asked quietly. "Certainly, when would you like it?" She replied. "No time like the present." Chad said and they waited for everyone else to disappear into their rooms. Then Chad began. "Do you remember talking to my bitch of a wife on Monday evening about Bonnie's suspicion that Grant was having an affair?" "Yes, but she never got the chance to say who it was that she suspected as she died so suddenly and tragically." "Very tragically and I had the thought that it was to silence her and get her out of the way.

I think that her suspicions were right about the affair and I think that I know who it is with, my wife. I now know that she has played me false from the moment that we first met. Could it be possible that she would go as far as to commit murder out of her desire for Grant? No, that is a silly thought or is it?" He looked at Greta. "So, you also think it is her? She whispered paused then continued. As far as wanting Bonnie out of the way, that could be true but – I would not want to say yes or no to committing murder –." "Are you saying that you had the same thought as me Greta?" "Bonnie did not say it in so many words but I had my suspicions and I have seen the way that Demmie looked at Bonnie and her eyes said to me that she wanted her gone. I have also been observing her and Grant closely for some time and to be hon-est, I was surprised when you two got married and have always thought that she was not right for you. There is something about her that reads false and she is an excellent liar. I have discovered that she is very devious and extremely deceitful. That much I do know and have gathered from the moment that we first meet. You have not been together that long only, about three years, so you should be in what they say is still the honeymoon period so what makes you think that of her Chad?" "To start with Greta, shall we say the bedroom was not too bad at first, not exception-al and I got the impression that when it did happen,she was not that interested. I have felt that she has not been interested in me for at least the past couple of years or so and it has been negligi-ble and even less since she has taken up running. She has always been far too tired, I told her that I would go running with her and that never happened as she would always come up with a rea-son why I should not. She was always home late and sometimes I could smell aftershave on her clothes – the same as the other day and there were always stains of some sort on her clothes." Chad said, "That must have been awful for you."

"Maybe at first but then I just gave up. It seemed the only thing to do. If I did question her, she always palmed it off by say-ing that someone must have laid something on her clothes to get the smell on them and someone had spilled something. The night that Bonnie died, she rushed out and jumped into his car before anyone else had a chance, shouting that he should not go alone. It was as though the whole event, even poor Bonnie dying, was pre-planned. I heard her whisper to him that everything would be alright, they didn't think that I would hear or notice that her hand was on his shoulder, and the way he smiled at her. I also noticed that he squeezed her hand affectionately and thought that it was not the action of a distressed husband who was watching his wife suffer and barely cling to her life. Malcolm took the family while we, the – shall we say 'not blood' family, stayed behind."

"I remember all of that."

"Well, I didn't think too much of it at the time and put it down to the situation but when they did not get back until well after midnight, almost one a.m. in fact, I began to wonder. I was feeling very dizzy and had a very strange feeling after my second coffee that she gave me. When she came to our room, her dress was torn with her zip caught up in it and that is not all. There was a suspicious stain there." He pointed to Greta's bottom. "I was feeling very sleepy and my eyes had begun to blur but in the haze, when her dress was ripped off, I could see that she was not wearing any underwear. Oh, she came up with a pretty sound and convincing reason but after several other little things that have been happening leading up to this week, with looks, smiles, glances, and what they thought was secret touching when they thought that no one was looking, I have become even more suspicious. I believe that I was taken in right from the start with her lies and falseness and that she only used me. Now, if we are correct, then I am sure that Cadiston will see that Bonnie was murdered and investigate." "That is if that horrible Standish does not stop him." Greta said. "I think that he is a very determined detective who wants to find the truth behind the sudden deaths that we have been faced with." "Just had another thought Chad, about his first wife and –." She put a finger to her lips. "We cannot talk anymore now, they are coming up the stairs." "Another time, then." "They stayed forty minutes after everyone else and they look a bit ruffled, night, Chad." Greta whispered. "Night, Greta."

Demmie noticed Greta walk away and heard her bedroom door close, then asked with suspicion in her voice. "That all looked very comfy, very cosy, so what did she want with you? You looked very pally so what were you two talking about with so much tenderness?" He did not like to lie but knew that it would be the only way to keep his and Greta's suspicions secret. "If you are referring to Greta, she was just saying how much she misses Malcolm and how lucky I am to have you. She said that it must be the same for Grant missing Bonnie, especially now that we all know that she was pregnant and how good it is to have all the family to support them. Her son and daughter are a big comfort to her as well. Lowell is so much like his father, it is almost like he is still here."

Her reply carried an air of bitterness. "For a start, Lowell is not her son. He was from Malcolm's first marriage, Greta is only his second wife." She snapped. "That is totally immaterial and a cruel thing to say. When Germelia died of cancer, he was at a loose end with a small child to look after and that was when Greta came into his life, as his childminder. It was not planned to be that way. The fact is, it did happen. She has been a good wife to him and an excellent mother to Lowell and their daughter, Jennifer, so there is no need to say such a nasty thing. What is it with you anyhow? You seem to have changed and become very bitter of late. Do I sense a touch of jealousy? Now, I would expect it from Grant and it is alright for you and Grant to be pally but, as for me, well, I thought that you were different." "Look on it however you want. However you look at it or wrap it up in fine lace, it is still the truth. And jealous of her? Pah, why should I be? This with Grant and me is totally different." "That is a hurtful and spiteful thing to say, even to me. A nasty attitude but I will not argue the point with you. You disappoint me greatly Demmie. Now, to change the subject, what do you think of Grant? You have been spending quite a bit of time with him so how is his mode?" She looked at him in a way that he had not seen her look before. "What are you getting at or implying?" He sensed anger and hostility in her voice. He smiled inwardly to himself because he felt that he had struck a raw nerve. He remained calm and spoke softly. "Implying, nothing at all, just concerned for Grant after the loss of his wife so suddenly and their unborn child. Unlike him, I do care and even though he is a complete ass to me, if you help him through his trauma, all the better." The tone of her voice changed from heavy and angry to soft, which made it clear to him that there was more to them than meets the eye and that the suspicions he and Greta had were probably very well-founded, "Grant is a real darling when you get to really know him and so misunderstood. He is handling it very well and I am the only one that can help him without asking a lot of silly, awkward questions. I am playing a major part in helping him recover." She said. "Alright, good enough Demmie, no more to be said on the subject. I am for bed after a quick shower." He turned and walked into the bathroom. Ten minutes later, he was climbing into bed and glanced toward his wife. "I'll just have a quick shower." She said. "Just don't fall asleep in the bath." "I said shower," she snapped in reply.

He refrained from answering her but in silence, he thought even more. He waited until he could hear the shower running then inspected her clothes. "Mm, that smell again." He was back in bed before she had left the bathroom. Moving around the bed, she noticed that her clothes were not how she had left them but said nothing. She stood for a few seconds and then climbed into bed. Just out of his curiosity, he turned and started to kiss and caress her but as had been the usual for a while now, he was pushed away. "Just go to sleep, Chad. I am far too exhausted for any of that sex stuff."

He turned over and was soon asleep but in his sleep, his mind remained very active. Her actions had almost confirmed to him that there was something between her and Grant. There was just one problem and that was how to prove it. Just as he knew that Cadiston needed evidence to prove murder, he also needed solid evidence to prove an affair. Sunday morning was soon upon them and once again, they were all up and about early. The September sun shone again, and with the gates open, the second

116

day of the Black Powder Gun Show had begun. Kevin had a massive interest in old weapons and was in his element when he got to talk about all the various types, from the very earliest examples to the very last black powder weapon produced before the change to the bullet and cartridge. Because of their delicacy, the originals could not be used and were only for display and no expense had been spared in reproducing exact replicas of every gun that he had and that had been made. His collection was extensive and to avoid an incident, it was with great care that he would help those that could afford to pay to take a shot with the weapon of their choice.

While giving his talk, he had spotted Cadiston in the audience and without hesitation, acknowledged his presence. There was also a young teenager sitting with his mother who asked if it would be possible to just feel the American Colt range of pistols on display as his mother could not afford to pay for him to have a shot. "Which of these weapons do you like, my boy?"

"All of them, sir. From the Colt Patterson, Colt Walker, Colt Dragoon, Colt Navy 36, the army 44, right up to the Colt 45 Peacemaker. Then there are the other makes like Remington's, Smith and Wesson, the Springfield and Sharps Carbine the Henry Repeating rifle and, of course, the famous Winchester." The boy said. "You know your guns, my lad."

He then explained how he had been brought up on westerns because his father was an avid fan of that era of American history and that had rubbed off onto him and he also had a massive interest in it. He also explained that his father had purchased almost every western movie there was, from the very earliest to the present day, and had a collection of plastic gun models of some of these weapons. The boy wiped a tear as he spoke. His desire was to be able to handle the real thing. It had been his father who had pre-booked the tickets and was looking forward to the show but had a sudden illness and sadly passed away five days ago. Before his last breath, he had insisted that he and his mother attend in memory of him. They both had tears in their eyes and wiped them continually until an elderly gentleman, showing his concern, passed his handkerchief for them to dry their eyes. The audience had listened intently to the lad's story and all agreed that if Kevin would allow it, they would all contribute to the cost to enable this lad to realise his father's dream of firing a real western pistol. Kevin was very moved by this story and thought for a moment before he spoke.

"I will not take your money although several of you have already paid for yourselves to use the available weapons. If you agree, I will give this young man and his mother a private viewing after the show with no charge in memory of their husband and father, what do you say?" There was a resounding cheer. "Very charitable, enjoy it, my boy, enjoy it for your father." Said the elderly gentleman. "Thank you all so very much, it means a great deal to us." Said the boy's mother, then they both resumed their seats so that the show could continue to the next stage. This interlude had totally relaxed Kevin even more than he already was. "That is sorted then so now, the show goes on." Every show that had taken place on Saturday was a great success and after chatting with this young lad, Kevin was filled with a new zeal and spring in his step. As he picked up the next gun, the show continued. Again, he held everyone's undivided attention. "For safety reasons, we cannot place a full charge into these weapons. Even the bullets and cartridges all have a smaller charge. But now, the first black powder pistol to be fired, is the wheel lock pistol." He continued to talk about the weapon as he loaded it and after it was fired safely, it was followed by several other black powder pistols with his full description of them – all without a single problem. From the flintlock pistols, he moved onto the percussion cap, then to the invention of the bullet. From the pistols, he moved onto black powder muzzleloader muskets and rifles, then the rifles that used bullets and with each show, he kept the rifle that he loved the most for his show's finale.

Kevin's son, James, was there to assist him and before the show had begun, had been introduced to the audience. James loved these weapons almost as much as his father and was learning about the various guns in his father's gun shop, where he worked. With his father's prompt, he disappeared into the marquee and returned with the final black powder muzzleloader to end the first show of the day. James knew that this weapon was the one his father loved the most of all the black powder weapons that he had. This was the famous Kentucky Long Rifle and he had his example of this weapon meticulously replicated. As he began his talk about the gun, his enthusiasm spilled into the audience. They could all see that he handled the weapon lovingly but to Cadiston's trained eye, it appeared that he went from being totally relaxed to a little bit tense as he was feeling the weight of this gun. He noticed that this was something he had not done with any other weapon that he had handled and fired. Kevin tried not to show his anxiousness and continued with his talk but Cadiston noticed the change in his facial expression. "You all know about the Battle of the Alamo that took place in 1836, from February 23rd to March 6th. You have probably seen several movies made about it." Heads were nodding. "Well, it was weapons like this, the Kentucky Long Rifle, that the handful of extremely brave defenders were using. They fought and died for their belief, to free Texas from the might of the Mexican army lead by General Santa Anna. There are, of course, names that you will all remember and can easily be called to mind who defended the Alamo to the last man. Brave men such as James Bowie, William B Travis, and of course David Crockett. There were many more whose names are not recalled so easily but if you look up the Alamo on the internet, you will find all their names there. You may be surprised to find the name of Daniel Bourne, who was born in England in 1810 I believe, who also fought and died in the Battle of the Alamo. Now, for safety reasons, as has been already explained, we are not allowed to place a full charge into these weapons. They would carry the shot for a surprisingly long distance. The charge placed in this weapon, as with all the other black powder and bullet weapons, has been carefully measured and will carry the shot just as far as the target that you see placed there. You have all seen in the movies, the rows of soldiers with their muzzleloaders, and when they are fired, the cloud of smoke that envelopes them. You have only seen the effect of one weapon at a time here. He smiled. "Just as well, otherwise I would lose sight of you all and you would be choking on it." The audience laughed and chuckled. "When this weapon is fired, there will be a large cloud and the air will be filled with the smell of gunpowder. Again, imagine if you can, twenty or thirty or even more of these all being fired at the same time. Now, to load." He appeared to be feeling the weight of his weapon and although no one else would notice this, Cadiston did. He watched Kevin's expression and whispered to his wife. "Samantha, he has been extremely relaxed until now, see how he is handling the Kentucky rifle? I have the feeling that he thinks, as I do, that something is wrong with it. Have you noticed that the mother and son who distracted him are no longer present? They left the second that weapon was brought out and that makes me very suspicious." "I saw them leave and wondered why especially after his chat. So what should we do?"

"Could we stop the show now because of a suspicion?" As they spoke, Kevin continued with his appraisal of the weapon and before continuing, slid the ramrod down the barrel and seemed satisfied that all was as it should be before he continued. This, as you know, is a powder horn. Later, they used the powder flask, and the amount of powder that goes into the barrel is measured by the mechanism. So, in goes the powder. The weapon is then tapped on the ground to help move the powder down the barrel. Next, in goes the lead shot wrapped in a small piece of wadding, almost there. Now, we use the ramrod to push the wadding down the barrel, taking care not to place too much pressure on it to avoid any distortion to the lead ball." The ramrod appeared to go to its full length. "Partly cock the weapon and open the pan, then place a measure of powder into it. Close the pan cover and pull the hammer all the way back until it locks. You are now ready to fire." He brought the rifle up to his shoulder and took aim. "When firing any gun such as this, it is important to squeeze the trigger gently and not to jerk it, that is if you want an accurate shot." Kevin continued.

"If we are going to stop him, we had best do it now before –."

In that second, the trigger was squeezed, followed by a large flash and a massive explosion, causing the barrel to split open and send pieces of splintered metal through the air. Panic immediately erupted in the spectators as they all tried to run from the horrific scene of a man who stood for a few seconds before collapsing to his knees and then onto his belly with his face gone and his head virtually blown off. "Oh my God, we are too late!" Cadiston shouted as they ran forward. James stood traumatised and could not move. He was just staring down at his father's lifeless body. Cadiston and his wife were quickly at Kevin's side. "Samantha, can you do anything for him?" Cadiston asked. Her experience told her the answer to the question.

"Sorry, Ashton, no, he is gone. The explosion removed his face and almost took his head off." "You can do nothing for Kevin but try and help his son, James, while I get the ambulance and forensics here. I will somehow cordon the area, get a collection of photographs and write my notes detailing every aspect, then pick up the gun, and start picking up the debris. I am convinced that this was no natural accident but was staged to look like one – just as Bonnie's and Malcolm's accidents were. This will be a massive job for our firearms boys, they will have a job on their hands sorting this one." But Cadiston was not daunted by the prospect, just dismayed and angry at himself because he had not acted quick enough to save Kevin.

Samantha had sat James down and was giving him a drink of water. He was in pieces and felt blame for what had just happened as he had passed the offending weapon to his father.

Samantha was trying to reassure him while Cadiston had been busy cordoning the area off around the site where pieces of the barrel could have flown. He knew that it was important to collect every single piece so he did not want them trampled into the ground.

After hearing the explosion and seeing the panic, the family had been quick to gather near Kevin's headless body. Lizabeth had screamed and burst into uncontrollable floods of tears while her son, Kansas, and sister-in-law, Greta, tried to console her. Lowell and Jennifer were beside their cousin, James, who just stood and stared at the body. When Sadie arrived at the scene, standing with her son, there was absolutely no consoling her. She began to scream and was physically sick seeing her husband's deformed body lying on the ground.

"Samantha, will you get something to cover the body, please. This is not a sight that anyone needs to see, especially his wife and son." Said Cadiston.

A cloth was quickly found and in seconds, Kevin's body was covered.

While Samantha was seeing to this, Cadiston had carefully photographed the damaged rifle and the surrounding area before he picked up the damaged rifle and powder horn that Kevin had used and nothing would be touched or moved until after he had finished photographing and documenting the scene carefully. With his photographs and documentation secure he then began to retrieve the larger and easily visible pieces of the splinted barrel placing them into an evidence bag as whatever he was doing he always carried several with him and feeler gloves, he took several photographs of Kevins body from different angles documenting each one as he had taken his picture, they did not make for a pleasant picture to look at but he knew it was necessary. He knew that there would be very small pieces that could not be seen with the naked eye and they would be collected by forensics. It was then that Grant turned up and seemed more concerned with the gun than his own brother's tragic death. "Hey, where are going with that weapon mate?" He shouted and demanded that it be handed to him. Cadiston just looked at him and instantly knew who it was. "Grant, isn't it?" He asked. "Not that it is any of your business but what of it? I ask you again, where are you going with that weapon, give it to me now?" Cadiston remained calm even though he could sense the hostility in Grant's voice. "And I will tell you, sir, to have it analysed by our firearms experts to see what went wrong." "Firearms experts? No need for that as I can tell you exactly what has just happened. It is quite simple, Kevin finally got careless and overloaded the weapon. He put far too much powder in the charge, it is as simple as that. I always knew he would do it one day so there you have it. Now, I will just take the weapon." Grant replied. "I think not, sir, this may well have been a tragic accident but without fail, our fire-arms experts will be checking this weapon over thoroughly and there will be no argument about it."

Grant did not like to be told and as Malcolm and Kevin were now out of the way he, was sure that he was to be the next Lord. Angrily, he shouted. "I am the next Lord Mandaten as the only remaining son and blood heir so just who the hell do you think you are to tell me what is to be done?! You have absolutely no right –." Cadiston raised his hand to silence him while he pulled out his warrant card. "I beg to differ, sir, I have every right." After looking at the card, Grant calmed down. "Of course." He snarled. "Should have realised and remembered you from the other day. You are that Cadiston, the detective. Not very good with faces but I should have recognised you. Well, take the dammed thing then and check it over and you will find that it was simply overloaded. I knew that Kevin would make a terrible, disastrous mistake one day." "I do not believe that, not for a single minute, Uncle Grant. My father was extremely careful with all these weapons and he fired it yesterday eight times without a single problem so there has to be another explanation." Said Kevin's son from the side. "What do you mean another explanation, such as, James? What other explanation could there be? Accept it, my boy. Your father finally got careless and overloaded the dammed thing." Cadiston could see how this was affecting Kevin's wife and son so stepped in. "Enough now, Grant. Kevin's wife and son have enough trauma to contend with without you adding to it. If you cannot be supportive, then I suggest that you leave right now. I will question you later. Our experts will examine the remains of this weapon and then we shall see what happened to it. By the way, Grant, it looks very much like you have been in a violent fist fight. You have a bleeding split lip, and looks like you have lost a tooth. And that is not all, your knuckles are also grazed and bleeding. If I am not mistaken, looks like you will end up with a black eye as well." Cadiston observed him carefully."- Fight? Not me. I guess that must have happened when I tripped over a guy rope and banged my head in my haste to get here after the explosion. What gives you the right to call us by our first names? Can I have the gun now?" "Personal touch. And sorry, no go, the weapon stays with me." Grant walked away in a huff. Cadiston's notebook was in his hand and he wrote a comment about Grant's actions and his lack of caring. He noted: Very insistent that he should have the weapon, why? Walked away in a huff saying. "Take the dammed thing then." Cadiston wrote down word for word of what had been said, then added a description of his appearance, including his cut and bleeding lip, missing tooth, grazed knuckles, and black eye. He added: Said that he tripped but looks more like he had been in a fight? Seemed more interested in the gun than his brother's tragic death. Why? This had all happened so fast and within minutes, the public information system had burst to life with a message.

"Ladies and gentlemen, unfortunately an accident has occurred at the Black Powder Show. This area will be closed to the public for the foreseeable future but ..." There was a slight pause. "All other activities will continue. Will all the spectators that were present at the time of the incident please report to the first aid station to ensure that there are no injuries, thank you for your cooperation." The system went silent. Shortly after, a carriage pulled up and Lord Mandaten stepped out with assistance. "We heard an explosion so what has happened here and where is my son Kevin?" James had gathered himself by now and was at his grandfather's side to help support him. "Take it, easy grandfather, I know it is hard for you but it will bring on another attack." Said James. "Never mind that, James, what has happened?" "It is my father, he ... he is dead." "Dead? It can't be. Kevin dead ... First Bonnie and her unborn child, then Malcolm and now Kevin ... But how? What happened?" Grant stepped forward before anyone else could answer. "How, I will tell you how, Father, he finally got careless and overloaded that Kentucky Rifle of his with black powder."

"I do not believe that, Grant. Kevin was very particular and very careful with all these weapons, especially that one. He used every weapon on Saturday and there was not a single mishap or accident of any sort, he used the Kentucky several times without incident so why should it have been any different today?" He then spotted Cadiston. "You got here quickly, Detective."

"I was already here, my Lord, to see the show." Informed Cadiston.

Lord Mandaten placed a hand onto his shoulder and whispered in his ear.

"I did not like that Standish fellow, Bradinham and I have now remembered when I first had dealings with him. It was four years ago when my brother's family was wiped out and he wanted the case closed without proper investigation, saying they were all killed in a tragic road accident. We thought differently then and that hasn't changed. No one has ever been found or prosecuted for dangerous driving on that day so now I ask you personally, investigate my son's death, Cadiston. I do not believe for one minute that it was an accident. He was far too careful and while you are at it, I ask you to investigate Bonnie's and Malcolm's death as well. I believe that it has started up again."

"Started up again? What do you mean by that remark, my Lord?" Asked Cadiston. "From the late sixteen hundreds and over the ensuing centuries, every so often members of our family have died mysteriously. There has never been a full investigation and that means no one has been found guilty for the murders. Now, according to Standish, since he has been on the scene of every single one, each one was deemed a tragic accident. I do not believe they were so investigate them for me, Cadiston. Get to the truth and bring the guilty to justice, whoever they are." Lord Mandaten pleaded. "It shall be done, my Lord and believe me, if it was not an accident, and that applies to any of your family that has passed away, I will somehow find out and bring the culprit to face the full penalty of the law." "Do it then, my man, whatever it takes and whoever it was, do it!" "You can rest assured of that, my Lord, I already have my suspicions on these current deaths in your family and I am determined to get them investigated fully, you have my word. I will get to the bottom of them all, if it is the last thing I do. I will not give up on the search for the truth, my Lord, and if I have to go against orders to get to the bottom of it and carry out my investigation in my own time, then I will." Cadiston said confidently. "Good man." Said Lord Mandaten.

Leaving Lord Mandaten with his family, Cadiston pocketed his phone and turned to his wife. "Ambulance and forensics are en route, Samantha, and should be here soon. I have started on it but now we just need to finish securing this area."

Ten minutes after the incident, Chadrick had arrived on the scene. "That was one hell of a loud bang. In fact, sounded like an explosion. What in heaven's name was it and what has happened? Oh my, who is it covered under that bloodied cloth?" Greta was the first to answer to him.

"It is your brother. Kevin and he is dead. His Kentucky rifle exploded in his face and almost took his head off. It was horrible. I had the misfortune to see him before he was covered." His face went pale and he looked stunned. Then placed a hand on her shoulder. "I can't believe it. Grant too? A horrible sight for you, Greta." He took her in his arms as it seemed the most natural thing to do and as he paused for a moment, their eyes met and were locked in a warm, caring gaze. He reached into his pocket and passed her his clean handkerchief. "To wipe your eyes, best you go help Sadie and James as their need is the greatest. I need to ask, did she see?" "She did, they both did."

"Not good, that picture of husband and father will stay in their memory, and in yours, forever now. Best go do what you can to give some comfort to them." While they spoke Demmie turned up.

"Wondered where you had got to. Most of the family is already here." Chad said. "I was in the little girl's room, now what has happened?" "Kevin's gun exploded in his face and he is dead." He sensed a half-smile come to her lips. "Greta is going to be with Sadie and James." "I will come with you, Greta, this is terrible. First Bonnie, then Malcolm and now Kevin … With all these accidents it makes you wonder who will be next. Terrible just terrible." Her eyes were on Grant as she spoke. "We must do all that we can to give our support to you, Grant, Sadie, and, of course, you, Greta. I see that all the family is here now apart from Sammie. I wonder where they are. It was a loud explosion and we all heard the bang. They must have, as it carried a long way but, well they are not here –."

"Not yet but they should be soon." Replied Greta. "The last time I saw them they were over in the children's play area with Sadie." Said Jennifer shaking as she had also seen the remains of her uncle Kevin. "Well, Sadie is here so they could not have been there with her at that time in the play zone, could they?" said Lizabeth through her tears. Chadrick began to look puzzled.

"They must have heard it, I was right over by the stable block, helping to saddle the western ponies and we all heard it. Lizabeth, followed soon after by her son and husband, were here not long after Greta and they all heard it so where could they be?" "I do not know where they were but they were not with us and we are here so does it really matter?" Lizabeth said with an attitude. "It matters, Lizabeth, all the family should be here. You three get over there with James and Sadie and I will call on the radio and get them here. Even though there is nothing anyone can do. By the way, Demmie, you have blood on your sleeve." Chad said and pointed at the stain. "Damn, it must have been when I changed for my monthlies." Demmie replied. "Ok, just thought I would let you know." He watched them walk away, then opened the channel and began to call. "Chadrick to Sammie, come in." The radio crackled. "Chadrick to Sammie, come in, do you read me?" There was still no reply. He changed the channel. "Come in Sammie, Walter, Gloria, anyone? Chadrick to Sammie, do you read me?"

There was still silence so he tried every channel that was available, just in case they had logged into the wrong one. Try as he may, their radio remained silent. At this point he became concerned. Herbert had walked up to join him. "You look worried, is there a problem?" He asked."Cannot reach Sammie." Chad said. "Maybe a flat battery." Herbert suggested. "Shouldn't be, they were all charged last night. I have tried every channel and she is not on any of them. All I can do is search for her but will need some help, Herbert." They had talked for long enough and knew that there was no time for any further delay and the time was now to put the search into fruition. Lowell walked calmly over to Cadiston and stood for a moment. He gazed around at the family before speaking.

"Detective, may I just say something to you? It may have absolutely no bearing on what has just occurred today but, well, you should know anyhow."

"And what may that be?" Asked Cadiston. "Well, I cannot be totally sure but after yesterday's show, we were on the way back to the Manor and I thought that I saw uncle Grant near the gun marquee." "Thank you. Lowell isn't it?"

"It is, I will get back to mother now." He turned and walked away, leaving Cadiston to continue picking up the visible metal fragments. After two hours, the searchers regrouped at the aid station. "We have searched this whole site and she is nowhere to be found Chad and that is worrying." said Jacob. "Jeremiah, will you check the Manor if no one has done so please?" Requested ChadThere were nods of the head to signal that no one had checked the Manor. "The rest of us will search the woods. It is out of bounds and cordoned off and they should not be there but as it is the only area that we have not searched yet, we had better check it out." Said Chad.

"Haven't checked the old Manor ruins either Chad." Said Jeremaih as he turned to leave for the manor.

"True but we will search the woods first. She would have no reason to be in there but I don't know where else to look apart from the old ruins." Said Chad. "Let's go then, Chad. With all these deaths that are happening in the family, the sooner we find her, the better and hopefully alive." "Don't even want to think that thought, Herbert." They made their way up to the woods and the search began. They were spread out and walked slowly forward through the cordoned area. Chad knew that it would take at least one and half hours to walk through the small forest and just twenty minutes into the search, a cry went up from Freddie. "Over here, all of you! Over here, I have found them, all three of them are here together and I hate to say but it is not good." A steady walk turned into a run and when they saw the tragic scene that greeted them, they all gasped. "Oh my giddy aunt!"

"Good Grief!" "Stone the crows." "Geeze man." "Alright everyone stay back and do not enter the crime sceme for fear of cross contamination, said Herbert extremely loud so that they could all hear him. "This is unbelievable, how in heaven's name could that have happened?" "A good question, Jacob, and one that will need answering. Freddie, I saw that police detective, Cadiston, was here today. Can you go and find him and bring him up here pronto please. He was down with Kevin at – Well, that area. So, if he is still there then he will be easy to find." Chad said."Saw an ambulance and more police arrive and go there so no problem." Freddie turned and began to run. "I am on the way, Chad." He shouted and sprinted away.

A few surprised expressions had been voiced but most of them had remained silent with their mouth agape, shocked at what they were seeing. Chad was the first to approach the bodies and issued orders straight away. Re-iterating what Herbert had already said, "The rest of you, hold your distance and do not disturb the scene or the surrounding area any more than absolutely necessary. Cadiston will need to examine it carefully." "What are you thinking, Chad?" Herbert asked. "Not sure, Herbert. First Bonnie, then Malcolm, a short time ago Kevin, and now on the same day Sammie, her daughter and her husband. I think an occasional accident, yes, but we now have seven deaths all within a week. Accidents or something more sinister?" "You mean – what we think and that is murder? But there are six not seven aren't there unless my maths are wrong?" Herbert looked puzzled. "Seven, counting Bonnie's unborn child. I am beginning to wonder about all these sudden deaths but here comes the real expert and if I am not mistaken, he will be the one who able to find out the truth." "Chadrick, you sent for me? The lad didn't say why, just that you needed me to be here in the woods and quickly. It took a bit longer to get here as I had to drop something off at my car." Cadiston said.

"No matter, you are here now. Sorry to drag you away from Kevin that was terrible, but you will certainly have to see this. Step aside, men, and let the detective through." They all stepped back. When he saw the three bodies, even Cadiston gasped. "Today of all days, this is not good but the first thing we must do is to secure this area. Can your men do that for me by attaching more ropes from that tree to that one? Then skirt around the perimeter and tie off the other end to that tree there, please." "There is some rope at the hut near the main gate that I can go get." Jason was gone before anyone could answer him.

"A young woman, I must say a very attractive young woman, is making her way up here, shall I stop her Detective?" Herbert asked.

"It's alright, Herbert, that is my wife Samantha."

As soon as she arrived, Cadiston addressed her. "Photographs and documentation first, then Samantha, will you look at the three bodies, please, and give me your opinion." "Three bodies? Surely not more deaths here today, Ashton, one death is one too many –." She trailed off. "Afraid so." Said Cadiston. "I have kept the area as undisturbed as possible for you. I was just saying that there are now seven deaths in the family, all within a week. It does not appear right to me, Detective, but then I am not an expert." Said Chad.

"Just between us, Chadrick, me neither. Now, while my wife inspects the bodies, a few questions." "Ask all you want, Detective, we will do all that we can to help you." Chad said. "Herbert, if my mind serves me correctly?" Herbert nodded. "Tell me what you can." "Not much, really. My sons, Jeremiah and Jason, and I were over at the market stall, that is where we have been all day until I joined Chad. Then we called the rest of the men."

"No need to question your sons then as you were all together." Said Caadiston. "Name's Jacob, and those are two of my sons.

Like Herbert, we were all together fetching and carrying supplies all day. We had gone to the warehouse to fetch more supplies as they were selling them out pretty quickly. When Herbert called for us, we came running."

"So how many more are there?"

"Just one, Anthony. I don't know for sure but have a pretty good idea where he was." His sons Freddie and Charles who were there smiled and giggled as if they also knew. "Alright you two. If I am correct, I think that he was doing a bit of courting with Rose, one of the kitchen helpers." "That will do then, Jacob." Chadrick's radio crackled into life. "Ambulance is seeing to Kevin and police forensics are securing and picking over the area." "who called for that?" asked Chadrick. "I did." Replied Cadiston. "You may be inexperienced Cadiston but you are certainly on the ball in arranging what you need." "Try to Chad, and it looks as though we will need more transport to move these unfortunate people and we had better get forensics up here also." His phone clicked and in seconds, they were en route to the Manor. "Will someone wait at the gate and direct them here?" "On it." Replied Jeremiah who had returned from checking the Manor for Sammie and her family. "Now, can you give me their names?" Asked Cadiston. "Sammie Mandaten, or rather Larkspere is her married name, she was married to Walter who lies there and the other poor victim, the young girl, is their daughter, Gloria. That is a whole family wiped out by some crazed archer." "Lord and Lady Mandaten's daughter, son in law, and their granddaughter." "Thank you for that, Herbert. Now, I will take a good look around and do my assessment before our forensic team arrives." The men watched in amazement as he carefully examined the area in minute' detail. "Glad you got some rope to cordon this place off Herbert." Said Cadiston "Jason has gone to get some more for you, he will be back in a jiffy." Herbert replied. He saw him heading away, first he began to walk, then jog, and finally broke into a full run. Cadiston was being very methodical and was busy taking photographs and notes as he required every detail to be documented, all the while at the same time he was mumbling to himself.

"Broken branch and twigs, crushed grass with some footprints in the soft ground, look identical to those observed at Devil's Dyke. Three bodies, all together, signs of dragging. Bushes and area show signs of a scuffle, possibly a fight. I wonder, could Grant and Walter have fought and was he protecting his family? This evidence could put Grant in the frame for murder. Ground disturbed and on this bush …" He had a closer look. "It looks like blood, need to get a sample." He produced a polythene bag and a penknife from his pocket, cut the piece of bush, and placed the blood-splattered leaves into it. "Deeper footprints, then just toe imprints, like someone running away."

"Ashton, can you come here?" "With you in a minute, Samantha. I would say a man going this way and in a mighty big hurry." He looked in the general direction. "Interesting, they appear to head back toward the black powder marquee. Now, that could be Grant and there appear to be three sets heading toward … Let me see … Yes, toward the main gate. Get forensics to confirm direction. One lighter and not so heavy on their feet, the other two deeper. Archery site over there and bodies appear to be in line with them. A fair distance for an arrow to travel. Can't see anything else at this point in time so let forensics check the area more thoroughly, now Cadders get to Samantha".

By now, Jason had returned with some more thick rope. "Good man, will you tie that end to the tree just there, then around this complete area, right up to that tree there?" Asked Cadiston. "Leave it to us and if there is not enough rope, then I will fetch some more." Said Jason. "Good man, I will leave it with you." Cadiston approached his wife and she stood up. "This is very strange, Ashton, all three have been killed with arrows. One accident I can understand but three? That is a tough pill to swallow. You were involved in checking the area for evidence while I checked the position of the archery targets. They are in line with the bodies. I also looked at the trajectory of an arrow fired from down there and it would need to be extremely high to reach this spot."

"Noticed that also precious but look at the distance from the firing line to the target, then the additional distance to the bodies and where they would be shot from. Needs a hell of a bow to achieve that sort of distance. If my memory serves me right, an English longbow in the right hands would achieve that distance but it would need to be in the hands of an expert to get the right height and trajectory to have the power to penetrate these bodies. From the marks on the ground, at least one of them was dragged from those bushes that have been been damaged in what I suspect was a violent fist fight and placed beside the other two." Cadiston said. "My thoughts also. After a quick examination of the three bodies, I will tell you my thoughts. The arrows on the man, Walter I believe is his name, they have been pushed into his body with great force. I would say by hand, not bow, because of their angle. By the look of his facial bruising and knuckles and without a post-mortem, I would say it indicates a fight just before death." Said Samantha.

"And I am sure that I know who the fight was with but that doesn't mean he murdered them." Said Cadiston. "A much gentler force was used with the two female bodies, Sammie and Gloria, and that tells me that there was no resistance when they were inserted but there is an unexplained gash to Sammie's head. To my mind, she was struck and unconscious before the arrows were planted. Possibly by a heavy stone that was thrown possibly into the bush to try and hide it from sight." She explained. "Saw it Samantha, There is a bloodied stone lying beneath that bush so well spotted," "It had better be taken for examination and my suspicion is that the blood on it will match Sammie's." Said Cadiston."Now back to the arrows. Again, the angle does not align with a falling arrow. In my estimation, without a full test, all three were killed by arrows that had been forced into their bodies by hand and not by a shot from a bow." Samantha speculated."I had that thought when I first saw them but you work in the forensic mortuary so you know a lot more about that side of it than I do, Samantha. If you are standing and get struck, the arrow would be in a downward angle, these are all straight. If the idea was to make it look like a tragic accident, one arrow would have been sufficient so why use two?" Cadiston wondered.

"Overkill, Ashton, and another interesting point, if you look at the arrows, they have all been placed in the exact same positions." Said Samantha.

"Now that is an interesting observation, it most certainly is. The transport is here so we will let them take the bodies away and Charles and you can carry out a full post-mortem, I think." "Absolutely, it will confirm the cause of death and the pressure used to plant the arrows." She said. "Excuse me butting in, Detective, but will that do?" Jacob asked. "Well done, Jacob, that will do just fine." "This is becoming a habit, Detective, fetching a body from here and now we have three and Pete has another." "You are right there, Dave. One thing, will you take special care not to disturb the arrows please? Very important to know the exact angle of their implantation." Cadiston added. "You got it, Sergeant." Said Dave. "Not me, Dave, just plain constable." "Well, the way you handle things, you should be. Bodies straight to the forensic mortuary?"

"Please." They stood and watched, and with them safely removed, Cadiston instructed the forensic team. Then, with his wife by his side, he made his way down to the Manor to break the sad news to the family.

With Kevin's body also removed and the forensic team searching the black powder area for any small fragment of the shattered gun with magnets, the family had all returned to the Manor, leaving the employees to continue with the show. Samantha rang the bell and Jonas was quickly in attendance. "We need to speak to Lord and Lady Mandaten please, Jonas." Said Samantha. "The family are in the long room, Detective Cadiston and this young lady is with you so go straight in, they have been expecting you." "I would rather speak to them alone and not with all the family present." Said Cadiston. "I will show you into the lounge then. I will leave you there and ask Lord and Lady Mandaten to join you, if that is acceptable?" Jonas asked. "Perfectly if it suits Lord and Lady Mandaten." Replied Cadiston and they followed him down the long hall. "Please take a seat while you wait and I am sure that the master and his wife will not mind at all, his lordship has taken a shine to you detective Cadiston."

A few minutes passed and when Lord and Lady Mandaten entered, they rose from their chairs. "Ah, Cadiston, and who is this lovely young lady with you? Is she a police detective?" Asked Lord Mandaten. "In some respect, she is a detective but does her detecting in a different way. May I introduce my wife, Samantha, my Lord my lady" "Hello Samantha, now, tell me, your husband says in some respect? Are you also a detective?" He asked.

"Not as Ashton is, my Lord, my work is with forensics and I carry out post-mortems to determine the cause and time of death. I also look for any other hidden evidence that is to be found on a body, unexplained bruising, and maybe drugs or other substances that should not be present." Samantha explained. "So, you will be carrying that out on my family then?" "I will, my Lord." "Now then, introductions over. You must have a very good reason for wanting to speak to us alone. What have you to tell us? What news have you about our missing daughter, Sammie, her husband, and our granddaughter. I pray that it is not bad news." While he spoke, both Samantha and Cadiston could sense the sadness in his voice. "I have a good reason for speaking with you both alone, my Lord. You already know about your son, Kevin, and that will be thoroughly investigated but we have news concerning your daughter, Sammie, and her family. That is why we are primarily here, sir. I regret that it is bad news, they have all been found and it is with a sad heart and my unpleasant task to inform you that they are also deceased." Said Cadiston.

"Deceased … Sammie deceased? Walter and Gloria also? All three? But how? It cannot be and not today of all days." "I am sorry to have to inform you of this, my Lord, and it is a great shock for you but sadly, they were all found dead together." Cadiston continued. "But how, Cadiston?" Lord Mandaten could hear that he had an air of sadness in his voice. "I cannot say at this point in time, only that I strongly suspect foul play. That is why I wanted to tell you without the rest of the family present. In my past visits to the Manor I have noticed the hostility between them and that is all I will say at this point. We will be able to confirm the cause of death after the post-mortem."

"Bonnie and her unborn child, Malcolm, Kevin, now Sammie, Walter, and Gloria, that is seven. When will these deaths end? Surely, they cannot possibly all be accidents as that nasty Standish would say? There must be foul play, it is the only explanation. I am beginning to understand your thinking, Cadiston, you are thinking along that line and of the opinion that somewhere a member of this family has a hand in these deaths. I charge you to find the killer, Cadiston. Find the killer or killers of our family, whoever they are, and see that they are brought to justice."

"I can only imagine how you are feeling at this moment but leave it to me, sir. I will investigate every aspect of each death and I assure you that I shall not be stopped or just allow them to be written off as a tragic accident as Standish would want to do. I assure you, my Lord, that I am determined not to be silenced or stopped in my pursuit of the truth and can tell you that my suspicions are far too great for that to be the case. I promise you that I will check and double-check every aspect of each individual case and if there is foul play, which I strongly suspect there is, these deaths were not tragic accidents but cover-ups of murder, then be assured that I will find that out, my Lord. I will not stop until I have found all the evidence. A murderer may think that they have covered their tracks very carefully and it may take time to find them but there is always a clue to be found somewhere. They can run but they cannot hide forever. You can rest assured that I will find them, whoever they are. I am a man of my word, my Lord, and even though I am still classed as a trainee detective constable and inexperienced, you have my word and my solemn promise that the culprit or culprits, whatever the case may be, will be found, tried, and convicted."

"Then you go and do it, Cadiston. Inexperienced they say you are and that you may be but I have great faith in you and your abilities. You find the culprit or culprits, whoever they are for all our sakes. And please do it before I succumb to this dammed illness. Only then will I be able to rest in peace." He pulled the bell cord. "Alfred, show these good people out." "Detective, this way, please." Said Alfred motioning toward the door. "Just one more thing, my Lord, please leave the two areas under investigation untouched until the forensic teams have completed their work." "It shall be so Cadiston." They turned and left, walking slowly to the car park.

Rejoining the family, Lord and Lady Mandaten broke the sad news about Sammie, Walter, and Gloria. Tears filled their eyes as they spoke after which Lord Mandaten collapsed and began to cough violently. A handkerchief was placed over his mouth and when it was removed it was clearly visible that he was coughing up blood. The rest of the family stood by and watched. Chadrick and Greta moved quickly to be at his side. They were supporting him on either side while his wife was replacing each bloodied handkerchief with a clean one. He was then given a glass of water and with their caring support, they managed to calm him. He could not speak but managed to pat their hands as a sign of appreciation and a thank you. They understood and did not need the spoken word. The doctor was called and told them to keep him warm, calm, and comfortable in the meantime, saying that he must on no account be stressed or over-excited. This was, in the current situation, near impossible. With his wife, Chad, and Greta beside him, Lord Mandaten sat as comfortably as possible while the rest of the family stayed in the background. Now all they could do was wait.

Chapter Five

The Suicide

"Nasty business all this, Samantha." "It certainly is, Ashton. I do believe you are thinking that you face a murder case on all six counts."

"Seven, my lovely, we must never forget and always include Bonnie's unborn child in the equation. My suspicions grow stronger with every incident and it certainly looks that way. Most of them have been very cleverly disguised to look like accidents, apart from the last three." He said. "Cleverly but not clever enough to fool you, Ashton." He smiled at his wife. "Definitely not, there was real venom in this attack and to achieve what? That is the question. I would say that there is a real hatred and another thing bothers me about these cases and the deaths –." "What is that, Ashton?" "Why did ... Or rather, why does Sergeant Standish want them all closed so quickly without a full investigation and classed as tragic accidents? He was the one that led the case of Lord Mandaten's brother and his entire family four years ago and that of Pedro Santos at Devil's Dyke. It makes me so angry knowing that if Standish had just listened to me after Malcolm's death, we may have prevented another one. I need to have a look, with or without permission, into each one of his cases concerning the Mandaten family to see if they were all classed as tragic accidents and without a full and proper investigation. I don't want to think it, let alone say it, but that leads me to believe that somewhere along the line, there is a cover-up of a murder and somehow Standish is implicated. Now, if we look at Bonnie and her unborn child, Standish had closed the case as an unfortunate accident even before he had read the post-mortem but as far as I am concerned, the post-mortem is more than enough proof that they could have been poisoned. That being the case, their deaths should be investigated. Finding the evidence and proving it is one thing but without further evidence, it willprobably be impossible to prove. Well, you know what I mean. Malcolm … Herbert said the horse was unsettled when he entered the stable to saddle him and he thinks he could have been spooked by someone that knows horses, especially Thundist. And that points to someone on the inside or someone employed by them to scare the animal before he rode it. Out on the ride, it could have been spooked by someone again who knew just how it would react to a situation. It happened up at the Devil's Dyke which has been labelled as haunted and incidents have happened there before. Could it be someone, possibly dressed up, to scare the horse? And instead of Malcolm falling, could he have been pulled from the back of Thundist, then struck with the masonry before being dragged and left to die? With everything carefully placed, it could be misconstrued as an accident by someone who is not looking properly at the evidence, for example, Standish who again has closed the case as a tragic riding accident. It makes me so angry because when you look at the evidence, it is clear that, in fact, it was a very clever murder cover-up. There were plenty of discrepancies at the site and I wanted forensics to be there to give the area a thorough examination but Standish stopped it. Why? Now, there is a question. Kevin had possible sabotage to his gun and when our firearms experts have examined it thoroughly and pieced it together, then we will know the answer to that. Now, Sammie, Walter and Gloria, seems an impossibility that all three would suffer the same fate of death by flying arrows. An accident with maybe one arrow but all of them were struck with two. Two arrows were all implanted into their bodies in the same location. By the signs in the area, it all looks very suspicious. Plus, they were in a restricted and out-of-bounds area. If Standish was here, he would try to say that they are all are very tragic accidents but, again, why? What motive could he have and why does he want to cover up a possible murder? That is something I aim to find out." "Charles said that you were very determined and given time, you will find the answers to all your questions." Said Samantha. "Once you and Charles have completed the post-mortems and Jooners has completed the forensic results, not discounting the result on the gun that Kevin used, I will have some ammunition to load up and with that, no one can deny the need for further investigation."

"You will not let this go, will you Ahton? Not one of them." She asked. "Not a chance, Samantha, even if I have to do it on my own time, against orders, I will continue, it is the only way to get to the truth. I gave Lord and Lady Mandaten my word and solemn promise and I will not break my word. Just because the evidence of a crime does not present itself easily, does not mean that it is not there or does not exist. Evidence presents itself in different forms it can be in a hidden item or in the spoken word, it can even be in someone's mannerisms and body language. The evidence is there and must be found."

"True enough but very difficult." "Never the less, I must keep searching. Anyhow, I have given my word to Lord and Lady Mandaten and when my word is given then I always keep it." "And I know that to be true, I will help you in any way that I can and I know full well that Charles will too." Samantha reassured him. "Goes without saying, Samantha, I already know that I can rely on your full support, my big stumbling block is Standish.

I need a way to bypass him as he has it in him to stop me dead in my tracks. I must find a way around him to get to the true results. As for Sammie and her family, I have a suspect in mind and believe that he has already lied to me. He may think he has me fooled but the truth will come out in his questioning about their deaths. Now let's get this gun back to the experts for a full and thorough examination. When they have completed their analysis, I will have the answer, accident or murder. It will have to be Monday morning now and I will be waiting on their doorstep." The car engine roared to life and they were on their way.

"I must somehow get another look up at the Devil's Dyke. It may be a while since the incident took place, never the less, I do strongly believe that there is some hidden evidence up there and I still need to have another look. I wanted to get our forensics on it straight away. Standish said no need to trouble them and that meant it did not happen, so I guess I will just have to do it myself."

Samantha looked at him and placed her hand onto his. "Not alone, Ashton, not without me. If you are going to risk everything, then we do it together."

He sent her a loving glance and squeezed her hand. "Wouldn't want it any other way." Then he smiled. Very early in the morning of Monday, 29th September, Cadiston was found waiting outside the firearms department. At eight a.m. Daniel arrived and was surprised to see him there.

"Morning Cadders, what brings you to my little abode so early?"

"This …" He carefully unwrapped the damaged rifle. "Need you to have a really good look at this and find out, with your skill and knowledge of firearms, whether it had been tampered with. If you cannot be sure, then get a second opinion." Said Cadiston. "Wow, by the looks of what is left, I would say an old black powder muzzleloader with far too heavy a load." "That is exactly what it was. The question is, can you tell from this if it was tampered with in any way?" He produced a polythene evidence bag. "I picked up these pieces from the site and forensics will be bringing you some more to put the barrel back together or at least into context." "It is in a right old mess and an extremely big job and my guess is that it will take a bit of time. Only then can I answer your question, only after I have taken a really good look and carried out a few tests on it. Only then will we know. By the way, Standish know you are here with this?"

"No, not yet and if it could be avoided, I would rather he did not. Sad to say but I doubt that." "You must have your reasons and they are not for me to question but I can understand as we have had dealings with him. Come to that, where did you get the gun in this condition and why the question?" "I was at the Black Powder Gun Show at Mandaten Manor on Sunday and Kevin Mandaten had his head virtually blown off when it exploded in his face." Cadiston explained. "Now, that name rings a bell. There have been two others from that family, if my memory serves me correctly. Now, let me think … Mmm, got it, Bonnie and Malcolm. But they were both accidents according to Standish or have you other ideas?" He just smiled. "Now this gun that you want us to

141

examine, what makes you think it is suspicious?" "The way that Kevin handled it before his shot and very strong suspicion, some would say a hunch. Plus, there were more deaths at Mandaten Manor yesterday and, as you can guess, I can say no more about them at this point in time. Tell me, Daniel, will you be able to see after your tests etcetera if it was tampered with?" "Leave it to me, Cadders, we have just finished with the shotgun report for Sergeant Folkes that was used in the jewel shop robbery so, my friend, we can get on to this immediately. I don't know why we are still standing on the doorstep, so to speak." He unlocked the door and they went in. "Now bring it over here for me and all those bits that you have." "What I need to know, if possible, is whether this weapon was loaded with an excessive amount of black powder prior to Kevin putting his own powder charge in the barrel. I have the powder horn that he used so can you check if the measurement has been tampered with? Look for any suspicious marks on the –" He smiled. "Well, you know what to look for."

"Leave it to me and it will be gone over very thoroughly. Ah, John is here now and between us, we should come up with your answer." "Ring me." Cadiston said. "Will do. John, come look at what we have to examine, this will prove to be a tough one." They both began to look at the mangled weapon. "You still here, Cadders? Don't worry, we will definitely ring you and not Standish as soon as we have it all analysed but it will take a bit of time to find out all that you need to know about it. Will be difficult to piece together as well but we will give it our best shot." With a wave he made his way up to the office.

"Quarter to nine, you are late, Cadiston." Snapped Standish.

"Not me, Standish, been here since before eight a.m. but had to drop something off." Cadiston said casually. "What and where?" Standish demanded. He was now accepting Cadiston caling him Standish and not sergeant. "Guess you will know at some point so no time like the present … I had to drop something in the firearms department." "Such as?" "Well, firearms, would signify a firearm, surely." "Don't get smart with me, boy! And don't forget before I retire, I have the final say in whether you will make a detective or be returned to the beat." Snapped Standish. "How could I forget that?"

"Now, what weapon and how did you come by it?" "From the Mandaten Black Powder Gun Show. A rifle exploded and killed Kevin Mandaten."

"Well, I am no firearms expert but sounds to me like an overload. Tragic accident again so don't go trying to make more of it than it is as you have tried to do with other incidents. Maybe I will take a stroll down to firearms and have a word with Daniel and John, don't want them wasting their time." Said Standish. "It is not a waste of time. Lord Mandaten himself was there and has requested to know exactly what went wrong with the gun so best let them check it out. His Lordship would not be very pleased if the investigation was halted before it got started or as before, the case was closed before a proper investigation had been carried out." He could see that this time, he had Standish backed into the corner and knew that he did not like this but continued. "We do not want to upset the family any more than they are already with all these deaths, now do we, Standish?" He gave Cadiston a long, cold stare. "Think you are so very clever, don't you? But suppose it can do no harm so we will let them look at it and see what they come up with. Understand this though, it is just for Lord Mandaten and his family and not for you. Even without seeing it, I know that it will be shown as a tragic accident."

Cadiston just smiled and thought, just like all your cases.

Monday arrived and as the exterior of the Manor was bathed in the early morning September sunshine, in the breakfast room the mode was bleak and dark. There was not a word to be said as the family was still numb after the tragic incident with Kevin, followed by the deaths of Sammie, Walter, and Gloria. The staff was all working as quietly as possible as they tried to continue with their daily duties. But as they had become close to the family, sadness filled every heart and it was with great difficulty that none of them burst into tears.

"I wonder if that detective, Cadiston, will be called here again today."

"I certainly hope not, Lizabeth, we have had to call him far too frequently so don't want to see him today, not unless it is a routine visit." Chad said.

"Didn't ask you, Chad, I was speaking to Grant. Anyhow, from all accounts, you and the detective are becoming bosom buddies, you allow him to call you Chad. Where is your protocol? He had better show it to me." Lizabeth said.

"You have all been told many times to change your attitude. Chadrick is one of us and a valued member of this family and I am becoming tired of repeatedly telling you all and in that respect, well, I may as well speak to that wall for all the good it does." Lord Mandaten exclaimed.

"Yes father, you are right. So, just for now, we will treat him as one of us but after … Well, no matter about that. Now, there is a deal of work to be done so we had better see to the clearing up after the weekend."

"I will help with that, Grant, you should not try to tackle it alone."

"No thanks, Chadrick, I don't need your help, I'd much rather do it myself."

"Stop it, Grant, you know fathers view and you do not want to antagonise him further. We will all help." Snapped Lizabeth.

"Not a job for the girls but thanks anyway, appreciated." Replied Grant.

"Let's get to it then." Said Lizabeth.

They left the breakfast room, returning to their bedrooms, and changed into some old work gear. Minutes later, they met outside and with jobs allocated, they prepared themselves for their day's toil.

"Let me see that eye of yours, Grant, it looks so painful. Now, how did you lose that tooth, get that black eye, and your cut lip?"

"I got clumsy, Lizabeth, and stepped onto a rake that someone had left the wrong way up."

Chadrick was quick to pick up on Grant's different story to the one that he had heard him tell Cadiston after Kevin's death. His thought was that he would remember the comment but for the sake of saving an argument, he would not challenge it.

"Well, the work gangs are all here and if we are going to get this place cleared up today, then we had better get on with it." Chad said.

"No one put you in charge, Chad, so button it! If there are any orders to give then I, as the only remaining male heir, will issue them." Grant snapped.

"Don't be so petty, Grant, one would think that you are jealous of Chad." Greta said softly.

"You can button it as well, Greta, you are nothing but a mere feeble woman and not a true blood Mandaten."

"No need for that kind of talk, Grant, but if you want to be the boss man, do so then and you are welcome." Chad said as he turned and walked away. Demmie stood and smiled but Greta turned to go after him.

"Greta, you may be a mere woman but stay here!" Snapped Grant. "He is not really one of us so leave him on his own. We can get on quite well without him."

She stood her ground and challenged him. "You may be the only remaining son and heir as sadly my husband and your brother, Kevin, are gone but I will not be ordered about by the likes of you. You may not like it but you do not own me so I will go where I like, when I like, and with whom I like. You will not tell me what I can and cannot do so I will do exactly as I wish." She then turned and followed Chad.

"You do not defy me, woman! I told you to stay here." He yelled. She ignored him.

"Let her go with him, Grant, we do not need either of them, now do we? They will both be gone from our lives for good soon, completely out of our way. And anyhow, we have each other and we will probably be better off without them." Said Demmie. "

But he is your husband." Said Lizabeth.

Demmie stared at her and snapped back. "So, what of it? He is my husband and it is in name only so what do you want to make of it?"

Lizabeth raised her hand as though she was protecting herself. "Not a thing, Demmie, not a thing." At that point, Lizabeth saw a different, nasty side to Demmie. A side that had not been present before and this made her a bit wary so thought the best thing was to remain silent.

"Let them both go and do whatever they want, Grant, we can manage quite well without them. Besides, the truth is neither of them belongs and are not of this family's bloodline." Demmie said, looking at Grant supportively.

"That is true, Demmie, they are just hangers-on, nobodies, just waiting to pick up the scraps from our table. He was an unwanted baby and is no brother of mine, just an adopted brat. And she was only here because she was the wife of Malcolm and now that he is dead, that makes her just a hanger-on."

Sadie was close to tears with all the bickering and insinuations. Before speaking, she wiped her eyes. "So that makes me a nobody and a hanger-on too then, does it, Grant? I was only Kevin's wife and the mother of his son and now that he is dead, that makes me ... Like Greta, not of the family blood and a hanger-on. We are both of family widows."

"Unwanted widows and hangers-on. Yep, guess that is right and not our family anymore. The sooner that you realise that and depart, the better it will be. Kevin and Malcolm are both dead and both got careless, one with his horse, the other with his gun. Soon you will all be gone from my sight as I will not tolerate any hangers-on when I am the master and Lord of the Manor, which will be very soon now. You, Sadie, were just a gold digger and latched onto Kevin for who he was and what he had. Just like Greta did with Malcolm. She took advantage of him after his first wife died for a free meal ticket but that is about to stop, and then you will all have nothing. As for you, Sadie, you saw a free meal ticket and you will soon be paying for that." Grant spat onto her feet. Sadie burst into tears. "Oh my, blub away. Go on, Sadie, go ahead and blub. The truth hurts and that is what you have been told. Kevin was a fool to be taken in by you but not me. Now, you can leave my Mandaten and never return." Said Grant in his usual cold and unfeeling tone of voice. "You, you are a beastly bully, you uncaring bafoon! I married Kevin because

I loved him for who he was, not for what he had but you would not understand that. But Kevin knew." Replied Sadie through her tears. "Go ahead and lie as much as you like, Sadie, you will not get the better of me, no one will and I will be the King of Mandaten. I will see to that." Grant said.

In floods of tears, she turned and ran away in the direction of Chad and Greta. He may have been walking away but had heard every word that Grant said and was disgusted by his attitude. He had disregarded so much over the years but now his anger was rising and was ready to explode like a volcano. Chad was a kind and gentle man and although he could defend himself, his gentle nature still hated violence of any description. Chad knew that Grant needed to be taught a lesson because this time he had gone too far with his unwarranted abuse of both Greta and Sadie and that had angered him greatly. He knew that this time, he could not stand by and do nothing. He quickly turned and faced up to him. With a glance of steel and with venom in his voice he spoke. "Grant, you are nothing but a despicable low life and if you insinuate that we should tolerate such diabolical impertinence from an undecided piece of humanity such as you, then you are sadly mistaken! You are a complete and total ass and should be ashamed of yourself. Sadie is in a state of deep depression and has just yesterday lost her husband, your brother Kevin, under tragic circumstances. Greta lost her husband a mere week ago and they have both put their grief aside to help today. You may not have cared about Bonnie and that was plain for all to see. Plus, she believed that you were having an affair and I have a pretty good idea who it is with and she is not far from where you are standing. But that is a different matter and, in time, will be dealt with accordingly. Ridicule me as much as you like because that is just water of a ducks back, but leave them alone and treat them with the kindness and consideration that they both deserve." "Oh yes or what big man? You throw out some big words for a nobody!" Grant said and then pushed Chad. "Bugger off and stop interfering!" "You are wrong to push me Grant, I am a gentle person, and I hate violence or confrontation of any sort but be warned, you do not want to push me too far. Apologise to Sadie and Greta and let that be sufficient." Chad said firmly. "Big talk, mister nobody with nothing to back it up! Go away and cry with your two little women, boo-hoo." Grant said childishly. Chad was beginning to fume inside as his rage rose but through it all, he still managed to remain calm. He shook his head. "You are totally unbelievable." Then he turned to walk away but Grant grabbed his arm, spinning him around to face him. "Cowards walk away men stand and fight." His hands were raised, forming fists. "So, what are you, man or mouse? Squeak, squeak, mouse I guess." Said Grant with a smirk on his face. "You are so wrong, Grant." Sadie said angrily through her tears. "It takes a real man to turn and walk away and only a fool will stay and fight when there is no need." "I agree with Sadie, only a fool would stand and fight when there is another way and that makes Chadrick a real man and it is you who is the mouse. Sadie was right you are nothing but a bully and a stupid idiotic creature!" said Greta through gritted teeth. Grant shook his head,) angrily.

"Come Sadie, we will leave them to stew." Said Chad. She then turned away. Grant did not like to be challenged, especially by a woman as he was a controller, a bully and to his mind, he was always right. He grabbed her arm, spinning Greta around to face him. "Shut your mouth, both of you! Sadie, you simpleton, Kevin was nothing compared to me and as for your son, he will go the same way as his father did! You can stop your sniffling too, Greta. Neither of you matters in the slightest anymore now that your husbands are dead and gone! You know nothing, Father still lives but not for much longer and if it were left to me, you would both pack your bags and go now –." Grant 's outburst was cut short because by this time, Chad had reached the end of his patience and was about to snap. "That is it, Grant! You have said much more than enough and now you have gone too far, I will not stand by and take any more of your foul abuse, no more of it. For that you can and will apologise to both Greta and Sadie or bare the full consequences!" Grant's fingers went up to his mouth as though chewing them in a frightened pose. "Oh my, I am so scared. Chad is standing up for the poor helpless, simpleton women." He said this in a mocking voice that was meant to ridicule him. "You WILL apologise, Grant, even if I have to beat it out of you, and believe me I can." He replied in a very strong voice. Grant retorted back in a smarmy manner. "Oh yeah? You and whose army Chad the interloper?" "I need no army to beat you, Grant, as a child I did it quite easily, the only difference is that now we are grown men." Chad said evenly. "As for that I most certainly am a man but you, squeak-squeak, is that a mouse that I hear again? Run away and crawl back under your stone or you will see that I can beat you with one arm tied behind my back." Chad shook his head again. "Quite honestly Grant, I would rather walk away but with your behavior –, hmm, let's just say you do not want to find out, now apologise to Greta and Sadie and let that be an end to it." Grant started to push Chad but even though his inner rage was at breaking point, he still managed to remain calm. He was doing everything possible to avoid a confrontation. "Don't push me, Grant, you do not want to get into another fight as you already have a black eye, a missing tooth and split lip from a previous one!" "Well that person will not trouble me again, that is for sure as he dead." He then ignored the warning and pushed again and again. The next time, Chad snapped and grabbed his wrist, twisted his arm up against his back, and pushed him as hard as he could. This action sent him sprawling and he fell flat on his face. He looked down at the figure that sprawled in the gravel and shook his head. "Come on Greta, Sadie, we will leave him lying there groveling in the dirt and go do our bit of clearing up. Your children will catch up later."

Chad now had his back to Grant, who had risen with the help of Demmie and was again on his feet. With a wild yell and like a raging bull, he charged at Chad, who was not surprised as he was expecting this to happen. He waited for the moment, then side-stepped, leaving a leg trailing that Grant tripped over and was again sprawling in the dirt. Chad placed a foot onto his back, keeping him pinned down. "It is done, Grant, now leave it before you really get hurt. I have no desire to fight you so we will go that way, you go your way and we will consider this fracas over." He removed his foot, turned, and began to walk away but Grant was not done. With a bit of help, he was on his feet once again. He picked up a piece of wood that had fallen from a lorry and struck Chad across his back. Chad reeled with the pain but maintained his balance. Turning, he faced his adversary, and when Grant saw the look of steel in his eyes, he began to regret his action but knew that he could not back down. The fight was on and as they exchanged blows, it was obvious that Chad was the better fighter. He was landing many more blows and it was easy for all to see that most of Grant's were being blocked or avoided. Knowing that he was losing the fight, Grant pulled a knife. Chad glanced at the blade and smiled. "You sure you want to use that?" "You will see when you are gutted like a fish Chad." Grant spat. "I was thinking more along the lines of you looking rather silly with that blade stuck in your backside." With the blade forward, Grant lunged at him but Chad was ready and within three moves, it was just as he had said. Move one: he side-stepped, allowing the blade to pass him. Move two: he grasped the arm that was holding the blade and twisted it up Grants back, forcing him to drop the blade. Move three: Grant's trousers were pulled partially down, then the retrieved blade was plunged not too deeply into his backside.

"I gave you fair warning, Grant, now apologise and let that be an end to it before you really get hurt." "Alright, I apologise." Grant squealed in pain.

"Come on, girls, let us get on. You coming with us, Demmie?" Chad asked.

"Better not, I will see to Grant so no, I will stay here you brute and bully." Demmie said. "As you please." Said Chad. "I will do as I please, don't worry yourself on that score." She snapped. "Not worried in the slightest, Demmie, in fact, you both deserve each other as you are cut from the same cloth, both cheats, she will cheat on you Grant because once a cheat always a cheat." "I will not cheat on Grant he is all I want". "You are welcome to her Grant", Chad with Greta and Sadie turned and walked away, leaving Grant and Demmie together. Demmie shouted after them, "You are a brute and a bully Chad". "You a brute and a bully, I think not, it is the other way around. Grant is the bully and Bonnie told me so. If he did not get his own way, he would hit her, and she did not lie." Said Greta in reply.

All that day, they were busy organizing the helpers and never gave Grant another thought. They were far too busy. They made a point of bypassing the area used for the Black Powder Show that was still under police investigation, as well as the archery area and the woodlands. Everywhere else they were removing every item that had been installed for the show, the marquees were down, the wild west town was dismantled, the jousting arena was cleared, everything apart from the two areas reserved. The whole showground was slowly returning to its grassy meadow and open space. "Always seems to be the case that it comes down quicker than it goes up." Greta said. "You are right there, a lot quicker coming down than when it was being built up." Sadie replied, Chad smiled.

Grant had been taken to the hospital by Demmie and had been treated for his stab wound to the backside. When they were asked how it had happened and to avoid any embarrassment, he lied and said that he had been cutting some string and had dropped the knife then had tripped and fallen onto the blade. This explanation was accepted. "Well, Mister Mandaten, it is not as bad as you may think. The blade was only short so was not too deep. Now, you will be a bit uncomfortable for a time but there will be no other complications. You have been given a tetanus injection and your wife can change the dressing for you in a couple of days. We have given you enough dressings for two weeks. You are free to go now, and next time be more careful." He just grunted at the nurse and left. Demmie followed him and as she whispered, she looked lovingly at him. "I like the sound of that, your wife can change the dressings. Now that Bonnie is dead and gone and Chad will soon follow her, make it soon, Grant." He did not return her glance and again, just grunted they left the hospital and returned to Mandaten.

With the grounds clear and the police forensics teams still busy examining every aspect of the two areas that had been reserved, Chad, Sadie and Greta took time out to watch them. The first team was taking careful measurements and shooting arrows toward the woods, while the second was crawling on hands and knees with magnets, searching for any small piece of Kevin's exploded rifle. When they had seen enough, joining the family they all began their return to the Manor. They had observed them taking careful measurements and several samples.

"Well, we have done nothing wrong, have we Tomas, Kansas? That being the case, this should not worry us." Remarked Lizabeth. "Rightly so, my dear, not at all." Replied Tomas. Kansas just smiled with his head moving just like a nodding dog toy. They had seen Grant's car return with Demmie at the wheel and the moment that she had dropped him at the Manor, she made her way up the field and joined Lizabeth and her family just as they had finished.

"They are still checking the area where Sammie, Walter, and Gloria died." Lizabeth said. "We don't know how they died, only that they are all dead. It was probably a tragic archery accident as it is that area they are covering." Replied Tomas. "It certainly looks that way." Kansas replied. "Well, sergeant Standish will soon have it sorted not that stupid young constable Cadiston." Replied Tomas. "Archery accident then." "You could be right, Demmie, it must be just that, otherwise they would be examining another area." Said Lizabeth.

"Looks like those three interlopers and their offspring are making their way back." Said Demmie. "Strange thing for you to say, especially as one of them is your husband." Replied Lizabeth. "Husband? Him? Not really and I will soon be shot of him and good riddance to him." She smiled. I will say nothing more than that." "Okay, shall we catch them up and walk back with them Demmie". "No thank's Lizabeth I hate them all," "I just hope that Grant is going to be alright." "I am sure that he will be, Lizabeth, as the hospital did not want to keep him in." "So, what did they do? You were there with him?"

"They removed the blade and cleaned the wound, putting a large padded dressing on it, then they gave him a tetanus shot. He has a ring to sit on as he will be in a little bit of discomfort when he sits down. They said it should take about two weeks to heal as it was not too deep." Said Demmie. "Not that bad then, he will not die from the wound." Tomas said. "Not that bad, Tomas, but bad enough." Replied Demmie. "Why did you stay and take him to the hospital when your husband is over there with Sadie and Greta the two other women?" Lizabeth asked. "Because I was more worried about Grant than him over there. Aren't you worried about Grant, Lizabeth? After all, he is your blood brother." "Of course I am, Chad need not have done that to him but Grant did push him too far and he said that he would we were close enough to hear the argument." "Well, even so, he should not have stuck the blade into his buttock." Demmie said. "I guess not, Demmie, but well, he did. Grant will not be able to sit very comfortable for a while so that will make him think twice before he challenges Chadrick your husband again and that you can be sure of." "Not my husband for much longer." Demmie spat. "Well, that is not our concern. Now, back to Grant, he hated Chad before this and now I guess he hates him even more. And after that event it has put him on a trail of revenge." Tomas added. "Probably, Tomas. Well, enough chat, the clock is ticking so let us get back. I feel filthy so a shower and change of clothes for me." "For us all, Lizabeth, now let us stride it out." They began to walk a lot quicker in their attempt to arrive at the Manor before Chad, Greta, Sadie and their respective children, Lowel, Jennifer and James.

When Demmie had left the wounded Grant sitting on the ring, he was angry at the fact that, yet again, he had been bested by a younger Chad. He glared at him with hate and said just seven words before blanking him for the rest of the evening. "You will get yours and very soon." "How is it now, Grant?" "Painful, Demmie, otherwise not as bad as expected." "And the arm?" "A bit sore but that is fine and can still be used easily without pain. Now, stop your fussing before someone notices." "Let them notice, I am not bothered if they do. As for your injury, that is good. I hate him as he should not have done what he did to you and standing up for those two widows when it was nothing to do with him."

"They will be dealt with in due course. Now, stop fussing before someone notices." Grant said more firmly. "So what if they do notice?! They will soon be told about us and it will be out in the open." She said impatiently. "Not until I say." "It does not matter now, it is done so why not tell them?" "Soon, my woman." He sent an evil glance across the room. "And as for Chad, the next time that we cross swords, he will get his comeuppance." His voice now changed and had taken on an air of sharpness and dominance. "And as for telling anyone about us, you just hold your tongue as that will be when I decide and if I decide and not a moment before! So keep your mouth shut if you know what is good for you." "What do you mean if you decide? I love you, Grant, and always have from our very first meeting. I want you so badly that I will do anything for you and stop at nothing to get you, I give myself to you freely." "You said do anything?" Grant looked at her. "Anything at all." She said. "Shut up then and say nothing." "Alright." She smiled and touched his arm affectionately which was noticed by Greta and Chad.

Sadie was very distraught and depressed, even before Grant's vial outburst and that did not help her state of mind. She was trembling from head to toe and her tears ran freely. Some of the family were trying to comfort her but to no avail and so, Doctor Mansen had been called because of the terrible condition that she was in. Although she was trying to hide it for the sake of her son, James, there were those around her that cared and could not help but notice her serious condition. The doctor had given her a course of Amitriptyline to calm her and help her to sleep and before he left, he had whispered to her son James. "Keep a close eye on your mother, my boy, she has been hit very hard. Now, tell me, are you alright?" "Thank you, I will be fine Doctor, my mother is my main worry and that takes up all my energy." "Of course, and if you are sure that you are alright then I will leave it there, you look after her, James." "No question of that, Doctor Mansen." "Call if you need me." The door closed behind him and a moment later, they heard his car driving up the long drive.

Sadie had remained quiet all day, still reeling from Grant's savage attack with his harmful words. Grant was building his anger toward her as he blamed her fully for Chad's intervention and his discomfort. James had noticed his mother's mood and hoped that after taking her medication, she would calm down and get some sleep. However, that was a little way away because now they all sat around the dinner table. There were no words spoken from her lips as she sat in silence. She hardly touched her meal and spent the whole time with her eyes glazed but the stare she gave was fixed on one person. James could see clearly that she stared with eyes that were filled with hatred and contempt for Grant.

"Our numbers at the table should have grown but sadly, now it has lessened. We have lost our Sammie and her family, our grandchildren Jennifer, Lowell, and James have lost their fathers and we have lost our sons so that makes you boys the head of your households. It is down to you to look after your mothers in their absence like I know that you will." Lord Mandaten said. "I will care for my mother, (Greta.) Grandfather, I have my sister Jennifer to help me. We will make sure that she is well cared for." Lowell said."You are a good lad, Lowell, and look so much like your father. I have no doubt that you and Jennifer will do your very best." Said the boy's grandfather.

"I intend to find out the truth behind my father's death, he was an excellent shot and extremely careful with all the black powder weapons. He knew every inch of every gun and every single risk and safety measure. Plus, the Kentucky Rifle was his pride and joy and had been fired safely on Saturday in each of his shows – eight in all. As had all the other black powder weapons. They had all been fired safely again in the Sunday show before the Kentucky exploded. I noticed that he seemed to hesitate and was feeling the gun with suspicion and that makes me think it had been tampered with." James said confidently. "Tampered with? That is nonsense, James. Your father became over-complacent and got careless just as the famous horseman, Malcolm, did." Grant had a type of arrogance about him.

"I do not believe that for one single minute, Uncle Grant, and I am determined to find out the truth." James protested. "Cadiston will arrive at the truth for you, James, your priority is to look after your mother (Sadie.) Now, if we are all done eating, we will retire to the lounge for coffee." Lord Mandaten said and they rose from their seats to leave the dining room. "Mother, you have been very quiet all evening, all day in fact, and have hardly touched your meal. I know that you are terribly depressed after Father's death, as Aunt Greta is over uncle Malcolm's, but when I caught up to you I noticed that you were distressed over something else and that has been playing on your mind all day and I can see that it still is. I know that we are sad because of Father but something else has upset you. I saw the way that you were staring at Uncle Grant." James looked concerned.

"You are a good son and I know that you are concerned for me but do not worry yourself over what happened, James. It is over and done now and your Uncle Chad made excellent recompense." Sadie said. "But what was it? Please tell me, Mother, I do not like to see you so sad." James pressed on. "It was something very hurtful that was said but, as I said, your Uncle Chad fought in my corner and made perfect recompense." He looked across the room. "It was that vile Uncle Grant that said hurtful things to you, wasn't it? That is why you fixed your stare on him so no need to say anything more. Now I understand why he went to the hospital with cuts and bruises and a blade stuck in his buttock. He and Uncle Chad must have had a massive fight and Chad won, good for him." James smiled. "Now, say no more about it, please son, as it is far too depressing." They continued to the coffee lounge but once there, James could not stop himself from setting his stare with hate in his eyes at Grant. he wanted to challenge him there and then but respected his mother's wishes.

The hour was getting late and the coffee and brandy had been free-flowing. Chad, who was not a heavy drinker, and had enjoyed the two small measures of brandy that had accompanied his coffee but now he began to feel strange again. "Demmie, I am suddenly feeling extremely tired, a weird feeling. Again, after the coffee you gave me – just like I did the other evening um, Monday. Yes must have been Monday, yes that was it. I am going up, are you coming with me as we need to talk in private?" "You go, I will just finish my coffee and brandy. I feel quite relaxed after all the excitement so will be up in a minute." Demmie said. "I will probably be asleep." Chad said slowly. "Good, I certainly hope so." Demmie mumbled. He queried what she had answered. "What was that you said? I didn't quite catch it" "I said good night be up in a minute." Demmie said a little louder. "Oh, night then."

Greta had not misheard and sent a glance toward her and Grant. Chad left the lounge and found it very difficult to climb the stairs. If Greta had not been following him with her children, he would surely have fallen without their support. As he spoke, his words were becoming muddled. "Thank you, all. I say must I feel most strange, my head, my spins and I can hardly keep my spins eyes open … Well, night all … See you in the morning." His bedroom door closed and without undressing and with his eyes closed, he flopped straight onto the bed and was out cold.

In the next room down the hall Sadie had taken her tablets, as prescribed by the doctor and James had made sure of that. James and his cousin, Jennifer, had sat beside her bed until his mother had finally cried herself to sleep. The Manor was now silent as it settled with its occupants to rest for the night. There were the usual groans and creaking sounds of an old house and maybe a few more creaks that were not so usual.

No one rose early on Tuesday morning and everyone arrived in the breakfast room in staggered times. The last to arrive was Chad who still looked half-asleep. "Morning Uncle Chad, I must say you still look extremely tired, are you feeling alright?"

"I wish that I could answer that, Kansas, but quite honestly I really don't know. My head feels like it has been hit by a sledge hammer, I feel dizziness, amnesia and a strange sickly feeling and my eyes are extremely heavy and my vision is blured. if I had had a lot of alcohol, I would say a serious hangover but two small measures with my coffee? I think not." Chad said confused. "Now then Uncle Chad, I am not an expert yet but let me look at your eyes." "As I said my eyes are heavy and my vision is blured". "Kansas looked carefully and pulled the eyes wide open to get a better look. "Well, I may be still in med-school and am not a doctor yet but from the look of your eyes that are blood shot I would say that you have been drugged but, I could be wrong." Demmie was quick to respond to this. "Drugged indeed, Kansas, that just shows your inexperience you cannot tell from looking in the eyes. Your Uncle Chad is not a drinker and he had two small glasses of brandy last night it is probably the effects of that. Drugged indeed, now that is a laugh."

The remark was noted by Greta who had witnessed his condition on the previous Monday and thought that being slipped a strong sleeping draught was the most probable explanation for his condition on both occasions. "I guess so, Aunt Demmie, it must be a reaction to the brandy, we will leave it at that." No more was said on the subject.

"Didn't hear you come up last night, Demmie, and you were not there when I woke this morning." "You were out cold. I did not want to wake you so –." She glanced toward him and smiled. "I came down with Grant this morning. I thought I would let you sleep in as you were feeling unwell last night." "Very considerate of you I am sure. So, you came down with Grant?" "So, what if I did? Just what are you implying?" She said defensively. "Nothing, Demmie. No need to be so touchy. So, you came down with Grant, not me, all there is to it. No need to make a song and dance about it." She glared at him but no more was said. "Good morning, James, and how is your mother this fine Tuesday morning? We may be sad at our losses but just listen to that beautiful bird song." Said Lizabeth.

"It is beautiful and as for Mother, I have not seen her this morning yet, and that being a fact I cannot answer that, Aunt Lizabeth. Jennifer, and myself were knocking on her door for at least six or seven minutes and as there was no reply, then we

158

went in. Her bed was made and strangely, the room was completely tidy as though not being used. We thought that she must be down here already." Said James. "She is not Here, James. Has anyone seen her this morning?" enquired Grant. Heads began to shake the bell cord was immediately pulled. "Bradinham, have you seen Miss Sadie this morning?" Grant asked. "No, Master Grant, I have not, shall I check with the other staff?"

"Yes, do it and be very quick. Well, as quickly as possible at your age.

Well, don't just stand there man, go on then." He turned and left. Nothing was said but Chad felt that it was unlike Grant to show some form of caring, especially for Sadie after she had stood up to him. While they waited for his return, breakfast was forgotten about and twenty minutes later, Alfred came in. "Mister Bradinham is not feeling well so he has asked me to take over for him and as requested, I have spoken to every member of the house staff. When Charlotte entered Miss Sadie's bedroom, she had already risen and had left the room tidy. She told me that the only strange thing was that she could not find her night attire. I am sorry to say that no one has seen Miss Sadie this morning." Alfred said with concern in his voice. "Thank you for that, Alfred." Chad said, he turned and left the breakfast room. "Right then, it appears that we have another problem. We need to find her and quickly. She was extremely depressed yesterday after losing Kevin and Grant's unwarranted outburst did not help." James sent Grant a hateful glance. "I do not want to think the worst but, we had better get a search going." Grant now spoke up. "For once, I have to agree with Chad, call all the hands in from the farm. There is not a moment to lose so let's get going." In that moment, Jacob burst into the breakfast room. "What is the meaning of this, man?! First we had Herbert and now you come bursting in, what is this an open house for the stable and farmhands? You are not allowed in here! Why, the very audacity! You are nothing at all, just a farmhand, so get out!" Snapped Grant.

"Thought his manners were too good to last." Whispered Greta to Chad. "Now, shut it, Grant, for once in your life, shut up! Just ignore him, Jacob. Now, what brings you in here in such a way?" enquired Chad. "You had better come quickly, Chad, the quicker, the better. It is not good." "Speak to me, man! I am the master here in my father's absence. We will all come. Now, what is it, man?" Grant insisted. "I told you to shut it, Grant! Jacob is talking to me." Grant opened his mouth to speak again but James spoke before he could get a word out. "Belt up, Uncle Grant, and let Jacob talk to Uncle Chad." He wanted to reply but James had a steely glare in his eyes and strangely, it silenced him. "I cannot tell you, not here, outside, Master. James had better stay here with the ladies if you please, Chad." Said Jacob.

"Direct your words to me, imbecile, I will not be ignored I am the master here in my father's absence." Said Grant angrily. "It is alright, Jacob, lead on and we will follow. James, stay here with the ladies. Tomas, Kansas, Lowell, with me." Said Chad, trying to keep a calmness in his voice even though he feared the worst. "But I –." James started to speak but, Chad interrupted him.

"Stay James! Llook after him, Greta, Lizabeth, and you, to Jennifer, please."

"Go, Chad. He will be alright with us." Replied Greta. Jacob was about to make his way to the back door when Chad stopped him. "This way, Jacob, front door will be quicker." He glanced toward Grant. "You sure, Chad?"

"Sure, and you need not say anything, Grant, we have another priority So, without question, let us get a move on."

Freddie was waiting with a pony and trap, which they all climbed into, and with a quick giddy-up, they were on their way. "Tell us now, Jacob, what is it that perplexes you?" Chad asked.

"It is most terrible, Chad, just terrible. We were heading up to the top field, the other side of the woods, and as we were passing the lake, Freddie –" He hesitated before continuing. "Terrible, just terrible." "In your own words, Jacob." Chad said encouragingly. "We got just as far as the lake when Charles noticed that the rowing boat was stuck way out in the middle."

"Make your mind up, man, just who was it, Freddie or Charles, that saw whatever –." Chad's angry stare silenced Grant. "Makes no difference who it was so please continue, Jacob." "At first glance, we thought it must have come adrift so we decided to bring it back in but everything has been calm so we could not understand why it had broken free. We went for a closer look — there was a bit of low mist still hanging over the water. That was when we saw her floating face down. We do not know who it is exactly. Only that it is the body of a female and Freddie thought it may be — I don't like to say but he felt sure by the — It is terrible." Jacob trailled off. "Yes, you have said it's terrible but what did he recognise?" "Shut up, Grant, and don't be so insensitive. Carry on, Jacob, in your own time." Chad said. "Freddie thought he knew who it was by the auburn hair — oh my! It is terrible, just terrible. We know that it is a female because she is wearing what looked like a dress. We thought about retrieving the body but decided against it and we came straight here." "I hope that I am wrong, Jacob, but I have my suspicion who it is as well." Chad said silently. "You can say it out loud, man, you mean Sadie. Well, not a big surprise there if it is her. She was mighty depressed last night. When we were all in bed, she must have crept out of the Manor, taken the boat out, and then thrown herself over the side and drowned. Must have taken her own life — simple Suicide, that is my guess." Said Grant in a devil may care attitude. "Grant, you have a filthy mouth and no suicide is a simple thing, and if you recall you did not help the situation with your cruelty toward her. I will tell you this, if we ever do get into the situation of crossing swords again, you will not get off so lightly, you are nothing but a despicable bully." Said Chad. "Have to agree with you in that, Chad, never a truer spoken word." Jacob agreed. "Who do you think you are, Jacob?! When I am the master of all this and the Manor, with all her holdings, you will be out of a job, you and all your family." Grant spat. "And I tell you this, if you were the master, then we would all leave of our own accord anyhow. Not one of us would want to stay with you at the helm of the estate." He did not have time to answer as they had arrived at the lake. "We are here, Chad, and there she is. It must be as you thought, Miss Sadie, as I cannot see how anyone else could be out here. Oh my, what of poor Master James? He has just lost his father and if it is his mother –. Terrible, just terrible." Remarked Jacob with sorrow in his voice.

Grant had a smirk on his face. "Well, if it is her, then nothing more than she deserves after humiliating me." Everyone was stunned at this outrageous comment. They all gazed at the floating body for a moment and then Chad began to remove some of his clothes. "Only one way to know for sure. Ring for an ambulance, Jacob, and best ring the police as well. Ask for Detective Cadiston." "Already done, Chad, you be very careful in there as there is a lot of weed that can tangle around your legs and drag you down." Jacob said. "That I know only too well, been in here before, remember Grant?" Said Chad. "Don't need to remember as everyone else is there to remind me." Grant grumbled."Wait a minute, Chad, I have an idea. Tie this rope around your waist, just in case." "Good idea, Freddie." The rope was tied around Chad's waist and moments later, he was in the cold water, swimming steadily toward the floating body. The closer that he got to the body, the more he was convinced that it was Sadie. She was face down with her long auburn hair floating on the surface as if being blown by the wind. He gulped hard for, in his heart, he hoped that it was not her. His mind told him otherwise. In a few strong strokes, he was there and as he turned her over, his heart slumped as his suspicion was confirmed. Tears welled in his eyes and he let out a loud cry of anguish. "No! Dear God, no, Sadie, Sadie, Sadie!" He gathered his thoughts and calmed himself. He then started looking around, climbed into the rowing boat, and then pulled her into it with him as gently as possible. She was wearing only a thin nightdress which hid nothing at all. He removed his shirt and arranged it to cover her body but to his dismay, this did not cover her nakedness. A slight frost still lay on the ground and mist still hung over the lake. It was still very cold but he ignored this and removed his t-shirt to place that over her in his attempt to cover her near-naked body. He wiped his eyes and whispered. "There you are, Sadie, you are covered well enough to hide you from prying eyes."

He had untied the rope from around his waist and retied it to the boat's ringlet and with a signal, those on the jetty pulled them in. He was now bare-chested and was shivering in the cold. This did not concern him, Sadie did. All the way in, he cradled her body in his arms and had fixed his stare onto her lifeless eyes. His own eyes were filled with tears. "Talk to me, Sadie, tell me who did this to you as I do not believe you would have done this to yourself. You would not put your son through this pain, not after just losing his father. If only you could tell me but maybe, in some way, you can tell Cadiston. I can but hope my dear Sadie, we are at the jetty so I need to get you out of this boat." He raised his voice and continued. "Jacob, boys, come and help me lift her and be very gentle and make sure that you keep her body covered, sadly it is our Sadie." "An extremely bad day, Chad, extremely bad day." Remarked Charles. "Terrible, just terrible, another family death for them to bare." Added Jacob.

They remained silent while they lifted her body carefully and, ignoring the early morning chill, took off their coats and covered her body as if to keep her warm while they waited for the ambulance and the police to arrive. Freddie had taken his warm sweater off and passed it to Chad. "Best you put this on before you freeze Chad." "Thanks Freddie, but what about you getting cold?" He asked.

"I still have warm clothes on, you are the one that is half-naked." He nodded then they all stood silently looking upon the still form of Sadie. All but four had tears in their eyes. They did not wait long as just three minutes after Chad had retrieved Sadie's body, the police arrived. "I was hoping that there would be no need to call you today, Detective Cadiston, but unfortunately for us, that is not the case as there is another death for you to investigate. This time, it is Sadie and it appears that she has drowned in the lake. That makes eight family deaths for us to deal with now so over to you." Chad said sadly.

"Alright, Chad, I will see what has happened and investigate for you. Judging by first appearance, it looks like a case of suicide by drowning but then things are not always what they seem, are they?" Said Cadiston. "Stand aside there and speak with me. I am in charge here, step aside and let the dog see the rabbit." Said Standish in a bullish fashion. "Sergeant Standish, I do not like your attitude and that is not very tactful considering what has transpired here." "Chadrick the adopted one is it? I could not care less. Now, what have we got then?" Said Standish.Grant smiled and answered. "Jacob and his sons saw the rowing boat in the middle of the lake and thought it strange. When they investigated, they saw a body floating face down. They called for us and Chad went in to retrieve the body and that is when we discovered that it was the wife of Kevin, Sadie." "Kevin was her husband? The chap that had his head blown off on Sunday?" Asked Standish. "Yes, that was him, Sergeant Standish, and again, I do not like your tone." Chad warned again.

"I have no problem with that. Now back to the case. Was, past tense, as he was the one who got careless and was blown up by the old musket. Another tragic accident." Standish said smugly."Rifle, it was a Kentucky Rifle Standish." Cadiston pointed out. "Musket, Rifle, makes little difference, he is still dead. Now, back to this latest event. Well, quite simple, as I see it a straight-forward case of suicide due to depression over the loss of her husband." "You are so rude and abrupt and very quick to reach a conclusion, Sergeant, without even examining the evidence and without an investigation. I do not like your attitude or your manners or the way in which you are handling this. So if you don't mind, step back as I would rather let Detective Cadiston investigate this case." Said Chad. Standish smiled and glanced toward him. "He is not a detective yet. Hasn't quite finished his training so he is still a novice at the game." "Well, even so, I would still rather he took the case." Chad remained adamant. "Not down to you, Chad, I am the eldest true blood son and the only true male heir left alive and that is discounting the only Mandaten named nephews. As for you, well, you are only adopted so down to me and Father. And I say that I agree with Sergeant Standish, a clear case of suicide."

Cadiston, who was always calm, had heard enough and was not about to be silenced or fobbed off again. He had promised Lord

Mandaten to investigate all the deaths that had occurred and now he was faced with another one. "Well, I entirely disagree with that and a full and proper conclusion cannot be reached without a full and proper investigation. Now, enough of this bickering over the poor young lady's body." They looked at Cadiston, wondering where this was coming from as he had always remained calm. "Now that you two have finished, this is a very serious moment. As I said, there should be no arguing over this poor young woman's body so all of you shut up and show some respect. To continue talking, we will move over there, away from this unfortunate young woman." Cadiston was now showing his strength of character. He had followed Standish on several cases prior to these at Mandaten Manor and he had always tried to silence him before and had always discredited his analysis of the case. This time, he had made up his mind that it would not happen anymore and, this time, he would not be silenced. "We will need the forensics to examine that boat so secure it for me please, Jacob. We will also need a post-mortem to be certain of the cause of death. There will be no questioning as it will most definitely be required and will take place for this. Even if you do not agree, Standish it is going to happen. It might appear on the surface that this was a tragic suicide but things beneath the surface are different and show discrepancies in the first thought, and while you could not be bothered to look further than your own nose Standish, I took the time and inspected the body of the deceased. Upon my inspection, I noticed something on the upper left arm. It is a small bruise with what looks like a tiny hole in the center of it. That is suspicious and will only be confirmed in a post-mortem." Cadiston said. "Small bruise, tiny hole, just how could you possibly see that, Cadiston?" asked an angry Standish.

"With this." He held up a pocket magnifying glass. "Handy piece of kit this. Now then, to continue, there have been a lot of deaths in this family in the past and from what I gather, all un-investigated, unexplained and those that you, Sergeant Standish, had anything to do with, have immediately been labelled as tragic accidents without a full and proper investigation. Now we have eight more deaths in the Mandaten family, all within two weeks, from the 22nd to the 30th. That is sufficient to create suspicion, even if you do not see it that way. I mean you no disrespect, Standish, but I will not be silenced by you anymore. We will need to carry out a full and thorough investigation to find out the truth behind this poor young woman's untimely death." Cadiston's tone was firm. Standish was astounded at the strength of character now being shown. He had not seen this before and had to gather himself before answering. "There you go again, Cadiston, trying to make something out of nothing and I don't like your implications. I have told you and warned you before that your future is in my hands and there you are, once again, making more of this incident than necessary. Plus, you are giving these folks a false impression. Look at them all logically: Bonnie, a tragic accident, death by natural causes, cardiac arrest or heart attack; Malcolm, well … I have no need to itemise the rest of them. You have no idea how to handle these cases, Cadiston, and this is not a classroom situation. Your inexperience is most certainly showing. Now take Malcolm's tragic riding accident, death by severe blood loss due to striking head. Kevin, once again, tragic accident, overloaded an old musket −." He caught Cadiston's glance. "Or rifle − So it exploded and now this, tragic but a straight forward suicide, no question about it." Standish was getting annoyed. "Thought you were not going to itemise them −. Anyhow, you are forgetting three others: Sammie, her husband, Walter, and their daughter, Gloria. Now, I may be the junior here and may be inexperienced but that does not alter the fact that I do know that all these cases show sufficient discrepancies to prove that they are not mere accidents. They all need to be and will be fully investigated." Cadiston reaffirmed.

"You are walking on very thin ice, Cadiston. You are really pushing your luck now and I can easily terminate your final training. They are all probably cases of tragic accidents but even so, just to satisfy your whim, do your thing. Just remember that I can take them from you at any time. I will be watching you very closely and it will be down to me to look at your evidence first and deal with it as I see fit. Remember it will be me that will determine the final conclusion and that has been done already, before you investigate. You will only find that they were all tragic accidents and when I have written the final report on this one, I will have the pleasure to say I told you so." "Well, this is not the time or place so, like it or not, we will have no more arguments and show respect for this poor young woman who I supect was murdered and did not commit suicide, and we will not discuss anything else anywhere near or over her body." Foulsham, their driver, had been observing their confrontations over the past months and had watched as they walked away to a quiet spot before Cadiston voiced his opinion and had made notes on the confrontation. "You are so wrong about all these deaths, Standish, and I will prove it to you. We may only have the post-mortem result that was carried out on Miss Bonnie and her unborn child and I know that there is other evidence to be found. That report has brought up very clear discrepancies which lead to my suspicions about the validity of her death having been a mere accident. I have taken the time to read and evaluate the report, which is a lot more than you have done, and that makes me question your methods. That is only the first case, the others which all need to be looked at and investigated properly before a conclusion can be met." Cadiston said."Told you, Cadiston, they are all tragic accidents and that is what will be recorded. Now, let these good people remove her body while we go and break the news to the family." Said Standish.

"I know that this is not the time or place to argue with you, Standish, you are so wrong about everything and I will not let the matter drop, your days of silencing me are done I have enough of it. I also intend to prove murder, with or without your authority." He had said his piece and turned, leaving Standish standing amazed at Cadiston's courage for speaking out. As Cadiston walked away, he heard words that were spoken just loud enough for his ears. "You upstart, bumptious young whelp, huh?" Think you can get the better of me? Well, think again and count your few remaining days for I will see to it that you go no further." He ignored these remarks as he had already stated that this was not the time or place. Foulsham was keeping a low profile but had also heard Standish's remarks and followed Cadiston over to where Chad stood in silence. "I must apologise for this unwarranted disruption, the lack of professionalism, and for his attitude. He makes me so angry with his quick one-look decision and I will personally see to it that a full and complete no-hole's-barred investigation is carried out. As I said, it may look like a simple case of suicide – but as I said and feel extremely strong about things are not always what they seem on the surface and we need to dig beneath that to arrive at the truth." Cadiston did not like the way in which his sergeant was behaving and how quick and ready he was to close Sadie's death as a suicide. This was not the first time he had challenged his method. He had a mind that ran on a single track and it would not deviate from its path and that was to close the case as quickly as possible and that did not sit well or suit Cadiston at all. He knew full well that by being the junior, he had to go along with it but he had seen and heard quite enough since being assigned to him and he could take it no longer. Now he had made his case clear and that was that he would no longer be fobbed off and silenced. Standish may have the upper hand for the moment but not for much longer. Things were about to change and now nothing was going to stop him from keeping his word and investigating these deaths, even if he had to conduct his investigations in his own time and unofficially. If that was what was forced upon him, making it totally necessary to arrive at the truth, then so be it. He looked at the transport crew that was waiting patiently. "Dave, you can remove the deceased and make sure that she remains covered. Take her directly to the forensic mortuary for me please." "You have it, Cadders. I must just say well done. It is about time someone stood up to Standish, never did like him." Cadiston just smiled. "Off to the Manor now to break the sad news to the family."

On their arrival, they were greeted by Alfred who was already waiting at the door and without delay, he showed them into the long room to await the arrival of the family. James was the first to enter and as soon as he had one foot inside the room, he had started to ask questions before everyone was there. "I know that you are the police and you are Cadiston so why are you here and why was the ambulance by the lake? And where is my mother, have you found her?" His voice was quivering as he spoke and it was clear that he was extremely distressed. "Calm yourself please, sir, calm yourself please sir, and we will tell you all that we know at this moment in time but first, I need to confirm that you are the son of Sadie Mandaten?" Said Cadiston.

"James, I am James and yes, I am her son. Now, have you found my mother?" Cadiston placed a hand on his shoulder. "If you would just calm yourself, James, and take a seat please, then we will tell you when all the family are here." His voice was soft and calming and James could Sense by his tone that he was a caring man, trying to act in his best interest. He did as had been requested and sat down. He waited quietly although his impatience was obvious as he shuffled about on his seat. His grandparents had been at the door and heard how Cadiston had spoken in such a way to calm James and they were both impressed with his handling of this traumatic situation. With all the family present, Standish stepped forward, ready to speak but Cadiston took his arm. "Let me do it, Standish, all good for the training."

"Be my guest but remember it is not for much longer so no insinuations and no voicing your suspicions, it was a tragic suicide so watch what you say." He replied. Cadiston looked around at the faces that stared back at him. He had been checking their body language and stance and after making his mental notes, he began with a soft, caring tone. "Sir, Lord, Lady Mandaten, with all due respect to you both, what I need to say should be directed at Master James as it is about his mother. James, it is with a heavy heart that I need to inform you that your mother has been found. She was found by Jacob and his sons Freddie and Charles. It was your Uncle Chadrick who unselfishly went into the cold water of the lake and recovered her body. Sadly, there was nothing that could be done as it was too late. Unfortunately, your mother could not be saved and is deceased." "Mother is dead? First Father, blown to pieces, now Mother – But how, Cadiston, how?" James was again on his feet but with Cadiston's voice remaining soft and calm, he continued, "Please James, sit down, I know that this is all very traumatic for you, especially after what happened to your father but when you have calmed down, I will continue." Chad was at his side with a comforting arm placed on his shoulder. "James, here, drink this." Said Greta as she passed him a measure of brandy which he swallowed in one gulp. "Thank you, Uncle Chadrick, Aunt Greta this is just too much to bare." All the while, the young detective was still observing the rest of the family and had made several mental notes on their reactions to the news of Sadie's death and they would be written in his note book at the first opportunity. With James settling thanks to his aunt and uncle, Cadiston continued.

"As I was saying, and again with a heavy heart, your mother's body was recovered from the lake. As I have already said to your Uncle Chadrick, it would appear at first glance that she has ended her life by committing suicide. It looks as though she had taken the rowing boat out into the center of the lake and slipped into the water, thereby drowning." Standish shot looks of daggers at him as he knew that he was doing what he had been told not to do. "But I do not go by first impressions and I am not convinced that this was what happened. Although I have no desire to cause you further grief, it is with that in mind that we will need to fully investigate the circumstances leading up to this tragedy before we can reach our conclusion." Standish sent him another hostile stare as he had blatantly defied him. Now that his hands were tied, he could not just write Sadie's death off as suicide. His hostile stare was also noticed by Lord Mandaten.

"I am sorry but there is no kind or soft or gentle way to report a family death, especially under such sad circumstances and after losing your father only a short while ago. This makes it even more unbearable for you." Cadiston continued.

While Cadiston was telling James the sad news about his mother, he listened but was not looking at him. Instead, he was glaring at his uncle, Grant, with a real hatred in his eyes which Cadiston noticed.

"As far as that goes, I beg to differ with you there young Cadiston, you had a very difficult task to perform and you have done it showing care and sensitivity and I applaud you for that, my boy. If I may ask, what follows now?" enquired Lord Mandaten. "Miss Sadie's body has been removed and there will be a requirement of a full forensic post-mortem which will confirm the cause of death —." Lord Mandaten interrupted. "Carried out by your good wife Samantha?" "It will be, my Lord, just as has been done with the other members of your family that have met with an untimely and suspicious death." He received another angry glare from Standish. Lord Mandaten noticed this but said nothing. "Now, I need to ask, can anyone shed any light on why Miss Sadie would have a reason to take her own life?" Cadiston asked. There was a lot of head nodding and face-pulling before Demmie spoke. "We all know that she was extremely depressed and had to have our family doctor out. He gave her some pills to calm her down and help her to sleep so maybe she overdosed and went for a walk in her sleep and ended up in the lake." "True, Aunt Demmie, the doctor did give her some medication but Jennifer and I sat with Mother after she had taken them and stayed with her at least an hour after she fell asleep. I looked in again an hour later and she was still asleep. I cannot believe that she would have done this, I cannot believe that she would take her own life because there is still me to live for and she would not have wanted to put me through all this pain." James said and turned. "You did this, Grant, you did this you murdered my mother with your foul tongue!" He then rushed forward and started to strike him. "You are responsible! You are a bad person, I hate you, I hate you." Grant went to strike James but Cadiston was quick to move between them, stopping his action. "Please, everyone, calm down." "Stupid boy, it is clear enough to me! So what are you suggesting there, James? That I killed her? Not possible as I have an alibi!" Cadiston thought why should Grant state that he had an alibi now.

James was in floods of tears. "I don't know about that, Uncle Grant, but I do not believe that she would have killed herself and would do this to me! She loved me and even though she was depressed, sad and – well, with everything that has happened, she would not do it and could not do it! I know of your rude outburst! I may not know what you said to Mother but I do know it upset her greatly. Even through all her pain, she could not have done this and taken her own life because she knows that is a sin. And what alibi would you need Uncle Grant? We were all in bed." "Indeed, all in bed. As for what was said, well, she should not have challenged me and I just told her some home truths, nothing more. So James, you think that someone helped her to take her life? Is that what you are implying? You are a foolish boy. Think clearly, boy, who would want to do such a dastardly thing? You are a son of Mandaten, she was your mother and a member of our family. We have lost far too many of them already over the years and that has made us few here that are left. I am the eldest and heir to the title and estate. You, James, and you, Lowell, are sons of Mandaten and if I did not have a son then you would be in line for the title." Grant said. "That is not what you said the other day about Sadie, Grant." Chad said. "Shut up, Chad, you are not family and you have no right to interfere, just keep out of this." Cadiston could see the hostility between these two and again his suspicions rose. "Gentlemen, please, think of James and how all this aggravation will affect him, this is a solemn occasion and families should unite at this sad time, not argue."

"The detective is right, Grant, and you have been told many times before to curb your tongue." Said Lord Mandaten sternly. "Yes, Father." Grant said softly. "There is nothing more I can say at this point, only that a full investigation will be implemented and in time, there will be questions to be asked and will need an answer. As for now, if there are no further questions for us then we will take our leave." The bell cord was pulled and after a few minutes, Alfred entered the room. He needed no instruction and led them to the front door. "A sad day, Detective. In fact, it has been a sad two weeks for the family." "Indeed, Alfred." He turned and walked to the police car, where Foulsham, their driver, waited. Once in the car, he looked back at the Manor as they

172

drove down the long driveway. They were on their way back to the station when Standish, who had remained silent until then, began. "You are a bloody fool, Cadiston. Fancy telling them that a full investigation would take place; giving them a false impression and false hope. Now all you have succeeded in is to upset the family even further with your handling of the situation. And the way you talked to them – Pa, I knew that I should have done it myself. Now there is a real problem. It was a clear case of suicide and that is all they should have been told and not that there will be a full investigation. You have really gone and done it this time and because of that you can kiss your career goodbye." "That is rather harsh, Sergeant Standish, and a bit hasty, isn't it? But then, hasty is your middle name." Foulsham said.

Standish snapped back angrily. "You keep out of it, PC Foulsham, all you have to do is keep your eyes on the road and drive." He did not answer but glared at Standish in the mirror. Cadiston did not answer but on the way back to the station he wrote his thoughts on the event into his notebook, itemising his suspicions.

"All right, now that the police have had their say and have gone, I will ask you, Uncle Grant, just where do I come into the equation? You said that James and Lowell are both Mandaten sons, so where does that put me?" "You, Kansas, you, my boy, are nowhere as you are not a son of Mandaten. You are a Kaysten by birth and that is the name that you carry, right from the moment that your mother spread her legs and conceived you then again spread her legs and popped you out. You were born a Kaysten, Kansas, and that is your name so, my boy, you will have absolutely no claim at all on the estate." Said Grant cooly. "You have absolutely no call to be so crude or disgusting, Grant." Lizabeth said angrily. "That's how he was born, sister, so just saying it how it is." "You can be so uncouth, Uncle Grant. The fact is that my mother is Mandaten born so that must stand for something." Said Kansas.

"Ha! You think it should stand for something, do you? Well, maybe if she had not married your father but she did so is no longer a Mandaten, she is now a Kaysten, just as you are, and will have no call on the estate. There is only me who is the senior and the only remaining one eligible for the title. The only ones that can stand in my way are Lowell and James and they would only be in the running if I was not here. I have no inclination of leaving, stepping aside or ending up dead so there you have it." Grant gloated. "So, you would write your sister off, would you?" Lizabeth glared at him. "Lizabeth, sweet Lizabeth, my darling sister, you did that for yourself, my dear, the moment and the day that you married Tomas and became a Kaysten." "That makes absolutely no difference and I am still of Mandaten blood and Mandaten born so –." Lizabeth started.

"That is enough, both of you, we have quite sufficient trauma without any further inner family squabble, especially as there are so few of us remaining." Lord Mandaten said firmly. "Yes Father, let us try to get on, shall we dear sweet sister of mine?" Grant said sarcastically. "You are a patronizing, ignorant, obnoxious oaf, Grant, and do not –." "I said enough!" Lord Mandated sounded strained. "Yes, Father, I apologise to you." She turned and walked away with her husband Tomas and son Kansas in tow.

Chapter Six

Cadiston Speaks Out

"Glad to see you are both back, I have got an urgent message from the chief, he wants a word with you two straight away." "What, right now, John? It is getting late in the day and he is usually away home by now?" Asked Standish.

"Not today, he has been waiting for you and said to inform you the instant that you walk through the door, Sergeant Standish." "Thanks, best we make our way up then." Standish said, leading the way as they headed to the superintendents office. "I don't know what the chief wants us both for and at this late hour my guess is something important –. I guess we will find out when we see him. I will do all the talking Cadiston and this time you keep silent, you have caused enough problems for one day, you hear me, Cadiston?" Standish snapped. "I hear you but I will tell you this, I have been silenced on far too many occasions by you and I have taken more than enough so maybe it is time that I spoke out." Cadiston said calmly. Standish glared at him and almost tripped which angered him even more. "Best you don't speak out, say just one word and that will be one word too much. Speak at your peril, Trainee Cadiston. Say just one word and you are finished as a detective the instant that you open your mouth." Standish threatened. "I take that as a threat, Sergeant." He grinned at him. "Take it however you like but keep silent now, we are at the chief's office." Standish straightened. The chief's p.a. was there and showed them straight in. "Ah good, you are back. Now then, Standish, I hear more problems at Mandaten. What has happened this time?" Asked the chief. "Not very much, Chief, a body in the lake and nothing at all suspicious about it, just a clear case of suicide if ever there was one, sir. But –." He sent a stare toward Cadiston. "I would just like to add, sir, that he, in my opinion, went too far and acted against my instructions." "I see, hmm –." He glanced at Cadiston, then back at Standish.

"We will discuss that in a moment but first things first, Sergeant. Now then, Cadiston, tell me what you think about this latest event?" He asked. "Is that really necessary, Chief to ask him as I have already told you what happened and –?" Standish started. "That will be quite enough, Standish. That sounds like you are disagreeing with me." The chief interrupted. "Not at all, sir, I just thought that it would waste of your time." The chief shook his head "Not at all, now go ahead, Cadiston, and give me your view on the latest death." The chief looked straight at Cadiston. "Standish thinks clear cut case of suicide. (He looked at Standish who had a fierce look on his face.) I am not so sure and have reservations, sir. After my examination of the body and my findings made my suspicions grow. I have no wish to go behind the sergeant's back but, if you are keeping count, this is the eighth death at the Manor in about two weeks and that to me raises questions and sounds extremely suspicious, sir. The first death was on Monday, 22nd September, and that, in fact, was a double death, Miss Bonnie and her unborn little girl child. On Tuesday, 23rd, it was Master Malcolm which was my first case and I was not allowed to carry out a full and proper investigation as I saw fit to, do sir. Then, on Sunday, 28th September, there were multiple deaths when the family lost Kevin and the family of their daughter, Sammie. Again, I attended. Now, today, Tuesday 30th September, Miss Sadie and all within ten days. With due respect, sir, if you go along with Sergeant Standish and his quick one-look conclusion, which I most definitely do not, then they are all tragic accidents. And if you want to take his word for it, instead of mine, then I would say, with all due respect, sir, that you are totally wrong and blinkered sir. Now, on the other hand, if you follow my suspicions and allow all these deaths to be investigated properly, then you are on the right path, sir. You did ask me what I think, sir, and I am telling you exactly as I see it." Standish was about to intervene but was stopped. "Sir really –." The chief raised a hand to silence him. "Let him finish, Standish, he is entitled to his opinion" "Thank you. Now, sir, the way I see it, these deaths were no accidents and the evidence that has been shown on the surface and in the post-mortem of Miss Bonnie serves to strengthen my suspicions. After having read that report carefully and assessing the contents –. Well, I am convinced that her death and that of her unborn child was no accident. That report adds fuel to the fire and makes every single one of these deaths carry a degree of suspicion and worthy of investigation. It will all be clearer with the subsequent post-mortems as they will provide the further evidence needed, creating more than enough cause for suspicion. As I have said, sir, all warrant a full and deep investigation. Unlike Sergeant Standish, I think that not one of these deaths should be labelled instantly as a tragic accident, sir. There are far too many discrepancies in them all. In Miss Bonnie and her unborn child's death, when the evidence produced in the post-mortem is looked at carefully, it raises questions. It all points to each subsequent death being more than a mere tragic accident. In my book, sir, they should all be deemed as suspicious deaths, possibly murders and with that in mind, investigated fully. You did ask, sir, and that is my view." The chief smiled. "You are young, eager, enthusiastic, and inexperienced, Cadiston, but you do make a very strong case. So, Sergeant Standish, what do you say in reply to that?"

"A complete over-exaggeration in my book, from the evidence that we have seen on the surface as Cadiston puts it, there is no requirement to dig beneath the surface sir, there is nothing suspicious and they are all sad cases of very tragic accidents, sir. I agree that it is sad that all these deaths are in one family but every single one of them, including this latest drowning which is a clear case of suicide, are nothing more than tragic incidents to befall the same family. This latest death, well, there is nothing more to it than a very distressed and depressed young woman who could not stand life any longer after all the tragedies that have befallen the family and the loss of her husband. To stop the pain, she took her own life and that is a clear case of suicide in my book and that is what my report will say." "And how do you answer that, Cadiston?" He shook his head in despair. "That is what you say, Standish, and I say that your method stinks. Why would a young mother want to leave her son to face the trauma of losing his father and then his mother all in a few days. There is another item that you failed to notice and that is there is no suicide note, it just does not make sense and that raises suspicion. If you had taken the time to look at the body, you would have seen the marks on it just as I did." Cadiston said. "Marks, boy, I needed to see no marks on the body." Standish snapped. "Because all you do is take a quick look and on first impressions you draw your conclusion." Again, he shook his head. "You have not looked at any of the evidence that is presented and is clearly visible. What is more, you have always shut me down and silenced me when I have pointed something out to you, from the very first case that I attended with you. We have been together for a while now and I have observed how you work from the first case that I attended with you right up to the latest that of Sadie Mandaten. On my very first case, you have refused to allow forensics to investigate the area for hidden evidence and tried to stop a post-mortem from being carried out, which I am certain would have lead to a full investigation. I may be young and inexperienced but as I have said, I still strongly disagree with you and do not like your methods. There are far too many discrepancies with all these Mandaten deaths, and if you take the time to look, which you most certainly do not. I ask you, sir, can we not wait until we get the post-mortem results on all these bodies before making any kind of decision? And should we not be looking at Bonnie and her unborn child's death with suspicion? Especially after what the post-mortem has shown us –. An indepth and complete post-mortem may bring something to light that would otherwise be missed and when it does, it will signify that a full and proper investigation is required. Not as you, Sergeant Standish, would want it just written off before that takes place. It would be a real travesty and, if I may say, criminal if they were all attempts to disguise murders. Think about it, if they are just written off as tragic accidents, then the perpetrators of these heinous crimes would go unpunished and walk free, sir. I mean no offence to you, sir, but as the way I see it, you did ask me for my opinion and I am tired of being silenced and I am repeating myself over and over sir. Lastly, sir, if he had listened to my suspicions about Malcolm Mandaten and acted on them instead of going with his single-thought-mind, I feel very strongly that some of these deaths could have been prevented." Standish went to speak but the chief raised his hand and stopped him. He sat silent for a moment, pondering over what had been said. "As I have said, you make a very strong case, Cadiston, and you have a very good point. Plus, your zeal and desire to arrive at the truth, no matter what, has not gone unnoticed. Now, I need you to leave us for a moment as I need to speak to Sergeant Standish alone. Wait in the outer office and I will call you back when I need to speak with you again." Without speaking, Cadiston stood and left the office. In the outer office, Cadiston sat down. J.J. smiled at him and whispered. "Don't look so worried, Cadders it will be fine." He smiled back at her. With the door firmly closed, the chief began. "Now then, Sergeant Standish, you have been with the force for quite a while and you retire soon, don't you?" "Yes, that I do, sir. Saturday in a week is the official day, 11th October. Work Friday and Saturday is a day off and, if I can sir, I would like to have all my cases closed before I retire. All of them, sir, including all Cadiston's cases at the Manor. I know that he is young and eager to make a detective and he tries hard to impress, sir, but –. Well, I have to say it, is he really going to make a good detective especially when he tries to read more into a case than there really is? All that stuff about evidence on the surface and digging beneath the surface to find hidden evidence waste of time sir. As his training sergeant, it is down to me to decide on that outcome make detective or not and quite honestly, sir –. Well, – I really don't know if I can recommend him, sir, as he has caused all sorts of problems and anxiety in the family with all these Mandaten deaths and his foolish suspicions. He oversteps the mark, sir, and goes against what I tell him to do. He creates falseness and although they are all extremely tragic in the way that they have come about, it is clear to see that they are nothing more than accidents. Tragic, yes, but accidents. As anyone with a trained eye can see, sir. Well, anyone except Cadiston that is. He wants to impress but in doing so, he keeps putting a spanner in the works, sir. I have serious reservations about his ability to become a fully qualified detective, sir, especially how he has just ranted and spoken out of turn. I must say that confirms my thoughts on the subject and just proves my point." The chief thought hard before speaking. "Hmm, this is very difficult for me Standish especially with your record b –. Well –." He paused briefly. "I have had a call from Lord Mandaten." Standish's mouth dropped open. "And he has specifically requested that young Cadiston investigates all the deaths and investigates every single one of them fully, from the first being Miss Bonnie and not forgetting her unborn child, to the latest one of Miss Sadie. He has taken a real liking to him and believes in his ability. After that call, I spoke with the superintendent who incidentally also had a call from him." Standish's face dropped at this revelation. "This was not an easy decision to make but, never the less, it has been made. Sergeant Standish, the powers that be have authorised this so as of five-thirty today, you are a retired police officer and an ordinary citizen. So your warrant card please then go home now and enjoy it."

The colour drained from the Standish's face as he passed his warrant card over. "But it is only 30th September, sir, and the cases need to be closed for the record sir." "Cadiston will do that. Your record is exemplary, Standish, you have served the force well and done enough. Now, you have been officially retired for thirty-five minutes so go home and enjoy your retirement."

Standish was stunned into silence and had nothing more to say but he was angry knowing that Cadiston had bested him. In the outer office, he sent a cold stare at Cadiston as he walked past. Cadiston could see the look of thunder on his face and wanted to smile but as he did not know what he now faced, he refrained. He watched Standish as he walked away with his head hung low, as though he had been scalded like a naughty child that had failed in his task and wondered just what had been said and taken place behind the closed door with the superintendent. Cadiston looked at Justine Jarvis or as she was nicknamed J.J. and wondered just what she knew of this meeting but he was soon to find out because, "Justine's phone rang and she answered it instantly. "Very well, sir." The phone was hung up. "You can go in now, Ashton." "Thanks' JJ". She smiled at him as he walked past her desk. "Come in and close the door Cadiston, then take a seat." There was a brief pause. "Now then, young Cadiston, what to do with you –. I have had you under surveillance for some time and have been watching you and Standish very closely from the moment that you were paired together. You may be surprised to hear that I am not alone in this. There are others in higher places that have watched also. We had a team assigned for that task and they have observed you both very closely." "P.C. Foulsham, sir, our driver, could he be one? I have observed him taking an interest in the proceedings and taking notes."

"He could indeed and that is very observant of you. I needed a pair of eyes close, that is why he was assigned as your driver. We can clearly see your enthusiasm and we could not help but notice hmm, – a bit of hostility from Standish towards you during your time with him. We did not want to lose a potentially good detective so now he is gone. The powers that be have declared him retired early so now you, young Cadiston, are on your own. It has been approved from the top that you have officially passed your probationary period and are now to be classified as a fully trained detective. Constable. It was expected that you would speak out at some point in time. It was expected to be much earlier than this but I guess that you had your reasons for the delay in voicing your opinion. Now, to the real business of the day, investigate, my boy. Investigate every single one of the Mandaten deaths with our full support. It is up to you now so go and get it done." Said the chief.

"Even those that have been closed by Standish, both past and present, sir? And the end reports written up?" Asked Cadiston. "I had a feeling that you would ask that and as I had anticipated that question, I have had the files pulled from records. They are all here for you to read and use as you see fit. That one is Lord

Mandaten's brother and his entire family from four years ago and other cases of Mandaten deaths that Standish had a hand in over the past fifteen years. All the cases are open and re-opened for you to investigate. Now then, as you are aware, this may all be a bit unorthodox in the way it has come about but it has come from the top. Lord Mandaten speaks very highly of you and it appears that you have found a friend in a very high place. He has put a lot of faith in your ability as a detective and although I could not show it in front of Standish, I do too. Sergeant Standish is from the old school and it has been hard for him to adapt to new ways of thinking. Now you, on the other hand, are from the new school and, what's more, you have come out top of your class in all areas so don't let me or the chief super down. Or his Lordship, come to think of it." The chief said.

"No sir, not a chance, I most certainly will not. If I may speak candidly, sir?" He asked. "Speak away then, Cadiston, it is only the two of us here." The Chief said. "I appreciate everything that you have said but I feel that this needs to be said also, even if it is very hard to say." Cadiston stalled.

"Just say it then, man, I do not want to be here all night. My wife is cooking steak for tea and I can already taste it." The chief said impatiently. "Over my time with him I have not been totally happy, At first everything was fine but then I gave some more thought to each case. I started getting the impression that Sergeant Standish wanted a quick closure on each of his cases, especially the Mandaten deaths, and all without any form of formal investigation and when I challenged his decision then he tried to shut me down and silence me. I also know that he closed the case on Lord Mandaten's brother and his family, who all perished together about four years ago, and some thought it should have been investigated further. I don't know how to say this, sir, but I have noticed that it is not just to have a closed book when he retired but there is an underlying reason. I cannot quite put my finger on it yet but there is something amiss with these cases at the Manor, sir, and I cannot think that it is just to have a closed file and a clear case book when he retires. I do not want to believe that it is anything sinister, never the less, an underlying reason and that reason needs to be found, sir." His Superintendent thought for a moment. "It is not so strange that you should say that and very commendable that even though supposedly inexperienced, you picked up on that fact because we have had suspicions about that for some time but could find nothing that incriminates him. Now, this goes no further than these four walls –. That is the reason why you were placed with him over all the other candidates because it was felt that if there were something amiss, then you would find it. You already have your suspicions about him so you are part of the way there. I charge you with this, Cadiston. Find the reason behind it for us and let me know what it is before anyone else, that is very important." Said the chief. "Understood, sir. That I will do gladly." Said Cadiston. "Good man. Now, get out of my office and get out there and solve these Mandaten deaths for me because as of now, they are all your cases. You have a task on your hands but, without a doubt, we feel that it is nothing that you cannot handle. They all need to be labelled correctly and if a murder was committed, the guilty party or parties involved in the crime will need to be apprehended as soon as possible. It is over to you then and don't forget the reopened cases from four years ago and all the other cold cases. That will be a task on its own merit but without reservation, we feel that you will be up to the challenge." The chief said eagerly. "It will be a real Pleasure, sir." Cadiston nodded. "Good, that concludes our meeting, and remember that you can ask for additional help when needed." The chief added. "Thank you, be assured, sir, that I will get onto the cases straight away." He turned and left the office with a broad smile on his face. All the way home, the massive, broad smile remained. He was delighted at the outcome of his talk with his chief and wondered why he had not spoken out before but he was glad it was done. He longed to tell his wife his good news. He was like a child the day before Christmas and although he was very suspicious of his methods, he still had a modicum of respect for Sergeant Standish. The one thing that was at the top of his list and a major concern, was his method of reaching a quick conclusion in the face of first impressions especially in regard to the deaths at the Mandaten Manor. He had watched him work and accompanied him on several cases and although he had dealt with those cases slightly differently, his method was the same. He had always made a quick decision in how to conclude the case. His main concern was why and in time, he would somehow find the reason behind his quickness for closing the Mandaten cases. It would not be easy but undeterred, he would still undertake the task. He was feeling relaxed now as, in a sense, he was free of his shackles and could work in his own way without hinderance. Now he would not be silenced and he had only himself to thank for this. It was only his tenacity that had made it happen. The instant that he walked in the door, Samantha could see that there was something that he wanted to tell her. She pretended not to notice but they knew each other so well and neither could hide it. "Alright then, spill Ashton, what is so important that you cannot wait to tell me?"

"I will give you three guesses, my sweet, and if you have not come up with it, then I will tell you." He said smiling broadly. "Can't you just tell me?" She asked."Play along with me, go on, have a guess." "One: you have passed your probationary period." He smiled at her. "Go on." "Two: Standish is coming around to your way of thinking." "And your third guess?" He nudged.

"The Mandaten files are to be reopened and you are to investigate them."

"You are just too good at this, two out of three is pretty good going. You were spot on with number one, I am now classed as a fully trained detective. You were also right with number three, the Mandaten files are reopened and I am to investigate every one of them by order of the Superintendent." He grinned.

"And what of guess two?" She asked. "Sergeant Standish, now, that is the crowning point. He has been retired early by order of the powers that be and that means I am on my own. I came to the end of my tether today and after being silenced for so long by him I could not allow it to happen anymore. It raised an eyebrow or two when I just spoke out and got all my frustration off my chest. It had been noticed by the chief and others that we did not get on too well from the very start of the association. It may have been a clash of our personalities or perhaps he had other motives to silence me. Either way, orders came directly from the top and there you have it. It is done now. I am completely free of him and free to investigate the Mandaten deaths properly. There was another reason that prompted the superintendents action and that was a call from Lord Mandaten himself. He never liked Standish, from his very first encounter with him. He had dealings with him in the past and was not satisfied with his decision. Anyhow, he is gone now, thank goodness, and I feel very relieved now that the shackles are removed so I have a free hand." Samantha smiled, "All I can say is that you must have made a really good impression on Lord Mandaten. It appears that you have a friend in a high place now and with this revelation, you can really get down to your investigating. I know that Standish has been a thorn in your side but now that he is gone, you will not be stopped or silenced so you can begin in earnest. You have Bonnie's post-mortem result to give you a good start and the way I know you, you will begin your investigation straight away and that makes it a very poignant case. I guess that you will require the other results as soon as possible. Charles and I have almost finished Malcolm's post-mortem. It would have been done sooner as per your request, we are being extremely thorough. Not that we aren't all the time as that is how we work. That's the way to find something that someone would prefer to remained hidden. Now with Malcolm's post-mortem, like you, we have found some major discrepancies. We have a small stumbling block, and it is a pity that we do not have the lump of Masonry used to cave his skull in as that would confirm what Charles and me are already thinking." She said. "That can be rectified very easily, my sweet, the area around the Devil's Dyke is still cordoned off, thanks to my insistence, so I will just go up there and get it for you. I know exactly where it is laying –. Unless it is as I suspected and –. If it was not an accident but a murder and the perpetrators have been back to the crime scene and have removed it."

He looked worried. "I hope not but would it be in order and legal to get it now? Would it be admissible evidence?" She asked.

"Required as part of an ongoing investigation, so yes, it would be legal. It is a vital piece of evidence and coupled with the post-mortem result, it is a very strong piece of visual evidence. Well, my precious one, there is no time like the present to strike but it is far too late in the day so first thing in the morning." He said. "True but you are not going back there alone, I am coming with you." She said and he smiled. "Thought that you would." He added.

Early on the morning of Wednesday, 1st October, one week and a day after Malcolm's death, Samantha sent a text message to Charles saying she would be in late and they were on their way to retrieve the piece of masonry. As they drove toward Mandaten Manor, he explained how Standish had been involved in the cases of Lord Mandaten's brother and his family, who all died four years ago. He was met with Lord Mandaten's wrath after labelling it as a tragic accident without a full and proper investigation. He now understoond how Standish had achieved so many closed cases. He also said that he had obtained all the files on Standish's cases that involved the Mandaten family. He told her how he has been given the go-ahead to get them all reopened even a case from France, and due to his suspicions, he was not convinced that they were all mere tragic accidents. Lord Mandaten himself had become suspicious.

Arriving at the Manor, he was wondering just how they would get in unobserved but luckily Jeremiah was there carrying out his routine maintenance and greasing the gate hinges. "Hello Detective, now what brings you back and with your good lady wife?" He asked as they approached.

"Hi Jeremiah, we need that piece of masonry that Malcolm struck his head on." "I told pops I thought it was strange that no evidence was taken away. We could all see that you wanted to do more but got stopped at every turn. None of us thought it was right and didn't like that sergeant bloke who was with you. He was – well, never mind that. I will open the gate and you can go get it, got to test the gate anyway. The area is still cordoned off, thanks to you, and I take it you would like this visit to be kept a secret?" "Very much so, Jeremiah, tight-lipped and not a soul to be told, not even your family. It will just be between us. What about the cctv camera?" Asked Cadiston.

"Turned off for maintenance so I haven't seen you, blind as a bat and deaf to boot." Jeremiah said looking around him. "Thanks, Jeremiah." They then drove slowly up the old road toward the ruins to retrieve the offending piece of masonry. Cadiston gave a sigh of relief when he saw that it was still there and without delay, he took another photograph of the offending object before it was carefully picked up and wrapped in an evidence bag. "If it was murder, they got careless. Or perhaps they thought that they had gotten away with it thanks to Standish as he is connected somehow and it had been covered up by him sufficiently to avoid further investigation. They probably thought that with me being silenced, it would go no further. Someone is in for a shock. While we are here, we might as well have a quick look around." Samantha watched him and wondered what her husband was doing "What is that you have there in your hand, Ashton?" She asked him. "I wanted to get a sample of the small footprints and I can see that they may not be as good now, should have been done last Tuesday and should also have had forensics here but Standish stopped that happening. I will have a go and see what I get." He made his plaster mix and poured it into the prints. While he was doing this, his wife was not standing idly by but was having a look around.

"Ashton, over here." She waved him over. "What have you found?" He looked down to where she was pointing. "See it? That white chalky substance, soil or something? It does not fit in with the area, the soil around the old Manor has a slight reddish hue and the Dyke is quite dark, almost black, so this white chalky substance is completely alien and out of place. To my mind, it would have been brought here on someone's foot and that leads me to believe that it is possible that there has been a crime committed here. They thought that they were clever and covered their tracks but then the perpetrator could have inadvertently carried it here on their feet. Best I take a sample as it could be possible evidence." Samantha got a bag from the boot of the car and took two samples, one of the chalky substance and one of the dyke's almost black, muddy soil for comparison. "I wonder what else we would find if we had a really good look around." At that moment, Jeremiah rode up. "Don't want to hurry you, Cadiston, but if I am taking too long, they will get suspicious and start asking awkward questions that you would not want to be answered." He said.

"Two minutes, Jeremiah, and we are gone." He retrieved his cast of the prints and before driving away, he said. "We need a much longer and better look at the old ruins and Devil's Dyke but –," he tapped his lips. "It needs to be kept a secret. I will speak to Jooners in forensics to see if he will come here with us." "I want to do all that I can to help catch whoever did this so take my mobile number and I will let you in whenever you need. The family – well, Lord and Lady Mandaten, have been extremely good to us all and our family before. In fact, they have treated us like their own family so anything any of us can do to help catch whoever did this, without reservation we want to help."

"Appreciate that, Jeremiah." With a wave, they were gone. "Maybe something can be sorted with him." "Maybe but for now we have what we came for and that will have to do for now. In the morning, I will make a call to the Manor and have a word with his Lordship and inform him of the situation, without the family being present as I have my suspicions about them."

Samantha smiled. "You have a new spring your step now, Ashton, it must feel good to be unchained from Standish." "Wonderful, my sweet." He said and smiled at her.

Back in the office, he began to write up his notebook and read through Bonnie's post-mortem again, taking in every aspect so that he had all the information at his fingertips to begin his investigation. Wednesday had passed by quickly and on this Thursday, ten days since Bonnie and her unborn child had died, he was keen to make a start on his investigation into their deaths. In fact, all the family deaths past and present. But wanted to speak to Lord and Lady Mandaten first to inform them of his plans. He had brought all Standish's reports home with the post-mortem result and had read them all very carefully on Wednesday evening. He did not agree at all with Standish's report and his closure of the case of Bonnie and her unborn child. As far as he was concerned, it could be shredded as it did not reflect the truth of what took place on that fateful evening. Now that he had been given a free hand, he would begin his full no-holes barred investigation. He was glad that he had finally spoken out and although he thought that it may go against him, it had the adverse effect and had worked to his advantage.

He was on his way but the first thing he needed to do was to inform the Lord and Lady of the Manor of his intentions, but not all the family. At this point in his investigations, they would all be deemed as a suspect and he would need to question them all individually on each of the suspected murders at some point to establish if any of them were guilty of the crime, either singularly or in conjunction with another party. He knew that if they were forewarned, they would be forearmed and that would prompt them to check if there was any evidence that could incriminate them and ensure that they had completely covered their tracks, therefore, making it extremely difficult to build his case.

When he arrived at the Manor, he was surprised to find that the gates were standing wide open and thought it was most unusual. He continued his journey down the long drive. With his car parked, he approached the front door, rang the bell, and then waited. Five minutes had passed before the door was opened by Jonas. "Detective Cadiston, now if you have come to see their Lord and Ladyship, you are out of luck on this day. Unfortunately, Detective, his Lordship took a turn for the worse last night and the family is at the hospital with him."

"I did need to have a word with them both in private today but it is not a problem, Jonas. Tell me, may I come in with their absence as there is something that I need to check on before I can finish my final report. I must make sure that it is totally accurate, you understand?" "Indeed, yes that I do, the t must be crossed and the i must be dotted with a full stop at the end, come in and do what you must. I am sure that they would not mind in the slightest." Said Jonas. "I may need a word with you and Alfred so will you be available?" Asked Cadiston. "If it will help, we will. This is a bad business, Detective, with all these deaths in the family so close together and only three, no correction, four years since his Lordships brother and family all died suspiciously. It was supposed to be a traffic accident and that Standish fellow handled the case and well – It left room for suspicion and no further action was ever taken but then you probably already know that. I do believe that they are not over that sad loss yet and now we have all these other deaths for them to deal with. A bad business, Detective, a very bad business." "It most certainly is and it is my aim to get to the bottom of each one of these deaths and find the truth of them all. There are a considerable number of cases and I must look at them one at a time if the truth is to be found but that will take time. Now then, can you show me exactly where the dessert trolley was on that fateful evening of Monday, 22nd September?" Asked Cadiston. "Follow me, Detective, and I will show you." He walked briskly toward the dining room and stopped in the hallway outside it. "The dessert trolley was exactly there where it is now." Jonas said.

"And apart from yourselves, did anyone come anywhere near it before the desserts were served?" "No one, no one at all, just Alfred, myself, and Mister Bradinham. Shall I get him to confirm that?" Asked Jonas. "If you wouldn't mind, thank you." Said Cadiston and waited.

Jonas turned and made his way down the hall and disappeared around the corner. Alone now, Cadiston began to look around the area and could not help but marvel at the magnificent old Chinese spice jar that was in an alcove. As he marveled at the antique piece, he also noted that it was close to the positioning of the dessert trolley and carefully measured the distance between where they would have been placed. He had a keen interest in history and antiquities that had been inherited from his parents. He had been brought up around them as they had their own antique shop. He inspected the old spice jar carefully and began to mumble to himself while he waited for Jonas and Alfred. "Beautiful old piece, wonder when it dates from. Maybe way back when the old spice road was in full swing around 410 AD. Be a miracle and priceless if it was so maybe not that old, 16th century copy maybe. Well, no matter, it is a beautiful thing and still has its cork. Now that must be a replacement or would cork last that many years?" His curiosity got the better of him and after he had touched it, was amazed that it moved. "Must be a replacement. Now, back to the subject on hand, trolley there, dining room there – Hmm – if it was tampered with, they would need to be prepared for that split-second opportunity. Who by and what with and who would benefit from her death? Think, Cadders, think!" Something kept his eye returning to the large spice jar that stood so prominently in the alcove. "I wonder – Could it be possible? The cork is loose but will it come off?" He used extreme caution and, sure enough, to his delight it did. "Now if it was used to hide something, it would already be prepared, hence the loose lid. Mighty dark in there and a long way down." He shone the small torch that he always carried in his pocket into the darkness and could see an object resting at the bottom. "Now, that looks remarkably like a syringe, how to get it out? Now that is the question. Too deep for my arm, I need something to get hold of it with – Something like a grabber." His fingers clicked as the thought came to him. "Of course, got one in the car. Thanks, Samantha, you knew it would prove to be a useful tool at some point." He replaced the lid just as the two footmen returned. "Alfred, Jonas tells me that this is where the dessert trolley stood on that fateful evening, is that correct?" Asked Cadiston. "It is." Alfred nodded.

"And no one other than yourselves were anywhere near it?" He asked.

"No one, just us and Mister Bradinham. Now, if there is nothing else you require of us …" Said Alfred. "Nothing, thank you." Said Cadiston. "Then we will get on with our duties."

They turned to walk away but halted abruptly. "No, wait a minute Detective, that is not altogether true. Remember Jonas, the three ladies went to the restroom and we had to wait for them to return to the table before we could serve dessert." Alfred said. "That's right, with all that has been happening, I had forgotten that. It w who hmm –. Now, let me think – Yes, Miss Lizabeth, Miss Greta and … Who else was it?" Said Jonas.

"I know, it was Chad's wife, Miss Demmie. That's it." Alfred said.

"One more question, then I am done. Was the trolley out of your sight when they went to the restroom?" Asked Cadiston.

"It would have been." Replied Alfred. "It would have been because we were busy clearing the main course table ware so, yes, it would have been but very briefly." Added Jonas. "I would say a minute at the very most but probably only seconds." Finished Alfred. "Thank you both, that is most helpful and fits in with my investigation. Now I can write my report." "Cross the t and dot the i, then full stop." Said Jonas with a smile. "Exactly Jonas, now I just need to fetch my camera from the car to take a couple of pics so if you have other duties, you can carry on and I will close the door on the way out. Thank you both for your help but keep my visit to yourselves, please, as I do not want to add any further stress for the family. Our little secret, just for now, until I have my full report written, understand?" Cadiston waited for a response.

"Implicitly, sir, our lips are sealed." Replied Jonas, giving a sign as through zipping his lips. They left him standing there and the instant they were out of sight, he hurried to the car and returned to the spice jar. With the lid off he shone the torch and reached in. When he brought his grabber out, it held securely as he had suspected: a syringe. With it placed safely into a sample bag, he carefully replaced the lid and took his photographs. He then made a final check to ensure that all was as he had found it and when satisfied, he then left.

Upon his return to the station, he went straight to the lab with his find. "Keith, Greg, got something here that I would like you to look at for me?"

"Well, in the bag Cadders it looks like a syringe with a small makeshift needle but not the sort a doctor would use." Answered Keith. "Very good, I can see why you have this job. Joking aside chaps, this may have been used to commit a murder, two in fact. But until you have analysed it, I will not know for certain. I need to know what the substance is it contained and any finger prints on it lifted." Said Cadiston. "Piece of cake, Cadders, leave it to us and we'll give you a call when we have the result for you." Answered Greg.

"Cannot ask you for anything more than that, thanks." He turned and walked away, returning to his office.

Picking up the desk phone, he dialed, and two minutes later the call was answered. "Forensic mortuary." "Hi Charles, did you get the piece of masonry you wanted from Samantha?" Cadiston asked.

"I most certainly did and, what is more, it is proving to be a real asset and an invaluable piece of evidence to aid our investigation. That was the missing link and has proved to be an essential part of the examination and with it, we are making good headway with the post-mortem. I have a strong feeling that your suspicions were well-founded as our report will show. We are working on it full time and it should be finalised sometime this afternoon so it will be in your hands by Friday morning." Charles said. "Friday, 2nd October, ten days after Malcolm was –. Well, as to that we will soon see. Sorry Charles, I am running on a bit but that will be great. I take it Samantha has told you the news?" Cadiston asked. "She has and no big surprise there, Standish was not a very popular or liked man and I know for a fact that he rattled too many people's cages with his method and bullishness. Now then, on that information, one copy only will be with you in the morning." Said Charles.

"Spot on, thanks." Cadiston hung up the phone and immediately started writing in his notebook. He began detailing the events of his visit to the Manor and his findings after talking with the two footmen. Then he began to look at a variety of scenarios to assess the murder of Bonnie and her unborn child. He looked at how it could be achieved and in doing so, making it look like a tragic accident. He ran through the incident over and over until he had arrived at the possible outcomes and he had three main suspects: Lizabeth, Greta, and Demmie. If one of them did commit murder, his question was, what could they possibly stand to gain? He was certain that at least one of them would gain something, but what? He did not stop analyzing the case until his mind was satisfied that he was very close to the truth. "Right, that is Bonnie and her unborn child's investigation underway. I will know more after the syringe has had a full analysis. Then I can start my questioning but for the moment, I can go no further. Not until I have that information in my hand. Time is a quarter to five and almost home time, I wonder if that report on Malcolm is done yet. Should I ring, should I wait, now there is a question." "Doing it again, Cadders." Said Mac. "Helps to keep me sane, Mac, what about you?"

"Me? Phew, most definitely, my friend, be nutty as a fruit cake if not." They both chuckled.

"Now then, Mister Standish, let me see just what you have written in your report about Bonnie and her unborn little girl child, even before the findings of the post-mortem or any form of investigation." He opened the report and read the very brief summary, shaking his head, in disgust, he closed it again. He sat back in his chair while he silently voiced his thoughts. "There is no way that I can see how you could possibly write a report with a conclusion without first having seen and read her post-mortem and gathering more information, just does not make sense. Why were you in such a hurry, Standish? Why did you insist on all these cases being closed without full forensics and a proper investigation before you retired? And why did you want to keep me silenced? I find it very hard to believe it was just to retire with a record number of cases and a closed book. There is something that does not ring true and smacks a little bit sinister. You can be sure that the reason will eventually come out. That will be then, as for now, I have some more reading to do when Malcolm's post-mortem report comes through." His head was full of suspicions as his fingers taped the closed file. "Now I am on my way and free of you but you can rest assured that it is not the end of this. Not until they have all been investigated fully. Now it is time for home and I will continue my analysis of these cases tomorrow." He felt good about himself with a touch of sadness because he knew that if he had spoken out a lot sooner, especially with Malcolm's case, there was a strong possibility that five lives might have been saved. Friday morning, 3rd October, Cadiston was at his desk, and in front of him was Standish's report on Malcolm. He thumbed the report and was half hesitant to open it as he was convinced that it would contain none of the truth about Malcolm's tragic death. "Ok, let's see what you have written." He opened the file and began to read:

Final Report on Malcolm Mandaten
Died on 23rd September

On arrival at the Manor, we were immediately taken to the site of the old Manor ruins, running close by is the Devil's Dyke and it was at this location that we found the body of Mister Malcolm Mandaten. The body was lying face down and he had been covered with a taupe by the men that had found him: Herbert and his sons, Jeremiah and Jason. Others present were Jacob and his sons Freddie, Charles, and Anthony. These men here named had collectively formed the search party and were the main people concerned in the search there were other workers but they had no active role to play other than to search for the missing Malcolm Mandaten.

When the body was uncovered, it was discovered that flies and the dyke rats had been on the body and it was quite apparent that he was deceased and there was nothing to be done for him. The ambulance had arrived and without hesitation, the doctor actively examined the deceased. In his expert opinion, we agreed that the presented evidence proved beyond all doubt that this was a tragic riding accident. He ascertained that Mister Mandaten had fallen from his horse after which he was dragged along the ground, thereby striking his head on a large piece of fallen masonry which resulted in fracturing his skull. It was determined by the doctor present at the scene that because there was no immediate help on hand, he sadly bled to death. The attending doctor put the time of death as between six a.m. and eight a.m. but due to the body being attacked by flies and rats, he could not be certain. The body was dually removed and transported to the mortuary but as is my experience, it was felt at the scene that a post-mortem would not be required as it is perfectly clear that the cause of death was from the fall and striking his head resulting in a massive skull fracture and severe blood loss.

Conclusion

As the evidence clearly portrayed and contrary to any other thoughts when the scene of the incident was examined, it is very clear that this was a very sad and tragic riding accident that resulted in the death of the named, Mister Malcolm Mandaten.

With these findings, there is no further need to continue with a lengthy, costly and unnecessary investigation.

Signed on this day by the investigating officer
Sergeant Standish.

Case Closed

"What a load of rubbish you have written, better not talk out loud but that will not stop me from thinking it." He re-read the report and thought that it portrayed a miscarriage of justice. "What rubbish and not a shred of truth, apart from the blood loss, but nothing else. Not much to go on there but I fail to see is how such a conclusion could be made without a full investigation and when the post-mortem result is in my hands, it will be a different story altogether. The truth will unfold for me, Mister Standish, as will the facts of his death and then it will all be disclosed. Sorry, Serge, but you are so wrong and there is much more behind all these deaths than meets the eye. When I have discovered the real, whole truth,

I can say to you I told you so. As I investigate this and other cases properly, I will also discover why you were so keen to keep me quiet and label them all as tragic accidents. It is as though you were trying to cover up something sinister. If only you had listened to me, Standish, and not been so pig-headed about everything, there would have been no delay in the investigation taking place and it would have been proven without a shadow of doubt and possibly saved further violent deaths. You wanted it all wrapped up quickly and without investigating but from what I have been told and what I have read, it is more than enough to throw some doubt on Bonnie and her unborn child being a case of someone's carelessness. From my way of thinking, I have multiple murders to investigate and all at the Manor. It is as though someone is trying to wipe the whole family out one at a time. Another day I must go to the library archives and search the complete family history or get those in the know to do it for me. Maybe the hospital records on births should be looked at also, especially Chadrick. He seems like a decent chap but looks can sometimes be deceiving and he is their adopted son so maybe after finding out about his birth, it will shed some light on the situation. A coffee would be nice −." He went to the machine and poured himself a cup and when he returned to his desk, he had no sooner sat down when the phone rang. "Detective Cadiston." "Morning Cadders, Charles here, just letting you know the post-mortem is complete and I think that you would like to see the result for yourself so can you come to the mortuary? I can promise you that it will not be a wasted trip and I think you will find it interesting as it supports all your suspicions." "Be there in twenty." Said Cadiston and the phone line went silent. This was what he wanted to hear and so he swallowed his coffee and wasted no time. On his way past the front desk, he spoke to the desk constable. "On my way to the forensic mortuary, John, I cannot say how long I will be only that it will be as quick as possible." "Not a problem." John replied and with that he left.

"Morning Charles, what have you got for me?" Cadiston said as he walked in. "Samantha is fetching the body from the chiller as we speak and when you see it I do not think that you will be surprised at the result." Said Charles. "What do you think then, Charles, tragic accident or murder?" "Easy answer, in our professional opinion, there is no question about it, murder without a shadow of doubt. Do you know what the missing link was." "I think that I can guess but go on, tell me." Cadiston said.

"The piece of masonry." Charles said with a smile. "Thought so." Cadiston said. "Have a read while we wait for the body to arrive." Samantha entered the viewing room but Cadiston continued to read. "Ok, I have read enough, and even without seeing the body and the damage caused, my suspicions rise. Excellent job both of you! Now show me what you have found, please."

Samantha began to uncover the body, slowly pulling the cover completely back, and exposing Malcolm Mandaten's body. "Now then Cadders, first take a look at the clothing, then at the torso. Then, when we turn him over, take a good look at the impact point." "That indentation was no simple collision with that piece of masonry, the indentation took some force." Cadiston noted.

"It certainly did and it is absolutely impossible for a blow like that to be caused to that area of the skull by being dragged into that piece of masonry. If it had been so, the force generated would have moved the masonry, leaving a grove in the ground. I believe you would have noticed that when you first saw it. When you returned to collect the weapon, it was just lying on the surface. I have also seen the photographs that Samantha took and combined they make powerful evidence. There is no doubt and, just as you suspected, this was a deliberate killing and they slipped up badly by leaving the murder weapon in the exact same position just lying on the surface." Charles said.

"Probably thinking that Standish would handle it and class it a tragic accident. They had not reckoned with me so they did get careless." Cadiston said.

"Standish? Do you think he was somehow mixed up in it?" Asked Charles.

"Forget I said that Charles as that is a separate issue for investigation."

"Forgotten Cadders. Now, if you look at this piece of masonry and the shape of it —." "Got it, Charles." Cadiston looked at the information. "Now, look at the indentation in the skull. If I place this object into it, as you can see, it is a perfect fit. By the amount of damage caused, as we have already said, this was no accident, Cadders, but a clever yet very clumsy cover-up. It is exactly how you had suspected in the first instance and it is safe to say that you have another murder on your hands." Charles concluded.

"I knew it, knew right from the start and forensics should have been up there to examine the area. Damn you, Standish! But it can still be done but any evidence that would have been clear on the day that this happened, will now be smudged. There still may be hidden evidence that only our expert forensic team can search out. Coming back to your report, this part is interesting about his extra thick skull. Whoever attacked him knew of this family trait. Murder, Charles, Samantha, murder. So that is two, no correction, three for me to investigate and when you have completed the other post-mortems, my guess is there will be more. Ok you two, I have taken up enough of your valuable time so, my friend and my wife, I will get back to the station and carry out my analysis and theory and begin my incidents board, then work out how Malcolm was murdered. See you at home, Samantha." With a wave, Cadiston was gone.

"Like I have said before, your husband is very determined." Samantha smiled, then said "Back to work then Charles."

Arriving back at the station, Cadiston was stopped at the front desk. "Cadders, I am glad that you came back here, message from the superintendent, he wants a word with you." "Thanks John, best that I do not hang about then and go straight up." Cadiston said. "Not right now, my friend, he has already gone for today. He has appointments so said first call for you on Monday morning at 9 a.m. sharp." "Monday, 6th it is then John." Cadiston said.

Sitting at his desk, he wondered what the super wanted him for and quickly pushed that to the back of his mind as he had other more important things to concentrate on. For the rest of today, he would put all his energy into his incidents board and concentrating on his analysis on Malcolm's death by studying the post-mortem report and reading his notes just as he had done with Bonnie and her unborn child. He had pieced together opportunity, method, and means, now all he needed to know was who benefitted from Bonnie's death. He opened his notebook and began to look at a variety of scenarios to ascertain just how the perpetrators of this second crime had achieved it. He forgot about the time he was spending on it and did not stop until he had a theory secure in his mind. All he required now was concrete evidence and suspects. According to his notes and to his way of thinking for the present moment, the whole family fitted that category. Friday also found him repeating this process with the cases of Kevin, Sammie, Walter, Gloria, and Sadie but to achieve a true theory he needed the post-mortem and forensic reports for all these untimely deaths. Fifteen days had already passed since the first untimely death and he fully appreciated that he had his work cut out for him and with so many cases to solve, he would need some help. He knew that he had to wait for all the results to be in his hands and although he had already gathered a lot of information to go on, there was still a lot more to find. He would not be idle over the weekend and he read and re-read every word that had been written. He went over all his reports, his analysis, and his theories, and with his mind so full of information, he was extremely restless. He felt that he had been held back long enough and now that he had a free hand. He wanted to get into his stride and get his investigation underway by asking his many questions to find the killer of these victims of what he declared were first-degree murders before they had the chance to strike again. His wife understood and kept him supplied with food and drinks and was sometimes sitting beside him reading the reports to aid his thinking. Saturday had come and gone and now, Sunday evening was upon him and it was only when he was in bed that he wondered what the superintendent wanted to see him for. He closed his eyes knowing that the morning would soon arrive and at nine a.m. his question would be fully answered.

On Monday morning, 6th October, at 9 a.m sharp, Cadiston entered the superintendent's outer office and the super's personal assistant, WPC Justien Jarvis, JJ for short, greeted him. "Good morning Ashton, please take a seat and I will inform the super that you are here." "Thank you J.J. Have you any idea why he wants to see me?" She just smiled, and after a brief call she said. "You can go straight in and good luck Detective Cadiston." She winked at him. He wondered what she meant by that statement and was even more baffled when he could hear voices in the office. He wondered who would be there to speak with him or if there had been a change in his position and he was off the case. A million scenarios raced through his mind. Upon walking into the office, he found his own superintendent, accompanied by the chief superintendent and the area commissioner there to greet him. "Come in, Ashton. I think that you know everyone present so take a seat and tell us how your investigation is progressing." Said the superintendent. "Good morning gentlemen, I am collecting and collating my evidence and formulating theories and scenarios. I can quite categorically state that it is as I have suspected all along, sir. I have some of the post-mortems carried out on the deceased and the lab report on an item that I found during a visit to the Mandaten Manor will be with me later today. Forensics has also provided me with some information that is all relevant and provides links to all the cases. I had strong suspicions before, sir, but with this added information, I have started building a case. Not wishing to talk out of turn but it needs to be said gentlemen – Detective Sergeant Standish was my training officer and if he had listened to me instead of silencing me and had taken more notice of my suspicions instead of just forming his own opinion straight away, a full investigation would have been underway directly after Malcolm Mandaten's incident. It annoys me, gentlemen, that I have been ignored and if he had taken the time and waited to read Bonnie Mandaten's post-mortem result, which clearly shows the cause of both her and her unborn child's death, maybe he would not have closed the case so quickly. After reading that report, my suspicions were aroused even more and the more information that comes into my hands, the more my suspicions are confirmed. We are dealing with a very cold and callous killer, or killers, who will stop at nothing to achieve their aim." Said Cadiston sternly.

"You appear to be very thorough, Cadiston, and have spoken out which tells us that you will not allow yourself to be silenced any longer and in doing so, you have begun walking your own path to reach the truth to all the Mandaten deaths". "No Commissioner, I will not be silenced any longer and the path that I now walk is the one that should have been taken long ago." Cadiston agreed. "So, young man, you are making headway and have it all in hand then?" asked the chief superintendent. "All in hand, sir, and when I have the report of the firearm on Kevin Mandaten's gun, I will be able to shed more light on his death. Not wishing to sound arrogant, sir, but if only I had been listened to instead of being silenced at every turn, there is a strong possibility that some of these deaths could have been prevented. The evidence that was presented at the time made it clear that there was more than enough doubt as to the validity of these deaths being mere tragic accidents. I said it before, sir, if these investigations had not been delayed and were started sooner, maybe lives could have been saved. It possibly would have stopped at Malcolm Mandaten's murder. I had written my suspicions and given them to Standish but it is very clear that he took no notice or further action. Now they all seem to have conveniently disappeared."He smiled. "It is just as well that I had the foresight to make a duplicate." "Just so Cadiston, and that has not gone unnoticed and that is one of the reasons he was retired early." Remarked his superintendent. The three officers looked at each other.

"All that you say is true, Cadiston, very true. Sadly, your suspicions were not listened to so that was not the case and did not happen. We understand your anger and frustration and will take the appropriate action now." Their heads were close together and he could hear their soft whispers but not the words spoken. There was a moment of silence as they all sat looking at him but he did not flinch. "Now, in view of your commitment, enthusiasm, and a great deal of determination to solve these deaths, it has been decided that to give you the necessary authority. You are to be promoted to temporary DCI with a detective sergeant to assist you and because of the magnitude of incidents, there will be other resources put at your disposal as and when required. Would you have anyone in mind to be your DS or should we just nominate one for you?" Asked the chief superintendent. He did not need time to think and answered straight away. "If there are no objections, sir, what about Trainee Detective Macswee?"

There was again a moment of silence while the three men whispered together. "Macswee, yes, he shows promise but lacks the edge." Said his immediate superintendent. "And you will be happy to have Macswee at your side?" asked the area commissioner. "Yes, sir." Said Cadiston. "Let us get him up here, then." The superindendent buzzed his phone. "Justien, can you get adam Macswee up here, please?" "Right away, sir." She dialed and after a short time, he was located and sent up to the super's office. "Ah, there you are Macswee, come in and take a seat. We have a proposition for you. Now tell us honestly, how do feel about working alongside acting DCI Cadiston as his DS?" "Work with Cadders? Sorry sir, I mean, with acting Detective Chief Inspector Cadiston, without hesitation sir." "You sound confident in your acceptance Macswee." The superintendent said. "Definitely sir, it would be a complete and real pleasure gentlemen." Macswee said. "Good man, that is that then. Now the you two go and solve the murder cases, DCI Cadiston. We are all looking to you and so is Lord Mandaten. You have quite a task on your hands and quite a job to do so go do it, the pair of you." Said the super.

"Yes sir." They both stood up and left the office. On their way downstairs, Mac could not help smiling. "Why did you pick me, Cadders? You could have had your choice of others, even a trained one." "True Mac, but I wanted you with me." Cadiston said simply. "Thanks, my friend, and I will not let you down. What now, DCI Cadiston? Seems strange calling you that, can it still be Cadders? But with due respect –." "That will be fine,

Mac, as long as it is remembered to use the correct name when the situation requires." Replied Cadiston smiling at his friend. "Got it." Mac said.

"I will tell you that we have a mountain of work to do if we are to solve these eight murders, for that is my suspicion. Are you still with me, Mac?" Cadiston asked. "All the way, Cadders, you take the lead and I will follow." Mac said enthusiastically. "Let's get to it then."

Back in Cadiston's office, the pair of them settled down. "Now, before anything else, let me bring you up to speed." Looking at the incidents board including some grisly photographs Cadiston went through every single piece of information that he had gathered. "And that is where I am at this present moment in time. Just waiting for the rest of the post-mortems and the report of the firearm." "You sure that you need me with you? It seems as though you can manage quite well on your own –." Mac concluded. "Wouldn't you like to be a detective then?" Asked Cadiston. "That is what I want to do but just failed the final exam by two points, unlike you who was top in every aspect." Mac replied smiling. "Stick with me, Mac, and continue your training. Then, when this is over, perhaps you can re-sit the exam." Said Cadiston encouragingly. "Six months they gave me and if it is another fail then back on the uniform beat for me." Said Mac. "Let's get these murders solved first, Mac, then we will see what we can do." Cadiston said. "If only." Mac replied.

"Ok Mac, I have filled you in this far and I can only tell you so much, the rest you will find out for yourself. These are the reports that we have to date so I suggest that you read them all through thoroughly, Mac, and form your own opinion, Then we will chat again. While you do the reading to bring you up to speed and know what is going on and what challenges we face, I have another small job to do." Cadiston said.

"Not a problem, DCI Cadiston." Mac said and picked up the first report.

"Well Mister Standish, let me see what you have written. I will keep an open mind as I read but my guess is that you are wrong and my friend DCI Cadiston is right in his judgement so here it goes." He opened the file and began to read.

Final report on the death of Bonnie Mandaten
Monday, 22ⁿᵈ September.

Mrs. Mandaten had been removed from the property and taken to the Royal Hospital where the medical team did everything within their power to save Mrs. Mandaten's life, sadly she had arrived too late and passed away.

It was because of the suddenness of her death that we were called upon to attend and a post-mortem was carried out. I saw no reason to suspect foul play as the result of the post-mortem confirms. The cause of death was a massive cardiac arrest (heart attack), possibly brought on by her illness of Anaphylaxis, (nut allergy syndrome.) She had suffered a massive anaphylactic shock due to her nut allergy which had triggered the tragic reaction. I looked carefully at this case and could find no possible reason to carry out a further investigation as it is clearly defined as death by natural causes. With this evidence, it led to the only possible conclusion.

Conclusion

There can be no doubt that this is a case of accidental death due to her allergy and the cause of her death is confirmed as a cardiac failure (heart attack). No further investigation is required.

Signed on this day by the investigating officer
Sergeant Standish

Case Closed

Mac did not speak his thoughts aloud. "Case closed my foot and not a single mention of the unfortunate unborn child. Another quick conclusion, no surprise there. Well, that is not good enough so case reopened and when Cadders and I have all the reports, we will take it to the next level. Now, report number two and

I guess that will give the wrong information as well. Makes me wonder just how you managed to stand being with him for so long my friend before speaking out, Cadders my friend, it must have been a real daily struggle for you but then you are much stronger than I am so perhaps that is how you managed to stand it before speaking out. Well, it is done now so watch out Standish, there are questions to be asked about these deaths and we DCI Cadiston and DS Macswee will be the ones to ensure that they are asked and then we will catch the killer. I am with my friend Cadiston now so if you were murdered, Miss Bonnie, with your unborn little girl child, which he and I are convinced that you both were, then we will find that out and bring your murderer to trial. Only when the guilty person is incarcerated and punished to the full letter of the law will you be able to rest peacefully. Finely Miss Bonnie, you have Cadiston's word that he will find your killer and he always keeps his word. I know him well enough to know that. Now you have mine also and, like him, when my word is given, I always keep it. There it is, Bonnie, we are on your case. Now for the next report written by Standish on Malcolm Mandaten. Once I have read that, I will read the post-mortems." He opened the file and began to read, and as he read, he began to see where Cadiston had his suspicions aroused. He muttered occasionally as he read the written words and was glad that from all the other choices available that Cadiston could have selected, he had picked him to be his accompanying Detective sergeant, hmm, DS Macswee that is me.

Chapter Seven

The Murder Trail Begins

It was now the middle of the morning on Monday, 6th October, and at Mandaten Manor the family, especially the grandchildren, were eagerly watching the private road and cheered when they saw the hospital vehicle approaching. They did not hesitate and moved quickly to the door and with it standing open, their eagerness was soon to be rewarded. "Welcome home, Grandfather, we have been waiting for you." Said an excited Jennifer as she planted a kiss onto his cheek. "It's good to be home, Jennifer, my little princess, I thought I would be home Friday but after a check, they said I had a bit of a high temperature and would not send me home and that meant they kept in for the weekend." Said Lord Mandaten. "No matter, you are home now, Grandfather." Lowell then directed his words to the transport attendant. "We will take it from here and thank you so much caring for our granfather." He said before Kansas had a chance to step in. He glared at him with hate in his eyes. "Very good, young sir and it was our pleasure." He turned and left and moments later, the transport was on its way up the drive. "Push me in now Lowell, please. I must say that this is very nice. My grandchildren are all here to welcome me home. Jennifer, James, Lowell and you, Kansas. Now, take me into the blue room, please. Then you can tell me what has been happening in my absence and of any new developments." Said Lord Mandaten. "We thought that is where you would want to go so the rest of the family are waiting in there for you. When we saw the transport arriving, Aunt Lizabeth ordered coffee for us and green tea for you, Grandma, as we know that you do not drink coffee." Said an excited Jennifer. "Thank you, Jennifer, and all of you are so thoughtful." Said Lady Mandaten smiling at them. "That is because we all love you both." Lowell said as he pushed his granfather's wheelchair. "And we love you all too, Lowell." Said Lady Mandaten with a smile. Again, Kansas scowled as he followed behind them. The door to the blue room was open and once they were all settled, the coffee and tea was served. "Now, what has been happening in our absence?" Asked Lord Mandaten. "The police have finished their long search and what are they called, James?" "Forensics grandfather, forensics." James said. "That's it. They were taking samples and measurements from the lake and grounds and there is one other thing to tell you. He was requested not to mention it but, well, he accidentally let it slip to me –. Detective Cadiston came here on Thursday to see you both but, of course, you were not here and we were all at the hospital with you. Anyhow, he had a look at where the sweet trolley was on the Monday evening that aunt Bonnie died and asked Jonas and Alfred a few questions about Monday, 22nd, also the day that Aunt Bonnie and her unborn baby died. Oh, I just said that –." At this remark Demmie looked sheepishly toward Grant who snapped and spoke harshly before anyone else had a chance to answer. "What's that you say, Jennifer? That detective was here snooping about without us being present? Why, the very audacity of the man, he should not have been allowed in by the servents." Shouted Grant extremely angrily. "Yes, Uncle Grant, he was here and only because he was doing his job thoroughly. We all need to know the truth about Aunt Bonnie and her unborn child and if you really cared about her, you would too." Answered an extremely brave Jennifer. "Why you, you are a cheeky little ten-year-old brat, and for that you deserve a slap." He took a step toward Jennifer with his hand raised, ready to strike but his path was quickly blocked by her uncle, Chadrick. Grant backed away. Jennifer continued. "Now, from what Jonas told me, he just wanted to look at where the dessert trolley was located on that fateful evening. He just needed to make a few notes and take a few pictures so that he could write up his final report, cross the t, dot the i, and put a full stop at the end, is how Jonas said it." With continued anger in his voice, Grant spoke out again. "Well, Jonas should not have allowed him to enter our home while we not present, plus he was out of order and had no right to enter these premises without us being present ("Repeating yourself Uncle Grant",) shut that tiny mouth of yours Jennifer before I fill it with my fist. Now to continue, and what is more, he could do nothing without a search warrant. Anyhow, what the hell has he got to do with it, thought Standish had already done that after he came and spoke to us. There is no need to drag it up again as we thought it was all done and finished with." Jennifer smiled. "Is it a problem for you then, Uncle Grant? You speak as though there was something to hide if you think that he needed a search warrant. Was there something you did not want him to see or find?" Asked Jennifer bravely and was prepared for his wrath. He was fired up and glared at Jennifer with his fist raised but after he had looked at Chadrick, he declined to answer her and put his fist down. "I will not converse with a mere snip of a girl." He said and stormed from the room only to return unseen a few seconds later. "Hmm, the truth hurts, and I think that you hit a raw nerve Jennifer, come stand by me." Said Chadrick as he placed his arm around Jennifer's shoulder. "Well, I think it possibly is juat as you said, Jennifer. He has been acting a bit strange since Aunt Bonnie died unless –." Stepping out from the shadow, Grant did not give James a chance to finish speaking before he snapped back. "Unless what, boy?" "I don't like to say." James said sheepishly. "Come now, if a ten year old snip of a girl can speak up you should beable to, just say it, boy, Uncle Chadrick is here to protect you." Grant glared at him. "Alright, I will. Unless there was something hidden and detective Cadiston did find something to make him suspicious about the way that Aunt Bonnie and her unborn baby died." Said James. "You three kids Jennifer, Lowell and you James are beginning to annoy me, it was due to natural causes cardiac arrest so what could he possibly have found?" Snapped Grant.

"Well, as to that I would not know as we were not here at the time of Aunt Bonnie's death. In fact, none of us were, only you grown ups. We did not arrive until Thursday. All we know is that it is very strange that all these deaths have occurred in less than three weeks and, what is more, we are all becoming even more suspicious about the death of our parents and not just Aunt

Bonnie." Said Jennifer. "You are a stupid little girl, suspicious my foot, there is nothing to be suspicious about, stupid girl!" Jennifer began to cry at Grant's angry outburst so Lowell stepped bravely forward. "There is no need for that attitude, Uncle Grant, and no need to speak to my sister in that way. You ranted at my cousin James mother and upset her greatly, now strangely she is dead." "I hate you Ungle Grant and blame you for my mothers death, you killed her with your bullish way. We are all entitled to have our opinion on the deaths of our family and what if he was here and what if he did find something? All the better I say, unless you −." Grant glared with hatred at James. "As Jennifer said, you have something to hide." James finished. Grant moved quickly toward James and stood so close to him that their faces were almost touching. "Why, you little swine! You have absolutely no idea, I have a good mind to deck you."

That was enough for Chadrick and without hesitation, he stepped between them before a blow could be struck. His voice remained calm. "If you want to deck someone, Grant, try me. But at least show some respect for their dead parents and to our parents who have only just arrived home from the hospital and I am sure that they do not want to hear you mouthing off yet again."

He knew that Chad, even though several years younger, had bested him before so with a grunt he turned and in a fit of incoherent mumbling, he left the room.

"Now what do you think that was all about? He was mighty rattled when it was mentioned that Cadiston might have found something." Remarked Jennifer. "Rattled and stormed out of the room and if you noticed, he was followed very closely by Aunt Demmie. They disappeared in the hall and they both look rattled at the thought of Cadiston being here and possibly finding something, so what is that all about?" Said Lowell. "I have absolutely no idea, we will just let them get on with it. More importantly, are you all alright, Jennifer, James, Lowell?" Chad asked. They all smiled at him and answered, "Yes, thank you, Uncle Chadrick. You stood up for our Mothers against him and now you have stood up for James, Lowell and me against the bully."

Jennifer said. "That is just what he is, Jennifer, he is nothing more than a big bully and can be very intimidating and frightening but I think he is afraid of your Uncle Chad." Chad smiled, and once again all was again calm.

"Chad the peacemaker, that is what you are, swifter than a sword, faster than a bullet, a peace maker." Said Greta. "Are you sure about that, Greta?" She turned her gaze toward Jennifer, Lowell and James who stood together, they all nodded their approval. "Absolutely, Chad, absolutely." Repeated Greta. A few minutes had passed and Demmie returned wiping her eyes. "Why Are you crying, Aunt Demmie?" Jennifer asked concerned. "Crying? Me? No Jennifer, I have something in my eye that is irritating." Demmie replied quickly. "There are some eye drops in the first aid cabinet, they may help." Said Lizabeth. "Yes, thank you and, I do know that and will go and use them." She turned and left. "Looks more like crying to me, my guess is that Grant has upset her Chad." Greta said softly. "Me too, Greta." Chad agreed. Ten minutes had passed before she returned, still wiping her eyes. This time she was followed by Grant, there was a lot of whispering between them and then they noticed that she had disappeared from the room again. "Both gone, hmm –." Whispered Greta. "Maybe nothing, just gone to get more eyewash." Said Lizabeth. Just then she returned but her facial expression denoted that she was not very happy. "You are in and out a lot, are you alright Demmie?" Asked Chad. She glared and snapped back at him. "Fine, why shouldn't I be?" Demmie snapped. "Ok, no need to bite my head off, just wondered where you went." "Only to wash my eyes and to the restroom, surely I don't have to say each time I am going there." "Not at all, my dear, not at all." She turned and left the room again. "Hmm." Said Lord Mandaten. "What is the hmm for, Grandfather?" asked Jennifer. "I was reflecting on your Uncle Grant's attitude and his behaviour. He did not like what you said Jennifer and that was extremely brave of you about having something to hide. Even so, he was out of order speaking to you in the way that he did. He did not like it one bit when James stood up to him and even less when you stepped in

Lowell, and if Chad had not been here who now's what he would have done, I believe he is capable of anything. I have watched him closely for some time and of late his attitude has seemed very strange. Then there is your wife, she also looked shifty and worried that something had been found. They disappeared down the hall, possibly near the dining room. Hmm –. Very interesting facts on both their parts. Now, to a detective that would be suspicious. In fact, there has been a lot of animosity and suspicious bickering for far too long so enough of that. Well family, my children, it is a lovely bright day and I have been kept inside for far too long so a turn around the garden with my family will be a real tonic after my time in the hospital. Now, what say you all to a nice calm walk around the garden and chat about nice things and we will speak no more of all the nasty unpleasantness and enjoy the sunshine while it still lasts." Said Lord Mandaten.

"You are very wise and right, Grandfather, there has been far too much unpleasantness around the Manor and, as you said, we shall put it all behind us. Let us go for that walk, shall we?" Kansas replied. "Those were not my words, Kansas, they are yours." His grandfather corrected. "Sorry, Grandfather, I only meant … Well, no matter, shall we go?" Kansas turned and headed for the door and quickly dissaperared from view. "Right behind you, Kansas." Said Jennifer. "But, I only have my slippers on, I will run to my room and get a pair of shoes so you all be going, I will soon catch you up." Jennifer added to her earlier observation. "The shoes that I have on are not really for walking in the garden, I will change mine as well."

"See you two in a minute, then." Said Kansas still out of everyones view.

Jennifer and James hurried to the stairs, watched by their cousin, Kansas from where he stood, and just as they were about to climb them on their way to their rooms, Jennifer said. "I will take a bit longer to choose my shoes than you James, it must be a female thing but wait for me at the top of the stairs so we can go down together." Even in his sadness of losing both his parents so close together, he still managed a smile. "Will do, Cousin

Jennifer." That was as far as they got because a shout stopped them in their tracks. "Wait you two, there is a car coming down the drive, best we see who it is before going for that walk." They returned to the blue room and watched the approaching vehicle.

When Cadiston returned to his office, Mac was still reading but looked up and said. "Bonnie and her unborn little girl child died on Monday, 22nd September, and it is now two p.m. on 6th October, that is fifteen days ago. It does not take a great deal of calculation but in that time, my friend, six other deaths have befallen the family. We certainly have our work cut out for us."

"So, my friend, you have worked that one out. We have an uphill battle on our hands, are you still sure that you want to be with me?" Cadiston asked.

"Even more so, you take the lead and I will follow, DCI Cadiston, as your lowly and faithful servant." Mac said. "Lowly and faithful servant, you say, want to know the next revelation?" Asked Cadiston. "Fire away." Mac replied.

"We are also to reinvestigate or rather to carry out an investigation into Lord Mandaten's brother and his family's deaths four years ago." Cadiston informed his partner. "Cold case, then?" Mac asked. "Not exactly, it was closed without a full and proper investigation by none other than good old Sergeant Standish." "From what I have read and heard, that sounds about right coming from him. He fooled a lot of people and now it is easy to see why not many liked him. Also how he has so many closed cases. Makes one wonder if he has put some innocent people away just to secure a conviction but not us, that is for sure. So what now?" Asked Mac. "Have you read everything?" Cadiston asked. He put the report down, "That is me done so what do we do now?" Mac looked up at Cadiston. "Now my friend, we make a start and begin by asking questions about the night that Bonnie Mandaten and her unborn little girl child died. The questions that are asked may lead to asking about Malcolm also as I strongly believe that all these deaths are somehow linked and we may find that we diversify into another case combined with the first." Cadiston was deep in thought.

"That means we head to the Manor then." Mac made his way out from behind his desk. "Mandaten Manor it is, Mac, and to help with the investigation, we will be taking blood, D.N.A., fingerprints, and shoe sizes so while you were reading, I have asked W.P.C.s Francis Rendham and Olito Paverson to join us." Cadiston informed.

"Both nice girls and good officers." Mac agreed. "That is why I chose them. Right servant, you can go fetch the car? In the car I will need to make a call before we leave or even on the way." Cadiston said. Mac smiled. "Lowly and faithful servant Macswee, that is me. Macswee the servant, suits me just fine." "Just one other thing Mac –." Cadiston said with a grin. "Only one other thing, Master?" Mac joked. "Just for now and that is do not forget to bow."

Mac complied "Yes, my Lord and Master." They both chuckled.

Settled in the car, Mac prepared to drive away. "What about your call to let them know that we are coming?" "Do it on the way as I don't want to give them a long forewarning." Cadiston explained. "Catch them unprepared, now I would have slipped up there and told them I was on the way, and by doing that they would have ample time to collaborate their stories. Just as well that you are the DCI, I would have blown it big time so I will stick to fetching the car and then drive on." The engine roared into life and they were away. Cadiston pressed his call button and in five rings, it was answered. "Hi detective, how can I help?" Asked Jeremiah. "Just a bit of information this time, is his Lordship back and are the gates open as we are on the way and should be there in about half an hour." "In answer to your questions, yes and yes." "Thanks, Jeremiah will give you a call if I need anything else." The phone went dead.: Mac did not bother to ask who he had called or who Jeremiah was, he was happy to be working with his friend so just accepted it. Cadiston and his new partner, Detective Sergeant Macswee, had been friends since joining the police force and had gone through a great deal of their training together. They had gelled from the beginning and they were both glad to be working together. Macswee always knew that

Cadiston had the edge on him and he had tried to follow his lead but that was then and now he was wasting no time and they were well on their way to the Manor and chattered as they travelled.

"I will let you do all the talking and questioning, Cadders, I will just sit back and take notes." Said Mac. "You can ask questions as well, Mac, we are a team now and I cannot think of anyone that I would rather be partnered with. We will work together as a team and not like the nameless one who remained an individual though he had someone to work with him." Said Cadiston. "Understood, I will add that, as far as I have heard, none of them liked being with him." Mac said. In the car riding with them were WPCs Francis Rendham and Olito Paverson who would be collecting the required samples from all the family for them.

"The nameless one, Sergeant? And may I ask who that is?" Asked Francis.

"Thought that you would know the answer to that, Francis." Said Cadiston.

"Can I answer that, DCI?" Olito asked eagerly. "Be my guest, Olito." Cadiston said and smiled. "Standish, there I have said it, sorry." Replied Olito. "Say no more, a nasty piece of work from all accounts. He was not a liked man and there was a lot of suspicion over how he managed to get so many convictions and close so many cases. There was also some talk about him securing convictions on innocent people which throws a lot of suspicion onto all his cases. I had the misfortune to be with him on a couple of his cases and did not like his methods and to this day I cannot be sure if any of my samples were ever used." Francis said. "Well he is retired now, Francis, and he will not get in the way or foul up an investigation again." Cadistoin assured her. "And a good job too. Now, I will say this to you for both of us, we can work with you, DCI Cadiston, and you, Sergant Macswee." "Very glad to hear it, Francis, and we are glad to be working with both of you. Now, we are almost at the Manor, the turn onto the private road is coming up". "All set, the pair of you, for what is up ahead?" Asked Cadiston. "All set, Mac has told us again what we need to take samples of so no problem." Replied Francis.

"Excellent, and I can assure you that the samples that you both are going to take will prove to be an invaluable asset. Now, should be there in about ten minutes, then to work." Cadiston said. "We talked about it after you had asked us to accompany you and both of us thought that would be the case, otherwise we would have declined to come with you. DCI Cadiston, just one more thing we would like to ask. Should we keep calling you DCI or can we call you Cadders like Mac does?" Asked Francis. Cadiston smiled, "As I am only acting for the time being and until all these cases are solved, it is fine to be like Mac and just call me Cadders, only call me DCI when the real need arises, you will all know when that is." "Thank you, that is so much more relaxing and makes us feel like we are also part of the team." Said Olito.

"As to that Olito, you both most certainly are and this is only the begining for you both. Now, the gates are in front of us and are already open so we are almost there. I will introduce you all and explain what you will be doing so that should put you at ease. We will start our questioning and leave you to get the samples, alright?" Cadiston said. "Not a problem." They were now passing through the gates and could see the Manor at the end of the long drive.

"Impressive looking place, how old is it?" enquired Olito. "Built in seventeenth century, that is mid to late sixteen hundred." Cadiston said looking out at the building. "Very old then."-said Olito.

With the car stationery, they all stepped out into the afternoon October sun, then Mac looked toward the Manor and smiled at the host of faces staring at them. "Looks like we have been observed." "Doesn't matter now that we are here." Cadiston said."You have the best view so who is it, Demmie?" Asked Grant. "Looks like that Detective Cadiston and he has two uniformed WPCs with him and another plain clothes man." Demmie answered. "Not that Standish, is it?" Enquired Lord Mandaten.

"No father, this one is much younger. I wonder what they are here for?" Demmie asked. "Maybe he did find something,

Aunt Demmie, when he visited the other day and wants to ask us about it." Jennifer said. "You are a silly little girl, Jennifer, what on earth would there be for him to find?" Demmie snapped in reply. "As to that, I do not know, Aunt Demmie, I do know that they are here now and already at the front door so I can safely say that we will soon know."

"DCI Cadiston to see you, my Lord, with three companions and he would like to speak with you and Lady Mandaten alone." "Thank you, Bradinham." Said Lord Mandaten. He turned and was gone. Lord Mandaten ushered the rest of the family away and it was with reluctance that they left. "We have a right to hear what he has to say so we should all stay." Grant said angrily. "Not so Grant, the officers want to speak with mother and me so leave the room now, all of you." They all left like scalded cats. With the family gone, Cadiston introduced his team. "My Lord, my Lady, may I introduce Detective Sergeant Macswee and WPCs Rendham and Paverson. My sergeant will accompany me with the questioning and my two WPCs will be taking the samples that are required. I do apologize for this intrusion, my Lord, and I can assure you it is all quite necessary."

"Of course, it goes without saying otherwise you would not be here. Now then young man, did I hear Bradinham call you DCI?" Said Lord Mandaten. "Indeed, you did hear correctly, my Lord, a temporary promotion while I investigate all the suspicious deaths that have occurred here at the Manor in the past two weeks." Cadiston then whispered in Lord Mandaten's ear. "I have also requested the reports on your late brother's family and will be reopening the case." "Detective, can I ask a simple question?" Lady Mandaten asked. "Please feel free to, my Lady." Said Cadiston. "It is about Bonnie, am I –. Are we to understand that you are now to fully investigate her death?" Asked Lady Mandaten. "You understand correctly, my Lady, I can say no more than that at this time but can confirm that a full investigation is to be held. In fact, that is why we are here today. I wanted to inform you before getting around to asking a lot of questions about that fateful evening and decided after what has

217

already been disclosed and what we already know, we must not be sidelined any further and need to begin to ask our questions and take our samples. It is today that we begin our questioning and it is from here that the trail to murder is set to begin that in turn will allow us to apprehend the murderer or murderess." Cadiston said confidently. "Correct me if I am wrong but I suspect that you believe that Bonnie's death was not just an oversight or carelessness on someone's part, and in fact, all these deaths were not accidents but something much more sinister?" Asked Lady Mandaten. "As to that, I cannot comment at this time, my Lady, as you know there have been eight deaths to date and it is our wish to hopefully prevent any more. Eight is more than enough. In fact, that is eight too many but sadly we are faced with them. Each one needs to be looked at individually and any suspicions dispersed before we can reach a conclusion and the final report can be written. Only then can the case be truly closed and with a satisfactory outcome." Cadiston replied.

"Now then my dear Florence, DCI Cadiston knows exactly what he is doing. There are things that he cannot disclose until his investigation is complete. Evidence can be found and to disclose it will pre-warn the guilty party so that they can cover their tracks. I had quite enough of that in my days in the army when evidence was cleverly hidden or disclosed too soon or false evidence brought forward and, sad to say, an innocent man was executed and it was not until much later that the real culprit slipped up and was found. Now then my dear, Cadiston knows just how to sort the truth from a lie and fact from fiction, that is why I requested that he investigate for us and not that Standish fellow, didn't like him at all. Now, when do you want to ask your questions about our Bonnie?" Lord Mandaten directed his question at Cadiston. "Now would be good but only if it would not be overly stressful for the family, especially after everything that has happened. Having said that, the questions must be asked." Said Cadiston.

"See my dear, thoughtful as well as thorough. You go ahead and ask your questions, Cadiston, you have my full approval." Said Lord Mandaten.

"Thank you. Now, if I can find the right page ... Ah, there it is. My two WPCs will be collecting the samples required so I need to ask, would you have a room that they could use? And another that we could use, please?" Cadiston asked. "The study is a small but functional room and what is said in there cannot be overheard so use that one. There is a small box room adjacent to it that you may find suitable for your WPCs to use. Now, should we call the family back?" Lord Mandaten looked towards the door. "If you would, sir, and if it is possible, keep them apart so that they do not talk to each other after they have been questioned." Cadiston said. "That will not be a problem, leave that to me, my boy." Lord Mandaten pulled the bell cord and seconds later, Jonas entered the room. "Will you ask the family to come back in here, please?" Asked Lord Mandaten. "Immediately, my Lord." Within ten minutes they were assembled.

"Lizabeth, my dear, will you show the detectives the way to the study and the room next to it?" Lord Mandaten asked.

"Certainly Father, will you follow me, please." They followed her down the hall and when Francis and Olito were settled, Mac and Cadiston followed her into the study. "Now, before you start, would you and your WPCs like some coffee or tea?" Asked Lizabeth. "Green tea for me, please, and coffee for my constables would be lovely, thank you." She pulled the bell cord and five minutes later, Jonas was there. "Can you bring a pot of coffee and another with green tea for the detectives and another pot of coffee for the WPCs, please Jonas?" "At once, Miss Lizabeth." He turned and was gone.

"Now, as I am already here with you and I expect it is to ask some questions, would you like to start asking them with me?" Lizabeth asked. "That will be fine, Miss Lizabeth, please take a seat. Seems strange asking you to do that in your own house, sorry, Manor." Said Cadiston. "Oh, it is not mine, Detective, it belongs to my parents and after they leave us, it will belong to whomever Father has passed the title of Lord to. We all know that he has made out his will but not what has been left to us or who will become the next Lord and own the estate and all that goes with it. As Grant is eldest and is now the only remaining living son, it sadly looks like it will have to be him." Said Lizabeth. "Why do you say that? It sounds as though you would not want him to be the Lord?" Asked Cadiston. "If I am totally honest detective, I do not and before you ask why I will tell you –. For a start he has no idea how to run the estate and in a matter of perhaps two years or less, he will have ruined it." Lizabeth said sternly. The person who would ensure the Estates future is Chadrick but he is not a Mandaten so cannot be the Lord." "As the only remaining sister, could you take on that role and own everything?" Asked Cadiston. She smiled. "A nice thought, Detective, but no, I could not. You are aware that I am a female and it must be a male heir. There are two Mandaten grandsons. Their fathers were Malcolm and Kevin. Lowell and James are their sons and it is they who would be named Lord before I would be considered to take over but with Grant there, they will not be considered." Lizabeth explained. "And what about Chadrick or your son?" Asked Cadiston.

"No, no, no, not him. As I already stated, for one thing, he is younger than Grant but mainly because he is nothing more than an unwanted baby and only an adopted child and not of the family bloodline. So there is absolutely no possibility of him becoming the next Lord although he is the best candiate for the role. As for my son, he is a Kaysten so he would not be considered at all." Lizabeth continued. "I am sorry to ask this but in the case scenario that there were no male heirs and as your sister, Sammie, sadly is also dead –. If that were the case, would it then go to you?" Cadiston asked. "It would go to me and I would own it all but my husband would be deemed as the honorary Lord but there would be a codicil to protect myself." A knock on the door saw Jonas enter with the provision of coffee, tea, and a selection of biscuits.

"Thank you, Jonas, and do my WPCs have some beverages also?" Cadiston asked. "They have, Detective, and are in the side room to do their work." Jonas informed Cadiston. "Thank you and we may have a word with you later." Cadiston said. "Call if you need me, Detective." He did not linger and was quickly gone. "Now then, Miss Lizabeth, we have diversified so back to the tragic day of Monday, 22nd September, and how the day progressed to include the evening dinner. Tell me all that you can remember of the day and include your movements, please?" Cadiston continued. "We arrived, now let me see –. Yes, it was mid-afternoon and with very little contact with the others, we went straight to our room to unpack and got settled. I had a long bath to relax as it was a long drive to get here, I had a short nap, then got dressed and we went down to the dining room. The time was then seven twenty-four. Our parents arrived at seven twenty-five and we all sat down. Father said grace and the meal began. Mother asked Bradinham if it had been remembered to cater for Bonnie's allergy to which he replied that it had. He also told her that Cook had taken extra special precautions. Everything was going well up to the dessert. There had been a few words in-between the courses which was not unusual and was all the usual family stuff. Demmie asked to be excused, as did myself and Greta. We all went to the restroom, then came back and had our dessert and that is when Bonnie collapsed, Chad used her Epipen but it did not work. The ambulance was immediately called for and she was taken away. We were all concerned and panicking but out of us all, strangely, Demmie managed to keep her cool as though taking control of the situation, she was acting like a different person to the one that we all know." Lizabeth said. "And how did that make you feel?" Cadiston asked. "I did not really give it much thought, my concerns were with Bonnie but I believe that she whispered to Grant in the hope that no one else would hear. She said 'It is done now so do not worry, it will be alright' or something like that. She jumped into Grant's car and Malcolm took the rest of the family, those that are blood family, the others stayed behind." Lizabeth said. "So Demmie was the only one, as you put it, non-blood family member, to be at the hospital?" Asked Cadiston. "Yes. Then, when we heard that poor Bonnie had died, Grant sent us all away but she stayed behind at his request to drive him home." Lizabeth said. "And what time did you all arrive home?" Asked Macswee. "We arrived home at about nine p.m. and Grant with Demmie nearer to one the next morning." Lizabeth answered. "Tuesday, 23rd, the day of your brother Malcolm's death –. Sorry to mention it as it must still be a painful memory for you. Now back to Bonnie, is there anything else that you can remember, however small?" Asked Cadiston. "Nothing, we waited until Grant was back home to know what had happened and then we all went to bed. Not much help I am afraid. Ah, one small thing I remember. Chad suddenly became very drowsy and started stumbling about as though drunk after having his last cup of coffee and was having trouble standing. He is not a drinker and I thought that was very strange." Lizabeth recalled. "Had there been any drinking?" Asked Macswee. "None at all, I know that because the drinks trolley had just been re-filled and none of the bottles had been opened until we arrived home from the hospital. Again, not much help." Lizabeth said.

"Can you tell me the order in which you came from the re-stroom?" Cadiston asked. "I think when I came out, Demmie and Greta were waiting for me. Sorry I can only be of so little help." Lizabeth said. "You would be surprised by how many people say that they have not been of much help but sometimes the smallest piece of information proves to be more helpful than a book full of testimonies." He finished what he was writing before looking up. "Who was it that served Chadrick his coffee?" "That was his wife, Demmie." She said.

"Three more questions for you, then we are done. Were the grandchildren here at that time?" Cadiston asked. "No, they did not arrive until Thursday evening." Said Lizabeth. "That would be the 25th. When you went to the restroom during dinner, did you pass the dessert trolley?" Cadiston asked.

"Yes, and it all looked so very deliciousGreta went away first then I followed her and Demmie entered the rest room a few seconds after me." Said Lizabeth. "Last question, what would you know about a syringe like this one?" He pointed to the syringe laying on the desk that he uncovered. She studied it and shook her head. "Syringe, I don't use one, neither does my husband, as far as I know, no family member is diabetic and it doesn't look like a normal syringe. Sorry I cannot shed any light on it, where was it found?" She asked.

"I did not say that one had been found so what makes you think that this one was?" Cadiston asked. "True, you did not say, I just assumed that you had because you were here the other day and have just asked about one and have shown me that one." Lizabeth said. "Thank you, Miss Lizabeth, perhaps you would go to see my WPCs in the adjacent room and then send your husband in for us, please. His name is?" "Tomas Kaysten, I will ask him to come down." Lizabeth said as she got up. "Thank you." Cadiston now turned to his partner and said. "Mac, put in your notebook to check what time Grant and Demmie left the hospital on that fateful evening." "Monday, September 22nd, will do." A few minutes later, there was a knock on the door and Tomas walked in. "Take a seat please, Tomas isn't it?" Said Cadiston. "It is, now what can I tell you about anything?" Asked Tomas. "I have not asked for anything yet so you are being a bit premature." Tomas looked a bit sheepish and went red in the face which was noted. "I would like to know all that you can remember about Monday, 22nd of September/" Cadiston said. "Everything?" Tomas asked. "Everything from the time you arrived at the Manor." Cadiston confirmed. "We got here in the afternoon and went to our room to unpack and freshen up as we had a long drive to get here. Lizabeth had a nap and I went for a walk before getting ready for dinner. We came down to the dining room at what must have been twenty-four minutes past seven. That is our usual time and it was only just before the parents arrived. We were all enjoying a delicious meal with some chat until the dessert when Bonnie collapsed. Chadrick used some sort of pen thing then the ambulance arrived, and after a few minutes, she was taken away. Grant and Demmie went after it, followed by Malcolm and the other family members, that is direct family, not husbands or spouses. They got back around nine and Grant and Demmie around one a.m. Tuesday morning." Tomas said. "Did anyone leave the table during the meal?" Asked Macswee. "No, no one did –. No, just a minute, yes, my wife, Greta, and Demmie. They had to go to the restroom, apart from that, no one. Once Grant was back with the news about Bonnie, we all went to bed." Tomas said. "And there is nothing else? Nothing said that may or may not be relevant?" Cadiston eyed him. "Can't think of anything. There was a lot of crying and sort of garbled shouting but nothing memorable. When we were all back, Chad was getting extra sleepy after his second cup of coffee but by then we were all tired. I do remember that it was after Grant and Demmie had got back and she had poured Chad's coffee. Oh yes, almost forgot, Malcolm asked Alfred to arrange to have his horse saddled for six a.m. Tuesday morning." Said Tomas. "And you all heard this request?" Cadiston asked.

"Well, we were all there so I guess we did." Tomas answered. "Thank you, if you should remember anything else while we are still here, come back to see us. Will you go next door to our WPCs, then ask –, Greta to come down next, please?" Cadiston requested.

"That I will do for you, Detective." Tomas stood up and left, leaving the door open. "Notice anything, Mac?" Cadiston asked his partner. "I may be wrong but he said Malcolm asked for a horse to be saddled but Lizabeth did not." Mac said. "Spot on, it is little things like that which throw suspicions and may require a second interview with that person to check on their story." Said Cadiston. A few minutes passed and then Greta appeared. "Please, come in and take a seat. Do you know why you are here?" Asked Cadiston. "I expect it has something to do with all the recent deaths." Said Greta. "At the moment we are concentrating on the first one. What can you tell us about the day of the fateful evening of Monday, 22nd of September?" Cadiston asked Greta. She began to cry. "It was horrible, just terrible to see Bonnie in so much agony and not be able to do anything to help her. I felt just so helpless, she was in so much pain. Chad tried to help and used her Epipen but it did not seem to work at all." "I know that this is difficult for you, especially after losing your husband the very next day, and so tragically. I am just trying to establish some facts about the events of that day and the fateful evening." Cadiston explained. She wiped her eyes and seemed to find inner strength. "And rightly so, Detective, I will be alright now so please go ahead with your questions." "In your own words, tell us all that you can remember from the time of your arrival, every detail however small or insignificant you may feel it is. All that you can remember ..." Said Cadiston.

"We arrived mid-afternoon and were travelling with Malcolm's brother, Grant, and his wife, Bonnie." She wiped a tear from her eye as she spoke her name. "They were both arguing, that is, Grant and Malcolm were but that was as usual. Bonnie and myself sat quietly in the back. The argument had started from the time that we left home and continued while we travelled. Bonnie asked them to stop as their arguing was a distraction for Malcolm's driving but Grant called her an interfering bitch and told her not to interfere in what she knows nothing about and to shut up. I hate him because he was such a bully to her. She also had suspicions that he was having an affair and wanted to tell us who she suspected after we had dinner that evening." Said Greta.

"Can you remember what they were arguing about?" Asked Cadiston.

"The usual, who should be the next Lord and what should happen to the estate. To say it was very heated would be an understatement." She paused and wiped her eyes again. Cadiston could sense her stress and was very compassionate. "Please, in your own time, continue, you had just arrived."

"We went straight to our rooms and unpacked, then bathed, and by then it was almost time to get to the dining room. We arrived at the dinner table only a few seconds before our parents, that would be about seven twenty-five. The meal was served and although there was some chat and snide remarks passed that father did not like, the best part of the meal was in silence." Greta continued. "What can you remember about the chat?" Cadiston asked, adjusting his notebook. "There was something about who should be the next Lord between the three brothers and the bitterness against Chadrick, who they said should not be there because as he is not of the family bloodline but adopted and that the discussion had nothing to do with him." She continued.

"Can you remember who said that remark?" Asked Cadiston. "Not really, there was so much hostility and banter going on. I think it was either Grant or maybe Kevin, I am sure it was not Malcolm." He could see that she was very distraught. "Please take a minute, then continue." She paused to gather her thoughts. "Lizabeth, Demmie, and I left the table and went to the restroom while the table was being cleared of the main course table ware and when we returned, the dessert was served." Mac now asked a question. "We Know that you, Lizabeth and Demmie left the table, my question is could anyone have had time to tamper with Bonnie's dessert in the time you went to the restroom?" "They may have but they would have needed to be very quick and be prepared. I think Demmie was last in and the first out –. Or was it Lizabeth? I really do not know who it was, only that I was the last and they were both in the hallway. As far as tampering with the dessert, I don't think so but maybe if someone did, they would need to be very quick as Jonas and Alfred were ferrying back and forth. As I said, if someone did tamper with it, then it would have to have been pre-planned and done in a very quick time, like seconds. I will just say that as far as my thoughts go, that is what I think happened as I know Cook is so very cautious when preparing Bonnie's meals." Greta said. "Now we already know that Demmie went with Grant to the hospital and your late husband took the other blood family members, leaving the spouses at the Manor. Can you remember the time that they arrived back?" Asked Cadiston. "Malcolm arrived back at about nine p.m. and Grant more like one a.m on Tuesday morning. We were all in the lounge having coffee while we waited for news and when it came, it was bad as poor Bonnie was gone with her unborn child." Greta said. "That sounds like you knew that she was pregnant?" Asked Cadiston. "Yes, I knew as she had told me. I was also with her when it was confirmed. We were not just sisters-in-law but best friends as well and we could tell each other anything in confidence and we talked a lot. I really miss her." As he could see that her small handkerchief was wet with her tears, Mac passed her his clean one and she wiped her eyes again. "I do not believe that Grant loved her as he did not seem at all that perturbed to lose his wife and unborn child." She said. Mac now asked another question. "So as I see it, you are of the opinion that someone may have tampered with Bonnie's dessert in the time you went to the restroom? Also, you knew that she was pregnant and of her suspicion that her husband was having an affair, could it be with Demmie?" "Yes, I do think it was tampered with as it is the only explanation. I suspect it was Demmie and Grant having the affair as it makes sense. As I said, I was with her when her pregnancy was confirmed and knew about her suspicion of an affair and someone wanted her out of the way and –." She wiped a tear again. "Now she is. Well, that is what I think, I wish that I could tell you who left the restroom first. I think Demmie was the first out or maybe Lizabeth, I really do not know who it was, only that I was the last and they were both waiting in the hallway. I do not want to think it was either of them but if I had to accuse someone, then it would be Demmie. I believe it is her that the affair is with as she and Grant have been very close with secret touching, smiles and –. Well, no matter. I will just say that, as far as my thoughts go, that is what happened as I know Cook is so very cautious when preparing Bonnie's meals but just how it was tampered with, I am at a loss." She said. "Now we already know that Demmie went with Grant to the hospital and your late husband took the other blood family Members, leaving the non-blood family at the Manor. Can you tell us again the time that they arrived back?" Asked Cadiston.

"Malcolm at about nine p.m and Grant with her more like one a.m. on Tuesday morning. We were all in the lounge having coffee while we waited for news. Grant seemed unfazed and seemed to be taking it very well but that could have been because the reality had not hit home yet. But I believe it was just a façade as his feelings were all false. Demmie poured us some coffee and that is all I can tell you. Oh! I have just remembered, it was after Bonnie collapsed that I overheard Demmie say to Grant 'It is done, it will be alright.'"

"And were those her exact words?" Asked Cadiston."Exact to the letter. Now where was I? Malcolm told Jonas to tell Herbert to saddle Thundist for him for six a.m. as he was going for an early ride. I believe that Grant asked him the route that he would take. I could be wrong, it may have been Tomas as by that time we were all very tired, especially Chad. He had begun to waver as though drunk and as we had not had a single drink apart from a glass of wine with our meal, he only had a half of a glass, it was very strange. He was struggling to get up the stairs and we had to help him, that is myself and Jonas. The next morning as I was worried about Malcolm going on his ride so I decided to go to the stable and to try and stop him but arrived just a few seconds too late so missed him. That is when Chad arrived. We saw the new foal, then hurried back to be in time for breakfast. He had only come out because when he woke, his wife was not beside him but when he went back to his room and into the bathroom, that was when he found her. She had fallen asleep in the bath. I can tell you no more than that, sorry." Greta said.

"One final question, what would you know about a syringe?" Asked Cadiston.

"Syringe? A strange thing to ask, and the only time I see one of those is at the doctor's surgery or hospital. Wait a minute, that is not quite right, I have seen one in Cook's utility box. Apart from that, I am sorry I can shed no light on a syringe. Bonnie was Grant's second wife but then you probably already know that. You probably also know that his first wife was murdered and now Bonnie has been. Find out who murdered my friend, Bonnie, and her unborn child, please! I believe it was murder and I feel that you do also otherwise I do not think that you would be here asking these questions. Bonnie was not only my sister-in-law but my very best friend and confidant. We could tell each other anything and we did, she was not happy with Grant and was going to tell me who she believed her husband was having an affair with on Monday evening after dinner but died before she could." Said Greta.

"Thank you, and I am sorry for distressing you. Now, would you go next door to our WPCs and then ask Chadrick to come in next, please. Again, Greta, thank you." Said Cadiston. "With pleasure, Detective Cadiston, Cadiston catch Bonnie's killer please." She smiled and wiped a tear, then held the handkerchief out to return it to Mac. He smiled and told her to keep it as her need was greater than his and he had another one. With a "thank you", she turned and left the study. "Gaining anything from this, Mac?" Cadiston looked at Mac. "Not really, I just haven't got your insight, you will have to enlighten me. So far, the thing I did pick up on is that Greta is very true and not a sign of falseness about her at all." Said Mac. "Well spotted, anything else?" Cadiston asked. "Ah yes, Lizabeth said that she and Demmie were waiting for Greta to leave the restroom, one is lying." Mac observed. "Now then, Demmie and Grant seem to be linked quite a lot. Why did she go while the rest of the non-blood family stayed behind? And why did she stay at the hospital instead of one of the family members? After what Greta has just disclosed about Grant having an affair, and believes it is with her, I can see things beginning to fall into place. I find it hard to believe that they were at the hospital all that time so when we leave here, you can take yourself there to check on that. Demmie was one of the three that left the table with Greta and Lizabeth and that raises one major suspicion with her and Grant. If they are having an affair and want to be together, then they would have a motive and I am certain that I have the means in the syringe that the lab is currently checking for me. If they wanted to be rid of her and make it look like natural causes, what better way than to plan it together? Chad suddenly felt very tired after drinking his coffee and it was after Demmie had poured it. He had to be helped up the stairs, if no one else was in that state, the question is why was he? Any ideas?" Asked Cadiston. "Only one that comes to mind is that he could have been drugged with a sleeping draught in his coffee by his wife." "You are starting to think, Mac. If Demmie spent the night in Grants bed what better alibi than being asleep in the bath. There is a lot at stake here and whoever becomes the next Lord will inherit this vast estate and a massive fortune and I strongly believe that they would all like to get their hands on that. Malcolm and Kevin are both deceased so that removes two male heirs and just leaves Grant which throws suspicion his way. Sammie is also deceased, removing one female heir so that leaves the door open for Lizabeth if Grant was not here. Then we also need to consider the male grandsons, two have the surname Mandaten, which could put them in danger. Plus, they can not be taken off the suspect list. All adds up to suspicious deaths in my book and from the little bit of evidence that we already have, not one of them died after a tragic accident, they all died in very suspicious circumstances, and from what Greta said Chad is an adopted son but that does not put him out of the equation. I told myself before at some point in time that I must go to the ancestry records library and check out the full family history and that includes all the husbands and wives as well. It may be better if we employ the services of someone that knows exactly where to look and find out all there is about all the family links and the derivatives there can be in a family tree. We must also have a look at the baby births and deaths register at the hospital where all the Mandaten children were born and that includes Chad". Cadiston said. The sound of footsteps signaled it was time to remain silent. "Come right in and take a seat, now then, Chad, tell us all that you can remember about the evening of Monday, 22nd of September –." Cadiston said. "A date that I will always remember, the night that Bonnie and her unborn child died. I know Cook and cannot believe that she was careless in any way. We have all dined here many times and there has never been a problem before so why now? That is what I would like to know. All these deaths in the family, Detective Cadiston, are very strange to me so you as a detective must sense that there is something amiss and something sinister going on. I know that there is no love lost between me and the three brothers or the two sisters, come to that, but even with their hostility toward me, I do not hate them. Lord and Lady Mandaten have given me a good life and helped to set me up in my own business so as far as I am concerned, without a doubt, they are my true parents. I am required to work very hard and it sometimes involves long hours but that is the joy of having one's own business." Said Chad. "And how does your wife look upon that?" Asked Macswee. "She has her moans, groans, and paddies but after time she usually calms down and knuckles down until the next time she blows. She says that she loves our quite simple life but sometimes it is hard for me to believe that she really means it and is just filling me with lies and falseness. I get the impression that she would like the high life and all the material things that the wealth of Mandaten would provide. We have been married for three years and went out for six months before that. I wanted to wait, it was her that pushed for us to get married in the first place. A few months into the marriage, she suddenly took up running and going to the gym two or three times a week, she also had long weekends away, allegedly to run in a half marathon. I would have gone with her but –." He paused for a moment "She always came up with some reason for me not to accompany her. Plus, the business keeps me occupied anyhow. I would have liked to know her a bit better first but hey, three years and we are still together even if at times it all gets a bit strained. In fact, most of the time. I have tried my hardest to get close to her but it was as though she did not want that and pushes me away. Anyhow, we are not here for my life history. You need to know about the night that Bonnie and her unborn child died. I am very worried about Greta as she and Bonnie were so close and losing her was a real blow. Then to lose her husband the very next day has dealt her a double blow very close together. Now back to your question, we arrived mid to late afternoon and left the taxi at the gate. I told Jeremiah to get back to his mare as she was about to have her foal. He left us there and we locked the gates for him and then walked the rest of the way. Went to our room and freshened up then came down to be ready for dinner at seven-thirty. All was going well until the dessert. Just before it was served, my wife, Lizabeth, and Greta left the table for the restroom and they were gone between five and maybe eight minutes. We ate our dessert and then Bonnie convulsed and collapsed. If only we had not had that dessert then she and her baby would still be alive, I tried using her Epipen but it failed to help her." Said Chad. "And you knew about her child and you all knew of her allergy?" Asked Cadiston.

"I only knew of the child recently, we all knew about her allergy syndrome, we were very careful not to have anything with nuts in it around her as that could have been fatal. Greta had whispered to me about Bonnie's pregnancy just before we entered the dining room, that is how I knew but I was sworn to secrecy. She was rushed to the Royal with Grant giving chase. My wife jumped in his car and went beside him which I thought was strange. Following close behind was Malcolm with the other family. Some of us stayed here, Malcolm got back around nine but Grant did not until one the next morning. We were all very tired at this point. Malcolm wanted an early morning ride so sorted that, then it got very strange as I was suddenly feeling very sleepy and had a hard job to stand. Now, if I had had a few drinks I would say that I was drunk but that could not be the case as I am not a drinker and we had had none apart from a glass of wine with our meal, I had half a glass. My head was spinning so I went upstairs to bed with help to stop me falling. I believe it was Greta and Jonas that assisted me. Oh yes, before we went up, Grant said to my wife, "Thanks for tonight." It was taken for her being with him at the hospital. Anyhow, in the bedroom, she got her zip stuck so I tried in my sleepy way to free it but the dress was already torn so she said rip it off and bin it, which I did. I was drifting more and more but noticed that she had no underwear on, no bra or knickers and questioned it. She reckoned she wet herself when she left the table so threw them away and the stain on her dress was from something spilled at the hospital. I was out of it by then so did not question why no bra. I may have been unusually tired but that much I can remember. She was not beside me when I woke the next morning so I just threw some clothes on and went to look for her. I met Greta who had gone to stop Malcolm but just missed him. That was about seven forty-five, then we went to see the new foal and after that back to the Manor. I found my wife asleep in the bath. If Bonnie and her child were murdered, then find out who did that to her Detective. Whoever it is, find them and if I can help in any way then I will. She was a dear sweet girl although she could be a bit snobby at times but even so, she deserved a better husband than Grant." Chad said. "One last question, what do you know about a syringe?" Asked Macswee. "Syringe? Strange thing to ask DS Macswee, but they are used sometimes in the kitchen to put delicate icing onto a cake. Cook has shown me how the icing was done, piping bags are used as well but I have seen cook use one, they are used in hospitals for giving injections, why do you ask?" Chad looked at Cadiston for an answer. "No matter, just curious. Will you go next door to our WPCs and then send you wife in next, please?" Asked Cadiston. "Consider it done." Said Chad and got up tp leave. "Now from what I have observed, Greta seems like a nice young woman and he seems like a decent chap but looks can be deceiving." Mac said to Cadiston when they were alone. "You are picking it up, Mac." His finger went to his lips. "Come in, Demmie, and take a seat. Now, what can you tell us about that fateful evening of Monday, 25th of September, the night that Bonnie died?" Cadiston noticed that she was very agitated and felt uncomfortable. He also noticed her body language and that she sat in a protective position. As she answered, there was a definite quiver in her voice and she could not look him in the eye. "Nothing that has not been said already, I should think." "Well, as you were not in the room, you cannot know what has already been said and what has not been said so in your own words, please?" Said Cadiston. "We came down to dinner and had a lovely meal, then Bonnie collapsed and was rushed to hospital. I went with Grant as I did not think it right that he should go alone and the family followed. After she had been declared dead, the family left while I waited with Grant to view the body. Then we left and returned to the Manor." Said Demmie. "And what time was that?" Asked Cadiston. "I don't know exactly, maybe eleven or twelve." She said.

"Are you sure about that?" Asked Macswee. "Well, I cannot be totally sure of the time as we had just been through a traumatic experience, perhaps it was a bit later." "So, if I said eleven-thirty?" Cadiston asked. "That must be it, then. Grant was beside himself and in a deep state of depression and I had to pull over to console him." She continued. "And what happened while you consoled him?" Cadiston asked. "He got out of the car and I followed him. He was going to jump into the river but when I tried to stop him, I slipped on the bank and almost fell in myself and it was him that saved me." Demmie said.

"And was that when you got the tear and stain on your dress?" She looked surprised at this question. "Oh yes, that was it." She said. "Now, after that episode, what then?" Cadiston asked. "We came back here and went to bed." She said. "Together?" Asked Cadiston. "Good gracious me, no, he went to his room and I went to mine and fell asleep in the bath." She said in a high-pitched tone. "Is there anything else that you can remember? Any small detail that you may have omitted?" Cadiston asked. "Not a thing, I was calm when it was all happening, then after in a state of trauma." She said. During the interview, Demmie jiggled in her seat which told Cadiston that she was not comfortable answering his question. From her actions he assessed that she had something to hide. "A state of trauma yet you managed to drive him home?" Her face went pale and she looked sheepish. "I pulled myself together for his sake." "I see, now, is there anything else that you need to tell us?" Mac could see that she wanted this to be over and had remained silent. He could see that she looked worried. "I don't think I have forgotten anything." Said Demmie. "Now, tell us what you know about a syringe?" Cadiston asked.

Her facial expression changed dramatically. "Nothing, why should I know about a syringe?" He then moved the piece of paper that was covering the one that he had purchased and again her face changed as she stared at it.

"Where did you find that?" She asked. "I never said I had found it, so why do you think that I did?" He asked. "Now you are trying to confuse me with all this talk of a syringe that I know nothing about." Demmie snapped. "You are quite sure that you can shed no light on a syringe?" Cadiston asked calmly.

"I have told you, nothing."She was getting extremely agitated by now so Cadiston closed the Questioning. "Thank you, now if you remember something later that you should have told us, please come back. Now, will you just go next door to see our WPCs but first please sign this just for the records." He handed her a pen with his notebook which she signed. "Thank you, one other thing before you go, your shoe size please?" "Shoe size, I do not see the importance or relevance of my shoe size but if you must know it is size six, in some shoes a five but mainly six." Demmie said. "Thank you. Now, if you should remember any other small detail while we are still here, please do not hesitate and come back to tell us. Will you go next door to see our WPCs and then we will call when the next person is required." She rose from her chair and left. "Why did you give her a different pen to the one that you are using? Come to think of it, you did not ask any of the others to sign, so why her?" Asked Mac. "False statement, Mac, and her fingerprints are on it, that is why I have just wrapped that pen." Cadiston explained. "But you did not get any others." Mac said. "We will, Mac, Francis and Olito are next door, remember? They will do that for us, then we will have all their prints along with their blood type, D.N.A and shoe size. Then we will have more evidence to either prove guilt or innocent but this one will do to start with. She evaded a lot in her statement and did not correct the date. Her body language was in the self-protection mode and she became very agitated when she saw the syringe. I am going to get the housemaid that looks after Chad and his wife's room." He pulled the bell cord and they waited. Six minutes later and Alfred came in. "You rang, Detective?"

"Alfred, I need you to do something for me. Can you send the housemaid that looks after Master Chadrick and his wife's room to us?" Asked Cadiston. "That would be Katrine, I will send her to you straight away and if I am not mistaken, she will be having a short break about now so shouldn't be long." He turned and was gone. "You did ask Demmie about the syringe and pushed it a bit more than the others." Observed Mac.

"Purposely, Mac, her story does not add up and if I had not asked about it, I believe that she would have covered up somehow that she knew of it. I could tell that she lied. If you were watching her closely, then you would have seen how she could not take her eyes off it. She is not to be believed as she already lied when she told her husband the stain on her dress was from the hospital and has just told us it was from slipping in the mud near the river. A lie, Mac, so how many other lies did she tell us?" Cadiston said. "True, I did notice all that and was going to mention it. So do you think she did it?" Asked Mac. "I have my suspicions about that. I see a strong case of desire and if she and Grant are having an affair, then she would want Bonnie out of the way so that she could have him to herself." Cadiston suggested. "And that gives her the motive. Plus, she knew of Bonnie's allergy and that makes her, in my opinion, some devilish kind of evil woman." Said Mac. "If, as I suspect, her fingerprints are on the syringe, we have her but that will only be answered after the fingerprint and syringe have been fully examined and we have the result." "You see a lot more than I do, Cadders, but in time I will catch up." He just smiled and poured another cup of his tea. They waited patiently for fifteen minutes before Katrine entered the study. "Come in and do not look so worried, we just need to ask you something and hopefully you can help us. Do you remember the morning of Tuesday, 23rd September?" Asked Cadiston. "I could not forget it, sir, that is the day after Miss Bonnie died and the day that Master Malcolm died." Said Katrine. "True but that is not why we need your help. Do you remember clearing the room of master Chadrick and his wife?" He asked.

"I can remember everything about that day, sir." Katrine answered quickly. "Good. Now, can you remember clearing the basket and the contents of it and where did it go?" Cadiston asked. "There were a few pieces of cotton wool that had been used to remove makeup and a lovely blue dress that was torn and stained, looked like a water stain and a bit of mudand smelt of something

236

sexual detective, if you know what I mean." Katrine said. "Exactly, now, it would be of immense help to us if we could retrieve that dress, is that a possibility?" Asked Cadiston. "Actually yes, instead of throwing it away, I was going to repair and clean it for my mother's charity shop for sick animals. It is still in my room as with everything that has been happening and the busy weekend that we have just had, I have done nothing with it." Answered Katrine. "Good, excellent, now can you bring it to us in secret? No one must know as it is to be used as part of our investigation and that will be a piece of evidence to clear an innocent person, can you do that for us, please Katrine?" Asked Cadiston.

"Lord and Lady Mandaten have always been very kind to me and my family and if by this small thing, I can repay some of that kindness, then very well if it will help them in any way. I fetch it now for you, in secret." She said. "Good girl, how long will it take you?" Cadiston looked at her. "Just five minutes, sir, if I go up the back stairs, my room is just next to them. I go, sir, and bring you the dress." Katrine said and got up. "Thank you." She hurried away to her room. "Now, that is a piece of luck, Cadders." Said Mac. "Need it sometimes, Mac." Said Cadiston. "Who else is there to speak to?" Asked Mac. "Apart from the staff, just Grant. Then we will see how his story ties in with Demmie's. When we have the dress, we will call for him." Katrine had returned quickly with the blue dress in a carrier bag. "As you are here, Katrine, what can you tell of the night that Miss Bonnie died?" "Nothing at all, sir. I finished my work at five-thirty and went to my parent's house. They live in the estate village just down the main road, twenty minutes away. I go on my cycle and did not come back until seven-thirty on Tuesday morning." Katrine said. "And the other maids?" Asked Cadiston.

"Charlotte was out with her boyfriend and I know that Angelica was with Jeremiah at the stable. I do not know what time they would be back." She recalled. "That is fine, thank you. Remember the dress is our secret." Said Cadiston. "I have forgotten already, sir." She stood and left the room. "Now we call for Grant." Said Cadiston. "I will go fetch him for you personally." Mac walked steadily down the corridor and into the lounge. "Master Grant, please." Without speaking, he stood and followed Mac into the study. "Come in, Grant, and take a seat." Said Cadiston. "Ok, let's cut the fancy frills, Cadiston, and get straight down to the chase so what is it you want to know?" He said in a boisterous, bossy manner. "Tell us all that you can remember about the evening of Monday, 23rd of September." Said Cadiston. "For starters, it was Monday, 22nd and not 23rd, that was Tuesday when Malcolm had his lot. Call yourself a detective and can't even get your dates right." Cadiston quickly thought to himself. "Now here is someone to watch carefully, he has done his homework and if I am not mistaken, covered his tracks. You may be innocent of the crime of murdering Bonnie but without a shadow of a doubt, I would think that you are guilty of another and that being the case, we need to find it." Grant continued. "We had our meal, then Bonnie collapsed and was taken to hospital. I followed the ambulance and Chad's wife came with me. The rest of the family was brought by Malcolm. Bonnie was declared dead ten minutes after reaching the hospital and as there was nothing anyone could do, I sent them back home and waited to see her body before leaving. I came home and went to bed and that's it." Said Grant. "As simple as that is it? I will ask you again to tell us all what happened on Monday, 22nd of September, when your wife and unborn child died. Now, is there anything else that you can tell us about that evening?" Asked Cadiston. "My wife died, isn't that enough for you?" Grant snapped. "Just trying to get all the facts, sir, every single little thing is of significance." Cadiston said. "Look here, Cadiston, your Sergeant Standish had finished with this case. I can see no reason why it needs to be dragged up and opened up again?" "Just answer the question please, sir, as we need to clear any suspicions and get the true facts of that fateful evening." Said Cadiston patiently. "Suspicions my foot, Standish told me that foul play was not suspected, she died of natural causes. Demmie was at the hospital with me and drove me back, got here about twelve-thirty onTuesday morning." Grant said. "You had quite a lengthy time at the hospital, then?" Cadiston asked. "Two or three hours or thereabout. Now that's it, I can tell you no more about it." Grant snapped. There was a moment's silence before Mac answered. "You are quite sure about that, sir?" "I don't like what you are implying, Detective." Grant snarled. "I am implying absolutely nothing, sir, just trying to get to the truth of that fateful evening. Now, is there anything that you would like to add?"said Macswee He looked at him straight in the eye noticing that Grant turned his gaze away. "I ask you again, sir, is there anything else that you can tell us about that evening because if there is, it will be better for you to disclose it now openly instead of us finding it out later and be assured that we will." Reiterated Macsawee. "My sergeant is correct in what he said, it is best to declare any information now as it will save you a lot of trouble later if you do not." Added Cadiston. "What's this then, DCI Cadiston? Good cop, bad cop routine?" He had a smirk on his face as he spoke. "So, what have the others had to say?" "That is nothing to concern you, sir, all I need from you is the truth and the whole truth about that evening." Said Cadiston.

"All right, so we stopped on the way home and she gave me some comfort after losing my wife." Grant said. "And by giving you comfort what do mean by that, sir?" Asked Macswee. "Geez, Detective, surely you do not need me to draw you a picture?" Grant said. "Hence the reason for the torn dress and no underwear? It must have been quite intense, this comfort as you put it, sir, as though in a hurry. Continue, please, and remember the whole truth. Was this the first time that she had, as you say, given you comfort?" Grant was now on his feet and angrily snapped his reply. "Yes it was, absolutely! Now, can I go?"

"Sit down, sir." Said Cadiston very sternly. "We have not finished with you yet. You are quite sure that this was the first time?" Reluctantly he sat down but by now Grant was becoming enraged and both detectives could see that his temper was rising. "Oh, for God's sake man, will you never let up?" "Not until we have the full truth." Cadiston said. "Alright, so it had happened before, what of it? She said her husband was no good and it was me that she loved, not him. It was like a gift horse as she was always up for it and I took advantage of the situation. No law against that, is there Detective?" He said snidely. "Only breaking the sacred law of marriage and so soon after losing your wife is very distasteful but I do not suppose that would bother you, would it?" Asked Cadiston.

"Not at all, Detective, not at all. Plus, I got one over on that adopted interloper, Chadrick." Said Grant with a smirk. "And when you had returned from the hospital, you then went to bed?" Asked Cadiston.

"Not alone if I am correct, sir?" Added Mac. "So, what of it? Think you are so clever, the pair of you? Alright, so she came to my room and we spent the night together. She had a plan worked out so that her husband wouldn't know. She left me early and made out to be asleep in the bath, satisfied now?" Grant snapped. "Almost, one more question, then you can go. Who apart from you stands to gain the title of Lord?" Asked Cadiston. "Apart from me there is no one, not unless you count Lowell and James as they carry the Mandaten name." Grant said. "You can go now, we will let you know when we require you to speak with us again concerning other incidents, especially when your brother, Kevin, died and your fight with Walter." Grant just glared at Cadiston. "Will you go next door to see our WPCs now?" Cadiston said and Grant stood and grumbled and after a long stare, he left.

"Now there is a nasty piece of work, I can see that he is a bully and likes to be in charge but in the back of my mind, I do not think that he killed his wife. My money is on Demmie but am I glad that I am with you, Cadders. Difficult and complex cases when they are all coupled together and there is no way that I would ever be able to solve any of them by myself. I am trying to follow but I must admit that I am a bit lost, I guess that we will need to look at every single one of the family members and eye them all with suspicion. That is all except Lord and Lady Mandaten, I guess." Said Mac. "Lesson one, Mac: no one is beyond suspicion. People can look very demure, likable, and look as though butter would not melt in their mouth but looks can be deceiving. In this instance, I am sure that we can make an exception and that would be Lord and Lady Mandaten. I said that this could be a power struggle but it could also be a case of hate killings. Lies, desire, jealousy, greed, and deception all play their part. It is very important that we do not discount any little thing, not even the grandchildren. If there were no immediate descendants to Lord Mandaten then a grandchild may stand to inherit and that must also be considered. Evidence, Mac, that is what we need, good solid hard evidence. We have the syringe that has hopefully been analyzed by now and we can be reasonably certain that it was used to murder Bonnie and her unborn child. What we do not know for sure is where it came from so a word with Cook will be a good place to start. We had better talk to her next." The bell cord was pulled and again, within a short space of time, Jonas arrived. "How can I help you, Detective?"

"Jonas, could you ask the cook to come and speak to us, please? But firstly, did you inadvertently mention that I was here the other day?" Asked Cadiston. "Sorry Detective, I was talking with Miss Jennifer and she was getting so upset about her Aunt Bonnie. Sorry, but to reassure her that it would all be alright, I did inadvertently let it slip." Said Jonas. "Not to worry, now Cook, please." Cadiston said. "Would that be Flora or Bernice, sir?" Jonas asked. "The head cook first." Said Cadiston. "That would be Flora, sir, I will send her to you." In a flash, he was on his way to the kitchen.

Her footsteps sounded very tired and sluggish as she made her way to the study. It was almost like her feet were dragging on the ground. "Come in, Cook, or may I call you Flora?" Said Cadiston. "Flora will be just fine, sir." She responded. "No need for the sir, my dear. I am DCI Cadiston, this is Detective Sergeant Macswee, Mac for short." Flora's head nodded in recognition. "I know it is hard for you and be assured that you are in no way a suspect or under any form of suspicion. All we need from you is some information. Do you ever have occasions where you use a syringe in the kitchen like this one?" She looked at it before answering. "Yes sir, it is used to put very fine decorations onto a cake instead of using a piping bag." "And has one been misplaced at any time?" Cadiston asked. "Actually, yes. About three months ago. I needed it to put the finishing touches onto a cake for one of the village children but could not find it anywhere so had to send Ruth out to purchase another one." Flora recalled. "One last question, when the syringe was misplaced, did anyone have access to it apart from yourself?" Cadiston asked. "Bernice would but only if she is decorating a cake. She had been away for three days and it was there when she left and was gone before she was back." Said Flora.

"Who else would be in the Manor during that time? The time it went missing –. Sorry, I said one question and that is another." Cadiston smiled. "The day before she was due back, the whole family were here. They all come to visit every three months and I must admit that I was not sure how I would cope with the extra people to feed without her." Said Flora. "Would any of the family need to visit the kitchen?" Asked Cadiston.

"Occasionally they may but not very often." Flora informed him. "And would they know where all such items are kept?" Asked Cadiston. "Yes, they would." Flora answered certainly. "Yet another question for you, was Bonnie present at that time, and did you cook for her?" He asked. "She was, sir, and I did cook for her without any problem. I just cannot understand what happened this time, I was so very careful." Tears began to fill her eyes. "Do not stress yourself, Flora, I am certain that you took every single precaution and there is some other explanation so there is no need to reproach yourself. All I will tell you is that we will get to the bottom of it. You have been very helpful so thank you and just one more question and after this, there will be no more questions. Have any members of the family visited the kitchen recently?"

"Miss Lizabeth and I think … Yes, Miss Demmie have both visited the kitchen within the last six-month period." Said Flora. "Thank you, that is all we need to know." Cadiston said. "Find out what happened, Detectives, she was a dear sweet child and the poor little baby and Grant was horrible to her." Flora said wiping her eyes. "That we intend to do." Said Cadiston and Flora smiled and as she left, wiping a tear from her eye.

"That was very informative. The family visits every three months and it was three months ago that the ghostly figure of the Lady Mary appeared. It was at that visit that the poor fellow, Pedro Santos, lost his life. How many other visits has she made over the years if she came every three months? We need to ask the question: was that coincidence or a fix to set the scene? The syringe must have been taken from the kitchen during that visit, ready to be used on 22nd of September to inject Bonnie's dessert with the deadly poison. Demmie had visited the kitchen so could it have been her all prepared when the opportunity presented?" Said Mac.

"You are thinking, Mac, and on the same line as myself." Said Cadiston.

"I have a suspect in mind, Cadders. Demmie is my prime suspect. She had motive, her desire for Grant, the opportunity when she left the table to go to the restroom, and the means. We just need to know how she got the contents of the syringe." Said Mac."See Mac, now you are really thinking." Cadiston praised Mac. "That is being with you. Now we know which family members were present at that time and it does not include the grandchildren." Mac looked proud. "It would appear that it had been pre-planned at least three months before the event and that makes it murder in the first degree. We have a suspect in mind, now all we need is the visual evidence?" Mac looked at Cadiston for confirmation. "It certainly does appear that way and maybe not an exact date set but pre-planned to act upon when the opportunity presented itself. Clever idea of yours to have that syringe on the table. I would never have thought of doing that." Said Mac.

"We just need to have a word with Lord and Lady Mandaten and then we are done here, for now." Said Cadiston. The bell cord was pulled and seconds later, Alfred had taken them into the sitting room. "We have questioned all the family members who were present at the dinner on that fateful day but just to need to ask if there is anything however small that you can add?" Cadiston asked Lord and Lady Mandaten. They went through the events of the evening and all that they remembered fitted in with the previous statements. "Just to conclude, DCI Cadiston, DS Macswee, I carried out my own questioning and I don't know if it will help but some of the remarks and actions made me suspicious." He opened his notebook. "I said that we may discover some evidence and Demmie said 'Or not as the case may be.' Then further on, she remarked in her words directed at Grant 'One thing that you can and must remember I am –.' She then hesitated and looked around and continued 'I mean, we are here for you, you will have my –.' She paused again to correct herself. 'our full love and support; And that was followed by a rather affectionate squeeze. This was directed at Grant and he replied 'I know that I have your love for all time.' I noticed that when he spoke, he was looking directly at Demmie and this leads me to believe that there is most probably something going on there. Well, that is it, our evidence. So now you can do with it what you will and hope it will help." "It will, sir, and thank you. Just between us, I know that Grant and Demmie are having an affair. She said that it is him that she loves and not her husband. He says that he just wanted to get one over on him. I get the feeling that lies and falseness are involved all around, desire on her part and lies on his. I also note that there is a lot of hatred there." Said Cadiston.

"You are quite right, Detective, we have tried our utmost to stop it but to no avail and so it continues. Lies on his part? Well, no big surprise there." Said Lord Mandaten. "Well, we have all that we need for now. Our WPCs have taken the samples and we have the statements so we will take our leave of you and thank you." Said Cadiston. "No, thank you, DCI Cadiston. Thank you for investigating, and congratulations on your quick promotion." Lord Mandaten said with a smile. "Only temporary, sir, just until we have solved all the deaths." Cadiston said humbly. "And you will, I –." Lord Mandaten then began to cough. "You rest easy, my Lord, the truth will soon be out and then you will have your answers, good day to you." They turned and left. "Ok Mac, back to the station. It's a bit late in the day but I would like to see if any of the results are back and if they are then tomorrow some more reading for us. You did a good job today, ladies, so well done both of you." Said Cadiston.

"Thank you, Cadders, nice to be appreciated." Mac drove steadily, and in next to no time they were back at the station. The instant that they had left, the family joined their parents in the sitting room. "That was a lot of unnecessary trauma that they have just put us through. Damn that Cadiston, asking all those unnecessary questions. The case was closed by Standish and should have stayed that way instead of stirring it all up again." Grant said grumpily. "Sounds like it worries you, Grant." Lizabeth said.

"Shut up, Lizabeth!" He snapped. "Well, they talked and wrote things down, then the WPCs took blood and DNA." Lizabeth said. "So that was why they were here with them, to get our blood and DNA. Well, they didn't get mine did they, I did not go in their little room." Grant said smugly. "They will be back, Grant, and then they will get your samples and there will no stopping them." Replied Lizabeth. Grant just grunted and swallowed his drink. "I was just thinking –." Tomas said. "Dangerous occupation that is, Tomas, too much thinking can damage your health." Grant mocked ."Now who is being silly?" Tomas said. "Just joking." Grant said. "Ha-ha, not very funny, Grant." Tomas said sheepishly. "Who cares? Damn that Cadiston! Bonnie's case was closed, he should leave things well alone and accept them for what they are instead of putting us through more unnecessary trauma." Grant said. "He is just doing his job, son, and we will leave him to do it.however he sees fit. If you do not like his investigating, that is your problem but your mother and myself want to know the truth and I hope that is the case with you all." Said Lord Mandaten.

"Problem? Of course it is a problem. Standish had sorted everything out so now it should be left alone instead of dragging it all up again. He was right when he said that Cadiston was young and eager to make a name for himself and now they have made him a DCI. Well, he is barking up the wrong tree now and we need to put an end to all this." Grant was getting annoyed.

"Why son? Why should we when he is certain that your Bonnie died in suspicious circumstances?" Said Lord Mandaten. "Dammit

Father, I have had all I can take on the death of Bonnie so just leave it alone and let her rest now plus –." Lord Mandaten began to choke, then collapsed into his chair. While the rest just stood and watched, Chad and Greta were at his side, supporting him. "Don't just stand there looking like a lot of idiotic fools! Father needs to get to the hospital so do something useful and call for an ambulance." Chad yelled. "Already done, Chad. I was about to clear the room and could see what was happening. I hope that I did act above my station and acted as I saw fit upon the situation instantly, I hope I did right?" Alfred said. "Absolutely Alfred and thank you." Said Chad. "Absolutely Alfred and thank you." Grant mimicked in a mocking manner. "Well, I blame that blasted interfering detective for Father's collapse, he had no right putting him through anymore –." "Shut up, Grant, you have always had plenty to say. Say nothing else, you have said far too much already, if anyone is to blame then take a good look at yourself with all your ranting." Grant could not answer his mother and slumped away into the lounge to pour himself another drink.

James had stood silently but followed Grant and watched as he downed one drink and then instantly poured another. "That is so typical of you, Uncle Grant! Whenever you cannot get your way, you just bury yourself in a bottle. I am ashamed to call you my uncle as you are nothing more than a drunken slob and it is you who is to blame for my mother's death." "Shut up, James, you know nothing. Now, run along and play with your toys before you end up like your father." Grant snarled. "What do you mean by that? End up like my father … Do you mean that I will be blown to pieces?" James pushed.

"Just go, boy, and leave it well alone –. Dam you, leave me alone, I mean nothing, it is just the drink and my depression." Grant said in an irritated manner.

"You depressed? Now that is a joke, you just do not care and about my –." "Leave it, boy! And clear off. Someone get this retch away from me before he says something he will regret." Grant now shouted. "Come on, James, leave him to drown himself in his liquor." Said Greta. "That's right, Greta, you take him away from me before I —. Well, nevermind that, just take him away out of my sight." She did not even bother to look at Grant and took James by the arm and led him back into the other room with the rest of the family.

The ambulance had arrived quickly and as they knew the case, a doctor came with it to be on-site to administer any treatment or medication needed. After his examination, the doctor declared that Lord Mandaten needed treatment that could not be carried out here so he was taken to the hospital again. There was sadness in the Manor on this evening. Some through worry and some because he still survived. The evening had passed slowly with very little conversation taking place but in their minds, the thoughts ran rampant. Night had fallen and now the Manor was silent but in the silence, the air of hostility was rife: and so ended Monday, the 6th day of October.

The instant that Cadiston and Macswee arrived home, they could not wait to inform their wives of their temporary promotions. "Acting DCI, Samantha, just until these cases are closed." Said Cadiston.

"It is no more than you deserve Ashton and who knows, when they are all solved, they may promote you officially." Samantha said enthusiastically.

"Bit quick for that." They both smiled and sat down to enjoy their meal. In Macswee's household, the conversation was very much the same.

Chapter Eight

The Fall

The morning of Tuesday, 7th October, saw Mac, as instructed, paying a visit to the hospital to check on Grant and Demmie's movements. Cadiston was sitting at his desk going through the statements that had been collected and his WPCs had taken their samples to be analyzed. Francis noticed Mac upon his return to the station and informed him that some samples were not taken as the people had bypassed them. Mac told Cadiston who was not happy at this news and decided to pay another unannounced visit to the Manor. Questions had been asked about Bonnie, now they would be asked concerning Malcolm's death.

"Grandfather has given us another scare but thankfully, it was not as serious as we first thought. I prayed that we were not about to lose him, prayed he would be alright. I cannot wait to see him well and he will be home today, thank goodness." Jennifer said. "You are right, Jennifer. Without a doubt, he did give us a scare." Said her brother Lowell.

"I don't think that he is ready to leave us, not just yet anyhow." Added Jennifer. "Do you know what I think?" James asked. "No but I do know that you will tell us, James." Said Kansas in a mocking fashion. "I think that he will want to hang on until Detective Cadiston has solved all the deaths and has discovered just what happened. I want to know, or rather need to know, the truth about my parents deaths and I am sure that you both will want to know the truth about your father." James continued."Goes without saying, James, and you could be right about Grandfather as he wants to know the truth about all these deaths in the family too and that is why he specifically asked for detective Cadiston to investigate them. He has made a start with our Aunt Bonnie and her unborn child and my guess is that there was more there than meets the eye, I suspect something is going on between Uncle Grant and Aunt Demmie." Jennifer said.

"You are very sensible, Jennifer, and it makes you wonder about Uncle Grant as he keeps trying to hush everything up." Lowell answered to his sister.

"You could be right, Lowell. The body and mind is a real marvel as I am finding out in med school. I just feel so sad for you all losing your parents and feel lucky that I still have mine."

"Lucky indeed, Kansas. James has lost both his parents and we have lost our father and if I read this right, Detective Cadiston believes they are all in suspicious circumstances. Those are our thoughts as well." Said Jennifer.

"Well, I know for a fact that my mother would not have taken her own life leaving me to bear the pain of losing both my parents within days of each other. I know that there is something suspicious about my father's death. He would most certainly not have overloaded his Kentucky Rifle, he was far too careful and cautious –." James paused briefly to wipe away a tear. "I strongly believe that they were both murdered. But why and what is there to gain by their deaths? More importantly, by whom, that is the question. As far as I know, they did no one any Harm. I know that there was rivalry between the brothers as they all want the title of Lord but would any of them stoop to murder to get it? Why my mother and Aunt Sammie with her family they have nothing to gain when the next Lord is announced? They were no threat and had no claim. Well, Aunt Sammie would if there were no other heirs. I do know that Father would have given his right arm as he wanted the title of Lord. He and Mother had talked about it when they thought I was not able to hear them. He knew that Malcolm and Grant would come before him as they were the eldest and I did hear some talk about a plan to discredit them both so that Father would gain the title for himself. I tried but I could not hear what it was to be. My mother was a gentle soul although she could be a bit materialistic and they are both gone now."

"Not one of us can answer why our parents have been so brutally murdered, James. and both Jennifer and I have our own suspicions about our father. He was an expert horseman and we cannot believe that he was thrown from the back of Thundist. We have watched him ride on many occasions, even on a spooked horse that was bucking and twisting, making it look like a wild west rodeo and he did not fall off. With his horsemanship, he brought the animal back under control and that convinces us that something else happened up there at the Devil's Dyke." He looked across at his cousin Kansas who sat quietly. "You are not saying much, Kansas, so what do you think?" "What do I think? Well, I think that you may all be putting yourselves through a lot of pain that is not needed. It is very sad that you, Lowell and Jennifer, and you, James, have lost parents but we were not there to see what happened to any of them so –." He paused and shrugged his shoulders. "Well, we just do not know what happened but that other policeman –. Now, what was his name?" Lowell thought for a minute."Standish." Said Lowell. Kansas then continued. "That's right, Lowell. Now, he said that they were all tragic accidents and I guess that must be what they were. So, that is what I think. You did ask and to my mind, you should all just accept that one suicide and the others just tragic accidents. Now, take this Cadiston, who I understand is not a fully qualified detective but is called a DCI, he is just stirring things up and is just trying to make something out of nothing. The bottom line is that we just need to wait and see, that is what I think." "That is easy for you to say, Kansas, as you have not been affected by these deaths and still have both your parents. What has happened to our parents was no accident and that makes us wonder about Aunt Bonnie, could she have somehow been murdered as well?" James said. "And she was pregnant, James, we must not forget that." Jennifer said. "A good point, Jennifer, so it does make us all wonder about Aunt Bonnie. I have noticed that Uncle Grant does not seem to be all that upset." Lowell remarked. "Maybe you three are thinking that but not me, Uncle Grant is just good at hiding his feelings." Kansas said.

"Does he have any? Even so, Kansas, it does make us wonder about Aunt Bonnie and all the other deaths." Replied Jennifer. While they were talking, a shadow lurked in the doorway trying to hear their conversation, and although unable to pick up on their every word had heard quite enough and interrupted. "What do you kids wonder about Aunt Bonnie?" Voiced Grant in a deep and sullen tone. "Hello Uncle Grant, we were just saying that after our parents' deaths, especially my mother and father were both murdered, could it be possible that Aunt Bonnie was murdered and that is why the detectives are asking questions, because it was not an accident after all?" stated James.

"Murder and suspicions, foolish young ones, have you nothing better to do with your time but surmise all sorts of false thoughts? You are all as bad as that dammed Detective Cadiston and his sidekick Macswee. All this talk and suspicion is all absolute nonsense. Sergeant Standish came and told me and your grandfather that the case of your Aunt Bonnie was closed. It was a very sad case of someone's carelessness, death by natural causes. It is only that dammed detective Cadiston who is stirring things up and causing us more grief so now all of you, let it go!" He said angrily. "We are sorry, Uncle Grant, the last thing that we want to do is to upset you." Jennifer said. "Upset? Me? Now, that is a laugh Jennifer. You have absolutely no idea so just drop your foolish way of thinking and accept that all these unfortunate deaths were nothing more than tragic accidents!" Grant said, then turned and left the room. "I have to agree with him and to persist in thinking otherwise only makes it more unbearable and adds to the stress." Kansas said. "As was already said, it is alright for you to say, Kansas, as you still have both your parents. Maybe if the shoe was on the other foot then you would think differently." Jennifer snapped. "Well said, Jennifer, you may be only ten years old but one thing is certain, you have a sensible head on your shoulders. I tell you all here and now that I, for one, will not drop it, rest or stop thinking it and will do what I can to discover just who it was that murdered both my parents. As far as I am concerned and will hold that in my thoughts, both my parents were murdered, you hear me uncle Grant?! Both my parents my father first then my mother who was a gentle soul and would not have taken her own life, so they were murdered and Cadiston will prove it to you somehow." James yelled. Jennifer placed her arm around his waist. "Calm yourself, James, Cadiston will find out the truth about all their deaths. I am glad to say the ambulance transport is here and that means that Grandfather is home again."

"At last." James said. "Brilliant." Lowell exclaimed and jumped up. "Smacks of déjà vu." Remarked Kansas in rather a cynical tone. At least three of the grandchildren were relieved that he had survived this latest attack and left the blue room heading for the door to greet and welcome him back to the family home.

"Welcome home again, Grandfather, you did give us a scare." Said Jennifer as she planted a kiss on his cheek. "Bless you, my little princess, you will be pleased to know that it was not as serious as was first thought so here I am. Now then, it is lovely and warm out today so let's take that walk around the garden that we missed out on yesterday." "As I just said, smacks of déjà vu." "That is rather cynical but who cares, Kansas, Grandfather is alright and is back home with us and that is all that matters." He turned his face to stare at James with hate in his eyes but said nothing. "Change of footwear, James." "Race you up the stairs, Jennifer, and hopefully no incidents to stop us today." She smiled and started running, reaching the top before her cousin.

"You cheated, James, you let me win." He found the strength to smile at his cousin before Speaking. "Let you win? Not a chance, I was slowed down with a stone in my shoe, that is why I need to change them." "A likely tail but I believe you, millions would not. Wait for me at the top of the stairs and we will go down together." Said Jennifer. "Alright Cousin, and I remember about the lady thing taking more time to decide, best we hurry up." They both smiled and made their way to their rooms. James had selected his shoes and had them changed in an instant while Jennifer could not decide which would be the best ones to wear. "These, no those –. Or maybe them. Oh dear, which pair shall I wear?" While making her decision, she heard a loud then muffled scream followed by a lot of lumping. Then before it went silent, a crash that she knew was the sound of metal. Pulling on the shoes that were in her hand, she was quick to investigate the unusual noise.

She thought that her cousin would be waiting for her and would be able to explain the noise but what greeted her, left her frozen at the top of the staircase. With her eyes wide open and fixed on the still body that lay at the bottom of the stairs and without thinking, her mouth dropped open and was emitting a loud scream. Her legs felt like jelly but as though in one step, she was at the bottom of the staircase kneeling beside the still body of her cousin, James. The old suit of medieval armour that had stood like a sentry at the bottom of the stairs was lying partly across his body. With her handkerchief, she began to dab at the blood that was running from his nose, ear, mouth, and from the gash to his head. She thought it must have been caused when he struck the old suit of metal: that is what she had called it. It was far too heavy for her to move and she was at a total loss. Not knowing what to do, she began to touch him, hoping that he would wake up and then she began to scream and shout his name. Even louder, she began calling for help, hoping that someone would hear and come to her aid.

Surprisingly, Grant appeared first, entering via the blue room door with a glass in his hand. "Whatever is all that noise and screaming about, Jennifer, it is enough to wake the dead." "It's James, he will not move. I –, I think that he was pushed and is dead, Uncle Grant!" He had a quick look at the still form and saw the untied shoelace. "Looks to me like he tripped on his untied shoelace and fell down the stairs and hit the old suit of metal. Only thing that could have happened. Got careless, just as his father did." Grant said coldly. In floods of tears, Jennifer replied. "That is a very cruel thing to say and I hate you for it." "As if I care, you are but a silly child." Said Grant.

By this time, Chad and Greta had arrived and the second they were in the hallway, they could see the still body and heard Grants remark. "You are doing no good being in here, so get out." Said Chad angrily, then knelt beside Jennifer. His head turned to footsteps from behind him and to his surprise, Kansas appeared as if from nowhere.

"Oh my lord, tell me what happened, Jennifer! This looks terrible. I heard you screaming and shouting for help." Kansas said. "It's James, Kansas, he has fallen down the stairs." Jennifer wailed. "Without question, he is dead. As I just said to the silly child, he tripped on his untied shoelace and fell down the stairs by all accounts." Said Grant before Jennifer could answer. "You are partially drunk already, Grant, at this early hour and were told to leave as your contribution is not required." Said Chad sternly. "Not required? Sounds familiar, so who gives a stuff?!" They were not surprised at Grant's devil-may-care attitude of another family death and with tears in her eyes, Greta answered. "You could be a bit more sympathetic, Grant. After all, he is your nephew." "Nephew or not, that makes absolutely no difference to me. He is just like his father, a careless one. I would say just like his father and that is a fact. He was very careless and should have tied his laces before coming down the stairs." Grant said coldly.

Chad sent him a look of anger and was about to stand but Grant had said his piece and knowing that, he could do nothing. Plus, he did not relish another confrontation with Chad, at least not yet so he turned and left.

Jennifer was sobbing and still prodding James in her attempt to wake him but this action, although it was well-meant, was having no effect. "Come away, Jennifer, and let your Cousin Kansas have a look. He knows a little bit about medical things." Greta said and gently moved her away. "But I must help him, Aunt Greta, I must." She said, still crying. "Come away, my girl, I know you are trying to help but there is nothing more you can do for him." Said Chad.

"Oh Uncle Chad, this is horrible! First his father was blown to pieces, then his mother drowned, and now Cousin James has fallen down the stairs. With everything else that has happened, it makes you wonder if he was pushed. Why is this all happening to us?" Jennifer sobbed. "I don't know, my little woman, but whatever the reason, it will be found out." Chad's voice was soft and gentle with a hint of sadness and Jennifer responded to this. As she stood up, although her body moved, her eyes remained on the still form of her cousin. "Well, I can say without a doubt that he is dead, it does not take a genius to see that. Don't know why

Jennifer is thinking he could have been pushed, you only need to look at the untied shoelace. It is as Uncle Grant said, he just tripped." Said Kansas. They were interrupted by Kansas's father. "Chad, something very strange has just happened." "Not in here, Tomas. This is tragic so what do you think is strange?" Chad asked. "The police are here already but can't possibly be to do with whatever has happened here, can it as it has only just happened?" Tomas said. "Perhaps that Cadiston fellow is a psychic, Father, and has pre-empted this." Said Kansas. "Don't be silly, Kansas. He has just turned up with that other chap and the two WPCs who were here yesterday so what do we do?" Said Tomas. "You are a fool, Tomas! Send them in here straight away!" Lizabeth snapped. "Yes, Lizabeth." Replied Tomas. "Tomas, after you send them in here keep the rest of the family in the blue room and stay out of the hallway." Said Chad. "Why, what is it that has happened this time and why was Jennifer screaming and shouting?" Asked Tomas. "It's James this time and from first impressions, it looks like he tripped and fell down the stairs but after everything else that has been happening of late, I have my doubts. We will leave it to Detective Cadiston and his colleagues as I am sure that he will sort it out and in doing that, he will find the truth". Said Chad.

"Looks like we have arrived at the right time, Mac. A routine visit has just escalated into another case. Francis, Olito, will you take the rest of the family in one room, probably the blue room, please. After we are done here we will come to ask some questions. Chad, would you stay a moment please?" "Would you all please move out of the hall and into the blue room, thank you." Said Olito, leaving Lizabeth to lead them, followed by the WPCs. "Now Chad, can you tell us what has transpired here please, and has anything been moved?" "Nothing has been moved, we have left him lying as he was and the suit of metal, as Jennifer calls it, is also as we found it. Jennifer was the first to find him and tried to prod him awake but –. Anyhow, she can tell you first-hand, Detective Cadiston, what she can." Said Chad.

Jennifer was still sobbing but managed to speak clearly. "I know this is hard for you so take your time, Jennifer." Said Mac.

"James and I went upstairs to change our shoes to get ready for a walk in the garden just like yesterday. I was in my room when I heard a scream, then a muffled scream, then a lot of thumping. There was a noise like a door closing, then silence and after a few seconds, the crash of metal. When I came to the top of the stairs, James was lying there at the bottom with the old metal suit on top of him. I ran down to his side and he would not wake so I called for help just as loud as I possibly could. He was going to wait for me so that we would come down together so why did he go without me?" Jennifer sobbed.

"Take a breath, Jennifer, you have done very well and all that you could do. Now, we will find that out and how he fell, alright?" Mac said quietly. "Is there anything else that you can tell us?" asked Cadiston. "Ambulance and forensics are on rout DCI." "Thanks, DS Macswee." "I don't think so, I think I have told everything." Said Jennifer.

"One more question, how long was it after you heard the first scream that you were at the top of the stairs?" Asked Cadiston. "Difficult to put an exact time on it. My room is the last down the hallway but couldn't have been more than two minutes, maybe a bit less." Jennifer sniffled. "Thank you, as DS Macswee said, you did very well. Will someone look after her please?" Cadiston said.

"She is my daughter, Detective, I will." Said Greta as she led her away from the scene and into the lounge. Cadiston whispered to Mac. "No more than two minutes or maybe a bit less, I have already noticed a discrepancy so could someone have committed another crime and disappeared that quickly, Mac? That is the major question." He looked up and raised his voice again. "Who was the first to arrive on the scene apart from the young lady?"

"After Jennifer, Grant, then her mother and myself and a few moments Later, Kansas arrived from back there out of the dark." Chad pointed in the direction. "And is Grant here now? If not, can someone get him, please?" Cadiston looked down at the lifeless body of the boy. "Greta, would you give Grant a call, he is wanted, please." Said Chadrick as she walked away.

"Alright." Greta answered without looking back. Kansas had been having a good look at the body of James and stood up turning towards Cadiston, "I am not yet qualified, Detective, but I do know enough to be sure that his neck is broken and that caused damage to the spinal cord he would have died instantly. My guess is that it happened when he fell and struck his head on that old suit of metal there. Jennifer has us calling it that now. Your proper examiner would know better than I do but it is my guess that is what killed him." "Two things, first your name, second is your thought?" Said Cadiston.

"My name is Kansas and we are cousins. It is obvious what happened here, even a blind man could see. Untied shoelace so he tripped and just look at the metal suit on him." Said Kansas. "An interesting theory of yours. Now, when did you arrive on the scene?" Asked Cadiston. "We were all outside in the garden and when I heard the screaming I came running in. Uncle Chad and Aunt Greta must also have heard Jennifer calling for help so ran back in to see what was wrong and were here just before me. They were definitely here when I came in. So was Uncle Grant." Said Kansas. "Thank you. Oh by the way, you have some fresh scratches on your neck that are bleeding, looks quite nasty and there is a chalky residue on your sleeve." His hand moved swiftly up to his neck his fingers feeling the warm blood. "In my haste to get in I tripped and fell so must have been from the pot and rose bush." Kansas said and turned to walk away. Cadiston turned to Mac with a look of suspicion on his face. "That will need checking out, those scratches look rather deep and too neat to be from a rose bush. Notice anything else in what he said, Mac?"

"He said he came in from the garden but Chadrick said he appeared from over there out of the dark, and there is no door that leads outside." Said Mac.

"Well spotted. Now, if James fell down those stairs, there will be evidence on them so go have a look and be careful not to step on anything like blood splats for example." Said Cadiston. "Understood." Mac said and made his way to the stairs, then carefully examined each one.

Grant had been found and was back in the hallway so Cadiston walked over to him. "Now then sir, I believe that after your niece, you were the first on the scene so what can you tell me?" Asked Cadiston. "Nothing really, I was in the blue room where everyone is now and heard her screaming, a thumping and the crash so came in to see what was wrong. Found her kneeling beside him, had a quick look, and could see straight away that he had tripped on his untied shoelace. And that is all I know, Detective, so there it is. Can I go now?" Grant asked.

"And where were you?" Cadiston continued. "Just told you, having a drink in the blue room." Grant grumbled. "Not in the garden with the rest of the family?" Asked Cadiston. "Nope, was having a drink first." Said Grant.

"Thank you, I will let you know if I require you again. Oh by the way, you have some white cobweb on the back of your jacket and something white on your sleeve." Cadiston said while scribbling in his notebook. "Must be from the garden where we were walking." Said Grant. "Thought you were having a drink first, sir?" Cadiston remaked. "Ah yes, I was but after the tragedy and a drink or two, I am just a bit confused." Grant said. "A bit confused, confused and a bit drunk, sir." He glared at Mac. "So, you don't pay for the alcohol drink, so what of it? Anyhow, I went to the garden first, then came in again for another drink while waiting for those two to join us. Well, James won't be, now will he?" Mumbled Grant.

"Thank you, that will be sufficient for now, we may need to talk again when you are sober." He glared at Cadiston again, then grunted and walked away leaving Mac and Cadiston with their thoughts.

"Jennifer was first on the scene, followed by Grant, then Chad and Greta, and lastly, by Kansas who appeared from over there in the dark. Hmm −. Very strange as there is no door. Three statements add up, one does not. Now I think a brief word with the rest of the family that were on the walk?" He knew the way so walked directly into the blue room. The family all sat in silence and once there, Cadiston noticed that Grant was missing again.

"When did Grant join you in the garden?" Cadiston asked. "Don't think he did, he left us and went into the blue room for a needed drink as he cannot manage without one. The next time we saw him was just now." Answered Lizabeth. "Can anyone add anything to what we have already been told?" Asked Cadiston. "I think that Grant went into the blue room and if I remember correctly, Lowell and Kansas were not with us straight away. In fact –. Yes, I did not see them until after the screaming of my niece." "Thank you for that, I have it in my notes that the only people that attended to James were first Jennifer, second was Grant, then Chad and Greta together, followed by Kansas, is that correct?" Cadiston tried to confirm. "Correct, Detective." Said Chadrick. "Thank you, I do not need to ask anything else at this stage of the investigation. I would like to just look at your backs and sleeves, please. One at a time." Cadiston requested.

They each stepped forward to allow him to inspect their clothes and then returned to their seat. "I see that you have brushed the white from your arm but along with the scratches on your neck, you still have some white chalky substance and cobweb on your back, Kansas, isn't it?" Cadiston noted. "It is and again, as I have already told you, it must have been when I tripped against the pot, that must have been it, from the pot that the rose that scratched my neck was in." Cadiston lightly brushed Kansas's jacket and collected a sample, it was so delicately done that he did not notice. "Thank you all, that is very helpful. Just one more question for you all, was there anyone else not with you or that joined you a bit later?" Asked Cadiston.

"Grant, I don't recall him being with us at all. He will not admit it but, just between us Detective, he has a major drinking problem and the whole family knows that. Jennifer had gone to change her shoes, as had James. Lowell disappeared for a short while, as did Kansas, maybe seven or eight minutes." Stated Lizabeth. Kansas quickly intervened. "I was not far away, just around the corner but could see you all waiting for those two to catch up."

Cadiston noticed a slight quiver in his voice which alerted him to suspect that it was another lie. "Grant was here until the argument, then he left in a mood and we did not see him until just now when you called for him." Said Tomas.

"And where he is now?" Asked Cadiston. "That is anyone's guess." Said Lizabeth. "Not much of a guess, Lizabeth, he is probably nursing another bottle in the other room." Added Tomas.

"Thank you all again, most helpful. Now when my WPCs were collecting the required samples yesterday, some of you inadvertently missed going to see them and that means they will be collecting them now and that will include everyone so if yours is taken again, it will not matter. Better twice than not at all." Said Cadiston and returned to the hallway to rejoin his waiting DS. "Talk to me, Mac, what have you found?"

"It all looks very strange, Cadders, so best you look for yourself. I have checked each stair and found traces of blood on only a few so they must be the ones that he most probably struck in the alleged fall. To me, it looks as though he did not fall but sort of rolled because to my knowledge, if you fall down stairs, you either slide down on your back or head first on your front and do not roll or tumble. Now, to my mind, when coming down stairs, you walk to one side and hold the rail. If you are falling, you try to hang on to try and stop yourself but there are no signs of that. These stairs are quite wide and when you look, the blood splats are all in the middle of the stair as if he came straight down. I thought to myself, if he was pushed, then there would be some scuff marks at the top of the stairs but I found none and that seemed suspicious. Well, to my mind anyhow. There were a few that probably came from his shoes but no other scuffs. Now this is what I wanted you to see ... What I did find was these marks on the floor against the wall that look like something had been dragged, thought them to look a bit strange."

"Good work, Mac, taken pictures, lots of pictures?" Asked Cadiston.

"I have and that sounds like the ambulance and a team of forensics arriving. That was the first thing I did seconds after we arrived so hope I did right." Said Mac. Cadiston smiled. "Make a detective of you yet, my friend."

"Hopefully but not as good and with such perception as you though." Said Mac. "You will get there. Now, before the ambulance team remove the body we had better get back downstairs as I want you to have a good look at the crime scene and tell me if you notice anything." Cadiston said.

"It does not seem that you are new to this as you have got it all mapped out like you have been doing for years." Mac said and smiled.

"Just takes thinking, Mac, photographs of the body done Mac." Asked Cadiston. Standing beside the body, he stared at James as he lay exactly how he had fallen. "Took pics from different angles to get every aspect. Sorry Cadders, I can see nothing untoward, you will have to tell me." "First, take a good look at the shoe laces. That is what I noticed when we first saw the body." Said Cadiston. Mac did this and after a long stare, he said. "One tied, the other one untied so looks like he may have tripped on it." "Notice anything else about the lace?" Asked Cadiston and Mac looked closer. "Nope, don't think so." "Look at the right lace, it is tied securely while the left lace is partially untied so why secure one and not the other if you are about to descend a staircase? Now look at how much lace is showing." Cadiston offered. "You have a good eye, I would not have spotted that small detail if you had not pointed it out to me. It looks as though it was untied after the fall and that throws suspicion straight away. Why tie one and leave the other partly untied especially if you are about to descend a stair case?" Mac said. "Make a note, Mac, that the untied lace is undamaged. If you look very closely at it, there is no sign of it being stood on or damaged in any way. If you stand heavily onto a lace, it will often break under the pressure and if it does not break, it will show signs of being crushed or frayed. These laces are still intact and if you look at the soles, you will notice that these shoes are brand new and I would say by the state of the soles, only worn once. There is a slight scuff mark which probably occurred at the top of the stairs where you spotted the scuffs. I do not think that young man is right in what he said, James did not die from falling and did not fall at all but was pushed down the stairs after his neck was broken up there." He pointed and continued. "At the top. He was already dead and therefore limp and that is why the body rolled. Now look closely at the suit of metal." Cadiston waited for Mac too have a good look.

"Correct me if I am wrong but the angle it is lying across the body tells me that he could not have struck his head on it and there is no blood or skin tissue on the metal." Mac said. "Spot on, Mac, and well observed. If he had struck it in the fall it would be in a different position. the way it lays across him it signifies that it was pushed over after he lay on the floor. As you rightly said, there is no blood or skin tissue on it." Cadiston tapped his pen on his notebook. "Look at the head wound." "On the right side, got it. If he had struck the armour, it would be on the left side." Mac said. "Well spotted, it takes a keen eye, Mac, to see what others miss. Now all we need to do is find out how it was done and by whom. Now we move on, look at the injury to his neck, Mac, and tell me what you see." He looked carefully, trying to see what Cadiston was seeing. "I agree, he may have been pushed but again, you are seeing something that I am missing." "Look carefully at the marks on his neck, stand here a moment and I will demonstrate. I think that someone struck him first, hence the scream and the injury to his head, then attacked him from behind like this, hence the muffled scream, and in the process snapping his neck. The body could not be left at the top so to make it look like it was an accident, they pushed him down the stairs and then somehow got down the stairs quickly and untied the lace after the fall. Whoever it was knew exactly how to break the neck and did it all within a two minute gateway, that tells me they must have known how long it would take Jennifer to get to the top of the stairs and as she did not see them, they had just disappeared and nice dark corner over there." Said Cadiston. "See Cadders, you have seen all that from just observing the scene –. And me? Well, still stumbling in the dark." Said Mac. "You will get there. Now look at the fingers, especially the nails." He knelt beside James and studied them.

262

"Looks like something under the nails on his right hand, could be –. Yes, I think it is skin or Flesh." Said Mac. "Well observed, forensics and a post-mortem will determine it but I think that you have cracked it. Now, who had scratches?" Asked Cadiston. "Kansas did and on the right side of his neck. I do not want to jump to any conclusion but looks suspicious. Something else, lack of scratches at the top of the stairs, Kansas is wearing soft shoes, trainers in fact." Observed Mac. "Good work, Mac. See, you can make a detective, all it takes is careful investigation and use of the eyes and sometimes the nose. Now we have done all that we can so best we hand over to Jooners and let the forensic team do their survey. All yours." Said Cadiston. "Thanks, Cadders." Said Jooners as he organised his team. Moving away from the area that the forensic team would investigate, Mac voiced his opinion on what he thought had occurred and smiled just before he spoke. "I think that he was attacked and killed at the top of the stairs. To try and make it look like an accident, the perpetrator pushed the lifeless body down the stairs and when he fell, he did not strike that old suit of metal so his assailant, who moved very quickly, then pushed it over onto him after the alleged fall and that could be his mistake."

"Well spotted, Mac, and why do you think that?" Asked Cadiston.

"The angle. If he had hit it in the –, I will say fall –, then it would be laying in a different position and not as it is directly on top of him. Plus, the injury to his head is on the right but if he had struck the suit of armour, it would be on the left. Someone deliberately pushed the metal suit over to make it look like it was that which had broken his neck." Mac said. "Well spotted." Said Cadiston.

The ambulance had arrived twenty minutes before the team of forensic officers and they had to wait before they could attend to the body. With forensics on the scene, they wasted no time in starting their investigation so that the body could be removed. "I would like to have a full post-mortem on the body, Jake, so if you can tell Charles for me." Cadiston said. "Will do, DCI"

Said Jake. With the body on board, they left. In the blue room, the family waited so he went to see them. "The forensic team are carrying out their investigation so no one must enter the hallway at this point in time. I see that Kansas is missing so one more thing, while the forensic team are carrying out their investigation we will take a walk in the garden to gather our thoughts before we leave so if you see us walking about, do not be alarmed it is all part of our ongoing investigation. I will speak with you again when our forensic team has completed their survey." He turned and with Olito and Francis taking the required samples, he with Mac at his side then went into the garden. "We will have plenty of reading and evaluations to do back at the station but a visit to the garden first." Cadiston said. "The garden, but why do we –. Don't answer that, the rose pots and bushes to see if Kansas was telling the truth and if he could see the family from his alleged position around the corner." Said Mac. "Exactly, I strongly believe that he was lying on all counts. I looked closely at the scratches on his neck and they looked far too deep and straight to be scratches from a thorny rose bush, too deep and too wide, to my thinking." Said Cadiston. "Maybe caused by fingers digging in." Mac suggested. "Precisely and that we will learn from the post-mortem, forensics, and the DNA that Francis and Olito have collected." Said Cadiston.

Without another word they walked briskly toward the front door but before going outside, Cadiston diverted and gazed at the family that were all sitting silently. "Look at them, Mac, and tell me that butter would not melt in their mouth." Said Cadiston. "Some maybe but not all of them and I think that if I had to, then I could pick them out." Replied Mac. "Good, we are gaining information and soon we will need to collate all the fingerprints, DNA, blood samples, and shoe sizes purely to eliminate the innocent from the guilty. WPC Rendham and WPC Paverson, will you remain with the family please until forensics have finished. Then, if we can think of nothing else that needs to be asked, we can leave." Said Cadiston. "Will do, Sir." "The garden, Mac." Then, while being carefully watched by Kansas, they made their way into the garden without saying another word. They walked slowly around the rose garden, inspecting every pot and every rose for signs of a major disturbance but found none. They inspected every pot and the ground where the contents would be spilled if a pot had been turned over, there was none, they took samples of the chalky residue on the pots for analysis. They then turned their attention to any other possible area where the incident could have occurred but there were none that had been disturbed. Also, the distance from the area to the foot of the stairs was too great. They checked where he had stood and again, this raised suspicion. "I think he told us a massive series of lies, Cadders, not one rose has been disturbed or broken and if they had been, there would be some soil debris on the ground. We have looked at every pot within the distance that would be needed to get inside quickly and further away and not one has been disturbed. From where he said he stood, he could not see the family." Said Cadiston. "Very true, Mac, and from the deepness of the scratches, a rose would need mighty large thorns to cause that much damage. Three straight lines, Mac, it says fingernails not rose bush to me. We will wait to get the DNA results and the result from under James's fingernails as that will provide us with what we need. Then Mac, we will have some real, concrete evidence, possibly enough to bring about a prosecution and conviction. While we wait for forensics to conduct their survey, let's return to the Manor and do some writing. As we used the study to carry out our interviews yesterday, I do not think that there will be any objection to us using it again." Cadiston said and they headed inside. They made their way to the study and once settled Cadiston said. "This a sad situation for the family. There were three sons and only one is still alive, they are being slowly cut down and if he is not connected to the murders then we must think that he is on the hit list. Two daughters and only one of them remaining alive so we have Grant Mandaten and Lizabeth Kaysten who are both blood family. One wife remains and that is Malcolm's wife, Greta, and one husband and that is Tomas who is Lizabeth's husband but a Kaysten, not a Mandaten. Seems strange that all the families apart from Lizabeth's have lost someone. Is it because she is behind it or because they are Kaysten. Now, for the grandchildren –. I believe that there would have been six but sadly three of them are deceased." "Six Cadders? I can recall only five with two deceased." Said Mac. "Three deceased, Mac. Gloria, James, and sadly Bonnie's unborn child. We must never forget that poor little infant who was not given the chance to live." Cadiston said. "That is very true and is so very sad but as you rightly said, the poor little infant must never be forgotten and another thing, the child's murderer must be brought to justice." Mac agreed. "Exactly." Said Cadiston and they finished writing their notes. "Well, there it is. As you said, so few Mandaten's left. Grant, Lizabeth, Lowell, and Jennifer, all born Mandaten. Just four blood kin so a very short list." Remarked Macswee. A knock on the door made them look up. "Sorry to disturb you, Cadders, but we have had a good look at the fall site now and we feel that there is a very strong likelyhood that the deceased did not fall but was pushed. By all the signs and marks that we have examined at the top, on the stairs, and at the bottom, we think that there was a minor struggle at the top of the stairs before the limp body fell. If someone trips and falls, they would do everything within their power to stop themselves from falling. There were no marks to indicate this. The blood splats on a few of the stairs, samples of which have been taken and will undoubtedly match the victims, were all central which again denotes that this was not a fall. We found no other blood. We examined the shoelaces and removed them for a full forensic examination before the body was taken away. First sight indicates no trip, we could find no sign of it being trodden on but as I said we have taken it for a closer examination in the lab. There are several scratch marks on the landing floor near the wall, possibly where a piece of furniture once stood and was dragged away. Hope that will help you, you will get a full written report but as you were here, we thought that you would like to know. Our guess and from the evidence that we have seen, it was no accident but murder, and the post-mortem will tell the cause of death so leave you with it. I will get the full report to you as soon as possible but as you know, we have got quite a few to write up. See you back at the station." Jooners turned and walked swiftly down the long corridor to his waiting colleagues. "No fall then according to our boys from forensics." Mac said. "Didn't think it was an accident. From the moment we saw the unfortunate lad and I had surveyed the crime scene, I instantly had my suspicions. We now have another murder on our hands, Mac." Cadiston said.

"Any suspects for this one, Cadders?" Asked Mac. "Possibly but we need much more evidence before we can put anyone in cuffs and when that happens, we can delve deeper to secure a conviction. I feel very strongly that all these family murders are linked and if we can find that link it will help lead us to the person or persons that we are looking for. It is my opinion that we are looking for at least two perpetrators of these heinous crimes and when there is so much wealth at stake in this estate, it points to someone in the family that stands to gain the most. Greed, Mac, is a key element in these cases and that is where we need to look first so let us take a close look at the family for starters. We will need to obtain a full and current family tree with those that are deceased and those that are still here. At some point, we will pay a visit to the ancestry library and get a list of the complete family with husbands, wives, and all the derivatives, plus any other name that may be of interest. As it is a long process, Mac, we need to get those in the know to do it for us. We must have a search for a full family history as there may be a skeleton or two in the closet. I think the hospital maternity records of infant births and deaths could bring up a clue so will need to make a full investigation into them as well. On the surface, this appears to be a case of desire, greed, jealousy, falseness, and lies and possibly a systematic annihilation of the whole Mandaten family." Said Cadiston. "So, to put it all in a nutshell, we have our work cut out for us." Mac said. "That we do so best we get the nutcrackers working. Still want to tag along, Mac?" Cadiston asked. "You bet I do, together we will crack it. Well, not quite right, you will crack it and I will just follow your lead." Mac's remark made Cadiston smile.

They made their way back to the lounge and as they entered, every eye was on them. Mac was becoming more aware of the hostile atmosphere between them and even though he was a police officer, it made him feel rather uncomfortable. "We are done for the time being so, we will leave now but be assured that we will return when we have collated all the evidence that has been gathered." Said Cadiston. Grant stood up and looking directly at Cadiston when he asked his question. "Evidence gathered? Such as, Cadiston? Be specific!" "As to that, I cannot answer but in time you will be told so we will leave it at that. WPCs Rendham and Paverson, have you taken the un-obtained samples for us?" Asked Cadiston. "With reluctance from three recipients, yes, we have them all. In fact, to ensure that none were missed, we have covered everyone." Said WPC Paverson. "Excellent work, WPC Paverson. Kansas, just one more question before we leave." Cadiston looked him in the eye. "What question? I have already told you everything." Said Kansas. "Just step over here, please." Kansas did as he was told. "You said you got the scratches from a rose when you knocked into a pot, is that correct?" Asked Cadiston. "It is so what are you getting at?" Kansas snapped.

"It is just that none are out of place." Cadiston said calmly. "No, they wouldn't be because the gardener was there and straightened it." Said Kansas.

"Of course, why didn't we think of that, sorry to have asked you again, sir." Said Cadiston. Kansas walked away feeling that all was good. "Thank you all for your time and as there is nothing more at present, we will leave now." He turned towards the door, followed by his team and they returned to their motor vehicle. Seconds later, they were driving up the long private road. Cadiston glanced at his watch. "Four forty-nine, been here all day, team. We have post-mortems being carried out and a lot of forensic, lab and a firearm's reports to be completed. When we have them to hand, we can move forward."

"Everything is a big help especially –." At that moment, his phone rang. He answered. "Cadiston." "Hi Cadders, Charles here, forensic mortuary. We have got your results on Malcolm

Mandaten's post-mortem and I can tell you that it makes for an interesting read. I appreciate that it is a bit late in the day but I know your keenness to have this result so can you get over here so I can show you?" "We have just left Mandaten Manor and will need to drop my WPCs at the station so if you can hang on, Mac and myself will be with you in about thirty-five to fifty minutes." Said Cadiston. "Be waiting," Said Charles and the phone line went dead.

"Drop the girls at the station and then on to the mortuary for us, Mac." Said Cadiston and they were on the way. This is what he had been waiting for from the moment that he first attended the site of Malcolm's death. He had always been convinced by what he had observed at Devil's Dyke and with the evidence that he had found there coupled with his suspicions, he knew that this was not a simple accident. Standish had sidelined and silenced him, therefore, delaying a full investigation but now he was free of him and would prove that Malcolm's death was not an accident but a very clever attempt to make it look like one, and now he would have his proof. He wanted to ask Mac to put his foot down on the accelerator pedal but thought better of it as he was a police officer and he had to observe the speed limit just as everyone else was required to do. At the mortuary, the car door was opened whilst the car was still moving. There was an air of excitement around him and he was out of the car before the ignition was switched off. He was in a hurry and with Mac close at his heels, he was almost in a run. He had waited for this and wanted to read the full report and see the body again and then the door would be wide open for him to concentrate on collecting more evidence to prove that his first suspicions were well-founded. "Hi Charles, Samantha, you already know Mac." Said Cadiston. "That we do." Said Samantha. "What have you got for us?" Asked Cadiston. "Samantha, can you bring the report from the office please?" Asked Charles. Thirty seconds passed and Cadiston held it in his hand. He gave his wife a quick peck on the cheek. "Thanks precious, now we will just have a quick read to establish the facts and we will read it fully later when we can sit quietly and take it all in. A quick read will suffice for now. After we have had a read, perhaps you can show us the body and exactly what you have found. Words and a visual combined will surely help to strengthen my suspicions about this death. If it were up to me, Mac would have been with me and an investigation would already have been started and lives could have been saved."

He then opened the file and they began to read, they did not go into great depth but skimmed the surface to enable them to get the facts and to form a picture. The report read:

In the examination of the body of Mr. Malcolm Mandaten, we noticed some bruising marks on his arms that were not concurrent with falling from his horse.

"Just as I suspected." Said Cadiston and they read on.

Certain phrases caught their eye.

... found to be caused by someone's fingers gripping his arms.

... did not fall but was pulled from his horse ...

"Also just as I suspected." Mumbled Cadiston.

... heavy bruising in the small of his back ... possibly made by a knee being pressed into it to hold him down.

"He was strong, they would need to do that."

... exact position to administer the death blows manually.

"All as I expected so far" Said Cadiston.

... not the result of him being dragged but struck repeatedly by the weapon used to cause his death.

"And thought you had got away with it, thought wrong! I am coming after you. Sorry Mac, we are coming after you, whoever you are."

... carried out a simulation and it was found after very careful examination of the piece of masonry and the head wound to determine the angle in which it was struck, that it could only have been administered manually and deliberately by a person unknown ...

"This all substantiates my suspicions that Malcolm's death was no accident, read on Mac." Said Cadiston.

... unusually thick skull and the extent of the damage denotes that there were a series of blows to cause the amount of damage to the bone.

We estimate a minimum of three, all directed deliberately and accurately at the same spot, namely the base of the skull.

"Extra thick skull ... Interesting and whoever did this must have known that fact." Said Cadiston.

"Points to family, friends, or someone in the medical profession." Said Mac. ... *the rear and near the base of the skull, struck with such force causing a large fracture and a massive bleed. The blows also damaged the spinal cord by cutting it with bone splinters, therefore, paralysing Mr. Mandaten. It is our findings that denote Mr. Mandaten was in fact dead before he was dragged to the spot where his body was found.*

"So, Charles, Samantha, you think he was dead before being dragged? If that is the case, it would explain the heavy bloodstain where he was pulled off and bludgeoned and the lesser amount where he ended up. What we are reading proves beyond any shadow of a doubt that being dragged most certainly did not cause the massive trauma to his head and before you ask, yes, I do have the rein. Mac has it on the investigation incidents board." Said Cadiston.

... examined a series of scenarios and none of the angles he could have been dragged matched or would have resulted in him being struck at the rear and base of his skull, as is the case. It could not possibly have happened accidentally and only by a series of blows being struck manually. Detective Cadiston retrieved the offending piece of masonry and upon examination of the skull indentation, it matches exactly with the said piece of masonry.

"And just as well we did as that is a major piece of evidence." Said Cadiston and they bypassed the conclusion going straight to the verdict:

Verdict

Mr. Malcolm Mandaten was the victim of a cold and calculated pre-meditated murder by a person or persons unknown.

Signed
Mr. Charles Dennasen – Mrs. Samantha Cadiston

"Damn you Standish! Any further evidence will be marred and smudged after the rain. It will not be easy but there is no doubt that we will have to get all the available evidence from that site. Samantha, can you think of anything you saw when we got the murder weapon, apart from the sample of white chalky soil?" Asked Cadiston.

"Not a thing, sorry." She said.

"Any fingerprints on the masonry?" Asked Cadiston.

"Plenty but none that are eligible, far too smudged in the blood and that is another thing, one strike would not leave it completely covered." Said Charles. "My thought also. Now, let us see just what we have got so far –. The murder weapon, namely a piece of bloodied masonry, a piece of rein that looks like it was cut, and a white chalky soil sample. There are my footprint casts but there has got to be more. There is something up there that is crucial to the case and we need to find it. We need to get up there and have a good search. Plus, we need to see Herbert at some point and get the rest of this rein, then it can be determined if it broke or was cut and my guess is it was cut. Fancy another drive to the Manor with Mac and me, Samantha? But only if Charles can spare you for a couple of hours." Cadiston looked at Charles.

"We have four more post-mortems to do so you may have to wait for them. Sadie, Sammie, Walter, and Gloria and another came in this afternoon but if you don't mind waiting a bit longer for them, be my guest." Said Charles.

"What do you think, Samantha?"Asked Cadiston. "I think that I can be far more productive here with Charles than up there at the Devil's Dyke. You have Mac to go with you so I think that is the best way to go." Said Samantha.

"You are right. Mac, at first light, we are going to Mandaten. Thanks both, see you at home Samantha." Said Cadiston and they left.

On the morning of Wednesday, 8th October, Mac was there to pick up Cadiston bright and early and on the way to the Manor, Cadiston made his call to Jeremiah. Jeremiah had expected another call at some point and with his quick thinking, came up with a good reason to be at the gate. Once inside, they made their way directly to the old ruins and Devil's Dyke. "Can I help in any way?" Asked Jeremiah. "Well if you like, you could make a search of the old ruins while we examine this area. You are looking for a bundle or package, maybe even a box but if you find such an item don't touch it under any circumstances! Come and get us." "Will do, Detective." Jeremiah turned and hurried away.

"Now then Mac, Malcolm would have ridden up from that direction so that is where we will start our search." They made their way back along the track until he was satisfied that they were far enough and then turned and walked slowly back toward the site where Malcolm was found.

"The signs are not as prominent now, we will continue to follow the hoof prints and look for any irregularities in their pattern." He said. As they followed the track, their eyes were fixed. "They all look pretty much the same as when I first looked so far. At least those that have not been obliterated. From what we can see, it looks like he was walking the horse at this point." They continued to walk forward when Mac stopped him in his tracks. "Not now, Cadders, over here they are getting smudged and uneven as though the horse sensed something." "We are close to where he supposedly fell and although smudged, these prints appear to be going around in a circle and they are difficult to pick out. But if I am not mistaken, there are footprints mixed in with them. I knew that we should have had forensics on the day. I had a word with Jooners, he said they could not do anything just now but would keep it in mind." Mac was on his knees and joining the sound of the constant bird song was the intermittent clicking of his camera. Cadiston was going to mix his plaster when he had all the photographs but knew it would be a waste of time. "That is the impression where he supposedly fell." He made the sign as if denoting inverted commas with his fingers. "Where he was pulled off his horse. At this point, he must have still been gripping the reins when the blows were struck." They carefully checked the indentation and even now they could clearly see a dark stain where the head would have been and knew that it could only be blood. "I did get a sample of that for analysis. After this the horse was forced to drag his dead body, leaving the trail in a dead straight and continuous line-up to the masonry. Now the old ruins are over there and if I am not mistaken, this is too far for it to fall unaided. There are a few footprints on the near side but not clear enough to take a mould of them. Would have been if it had been done when I first asked." Said Cadiston."I have photographs of them but as you said, not as clear.I have taken plenty of pics so that they overlap and once they are in the computer and pieced together with your Samantha's pictures, maybe we will be able to see a clearer aspect." Said Mac. They continued to search the area. "This is where I took the casts of the small prints the other day, now they are virtually ineligible, and just look at the hoofprints from this point. Much deeper and much more prominent. I will ask Jeremiah when he gets back as he knows horses." Said Cadiston. Mac continued to take his pictures while Cadiston looked around the area of what he strongly suspected was the scene of a murder. Satisfied that he had taken enough pictures, he rejoined him and for a few minutes. They summed up their findings and their thoughts.

"Now then, I think that he rode up here from that direction and was met by a person or persons unknown to us but someone that he knew, hence the horse is only walking." Suggested Cadiston."He did not suspect but on the other hand it was early in the morning so may have been surprised to find them Here." Continued Mac. "He was going to ride on but they grabbed his rein hence the reason the horse went in circles." Cadiston said. "He was then grabbed and pulled from his horse, landing heavily there on his face right where you are taking your cast." Mac added. "A knee in the back made sure that he was not about to get up and hopefully the cast will be good enough to show his face." Cadiston went on. "Then, whack! And his skull was crushed. They led the horse with him still gripping the reins." Mac clapped his hands for emphasis."Instead of forcing his dead hand open, probably for fear of breaking a finger or two, they cut the reins." Cadiston said.

"Then someone really spooked the horse, sending it in a panic down the road onto Rudslip meadow and back riderless to the stable." Mac finished.

"You know Mac, I think between us, we have discovered how it was done. Now comes the task of discovering who carried it out and it is not impossible that two or possibly more of these cases can be solved together." Said Cadiston. "I have not got very good plaster casts but at least the guilty parties are not to know that and this facial cast has come out far better than I expected. Now, Jeremiah is on his way back. Maybe he has found something." Said Mac. "Have you found anything suspicious-looking?" Asked Cadiston. "Sorry, not a thing. I went as far into the old ruin as was safe to do as the old masonry is very unstable. I looked for any sign of the pieces of fallen masonry being moved to hide something underneath but the way the ivy and moss have taken over there was not a stone out of place, so to speak. At least none that I could see but then I do not have a trained eye." Said Jeremiah.

"No matter, now tell us what do you make of these hoofprints?" Asked Cadiston. He followed them for a good distance, then returned to where they were waiting. "Even though they are faded, it is clear to see, from back there they are as a calm walking horse. Then there they get jumbled up as though circling, then again walking from the indentation to where Malcolm was found lying. They start here at a walk, then held here stationary. I can tell that by the ground disturbance that they moved a bit and from here the tracks are that of a horse in a full panic. You can see how the ground is disturbed. The horse must have been released when it got too hard to hold and going on what Jacob said, Rudslip has signs of a panicking bolting animal. Whatever put the frighteners into Thundist did the trick and going by what Pops said, he was like a mad horse when he found him." Said Jeremiah. "Thanks Jeremiah, that is very helpful. Now, there is one more thing before we leave, I need the reins that were on Thundist when Malcolm was riding him. Said Cadiston.

"Thought you might so I brought it with me and got it here." Jeremiah said and unhooked a bag from his saddle and passed it to Mac. "That is us done then, we will keep this area cordoned off for now as I have not given up on our forensic team giving it the once over. Thanks for your help, Jeremiah, and remember keep it to yourself." He gestureded closing a zip on his lips and a thumbs-up to signify that he understood. The car moved slowly down the old road and did not speed up until it was on the private road that led from the Manor. Seconds later, they were on the main road.

"We have gathered some evidence, Mac, but I feel there is more to be found, something really scared that horse, a waved blanket maybe?" "Or someone dressed as a ghostly figure, maybe the Lady Mary?" Suggested Mac. "We can rule nothing out, Mac, and if there were two people, it would need to be a larger man and a smaller man or woman working together by the size of the small footprints." Cadiston said. "But who? That will be the hardest thing to find out." Said Mac.

"Maybe, Mac, but when there is an amount of evidence on hand and the guilty party or parties know that we hold this, that is when they can easily slip up. I am not completely certain where to look for suspects although I do have my suspicions." Said Cadiston. "What have we got then? The casts of the hoof, face and footprints, the piece of masonry, which is a major piece of evidence, the two stained soil samples that are more than likely Malcolm's blood, and the chalky white soil sample." Said Mac. "Now, that last one is possibly the best one. All we need to know is where it comes from and that on its own could lead us to the culprit. We now have clear evidence and proof that at least two, no, three murders have been committed here at Mandaten Manor: Bonnie and her unborn child and Malcolm." Said Cadiston.

"When the post-mortem results are complete on Sammie, Walter, Gloria, and Sadie, I am sure that we will have four more murders to investigate. When Kevin's gun is fully examined, possibly another one and that will make eight in total." Said Mac. "Nine, Mac, James has unfortunately just joined the headcount. We had better get our investigation going in-depth and start asking many more of the right questions if we are to find the murderer or murderers. Back to the station and let us see if any of those reports are ready for us."

For the rest of the day, Mac and Cadiston reviewed all that they had found and knew so far but waited eagerly for more reports to reach them so that they could investigate, question, and possibly make an early arrest. They both wondered what the next day, Thursday 9th of October, would bring to help them along.

"Mother, I cannot be sure but while I was walking the dogs through the woods, there was activity going on up at the Old Manor. I think it could have been the police again. I saw Jeremiah riding across the field and watched him open the gates, then saw a car driving through them onto the Old Manor Road. What do you think they were doing if it was them?" Asked Kansas. "I don't know, Kansas, what could possibly be there for them to continue looking for? That Standish said an accident so there can be nothing for them to find. They were probably opening the area up again as the case is to be closed so it is probably nothing at all." Lizabeth said. "What is that you say, Son?" Tomas asked. "Maybe another visit from the police up at the Old Manor, Father." Kansas answered. "What could that be for, Son? Harry Standish had closed the case and there is nothing for them to find, is there?" Said Tomas. "Find? What could there possibly be for them to find, Tomas? It was an accident." Said Lizabeth. "Err, nothing Lizabeth. I should think there is nothing, is there Son?" Said Tomas looking at Kansas. "Not a thing, Father, nothing for them to find. Just that young detective trying to find what there is not. Now, say nothing more about it. I can hear footsteps and we are about to be joined." Said Kansas and they fell silent.

Chapter Nine

Steadily They Fall

"Hello Aunt Lizabeth, have you had a nice walk with the dogs?" Asked Jennifer.

"Kansas took the dogs while I had a leisurely stroll with your uncle but yes, it was very pleasant Jennifer, thank you."

"Good." Said Jennifer. They were now being joined by the rest of the family. "I was wondering if you could tell me, Grandfather, what do you think they have discovered so far about Aunt Bonnie? They were here a long while." Jennifer asked.

"To that, I do not know, Jennifer, but what I do know is that Cadiston may be a young, eager new detective and he may be inexperienced but he is a natural and a very clever detective. I, for one, know that he will search out and find the truth behind all these deaths for us. He has the right aptitude and looks at everything, however small, then he deciphers it and holds onto the relevant and discards the none-relevant. You can be sure that he will sort out the truth from the lies and fact from fiction. He will discover what has been happening to our family, then he will eventually arrive at the correct result. There can be no instant fix, these things do take time." Said Lord Mandaten.

"Even if it is or they have been covered up, he will need evidence so what if he finds none?" Asked Lowell.

"I am positive, my dear boy, that he will find the evidence that he needs, however small. He has a trained eye, Lowell, and he sees what we do not and if your father was murdered, in fact, it may be the case in all the recent deaths that we have had recently, then Cadiston will solve them all. He will find that out and bringing the guilty party to trial, whoever they are and in doing so, will get his conviction." Said Lord Mandaten.

"I agree, Grandfather." Said Lowell.

"Conviction, evidence … Bah! Everything was settled with Standish and now we are being put through more hell by this Cadiston chap. He should have left it well alone." Said Grant.

"That is what you say, Grant. That may satisfy you but not us. We want the truth, no matter how painful it is. If these deaths were accidents, he will discover that and if these deaths were murders, then he will discover that. To my mind, the only ones who want it all hushed-up are those with something to hide." Said Lowell.

"Lowell, you are a stupid boy! We all know that if we faced the truth, these deaths were all accidents so why drag it out further?" Snapped Grant.

"To find the truth." Lowell snapped back.

"Father, should we be talking like that especially in front of Jennifer? Surely they could not all be murders and I am afraid if they are –, Oh! I do not want to think that they are." Lizabeth said.

"You can have your thoughts, Lizabeth, and we will have ours and Cadiston will have his." Said Jennifer. "Well, let us hope if they are murders, he hurries up and finds the killer. Aunt Bonnie died on Monday, 22nd of September, and today is Wednesday, 8th October, that is just over two weeks ago." Said Lowell.

"Do you think he has found any evidence or if he comes up with a solution for Aunt Bonnie then the other deaths may well have a quick conclusion? And do not worry for me, Aunt Lizabeth, I am involved in all this just as much as the rest of you are." Said Jennifer.

"Well said and to answer your question, we can but hope that is the case, Jennifer. You may only be ten but you are very sensible and have a very mature head on your shoulders, my dear girl. But now it is almost time for our evening meal so best we all get ready." Said Lord Mandaten.

"Just for once my dear husband, especially after what has occurred and there are so few of us, will you not allow a bit less formality just for tonight?" Lady Mandaten said.

Lord Mandaten thought for a moment, then smiled. "Just for tonight then Florence, no formality tonight, family. By the grace of your loving mother and grandmother. Bradinham, some aperitifs before dinner please."

"Certainly my Lord." Said Bradinham and a selection was produced. After they had all made their choice, they sat quietly with their thoughts. There were fewer now but they eyed each other with suspicion, each remembering the events of the past two weeks. There was no idle chatter as they each had their own thoughts on what had taken place in such a short space of time.

"We are being whittled down one at a time, Grandfather. First we lost Aunt Bonnie and her unborn baby and the very next day, our father, then on the day of the show we lost Uncle Kevin, Aunt Sammie, Uncle Walter, and Cousin Gloria. Then Aunt Sadie and now we have lost Cousin James. That makes eight, no, nine." Jennifer said.

"One at a time you say, Jennifer, all except Sammie and her family, they all died horribly together." Lizabeth said.

"That is true, Aunt Lizabeth, but Cadiston will discover the truth and solve it." Jennifer said.

"Just listen to you all, talk and more talk and always the same thing, Cadiston will solve it. Why can't you get it into your thick skulls that there is nothing to solve, nothing at all?! Just take a good look at them, James was a stupid boy and had a careless accident. He tripped on his untied shoelace, anyone could see that he just got careless like his father. No need to itemize them all but from a straightforward suicide they all amount to tragic accidents, from Bonnie to James. That is all I can see and nothing more sinister than that. At least Standish had the right idea and got on with the job and concluded the case straight away to alleviate additional pain for the bereaving family. But as for this Cadiston, he is just dragging things out and trying to make a name for himself and make something out of nothing. Young and inexperienced Father said, well I think that he is just out to make a name for himself at our expense." Said Grant.

"I suppose you think that all these deaths in the family, including past and present, in fact every one of them that appear suspicious, were all just accidents then, Grant?" Lizabeth asked.

"Accidents? Sure they were all accidents. Except Sadie's and that was suicide. It sticks out like a sore thumb so of course, they are all accidents, Lizabeth." He swallowed his drink and belched Before continuing. "Just a mere coincidence that they have all happened within two weeks. Nothing sinister at all, just a co-incidence. They should have left Standish to deal with them all, then it would all be over. I am sick of hearing about it so now let us forget about the dead and concentrate on the living. We can do nothing for the dead, they are gone but the rest of us are the living remnants of the Mandaten clan, and at least for us we can." Said Grant.

"That is very cold and callous, Grant. We have had most of our family wiped out over the years and all under suspicious cir-cumstances. More recently, two of our immediate family members have been wiped out, your brother Kevin and your sister Sammie, all within two weeks. We have lost your brother, Malcolm, and your wife, Bonnie, with her unborn child. Nine deaths, Grant, do you feel nothing for any of them?! What about those of us that are left? Have you no feelings for them and for their safe-ty if a killer or killers is on the loose? Or are you so cold-heart-ed?" Lizabeth said.

"I do not know how I feel, Lizabeth, all I know is that I am sick and tired of all the talking about it. What has happened can-not be undone and we can do nothing for them as they are dead so leave it at that." Said Grant coldly.

"It is hard for us all but none of us are without feelings for the family that we have lost and are not afraid to show that we care. You do not have to act big and tough, Grant, for that will surely be your downfall. Believe me, son, I have many more years un-der my belt than you and have seen the result of false bravado." Said Lord Mandaten.

"Alright Father, I do not need a lecture or to hear about your time in the army. I care but all this talk about it will not bring any of them back and it gets me down. I do believe that all the deaths were accidents but I also wonder who the next family member will be to fall victim to an accident. It only takes a moment's lapse in concentration like Malcolm, Kevin, James … In fact, all of them. A moment's lapse by riding when he should not have been, overloading a rifle and not tying a shoelace. Sammie and her family were in the wrong place at the wrong time and shouldn't have been anywhere near the archery area or those flying arrows so their own stupid faults. All accidents and one suicide but I have no desire to talk about them anymore." Grant said.

"I agree with Grant, we should accept what has happened openly and not keep harping on it." Said Demmie. "Thought you might, Demmie." Said Chad.

"So, what if I do?" She snapped in reply. "Not a thing, not a single thing." Said her husband.

"Well, our dinner is ready so to the table, family, and let us enjoy our meal in peace and in silence. Fresh salmon tonight so in we go." Said Lord Mandaten. They followed their parents in and once seated, the meal service began. They looked around the table, counting the empty chairs. Now only eleven seats were taken up, the vacant chairs tipped onto the table as a sign of respect. "Eight down, eleven to go." Said Grant in a joking manner.

"That is not funny, not funny at all." Said Greta.

"So, who is laughing? I was merely stating a fact, Greta." Said Grant. "In very poor taste, son, now silence while we eat." Said Lord Mandaten. They all obeyed their father's instruction and the complete meal was then eaten in enforced silence. The clatter of cutlery was the only sound heard. No one had a word to say, it appeared that it had all been said before the meal had started. Even in the lounge, nothing was being said, giving the outward appearance that the family had all been dumb struck. It may have been silent but for some, the looks of evil continued.

It was now ten p.m and with their parents having already retired, the silence was finally broken. "I have had enough for one day and I am off to bed, night all." Said Lizabeth. Her husband agreed and rose, ready to leave with her. "Night Lizabeth, night Tomas." Said Chad. With a hand raised in a half-wave, they left. "I am done for as well, are you coming up with me, Demmie?" Asked Chad. She glanced toward Grant who nodded and gestured with his hand for her to go away. "Right with you, Chad, night then." She waited but all she received was a half-hearted wave.

"Well I am not a bit tired and it is a lovely clear evening so not bed for me. I think I will go for a walk. Anyone want to come along? Jennifer? Uncle Grant? Kansas? Anyone?" Asked Lowell. "Not a chance, Lowell." Replied his sister. "I am going up, are you coming, Mother?" Feeling the pain of losing her husband and sick of all the bickering, Greta did not reply but stood in silence ready to follow her daughter up the staircase.

"I am going to sit here and finish this bottle of brandy, you are on your own nephew." Said Grant. "Guess so." Said Lowell.

"Haven't you had sufficient brandy, Grant?" Greta asked. "Mind your own business, Greta." Snapped Grant. "Come, Mother, we will let him drink himself into a state of intoxication." Said Jennifer. "Shut up, Jennifer, and toddle off to bed with mummy." Grant moaned. Greta just shook her head and holding her daughter's hand, they turned to leave.

"Where will you walk, Lowell?" Asked Greta. "The usual mother, think I will head toward the stable block barn and the meadow behind it to see our resident barn owls and with a bit of luck, I may get some photographs of them." Said Lowell.

"They are a beautiful birds, son. Enjoy your walk. Now come along, Jennifer, unless you want to change your mind and go walk with your brother?" Greta asked. "Not a chance, Mother, my bed is calling me. Night Lowell, see you in the morning. Night Kansas, Uncle Grant." Said Jennifer.

There was no reply. They turned and left, leaving Grant with an empty brandy bottle on the table beside him and desperately hugging the nearly full bottle close to his chest to stop anyone taking it from him. Kansas was downing his Drambuie and had a serious look on his face.

"Are you sure that you won't come to see the birds, Kansas?" Asked Lowell.

"No thanks, Cousin, the only birds I want to see have two legs, arms and eyes but don't have feathers. Just going to finish this tipple, then I am off to my bed also."

Lowell left the lounge and after putting on his coat, he made his way to the side door. With the bolts undone and the key turned, he stepped outside and took a long deep breath of the cool night air.

"Right Mr. and Mrs. Barn Owl, my camera is loaded. Night vision is set so let us pay you a visit." And he was on his way.

Thursday morning seemed to come around slowly to them. As they stirred from their slumbers, they all felt refreshed. Once dressed, they made their way down to the breakfast room.

"Good morning, Jennifer." Chad said.

"Morning, Uncle Chadrick. I wondered, have you seen Uncle Grant this morning?" Then she sniggered.

"That I did, he is sleeping it off in the lounge and it smells just like the estate brewery in there. I think he finished the bottle he was cradling when we went up to bed and then got another so that means he drank a third one. There is an empty bottle on the floor beside his chair, another on the table, and he is still hugging the other empty one. We will let him sleep." Said Chad.

"Best thing. In my medical opinion If we wake him in his state, he will be like a bear with a very sore head and I, for one, do not wish to face an angry bear that." Said Kansas. "I think that applies to us all, Kansas." Replied Chad. With all the family in the breakfast room, Chad noticed that Kansas winced when he raised his right arm. "Problem with your arm Kansas?" Asked Chad.

"My arm? Oh yes, woke up this morning with it, a bit stiff. I must have laid awkwardly." Said Kansas. "You have some nasty looking scratches on your neck and your hand is cut but looks more like a rough gash. It also looks rather red and inflamed, you had better let someone have a look at that." Said Chad."Rose bushes did my neck and should have stuck to an electric razor instead of a wet shave." He then quickly changed the subject. "Cannot help but notice that Lowell is not down yet, he must have overslept. Wanted to ask about the barn owls, anyone seen him this morning?" Heads were shaking to signify no. "Not like my brother to be late for breakfast, I will go and knock on his door. Like you said, Kansas, he must have overslept after his

284

walk last night." Jennifer said and smiled as she almost skipped away. He called after her. "Hey Jennifer, tell him his breakfast is getting cold, if nothing else would get him up then that should make him hurry." They continued to chat while Jennifer went to raise her missing brother. Eight minutes later, she returned. "Knocked on the door for a while and as there was no reply, I went in. His bed looks like it has not been slept in just like with aunt Sadie which makes me worry so where is he, that is the question?" "Anyone know where he was going to walk last night?" asked Chad. "He said he wanted to see the resident barn owls." Said Kansas. "That is right, Kansas, he did just as we were about to go upstairs." Said Jennifer. "The owls, Jennifer of course, he always paid them a visit when we were all here?" said Chad. "Yes, he went to see them. Now I wish that I had gone with him." Said Jennifer. "Me also Jennifer, I am sure that he will be alright, Cousin." Kansas said. "I hope so, Kansas." Said Jennifer looking worried. "So that means the stable block barn and the meadow beyond so that is where we will look first. Maybe he fell asleep on a bale of straw while he was watching them. You coming with us to find him, Tomas?" enquired Chad looking at Tomas who sat listening but refraining to speak. "Of course, aren't you, Father? Kansas said in a domineering tone. "And I will be right with you, Uncle Chad. We wouldn't miss it for the world, would we Father?, Replied Kansas. This remark did not sit right with Chad. He thought for a moment but he did not challenge it and continued to think about the remark. They were about to leave when Alfred came in. "Sorry to disturb you at breakfast, Chad, but Herbert is at the side door and has asked to see you urgently. He is terribly distressed." "Be right there, Alfred." He did not hesitate and forgetting about his breakfast, he went straight away. When he set eyes on Herbert, he could see in an instant what Alfred had said was true. "Herbert, what is it that troubles you? Must be bad because normally you have a good glow in your cheeks but today your pallor is unusually pale. Plus, you have a worried frown on your brow." Said Chad. "It is terrible, Chad, just terrible but what in the blue blazes was

285

he doing alone in the stables especially with his fear of horses and especially at night?" Herbert stuttered.

"Fear of horses, that tells me everything! Only one person has that phobia so I guess that you are referring to nephew Lowell." Said Chad. "Aye, it is Master Lowell, Chad. You had better come and see but not the ladies, it is just too horrible for words." With Kansas and Tomas following close behind them, they hurried toward the stables. Along the way Chad asked. "Is he –." "Oh yes, he is quite dead, Chad. Hardly recognisable. In fact, totally unrecognisable, he is in one hell of a mess. The only way that I know it is him for sure is his name bracelet that had come off his wrist. What was he doing in the stable at night? There is nothing to see in there, only the horses. I just cannot understand why he went in there, what reason would he have? We all know that since his accident with that pony when he was only five years old, well, like I said –. We all know that since then he has this built-in fear and keeps well clear of them. It just makes no sense at all but if he wanted to see the horses to try and beat his fear, then he could see them during the day when we were all there to help him. Just makes no sense, no sense at all." Herbert rambled.

"He came out last night and went to see the barn owls and I just cannot see or understand him being in the stables either. As you said, after his incident with the pony when he was just five years old, he has not wanted to be anywhere near horses at all. Not hardly close enough to be in the adjacent field. The owl nest box is located on the end of the barn so if he went into the barn, understandable but there is absolutely no need to go inside the stable so why did he? We are here now so we had better prepare ourselves for this." Said Chad. "I don't think anyone could possibly prepare themselves for this mess, Chad, it is just far too horrible." Herbert said and lead them to the stall. When Chad looked in, the colour drained from his cheeks, turning his face instantly white and he also felt sick. He turned sharply away and swallowed hard. Kansas smiled and gave a chuckle. "Are you that squeamish, Uncle Chadrick? You look terrible, is it really that bad?" Chad attempted to raise his arm across the doorway to avoid anyone else seeing what he had just experienced. "There is nothing to smile or giggle about, Kansas. It is not a case of being squeamish, it really is a terrible sight in there and it would be best if you two don't look." "Well, we are here now so may as well." Said Tomas as he pushed his way past to look inside but he promptly retreated and vomited. "Oh, come now Father, is it really that bad?" Kansas asked.

"It really is, Son, worse than that bad." Said Tomas. "I will have a look anyway. If I am going to be a doctor –." Chad glanced at him as he already knew that he had been expelled from medical college and that he still tried to keep up the pretense that he was studying. "I will have more than my share of ghastly, grisly sights to see." He peered through the open door. "I see what you mean. Now, that is one hell of a mess. Poor Cousin Lowell, what a way to go, getting stomped to death by a mad horse. But my oh my, whatever could have possessed him to enter here?" Chad could not help noticing that his speech was very casual, almost as though all this tragedy was a joke to him. He also noticed that his reaction was as though he had known what to expect. Kansas continued. "In my reckoning, and for whatever reason, he must have come into the stable and into Star's stall. She did not know him so thought he was a threat to her foal and did what any mother would do, she protected her foal and stomped him and well, there is the result." "And that is your theory, is it Kansas?" Said Chad. "Doesn't take a genius to see that, now does it? It certainly looks that way and stands to reason by the state of him." Kansas said. "Maybe but I doubt it was the case and I cannot understand the ferocity of her attack. She is such a gentle creature and knowing her the way we do, she would more than likely have just put herself between Diamond and Lowell and slowly forced him out of their stall." Said Chad. "My Lord, Diamond! Herbert, is he alright after this ghastly experience?" Asked Chad.

"Best you come and look at him for yourself, Chad." Out of earshot, he whispered to him. "That is another strange thing, he seems to be unaffected."

"He must be blood-splattered but we cannot clean him until the police have been here." Said Chad. "Now there is the strange thing, have a good look and you will see what I mean." Said Herbert. Chad looked closely at the foal. "He has no blood on him at all." "None." Said Herbert. "Not one drop, I have checked him over as you must have done and not a single drop on him. It is as though he was not in the stall when this tragedy took place." Said Chad.

"Strange occurrence, wouldn't you think?" Herbert said. "Very strange. Just a theory, Herbert, but with everything that has been happening, what if someone took Diamond out of the stall and then pushed Lowell in, how would Star react to that?" Chad asked. "She would not like it at all and would do everything that she could to get back to her foal but not stomp anyone like that. She would use her body to push the intruder away." Said Herbert.

"That is just what I thought." Said Chad. Kansas had slowly and silently followed them and was standing in the doorway to the stall listening. "What are you trying to say, Uncle Chad, that someone did this but it all points to him coming in here and getting stomped on by Star?" "Well, whatever we surmise is of no matter. It is Detective Cadiston that will find out the truth along with all the other deaths. We had better call him right now and an ambulance." Said Chad. "Jeremiah has already done that and Jason is up at the gate waiting for them to arrive and by the sound of it, they are already here." They all retreated outside to meet them. "Well, well, well, if it is not our very own Detective Cadiston and his sidekick DS –. Now, what is his name? Ah yes, I have it, Macswee. This is becoming a serious habit, you keep coming here so perhaps we should put you up in one of the holiday lodges and save on the journey." Kansas said. "Stop being so flippant, Kansas, this is nothing to joke about. Your cousin is lying in there dead and that makes this very serious." Snapped Chad. "Yes, of course it is Uncle Chad. Sorry, I wasn't thinking." Said Kansas. "You never do think, now stay out of the way." Chad said impatiently. "Death is nothing to be flippant about, sir, it is always an extremely serious matter." Said Mac. "Truly spoken so now what has happened this time? We were called as a matter of urgency and after what you have just said, it is another death." Said Cadiston. "You are right, Detective, another death and this time it is my nephew, young Lowell. Judging by first appearances, it gives the impression that he was stomped by a horse and it is not a pretty sight to see." Said Chad. "Stomped by a horse, you say? But pretty or not, best we have a look." They followed Herbert as he led them to the stall and they looked in. "I see what you mean, never encountered anything like this before. It certainly is a mess." Mac had taken one look and beat a hasty retreat. "Our forensic boys will have a job to sort this one out. Not very nice for Charles and Samantha when they carry out the post-mortem on the poor lad either." Cadiston continued. "Post-mortem, you say? What do you mean post-mortem? Surely that is not required for this, is it? Surely you can see the mad horse stomped him to death. That is clear enough even for me to see and you as the detective, you must see it too?" Kansas said.

He sensed anxiety in his voice but Cadiston remained calm. "With so many deaths happening in such a short space of time and even though it may look straight forward, I am still having one carried out." "But –." Kansas started but got cut off. "But nothing, Cadiston knows what he is doing, Kansas, and if he thinks it is necessary then it is. It is so soon after James allegedly fell so why are you worried about that happening?" "Err –. Not worried, Uncle Chad, but look at the state of him. Surely no more pulling about will be necessary as it all looks cut and dried." Said Kansas. "I have already said that Cadiston knows what he is doing so again I ask you, do you have a problem with that?" Chad asked sternly. "Err, well, no. Guess you are right so no, not a problem. I was just thinking of poor Aunt Greta and his sister cousin Jennifer. It was bad enough for them with Uncle Malcolm." Stuttered Kansas. "No more for you to say then, Kansas, is there? So stay out of the way until called. Detective, have you any questions for us before we go and leave you to do your job?" Cadiston looked at Mac. "Who found the body?" "I did, Detective, and wish I hadn't. That sight will haunt me forever." Said Herbert.

Cadiston now took over. "Tell us what you can then, Herbert." "Came down here at eight-fifteen and wondered why the outside door was open. I came in and found Star and her foal out of the stall and the poor lad in it." Said Herbert.

"And that is when you fetched Chad?" Asked Cadiston. "It is." Answered Herrbert. "Can we see the horse in question, please?" Asked Cadiston.

"I will show you where she is." Said Herbert. Tomas and Kansas made ready to follow but Mac raised his hand to stop them. "No need for anyone else to follow us, thank you. Just wait here and we will question you in a moment." He sounded very assertive and this confirmed Cadiston's decision to have Mac as his DS not constable. Herbert took him to the stall where she had been placed. "Have you cleaned her up at all?" Asked Cadiston. "Not a bit, Detective. Now this bemused me and well, I still cannot see the possibility of this being right. You will probably notice it without me saying but the state of young Master Lowell's body and the amount of blood sprayed around the stall compared to the blood splats on Star –. Well, you would think there would be a lot more with so much damage to the body. You are the detectives and you can draw your own conclusion on that one. What is more surprising, her foal has not one drop on it." Said Herbert. "None at all?" Asked Cadiston. "None at all." Confirmed Herbert. "So that means he was not in the stall when Master Lowell was allegedly stomped by this animal? Now, that is a very interesting fact so what do you think, Mac?" Cadiston looked at Mac.

"From the mess in the stall, the horse should be covered in the young man's blood and brain tissue but there is hardly any blood and from what little I could look at, no brain tissue and that makes it very suspicious." Mac said.

"Thank you. Now, Herbert –." He put a finger to his lips. "Please keep it to yourself for now." Herbert made a zip sign across his lips. "If someone entered the stall and removed the foal how would the mother react to that person"? "She would push her body against them and in between her foal and them". "Would they receive an injury"? "Yes, possibly a few bruses and a shoulder injury as they tried to push her away". "Thank you Herbert and just as I suspected."

The forensic team had arrived in good time and had wasted no time in starting their investigation of the site. The name bracelet had been photographed where it lay before being bagged, as had the position of the body. "This is a real messy one, Cadders. I would put an estimated time of death between eleven p.m. and three a.m. by the rigor mortis but Charles and Samantha will give a more accurate time. Thought you would like to know that." Said Jooners. "Thanks, Jooners, while you are here, have a look at the horse that is supposed to have stomped the poor lad." He followed Cadiston into the stall and studied Star, then shook his head. "Not that horse, Cadders, it must have been another one. I had a stomping to deal with a while back and the horse was a mess but not this one. Not enough blood on it so if he was stomped then another horse was responsible." Said Jooners. "Our thoughts match, thanks Jooners." He went back into the stall to continue with his team of forensic officers.

The two detectives now walked to where the men stood waiting for them. Cadiston eyed them all carefully with Mac following his lead. "Same question to you all, where were you and what were you doing between the hours of eleven p.m. and three a.m.?" Kansas was quick to answer the question. "Well, I was in bed asleep." "Alone, sir?" Asked Cadiston. "What do you take me for? Of course alone, what do you take me for?" He snapped in reply. "Steady on there, Son, Detective Cadiston is only asking where you were, not accusing you of anything. As for myself, I was in bed with my wife." Said Tomas. "See Father, you have a witness, I do not. He may think that I had something to do with it because I was careless and cut myself." His voice was very jittery, his feet were shuffling, and he was very agitated, and had a worried look on his face that was noticed by both Cadiston and Mac. "Now why would the detective have reason to think that?" Asked Chad. Kansas began to panic and stammer as he replied. "Well, f-f-for a start, there is n-n-no one to confirm m-m-my alibi until Charlotte came i-i-into my room at about twenty past eight to wake me this morning –." "Deep breaths, Kansas, breathe and just calm yourself. If you have nothing to hide then you have nothing to worry about, do you? From what I know about providing an alibi, which is not very much, just because a wife says that her husband was in bed with her, does not necessarily prove to be true, isn't that correct Detective Cadiston?" Said Chad. Kansas was now breathing steadily and had calmed but the worried frown on his face remained. "It is, sir." Confirmed Cadiston. Tomas now gave him a worried glance and wondered why Chad had said this. "Guess not, Uncle Chad, but I don't want to be in the frame for something I did not do." Kansas said quickly.

"From what you have just said, you think that this was not an accident and someone did this?" His eyes rolled and he again began to panic but Chad managed to calm him and regulate his breathing. "Didn't say that but Uncle Chad did, he said it was just a theory but what if someone took Diamond out of the stall then pushed Lowell in, how would Star react to that. And Herbert replied that she would not like it at all and would do everything that she could to get back to her foal." Said Kansas. "And is that what you think happened here, Kansas?" Asked Cadiston. "Ye –. Er, no, oh I don't know. All I know is that he stupidly came in and got himself trampled by the mare. That is clear for all to see, even you two detectives." Snapped Kansas. Cadiston knew that to continue questioning Kansas would achieve nothing at this stage so he moved his questions on to the next person. "Thank you, Kansas, and where were you, Chad?" "Like Tomas, I was in bed with my wife." Answered Chad.

Mac then asked his question. "Can anyone shed light on why this young man would want to enter the stable alone and especially at night?" "I can answer that for you, Detective, there is absolutely no reason, no reason at all. When he was just five years old, he had a bad accident with a pony. He has hated horses from that moment on to the present day. He could not even stand them being in the next field so it is a complete mystery to me why he was in the stable at all." Said Chad. Cadiston spoke again. "Hated horses, now that is an interesting fact – Thank you, Chad, that is all for now and you may all leave. Sorry Herbert, but until forensics have finished, the stables are off-limits." "Understood Detective, but may we be allowed to remove the horses and put them in the paddock? They can sense death and are all very jittery, especially Thundist." Said Herbert. "Any problem with that, Jooners?" Asked Cadiston.

"Just let us have a look out there first, I saw some blood that we will need a sample of, and can you tell us where that trap door goes?" Asked Jooners. "That is the old hiding place for contraband. Back in the day, there was a bit of smuggling or rather receiving stolen goods or probably both." Said Herbert. "And that is the only way in and out?" Asked Jooners.

"Only way as far as I know, Officer, but this a very old manor house and quite a few of them I believe had secret passages included in their construction." Said Herbert. Tomas and Kansas sent worrying glances to each other at this remark which was noticed by both detectives. "Pictures and samples are all done, Chief." Said Sharon. "You can take your horses out then, Herbert, and the rest of you can leave now." Said Cadiston. With his two sons to help, the stable was soon empty leaving a clear field for the team of forensic officers to do their work. "What are you thinking, Jooners?" Asked Cadiston. "Well, Cadders, this is a strange one from what I have seen so far. Charles and your good lady are the experts but from what I have seen of the lad's body, I think that the incident was staged and that means the horse was forced to trample on him. From the blood splats on the horse and the state of the poor lad, my guess is that he was already dead before that happened. His skull is severely damaged and again, they will know better but to my mind, it was not the horse that did the damage but something that has the appearance of a horse's hoof. Someone cold-bloodedly caved his skull and chest in making it look like it was the horse." Said Jooners. "A clever cover-up then?" Asked Mac. "A clever try at a cover-up, Mac, and did you hear Herbert say that a lot of these old Mansions were built with secret passageways?" Cadiston looked around. "That I did, we will be looking deeper into that. Thanks Jooners, leave you to it. Come Mac, we had better go to the Manor." Said Cadiston.

As they made their way up the path, they talked about this latest incident. "Ok Mac, give me your thoughts, tell me what you think." "Murder and I have a suspect in my mind." Said Mac. "And who might that be?" Asked Cadiston. "I watched them all and deduced from the suspect's mannerisms that he was the only one that was trying to force the issue. I also noticed that he had a nasty gash to his hand and was favouring his right arm and shoulder and that is not forgetting the deep scratches on his neck that he had undoubtedly lied about that is my thought Cadders." Mac explained. "Well spotted and a good deduction so your suspect is?" Asked Cadiston. "Has to be Kansas but to do that he would have to be very cold and violent." Deduced Mac. "My thoughts exactly. Now, we are at the Manor and if my memory serves me right, looks like Alfred waiting at the door." Said Cadiston. "Come in detectives, the family is waiting in the blue room. Master Chad has briefly explained but would not say too much." He left them at the door and without hesitation, they walked in.

"Once more we are here and we must see you all under extremely sad circumstances. I am sure that Chad has already informed you of what was found in the stable." Said Cadiston. "My son, Cadiston, my son, Lowell, battered to death. First my husband, Malcolm, and now my son, Lowell. Both supposedly killed by a horse. Now I live in fear for my daughter and myself. When are you going to stop all these deaths?" Greta was near hysterics.

"Steady on there, Greta. Chad didn't say much, only that he had been found but from what Kansas and Tomas said this one really was just a dreadful accident." Said Grant. "You have absolutely no idea about it, Grant, and you are still very drunk." "That I may be but –." Grant belched and continued. "I still heard them say that they found Lowell in the stall of Star and that new foal of hers. The question is why did the silly fool of a boy go in there on his own?" Chad was ready to respond but Greta was on her feet and had crossed the room in a few long strides and the slap that she gave Grant across his face rang out loudly. "How dare you call my son a fool? He was much smarter than you could ever be! He was making something of himself while you are nothing short of a drunken bum who just sits back on his haunches and feeds off Mother, Father, and the estate. Bonnie rued the day that she married you! She was far too good for you, she would not admit it or openly say the words but –." Greta wiped her eyes. "She could not hide it from me and we know that you treated her abysmally. Why she loved you only she knew. You did not really want her and what is more, we could all see it! She knew that you were having an affair because she had told Lizabeth and me and would have disclosed just who it was if she had not died so horribly that night. We have had a lot of death in the family and if you dare ever say anything like that again about my son, there will be another death and that, Grant, will be you. Now you have two dead wives on your conscience … I doubt that will bother you." "Shut up, Greta! You bitch, sit down, you know absolutely nothing. You are not even real family and are only here because you were Malcolm's wife and he is dead so in my book, that makes you a hanger-on." While everyone else stood in silence, allowing Grant to abuse Greta, Chad was not about to and spoke angrily. "That will do, Grant! It is you who needs to shut up so not another word from you. Just sit down and keep your mouth closed. What Greta said is the truth and the truth always hurts and remember you do not want to push me again." "You may have bested me once or twice but if we ever cross real swords –." Grant made the action of sword fighting. "Then we will see –." "Any time you are ready, Grant, I will be there to ac- commodate you. Now shut up and sit down, Detective Cadiston is here to find out what happened to our nephew, Lowell, and you are being just a total ass and a waste of space. Now sit down and shut up!" Said Chad. Grant knew that Chad had already bested him but in his mind, he was seeking his revenge for the past hu- miliation and waiting for the right time to strike. For now, he sat down. "If you are all settled after that outburst, I will continue. I know how families can fall out with each other but under these circumstances you should all be pulling together. Chad, it may not be relevant to the current situation but can you tell me why Grant should not push you again?" Cadiston asked. "It was days ago −. In fact, the day before Sadie died. That would be 29th of September I believe. We were starting to clear the grounds after the show and he made some hurtful remarks to both Greta and Sadie." Said Chad. "That is correct, Detective Cadiston, very hurtful." Greta added. "I could not stand by and watch these two ladies be abused especially after what had happened to their husbands and I had reached the end of my patience so I stepped in and put him straight." Chad continued. "Put him straight, you brute? You mean you put him in hospital, Chad, so get it right." Demmie interrupted. "Yes, thank you for your input, Demmie, I was getting to that. We had a fight and he in his foolishness and anger pulled a knife. I warned him that he would look very silly with it stuck in his backside but he ignored it and well −. He ended up with it in his buttock. Nothing harmful just another of those family ruckuses." Said Chad. "It is a criminal offense to pull a weapon with intent to use it followed by a malicious wounding." Said Cadiston. "True Detective, that it is but no real harm was done. I am sure that he has learned his lesson so can it on this occasion just stay within the family? We have enough to cope with at present with all these deaths so please can we discuss that action later. And if you wish to press any form of charge then maybe when they are all settled." Said Chad. "It is against my better judgement but for now we will look past that event and raise it again in the future. Both of you be assured that it will not go unpunished. Now, I need to know if any of you know what possible reason Lowell would have had to enter the stable block alone and especially at night?" Asked Cadiston.

"None, Detective. The only way you would get my son in there was either kicking and screaming or unconscious." Answered Greta. Mac sat up straight at the word 'unconscious' and thought that must have been how he got him in there. Greta continued. "Lowell had an accident with a pony when he was just five years old and if it had not been for Chadrick's quick intervention, he may have died on that day. From that day forward, he has never wanted to be anywhere near a horse. We tried desperately, he even had therapy but nothing would make him change his mind." All the while she spoke, her tears fell and Chad was there by her side trying to comfort her and to pass a dry handkerchief. "Thank you, I appreciate that this is very stressful for you and that has confirmed what has already been stated. Now, has anyone else got a further comment?" Asked Cadiston.

"All I know is that when we were all going to bed, that is except uncle Grant who was very drunk and nursing a bottle of brandy, Lowell went for a walk. He told me that he wanted to see the barn owls. We call them our residents and they were his favourite and if I had walked with him then he would still be alive." Said Jennifer. She was also in tears and Chad was hugging her. When he spoke it was soft, the tone of his voice showed that he was a caring man. "It is not your fault, Jennifer, and if you had gone with your brother on that walk then maybe –, Well, we have no need to think of the maybe."

"Definitely not, sir, and I can see where your thought was going." Said Mac.

"He hated horses and would not, on any account, have entered the stable with someone and definitely not alone. The only way he would go in there was if he were unconscious. Hmm –. I saw the owl's nest box and he would have no cause to be in the stable to see the owls as the box is on the barn beside the stable block and easily visible. To my mind, he would have viewed them searching for their food around and across the open meadow, nowhere near the stables." Observed Cadiston speaking quietly. "Well on this occasion, he was a blind fool and probably thought that at night he would be safe in there. An Owl may have flown in there and he went to look for it." Said Kansas. "That is a possibility, Kansas, and we will keep that in mind. That will be all for now. I will know more when I have the full forensic and post-mortem results. Then I will be able to tell you more. With all that has happened here, my investigations are on-going. Headway is being made, that is all that I can say at this time. There are a few more details to clear up, then we will pay you another visit and maybe then we will be able to give you more information. As you know, we have made a start but there will be the need to question you all on every incident without exception. I have already spoken to you all about Bonnie and her unborn child so if you will all bear with me then I will do my level best to bring a speedy conclusion to all these tragedies which have to be proven to be accidents as was the previous suggestion." Said Cadiston. "All of them proven to be accidents? What makes you think they are anything different to that, Cadiston? When Srgeant Standish was on the case, well, he did not mess about and had them sorted in a flash and knew they were accidents." Said Grant snidely. "Sergeant Standish is now retired, sir, and I am acting DCI with Detective Sergeant Macswee as my assistant. It is very clear that Sergeant Standish did not look at all the evidence before drawing his conclusion. That is why the case of Miss Bonnie and her unborn child has been reopened and is being investigated." Said Cadiston. He noticed a sheepish, worried stare between Demmie and Grant before continuing. "At this point in time that is all I am prepared to say. There is a lot of work still to be done but progress is being made. I must ask you all not to leave the vicinity so if there are no further questions, we will take our leave."

"Questions, a waste of time and money." Said Grant; then walked away to get another drink. There was a nodding of heads as he looked at each of them.

"Nothing Detective, nothing at all." Said Kansas. "I could not help but notice in the stable that you were favouring your right arm and shoulder and continue to do so. There is also a nasty gash to your hand, can you tell me why that is?" Cadiston tilted his head slightly to have a better look at the gash. "Must have pulled my shoulder when I tripped into the rose bush." Said Kansas. Chad picked up on his explanation and knew that he needed to inform Cadiston of his different story and knew that he had lied. He also knew that he had to do it without Kansas knowing. "And what is the explanation for the gash on your hand?" Asked Cadiston, now shifting his gaze. "Must be the same thing." Said Kansas. "Sounds to me like the roses are rather violent and have a lot to answer for, sir." Remarked Mac. "What do you mean by that remark, Detective?" He snapped in answer. "Nothing at all, sir, I know just how vicious roses can be with their sharp thorns." Mac said smiling. "Now, if there is nothing further then we will take our leave." Said Cadiston. Chad whispered to him. "Can't talk now, too many ears but I have something that you should know so I will call you later." Cadiston nodded, then without waiting to be shown out and with his DS close by, made his own way to the front door. Lord and Lady Mandaten had sat silently during the questioning and only when the detectives had left did Lady Mandaten speak. "This is getting far too much for us to bare, I hate to think what could have happened if Jennifer had gone with her brother and we are so few now it is easier to count and name those that are left in the family than those who have died. The few of us that remain here are all that is left of the Mandaten dynasty." "Very true, Mother, as Jennifer said, we are being whittled down one at a time. Apart from poor Uncle Laseroie and his family and more recently, Aunt Sammie and her family. Now just what Mandatens do we have left? There is Uncle Grant and Cousin Jennifer, my mother, and grandfather −. All true Mandaten blood runs through their veins. I could be deemed Mandaten because of my mother's birth blood. There are so few of us left, it is getting to be very scary. If someone is slowly murdering us, who could it be and why now?" Kansas said. Grant blew in exasperation. "Someone murdering us? Phew, what a lot of dramatists you all are. Accidents, Kansas, all accidents, now that is −." "Shut up Grant and go back to your bottle." Snapped his sister Lizabeth. "Yes, that I will my sister dear." He walked away. "What you just said now, that is the leading question, Kansas. It is getting very scary to be in my room alone." Said Jennifer. "What if we all take a gun to bed with us, Jennifer, would that make you feel safer?" Replied Kansas jokingly. "It might but it would need to be only a small pistol a shotgun would be far too big and clumsy for me." Said Jennifer. "What about if I stand guard at your door, Cousin, would you feel safe then?" Asked Kansas. "Yes, but then you would get no sleep." Replied Jennifer. "Stop it, the pair of you. With that kind of talk you are frightening all of us. Jennifer can come and sleep in with me." Said her mother Greta. "Sorry Aunt Greta, good solution that is so that will just leave Uncle Grant and myself on our own. Mother and father have each other, Chad and Demmie have each other but then they are not at any real risk because they are not true blood-family. And then gramps is with grandma –." Said Jennifer.

"Well, no one had better try to kill me as I have my very own protector." Said Grant. "And just what might that be, Uncle Grant?" Asked Jennifer."My nice little snub nose thirty-eight caliber pistol so anyone that comes after me will get blown away." Grant smiled. "Is that legal then, to have that gun at home Grant?" asked Lizabeth. "Who cares, I brought it from the gun club after Malcolm met his end, just in case." Said Grant. "But you have always maintained that his death was an accident." Said Chad. "And it was but better to be prepared –." He belched before continuing. "Be warned, I have it and it is loaded and I am not afraid to use it." "Can I see it?" Asked Tomas. Grant lifted his shirt to expose the holster containing the pistol. "There, satisfied Tomas?" He asked. "Only leaves me to say that there is no more problem. It is all sorted now I am feeling hungry. It has been another long day with what has happened. I don't think any of us have eaten or thought about eating since breakfast and that was cut short." "It is another hour before dinner at seven-thirty so what have you in mind, Kansas?" Asked Lizabeth. "Bring dinner forward, of course, but only if Grandfather agrees." Replied Kansas to his mother. "Getting a bit above your station, aren't you Kansas? Or are you trying to take over?" Grant said. "Not at all, Uncle Grant, just thought it would make good sense." Kansas said."Enough! All of you. I cannot stand any more of the bickering, Everything is already topsy-turvy so Grandfather has no objections." Said their mother Lady Mandaten almost shouting. "Thank you for that, Grandfather." Replied Kansas. "I will go to the kitchen and ask Cook if it is possible." Said Lady Mandaten. "Yes Mother, thank you." Replied Lizabeth. Lady Mandaten was gone for twenty minutes and upon her return Announced. "Cook said that we could eat in fifteen minutes. The starters are ready Prawn Coctails and as we are having steak. They are cooked as we like them, well done, medium, rare or somewhere in between. There is no problem so let us get to the dining room."

They made their way there but because the meal was brought forward, the table was in a state of preparation and this worried the old butler, Bradinham, who began to panic. Kansas was quick to step in and spoke to the old butler in a very patronizing fashion. "Calm yourself, Bradders old man. On this occasion, it is alright so no need to get yourself all worked up and your knickers in a twist over it. Just put the cutlery down as each course is served". Bradinham had been instructed and trained in protocol and had served the family well for many years, he did not take his instructions from one of the grandchildren and especially not from Kansas as he was not a Mandaten by birth but a Kaysten. This was way beyond his endurance so he looked toward Lord Mandaten for guidance. "It will be alright on this occasion, Bradinham, thank you. Just carry on and we will make do for tonight." Said Lord Mandaten. With their instructions clear, the meal was eaten. Before they retired to the lounge for their coffee, Lord Mandaten spoke. "A word, Kansas?" "Yes, Grandfather." Said Kansas.

"Never, and I mean never, speak to Mister Bradinham like that again. When you address him, it is Mister Bradinham, not Bradders and your statement of not getting his knickers in a twist is almost obscene and I will not have it not in my home do you understand me boy?" said Lord Mandaten sngrily. Kansas cowered and hung his head as though in shame. "Yes, Grandfather. I am sorry I meant no offense." "Well, it was very offensive so never again." Said Lord Mandaten. "It will not happen again, Grandfather, sorry." Said Kansas. "It is Mister Bradinham that needs the apology so best you go and get it done." Said Lord Mandaten glaring at his grandson in disgust.

"What, right now?" Asked Kansas. "Right now, without delay." Lord Mandaten gestured towards Bradinham. Kansas walked away and made a half-hearted attempt at making his apology.

He felt belittled and small and hated to grovel to one of the staff members, regardless of who it was. His grandfather knew this would be the case.

The night had passed with some restlessness and now it was the morning of Friday, 10th of October, and everyone was down to breakfast. "I see that everyone is here this morning so no one died in the night then." Grant remarked. "That is not funny, Grant, not funny at all." Lizabeth said angrily. "Well pardon me for speaking, Lizabeth. I see the police are still looking at the stable so there must be something there for them to find." Said Grant. "Cannot imagine what. Lowell got stomped on by that mad horse and that is all there is to it." Replied Kansas. "Lizabeth, I think they are packing up to leave. Yes, I can just see where they are parked and if I am correct −. Yes, they are getting into their van." Remarked Demmie. "They were either there all night or got here very early this morning, what do you think Greta?"asked Demmie. An answer came before she had a chance to speak. "Well, no matter, they have done all they wanted to do so now we can get back to normal." Kansas said."Normal Kansas? What are you calling normal? From Monday, 22nd of September, up to today, Friday, 10th of October − nineteen days, almost three weeks − hardly a day has passed without a death, all our families have suffered apart from yours Kansas." Said Greta. "Maybe because we are not Mandaten but Kaysten. Well, maybe it will quieten down now for a while until Cadiston sorts the mess out and they are declared accidents just like that Sergeant Standish would have done. After breakfast I will go and have a word with Herbert, to see if he can tell us anything about what happened at the stable". Said Kansas. "I would not expect that he can tell you much but do what you think fit, Son."Lizabeth said.

"As to that, I most certainly will, Mother." His father went to speak but a glance stopped him and Kansas continued. "With or without either of your permission." His father shrank back into his chair and his mother said. "Find out all that you can, Kansas." "I will do just that, Mother. Would you or Father, as head of the family, like to join me?" Asked Kansas. "I think that you can handle it perfectly well on your own, Son." Said Lizabeth. "You are so right, Mother." Kansas was quick with his breakfast and hardly before his coffee cup was back on its saucer, he was gone. "He is in a mighty big hurry, Mother." Said Jennifer. Greta whispered in her daughter's ear. "Pay no mind, Jennifer, Kansas likes to think he is the boss and better than his father or mother, come to that. You can thank your Aunt Lizabeth for that as she has always favoured him over her husband." Kansas arrived at the stables and saw Herbert with Jason coming toward him. "Morning Master Kansas, nasty business but what brings you down here?" Asked Herbert. "We all were wondering if you could tell us anything about what the police were doing here so long?" Asked Kansas. "The forensics team you mean?" Asked Herbert.

"Just so man. Well, can you?" Kansas pushed. "I did speak to one of the policemen –. Well, it was actually a policewoman. She could not tell me much as it is an ongoing investigation." Said Herbert. Kansas was beginning to lose his patience and snapped at Herbert. "Never mind all that man, just tell me what she said!" "Not very much at all, they had taken plenty of samples and measured and photographed the blood splats on the walls and on the horses. She could not say anything else as it is an ongoing investigation." Said Herbert. "Did they find anything or take anything away with them?" Kansas asked. "Plenty of samples." Said Herbert. "I know samples, I saw them taking them. I mean anything else?" Kansas snapped impatiently. "If they did then they did not tell me and –." He shrugged his shoulders. "I saw nothing. They had a good look at Star and photographed her from the knee down as that is where the blood had splattered her. Oh yes, had a quick look down the old contraband hiding place." Said Herbert.

"Why down there and did they find anything down there? And what was wrapped up?" Kansas started to speak faster. "Well, if they did find something, they didn't tell me, why should they? Maybe they took a sample of the straw and I saw nothing wrapped up, did you Son?" Herbert looked at his son. "Not a thing, Pops. What do you think they had wrapped up then, Master Kansas, you must have seen what we did not?" Asked Jason. "Nothing in particular but there was nothing found so that is good, and nothing was taken away?" Asked Kansas. "I do not know, I was not here watching them. That is all, Master Kansas, some of them were here all night and all I know is that they were being very thorough. The van came back this morning about six-thirty, they put their stuff in it and left just a short while ago. They told me the stables could be used again but that stall will be given a good clean before a horse will step into it again." Said Herbert. "So, in effect, you have not told me anything more than I already knew, you have asked more questions, of course –." Kansas said. "It is not up to me or my place, Master Kansas, and even if you had asked more questions, I doubt that you would have got any more of an answer than I would have." Herbert said. "Well as to that, we will have no answer, will we?" Kansas said arrogantly. Herbert could not help noticing that Kansas kept holding his right shoulder as he turned abruptly and walked away. When he was well out of earshot Jason shook his head. "You know what Pops? He is one very worried boy, I think he has something to hide and that is why he wants to know what they found." "Just between us Son, they had something wrapped up which they removed but the officer could not say what it was. I did not see what they found before it was wrapped but was not about to tell him. Now, if Chad had asked then I would have." Said Herbert and after a short silence he continued. Did you notice him holding his shoulder, now if he had been in the stall and Star was pushing him, well, only supposition but, I do not like that boy.?" "I did notice but was not about to ask why. I noticed the deep gash on his hand as well and that looked very much like it was caused by something that ripped rather than cut. He is nothing but a spoilt brat, he is such an arrogant upstart and I have no liking for him." Said Jason. "Me neither, Son, me neither. Now let us get that stall cleaned out very thoroughly. It will probably take us a couple of days to get it done right." With their cleaning materials at hand, they began their task.

About ten-thirty, Chad came into the stable block and called out. "Herbert, are you in here?" "In Stars' stall, Chad." Herbert called back and he walked steadily down the walkway and stood in the doorway. "It will be a hard task to scrub the smell of death from these walls but that is not why I am here. My concern is for Star and her foal, are they both alright? As well as the other horses?" Asked Chad. "Go see for yourself, they are all out in the paddock." Said Herbert and with a wave he left them to their massive task. "Didn't want to know anything about the forensic search, his first concern was for the horses. Only one to come down here to see them. Kansas never mentioned them when he was down here, more interested in what the police had been doing and if they had found anything. I know his Lordship cannot come down here but at least he phoned to make sure they were all right." Said Jason. "A good person that Chadrick, Son, takes after the Lord and is more like him than his own blood sons are or were. As for Grant, nothing like any of the Mandatens at all and extremely hard to believe that he is Malcolm's twin, they did not look anything alike. It did not make sense and was a strange thing because when they were born, Lady Mandaten did not even know that she was having twins." Said Herbert.

"Well, we can't think about that now, Father. That was some forty-odd years ago, before I was born. Now we have some serious cleaning to do." Said Jason and went back to scrubbing. "Indeed, that we have Son, that we have."

Chad had arrived at the paddock and without hesitation, entered it straight away. he could see Star with her foal close by so he called to her in his soft, gentle voice. "Hello Star, my lovely girl." She looked up and immediately responded by walking toward him. "There you are my beauty, what a trauma for and your little Diamond to go through. If only you could talk then you could tell me who was responsible for the horrible deed as I know that you would not do such a thing. Oh Star, my beautiful girl, if only you could talk –. Now there is a thought, you may not be able to talk in actual words but in actions –. Now, that is possible and I bet that you remember who it was that so brutally murdered young Lowell and if they walked into this paddock, you would take your baby and run away from them. I wonder if that would work, it would certainly tell me something and in turn I would let Cadiston know I could then tell him of Kansas telling two different versions of his shoulder injury and the gash to his hand. Not a straight cut but jagged and inflamed. There's my girl." It was as though she was listening to his every word. "The next thing is to sort out who to bring in here first. Grant –. No, he was out of it and totally drunk. Tomas or Kansas –. It must have been one of them but why murder Lowell? What could they possibly gain from his death? I know that the two boys did not get on and that Kansas was extremely jealous of Lowell but would he go as far as murder? I wonder –. Could they be –. Are they responsible for all these deaths? But if it is Tomas and Kansas committing these murders, why would Lizabeth want her own family dead? Unless she is unaware of their actions. No, silly idea. It just does not make any sense, Tomas is a weedy thing and almost afraid of his own shadow, best to leave it to the professionals but I wonder if Cadiston is thinking on those lines though. Could it be someone in the family? But why are there so few of us left, a thought, Lizabeths family have not been touched and she is Mandaten blood, and what is there to gain by murdering everyone? What do you think, Star, my beauty, are all these deaths due to greed, lies, falseness, and jealousy? I know for certain that all of them desire the family fortune. Well, they can have it all and whoever gets it, I hope it makes them happy." He shook his head. "I doubt that. There is one name –. Grant wants to be the Lord –. We will see. Now my plan –. Do I bring them both together or separately? What do you say, Star? Will you help me to find the murderer of Lowell?" She placed her head onto his shoulder and he affectionately rubbed her nose and neck. "Right, I will go back and speak to Tomas and bring him to see you first." He gave her a few more pats then headed back toward the Manor.

The family was in the breakfast room where a lunch snack had been prepared and set out for them. "There you are, Chadrick, thank goodness. With all that has been happening of late we were beginning to get worried. You have been gone for quite a long while." Said Greta with Jennifer at her side and she took hold of

Chads hand. "You may have been worried, Greta, but do not include us in that. We were not worried, not me or the rest of us as I could not care less about him. As far as I am concerned, the sooner that he is out of my life the better it will be." Said Grant. "Well, we are not all like you, Grant. There are those amongst us that care." Said Greta. "Leave it, Greta. He is not worth wasting your breath on." They moved away from him and he lowered his voice to whisper. "I have just been to the stables to see that the horses are alright after what had happened there. They are all out in the paddocks while Herbert and his son clean the stall and that is quite a task for them. I wish they did not need to do it. I saw Kansas on his way back from the stables. I hid so that he didn't see me. Now, there is something that I need to do. I have a theory and I need to act on. I have no desire to ignore you so please bare with me." She smiled at him, then left him to gaze toward Tomas and then around the room looking for Kansas. He could not see him, then walked over to where Tomas was standing and approached him He began to shuffle his feet and looked rather sheepish. "Got something on my mind so thought you might like a walk after lunch, Tomas, so that we can have a quiet word without prying ears." He said. "That sounds a bit ominous, Chad, can't we discuss it here and now?" Tomas looked uncomfortable. "Bit personal so rather not if you don't mind." Said Chad. "Ok, after lunch then." Said Tomas. Chad nodded and smiled, then walked away. He had achieved his first aim and part two of his plan would soon follow. Satisfied with this, he approached the luncheon table and helped himself to some food and a glass of fruit juice, then sat quietly in the corner with his thoughts: "Could it be him? Last night I saw him go upstairs with Lizabeth but there was not a thing to stop him from coming back down and there have been a lot of strange creaks at night. He could have come back down later and followed Lowell to the stables but to what ends and what would he gain? And was Grant just pretending to be drunk so he could kill Lowell and be provided with a perfect alibi? He has appeared drunk before but has been very coherent with it. What a good alibi he would have, just like when his first wife was found murdered and we would all be backing him up. They were talking about protecting themselves when I came in and he was lowering his shirt so what has he got to hide under it? Then there is Kansas, he was still down when we all went up and I know that there was no love lost between him and Lowell. Lowell was getting on very well at university and Kansas was thrown out of med school although hearing him talk you would think that he was still studying. He has scratches, a gash on his hand, and a painful arm and shoulder and changed his story on how it happened. In other words, he lied to the police but would he go to those lengths because of hatred? Would he go as far as murder? To see Lowell in that state turned my stomach but not him –. He was not phased at all by what he saw so could he have committed the crime? It did look as though he knew what to expect. Lizabeth, now she can be a real bitch and is very money orientated but I cannot see her having the stomach to carry out such a vicious attack. Lastly, Greta and Jennifer –. In my mind most definitely not. That leaves just me and Demmie. I know that I am innocent and as for Demmie –. I don't trust her anymore. I was a fool and blinded by her beauty but now I know just how false she is and what is worse, I fell for her lies and falseness. It has taken a while to get me to open my eyes but she is very devious and deceitful. I do believe that she has been lying about many things from the moment that we first met and if she and Grant are having an affair and she wants to be with him, well, he can have her. Good riddance, they deserve each other. Now back to the problem at hand –. If my little scheme works, and I am sure that it will, then Star will tell me who killed Lowell and I will soon know. She is a clever girl and is the only one that can tell me. If it is as I believe, then Star will confirm my theory and I will let Cadiston know instantly. Then it will be up to him to act on the information. Right, sorted, now the next step is put it into operation." Chad then sat in the corner and ate his lunch in silent thought.

Chapter Ten

Murder in the First Degree

After they had finished their lunch, Chad glanced toward Tomas and gave him a nod then left the room to wait for him outside. He did not wait long because a few minutes later, Tomas followed. He wanted to talk but Chad was on a mission and wanted to know the answer to his question and was walking very briskly. "Slow down, Chad, this is not a race so why are you in such a hurry? I can hardly keep pace with you." Said Tomas. "Sorry Tomas, there is just something that I need to get off my chest and we need to be far away from the Manor to stop prying ears so step it out please." Said Chad. The pace was increased and within fifteen minutes, they were at the paddock. "Why are we here, Chad? I really don't like being so close to the stables where Lowell was killed, stomped to death by that mad horse. Up until now you haven't said much so what do you want to talk about?" Asked Tomas. Before he answered, he had entered the paddock where Star and her foal were having a run around the perimeter. "Come on in Tomas, unless you are afraid too, then we can talk without being disturbed." Said Chad. "Why should I be afraid, Chad? I love the horses at least all but that one, she is a mad killer. It was her that killed my nephew and should be destroyed now. If you do not mind, I will just stand safely by the gate." Said Tomas. Chad walked toward him and leaning on the gate, he began to speak. "That is what I want to talk about, just between us, Tomas. I am not sure that Star did kill Lowell."

Tomas swallowed hard and the colour in his cheeks drained, turning into a very pale white. "Are you alright, Tomas?" Asked Chad. "Fine. Must be because that mad horse has it's head is on your shoulder." Said Tomas. He stood stationary for a few seconds wondering just what it was that Chad was up to and although he partly wanted to enter the paddock, he hesitated.

"You have brought me here to talk so what do you want to talk about? Surely it is cut and dried or have you got your own theory about our nephew's sad and brutal death?" Said Tomas. "Just a theory, Tomas, and I wanted to get your view on it." Said Chad. By now with Star's head on his shoulder and her foal close to them and with a few gentle words from Chad, he approached and without hesitation, he began to stroke her neck as he whispered into her ear. "There you are my little beauty, I have brought Tomas to see you Diamond. Go ahead then, Tomas, it is quite safe to stroke her. She is not the vicious beast that someone would have us believe but a much gentler creature." Said Chad smiling. "I cannot see what stroking a horse, especially this one, has to do with Lowell's death or finding out what happened to him. As you do not seem to have a lot to say and are just wasting my time, I am going back to the Manor." He said angrily. "Sorry Tomas, I thought I could talk to you about it but I was wrong. No matter, I will come back with you. It was just something I had to try to be sure about it but well, it was of no use. No matter now, sorry to have wasted your time." They walked back in silence. There was coffee and tea in the lounge when they arrived and all the way, back Chad had been pondering over his next move. First, it was imperative to keep Tomas away from his son. He gazed around the room and to his relief, Kansas was not present which he thought was a bit of luck. But what if he came in and spoke with his father? If he did that then all would be lost. It was imperative to keep them apart and not be able to talk to each other otherwise his plan would then be rendered inoperative. He needed to action his plan quickly but how was he going to get Kansas to walk with him to the paddock without throwing any kind of suspicion? He sat quietly on his own thinking about how he could achieve his next move.

"You look confused so, what did Chadrick want you for Tomas?" Asked Lizabeth. "Blessed if I know, Lizabeth. He said he wanted to talk, then hardly said a word. We just walked and ended up at the paddock, then he wanted me to get in the paddock and stroke that dammed horse; the one that killed Lowell. I think that he is either losing his marbles or is up to something." Said Tomas. "Very strange behaviour, maybe he is our family killer, we will need to keep a close eye on him Tomas." Then they went to collect their beverage.

Chad never moved and sat quietly in the corner, sipping his coffee and setting his stare into open space as though he was not totally with it. "You look rather perturbed, Chad, what is it that troubles you? Is it to do with Grant and Demmie?" Asked Greta. "Not them, Greta, they are wlcome to each other, I don't give them a second thought as they are welcome to each other, opps, said that twice. I have a hunch. It is just a hunch but I do not want to bother you with it as you have enough to think about after losing Malcolm and now Lowell so tragically. I may be wrong but it just does not add up and I am pretty sure that Star did not do the killing. I need to play my hand and if I am right, then Cadiston will need to know what I have discovered. Pity I had not thought it out earlier in the day and had it done then I could have told Cadiston while he was here this morning." Said Chad.

"Is it to do with Lowell's death? If it is then there must be something we can help with. Jennifer and I will be only too glad to help solve his murder for we believe that is what it was." Said Greta. "Just as I do, maybe both of you can but only if you are sure and it will not distress you too much. I need to get Kansas to the paddock on his own and it is imperative that he does not see or speak with his parents, especially his father that is. If he does then my plan goes out of the window. If my theory is correct and I believe that it is, then someone else killed Lowell and tried to make it look like it was Star. Star will talk to me. No, I am not mad. She will not use words but actions and if my hunch is correct, it may lead us to Lowell's murderer." Said Chad. "If we can help to bring Lowell's killer to prison, then we will. You go back to the paddock and Jennifer and I will get him there for you. Just leave it to us." Said Greta.

"Alright but please be very careful. If my hunch is correct, he is an extremely dangerous person. I will make my way back to the paddock and stay there until you arrive." Said Chad.

He stood slowly, waited a few seconds and under the watchful eyes of Tomas and Lizabeth, left the room. "He is definitely up to something, Tomas, so as I said, we need to keep a close eye on him." Said Lizabeth as she watched Chad leave. "Do you think that I should I follow him now?" Asked Tomas. "No, that would look suspicious as we are being watched at the moment by Greta and her snivelling daughter but what I will do is ask what they were talking about." Said Lizabeth. She waited until Greta had left her daughter's side, then Lizabeth walked slowly across the room and sat down beside her. "Jennifer my dear girl, we are concerned for you and your mother so can you tell me what were you, your mother, and Uncle Chad whispering about?" "Nothing really Aunt Lizabeth. To be quite honest, he was not making any sense, no sense at all and I think that he may be –. Now, what is the saying? Umm –. Losing it? Yes, that is it, losing it. We are quite worried about him and wondered whether we should call the doctor." Said Jennifer. "Well, with all that has been happening of late it is not surprising, now is it?" Said Lizabeth. "I suppose not but then I am only ten years old so what do I know." She stood and walked to her mother who was waiting by the door. "Nosey, very nosey, wanted to know what we had been talking about, Mother. Well she can just keep guessing. Now tell me again about Uncle Chad?" Said Jennifer. "He has a theory concerning your brother's death and we are going to help him prove it." Said Greta. "Help him, how do we do that, Mother?" Enquired Jennifer. "By getting Kansas to the paddock so that a horse can talk to Chad. I know it sounds silly but he knows what he is doing." Said Greta. "Does he think that Kansas killed Lowell?" Jennifer asked. "I don't know but he has a theory and needs us to bring him to the paddock." Said Greta. "He is outside, I will go and find him and if you are going to the paddock then I will bring him to you." Jennifer replied smiling. "See you at the paddock but be very careful, Jennifer. If Chad is right then Kansas is a very dangerous person." Said Greta. "I will be very careful, Mother." Greta went in one direction while her daughter went in another to begin the search for her cousin.

"Now where are those two going? Greta was speaking to Chad before he left and why has she gone that way and her daughter the other. This is all very suspicious. We had better find Kansas and tell him to be very wary of them all." Said Lizabeth. "I saw him go upstairs a while ago and have not seen him come back down so I assume that he is still up there." Said Tomas.

"Then best we go up and find him before they do." Said Lizabeth. "No fear of that my dear, they are both going out-side." Said Tomas.

Jennifer did not need to search long before she had found him. "Hello Kansas." "Hello cousin, you look sad, can I help you in any way?" Asked Kansas. "I feel lost without my broth-er and you are the nearest to him that I have so will you walk with me a while, just to keep me company?" Asked Jenifer softly. "Glad to, Jennifer, just walk wherever you want to go because I will be at your side." Said Kansas and she took his hand as they began their walk. "Where are we going then?" Asked Kansas. "Nowhere in particular, I don't want to talk just walk. That is what I used to do with Lowell." Said Jennifer. "Alright." They walked on in silence. She led him around the garden then around the Manor, slowly bringing him toward the paddock where Chad and her mother waited.

"That is the way to the stables, are you sure you want to go there?" Asked Kansas. "Please Kansas, I need to see the horse that was responsible for killing my brother. I feel that I want to throw a stone at it." Said Jennifer.

"If you are sure." She gripped his hand tighter and they walked on. Nearer and nearer they came to the paddock and now they could see Chad and Greta fussing over Star and her foal. She led him right up to the gate, and the second that Star saw him, her eyes changed from their softness to a wild frightened look. She then whinnied loudly as though saying "It is him!" and with her foal following closely, she galloped away from them. "See, that proves it! That is one mad killer horse, Jennifer, and that cer-tainly proves it beyond all doubt. Let us be away from here be-fore someone else gets stomped by the mad beast of an animal. I certainly do not want it to be me." He raised his voice directing his words at Chad and Greta. "Mad, both of you are completely mad being in there with that murderous creature! That is a killer horse and should be put down and if I had Uncle Grant's handgun, I would do it. I am surprised at you, Aunt Greta, being in the paddock with that thing especially after it killed your son, my cousin." "Just trying to understand her behaviour, Kansas, will you not come in here with her?" Said Chad.

"You must be joking, there is no way that you will get me in there with that mad killer horse! Absolutely no chance, no chance at all. A herd of wild horses could not drag me in with that damned thing." Jennifer had already entered the paddock and was standing beside her mother and uncle. "Well Jennifer, all I can say is that you are just as mad as they are so when you all get stomped don't come crying to me. You have Chad and your mother here with you now so I will be going. There is something I have just remembered that I should have done earlier. See you later." He turned and left almost in a run.

Chad shook his head while they watched him running away. "I hoped that I was wrong, Greta, but Star's reaction to him has just proved it." "You mean that he is the one, it was Kansas who killed Lowell in such a brutal way? And Jennifer was alone with him? Oh my, we could have put her in danger!" Greta looked horrified. "If I am right about him then he would not harm Jennifer in broad daylight with people about everywhere, too many witnesses." Said Chad. Her face softened and she said. "I know that you would not put her in any kind of danger but I will have –." He placed his hand onto her shoulder. "Patience Greta, what you said is true, I would not put Jennifer in any kind of danger. She was perfectly safe with him and it is not proven yet but Cadiston will need to know this additional piece of information that I have found out. There is also something else that he should know, something that Kansas said and Cadiston will know how to deal with it. It does make you wonder if he was behind all the murders but why would he be and what would he stand to gain from all their deaths? He is not a Mandaten by birth so he has no claim to the estate. If it was him then it is just a senseless murder based on his jealousy." Said Chad. "By saying that I am sure that you know he was extremely jealous of Lowell and he would often jibe at him. I would not have thought that on its own was enough to make him kill but then we don't know what goes on in his mind." Said Greta and shivered.

"That is true, Greta. I have always had my suspicions about his state of mind and have observed some strange behaviour. I often wondered just what he would be capable of. It does puzzle me though because if he was somehow connected to all the deaths and he is not in line to become the next Lord or have a claim to the estate, what could he hope to gain? If he did take part in killing Malcolm and Kevin, as two of the three male heirs –. I am sure that he would need help to attempt to take Grant's life next. James and Lowell both carried the family's surname and would be considered if Grant were not alive but they are both gone. It makes absolutely no sense, there is nothing for him to gain. Are we heading in the wrong direction and have got it all wrong? Anyhow, whatever we do now, it is imperative to keep this information to ourselves.We must not let on that we suspect Kansas of Lowell's death in any way." Said Chad.

"I will try Chad but it will be an extremely difficult task and I am sure for Jennifer also." Said Greta. "It will, Mother, but if we are to catch him then we must try really hard to pretend that everything is normal with him." Jennifer replied. "You are so grown up, Jennifer, and you make perfect sense. I will say that it is to be the same for me, Greta. If it is him, then I would like to –. Well, never mind that. I need to tell Cadiston straight away as he is the one who will know how to deal with this information. There is something else, it was when Kansas was down here and he said that if he had Grant's gun then he would shoot her. Grant's first wife was shot, now that certainly makes you wonder. I will tell Cadiston that as well, there is quite a bit to disclose." Said Chad.

The instant that Kansas had gone, Star and her new foal had returned to be at their side and as Jennifer stroked Diamond's neck, she asked. "Tell me Uncle Chad, did Star speak to you?" He smiled and patted the mare. "She certainly did, Jennifer, but that is just between us and must remain so." Mum's the word then." Said Jennifer smiling.

"Absolutely, now we will head slowly back to the Manor and then I will go to my room and ring Cadiston to tell him my theory. Now, we all need to put on a very good act." He said and went into the barn, returning with an onion. "This will not be very pleasant for you both but will help to add some authenticity." He cut the onion and it instantly made their eyes smart. They then left the paddock and walked very slowly, dragging their feet as if they were weighted with deep-sea diver's boots. With Jennifer and Greta both having red eyes and tears running down their face, it was giving the impression that the sorrow they felt at their sad loss and by going to the paddock had increased their pain and had overwhelmed them. They had made their plan of action and when they arrived back and the instant that they were inside it would be acted upon leaving Chad free to make his phone call.

Later that Friday morning, 10th of October, and after their early visit to Mandaten Manor to watch the forensic team complete their survey of the stables, Cadiston, Mac, and WPC Rendham were again back at the station.

"First thing, Mac, we need to get a team searching the whole Mandaten family tree. We only need to find out all the spouse's surnames before they were married so that we have their partners and their family trees. We know that one of them is Kaysten and he is married to Lizabeth, we need that investigated to see if we can find a link. We need as much family tree info as possible. Also, we need to check on the Standish family line." Mac was about to ask why but Cadiston spoke first. "Don't ask, Mac. It is just something that I personally need to do." "Leave that one to me then and I will ask my friend, who is the library ancestral researcher, to find out for us." Said Mac.

"You will need to tell them why we require the information but don't tell them everything." Said Cadiston. "Got it." Mac picked up the phone and dialled his friend's number. While he did this, Cadiston had begun sifting through the evidence that they had just gathered. On Monday, the pen with the fingerprints on it had been sent to the lab to enable them to lift the print from it and they were waiting for that to be analysed. When the internal postal clerk came into the office, he was whistling merrily as usual and said. "Hi both. Shush, sorry, Mac is on the phone but got internal mail for you DCI, from the lab."

"Thanks Bennie, appreciated. Surely can't be from what we left on Monday, they haven't had time." Said Cadiston. Mac was back with him after his call and was looking rather pleased with himself. "All sorted, there will be two of their team working on the information that we require. There will be Richard Foxall and Hattie Morset, she is a family friend and what is better, they can make a start straight away." "Well done, Mac. Now, for the post –." He eagerly ripped the envelope open and began to read. "Well there is a surprise, they have lifted the print from the pen already and have also collated Francis and Olito's prints that they obtained and that is an excellent result. It supports our suspicion, Mac, so the result is just perfect and as we had thought. The fingerprints have been matched and belong to non-other than Demmie Mandaten. That confirms that she stole the syringe from the kitchen and with the deadly mixture filling in it, she waited for an opportunity to arise, then used it to inject Bonnie's dessert and, in effect, murdered both her and her unborn little girl child." Said Cadiston. "We have our double-murderess bang to rights, Cadders. On this evidence alone we can arrest her but what if she is involved in any of the other murders? If we go ahead and arrest her now wouldn't that alert her accomplice?" Asked Mac. "You are beginning to think like a detective, Mac, and a very valid point. For the double murder of Bonnie and her child, we have her bang to rights and there is no way that she can wriggle out of it but if she was involved in all the other murders, there is an accomplice, and as you said they would be alerted if we arrest her. My strong hunch and suspicions all point to Grant, apart from James and Lowell. Demmie and Grant are having an affair which is probably deeper than he let's on and Grant wants to own Mandaten and be the next Lord. So my friend, if they are the guilty parties, then we have motive, opportunity, and the means to commit the crimes. Now, before we can arrest her, we need to have the results of all the fingerprints, D.N.A and, blood samples that were collected by Francis and Olito. They need to be matched with those from forensics at the scene of the crime and the D.N.A. from the skin or flesh samples taken from beneath the nails of James and Gloria. When they returned with us to the Manor on our latest visit, were you observant enough to notice that Kansas was a bit sheepish and was not keen to supply his prints or D.N.A.? And how he was still shielding his right arm and shoulder? There are also the scratches and I am not convinced at all about how he says he got them on his neck. And now he has another gash on his hand, not a clean-cut but a jagged gash that is inflamed. Not clean so possibly from a rusty nail so why do you think that is Mac?" Asked Cadiston. "That one is easy. When we checked out the garden, there was not a single pot out of place, tipped over or broken and not a rose bush broken or crushed which would have been the case if he had fallen into one. Even if it had been cleaned up by the gardener, it would still be broken and none were. Another thing, the chalky debris on his sleeve and his back, which you took a crafty sample of, did not match any of that on the containers, urns, pots, or anything else they are in. We have his DNA and when the analysis is done on what was under James and Gloria's fingernails, they may match up. There is the other thing about him favouring his right arm and I noticed a few nails in the stable that could have caused an injury like that gash. As they were all dirty or rusty, that would account for it being inflamed. My guess is that he injured his arm in an attack and likewise the gash to his hand. D.N.A. will itemise if his is at the scene of a crime." Mac said. "Well done, keep thinking like that and you will become a full detective sergeant instead of acting Mac. Right, that is him but Grant was also rather reluctant to provide samples. I am certain that Grant's will match those found on the oars and on the boat which in itself is not evidence enough but is he a good swimmer? That is something that we need to find out. I know that Chad's prints will also be on the boat but he still cannot be excluded as I still don't know if he is innocent of all crimes. I am a bit foxed about the small footprints that I took the casts of at the Devil's Dyke and those that the forensics sampled at the woods near the archery site. Demmie is a size six but these were only a size four, we still need to look at everyone's shoe size as well. Francis and Olito should have done that when they collected the other Samples." Said Cadiston. "My fault there, I forgot to ask them to get them, I only told them to get fingerprints, blood, and D.N.A. I'm sorry." Said Mac. "Not a major error, Mac, and soon corrected without causing a real problem." Said Cadiston. He was about to ask for the car to be brought around when the phone rang. "Cadiston." He answered. "Hello Ashton, we have finished the post-mortems on the family Larkspere, that is the results on Sammie and her family. Charles thinks that you should be here to see the bodies so can you come over now?" Asked Samantha. "We were just going to pay another visit to the Manor as we have a major lead but that can wait a bit longer as they are going nowhere. So I'll be with you in twenty minutes, Samantha." The phone went dead. "Go bring the car around, Mac, we are taking a trip to the mortuary. The results are done on Sammie and her family and Charles wants us to have a look at the bodies." Said Cadiston. "On the way boss." Mac said and made his way to the car.

On the way past the front desk, Cadiston spoke to John. "On our way to the mortuary, John, we have a few bodies to look at. I expect to be there for some time, probably until late this afternoon. We will go straight home from there. If there are any real emergencies, get me on the mobile otherwise –. I will have a quiet weekend with the wife. I have a strong feeling that from Monday morning, things will start to get a bit more hectic as we delve deeper into all the Mandaten deaths and uncover more and more evidence." "Right you are, have a good weekend and build up your strength for next week." Said John. "Do my best,

John, see you on Monday." After leaving the police station, they drove straight to the forensics mortuary and as Cadiston had suspected, they spent the remainder of the afternoon there, reading and inspecting the bodies.

After arriving back at the Manor and before entering, Greta, Jennifer, and Chad had a look in the lounge where they saw Kansas talking with his mother. "There is Kansas but where is his father? They have not seen or heard us yet so make it look really good, and don't hold back Greta. It has to look real." Said Chad. She ran her hand lovingly across his cheek and he smiled at her. Entering the lounge, Lizabeth and Kansas's heads turned and they could see that real tears were flowing. Now it was time for action so Greta shouted at Chad and yellled, "You are a bloody fool Chad." She then slapped Chad really hard across the face and while it rang out, Lizabeth smiled. Then Greta said very loudly so that they could hear clearly. "I detest swearing and you have made me swear. Damn you Chadrick, that was a silly and stupid thing you made us do. I just cannot come at your reasoning, it was bad enough for me but especially bad for Jennifer." "I am so sorry Greta, I thought it might help but in hindsight, it would have been better for you both not to have come to the paddock or anywhere near the stables, it was far too painful for you." Chad said and turned toward his nephew. "Kansas, I am surprised that you brought Jennifer there or allowed her anywhere near the place." He turned and left before he had the time to answer. Greta and her daughter were really sobbing, they did not need to pretend as they were both distraught after Lowell's untimely death and the strong onion was also playing its part making their eyes extremely red. They were holding on to each other for comfort. Chad lingered and the next part of the plan was executed. She snapped at him again. "For goodness' sake, Chad, just get out of my sight I have had enough of you for one day."

With his head held low he turned and left. When he walked away, his head hung lower. He then went up to his room and immediately rang the police station. "Station here, Constable Cutting speaking." "Chadrick Mandaten here, can you put me through to

DCI Cadiston, please?" Asked Chad. "Sorry sir, he is not in the office and I do not expect him back today so not until Monday morning. Is your call urgent, sir?" Asked Constable Cutting.

"Urgent enough, Constable Cutting, but nothing that will not keep until Monday morning. I have some new information and a theory for him regarding the death of Lowell Mandaten and need to run it by him. it would be best if I told him now –. I guess that I can sit on it until Monday. If he does come back in or you have any contact with him at any time over the weekend, tell him to call me but not on the landline, on my mobile. It is imperative to make sure it is not the landline. My number is 07771110023. If not, I will call back 8.30 sharp on Monday morning have –." The phone line went suddenly silent.

"Hello? Hello? Hello? Hello sir? I cannot hear you, are you still there?" Constable Cutting received no response so checked the number and found it to be Mandaten Manor. Without delay, he dialled the number and after several rings heard. "The number that you are calling is currently unavailable." He then expected to hear. "If you would like to leave a message, please speak after the tone –. Beep." But on this occasion, the second part of the message did not come. "There must be a problem with the landline. It happens –. He didn't say it was desperately urgent so just leave the number and message for Cadders when he comes in on Monday. Ah Bennie, just before you go, can you pop this message onto DCI Cadiston's desk, please?" Said Constable Cutting.

"No problem, John, will do. Looking forward to the weekend off. It is almost twenty minutes to five and I have done 9 minutes overtime already so two more minutes will not hurt, now will it? See you on Monday morning, night John."

Chad had tried to redial the number and had found that he could not raise a dialling tone so guessed that there was a fault on the line. He had passed on his message and that meant that his theory was in hand but he would need to hold on to his information until Monday. For the rest of the day, Greta, Jennifer, and Chad avoided each other as part of the plan. The moment that Greta saw Chad on Saturday morning, 11th of October, and before anyone else was present, she quietly asked him. "Did you get through to Cadiston Friday afternoon?" "No, he was out and as I was talking to the constable that took my call, the phone line went suddenly dead. What is even more strange, I could not redial and even more so, I cannot find my mobile phone anywhere. I remember going to bed and leaving it in the lounge on Wednesday evening but the next morning it was gone and that was Thursday, the morning that Lowell was murdered. I have asked everyone apart from you and Jennifer if they had seen it they all said no. I have searched and looked everywhere but it is not to be found." Said Chad. "Those two seem to be very cosy over there with their heads together again and whispering. Makes you wonder about yesterday's little episode." Said Lizabeth. "Strange thing about yesterday, he wanted to talk then said nothing that made any sense, and why take me and Kansas to the paddock, very strange behaviour." "Say no more about that Tomas, now after yesterday's incident and the slap Greta planted on Chads face they look very cosy whispering in the corner together today." Chad saw Lizabeth watching them so left Greta and walked away. Thankfully, Friday had passed by without any further incidents at Mandaten Manor, much to the relief of the surviving members of the family. Saturday morning had seen them all rise as usual and now in the afternoon, they were all feeling relaxed. Grant and Demmie had, once again, disappeared. Greta and Jennifer had left the lounge and were walking in the garden. Chad was with the horses, leaving Lizabeth with her husband and son snuggling close together and whispering. "Something I ought to tell you, Lizabeth. When I was upstairs on Friday afternoon after Chad's strange behaviour, I overheard him calling the police station. That was after he had taken me to the paddocks on the pretence of wanting to talk and said nothing that would make sense. Later, Jennifer took Kansas there. It all seems very strange and thereafter, he called them. Why would he do that after we had been to the paddock and seen that murderous horse and not before? Don't know why he wanted to but I heard him say that he wanted to speak to that new detective, Cadiston, the one that keeps coming here." Said Tomas. "On Friday you say? So what was that about I wonder –. I told you that we needed to watch him closely as he was up to something. Wait, it is just a thought but if he killed Lowell, then he may want to incriminate Kansas or you somehow. Maybe that is why he took you both to the stable and paddock, all that crying from Greta and Jennifer and the slap in the face were to fool us. You are a fool, Tomas! Why did you leave it until now to tell us about the phone call?" Said Lizabeth angrily. "Sorry Lizabeth, it just slipped my mind. What do you think and suggest that we do then?" Asked Tomas.

"More to the point, did he get to speak to Cadiston and what did he say?" Asked Lizabeth. "He could not speak to him, that much I do know. To stop him from talking any further I pulled the phone line out and broke the lead. I made it look like an accident with moving a table that was near the junction box." Said Tomas. "Good thinking, for once! Now leave it with me and I will think of something. Go on, leave me to think this out." Said Lizabeth. "Come Kansas." Tomas and Kansas then went upstairs to talk in private. When Chad came in from the stables and saw Lizabeth sitting on her own, he smiled at her before speaking. "Don't suppose you have seen my Demmie, have you? She disappeared early this morning and I haven't seen her since just after breakfast. I have looked but cannot seem to find her anywhere." Said Chad.

"Sorry Chad, no. I haven't seen her for quite a while –. Or Grant, come to that and his car is gone." Said Lizabeth. "Do you think that they could be together?" He asked. She looked at him and tried to hide her sly grin, this was her chance to stir up a real problem for him. "Who can say? You know that they have seen a lot of each other lately and for some time. Bonnie had her suspicions about Grant having an affair so maybe she was right all along. Perhaps it is them together so all I know is they are both missing and at the same time and that could be suspicious but well –. You can draw your own conclusion from that." Said Lizabeth slyly. He shrugged his shoulders. "No problem, she mostly does her own thing these days anyhow. In fact, has done so for quite a while now but if they are together, then they are welcome to each other. If she comes in, will you tell her I need to speak to her? I've got something I need to discuss so I will be upstairs in our room." Said Chad.

"I will tell her." Said Lizabeth, with no reply to her Chad turned and went upstairs. Lizabeth then ordered some afternoon tea and a pot of coffee. With her tea poured, she sat sipping it while she waited deep within her thoughts to contemplate what the next step would be to stir up trouble. Minutes later, she was on her mobile phone. Thirty minutes had passed when she heard a car pull up. Looking outside, she could see that it was a taxi. Just as quickly as it had arrived it drove away. A few moments later, Demmie came into the lounge with a real swank in her step and a broad grin on her face. She was carrying some shopping bags and without waiting, Lizabeth pitched her voice to make her sound worried. "Oh! there you are Demmie my dear! Thank goodness that you are back, you had better see what is wrong with your husband. He sounded quite angry and went to your room, he wants to talk with you desperately and he did not sound very happy." "Well, he is not going to spoil my day as I have just received some wonderful news so he can go whistle and wait." Said Demmie in reply. "I must say that you look rather pleased with yourself." Remarked Lizabeth. "I am, and I have something much more important to deal with than him. Now, have you seen Grant anywhere? There is something very, very important that I need to tell him before anything else." Said Demmie. "You may pour the coffee, Alfred, my son and husband will be down presently." Said Lizabeth. "Yes, Miss Lizabeth." Said Alfred and Lizabeth turned her attention back to Demmie. "I thought that Grant and you were b –. Well, it does not matter I was wrong in that assumption. His car is gone but he quite obviously is not with you." "No, he is not. I had something to do but what makes you think that he was?" Asked Demmie. "No reason. So no, I haven't seen him all the morning but I do think you should go to see what your husband wanted you for, he did sound rather angry." Said Lizabeth. At that moment Kansas entered the lounge and spoke in a hurried and frightened way. "Oh, Aunt Demmie, you are here. I am I glad I have seen you before you go to your room. I have just overheard Uncle Chad ranting and cursing, he sounds extremely angry. I am afraid I stood and listened to him and he was saying something about you having an affair with Uncle Grant." "Dear, oh dear. It would come out now and before I have seen Grant to tell him my news –. It was not supposed to come out yet but with what I have to disclose, I had better go up and get it over with." She then made her way slowly up the stairs. Lizabeth smiled and Whispered. "Well done, Son. With my prompt, you timed that perfectly. Now, that will stir up a hornet's nest between them two and involve Grant." "What was that you just said about Chadrick? Did I hear you right that he is ranting and cursing in their room about an affair that Demmie is having and it will stir up a hornet's nest?" Asked Greta. "You must have crept in as silent as a mouse, I didn't even hear you come back but yes, that's right Greta. He knows about the affair and Kansas said that he sounded really angry." Said Lizabeth. "That's right, Aunt Greta, and I can't be sure as I may have misheard but I thought I heard him say that he was going to beat her for all the years of falseness and lies that she has spun him since they have been together." Said Kansas. "I know that Bonnie spoke to you about an affair as she did to me. It must be true then that she and Grant are having an affair. Surely you thought it too, Lizabeth, especially after talking to Bonnie and how did Chad find out?" Asked Greta. "Maybe I did or maybe I did not. It is nothing to do with me so I didn't want to get involved with it. I may have hinted something to that effect to Chad but who cares how he found out." Said Lizabeth smiling. "That is so very typical of you, Lizabeth. If it did not involve a benefit for you then you did not want to know. Now you have managed to stir up trouble and I do not believe it is as you and Kansas are saying. Now where is Grant?" Asked Greta. "I have absolutely no idea and I do not care where he is. His car went out early this morning after she had left in a taxi, who cares anyhow and he hasn't been seen all day." Said Lizabeth.

"Well, his car is not there so he must still be out somewhere." Said Greta. Lizabeth looked at Greta and smiled. "Well, who cares Greta?" "I do, for one." replied Greta. "And you are not alone, so do I Mother." Said Jennifer.

"I am going back up to see what is going on, Mother. Said Kansas. "Be very careful, Kansas." Said Lizabeth. "Don't worry so, Mother, I will be fine." He winked at her, turned, and was gone. Just then, two gunshots rang out, and then it was quiet. A few seconds later, Kansas came running back down the stairs and into the lounge. This time, the smug look on his face had disappeared. He had turned white and now he looked really scared. "Quick Mother, you had better ring the police! Those gunshots came from their bedroom. I thought that we −. Well, no matter what I thought. It must be Uncle Chad and I think that he has gone completely mad. I think that he may have a gun in there and has shot and killed Aunt Demmie. I was listening to the arguing and was just coming back down when I heard the shots."

Lizabeth was not a bit flustered by this and after calmly picking up the phone, she dialed 999. The line was dead. "That is strange." She then remembered that Tomas had broken the cable. Without speaking, she picked up her mobile and dialled. "Emergency which service do you require?" "Police and be quick there is a mad gunman in the house!" She said very calmly and seconds later, the connection was made. She now changed the tone of her voice from calm to panicking, this was noticed by Greta who thought it was strange.

"You need to hurry to Mandaten Manor, I fear for all our lives! It's Chadrick and he has gone completely mad and was threatening to kill his wife and we have just heard shots fired." Kansas took the phone from his mother, "Sorry mother is too frightened so I have taken over the call, I am her son Kansas, he said he had killed before and this would be easy, now hurry, please hurry!" Lizabeth screamed and sounded almost hysterical. "I hear you". Greta thought that those words were strange as she knew Chad well and the word kill had not been spoken before. "A car has been dispatched, now try to remain calm. Can you see him and are you under immediate threat?" Asked the voice on the other end of the phone. Lizabeth now held the phone again, "Stay calm you say? With a mad gunman on the loose? In answer to your question, no he is in their room and –." Ten minutes had passed since the first gunshots sounded and there was then the sound of two more blasts. "Oh! My goodness, that was gunshots again! I believe he has done it, what should we do?" Then there was the sound of someone running down the stairs. Within seconds, Tomas was standing by her side. "If there is any danger to you, can you vacate the building easily and safely?" The operator asked.

"Yes, we can as he is still upstairs so shall we get out?" Asked Lizabeth and Tomas was hovering and waving his hand to indicate that he wanted the phone. "No, wait a minute, my husband wants to speak to you." All the time that he was speaking, his eyes were fixed on Lizabeth. "This is Tomas Kaysten and we are not in any immediate danger as I have just had to hit Chadrick hard over the head to stop him but sadly not before he had shot and killed his wife. He shot at her twice and she is in a hell of a mess. From what little I could see it looks like she has been shot in the chest. I do believe that he may have been coming to kill us all but now I have stopped him. I had no choice but to hit him in self-defence and to stop him, I also had to save my wife, my son, and the rest of the family! I don't know but he may have been the one that was killing the family so please hurry and get here. We are safe now and he is knocked unconscious but get here quickly." Then, very strangely, they heard two more shots fired and they began to panic. "The car is en route and will be there in a short while, sir." The operator had heard the shots. "That sounded very much like more gunshots, sir. If you can keep an eye on him, do so. If not, vacate the premises but stay safe." Continued the operator. "Stay safe you say? That I intend to do but that was two more shots fired." Said Tomas. "I heard you say that you had rendered him unconscious, sir. It seems strange that two more shots have been fired. Just stay away from him and if he starts to come down the stairs, vacate the premises." Said the operator.

"Probably nervous reflex and as far as staying safe, that we will do! I think the police are here now." The phone was hung up. With the police officers moving slowly up the stairs, Lizabeth looked first at Kansas, then at Tomas. As he spun his story to the police phone operator, he had winked at her. Kansas saw this and smiled but this action was also seen by Greta.

"I thought he was unconscious so how could there be two more shots fired?" Asked Greta. "Probably nervous reaction, Greta." Then he smiled.

"I cannot imagine what there is to wink and smile about any of you and I cannot believe that Chad would do such a thing. He has always been very protective of the family, all the family, and would not murder the people that he loves and cares for! Definitely not the family he was taken into and given a life, he is not like that, plus, he hates violence of any sort." Said Greta.

At this point, they heard another car on the gravel but did not hear the bell ring or the door open. "Strange." Said Lizabeth, then jumped as Grant suddenly appeared from out of nowhere. "That is very silly talk, Greta! How do we know what he is really like as he is not a Mandaten. For all we know, he probably has bad blood coursing through his veins and probably comes from an evil family of murders." Said Grant. "Where did you just spring from? Surely not from the car that just pulled up. One minute not there, then as if by magic, you appear. You did not drive up and come in through the front door so where did you spring from?" Asked Greta. "None of your business where I have been or where I sprang from, leave it alone, Greta!" Snapped Grant.

"Well, wherever you where will come out but what you said is absolute nonsense Uncle Grant! Uncle Chadrick is a very kind and considerate man and I love him." Said Jennifer. "You are nothing more than just a silly little child, Jennifer,and you know absolutely nothing about life. Now, the police are here so –." He paused briefly. "Well, we need to let them do their work and talk to them when they want us to." He then disappeared again. Tomas had followed them to the base of the stairs and stepped forward to speak to the officers. "Take care, officers, he is armed with a shotgun." "Just stay back, sir. We understand that the gunman had been rendered unconscious by you, and two more shots were fired after that so how could he reload and fire the weapon if he were unconscious, well our detective will sort that one out, but do not worry, sir, our firearms unit is on the way. We will just have a quick look and be very cautious, you need have no fear of that." Said an officer.

The arriving officers continued moving slowly up the stairs, watching the bedroom door for any sign of the gunman leaving the room. Although knowing that he had been rendered unconscious, they were still prepared to be confronted by an armed man. They approached the door with caution, then hesitated while listening for any sound. There was only silence so they slowly pushed the door open and then just stood in the doorway staring at a scene of carnage.

"Good grief man, what carnage! Just look at the mess that poor woman is in, she is almost cut in half." Said one officer named Jake.

"Looks like there is blood everywhere so I, for one, am not going in there." Said another officer named Steve. "Me neither, this is quite close enough, thank you." Said a third officer Ted. "From the doorway it looks like she was over there by the bathroom and he had his back to the door and blasted her from where he stood. The impact of the double shot must have carried her in the air onto the wall and on impact she slid to the ground. Looks like a cold-blooded murder in the first degree to me." Said Jake. "Have to agree with you there but from what I know about shotguns, to shoot from here and the victim is laying over there –. Must have been one hell of a load and a big blast. The gun is near him, in fact, it is in his hands and that leads me to believe that he is the shooter and must be unconscious as he has not moved at all, Jake. He is bleeding from the head wound." Said Steve. "Guess that chap must have hit him pretty hard to stop him, probably with that old hammer thing laying there. We had better stand down the firearms boys as they will not be needed now. We can leave it all to the newly promoted DCI Cadiston, now that he is here." Said Ted. "Acting DCI, Ted, not got his stripes fully yet." Steve announced. Cadiston appeared and asked. "Has anyone called for an ambulance?" "One was dispatched with the initial emergency call and we have called for a second when we found there were two bodies, one for each of them." Said Jake. "Two bodies?" Asked Cadiston. "Yes, two bodies, the shooter and his victim." Answered Jake. "Anyone been inside the room?" Asked Cadiston. "No one, DCI Cadiston. We can see quite enough of the blood bath from the doorway, thank you." Said Steve. "Steve is right, it looks like a real blood bath in there." Said Ted, I had to use the bathroom to be sick.

"So, I can safely say that no one has checked on either body to see if there is any sign of life?" Asked Cadiston. "Nope, left it all for you just as we found it." Affirmed Steve. The ambulances had arrived and Jooners and his forensic team were also there and waiting to get into the room to analyse the scene. Mac had thought quickly and acted instantly. He had assessed there was no danger from the shooter and told firearms to stand down. "Has the shooter moved at all since you got here?" Asked Mac. "Not at all, I think that other chap must have hit him pretty hard." Said Steve. "Check him out for me first, please Jooners." Jooners walked over and did this and was shaking his head when he came back to Cadiston. "Skull is badly fractured, he has lost a lot of blood but is still alive. He needs to get to the hospital pronto if he is to be saved, even then it will be touch and go." "Mac, get that first ambulance crew up here in double time and get Chadrick to the hospital and be quick about it!" Ordered Cadiston. The first crew ran up the stairs and within seconds, had Chad's still body on the stretcher and with a blood-soaked bandage around his head, they were on their way to the Royal with their lights flashing and the siren blasting. "Tell me, Jake, was the gun still in his hands when you saw him?" Asked Cadiston. "Told you, Cadders, we left everything just as it was for you to see. With that much blood about, we were not going in there were we Ted, Steve." Replied Jake.

"Hmm, very strange that one, so he was unconscious after being struck and still holding the gun as though ready to take another shot? Now that is interesting but does not ring true. Ok Jake, Steve, Ted just keep everyone in the lounge please and I will be there in a minute to speak with them when I have finished here." Said Cadiston.

"Will do." The three officers went downstairs. For fifteen minutes, he watched the forensic team at work while he and Mac conducted their own survey of the room. "Gun was still in his hand after a crushing blow to the skull, is that possible? Not in my book. Live cartridges scattered all around him, does not look right. If he had intended on murdering the rest of the family, they would be in a cartridge belt or pocket for easy access –. He shot from here and that hit the victim with enough force to carry her through the air and smash her against the wall. Back to the door, shot both barrels into victim's chest, sending her crashing into the wall near the bathroom. I am not a firearms expert but even I know the distance is too far. Reloaded, two more shots fired, this time under the bed –. Very interesting but it somehow does not fit, Mac. There are far too many discrepancies already. We are being led falsely again Mac, what we need to know is what really took place here. Chadrick Mandaten, you are the only one who can tell me that." Speculated Cadiston.

He looked toward his forensic team's leader for a few minutes before speaking. "Jooners, you have seen the victim's body and the alleged shooter's body and have assessed their positions –. So, what do you think so far?" "First impression Cadders, without looking too close, cold blooded first-degree murder, of that we can be sure of. Now, good old Standish would jump for joy and settle for that verdict without looking any further but he is not here now but you are. I know for a fact that you will not be satisfied with first impressions and will want to search out the truth." Said Jooners. "True, and after you have had a look?" Asked Cadiston. "Well first thing, he stood there with his back to the door so that chap who hit him came up from behind. From the wound that he received, he hit him very hard and not just once. He was struck at least twice at the base of the skull. My guess is that he was struck twice while he was probably semi-conscious on the floor." Said Jooners.

"That sounds like he was struck three times." Concluded Cadiston.

"Indeed, that he was. Sandy, Shirly come over here a minute, need you two to act this out for us." Said Jooners. "Be right there, Boss." Said Sandy.

"Now then Sandy, you are the shooter so carefully take the gun and aim over there where the victim would have been standing. Shirly, here –." They moved accordingly. "Now I come in behind the shooter and whack him on the top of his head but as you can see that is not feasible. I would need to be very tall to strike him there. Ok, drop down as though you have been struck as realistically as possible." Sandy did this. "See, Cadders, the gun would not still be in the hand with your finger on the trigger so that leads me to believe that it was placed there after he was unconscious. Now, my guess is that he was not totally unconscious from the first strike so this is my thought –. I believe that a second person came in and whacked him again and from what I saw the blow was aimed at the same spot that killed Malcolm Mandaten, the only difference is that he was struck several times and this chap only twice but in the same spot." Continued Jooners. "That would mean that there was someone else in this room." Said Cadiston. "That is my assumption but after we have carried out a series of re-enactments, I will be able to define that much clearer. I know from the skull injury that he was hit three times, once on the top of his head and twice at the base of his skull which denotes that someone was above him when the first blow was struck. I may be repeating myself, Cadders, but –. Well, I was very curious as to why there was no call for forensics when Malcolm Mandaten was found. Well, my curiosity got the better of me and that set me thinking. A little while later, I asked Foulsham, your driver, and found out that when you asked if I could attend, your request was denied. It became even clearer when I found out that Standish was there with you and would not call us. Anyhow, I had my doubts from what your driver had told me and following your lead, I called Charles and went to the mortuary and he accommodated me by letting me see the body." Said Jooners. "Now that is very interesting Jooners, I was getting ready to put Grant in the frame for that murder but now I may have to think again." Said Cadiston. "Now another point, the evidence just does not fit. The distance from where the alleged shooter was standing and where the deceased was laying over by the bathroom –. Not a chance, the distance is far to great. Sandy again please. For the deceased to end up there, the shooter would need to be where Sandy is standing now and not just inside the bedroom door. After our full survey of the scene and investigation, I will be more accurate but without that, will it do you for now?" Asked Jooners.

"Didn't think this was a simple case, Jooners, and you have just confirmed my own thoughts. What say you Mac?" Cadiston turned to Mac. "Murder in the first degree, absolutely, but not by the person who we know as Chadrick Mandaten who I believe is a victim in this also." Said Mac. "Good thinking, Mac. Now you are beginning to see what some would miss." Said Cadiston.

"Only because I am with you, Cadders." Again Mac's comment made Cadiston smile. "Thanks Jooners, leave you to get on and be back in a while but now I will go and speak to the family." He stood for a moment in the doorway, weighing the event up in his mind, then followed by his DS, went downstairs. On the way down, he saw Alfred carrying a tray and followed him.

"Good, you are all here apart from Grant I believe. Do you know where he is?" Asked Cadiston. "Have not got a clue, Cadiston. He has been missing since early this morning just after breakfast, in fact. He appeared briefly after the shots had been fired, then disappeared again. Now if I have this right, you two are the detectives so you find him." Said Tomas very sarcastically.

"You need have no fear of that, sir, we most certainly will. DS Macswee, go have a look around outside." Said Cadiston. "Will do sir." They watched him leave. "Now then, who was it that made the initial 999 emergency call?" Asked Cadiston.

"That would be me, detective, Lizabeth Kaysten, I am –."

"The daughter of Lord and Lady Mandaten and married to Tomas Kaysten, you have a son named Kansas, yes that I remember.

Now, can you tell us exactly what was happening to make you call 999." "I was upstairs changing clothes and on the way down I heard Chadrick ranting and cursing in his room. He had found out that Demmie, that is his wife, was having an affair. I came down and went over to her and told her she had better see what is wrong with Chadrick as I heard him ranting and cursing in their room. He sounded extremely angry and was saying something about Demmie having an affair."Demmie's reply was 'It should not have come out yet, I had better get it sorted' and she went upstairs. I stayed down here in the lounge. It was a short while later that my son came running down and said that he was threatening to kill her. I believe I heard him say that he would kill them both, he had killed before so it would be easy to kill again but I just thought it was talk at first. But when Kansas came running in, I picked up the phone and rang. The rest you know." Said Lizabeth. "Kansas, now what did you hear?" Asked Cadiston. "I ran downstairs and shouted 'Quick someone ring the police, Uncle Chad has got a shotgun and is ranting at Demmie and threatening to shoot her if she doesn't say who the affair is with' and that is it. Then shots were fired and mother phoned." Said Kansas. "One more question, did you see the shotgun in his hands?" Asked Cadiston.

"Err, well umm –. Not exactly, I was not going in to face a loaded gun now was I? But –." He looked at his mother. "I did hear it click." He stammered.

"Thank you, then you came running down, Tomas?" Asked Cadiston. "He had already shot twice so I had to hit him to stop him doing anymore killing. He said that he had killed before and it would be easy to kill again. He then said 'now for the rest of you.' He had already shot his wife and reloaded so I was protecting my family." Said Tomas. "You struck him hard then?" Asked Cadiston. "Just as hard as I could detective." Said Tomas. "And how many times did you strike him?" Continued Cadiston. "Only the once, that was quite sufficient. He fell straight away and did not get up." Said Tomas. "And where on the head did you strike him, illustrate for me please Tomas?" Asked Cadiston.

He made the action of striking down and pointed to the top of the skull. "And what weapon did you use, sir?" Asked Cadiston. "Weapon? An old fashion knight's hammer, and after I dropped it on the floor and ran straight down the stairs. I came downstairs and took over the phone call to the police from my wife telling them what had happened." Said Tomas. "And that call will have been recorded, sir, and I will listen to it later. Is there anything else that you can tell me?" Asked Cadiston. "Not a thing, Detective, but I think this shows who the killer of our family is. He is not really one of us, just an adopted, unwanted child who has been sponging off us for many years." Tomas added. He did not answer but watched them and noted their body language. He noted their feet shuffling, no direct eye contact while giving evidence, hands wringing, arms folded across the body, Which is a classic mode of lying and self-protection. "One more question, sir, did you actually see the gun in his hands before you struck him?" Asked Cadiston. "Oh yes, I saw it alright. Just before I hit him." At this point he looked toward his wife. "He was turning and as I didn't want to get shot as his wife had, I hit him just as hard as I could." Said Tomas. "And that was here?" He pointed to the base of his skull and Tomas just nodded. "Thank you –." He had written down every word and all the body language movements and their eyes, he knew that the eyes can tell a lot. "That will be all for now." He then finished writing his notes. He could see that Jennifer was agitated so decided to ask her his questions next. "Now to you, Miss Jennifer, can you shed any light on what has happened?" "None at all, only that lies have been told, I was in the garden with Mother and when we came back in, Aunt Lizabeth and Kansas were talking. Then Uncle Tomas came running down but –." She hesitated.

"Go on, Miss, you were about to say something else." Cadiston encouraged her. She looked at her aunt. "It is what Aunt Lizabeth said and I know that it is not correct so why did she lie to you?" "How dare you call my wife a liar? And what do mean, Jennifer, what she said is not correct? You were outside." Said Tomas outraged. "That part is true, Uncle Tomas but she was not upstairs

335

changing, you were all sitting in the lounge when we went into the garden and then you and Kansas went away. That must have been upstairs. Then aunt Demmie came in, no −. That is not right, Uncle Chadrick came in and after speaking to you Aunt Lizabeth he went upstairs.Then Aunt Demmie came in and after speaking with you, she also went upstairs. We came back in and Lizabeth was still sitting in the same spot and in the same clothes, she had not changed. We could see you all from the garden and saw you and Kansas leave her still sitting in the same chair and then she made a call on her phone. Mother and I walked beneath Uncle Chadrick's window which was open and did not hear any of the shouting and arguing or anything else that you say was happening. Not until the gun shots." Said Jennifer. Tomas looked sheepishly at Lizabeth before answering. "You are a silly little child, Jennifer, and know nothing. You are the one that is telling lies just to protect your murderous Uncle Chadrick." Tomas stated. Jennifer was finding an inner strength as she again answered. "I may be ten years old, Uncle Tomas, but I do not lie, unlike all of you." "Why, you little −." Tomas started. "That will be quite sufficient, thank you sir." Said Mac, stepping between them. "We will find who is telling the truth and who is telling a lie so all you are required to do is answer our questions. Now then, Jennifer, you said that you had heard nothing until the gunshots and how many were there?" "Six. Two very close together, like both triggers were pulled simultaneously, then there was a space of maybe four or even five minutes. It may have been a bit longer but by that time we had come in before the next two were fired. After that, Tomas came running down the stairs, then there was a further time lapse of maybe five minutes or it may have been a bit longer and then there were a further two. The last two came while they were on the phone, now I do not know much about guns but if Uncle Chad was unconscious as Uncle Tomas has said how could he reload and fire two more shots to total six." "Stupid girl, that must have been while he reloaded after his first two shots and before I had knocked him unconscious." Said Tomas. "That will be quite sufficient of that talk, thank you, and I think that you all need to think again about what actually happened and your version of the story. Now then Jennifer, you said two shots close together, then a gap of maybe five minutes before the next two, then another gap of about the same duration before the final two shots, making six in total." Cadiston thought to himself. "Hmm, two shots after he was unconscious, interesting." "So six blasts in total?" Cadiston asked Jennifer. "Yes, I think that is accurate, it was all happening quickly. The shots came when we were all downstairs and they came very close together."

While Jennifer was talking, Cadiston caught the sheepish glance between Tomas, his wife, and son. This went into his notebook. Tomas spoke first. "You were not in here all the time, Jennifer, you were outside in the Garden. You cannot really tell where your Aunt Lizabeth was or where we were or, come to that, what really happened today, I ask —." "Thank you but we will ask the questions, sir, and will speak with you in a moment. Thank you, Jennifer, is there any other little thing that may help?" Cadiston asked.

"Only that I do not believe that Uncle Chadrick has it in him to do this terrible thing. Oh, he could defend himself well enough and I know that he hated violence and no matter what she had done, he would not and could not have done this." Jennifer said shaking her head. "Thank you, and Miss Greta, where were you?" Asked Cadiston, directing his gaze at Greta. "Walking in the garden with my daughter, then here in the lounge and I agree totally with what Jennifer has said. There is a lot of hate for Chadrick and none of you can deny that. He has done nothing but give love to all the family irrespective of how you treated him. Like my daughter, I heard nothing, no raised voices, arguing, or anything until the gun shots. The first two then a time lapse before the second two after which Tomas ran down the stairs, then a third two totaling six shots fired. Like my daughter said, I also noticed a discrepancy in Lizabeth's statement. She was or rather is still wearing the same clothes. I agree with my daughter. I cannot believe this of Chadrick. He is a very gentle and kind man and to be honest, I have never heard him raise his voice in anger toward

337

anyone although he has been given just cause on many occasions and sometimes pushed beyond many other people's limits but he has always remained calm." Said Greta. Tomas started speaking in an annoyed tone. "My God Greta, you two must be blind then and speak of him as though you are in love with the murderer. He was found with the gun still hot and smoking in his hands and that is irrefutable evidence." "That will do, thank you, sir. It does –. Well, that is of no concern." Just then, Mac came in with Grant. "Good, you have found him. Now Grant, I just need to know your whereabouts for the day." Cadiston continued. "I have been out from early and when I came back, I went to my room. Then after the commotion, I went out again and have only just arrived back. Your DS here nabbed me before I had even turned the engine off." Said Grant. "And is there someone that can collaborate your story?" Asked Cadiston. "There is but I will not say it here in front of them. I have already informed your DS and I am sure you do not need to hear it from me again." Snapped Grant. "DS Macswee, over here a moment please." Mac whispered in Cadiston's ear. "He does not want it broadcast as this young lady works here." "You have her name?" Asked Cadiston. "I do." Said Mac. "And it is my guess the name is not that of Demmie." Said Cadiston. "Nope, not this one." Confirmed Mac. "You say that you have been out all day until just now when my DS saw you?" Asked Cadiston. "That's right." Said Grant. "Thank you, that will be all for now, Grant, apart from the fact that you have some blood on your sleeve and we will need a sample of that." Said Cadiston calmly. "Why should you? It must be from the pheasant that I shot." Grant said smugly. "Nevertheless, we will take a sample." Mac had already gone to the car and had returned with the sample kit and although Grant was reluctant, Mac took his sample. Cadiston then continued. "All of you, please stay in this room as I may need to speak to you all further. Mac, with me. We will go up and have a word with Jooners, Pcs Jakeson, Stevens, Tedlow keep them all here please." "Will do chief." Said Jake.

The moment they had left the room, Grant stood up to speak. "Why the hell is he here again and who will fill me in on what has been going on while I have been absent? What have I missed?" "Demmie has been shot dead and Chadrick did it. Tomas hit him." Said Lizabeth. Grant looked surprised and said. "Tomas did?" Lizabeth continued. "Yes and knocked him unconscious before he could kill the rest of us. Oh yes, then that Cadiston arrived and he was taken to the hospital." "So, you say that Chad killed Demmie and Tomas knocked him unconscious. After that, he was taken to hospital. Now there is a turn up for the book. Well, can't say I am sorry because that means he has finally got his comeuppance and gets them both out of my hair. You say she is dead –. Question is, is he dead or alive? Dead, I hope." Said Grant. "What do you mean by that remark Grant?" Asked Greta. "It is of no importance, Greta, so let it drop." Snapped Grant. "Of no importance you say? Well, it may be to the police and they may be interested to know that you came in for short time appearing from nowhere, then went out again until the police DS brought you back in." Said Greta. "Well, I will not be telling them any of that so leave it there for your own sake and the sake of your silly little child if you know what is good for you." Threatened Grant. "That sounds very much like a threat against my mother, Uncle Grant, and for that alone, I could go and tell Detective Cadiston or the constables that are outside the door if they did not hear your words." Jennifer said. "Sit down, Jennifer! You are nothing but a silly little child and only ten years old. Do not interfere in what is not your concern or in things that you know nothing about! Go and do some little girlie things like play with a doll or something." Said Grant mockingly. "I am getting tired of being told that I am a silly little child and only ten years old, I know exactly what is going on here and am a part of it as much as you are." Jennifer said pragmatically. "Whoopee for you, now shut up."Grant snarled.

"I do not like your tone, Grant, and Jennifer may only be ten but that does not give you the right and you have no call to speak to her in that way. I suggest that you are the one who needs to sit down and do not forget that the police are still here and may need to ask some more questions before they are finished with their investigation and words can slip out." Said Greta. "Hmm." He went to speak but then surprisingly he sat down. Cadiston and Mac had left the lounge and proceeded to walk up the stairs and just at the same time, Jooners had left the scene of the crime. "Ok chaps, you can fetch the second body now." The ambulance transport team walked past them. "Mortuary lads, post-mortem, please. Tell Charles and Samantha." Said Cadiston. "Thought so, Cadders." Said Greg of the transport. Ten minutes, later they were carrying the lifeless body of Demmie to the waiting vehicle. "Interesting one this, Cadders. Come in and see what you think of our re-enacting."

Cadiston had a look down the stairs and could see some of the family at the bottom, taking a good look at the proceedings. He made a note of who they were. "PC Jakeson, take these people back into the lounge please and keep them there. DS Macswee, see that it is done then get back up here. Stay by the top of the stairs and do not let anyone up here." Said Cadiston.

"You have it, sir." Said PC Jakeson.

Cadiston then followed Jooners into the bedroom, the scene of this latest atrocity. He heard Mac tell the family to return to the lounge until needed further for questioning and smiled. Seconds later, he was back at his side. "We will start from here. Sandy, I will use you again as the alleged shooter as you did it so well before. Sally, you can be the victim and Lang, the real assailant. Now, we know from the way that the blood has spread and the position of the body that the victim was standing here near the bathroom and that makes it absolutely impossible for so much damage to have been caused to the body if the shooter had been standing near the door. The spread of the shot makes it impossible if he was standing there when he shot her. To cause that much damage to the body, she would have been about here." Sally moved into position. "Then she would have been lying there." Again, Sally moved into position. "There is not the slightest chance that the shots came from someone standing over there by the door and the body ended up against the wall over there. For starters, the spread and pattern of the shot would be different and much of it would not have made any form of contact with the victim and the pellets would be strewn all about but there are none. The victim was facing the shooter when she was shot but there is no possible way that she was standing over there or that he was over here. Not for her to end up against the bathroom door. Sally, please stand in the position as we tried earlier. That is where the first suspicion strikes. It was a chest shot so the angle of the shots would need to be there and the body would then be forced back onto the bed or possibly rolled onto the floor beside it. If that was the case, then blood would have sprayed all over here." He pointed and gestured. "And the bed would be covered, it is not. Next, by the state of the body, they were not standing that far apart but reasonably close together. Now, if someone had a shotgun on you, would you stand still? No, you would back away and that is what I believe she did until she was against the bathroom door and could go no further. Ok Sally, Sandy action ..." They began to move accordingly but slowly in the direction Jooners had pointed. "The shooter would have had to follow her. When she was shot, she would have had to be standing there and that is determined by the blood spread. If it is as we are wanted to believe, he was knocked unconscious by the door by who was it?" Asked Jooners. "Tomas." They answered in unison.

"Then there is no way that he was the shooter, the alleged shooter would be lying unconscious here, not where he was found by the door. Two shots were fired that killed the victim, of that we can be sure. They were followed by two more. Do you know how far they were apart?" Asked Jooners. "Four or five minutes, possibly a bit longer." Said Cadiston. "Interesting point. So if Tomas hit him, could he have put the gun back into his hands but inadvertently fired the shots before running downstairs? Sandy, go back to where the alleged shooter was found and go through the motion, but this time use the shotgun." Said Jooners. "What about the fingerprints." Asked Cadiston. "Already taken, Cadders, but as you see he has gloves on." He put two used cartridges into the chambers and pulled the trigger twice, then ejected the used cartridges and reloaded, ready to fire again. He then went through the motion of being struck. "Maximum time, eight seconds to reload. So this is what I believe happened. The alleged shooter came into the room and someone was already there waiting for him. The instant that he came in, they struck but on the top of his head. Now he was already lying on the floor just inside the door when the victim came in. If we are to believe what has been said, they were arguing but if he had already been struck, that is a fallacy and not at all possible. Now, I believe that he did not have the gun and the real shooter was hidden behind the door. The victim went to the bathroom to get a towel to stop the blood from the first blow to the top of his head, hence the towel by her body. Upon leaving the bathroom, she was faced with the real shooter who had come out of hiding and she was forced to face him or her. She backed away, then they shot her twice at close range. Now they had to be quick because they heard Tomas who was easing the door open. They threw the gun down and hid and I believe that it was after they hid that shots three and four were fired as we found the lead pellets under the bed and in the skirting. Now they only had seconds to hide and I believe that was in the wardrobe because of the bloodied footprints going up to it, we checked inside and there are smudged bloodied prints in there but not eligible enough to get a sample but we are certain that the blood will be that of the deceased. I think that Chad was then regaining consciousness when Tomas was entering the room. When you think about it, if Tomas thought that there was a crazed gunman in the room, would he have attempted to enter? Simple answer is no, not on your life. That is why I believe that someone else had already struck Chad and Tomas then struck for the second time with that heavy weapon. After Tomas checked that Chad was unconscious and bleeding, he saw the situation and to make his story good, tried to replace the gun into Chad's hand hence a five-minute plus delay in the second pair of shots. He then ran down the stairs and took over the phone call. The real shooter then reappeared and loaded the shotgun again but in placing it in his hands the trigger was again pulled and of course, it went off. Hence the long delay before shots five and six, also after Chadrick was unconscious. Now a big question, the alleged shooter was unconscious after he had been struck so that raises a question, how could he have taken four more shots? When you questioned this Tomas, tell me, how many times did he strike Chad?" Asked Jooners.

"He said only once on the top of his head but after asking again, it had moved to the back of the head which indicates that he lied." Said Cadiston.

"True, he is not speaking the truth which I suspected. From my examination, Chadrick was struck three times, once on top and twice at the base of the skull and those two while he was partially conscious on the floor without the shotgun in his hands. The position and angle in which he was struck makes me think that the person who struck him also struck Malcolm. I think you will probably be thinking the same." Said Jooners. "You have that correct, Jooners, and based on this, I believe that we may have our killer in our sights."

"We will make one final attempt at a re-enactment of what we think really took place here. Sandy, Sally, Lang, will do the acting and I will commentate. If you please –. Positions, camera roll, and action. Chad came in and someone was waiting for him standing on the chair behind the door and whack on the top of his head. If he had been struck here with the loaded gun, the shots would go either into the bed or into the wall, as you can see by the way that Sandy falls and where the shotgun lands. That tells me that the gun was not in his hands when he was struck. In came the victim and seeing him on the floor with a head wound, she ran to the bathroom and came out with a towel. She was then faced by the real shooter, they approached while she backed away until she could go no further, then came the first two shots. The gun is covered in the victim's blood which again denotes that the real shooter was very close to her. Now the shooter hears footsteps so hides, leaving the gun on the floor. Hearing the gunshots, Tomas looks carefully in and sees Chad lying on the floor semi-conscious and the gun lying not too far away from him. Without thinking that there might be someone else in the room, he then picks up the old hammer and strikes him twice in the same position of the skull as Malcolm was struck and, to my mind, in the hope of killing him. He then tries to replace the gun in his hands to make his story look good. He knew that he had to be quick and in his haste, he slips up and the gun fires. In a panic, he runs downstairs and takes over the call. That is when shots two and three are heard. The real shooter returned from their hiding place in the wardrobe and placed the loaded gun into Chad's hands but it had already been fired when Tomas tried to do the same and that meant they had to reload again, leaving live cartridges in the gun but again, they fired so they left the empty gun in his hands and made their escape unseen. Another thing, if you were that close, you would get blood splats onto yourself." Explained Jooners. "True." Agreed Cadiston. "Well, apart from the alleged shooter's own blood, we found that he had none of the victims on him. I am certain that he did not pull the trigger, Cadders. Someone else did and for whatever reason, are trying to pin it onto him. As for Tomas striking him, that tells me that something is underlying, some reason why he wants him out of the way and silenced. We have the old antique knight's hammer we will remove the fingerprints from that and from every used cartridge that was scattered about as well. We need to keep repeating the scenario to get it reasonably accurate although we all feel that we are very close to the truth. Right, all set for this, our final full scenario. Now gang, for the last time, action." He then watched as the forensic team re-enacted the shooting as they had analyzed it and Jooners told the story while his team played the parts. "Chad came into the room and was struck by the hidden person on the top of his head by someone that was standing on the chair. He fell and lay there motionless while the attacker hid. But if you disagree, Cadders, just cut in."

"All fits with my thinking this far so please, continue." Said Cadiston.

"Demmie entered and seeing that her husband was lying on the floor bleeding from the head wound, she ran to the bathroom to get a towel. When she came out, she was faced with the real shooter. She backed away until she could go no further and almost at point-blank range, the gun was fired. Hearing the door opening, the shooter then retreated and hid in the wardrobe after throwing the gun down. Tomas saw the gun and Chad lying there and he was possibly coming around or moving so he took the hammer that was already lying on the floor beside him and struck him again very hard with the hope of killing him. He then tried to place the gun back into his hands but because he was hasty, he slipped up and it fired. He left, running downstairs to take over the call. He then concluded the scenario with the real shooter −. I think that there is a lot more to this case than meets the eye and more questions need to be asked to discover the whole truth. We have done our bit so over to you now, Cadders." Said Jooners.

"Thanks, when I first came into the room and saw the scene my instant opinion was that the distance was far too great between where Chad and his wife's body was laying. We have both been on the same wavelength and it was already in my mind that this was a complete sham and a fix to make it appear that Chad had shot his wife before being clubbed. Someone is trying to incriminate him to remove him from Mandaten or someone wanted Demmie out of the way or it could be a combination of both. I have my suspicions about the testimonies that were given but my main suspect was not here or … At least, that is what he wants us to think but I have my suspicions on that score. If he was not on site, then that lets him off the hook for this one. I have a pretty good idea who is the real shooter but I may be wrong so first I will need to speak with Chad. Unless the double whack on his head has done it for him." Said Cadiston. "He was still alive when he left here, Cadders, weak but alive so fingers crossed for him." Said Jooners. "Absolutely Jooners, let me have your official report, fingerprints, and other findings as soon as you can, please." Said Cadiston.

"Goes without saying, DCI Cadiston, solve this mess and you could keep that title. We will just tidy up here, bag any evidence, then make our final check and if there is nothing else for us, then we will be away but keep this room sealed and off-limits just in case we need to come back." Said Jooners.

Official police tape was produced, ready to place over the doorway. With Jooners and the forensic team finishing their work, Cadiston and Mac returned to the lounge.

"Tomas and Kansas, would you stand please as you were in the room I just need to check if you have any blood on your shoes or clothes." Said Cadiston. "Well I did not go in so should be none on mine." Said Kansas and Mac checked over the clothes of Kansas.

"He is clean, now you sir, please." Mac checked over Tomas. "Clean, very clean like a fresh clean ironed shirt just put on. Apart from some blood on the shoes, no other signs." Said Mac. "Well, we had been up to our room to change hence the clean shirt and after what I had just witnessed, well, I did not give it a thought to wipe my shoes." Said Tomas. "Remove them please, sir, and place them into this bag." Said Mac. "Whatever for, Detective? They can tell you nothing." Said Tomas. "Just do it, please." Said Mac in a very demanding manner and Tomas complied.

"Did you go over to the deceased body?" Asked Cadiston. "Not a chance, just looking at it was more than enough for me." Said Tomas. "So that being the case, then the blood on your shoes should be that of Chadrick, and if that is then you have nothing to worry about. The fact remains that you should have removed them and put them into the evidence bag when first asked by my sergeant." Said Cadiston.

"So why do you want my shoes? They can tell you nothing." Tomas said again. "A process of elimination, so why did you all come down separately, why not come down together?" Asked Cadiston.

"I took longer because I had to use the bathroom." Replied Tomas. "A quick, snappy answer." thought Cadiston. "Thank you, Tomas, and just to get the facts straight, how many shots were fired?" Asked Cadiston.

"Four shots, Detective. No wait, not four, it was six." Said Tomas nervously.

"And the last two appear to have been fired after you had knocked him unconscious. Not a problem as it will be recorded on your emergency call. Now, would any of you like to change your statement because if you do, now is the time –." He paused "No one, right we will move on and have another word with you, Grant, in private please." He took them into the long room.

"Alright Cadiston, you are beginning to annoy me so what do you need to ask me now? I have already given my alibi at the time of the shooting. I was not here so there should be nothing else for me." Snapped Grant. "Sit down, please. Now, tell us just how long were you having the affair with Demmie for." Grant looked surprised that Cadiston knew about this. "I was not having an affair with her as such." Said Grant. "Not an affair so what was it then? Giving you comfort in your hour of need as you put it –. If it was not an affair, was it just an occasional fling?" Asked Cadiston.

"That is exactly what it was, an occasional fling and nothing more for me. Look detectives, you must know how it is, now don't you? Look at it from my side … If you can. Who would refuse the advances of a woman such as her with all the curves in the right places well." He made gestures with his hands and continued. "Come on now, I surely have no need to paint you a picture, surely not? The truth is that we got together a few times but that was it." "Before you told us that she had given you comfort, as you put it, after your wife had died and you were on the way back from the hospital. The truth now, just how many times before that and while your wife was still alive did it happen, sir?" Asked Mac. "Alright, six or seven or maybe more, I was not counting but it was always her pestering me. I wanted to get one over on Chad so went for it on every possible occasion. I was only doing it out of spite and well, a bit of fun. She was not satisfied with that and wanted it to be much more. You could say that her desire was the ruling factor and she would not take no for an answer. She told me that she would not just be used as a sex slave and a bit on the side and wanted us to get married. When she asked me to divorce Bonnie I said no. She told me that she did not love Chad and never had, she only married him to get into the family circle so that she could get closer to me. She said it was me that was her true love and always had been from the first time that she saw me and that was before they were married. She hated her life with him and felt like she was living the life of a pauper when there was a world of riches to be had. She craved for the high life and the riches that would go with being the Lady of Mandaten Manor but not with him, with me, and would do anything to help me to gain the title of Lord. She said that she would do whatever it took, even go as far as killing, to ensure that the title went to me. Kill for me –. Oh my God, Bonnie –. Surely not Demmie – D-d-did – No, she died of natural causes. Sergeant Standish confirmed that. She was a bit overpowering and at times, rather frightening, even to me. She was also very devious and to be honest, I did not know just what she would be capable of. I had already found the one that I intend to be my wife after Bonnie and it most definitely was not her." Said Grant. "So now you are saying that your liaison was going on for a long period of time, was it not? Remember, the truth because I will find out." Warned Cadiston. "Damn you, Cadiston! You just will not let it go, will you?" Grant snapped. "Not a chance, now the whole truth and nothing but." Said Cadiston. "All right so we had been fucking for the past two and a half years, satisfied now?" Grant all but yelled. Cadiston looked Grant straight in the eyes. "Not until the whole truth is declared, now did you help to plan or have knowledge of your wife's murder and why did you lie before? The time is now to tell the whole truth as you have told lies from the start. So the truth now and you may belay any of my suspicions." Said Cadiston. "Nothing but the truth you say? Well, the complete and honest truth is that I had nothing to do with Bonnie's or Malcolm's deaths and there is no way that you can pin either of them onto me." Said Grant sourly.

"At the moment we are dealing with your wife, we will get to the others in due course and then there will be a multitude of questions to answer." Said Cadiston. "As I said, you will not just roll over and let it go, will you? So alright then, the whole truth.

I had nothing to do with Bonnie's death and I knew nothing and had no idea about the child that Bonnie was carrying. Anyway, why should I want them dead, they were my smoke screen to get what I wanted and that was the Lordship. Alright, I had a plan to win the title but that did not include murdering my brothers or my wife and that really is the whole truth, so help me, it is." Said Grant. "Now let me get this straight, you were not having an affair with Demmie, just a liaison for two and half years but you are having an affair with this other woman?" Asked Cadiston. "Ok so I had more than a few times with Demmie after she threw herself at me and I am not having an affair with this girl, this one I love her to distraction. I did not love Bonnie and I swear that I did not kill her or have any part in her death. The truth is that I wanted her out of my life completely but I did not want her dead. After the announcement that I would be the next Lord Mandaten and it had been fully declared, I was going to get a divorce and had already seen my solicitor who has the divorce papers drawn up ready for me to sign. You can check on that. My solicitor is Woods, Gray and Stemmings." Said Grant.

"And believe me, we will. You did not murder your wife directly and that, we know to be true but you should not have lied to me about your fling with Demmie or lead her on. You gave her a false impression and that, in effect, led to the murder of your wife. You may not have directly had anything to do with her death and the unborn child that she carried but indirectly you most certainly did and that was because of your falseness and lies. As for your affair or not as the case may be with the lady in question, her name will not be disclosed unless it is found to be necessary to help in our investigation to solve any of the cases of murder in the first degree. You now have two murdered wives on your conscience." Grant looked stunned at this remark. "Now, is there anything else that we should know? If so, tell us now." Added Cadiston.

"Only that the lady in question was becoming jealous of Demmie and wanted me to end the association once and for all but as I said, she was a very devious woman and I did not know just how to get rid of her but I did not kill her either and that is God's truth, Detective. Anyhow, I was not here at the Manor when she was killed, now was I?" Said Grant smugly and Cadiston noticed that he had a slight grin on his face as he spoke. "Alright Grant, if there is nothing else to tell us, you can go now but we will require you again at a later date as our investigations deepen. A bit of advice for you, no more lying because, believe me, I will find the truth and all the lies." He said. Grant stood up and walked slowly back to the lounge with his head hung low like a scalded child that had been found out. He was again mumbling incoherently as he picked up an unopened bottle of Scotch Whisky, then sat in the corner drinking it directly from the bottle.

"He did not kill his wife directly, Cadders. We know that because Demmie did but now she is dead and dead people don't talk. That is very convenient. She may have acted out of desire and carried Bonnie and her child's murder out on her own in her attempt to get what she wanted and that would be Grant. I am thinking that, on the other hand, he may have known something of her plan but did nothing to stop her. That would, to my way of thinking, make him an accessory by association. Now, with maybe he had a hand in Demmie's murder even though he was not here according to his alibi. There is that but again, he could have employed someone to do it for him to shut her up out of fear that she might incriminate him under heavy questioning. Do you think he knew all about her plan to murder Bonnie and did nothing to stop her as it fitted into his longterm plan? Although if I remember correctly, he had said that Bonnie was an integral part of his master-plan to help him to gain the title of Lord Mandaten. What about all the other murders? There are eleven in total and another thought they could have been committing them together. I tried to work it all out but I cannot see how it would all piece together. I may not have your skill of perception or deduction but to me, he is a prime suspect." Said Mac.

"A suspect yes, Mac, but not a prime suspect for all the murders. I feel very strongly that we are dealing with more than one murderer or murderess. There is a great deal at stake here and a large fortune to take control of. We need to get all the forensic reports together and read them all through again and we need the report on the chalky soil substance including the one taken from Kansas. If it comes from the same place, which I think it does, then we need to find out where that place is and that will tell us how they moved about freely without being seen, a secret passageway comes to mind. When we have the forensic report on the stable block, we will see what was found in the contraband storage pit and if there is another way in and out of it. The blood and DNA will also be prime evidence." Said Cadiston. "I said it before, this is not going to be an easy case or cases to solve but we are making headway." Said Mac. "That we are Mac. Now from here, our first port of call will be the hospital to see if Chad is alive or dead. If he is dead, then the person that killed him is going to say that it was a necessary action to protect his wife and family. That person is Tomas but I have my suspicions that he is lying and there is an underlying reason for wanting Chad silenced. In fact, I believe that they are all lying apart from young Jennifer. Eleven murders Mac, that is what we have and every one of them was murder in the first degree, and not one of them is a tragic accident. Carefully planned and executed to look like an accident and one made to look like a suicide but not quite clever enough. We have a mammoth task on our hands, Mac." Cadiston said.

"I have confidence in you, Cadders, and so does the chief and super, not to mention Lord Mandaten and I am proud to be working with you. I am learning more with you than with my training sergeant." Said Mac.

"Just as well Lord and Lady Mandaten were not present today, they have had quite sufficient trauma to deal with over the past couple of weeks. These murders all started on Monday, 22nd September, and have been happening until Saturday, 11th October, today. One thing is for certain, we need to pull our fingers out and get the culprits caged before anyone else loses their life." Said Cadiston.

"Do we need to ask the family any more questions now?" Asked Mac. "Not just now but we most certainly will later. I strongly believe that we were told a cock and bull story by Lizabeth, Kansas, and Tomas about the argument between Demmie and Chad and I have a strong suspicion about their son, Kansas. Our priority now is to get to the hospital and see what is happening with Chad." Said Cadiston. "I will go get the car running while you tell the family we are leaving and not to enter the murder scene in the Bedroom." Mac said and opened the front door, leaving Cadiston in the hallway. In the lounge, the family waited and only one rose to their feet when Cadiston walked in. "We are leaving now but on no account must anyone enter the Lowell suite bedroom. The door has been sealed and it is taped over and if anyone enters it, they are in breach of a clear directive and may disturb some piece of vital evidence for which they can be prosecuted. We will be needing to question you all again further about today's incident and all the other incidents that have taken place over the past weeks. That being the case, you all need to stay here or in the vicinity." Said Cadiston.

"I see absolutely no reason for any further questions about today's events, Detective. We have told you everything so there is no more to tell, now is there?" Said Tomas. "Is that so Tomas? You may think that but I am not at all convinced about the stories told so further questioning will take place, of that you can be sure. Now, is there anything else that you should tell us or are there any more questions for us before we leave?" Asked Cadiston. "I have one, Detective Cadiston." Said Greta. Grant sent her a look of anxiety.

"Please ask it then, Greta." Said Cadiston. She moved him further away from the family and whispered her question to him. "I was just wondering, would it be in order and permitted to go and visit Chadrick in the hospital?" She asked.

"He will be under a constant police guard but I can see no problem with you visiting him. That is if –. If he is still alive. He was hit pretty hard with that old medieval knight's hammer and the injury he received was very serious. We do not know yet if he is dead or alive. We are now going to the hospital to find the answer to that question and if you like, I will let you know the outcome, but, – keep the result to yourself please. The fewer people that now what happened the better it will be for our investigations." Said Cadiston. "I understand that fully, and swear to keep it a secret and that would be very much appreciated, thank you. However there is one other thing that you should know –. Before this terrible thing happened to him and he was attacked, he had something to tell you about my son's death and some other evidence that he had discovered. He telephoned you on Friday but did not reach you and now this has happened so do you think it was done to silence him as we do." "I cannot comment on that but I will keep that in mind. Now, how many do you think would want to visit him?" He gazed around the room, taking in the body language of each of the family. They all sat in silence with blank expressions on their faces. "Just myself and my daughter, Jennifer. I do not care what they think or what the evidence may show, it is just like them, all false and I am sure it was fixed in an attempt to make him look guilty off shooting Demmie just to get rid of him and I still do not believe that he could do such a thing or murder any of the family." Said Greta sternly. "Well at this point in time and the first impressions confirm that this was indeed murder in the first degree and as far as who pulled the trigger, that has yet to be established and confirmed. I will let you know if it is possible and when you can visit so give me your number then I can contact you directly." Said Cadiston and pulled out his notepad."There you are, I have written it down for you." Said Greta. "Then, if there is nothing else –." He looked at them. "No? Then I will be on my way." He turned and left. Walking to the waiting car, he heard the heavy door close behind him. With the car on its way up the drive and the family on their own, stares of disgust were now being thrown at Greta and Jennifer. "What was all the whispering with Cadiston about then? I hope you did not say anything about me." Grant said bitterly. "No Grant, not about you. Cadiston does not need me to tell him anything because he will discover it all for himself. If you must know what I asked him it was, if Chadrick is still alive and whether we could visit him, not that it has anything to do with you." Said Greta. "Hear that, Lizabeth? She wants to visit the family murderer." Said Grant. Speaking with a disgusted tone in her voice, the condemnation began by Lizabeth. "I am lost for words, Greta. My goodness, fancy you wanting to see a cold-blooded murderer, are you mad and have you lost your senses and all sense of decorum? My God Greta, whatever are you thinking? My, my, my –. Why he was probably the one responsible for all these family deaths, including your husbands. Well on my part, and I speak for my husband and son also, I hope he is dead." "Well, for someone who was lost for words you certainly had plenty to say, and no Lizabeth, I have not lost my senses I just do not believe that he could be a cold-blooded murderer." Said Greta defensively. "Well, you did not see what I saw. I saw what he had done to his wife and if I had not knocked him unconscious when I did, we may all be dead now and you included. He did it alright of that there can be no doubt as he was the only person in the room apart from Demmie, of course. Stands to reason that he did it just before I stopped him, he did it alright. You should all be thanking me for saving your lives and putting the murderer of our family away. All of you should, including you, Grant! And you, Greta, and your daughter! My wife and son! You all owe your lives to me and that makes me a hero, the hero of the hour!" Again, Grant gave Tomas a strange look. "So, you were the one that knocked him unconscious, were you Tomas? And you think that you are the hero of the hour, do you?" Asked Grant. "That is right." Said Tomas. Grant just chuckled. "Well, for all that you say I still believe in him, and as to that I have absolutely no doubts Tomas, not one. Said Greta.

"Always thought that you were not all there, Greta. I must say that this just proves it. We all know that he was the killer of our family and that makes you the only one that thinks he didn't do it, you have lost the plot then, Aunt Greta." Said Kansas. "My mother has not lost the plot, Kansas, and she is not alone as I have not either and believe in Uncle Chadrick. If Mother wants to visit him, that is if he is still alive after Tomas's vicious attack on him, then it is up to her." Said Jennifer. "My vicious attack? I saved your life and your mother's life, you are nothing but a silly child Jennifer." Said Tomas mockingly. "I am getting very tired of Jennifer being called a silly child. She has got more brain and intelligence than any of you." Said Greta angrily. "For goodness' sake, go then, Greta! Go with your snivelling brat and visit the murderer of our family if he is alive but none of us will be with you so you will be totally on your own. Believe me, when this is all over and he is found guilty of all the murders and even if he is already dead, you will be written out of our family and get nothing, I will see to that. Even if Father has put you in his will, I will contest it and I will win the day. Go to your murderer and forget about us and having anything from the estate, you may as well give up now." Snarled Grant. "With your opinion and attitude, Uncle Grant, my mother would not want you to come with her. Come to that, she would not want any of you to be with her. Plus, there is no need for any of you to be with her as she will not be alone because I will be going with her." Said a feisty Jennifer. "Just as I thought, Greta and Jennifer, a pair of Jezebels together." Said Kansas. "Say what you like Kansas, but remember that none of you are shinny white and we both know of your falseness and the lies that you have all told when you spoke to Detective Cadiston or his sergeant." Said Jennifer. "Be very careful little girl, one killer may be caught but what if there is more than one? They may hear you, and if there is a second murderer on the loose then you are not safe while you live here. Plus; you are not wanted so the sooner that you are both gone from here the better for us all." Said Kansas abruptly. "I have as much right to be here as you, Kansas, and you do not frighten me with that kind of talk either. If that is true, have you thought about your own safety? What is there to say that you are not on their hit list, bet you have not thought of that?" Said Jennifer smiling. "Why you –." Kansas started but Greta quickly interrupted. "Come, Jennifer, they are not worth wasting your breath on. It is useless to argue the point with them as your words just go in one ear and straight out of the other as there is nothing between the ears to stop it. Come Jennifer, we will leave them all to wallow in their own rottenness and we will see that their greed, jealousy, falseness, and lies will be their downfall eventually. Because they may not believe it but DCI Cadiston with DS Macswee will uncover the lies and discover the truth about them all. As to that, we may not be here to see them fall but we will certainly hear all about it and read it in the papers probably in one of Simon Cauldwell's articles," "And we will be well rid of them mother." Said Jennifer. Jennifer then stuck her tongue out at them then together they turned and retired to their room. "Well get her and her brat," remarked Grant then settled back with his bottle of brandy.

Chapter Eleven

The Long Vigil Begins

From Mandaten Manor, Cadiston and Mac went straight to the hospital and by the time they arrived, it was early evening on Saturday, 11th October. Other visitors watched when they saw the two detectives entering the doors and making their way to the reception desk. They were both eager to know what was happening and walked straight up to the reception desk, they both had their warrant cards in their hands and wasted no time in showing them.

"DCI Cadiston, DS Macswee, good evening, how can I help you?" Asked the receptionist behind the desk. "A short while ago a patient by the name of Mr. Chadrick Mandaten was brought in with a severe head wound and I need to know if he is dead or alive, where he is now and what is happening with this patient, please." Said Cadiston. The receptionist tapped on her keyboard and said. "Over an hour ago, a Mr Chadrick Mandaten was brought in to accident and emergency, and after a quick examination, the seriousness of his injury were discovered and he was rushed straight into the theatre for an emergency cranial operation." Said the receptionist "And who will know how it is going?" Asked Cadiston. "Only the surgeon performing the operation, if you would like to wait then I will get in touch with the recovery room and ask them to contact me when he is out of surgery. Then you may be able to talk to the surgeon carrying out the emergency surgery and that is our Mister Doctor. Mafidsen." Said the receptionist. "Thank you, we will be in the waiting room then." Said Cadiston. "I must warn you, Detective, it could be a very long wait. These operations can take several hours depending on the severity. I can tell you that a room has been reserved for him on the critical care ward and if he survives the operation, he will be transferred there." The receptionist said with a sad smile. "The wait is not a problem and thank you,

Janice, for the additional information, we will be in the waiting room." Said Macswee. "How did you know that was my name?" Asked the receptionist. "On the staff recognition photo board behind you." Answered Macswee pointing at the board with a smile. "Of course, I should have thought of that but most people ignore it but, – then you are a detective and trained to spot things that others ignore." She replied smiling. "Something like that, we will be in the waiting room." Said Cadiston and then turned to Mac and said.

"A coffee would be nice and maybe a sandwich, DS Macswee, as I missed my quiet meal with the wife. I think we could be in for a long wait so best we make ourselves comfortable." "I will go to the café and get us a few sandwiches and some coffee to keep us going while we start our long vigil." Said Mac. "Here take this." Cadiston passed him a ten-pound note. "Can I keep the change, sir?" Asked Mac with a cheeky grin. "On your bike, DS Macswee." Said Cadiston and they both chuckled as Mac left the waiting room. While he was away, Cadiston arranged for an officer to be positioned outside the room that had been reserved for Chad in the hope that he survived the major surgery that he was now undergoing. They had eaten their food and drank their coffee but sat quietly waiting for any news of Chad's operation. "22:35 – Cadders. We have been here since 18:20 so we have been here for four hours and fifteen minutes. It sure is a long operation that he is undergoing so it must be a serious injury and a lot of damage must have been done when Tomas struck him with the old knights war hammer, it was already on the floor beside Chad so someone else made the first heavy skull crushing blow." Said Mac.

"Thanks for the time check, and you are spot on with your analygy. I would not be surprised at all to hear that there was extensive damage especially after looking at that old medieval knight's hammer. Imagine going into battle and receiving a whack across the skull with that weapon. I would think in the medieval period when this weapon was being used, the survival rate was nil." Said Cadiston. "From on top of a horse, striking that down, it would crush the skull and even on foot it would do a lot of damage. Nasty weapons they used in those days. That confirms that someone was standing on the chair behind the door to strike down, just as Jooners and his team re-enacted the scenario." Said Mac. "See Mac, you are thinking like a detective now. Nasty weapons indeed, Mac, and there are a lot of them displayed in the Manor especially in the long room and on the walls all the way up the staircase. There are swords, maces, battleaxes, pikes, battle hammers, and the like. Nearly everywhere that you look, there are collections of muskets, pistols, swords, and pikes not to mention the various suits of armour." Said Cadiston.

"Suits of metal is what young Jennifer calls them. I wonder if they are all family heirlooms." Enquired Mac. "From what I know of the family, they first hit our shores in 1066 with William the Conqueror at what we know as the battle of Hastings, and as the years progressed, the Lord formed his own regiments and probably armed them from his own pocket. During the first world war, Lord Mandaten had his own regiment and sadly he lost most of his men over the 1914 to 1918 war years. They were engaged in the battles of Ypres, Arras, the Somme, and Passchendaele just to mention some of the many battles they were involved in. Although there is the main armistice day of remembrance, Lord Mandaten holds his own to remember all those that had fallen in the family chapel where every name has been recorded and his own battle flag, there is also a list of every battle that his family were involved in through the centuries." Said Cadiston. "Done your homework on the Mandaten's then Cadders –." They continued with their idle banter for another hour, watching the clock all the time. "That is another hour gone." Said Mac. "Just had a thought, Mac, neither of us have contacted our wives to let them know where we are, best we do that this instant." Said Cadiston. They both had their phones out and within seconds, they were talking to their wives. "At the hospital, Samantha." Said Cadiston. "Hospital? Are you alright?" Asked Samantha. "Don't panic my precious woman, I am fine. We are waiting to hear how Chad Mandaten is, sorry, should have phoned you earlier." Said

Cadiston. "Don't worry about that but what happened to him?" Asked Samantha. "Without going into too much detail, he was struck very hard on the head and is undergoing emergency surgery. In fact, since just after six p.m. I cannot leave until I know if he survives." Said Cadiston. "I understand that, Ashton, this kind of operation can take several hours to complete so it will be a long wait and an extremely long vigil after the operation." Replied Samantha. "I will let you know the outcome as long as it is not too late tonight, if not in the morning. Sleep tight and remember I love you." Said Cadiston blowing a kiss down the phone. "Love you too my lovely man." With the sound of kisses being returned. Seconds later the phone line went dead. "Everything alright with you, Mac?" Enquired Cadiston. "All is good, Angela is very good and understands." Said Mac. "I was thinking, there is no need for us both to be here so if you want, you can go home. That way at least one of us will get some sleep tonight." Said Cadiston. "Are you sure Cadders? I don't mind waiting." Said Mac. "Go home, Mac. You have the car and I will see you Monday morning. If I am not in the office, come back here because that is where I will be." Said Cadiston. "If you are sure". "Go home Mac, and I am sure". "Night then Cadders, and see you Monday." Said Mac.

"Night Mac." Said Cadiston and the door creaked as it was opened and slowly self closed on its sprung hinges.

It was now three a.m. on the morning of Sunday, 12th of October. Cadiiston had been there all night and was fighting to keep awake but when the nurse entered the waiting room, it was like throwing a bucket of cold water over him and he was instantly alert. "DCI Cadiston?" "Yes nurse, that is me." Cadiston said standing. "We got the message earlier from Janice that you needed to know the outcome of Mr. Chadrick Mandaten's operation." Said the nurse. "That is right. Can you tell me now nurse, is he still alive?" "The operation was conducted by our Mister Doctor Mafidsen and as you can imagine after such a long operation, he has now gone to bed. There were two injuries to his skull, he was struck once on the top of his head that caused a fracture and at least twice at the base of his skull so three times and we can tell this from the extent of the damage caused. The first was almost certainly on the top of his head causing a fracture but the most severe was the second and third strike which caused a lot of damage to the base of the skull. This area caused the biggest problem but Mister Mafidsen was able to remove the tiny fragments of bone and release the pressure on Mr Mandaten's brain and spinal cord. He had suffered considerable blood loss so has had a blood transfusion. Even so, it was touch and go. If he had not got here when he did, it would have been too late to save him. He is very lucky to still be alive and is not out of the woods yet, not by a long shot, even though the operation was successful. He will be kept in a side room on the high dependency critical care ward for a considerable time. Dr. Mafidsen had to put him into an induced coma to ensure that he remains perfectly still as part of his skull is missing and will be rebuilt when his brain swelling has reduced back to normal. Where the bone cannot be replaced, a metal plate will be inserted to protect the brain. He has a long, slow recovery ahead of him and the next twenty-four to forty-eight hours are the most critical. He may be in a coma now and it is after that time that Dr. Mafidsen will be able to assess if he will make the suspected and hoped-for recovery. All injuries to the head are life-threatening and a lot of them are life-changing so let us hope that in this case, it is neither." Explained the nurse. "Can you tell if he will suffer any permanent brain damage?" Asked Cadiston. "As I have said, the next twenty-four to forty-eight hours are the most critical but we are hopeful and that is why he had part of his skull removed and is in an induced coma, to give it time to heal and that is a very slow process. Now if there are no further questions for the moment, I will get back to my patient. He is a very sick man, Detective Cadiston and has to be kept under constant monitoring." "Thank you, nurse, that is a very detailed report, I suppose to see him is out of the question?" Asked Cadiston. "At the moment, yes but maybe in a couple of days. He will probably still be in the induced coma. A lot depends on his recovery speed. He is young, fit, and healthy so although we cannot be certain, we are hoping that he will make a full recovery. Time, Detective, that is what he needs time and that means a long vigil begins starting now but with sufficient care, he should hopefully be back to normal in due course. Now I must go as I have to relieve nurse Skelling." Said the nurse. "Thank you again and I will be in every day without fail to see how he is and there will also be a police officer stationed outside his room at all times." Said Cadiston. "He is already at his station, DCI." She smiled and walked away.

He sat down to give himself time to reflect on what the nurse had told him and when he glanced at his watch, it was "Six a.m. Sunday, 12th of October." He said and took a deep breath, then let it blow out slowly. "I have been here almost twelve hours so do I go home now or stay here? I will give Samantha a ring, she will be awake even if she is not up yet." His phone was in his hand and after two rings, Samantha answered. "Morning my sweet." He said. "Morning adorable man, what a night you have had. At a guess I would say that you are still there at the hospital?" She said. "I am but the operation went well and thankfully he is still alive. That is the good bit, now we are in for a long vigil as it will just take time for the healing process. He is in an induced coma and has part of his skull removed and that may need to be repaired with a metal plate at some point in the future." Said Cadiston. "I thought that he would, who was his surgeon?" She asked.

"A Mister Doctor. Mafidsen." Said Cadiston. "He was in excellent hands then as he is one of the very best in cranial surgery and I know that it will be an excellent job that he has done but as you said, now comes the long vigil, waiting for him to recover." Said Samantha. "I will not be able to proceed with his case until I can speak with him as only then will I know the true facts although I already have a good idea of what happened. In the meantime I will be pursuing the others and already have some strong suspicions about certain parties but not over the phone. I thought that I may stay here but I am shattered." Said Cadiston.

"I could pick you up now, Ashton. If you like you can have a shower to freshen up and get some much-needed sleep unless there is anything else that you need to do?" She replied careingly. "Nothing that will not wait until Monday so see you in about thirty minutes, my sweet." The phone went dead and he sent a message to Mac telling him what was happening. Thirty seconds later, he received a reply from Mac's wife who was using his phone. It read: Mac still asleep, was about to wake him but will belay that now. Thanks for your message, I will pass it on when he wakes. Angela for Mac. "That's it then, may as well wait outside for Samantha and come back here later in the day to see if there is any change." Cadiston said and the door creaked again as it opened and again as it closed but he was not bothered. He was going home for a shower and a short sleep but would be back to check on Chad later in the Day.

Samantha was there in twenty-five minutes and as he sat in the car seat, his eyes closed. "It has been a long night for us both but now I need a shower and a few hours of sleep, then back to the hospital." Said Cadiston. "Back again today?" Asked Samantha.

"Today and every day until he is out of the woods and well on the road to recovery. As was said, my sweet, now comes the long vigil. I need to be with him the moment that he can talk because he has something important to tell me. Greta said that he tried to call me on Friday afternoon but, as you know, I was at the mortuary and then came home with you so I missed his call. It must have been of some great importance and maybe to do with all the killings at Mandaten so just maybe the murderer has tried to silence him." Said Cadiston. "Already thought of that." Said Samantha. Cadiston yawned and stretched as much as the car would allow. He dozed for the next fifteen minutes but was awake the instant that the engine was turned off. Once indoors, he went straight to the bathroom. "Just throw your clothes on the floor and don't worry to pick them up, you just get your shower and tumble into bed and I will wake you at two. I will aim to have a meal ready for two thirty so that will give you time to get up and mobile." Said Samantha.

"That sounds good to me, what would I do without you, Samantha? Thanks." Said Cadiston. "Have someone else to do it for you." Said Samantha.

"Not a chance, my precious one. There is one of you and that is all −." He yawned before continuing. "Is all I need. No one could hold a candle to you, my precious and the little bundle that is inside you. Now, a shower and some sleep." His clothes were scattered on the floor and after his shower, he did as his wife had instructed and just tumbled into bed and went directly into a relaxed mode and was soon sleeping.

At two sharp he was called and at two-thirty he was sitting at the table and enjoying the meal that his devoted wife had prepared. "I thought back to the hospital at three-thirty. I know that there will probably be no change in his condition but no matter, I must keep going so the instant that he can speak, I can get his side of the story which will probably be completely different from what has already been said. They have tried to fill me with lies and more lies when they tried to feed me false information. I instantly realized that was their game and the recorded emergency call will sort the wood from the chaff." Said Cadiston. "No fooling you, Ashton." Said Samantha with a smile. "Not a chance, I am onto them and I know that there is something that they are trying to cover up. They may think that they are being clever but I know better. I will find out what it is they are covering up and believe me, I am reasonably certain that I already know the answer to that. First things first and that is that I need the evidence and that is very close." Said Cadiston. "Can you tell me what happened now?" Asked Samantha. "Shouldn't really discuss a case −." He paused for a moment. "In some respect, you are already involved in the investigations as you and Charles will be looking at Demmie's body and I can tell you it is a mess. I guess you are involved so no harm can be done. How we see it – that is Jooners, Mac, and me – when Chad went to his room, there was someone hiding there waiting for him. This person had the first blow and knocked him down. Demmie came in soon after him and saw him lying there bleeding so went to fetch a towel from the bathroom. When leaving the bathroom she was confronted by the real shooter who shot her twice at close range in the chest. Then the real shooter, who had already shot Demmie and thrown the gun onto the floor to be seen when Chad was struck again by Tomas, waited for the coast to be clear and then placed the gun in Chad's hands to make it look like he had shot her but the gun fired again as Tomas was placing it into Chads hands, he panicked and ran downstairs, then the real shooted re-imerged from the hiding place and tried to put the gunback into Chads hands but again it fired. How can an unconscious man reload and fire a gun? and there you have it." Cadiston summarised as best he could. "Answer not possible, someone else was in the room, got it in one." Said Samantha.

"Grant was not seen all day but I am not so sure that he did not have a hand in striking Chad the first time. When the full report is complete, I will have my evidence and will start to question my main suspect to the shooting in length and that is not Chad. I feel certain that he is being fitted up. The victim was his wife, Demmie, shot with his own shotgun at close range with both barrels and it was a mess." Said Cadiston. "I can imagine. Just completed one of those for DI Folkes from the Crabets jewellery shop robbery. You will require a post-mortem on Demmie but this will not be required to authenticate the cause of death so is there some other reason that you want her body checked?" Asked Samantha. "A strong suspicion Sam, I have observed them all extremely carefully and my suspicion is that Demmie is pregnant with Grants child just as Bonnie was." Said Cadiston. "And I know your suspicions are well-founded. Poor Chad, I will come to the hospital as I would like to be there with you." Said Samantha. "That will be good, I was hoping that you would come along and my sweet, you never let me down." She blew him a kiss. "As for Demmie's body being checked, as I said but then I could be wrong but I think that she may have been pregnant by Grant, just as Bonnie was, and he did not want that as he did not want her and was just using her to get at Chad. If she is, it could be the motive to have her killed. She was a thorn in his side and wanted them to marry but he has a new love so the fling he was having with her had run its course and as I said, it was to get one over on Chad. It may have got out of hand and the other woman's jealousy, that little green monster, may have reared its ugly head." Said Cadiston.

"Well, switch your brain off and forget all that for the time being and eat your meal while it is fresh and before it gets stone cold. I don't want to reheat it." She smiled. "Come on, let us finish our meal." Three-thirty saw Cadiston and Samantha at the Royal Hospital heading toward the critical care ward.

"Can I help you, sir? You know that you should not be up here, the visiting on this ward is restricted and is by appointment only and then only in severe cases." Said the nurse behind the desk. His warrant card was in his hand as he Spoke. "It is alright, nurse. I am DCI Cadiston, this is my wife, WPC Cadiston, we are just checking on the progress of Mr. Chadrick Mandaten."

"Ah yes. He is my patient but he only had his major operation this morning, well, through Saturday night into this morning, in fact. There is no change to his condition." Said the nurse. "I did not think there would be this soon after his surgery and change or not, I will be in here every day to make sure." Replied Cadiston. "That may be a real waste of your time, Detective. Well, it is your prerogative." Said the nurse.

"Let us go home, Samantha, be back tomorrow, Nurse Lynn." Said Cadiston. They were leaving when they heard his name called. "Detective Cadiston!" They both turned. "I thought it was you. If you have come to see if there is any change in Mr. Mandaten, it is far too soon to tell." Said Nurse Francis. "We have just found that out, Nurse Francis, from nurse Lynn but thank you. Look after him please, he may be the innocent victim of a serious and vicious crime and not the guilty party but to that end, we need to speak with him." Said Cadiston. "He had the best surgeon and his aftercare will be second to none and anything said here, will remain here." Said Nurse Francis. "To that, I have no doubt." Said Cadiston, and Francis smiled at them and then went back into the ward.

"How did that nurse know you?" Asked Samantha. "She was the one that was in attendance after the operation and gave me all the details last night. Well, early this morning just before I called you. Now home, me thinks, as there is nothing we can do until Monday. I will still pay the Royal a visit tomorrow and every tomorrow after that until he is off the danger list and can talk to me –." Said Cadiston. They entered the lift and in minutes were on their way home.

At home with his wife, Cadiston could not settle. He had been told that Chad had some information for him and a theory about Lowell's death. He wanted to hear his theory as soon as he was able to talk so Sunday evening saw Cadiston at the hospital again. He had spoken with the nurses that were caring for him and this time, he had been allowed to sit by Chad's bed. He looked at the wires and tubes that were placed all over his body and all the apparatus in his room that was being used to keep him alive."

Nurse Francis was on duty again and spoke to him. "Mister Doctor Mafidsen came in this morning to check on him and was very happy with how he is progressing. He said that someone that had been struck so viciously three times where he had and with the extent of damage caused, would normally be dead. He was extremely lucky because Mr. Mandaten had exceptionally strong bones and that is what saved him. The first blow was on the top of his skull and had fractured it and although it was serious, it was not a killer blow. Now the second and possibly third blows had shattered the bone at the base of his skull. He was struck even harder there and by his facial injury, we suspect that he was already lying on the ground face down. Now comes his life saver: his skull, especially at the base where he was struck, is exceptionally thick and because of its strength and although severely damaged, it had protected his brain and spinal cord. He is an extremely lucky young man, Detective, and if he had been struck twice more with such ferocity, it would have been a different story. You have heard the saying 'You have a thick skull'? Well, in his case, he does. I can see that you have a major concern for him and although early days, the signs are looking good. Now then, can I get you a tea or coffee while you are here?" Asked Nurse Francis. "How long can I stay first?" Asked Cadiston. "A maximum of two hours." Said Nurse Francis. "Then I will forgo the offer of a drink, thank you, as I have already been here two and a half hours." Said Cadiston. "I know that as I saw you come in." Said Nurse Francis and smiled."Well, I guess that I will be on my way. Here is my mobile number so if there is any sign of change before I come back tomorrow, will you give me a call please?" Asked Cadiston. "I will do it for you personally, Detective." She walked with him to the door and watched him and Samantha until they were in the lift, he turned and waved as the doors closed. Monday morning, 13th of October, at eight-thirty, Cadiston was in the office. Two minutes later, Mac arrived and said.

"Morning boss, is there any news on Chad?" "Saw him Sunday afternoon and again in the evening, according to his surgeon, he is lucky to be alive. You have heard of people saying that someone has a thick skull? Well, apparently that is just what Chad has and that is what saved his life. He had to remove a lot of splintered bone but luckily the brain and spinal cord escaped serious damage. It will be a long healing process and maybe it could be months before he is back with us but from what has been said, he is already on the mend." Said Cadiston. "That is great news, boss. Any of the family been in to see him?" Asked Mac. "Not yet but I know of two that will want to when they can. I think that a phone call is on the agenda now." He pressed the numbers and after two rings, it was answered. "Greta? It's Cadiston, can you talk?" He said. "I can." Said Greta.

"I thought that you would like to know that Chad had a major operation and a blood transfusion but is doing well. You will not be allowed to visit yet as he is still very seriously ill and on the critical list. He is in an induced coma to keep him still while his skull and brain heal but there is every chance that he will make a full recovery. Keep it to yourself as there may be more to this incident than people think." "Someone coming. Thank you, Chandra, but I do not require any so please take me off your call list." Said Greta. "Got it, will ring when I know more." Said

Cadiston. The phone line went dead. "Who was that you were talking to, Greta? You said Chandra?" Asked Tomas. "No one of importance, just one of those cold callers." Said Greta. "You will not object to me checking your phone then?" Said Tomas. "My phone has nothing to do with you, Tomas, but if you must then go ahead."Said Greta, and she passed him her phone so that he could check the last call. Although a little bit worried she did not show it. He opened her call log and saw that the last call was listed withheld, international, he passed the phone back with a grunt.

"Why did Uncle Tomas want your phone, Mother?" Asked Jennifer. "To check my last call." Greta showed her daughter. "One of those cold calls then." Her mother smiled and whispered. "It was about Chad but shush, must keep it quiet." "Mum's the word, then." She smiled again. "What are you two smiling about?" Grant asked. "No law against smiling, is there Grant?" Said Greta.

"I suppose not but with losing your husband and your son, for the life of me, I cannot see anything for you to smile about. Especially when very soon now you will be penny-less. Not unless you have heard we are now all safe because the killer of the family is dead. More coffee, Lizabeth?" "Well thank you, Grant, I would like another cup." Said Lizabeth.

"What is on the agenda for today, Cadders?" Asked Mac. "We have read a lot and deciphered what we have to date so now we need to get all the evidence so far into Perspective, then we will have a much better idea in which direction we are travelling. A visit to the Royal this afternoon to check on Chad and after that, a visit to the Manor. We will line the murders up as they have happened and try to work out everyone's whereabouts and movements on those days and at those times. We have some of the post-mortem results and most of the forensic reports but I will be glad when the rest are in. Then we can really piece things and events together. Now Mac, my buddy, we had better get to work and itemize each case."

A second large pinboard was brought into the office and the task of putting the murders into a time and date order began.

The morning passed quickly and between them they had begun to make headway. As they both stared at the evidence and case board, Cadiston realized it was now time to visit the hospital again. Together they arrived and were taken into Chad's room. "Hello again, Nurse Lynn. and how is the patient today?" Asked Cadiston. "Mister Doctor Mafidsen is surprised at how well he is doing in such a short time. He is talking about slowly bringing him out of the coma maybe on Wednesday, that would be the 15th. He has a remarkable healing aptitude and even though he has been through major surgery and suffered a massive trauma, he is surprising us all." Said Nurse Lynn. "Have there been any calls from the family to ask how he is doing?" Asked Cadiston. "His father, Lord Mandaten, has called and we informed him of the secrecy but apart from that no one." Said Nurse Lynn. "Well, I know of two people who would dearly like to see him, and who knows, it may help in his recovery if it was arranged and they were to visit. I have heard of people being helped in this way." Said Cadiston. "That is very true but I cannot authorise it my-self, only Mister Doctor Mafidsen can do that, and only if it is in the patient's best interest." Said Nurse Lynn. "Well as to that, I am sure that it would be as love is a great healer combined with all the medical requirements. Is he still here? If he is, then per-haps I can have a quick word with him?" Said Cadiston. "Leave it with me, Detective, you go and sit with him and I will make the call." Said Nurse Lynn. "Thank you." Said Cadiston. Sitting beside Chad's bed, Cadiston spoke quietly to him. "Cadiston here, Chad. Got yourself in a bit of a fix, haven't you? Have no fear, I will get you out of it. I am not going to tell you much for the moment as I do not want to overload you with informa-tion. I understand that you have something that you need to tell me so as soon as you can talk about what happened on Saturday, we can bring the culprit to justice. I strongly believe that you are an innocent victim of someone's vendetta against the family and there is more than likely an internal wrangle also but I do not want to burden you with all that just now. You get better, Chad, that is what we all want for you and I know that Greta and −." He noticed a slight twitch when he mentioned Greta − "and Jennifer are longing to visit you. Greta −." Again, the same twitch at the mention of her name. "She is very worried about you so I am trying to get permission for her to visit. Would you like that? Would you like Greta and Jennifer to pay you a visit?" He purposely used her name again to see if there was a reaction and to his delight, there was a slight twitch as though he had heard his every word and understood. "You will make a full recovery, then you can tell me what it was that you wanted me to know but that can wait for now. I know that you can do it, Chad. You are young and strong I am sure that you are not going to allow a little old bump on the head to stop you from hearing the truth, now are you my friend?" At that moment, Nurse Lynn returned. "I have had a word with Mister Doctor Mafidsen for you and he has agreed that Greta can visit." Again, at the mention of her name, Chad twitched. "Did you notice that, Nurse Lynn? At the mention of her name?" Asked Cadiston, "I most certainly did and as you said, it will be a good thing for her to visit. I will inform Doctor. Mafidsen of the response at the mention of her name as this is a positive sign that even in his induced coma, he can still hear and understand. Talk to him, it will be good for his healing process." Said Nurse Lynn. "I have been, nurse, and we have had a good chat but sadly, I think our two hours are up. I will be in touch with Greta and bring her to visit." Cadiston said and again, the same response was noticed. "Then I will leave it with you, Detective Cadiston. I have here for you a pass which will allow her admission and you and your DS do not need one." Said Nurse Lynn. "Thanks again, nurse, and see you again tomorrow." Said Cadiston. "Not me tomorrow, Detective. Nurse Francis will be on shift and you have already met her, haven't you?" Said Nurse Lynn. "That I have so thank you again and see you when you are next on shift." Said Cadiston and they left the ward feeling very positive and possibly joyous about Chad's recovery. "See Mac, a vist from someone who loves him will have a power of good to assist his recovery". "Greta Cadders, great".

371

"Now where or do I already know the answer to that Cadders," "Mandaten Manor for us now, Mac. We need to have a word with his Lordship and with Greta." Said Cadiston. With the engine fired up and the gear selected, Mac said. "Map set so Mandaten it is."

"You know the way Mac, without help from a map." Said Cadiston. "Set in my head. I have a map of our area built in so just tell me where you want to be and when you want to be there and I will take you. Now, you want to be at the Manor so Mandaten, here we come." Said Mac.

At the gates, Cadiston announced himself and as he spoke, the gates opened automatically. "Drive straight in, Detective, we saw it was you so come in, we have been expecting you to call." Mac drove steadily down the long drive and pulled up in front of the great Manor House. The front door stood open and Alfred was waiting to show them in. "The family is in the lounge, DCI Cadiston. I will announce you to them." Mr. Bradinham was in the hall and took over from Alfred. "His Lordship is waiting for you in the lounge, Detective, if you would follow me please." Said Bradinham. They knew the way but observed the protocol and walked slowly behind the old butler.

"DCI Cadiston and Sergeant Macswee to see you, my Lord." Said Bradinham.

"Thank you, Bradinham, that will be all." Said Lord Mandaten. The old butler gave a half bow; "My Lord." He said and left. "Come in, Cadiston, and tell me your news but first, there is tea and coffee on the sideboard so please help yourself to whatever you prefer." With their drinks selected, they sat down in front of Lord Mandaten.

"Now then, do you want the rest of the family here or just us?" Asked Lord Mandaten. "Just you, my Lord, with your good lady and then a quiet word with Miss Greta before we leave." Said Cadiston. "Then that is what you shall have, now begin." Said Lord Mandaten. "I will speak softly as walls have ears and this is for yours only. You have probably heard some tall tale spun about Chad and Demmie by a member of the family. In our mind it was a good thing that you were not here at that time." Said Cadiston.

"Heard what Tomas said had occurred but did not believe him and he appeared very shifty, I may be old Cadiston, that does not stop me from picking up on some ones lies. He was perspiring rather heavily so I told him to stop as I would rather hear it from you." Said Lord Mandaten.

"According to what we have been told by Lizabeth, she heard Chad ranting about Demmie having an affair and she sent her up to their room to speak with her husband to get the problem sorted. While she was in the bedroom with him, Kansas allegedly heard him say that he was going to kill her so rushed downstairs and told his mother that Chad had a shotgun and was going to kill Demmie and to phone the police which she did. While she was on the phone, there were two gunshots, then a delay of up to five minutes and then two more. Now after the second two and before the final two shots, Tomas had run downstairs after allegedly knocking Chad unconscious and taking the phone from Lizabeth who was talking to the call operative explaining what had happened. We were on the scene quickly and our forensic's team has examined the crime scene thoroughly. Now, just for you alone to know, from the evidence and suspected lies that were told to us, we are convinced that Chad did not pull the trigger. We could say that he was sort of an innocent bystander. He was in the room and can possibly identify the real shooter who had already struck him. When Tomas entered the room, Chad was on the floor half-conscious, and instead of helping him, which any decent person would do, he struck him for a second time. There was someone else present, the real killer, but Tomas could see no one as they had hidden in the wardrobe. With Chad lying unconscious on the floor now, because of the time delay, we believe that Tomas reloaded the gun and tried to place it into Chad's hands to add to the incrimination but it was inadvertently fired so he left the gun and ran downstairs with his false story. The third-party, that shot and murdered Demmie, now reappeared, reloaded the gun, and placed it into Chad's hands but when they put his finger on the trigger, it fired again. Fearing that someone, namely the police, would investigate, they magically disappeared.

I still need to listen to the recorded phone call and that will tell me more about the case but as to that, I can say no more." "You appear to have an inner sense, young Cadiston, and it sounds to me that you have it sorted. All you need is the evidence and that will lead to the assailant. I knew he could not have carried out such a callous act. It may seem strange to you, especially because he is our adopted son but we both feel that we have a stronger bond with him than our other three sons, of which the worst of the three is the only one remaining." Said Lord Mandaten, Cadiston smiled. "We cannot disclose anything further for the moment as it is an ongoing investigation but I will say that we have our suspect in our sights. Now, if we turn the clock back to the night of Monday, 22nd of September, the night that Bonnie and her unborn little girl child died, or rather were murdered −. We now know conclusively who committed the crime. Upon a visit to the Manor, it was at the time when you had been rushed to the hospital, I took the liberty of having a look around the place where the dessert trolley was on that fateful evening. While looking around, I was admiring the old spice jar and noticed that the cork lid was loose. I removed it and recovered a syringe that turned out to be the one that Cook had lost about three months before which coincided with the last family visit. When it was analysed, it was found to have contained a very high concentration of odourless and tasteless pure peanut and this was injected into Bonnie's dessert. The perpetrator only had seconds to complete this act and dropped the syringe into the jar to be retrieved later for disposal but I got there first. A fingerprint was lifted from it and following my suspicions, I obtained a further print from my main suspect and a match was found. It was the print of Chad's wife, Demmie. We later found out that she and your son, Grant, had been having a liaison and she wanted it to be a permanent thing. She would leave and divorce Chad and wanted him to divorce Bonnie which he refused to do. He did not really want Demmie and was only carrying on with the affair to get one over on Chad. We believe that there is a lot of jealousy between them. We also found out that he was having another affair and he said that he loved this lady to distraction and that he was going to set up home with her once he had secured the title of Lord Mandaten. We know this lady's name but again, at this point, we cannot disclose it. Demmie is now dead so we will never know her true motive for killing Bonnie and can only surmise that she was driven by desire as she wanted Bonnie out of the way to free Grant up for herself and as he would not divorce her, murder was her answer. It is very sad because Bonnie and her unborn child were murdered by Demmie in cold blood for no reason at all, as it turned out that Grant did not want her and was purely using her. We are still looking at her death with suspicion because what we do not know is whether Grant knew about the plan. We are making good headway with the other murders and once we have all the post-mortem reports on hand and when coupled with the forensic reports, D.N.A., and blood, things will really begin to be pieced together and it is safe to say that after this, my suspicions may be confirmed." Said Cadiston. "So, you have confirmed that our Bonnie and her unborn little girl child were murdered by Demmie and all because of her desire to have what she could not? She was having a liaison with Grant and now someone has murdered her. One could say that is justice but not at the expense of our son, Chadrick. Now then, regarding him, Cadiston, how is our son?" Asked Lord Mandaten. "We have a long vigil ahead of us and I do not want it broadcast as I would like the suspect or suspects to believe that he will not recover. He is on death's door if they ask. He is doing much better than his surgeon expected and we have a long vigil ahead of us. There is a long way to go and it will most likely be several months before he is fully recovered. Apparently, he had an unusually thick skull and that in effect, was what saved his life." Lord Mandaten looked at his wife, then back at Cadiston. "Would you repeat that last statement please – please? What was that you just said about Chadrick and his skull?" "An unusually thick skull and that is what saved his life." Repeated Cadiston.

"That is what I thought you said. We have always understood him more than our other sons and to be honest, he has a lot more

Mandaten in him than Grant ever had and now you tell us that he has an unusually thick skull." Lord Mandaten again looked toward his wife. "Now, that is very strange and an interesting fact that you tell us as we have a trait in the Mandaten family of unusually thick skulls. We have not heard of it in any other families so how come he has it?" Said Lord Mandaten. "That is a very good question and one that we will investigate fully to give you the answer. There are a few more things that we need to look at in-depth if we are to form a full picture and if we are going to reach the truth and a final closure to all of these cases. As you are aware, they all take time. I was not happy before with how things were and it has been approved and I can let you know that we are not going to overlook the case of your brother, Baron Laseroie Mandaten and his family. I already have the case file in my possession. As you may be aware, one piece of evidence may be enough to make an arrest but not necessarily to gain a conviction. We are moving as quickly as possible. We are gathering vital evidence and as I said, we are working as quickly as possible but if we were to try and rush things forward, then we could miss something vital and an innocent person could go through an ordeal that was not necessary. Likewise, to make an arrest too soon before sufficient evidence has been gathered, in other words, sufficient to secure a conviction, may result in a guilty person having to be released and that is the one thing that we wish to avoid." Said Cadiston. "That is understood, Cadiston. Now, if you are done with us, I believe that you wanted a word with our Greta." Said Lord Mandaten. "I do, sir, if it is convenient." Said Cadiston. The bell cord was pulled and two minutes later Jonas entered. "You rang, my Lord." "Jonas, will you find Miss Greta and bring her here please." Requested Lord Mandaten. "At once, sir." Jonas turned and was gone. "I suppose that you are not allowed to tell me who you suspect?" Asked Lord Mandaten. "At this point in time, sir, I cannot." Said Cadiston.

"Understood. Ah, here is Greta for you." Said Lord Mandaten as Greta entered the room. "You have kept to your word, Detective Cadiston, thank you." Greta said. "Not a problem, Miss Greta, and I strongly believe that when your word is given, then it must be one's bond." Said Cadiston. "Indeed Cadiston, now what did you require of Greta?" Asked Lord Mandaten.

Cadiston turned to face her. "It has been arranged for you to visit Chad but even though you visit him, you must let everyone believe that he is not recovering. I cannot tell you why but it must remain a secret so can you do that for me?" Asked Cadiston. "Easily, Cadiston. I have lost my husband and son and do not want to lose him also. None of the others have any interest in seeing him and they think that I have lost all my senses wanting to visit a murderer. I know him or rather we know him well and I do not believe that he is responsible for all these atrocities and neither do his parents. Can I take Jennifer with me as I do not want to leave her alone and she would like to see him also." Said Greta. "You will need to present this pass because visiting is strictly controlled but I see no problem with that." Said Cadiston. "Thank you." She turned and left.

"Means a lot these days to have a man who sticks to his word, Cadiston. Sadly a trait that I am afraid is missing in a lot of people and sadly in my sons apart from one and he now lays on death's doorstep. Now, as for what Greta just said, his mother and I do not believe that he is a murderer either. Well now, if there is nothing else then I must have my afternoon nap, a bit later than usual but never mind as the news that you have passed to us has given me a new zest and desire to live a lot longer." Said Lord Mandaten smiling.

"Then we will take our leave of you, my Lord. We will probably be calling back here quite regularly as there are many questions to be asked until these cases are solved. There are also outside sources that are to be investigated so on our visits, we will try not to disturb you." Said Cadiston. "Disturb me? Nonsense man, I would not have it any other way. You disturb me when you like." Said Lord Mandaten. "Very well, sir, and now enjoy your nap." Said Cadiston. "That I shall, my boy, that I shall as I can rest a lot easier." Lord Mandaten. Alfred was waiting for the meeting to end and they watched as he wheeled Lord Mandaten from the room.

"It is a bit late in the day to return to the station. There is nothing that we can do constructively there anyhow so home for us, Mac." Said Cadiston. "Home it is, then." Said Mac and they left the Manor, driving slowly up the long drive. The gates opened automatically and closed the second they drove through them.

"Pick you up in the morning Cadders." Asked Mac. "No need, Samantha will drop me off." Said Cadiston. The instant that Cadiston had left and just as Alfred was wheeling their father from the room, the rest of the family entered and before anyone else could speak, Grant pounced. "He is here again, blast him ready to cause more upsets for us especially you Mother, Father, so what did that snooping detective want to see you about that was so important that we could not hear it?" His father gave him a stern look. "That has absolutely nothing to do with you Grant. If he had wanted you to know, then he would have spoken with you."

"And why should he speak to you alone Greta, now that has me puzzled as you are not even family so what is so special about you and not us, besides you are not real family?" Lizabeth said bitterly. "You are repeating yourself and I do not like your tone, Lizabeth, and again Greta has no need to answer you. You seem to forget that she has only recently lost both her husband and her son." Said Lord Mandaten even more sternly.

"It is alright, Father. They will know soon enough so I will put them all at ease and answer her question. As I was the only one who asked if I could visit Chadrick, he wanted to let me know that there is very little hope of him surviving but if I wanted to, then I could go and sit by his bed. That was all, not that it has anything to do with any of you, satisfied Lizabeth?" Said Greta.

"Excellent news and let us hope that he dies and soon, that is what I say. At last we are rid of that interloping murderer and good riddance." Said Grant.

"That is just what I would expect from you, Grant." Greta shook her head, turned and walked away, following Alfred down the long hallway. Tuesday, 14th of October, arrived and after a morning of reading and rewriting, it was time for a visit to the hospital.

"Good afternoon DCI Cadiston, DS Macswee. Mr. Mandaten has already got two visitors with him." Said the nurse. "And who might that be, Nurse Skelling?" Asked Cadiston. "The young lady had a pass and said her name was Greta Mandaten and her daughter, Jennifer, accompanied her. I thought at first that she was his wife with their daughter. She said that she was his sister-in-law and Jennifer his niece. I said it was alright as they had a pass." Said the nurse and Cadiston smiled at her. "I know that as I arranged it for them and now how is he today?" He asked. "Mister Doctor. Mafidsen is thinking that he may be going to start bringing him out of the coma tomorrow so a very good sign." Answered Nurse Skelling. "And is there any response to Greta and her daughter?" Asked Cadiston. "There is quite a lot and again, a very good sign as it is only three days since his operation." Replied Nurse Skelling. "Can I just pop in to say hello and to let him know that I have been in to see him?" Asked Cadiston. "Hmm, – Should not really as there are already two visitors but as it is you, go on then." She said. He squeezed her hand and entered the room. "DCI Cadiston, you are here to visit as well so shall we step outside?" Asked Greta. "Here every day, Greta, and no need for that, you stay put. Hi Chad my friend, see what I do for you to help you get better? Told you that I would help to get you sorted. Now, what more could you want than an attractive young lady, in fact, two attractive young ladies to be here and hold your hands." Chad twitched as he had before in recognition. "The rule is only two visitors at a time and as I do not want to get nurse Skelling into trouble, I will leave you with Greta and her daughter Jennifer. As they will have a power of good on you, anyhow, I am sure that you would much rather have them here than me. I will be back, you can count on that and tomorrow is possibly going to be a big day for you so, my friend, you hurry up and get out of that bed." Chad's hand twitched as though he understood. "See you tomorrow, Chad." Cadiston said and he turned and left the room.

"Back to the station, Mac, and let us see if any of those reports are ready yet." Said Cadiston. While Mac parked the car,

Cadiston went straight into his office. He was pleased to see an envelope on his desk and before opening it, read the note again that John had left informing him that Chadrick Mandaten had called to speak with him on Friday, 10th of October, as he had some relevant information about Lowell Mandaten's death.

"Now I wonder if his getting attacked has any bearing on the information he wanted to give me. Good way to silence someone, they cannot speak if they are dead. It poses the question, did Tomas want to kill him? They think the dead cannot talk,how wrong they are, just as Demmie is dead and let them think that Chad is also dead, well they are wrong the dead can talk thanks to forensic science. What possible information would he have on Tomas or Kansas? It must be tangible but whatever it was, would it be strong enough to make them kill to prevent it coming out. We may have a long vigil ahead of us but best you recover quickly, Chadrick my friend, so we can get this sorted. If only I had returned to the office from the mortuary, then maybe Demmie's death and Chad's attack would have been avoided."

"Talking to yourself, Cadders?" Asked Mac. "Thinking out loud, Mac. Now we will see what the boys have given us." He turned to the envelope and was quick to open it. With the contents in his hand, they skipped the introduction and began to read:

After checking all the chalky samples, we have concluded that this is a form of thick chalky whitewash and was used to act as a sealant on the walls of tunnels that had been dug in years past, for example a means of escape from churches and or cathedrals. In many old Manors these means of escape were incorporated into the building and Mandaten may be an example of this. All three samples matched, as did the sample you collected from a suspect's coat. After conducting a series of test experiments on the object, it is our conclusion that they did come from the same source.

"Looks like we have to find a secret passage at the Manor, Mac, so that calls for a trip to the buildings archive as that may help. If we find the answer there, much the better. I noticed that Grant also had a chalky residue on his jacket and some cobwebs on his back. Now, if we had that jacket and it matches these samples –. Well, never mind that. Now I have a special job for you, Mac, and one of great importance. I want you to do a thorough background check on Grant. There is rivalry between brothers in some families especially when there is a fortune at stake but this is unusually aggressive between him and Chad. We know that as a child, Chad saved him from drowning which was a real embarrassment as he was quite a bit older. I have not been told directly but from what I have heard in passing, Grant is supposed to have a fear of the water and cannot swim." Mac interrupted. "There it is again, Cadders, you get a snippet of information from whatever source and hang onto it. You are the master at that because I did not pick it up." "You will you, Mac, you will learn to listen to everything that is being said even if you think it is not relevant. Now if he was responsible for Sadie's death, he would need to swim after leaving her body in the lake so check everywhere to see if he had swimming lessons. Also check if he has been training at a running club or a keep fit gym as that will tie in with Demmie. Take these photographs with you, it will help to identify him in case he has been using a false name to hide his true identity and that I suspect." Said Cadiston. "I didn't know that we had a photograph of him or any of them, come to that, so how come?" Asked Mac.

"Got photographs of the whole family, Mac, including Demmie. I had copies made of the family photos on the sideboard before putting them back as there is so much happening they did not notice that they were missing so they were not even aware they were being copied. The rest I snapped with my phone." Said Cadiston. "That was either clever or sneaky, Boss." Cadiston smiled. "A bit of both. Now, back to the subject, be very thorough and leave no stone unturned as we need to know everything about him. My suspicion s tell me that he is not who everyone thinks he is. It will not be an easy task but one that I am confident that you can carry out. You will need to check out not just the main venues but the backstreet ones also, he may have wanted to do it in secret. See if there are private tutors that he could have used. Detective Sergeant

Macswee, that is your task. It will take you a few days and when you come back and if my suspicions are correct, you will find that he used a name that I may already have written down. Go and do it, my friend, and have me the answers that I want. Bring me the names used and all the relevant information, Mac. You can make your start on that investigation on Wednesday morning, 15th of October, to Sunday, 19th of October, should be long enough as that is five days. Go home now, Detective Sergeant Macswee and remember that you may need to spread a wide loop as he probably did not use anyone local. I have confidence in you so off you go and see you back here on Monday, 20th at eight-thirty on the dot with your results. One more thing, I did not want you to be alone on this investigation and so I have arranged for WPC Olito Paverson to go with you." Said Cadiston. "Olito, that is fine, She is a good officer and pretty acute so may pick up on something that I may miss. I'll do my best for you, Boss, and see you Monday with the information. I won't let you down, Cadders, and I will have the information you need." Said Mac with a salute, and with his hand raised in a wave he was gone. Cadiston looked at his watch. "Time for home myself now that Mac has his assignment with Olito. So what is Wednesday's plan?

1: In the morning to the archive of building plans.

2: The hospital to see how Chad is doing and if he is coming out of the coma alright. That will do for Wednesday, may need to flit between the two depending on what I find and how long I will need to stay at the hospital but as for now, home." Cadiston thought out loud.

Wednesday morning, 15th of October, at 08:59 and Cadiston was waiting outside the Museum and Archive of Building Plans. He tapped his watch at 09:00 and said. "Come on, the door should be unlocked so I can access the building records of Mandaten Manor."

At 09:01, the large old lock clunked as the key turned and the door was opened. "Good morning, sir. You are about early, we usually do not have anyone in until 11 a.m. at the earliest." Said the clerk as Cadiston entered.

"DCI Cadiston and I need to look at some very old building plans of Mandaten Manor, built and then burnt down in the sixteenth century. The present Manor was being built around the thirteenth century and added on to over the years."

"Mandaten you say? That rings a bell. Now let me think, thirteenth century – Ah yes, that will be in the King Henry III room. Follow me, please. I will take you there and help you to find them." They had entered the designated section and with the information on hand, he could begin his search.

"Please take a seat, Detective, and I will bring them to you." He waited patiently for the clerk's return and fifteen minutes had passed before he stood beside him. "Now then, because of the delicate nature of the original plans that have been kindly donated by the current Lord Mandaten, I cannot show you the original plan on paper. As you say, the work was started in the thirteenth century but the Manor that stands today or at least the main part of it was built in the seventeenth century. It took many years to complete and at that time, there was a lot of turmoil in the country as that was the time of the English Cicil War, a terrible time. Now as I said, original plans are delicate and because of that, it has been transcribed onto this computer disc. The computer is ready for use and when you have the disc inserted it will be displayed onto the screen just there. It is much easier to see when it is enlarged." Said the Clerk. The disc was quickly inserted, the computer whirred into action and in a few seconds, the plans were displayed. With the mouse, he carefully scrolled over them and at first, found nothing. He was beginning to think that he was wrong and muttered. "Come on now, don't let me down, be there." The curator, who was still there, asked him if he was looking for anything specific. "It may sound silly but secret underground escape passageways." Said Cadiston. "Now that is strange because you are the third person to look at these plans and ask the exact same question." Said the curator. "The third, now that is interesting and have you their names?" Asked Cadiston. "They will be in the visitor book. When we go back to the front desk, I will look them up for you, Detective.

Now, if I may." He took control of the mouse and soon found what Cadiston was looking for. He said. "The passageways are mainly in the oldest part of the Manor, as you can see, but links were made to the new building as it was erected through the six-teenth and seventeenth centuries. You can see there that from the oldest part of the Manor, they lead away from it and emerge near the woods."

"And that is not far from the lake." Said Cadiston. "Not far at all, about two hundred yards to me but to the young ones about sixty metres. There are also connecting tunnels that go to the sta-bles. The builders were very clever and incorporated them from upstairs behind the panelling but if you do not know where to look, you would not find them. Does that help you?"Asked the curator. "It most certainly does. Now, is there any way to get a copy of these tunnels?" Asked Cadiston. "Just give me two minutes." He began to hum a tune while Cadiston stood and watched. "Sorry, it took three minutes but there you are, will they do?" Cadiston looked at the prints. "Excellent, thank you. Now, those names please." The disc was removed and replaced in its allocated file and the computer shut down. "Follow me please, DCI." Said the curator and Cadiston obliged him without saying a word. "We would not normally allow anyone to look at this book due to data protection but as you are a detective, we can make an exception. Here we are." Said the curator. Back at the front desk, the visitor's book was produced and the pages were then slowly turned. "There you are, Detective, that is the entry. The first was over six months ago and that was a Mr. Grenville. Then again, now let me see –." He flipped the pages over as he spoke. "There. Six weeks later by a Miss Hurdshaw, said she was a student at the Amptil University studying architecture." "Are these their addresses?" "The ones they gave us but because of your interest in them, I have a feeling that they are false." Said the curator. "Probably but they will be checked. I don't suppose you could give me a description of them?" Asked Cadiston. "Let me think, it was a while ago. Now, if I remember correctly, the man was about six feet tall and well built, brown hair but I can go one better for you. He would be on our CCTV. In fact, they will both be caught on camera. We do not let people know that we have it but with so many rare plans, it pays to be extra careful. In fact, it was the police that installed them for us a sergeant Folkes organised it." Said the curator. "And can you get me copies of them?" Asked Cadiston. "I will run you copies if you will bare with me." He disappeared into a back room while his assistant stayed at the front desk. "It was a while ago, Detective, and I can remember the lady as we do not get many of them in here and when we do, they are all elderly or college students but not this one. She was very attractive and had auburn hair with hazel eyes, a lovely complexion and I would even say skin as smooth as silk." Said the clerk. "And if you saw her again you would recognise her?" Asked Cadiston. "In an instant, detective. We do not usually get attractive young women in here, they are usually men fifty and upwards. The one you are asking about, he was only in his late thirties or maybe early forties. We do have a run on students who are studying architecture and building methods." Replied the clerk. "You have a good memory then." Said Cadiston. "Not really, it was only that they were so different from our normal visitors." Said the clerk. Thirty minutes had passed before the curator returned. "There you are, Detective Cadiston, I hope it will help you." "Thank you and I am sure that it will but before I go, would you look at these photographs and tell me if you recognise any one of them." He laid them onto the counter for them to see. "That one, that is Mr. Grenville but not any of the others." Said the curator. "That is a great help, many thanks." He left the archive of building plans and as it was only half-past eleven, went back to his office with the objective of watching the two CCTV discs. His computer whirred as it loaded and then he began to watch disc one and after ten minutes, it was at the place that he needed. "Now let us have a good look at you. Hmm, need to bring you up a bit larger." He mumbled to himself.

"CCTV footage, now that looks interesting and I guess that you need it enlarged?" Said DI Richard Folkes. "That I do, Richard." Said Cadiston.

"Bring the disc over here, my computer has the right programme so will be better for that than yours." Said Richard. "With the cases you are on, have you the time?" Asked Cadiston. "Shouldn't take long." Said Richard and with the disc inserted, they searched to find the correct spot which Richard enlarged. The scene was paused and Cadiston could easily see who Mr. Grenville was. The disc was removed and disc two was inserted. Again, the correct time stamp was searched and paused, and the picture was enlarged.

"Now there is a turn up for the book, so you are Miss Hurdshaw. I never suspected you. Thanks Richard, I owe you a big one." Said Cadiston.

"Not a problem, Cadders. I am a bit stuck on this missing person's case and the Crabets jewel shop robbery even though we have the shotgun they used and may appreciate a bit of help later with it." Said Richard Folkes. "You will have it." Said Cadiston. "I take it you recognise these two characters?" Asked Richard. "That I do but they are not who I thought they would be. Never the less, I have their card marked." Said Cadiston. "Making progress on the Mandaten murders then, Cadiston?" He turned to see his chief behind him.

"Yes sir, making some good headway and Macswee is off to find another major link in the chain so the net is closing in. One murder has already been solved – that of Bonnie and her unborn little girl child –- so, chief there are nine more to go." Said Cadiston. "Stick with it then, Cadiston, and get the result and don't forget to call on others to help if need be." Said the chief.

"That I will, sir, and already have." Cadiston assured him. "Good man." His inspector turned and walked away.

"Thanks again, Richard, that was a great help. I will return the favour one day, now I am off to the hospital to see how one of the victims is doing. He could possibly be brought out of the induced coma today if all is well with him so fingers crossed. Thanks again and catch you later." He was gone before DI Richard Folkes could reply.

"Welcome back, Detective Cadiston, and no Sergeant Macswee today?" Said Nurse Francis.

"He is off on a special mission." Said Cadiston. "Say no more. Dr. Mafidsen would like a word with you, and do not worry, Chadrick has two visitors in there with him." He peeped through the window in the door and smiled.

"Greta and her daughter, Jennifer. That is good, I hope they are helping him." Said Cadiston. "Of that, you can be sure. Greta would like a word with you when you are finished with Mister Doctor. Mafidsen." Said Nurse Francis.

"Right you are, Nurse. Now, where do I find Mister Doctor. Mafidsen, Nurse Francis?" Asked Cadiston. "He is in the office just there." She pointed in the direction. "You can go straight in as he is expecting you." Said Nurse Francis and smiled. Walking toward the office, he was wondering what the surgeon wanted with him and hoped that it was not to be bad news. "Good afternoon. Now, then if I am not mistaken you are Cadiston, the detective?" Asked Doctor. Mafidsen. "That I am, and you are Mister Doctor Mafidsen, unusual to be called both, now what did you need to see me about?" Asked Cadiston.

"Just my own little fetish, now then about Mister Mandaten. I have checked him every day and will continue to do so but I am delaying bringing him out of the coma for a few more days, probably untill next Monday, the 20th. There is nothing to worry about but after examining him, I feel that I was being a little bit over presumptuous and if I bring him out of the coma too soon, it will do more harm than good." "He is in your hands, Mister Doctor Mafidsen, and I support your decision. I know that you have his best interest in mind and, well, I am going nowhere, neither is he. When would you expect to bring him out of it if not on Monday?" Asked Cadiston. "Maybe Tuesday, 21st or Wednesday, 22nd. I will decide after a further examination of his progress. He wrote the dates in his notebook. "But you will know what is decided as you are in here every day to check on him and why that is, is entirely your business or why he has a police officer sitting permanently by his door is none of mine. My main concern is for my patient's health and welfare. Your concern is to abide by the law but I believe that you are concerned for the patient's welfare also. Now, if there are no questions for me then I must get going because I have another operation to perform in forty minutes on a young motorcyclist who lost a leg in the accident and has a serious head injury which would have been far worse if she had not been wearing a crash helmet." Said Doctor Mafidsen.

"I will not delay you then as your time is precious and seconds are the difference between life and death." Said Cadiston. "Exactly Detective. I will just say that allowing the two ladies to visit has done the power of good to Mr. Mandaten and as you requested it, I think that you definitely have his best interest at heart as well, Detective, and it is not just a matter of law." Said Mister Doctor Mafidsen. "You could be right there, Mister Doctor Mafidsen." They both smiled and Cadiston went to visit Chad again. "Hello again, Greta and Jennifer. How is the patient today?" Enquired Cadiston. "I am sure that he knows we are here and Doctor Mafidsen, his consultant surgeon, thinks so as well. He is coming along nicely but will not be back with us properly for a few more days." Said Greta. "I get the feeling that you both think a lot of Chad." Said Cadiston. "We do and so did my son, Lowell." At the thought of her dead son, she shed a tear. "He was more like a father to him than my husband was. He stood up for us while others stood by and did nothing. We will always be thankful to him but it is not for that reason or just at that particular time so we will leave it there, shall we." Said Greta smiling and also blushing. "We shall and do not worry, I am not going to press you for a deeper explanation. I can draw my own conclusions. What you want is for Chad to get better and that means a long vigil for you both but when you love someone as much as you both love Chad, it does not matter does it? And it does not matter what others say." Said Cadiston.

"Not at all, we will both be beside him every step of the way and help him to recover." Said Greta. "Good enough for me. Now, before I go, is there anything that I should know as the nurse said that you wanted a word with me." Said Cadiston. She moved away from the bed. "Stay with Chad, Jennifer, while I have word with Detective Cadiston." Said Greta. "Alright, Mother." Said Jennifer. They then moved outside the room before Greta began. "You ask if there is anything that you need to know and if by that you mean are awkward questions being asked, then the answer is yes." Said Greta. "And by whom?" Asked Cadiston. "Strangely, not by who I thought would ask. It was mainly Tomas with Kansas, they were asking what we were doing and where we were going every day. Grant appears to have lost all interest but listens in when they ask about Chadrick. They have all been enquiring but not in a nice way. I just say that he is in a coma and in an extremely bad way and is not expected to survive but I do not want him dying alone so we sit quietly beside his bed waiting. I am certain that they do not seem to ask in a caring way but as though they all want him dead. They also say that we must be totally mad to visit a family murderer even if he is at death's door." Said Greta. "Not in my book, Greta, but that is just between us. I will see you tomorrow unless there is something else?" He asked. "You remember when you questioned them about Chadrick and Demmie being shot?" Asked Greta. "Very clearly and it is all documented." Said Cadiston.

"Well it was not totally the truth that they told you. Lizabeth told you that she was upstairs changing and on the way down heard Chad ranting and cursing in his room That was a lie. She never went upstairs and although Jennifer and I were in the garden, we could still see the lounge window and she was there all the time. She said that she had changed her clothes, another complete lie as she was wearing the same ones when we went outside and when we returned. We saw Tomas and Kansas both talking with her then they went upstairs but she stayed down so why lie to you? She then used her mobile phone and then Kansas came running down and said he had heard them arguing. Again I say that we were right beneath their window and heard none of that so why are they all telling lies? Is it to get Chadrick into trouble and get him out of the way? Another thing crossed my mind –. Chadrick had a theory that would lead to Lowell's murderer. He took Kansas or rather we helped to get him to the paddock and when Star saw him, she bolted with her foal which led him to believe that Kansas was Lowell's murderer and he wanted to tell you that with something else that he had discovered. So did Tomas try to kill him when he struck him to silence him?" He took hold of her hand. "Thank you, Greta. That is a possibility that I already have locked in here." He pointed to his head. "Be assured I will get to the bottom of it. Now, was there anything else that you can remember?" He asked. "Only something that was said by Kansas. He said that if he had his Uncle Grant's handgun, then he would shoot the mad horse himself." This remark was instantly written into Cadiston's notebook. "Thank you. Now best you get back to him as I think that he will be missing you." Said Cadiston. Greta returned to her seat while Cadiston stood by the door. "There you are Chad, I didn't keep her from you long, did I my friend? Now, you listen to me, you get better for these two ladies that love you." Chad twitched and Cadiston thought that he saw him smile. Without another word, he opened the door but before he walked away, he turned and smiled at Greta and Jennifer who sat on either side of his bed holding his hands.

Thursday, 16th of October, Cadiston began to assemble his team of extra help to find out some information to help with his investigation. On his list were WPCs Janet Crowth and Grace Jorde, PC Howie Julip, and WPC Nadine Crown, WPC Francis Rendham and WPC Olito Paverson, who had already been there to help and Olito was with Mac investigating Grant, and PC Peter Roland and WPC Jenny Borrows. This was his team and they were all eager to assist in searching out information and evidence for his investigation. He informed them that their assignments would be complex and would produce major evidence in the investigations into the deaths at Mandaten Manor and the information that they gained might lead to the arrest and conviction of a murderer and every detail that they collected would be of vital importance. He also asked if any of them would rather not be on his team and he would assign someone else without prejudice. Not one of them refused.

"I think that I can speak for us all. Myself and Olito have already started working with you DCI Cadiston and DS Macswee and are proud to do so" "Well said, Francis, and that goes for us all, acting DCI Cadiston, and we do not care about the acting one bit, we are all proud to be on your team." Added WPC Jenny Borrows. "One question, sir, are we in uniform or plain clothes?" Asked WPC Amelia Stroud. "Entirely your choice." Replied Cadiston. "Leave it to us then, sir, and we will tackle our task with enthusiasm and bring you the evidence that you require." Added WPC Francis Rendham. "Thank you all, time is of the essence in finding the evidence and I know that you will work hard to find it. With that said, I will sort out your assignments as quickly as possible so stand by and be ready for action." Said Cadiston. "On it sir." Said WPC Amelia Stroud They turned and were gone.

He spent the rest of the day looking at the evidence that had been collected and visiting the hospital. Friday just flew by with Cadiston visiting the hospital twice a day. He was happy to see that Greta and Jennifer were also there and that she had totally ignored the rest of the family, apart from the parents that condoned her visits. Saturday and Sunday passed quietly with the visits as a fixture but on each one, Chad appeared to be more aware even though he remained in the coma. Mister Doctor Mafidsen checked him on the morning of Monday, 20th of October, nine days after his operation and was extremely pleased with his progress. When leaving, he met Greta and Jennifer on their way to sit with him so stopped to speak with them.

"Good morning Greta and Jennifer. It is good that you visit Mister Mandaten and I am more than convinced that it is due to your visits that he is doing so well. Many would have died from the extent of injuries that he received but I believe that he is fighting extremely hard to get better because of the connection with the both of you. I have no idea what your relationship is but that is immaterial and between you both, the fact is that your visiting is much better than all the medicine. You most certainly are a real tonic for him. I have no idea what it is you are doing but just keep doing it and I have decided that because of his progress, I will bring him out of the induced coma on Wednesday, 22nd October, and that is just eleven days after his operation." "If it is permissible, can we be present when that happens?" Asked Greta. "It is very unorthodox and has never happened before but you are here every day so be here for ten-thirty and I will decide then." Said Doctor. Mafidsen."Thank you – I was about to say doctor but that would be wrong so thank you Mister Doctor Mafidsen." Said Greta. "Excellent, see you on Wednesday, 22nd, at 10:30." Said Doctor Mafidsen as he turned and disappeared into the office. When they entered Chad's room, Nurse Francis was just finishing her treatment routine. "There you are, Mister Mandaten, your lady visitors are here again, Greta and Jennifer. His fingers twitched. "Wednesday is going to be a big day for him and only eleven days after his major surgery and inducement. Now, if you need anything at all I will be in the room next door." Said Nurse Francis. "Thank you, nurse Francis. He hates all the formality and I am sure that he would not mind in the slightest if you dropped the Mister and just called him Chad." She smiled and left. Cadiston had been informed of the decision to bring Chad out of his coma. Doctor Mafidsen's secretary had phoned Cadiston so that he was there during his visit and examination. The instant that he arrived, Doctor Mafidsen had been waiting in the office for him. The date was set for Wednesday, 22nd, eleven days after his surgery. He was told that Chad had progressed extremely well and that was partly due to the two ladies that have put all else aside and have shown such devotion by visiting him every day and that was due to Cadiston's request. The process would be slow and was scheduled to begin at eleven a.m and Cadiston should arrive by ten-thirty a.m. Greta and Jennifer had requested to be present as he comes around and were waiting for the decision whether it would be allowed. After being informed, Doctor Mafidsen had left to attend his other patients. Cadiston spoke to the nurse. "There walks a good man nurse." "One of the very best cranial surgeons in the business, Detective, he is not just a brilliant surgeon but an extremely nice man." Said the nurse.

"Do I detect a hint of a crush, Nurse Lynn?" Asked Cadiston.

"Detective really, he is a married man and I am a married woman. Why, the very thought –." She smiled at him. "Well, maybe a tad." "Our secret then, Nurse." said, Cadiston and tapped his nose so they both smiled.

"Will you return again this afternoon to visit?" Asked Nurse Lynn.

"Not today, Nurse Lynn. It has been a long vigil. I will definitely be here tomorrow and without fail at ten-thirty on Wednesday morning. Now I am back to the station to see what information my busy DS has for me." Said Cadiston.

"I will see you on Wednesday morning then. In fact, I have a feeling that all the nurses that have cared for him will want to be here even if they are not on shift." Said Nurse Lynn. "That is nice and shows how you all care for your patients." With a wave, Cadiston was on his way.

Cadiston was pleased with how the investigations were progressing and knew that with the help of his new team members, other vital evidence would be found and used to bring the guilty to trial and secure a conviction. Mac had previously phoned the station, leaving a message for his DCI to tell him that his search had taken him and Olito far and wide and he had not completed it until late Sunday evening but the final piece of information he would not be able to obtain until Monday morning. He believed that he had secured all the evidence required but had a difficult time getting the last piece of evidence so was sleeping over and would not be back until early to mid-afternoon. However, when Cadiston arrived back at the station he was already there waiting for him. He was keen to divulge the information that he and Olito had gathered about Grant and he also wondered what his DCI and friend had been doing. He knew that he would not have been idle. He had names, locations, and news that he hoped was what Cadiston required and had surmised that some of the information that he had would possibly be as his DCI had suspected.

"Afternoon Mac, you and Olito had a busy time then?" Asked Cadiston. "You could say that but following your lead, I feel that we have got all that was required and maybe a little bit more thanks to Olito's invaluable help." Said Mac."Well done both of you! While you have been busy and working hard to gain the evidence, I have not sat idly by and have done some investigating myself. I have set up a team to give us a hand and I am anxious to hear all your information and what you have discovered but for the moment, we will belay all that as Bennie is on the way and I have a strong feeling that he will have a great deal of post for us to sift through. With the information you and Olito have gathered, plus my own to run through and asses, we are in for a busy time." Said Cadiston smiling.

Chapter Twelve

The Post-Mortem, Forensic and Lab Reports

"Afternoon DCI Cadiston, afternoon DS Macswee." Said Bennie.

"And good afternoon to you, Bennie." Said Cadiston. "Lots of internal post for you today: lab, forensics and post-mortems, real heavy bag full. Well, cannot stand here and pass the time of day with idle banter, got lots more post to deliver." Said Bennie. "Thanks, Bennie." As he left, he closed the door.

"Quite a pile for us so we had best make a start. We will go through them all, from the very first and that was Bonnie and her unborn little girl child, to the last that has only just happened and that being Demmie. Let us hope that it is the last death this family will have to suffer. The Mandaten family has suffered very heavily with this number of deaths in such a short time, eleven in fact. From what I have observed, all these deaths are rooted in desire, twisted minds, jealousy, greed, falseness, and lies. There may also be another cause and that I have in the back of my mind, is revenge. One thing is for certain though, they all add up to cold-blooded, pre-planned murder. Whichever way you look at them or try to dress them up as tragic accidents, they all equate to murder in the first degree. Now, we have a lot to go through, Mac, so we will get these read through first and then you can tell me all the information that you and Olito have gained about Grant. Thereafter I will fill you in with mine and following that, we will set our team on finding out other vital evidence that we need, plenty to occupy us so best we make a start." Said Cadiston.

The files were lined up and the first one opened. "Right, we have our pinboard with all the information on it, we have the family photographs so here we go then." Said Cadiston and they began.

Mrs. Mandaten suffered from anaphylaxis which is a complaint that affects the body's immune system and means that certain foods must be avoided at all costs. On the night in question, Mrs. Mandaten ingested a substance that we now know as a concentrated solution of pure peanut and after ingesting the said substance, she was placed into a severe anaphylactic shock which, in turn, led to her having a series of cardiac arrests, (heart attacks.)

In taking the necessary samples of blood and tissue, it was found when tested that her system contained an exceptionally high level of peanut which she should avoid at all cost and the dose that was ingested by the deceased was more than a sufficient amount to induce the shock, placing her into a coma and this, in turn, would lead to the cardiac failure. At face value and without a post-mortem, it would appear that Mrs. Mandaten died of natural causes being a massive heart attack which led to cardiac failure and would have been deemed to be the cause of death by natural causes. It was the persistence of Detective Cadiston and his insistence to carry out an investigation into her death. We can confirm that had this not been requested, the true cause of death would have been missed.

After carrying out a series of tests on Mrs. Mandaten's blood and tissue samples that were found to contain an excessive amount of a solution of pure peanut it is our professional opinion that such a high quantity of peanut in the system would need to be introduced involuntarily, therefore, we cannot justifiably state that Mrs. Mandaten died of natural causes but was the victim of foul play. In carrying out our post-mortem, it was also discovered that Mrs. Mandaten was two months and three weeks pregnant therefore her death has led to a second death, that is of her unborn child.

Conclusion

Although at face value Mrs. Mandaten died from cardiac failure that was the result of her condition of Anaphylaxis, we were not convinced that her death was due to natural causes. Her blood and tissue samples contained an unusually high amount of peanut to which she was allergic. The question arose as to how such a high quantity of pure peanut had entered her system when everyone knew of her allergy. In our professional opinion, it was introduced into her food by a person unknown and I conclude that Mrs. Mandaten did not die from natural causes but lost her life and the life of her unborn infant involuntarily. Knowing of her condition this was a callous and cold-blooded act and would have caused Mrs. Mandaten to die in extreme agony.

Verdict
Mrs. Mandaten and her unborn infant that was a little girl were the victims of a pre-meditated act of murder on both counts and this act was carried out by a person or persons unknown.

Signed
Mr. Charles Dennasen – Mrs. Samantha Cadiston

"Now for the Lab report which will only serve to confirm the findings in the post-mortem and my own suspicions. I feel very strongly that this young woman and her unborn child, for the child must never be forgotten, have died needlessly, Mac." Said Cadiston.

"I have not been on the cases as long as you, Cadders, and I have to agree, their deaths were an unnecessary loss of life." Agreed Mac.

"And for that, the murderess has paid the ultimate price but sadly not her accomplice so we still have work to do in finding that accomplice. Now, the next report."

For the Attention of Detective Cadiston
From Laboratory Friday 3rd October

Result of tests on syringe left by Detective Cadiston on 1st October.

The syringe was not the usual type used for administering an injection but one that would be used in a kitchen. In conducting our requested examination to analyse the contents, we found it to be an extremely highly concentrated solution of pure peanut. This product would not be readily available on the open market therefore it must have been specifically produced by parties unknown and these parties would need to have a sound knowledge of the chemical composition of the food and would need the facilities of a laboratory if they were going to produce such a product.

The solution had been produced to be tasteless and odourless so it could only have been produced by a skilled food technician. Because of the high concentration of peanut in this product, it would without a doubt be signing the death warrant of a person that suffers from the allergy syndrome of Anaphylaxis should it be ingested unknowingly by this person.

We examined the syringe and found that there was a partial fingerprint. This was lifted and is enclosed. With the use of a computer and although the print is only partial it may still be possible to match this with prints taken at the scene or from interested parties to either eliminate them from your inquiries or give cause for further questioning and investigation.

We have also returned the syringe for your evidence file.

Hope this helps with your case and inquiries.

Signed
Keith Mansun senior lab technician

Just as we thought, you were definitely poisoned, Bonnie, poisoned both you and your unborn little girl child. You cannot hear us but we know who did this to you and she has also been murdered. Now we need to find her accomplice so that is not a case closure as Standish wanted but an case open and that is a solemn promise. Now for Malcolm Mandaten, let us see what that brings up." With the report open, they read on.

The Post-Mortem Result on Mr. Malcolm Mandaten:
Date of Death Tuesday, 23rd September:

Upon the insistence and request of Detective Constable Cadiston, we carried out a full examination on the body of Mr. Malcolm Mandaten and during that examination, we noticed some severe bruising marks on his right arm that were not concurrent with falling from his horse. When we examined them closely, the marks were found to be finger imprints caused by someone gripping his arm very tightly. It is our thought that by using great force and in our professional opinion, they denote that he did not accidentally fall or was thrown but was forcibly pulled from his horse.

We found that there was heavy bruising in one place on the rear of the body and the location of this was in the small of his back, again not concurrent with the alleged fall. We carried out a full examination of the area and we found that it was possibly made by a knee being pressed into him to hold him down. Being held down in this way placed him in the exact position to administer the blows to his head manually and during our investigation, this was found to be the case. Therefore his death did not result in him being dragged onto the fallen piece of masonry although without a doubt this was the weapon that was used to end his life.

When we carried out our examination of the piece of masonry and the head wound to determine the angle in which it was struck, we discovered that the theory of being dragged is not a possibility and denotes that it could only have been done manually and deliberately by a person or persons unknown.

During the examination, we found that Mr. Mandaten had an unusually thick skull and the extent of the damage denotes that there were a series of blows directed to the same spot at the base of the skull to cause the amount of damage that was sustained therefore an impossibility that this was a single strike. Because of the density of the skull, we estimate a minimum of three possibly more, blows were administered to ensure that a severe fracture was the result. We also can confirm that to cause this amount of damage to the skull, each blow was directed perfectly, deliberately and accurately at the same spot being at the base to inflict maximum damage with the hope that the spinal cord would be severed by the bone fragments which would leave the victim afflicted with severe paralysis from the neck down therefor making the victim completely incapable of movement, if not dead. This act was committed by a person or persons unknown that have a knowledge of the human body and the function of the spinal cord and was most definitely not after being dragged by a bolting horse.

It also became completely clear that whoever struck these blows knew of Mr. Mandaten's unusually thick bone structure. As has already been stated, the blows were to the rear and near the base of the skull and were struck with such force causing a large fracture and an intended massive bleed. Because of the severity of the blows struck, the bone splinter also damaged the spinal cord therefore even if he had survived this violent onslaught, Mr. Mandaten would have ended up completely paralysed.

With other evidence presented to aid our examination and investigation, it is safe to state that in our professional opinion, Mr. Mandaten was dead before he was dragged to the spot where his body was found.

We then examined his clothing and found by the tears and the marks on the front of his legs, face, and torso that he was dragged on his belly which denotes that the blows to his head were not caused by being dragged by a frightened, bolting horse but were inflicted by a person unknown. It is probable that his horse dragged him but this was not in our opinion a bolting animal but one that was being calmly led. He had maintained his tight grip on the rein due to the paralysis caused when his spinal cord was severed and damaged and a small piece of the rein was found in his hand. Detective Cadiston has this in his possession. If Mr. Mandaten had been dragged on his stomach at full force onto the piece of masonry, in this scenario he would have been looking up, then it would have struck him full in the face. If he was face down, his facial injuries would have been very severe, which they were not. If he had been dragged on his back and was looking up, which we know he was not as there were no injuries to his back apart from the single bruising, the top of his head would have been struck.

We examined a series of scenarios and whichever angle we placed the body to denote how he could have been dragged into the piece of masonry, none of them matched or would have resulted in him being struck at the rear and base of his skull multiple times, as is the case. As we have stated, we looked at every possible scenario and from every possible angle and from the site of the impact at the rear and base of the skull and with the amount of damage caused it could not possibly have happened accidentally. The examination proved that the amount of damage caused was most definitely not a single blow but a series of blows being struck manually.

We had examined the body for other bruising that was concurrent with falling from his horse and had found none. The only bruising sustained was to the arms and small of the back that has already been explained. We measured and re-checked the shape of the said bruising and our findings show that on the arms were fingerprints and it was the assailant's knee being pressed into the small of his back to hold him down that had caused this bruising. To be certain, the bruising to the arm and small of the back was retested and we can confirm that our previous findings are correct.

We requested the murder weapon and Detective Cadiston retrieved the offending piece of masonry to aid our investigation and upon examination of the said masonry and the angle of the skull indentation, it matches exactly with the said piece of masonry in fact it fits as if a piece from a jigsaw, and confirms that the injury sustained to the skull was actioned manually with the piece of masonary fitting into the skull indentation. We also removed a quantity of soil and grass from the victim's mouth which denotes that he was being held down to position the head ready for the series of blows to be struck.

All other injuries to the body do not coincide with those that would have occurred if Mr. Mandaten had been thrown or had fallen and then had been dragged violently by a frightened, bolting horse.

Conclusion

From the evidence gathered during the post-mortem, it is our combined and professional opinion that it was not at all possible that Mr. Mandaten died from a tragic riding accident, there are far too many discrepancies. We, therefore, declare that there is reasonable doubt that rules out that this was a tragic riding accident but gives cause for our suspicion that foul play is to be suspected and to this end, we investigated further and repeatedly.

We now checked the body for signs of severe damage caused by the deceased being dragged by his horse, here follow our findings:

Front – There were a few scratches to the shins and face, the main torso was relatively undamaged.

Back – There were no visible signs that the body had been dragged on its back.

We now re-checked the clothing worn and after a careful examination, we found that there was insufficient damage and there were no visible signs that Mr. Mandaten wearing these clothes was dragged violently by a bolting horse. There was an occasional tear but there are very few visible signs or damage to the said clothes that denote that he was dragged violently by a bolting horse. The lack of damage to the clothing was more defined as deliberately but moderately being dragged slowly by the horse being led.

We now re-examined the head:

Face: Upon examining the face, we found several teeth had been broken. The broken teeth were supplied to us by Detective Cadiston. We removed from the mouth an amount of grass and soil. This evidence denotes that the head was being held firmly down, forcing it into the soft ground. It would sink further in whilst being struck. This promotes the theory that more than one person was involved in this violent attack upon Mr. Mandaten.

Skull: Primarily the strike site:

The strike site, the position, and the angle of the blows to the base of the skull were cause for us to have major concerns over the way that it had transpired. Upon close examination, it was found that it could not possibly have been the result of Mr. Mandaten being dragged violently and at speed onto the fallen piece of masonry.

Reason one: The position of the strike did not match such an action and the damage caused to the base of the skull was so severe that it would be impossible to cause such an injury. It was found after careful examination of the offending piece of masonry and the head wound – to determine the angle in which it was struck – that it could not possibly have been done by the deceased being dragged violently into it, this is defined by more than a single blow.

Reason two: The shape of the blows, were all found to be struck near the base of the skull and aimed in the exact same spot. If Mr. Mandaten had fallen from his horse by being thrown and was then dragged by the animal, as we were led to believe happened, he would have had to angle his own head in a certain way to receive the injury that was caused and would need to be dragged and struck more than once.

We have just cause and reason to believe that a minimum of three blows, if not more, were struck all exactly on the same spot at the rear and near the base of the skull. They were struck with such force to cause a large fracture and a massive bleed. The blows were so intense that the spinal cord was damaged and in the event that Mr. Mandaten had survived the skull fracture and the loss of blood, he would have been permanently paralysed from the neck down. It is our strong belief that Mr. Mandaten had been forcibly removed from his horse, then violently struck, rendering him into a state of unconsciousness and if not already dead, was close to death before he was dragged to the spot where his body was eventually found. We know this to be true from the two blood samples and photographs of the bloodstains provided by Detective Cadiston. One sample from the fall site and one from the site where the body was found. The photographs show the spread of blood clearly and upon analysis, both blood samples were found to be from the deceased, Mr. Malcolm Mandaten.

Because of the discrepancies, we re-examined every aspect three times. Upon each examination, we could find nothing to change the outcome and they all concluded the exact same results. It took multiple strikes to inflict the amount of damage sustained. We looked very carefully at every possible scenario and from every angle and from the site of the actual impact that fractured his skull and failed to find any other feasible answer.

With all the evidence that has been produced in the lengthy and thorough post-mortem examination, it is very clear that Mr. Malcolm Mandaten was the victim of an act of aggression toward him by a person or persons unknown. It is our professional opinion Mr. Malcolm Mandaten was already deceased before he was dragged to the spot where his body was eventually found.

After collating all the post-mortem evidence, reaching our final verdict was made a lot easier. I would also state that after the findings of the post-mortem examination, a full forensic investigation of the site, as was requested by Detective Constable Cadiston, at the scene and at the time of the incident should have taken place and would have secured the site for a further and deeper investigation, enabling vital evidence to be gathered.

Verdict
Mr. Malcolm Mandaten was the victim of a premeditated act of violence upon him which was committed by a person or persons unknown and resulted in his untimely death.

Signed
Mr. Charles Dennasen – Mrs. Samantha Cadiston

"That was quite a read and what an in-depth post-mortem. It only goes to prove what you have said all along, Cadders. To my way of thinking, ex-Sergeant Standish has something to answer for denying you the forensic examination of the old Manor and Devil's Dyke." Said Mac.

Cadiston smiled and said. "We will not go there as it is in hand now. Next case is that of Kevin Mandaten, and for this, there is no post-mortem, just a confirmation of death as it was not necessary. I was there at the time of the incident and I will go as far as to say 'at the time of the murder'. No post-mortem but we do have a detailed report from Daniel and John in the firearms department about the gun and from Jooners in forensics. Without Standish, there was no delay in getting them there this time."

"Before we read that report, I just need a break to the little boy's room. I will bring us some coffee when I come back, be five minutes." Said Mac.

"Ok Mac, I will just stretch my legs." Said Cadiston.

Sure enough, five minutes passed and they were again sitting with their heads together reading the next report.

Confirmation of the death of Mr. Kevin Mandaten
On Sunday, 28th September

Although a full post-mortem was not required to establish the cause of death, we still examined the body for any irregularities. Mr. Kevin Mandaten did indeed die from the explosion of his firearm which damaged his face and head so severely, in fact, almost removing it from his shoulders so there is no hesitancy in confirming that he died instantly at the scene. In examining the remains of his head and face, a quantity of gunpowder was embedded in the flesh. There were small fragments of metal from the exploding weapon that had been embedded with such ferocity, they had penetrated the bones through the flesh. These fragments were removed and were passed on to the firearms department.

Other than the severe damage to Mr. Kevin Mandaten's head, the body had suffered no further trauma. The blood and tissue samples were normal.

Conclusion

As the cause of death is undeniably obvious and was unmistakably due to the weapon exploding in the face of Mr. Kevin Mandaten, a verdict of accidental death would normally be registered. However, due to other mitigating circumstances pointed out by Detective Cadiston regarding this case, a conclusion at this point in time cannot be reached and, therefore, a closing verdict cannot be announced and recorded. Although it is clear what caused the untimely death of Mr. Kevin Mandaten, namely the explosion of the firearm, there is also a strong suspicion placing doubt as to the validity of his death. As we already stated, there is no doubt as to the cause and although it is known that the death occurred by the weapon exploding, there are a considerable number of concerns to warrant an investigation so this has been deemed to be death under very suspicious circumstances.

Verdict

There can be no closure or verdict as this incident is pending further investigation. It is therefore necessary and we are recording this as a death under suspicious circumstances.

Signed
Mr. Charles Dennasen – Mrs. Samantha Cadiston

"That is pretty straightforward as the cause of death is known and cannot be reputed. But now we will read the report from the firearms department regarding the explosion of Kevin's Kentucky rifle. I have already seen it and know of its contents. In my book, it never hurts to re-read a report as the first time it is possible that the reader could miss something that could turn out to be a vital clue and it will be the first time for you. We will also read the forensic report so there is the file, let us do some more reading." Said Cadiston while the file was opened and they read in silence.

For the Attention of Detective Cadiston
From
Forensics Friday, 3rd October

Results found in the examination of the site of Mr. Kevin Mandaten's reserved area by request of Detective Cadiston on Sunday, 28th September.

After a careful search of the area, the pieces of the damaged weapon found were taken to the firearms department. We also proceeded to carry out a routine search of the designated area and upon investigating and conducting a search in the marquee, we found traces of a white chalky soil that did not match those of the area. The marquee was pitched on grass so when we found an amount of the white chalky soil, we immediately knew that this was alien to the surroundings and these were bagged and are enclosed.

We ran a thorough examination of the designated area and apart from the metal fragments from the exploded weapon and the white chalky soil, nothing more was found.

Signed
Sergeant Jooners Forensic Scientist

"When I first received the report from Jooners, I thought it was a rather large envelope and again, that chalky soil has turned up and looked just like that which Samantha found up by the old ruins and Devil's Dyke. Suspicious or not, Mac, why that chalky soil again. Now it has been found in two different places, question is where does it originate from? That question we must answer, Mac. The soil that is seen in the ploughed fields has a reddish colour to it and not a sign of any chalkiness. Find where it comes from and it may help to lead to the guilty party or parties." Said Cadiston.

"Now we know what it is, thanks to our lab boys so a good clue and evidence, if I am not mistaken." Said Mac.

"You are not mistaken, Mac, and I may have the answer. We will get to that later. Now let us read the next one and that is from the firearms report."

Firearms report on Exploded Kentucky Rifle
Left by Detective Cadiston
Monday, 29th September

Examination completed on Wednesday, 8th October

Upon receiving an exploded firearm, a replica Kentucky Rifle, from Detective Constable Cadiston on Monday, 29th September, we began our investigation into the possible cause of the barrel exploding.

We also received many fragments of the exploded barrel from Detective Cadiston and more arrived with Sergeant Jooners of forensics and Charles Dennasen of the forensic mortuary. In due course, we would attempt to reconstruct the exploded barrel to ascertain the cause of the explosion.

After a very careful and thorough examination of the remaining portion of the barrel and the design of the weapon, we noticed some discrepancies in the colouration at the base end of the barrel. Upon further examination, it was made clear that a large quantity of black powder had been held in this section and this led us to believe that an overload had caused the explosion. It was at this stage that we began to piece together all the fragments that had been found, allowing us to rebuild the barrel as far as the explosion would allow. Upon its completion, we were then baffled by a small round disc that had been brought in by forensics and did not appear to belong to any part of the weapon's barrel or mechanism. We had at first thought to discard it but as it had been brought in by forensics with other pieces of the weapon. It was then decided to keep looking for its place in the reconstruction process.

With careful and extreme micro examination, connected to the computer, we were able to determine the burn of the powder. It was a difficult task and we discovered that there had been a significant amount of black powder placed in the barrel prior to Mr. Mandaten's own smaller measured load but were still confused as to how it was contained there. We carried out a series of computerised tests to discover the effects of an overload of black powder and in our opinion, this weapon had most definitely been tampered with prior to Mr. Kevin Mandaten using it. As the weapon was used safely during Saturday's shows, we assume that the weapon was tampered with after the closure of the show on Saturday and the opening of Sunday's show.

As the weapon would have been thoroughly cleaned after Saturday's show closure, we can ascertain by the mark on the barrel that the initial load would have been placed there the day before use and would have rested there all night. After all our rigorous testing, we can confirm that the weapon was tampered with and pre-loaded on the evening of Saturday, 27th September, in advance to its use on Sunday, 28th September.

We also carried out an examination of the ramrod used to push the load securely down the barrel and found that it had been very carefully cut. To the naked eye, it would not have been visible. We carried out another test on the ramrod and this was only noticed under a microscopic examination. The tip was much paler than a rod that had been used on many occasions as it would have been stained by and would also contain a small amount of powder whereas none was found to be present. In use, it would have appeared that the ramrod had gone the full length of the barrel, thereby making it suspicioous. After taking a measurement, it was found to be almost one and a half centimeters short. Again, this is a major cause for suspicion.

Upon our inspection of the powder horn, it was found that there was no tampering with this item and the measurement was of a lesser amount to be certain that a full charge was not loaded.

At this point, we could now confirm that the weapon had been tampered with and a pre-load had been placed in the barrel prior to the load of Mr. Kevin Mandaten because we could not confirm how a large charge would be held in position waiting to be ignited. However, we were still baffled by the small round disc that appeared to play no part. At this point, I was called away with the small round disc leaving me baffled as it appeared to fit no part of the weapon John eventually came up with an idea and experimented. To our delight, we found that this small disc was not waste after all but was very cleverly used in tampering with the weapon. As you may be aware, every single gun barrel has its own fingerprint in the rifling so we can be certain that the weapon in question was in the hands of an expert quality machinist to enable him to produce such a perfectly machined disc.

With this information, we could then examine the pre-load amount and we estimate that a charge to cause this amount of damage must have been at least five times more than the full amount that the barrel would bear.Our experiment and testing gave the answer: After the quantity of black powder had been poured into the barrel, the powder would be poured out if the weapon was tipped barrel facing down but this could not happen as it was held in place by this well machined small round disc. After discovering this we then carried out further tests on the disc itself and found that it had been very carefully machined to fit the exact shape of the barrel's rifling so it could only have been made by an expert machinist. The only way that this perfect fit could be achieved, was if the machinist of the said disc had the weapon itself. We estimate that the person that placed the pre-load into the weapon was the person that had taken the rifle to the person that manufactured the disc.

After the load had been poured and the securing disc pushed into place, the ramrod would then be too long so would have been cut to its new perfect size hence the lack of discolouration. With the powder charge and the disc in place, the weight of the rifle would be fractionally heavier and in the hands of an expert, this would be noticed. As other elements of the day were in full force, it possibly went unnoticed.

If you can pop down to the firearm's department, then we can show you.

Test and investigation carried out by
Daniel Gardener – John Granster

"I paid them a visit and would like you to see for yourself the destruction caused so when we have read all the reports and if it is not too late in the day, we can go down to the firearm's department for you to see the evidence first hand." Said Cadiston.

"That would be good. Now case four, the triple murder." Said Mac. Three post-mortem files were laid before them and once open, they began to read:

The Post-Mortem Result on
Mrs. Sammie Larkspere Nee Mandaten:
Requested by Detective Cadiston
Date of Death Sunday, 28th September:

We began the post-mortem on Mrs. Sammie Larkspere on Monday, 29th September. There were two arrows that had been forced into her body and it was found that the first had entered the right side of her chest in an upward movement, passing beneath her ribs, scraping her sternum, and had punctured her right lung. The second had squeezed between her ribs on the left side of her chest and had punctured her heart. In the examination of her body, we also found that she had been struck on the left side of her head with such force that had fractured her skull and that could possibly have rendered her totally unconscious.

We asked for the forensic analysis of the area where the body was located and after reading their report, it enabled us to determine that the angle of the two arrows could only have been forcibly placed into her body by hand. It was also found that they were placed specifically and with gentle force as the surrounding area was not heavily bruised as it would have been had the arrows struck from the force of a bow or free-falling after being fired. There was also the depth of the thrust. It is clear to see and evident from the angle of the arrow's insertion into Mrs. Sammie Larkspere's body that they were both inserted by hand and this led us to believe that the attacker knew exactly where to place the arrows for maximum effect. This again denotes that the victim was already unconscious when the arrows were inserted into her body as there was no resistance or tearing of the flesh at the entry point. It is not known which arrow was inserted into the body first but either would have led to death, one very slow choking on her own blood the other when the heart had bled out.

Upon our full examination of Mrs. Larkspere's body, we found that apart from the blow to the head, the body had no other signs of a struggle. It is our opinion that she knew her assailant and because of this, she was relaxed in their company and caught completely off guard being unaware of the impending violent attack.

Conclusion
From the evidence during the post-mortem examination, we can conclude that Mrs. Larkspere received a sharp blow to the left temple so severe that it fractured her skull thus rendering her unconscious. In this state there was no resistance when two arrows were forcibly placed into her body. We can also confirm that Mrs. Sammie Larkspere died from the wounds that she received by the insertion of either of the two arrows and we can also confirm that these arrows were deliberately and specifically placed. We cannot be certain which arrow was inserted first but either would have been responsible to cause her death. Arrow one was inserted beneath the ribs on the right side of the chest and after scraping the sternum, was angled to puncture the right lung. The second was forced between the ribs on the left of the chest, puncturing her heart.

Arrow one punctured the lung and this would have led to a slow death choking on her own blood. Arrow two punctured the heart and this would have led to death when the heart had finally bled out. Both deaths independently would see Mrs. Sammie Larkspere suffering and in great pain had she not been unconscious.

The large stone that was used to inflict the head wound had been deliberately placed to give the impression that she struck her head after falling: this we know from the forensic report. The positioning of each arrow denotes that they were positioned deliberately and were inserted by a person or under the guidance of a person that knew the human body and was placed to give maximum effect. Apart from the skull fracture and the wounds inflicted by the two arrows, there was a lack of any other injuries that would have been sustained if a struggle for survival had taken place. Due to the lack of such a struggle in defence of her life, it is our professional opinion that Mrs. Larkspere was undoubtedly the victim of a person that she possibly knew and because of this felt no threat from them.

The evidence gained in the examination leads us to believe that Mrs. Sammie Larkspere was the victim of a vicious attack that led to our verdict.

Verdict
Mrs. Sammie Larkspere was the victim of a pre-meditated act of murder by a person unknown.

Signed
Mr. Charles Dennasen – Mrs. Samantha Cadiston

"How could someone be so –" Mac shook his head. "Words fail me, Cadders.

We most defiantly must catch these vicious people as I am sure that there is more than one perpetrator of these heinous crimes."

"You have that right, Mac, and as I have already said multiple murders and multiple murderers. I am confident that together we will put an end to their reign of terror, now we read on." Said Cadiston.

They did not hesitate and moved directly to the second report:

The Post-Mortem Result on Mr. Walter Larkspere:
Requested by Detective Cadiston
Date of Death Sunday, 28th September

We began the post-mortem on Mr. Walter Larkspere on Monday, 29th September, and completed it on Tuesday, 30th September. Upon our examination of the body, we found that there were two arrows that had been implanted violently and with great force into the body. We also noted that Mr. Walter Larkspere had severe facial injuries and other bruising about his torso which led us to believe that he had also been involved in a violent altercation and was possibly fighting for his life. One arrow had penetrated the larynx, passing completely through the throat to exit at the rear of the neck and damaging the spinal cord. The force used was so great that it had shattered the vertebra in the neck. This single wound would have made it very difficult to breathe and because of the spinal cord damage, he would then be incapable of further defensive actions. A second arrow was forced into the lower abdomen which had passed through the stomach and the liver and was inserted with such force that it excited through Mr. Larkspere's back. Both these arrows had been placed violently, with great force and haphazardly unlike Mrs. Larkspere's. This gave rise to our thought that after seeing his wife attacked and struck down, he possibly put up a very brave but fruitless fight for the survival of his family and was violently and maliciously struck down. Both arrows individually would have led to a very painful and slow death. One from asphyxiation as he gasped for breath, the other from the loss of blood.

There was heavy bruising and tears to the flesh around the entrance sites of the arrows which denote that force was used to puncture the clothing and the body. Fibres of clothing were found on the arrow points, also force was detected in the depth that they had travelled into the body.

Upon examining M.r Walter Larkspere's body, we found a number of cuts, abrasions, and bruising to his face and hands that denotes that he had been involved in a violent fistfight that we believe was prior to the altercation with his killer. In his weakened state, he would have attempted to fight for the survival of his family, great force was used and this would have only ceased after being overpowered and the insertion of the arrows. We found other injuries that his body had sustained which were possibly attained in his struggle for survival with his killer. During the post-mortem and examination of the internal organs it was then discovered that Mr. Larkspear had a heart condition and had experienced a series of minor heart attacks. These attacks had caused scar tissue to the heart wall and this condition meant that he would have died within six months. Due to the additional exertion used in his altercation, a massive heart attack was induced which would have led to his death. This being the case, the insertion of two arrows was not required to end his life making which made his attack unnecessary.

We re-examined the body due to the number of injuries it had received and can confirm that Mr. Walter Larkspere was involved in two separate altercations. One was with a person unknown in which one of his teeth was broken. The broken tooth with a whole tooth were given to us by forensics. The broken tooth was matched to Mr. Larkspere, the whole tooth is to be identified. The second altercation was with his killer. There were heavy facial injuries that denote that the first fight was extremely fierce and because of his weakened state, the second altercation was slight.

We already had the forensic analysis of the area and as already stated, we were able to marry one broken tooth to Mr. Larkspere. The other whole tooth we can be certain was from his first assailant. From the report, can confirm that the arrows implanted into Mr. Walter Larkspere's body, and by the angle of their insertion, were placed very violently and haphazardly by hand and were most certainly not fired from a bow.

Conclusion

Mr. Walter Larkspere died from a massive induced heart attack and the wounds received by the insertion of two arrows in varying positions into his body were unnecessary to end his life. From the angle of each strike, it is assessed that these were haphazardly placed with such force to cause maximum pain and would therefore result in a painful death.

One arrow was inserted with such force that it penetrated through the larynx, exiting the spine and shattering the vertebrae, therefore, damaging the spinal cord and rendering the victim unable to defend himself further. Another arrow was inserted into the lower abdomen, passing through the stomach and entering the liver causing a slow internal bleed. The force used was so great that the arrow tip had exited the body.

Both these wounds individually would have resulted in a painful death and singly either one would have proved fateful. Sadly, Mr. Larkspear was put through an unnecessary trauma as he would have passed away within six months due to his heart condition. It is our professional opinion that the killer or killers were at the scene watching the first altercation between Mr. Larkspere and the unknown assailant and unaware of his condition struck ensuring that the maximum amount of pain would be endured before death. We had been informed by detective Cadiston that Mr. Larkspere had been involved in a confrontation prior to his death. Because of the first attack and the ensuing fight detective Cadiston was suspicious of the circumstances and felt that the real killer had witnessed the first confrontation and was of the thought that the first attacker who had fled the scene would be found and then blamed for their deaths and as they were aware of this person's identity then they would disclose it at the right time to the police. It is our opinion from the evidence gained in the post-mortem, that as with his wife, Mrs. Sammie Larkspere, Mr. Walter Larkspere also knew his attacker and was also caught completely off-guard, thinking that they would help him in his state and was feeling safe in their presence.

It is with the evidence that has been gathered from the post-mortem examination coupled with the forensic evidence and the information gained from detective Cadiston that has made it possible and led us to our verdict.

Verdict

Mister Walter Larkspere was the victim of a pre-meditated and violent attack and died from a massive induced heart attack. Even though the death was of natural causes because of the violent attack and insertion of two arrows, Mr. Larkspear was still the victim of an act of murder by a person unknown.

Signed
Mr. Charles Dennasen – Mrs. Samantha Cadiston

"I have no words, there are no words. That poor man, to see his wife and daughter murdered so brutally in front of him – We must get them, Cadders." Said Mac.

"We will, Mac. After seeing these photographs of the bodies and reading these reports, do you still want to be a detective?" Asked Cadiston.

"If it involves putting people like these undesirable pieces of sh ... They need to be flushed down the pan, in other words, put away where they belong or better still strung up. You ask if I still want to be a detective, if I can help to action that then yes even more so and what is more with you as my DCI – I will be more than happy." Said Mac. "Thought you would say that, Mac, and each day brings us a step closer to them.

When Chad has recovered sufficiently to be able to tell us his findings and we have assessed it, then we will be closer still. Greta told me that it has something to do with Lowell's death and Kansas. She also told me that Kansas had said if he had his

Uncle Grant's handgun ... Remember that Mac, he would shoot the mad horse himself." Said Cadiston.

"Wednesday 22nd is the big day for Chad, isn't it?" Asked Mac.

"That is the day and we will both be there to see it take place, but he will still need a few more days to come fully round and possibly months to fully recover so the vigil will not be over as it is not just as simple as 'wake up and talk'. Chad is our secret weapon, Mac, and we will have to play a charade with him. We must let them all think that he is dead and for that we will need some extra help and I think that we will have two very good actresses to pull that off." Said Cadiston. "And I know who you have in mind, Greta and her daughter, Jennifer." Mac said and smiled. "Just so, Mac. They will do a sterling job for us but now more reading. W have the third in the multiple murder, that of their daughter, Gloria." Said Cadiston. As before, there was no hesitation and the report for Gloria was opened.

The Post-Mortem Result on Miss Gloria Larkspere:
Requested by Detective Cadiston
Date of Death Sunday, 28th September:

We began the post-mortem on Miss Gloria Larkspere on Tuesday, 30th September and completed it on Wednesday, 1st October. This was a traumatic experience for us as this was the third member of the same family and was a young lady of just nineteen years of age who has been brutally cut down and robbed of the chance of a good life.

Uopn examining the body of Miss Larkspere, we found that there had been two arrows very carefully and deliberately inserted into her body. The first had entered her body and punctured her right lung and the second had penetrated her ribs, puncturing her heart. Note: Both arrows had been inserted in the exact same positions as Mrs. Sammie Larkspere.

We carried out a further examination and apart from the two arrow sites, we also found a number of injuries, namely bruising and abrasions that denote that she had been involved in a violent struggle. She had also been struck with a heavy object possibly a stone, and we were informed by forensics that apart from the stone beneath Sammie Larksperes head a second was discovered beneath a bush and the blood on it matches Glorias. These injuries were most probably obtained as she attempted to protect her life. From the marks and bruising to her torso, and the blow to her head we concluded that after her struggle she had been forced to the ground and was then sat on to hold her down and render her virtually immobile. We inspected her hands and found marks that are reminiscent with someone holding and gripping an object very tightly. Upon further examination, it was found that beneath the fingernails of the right hand was a quantity of skin/flesh. This was removed, the DNA will be extracted to identify the owner. The marks on her hands denote that she had taken a tight grip onto the arrow as it was being forced into her body in the failed attempt to defend herself. There was a number of bruising around the first entry site and slight tears in the flesh. The lack of bruising around the second site denotes that the second arrow was inserted without a struggle. Her face was found to have the imprint of fingers showing that she had been slapped very violently.

We already had the forensic analysis of the area and following their report, we determined that the angle of the two arrows could only have been placed by hand. It was also found, just as with Mrs. Sammie Larkspere, that they were placed specifically. Although Miss Gloria Larkspere had attempted to stop the insertion of the arrow into her chest, it was still with gentle force. If these arrows had struck from the force of being shot from a longbow, then there would be more bruising and tearing of the flesh also from the depth of the thrust. This denotes that although the victim attempted to stop the insertion of the first arrow, it would be a halfhearted attempt as she was already partially unconscious if not fully unconscious when the second was implanted. It is not known which arrow was inserted first but either would have led to death, one causing her to slowly choke on her own blood and the other when the heart had bled out. Again, exactly as Mrs. Sammie Larkspere.

The body had a lot of signs of a violent struggle and we removed some samples of flesh from beneath her nails and believe this to be from her attacker. We also believe that her fight for survival came possibly after her mother had been knocked unconscious and her father was fighting for them also. It is our opinion that she also knew her attacker, just as Mrs. Sammie Larkspere and Mr. Walter Larkspere did, and was caught completely off guard and unaware of the impending violent attack. We believe that she had witnessed her father's first fight and knew this person and it was after the assailant had fled the scene that their killers, who also possibly witnessed this fight, appeared. After seeing her mother knocked unconscious and her father again engaged in combat and struggling as he would have severe chest pain, it was only then that she was forced to fight/struggle to protect not only her own life but also that of her parents.

Conclusion
Miss Gloria Larkspere died from the wounds received by the insertion of two arrows. These were both deliberately placed, one to puncture a lung and the other the heart but either would cause death. The positioning was exactly as Mrs. Sammie Larkspere which led us to believe that they were inserted by the same person. Due to the injuries on her body which show signs of a struggle and in our professional opinion Miss Larkspere fought furiously in the defence
of her own life.

Verdict
Miss Gloria Larkspere was the victim of a pre-meditated act of murder by a person unknown

Signed
Mr. Charles Dennasen – Mrs. Samantha Cadiston

"This is totally beyond belief, Cadders. The mother and father both murdered in front of their nineteen-year-old daughter then she too was brutally killed. Something I read there makes me think of what you suspect is another reason for all these deaths. You said twisted minds, greed, jealousy, falseness, and lies and if I am not mistaken, your other thought is a vendetta against the complete Mandaten family." Said Mac.

"Make a detective of you yet, Mac. You are spot on and I have a suspicion that I already know who Walter's first fight was with and this person has already told plenty of lies. We will have the DNA from the tooth and if my suspicion serves me right then I know the mouth in which it will fit. Well, we move on so now we need to look at the forensic report." Said Cadiston.

Forensic report on the events and death
of the family Larspeare that took place on
Sunday, September 28th
For the Attention of Detective Cadiston

Arriving at the scene, we found that it already had been cordoned off and set to work with our investigation.

We found evidence that there had been an altercation in two separate areas so investigated them as a separate identity.

Area One: In this area, we found that some of the bushes had been damaged by a person or persons falling into them. There were several broken branches and the surrounding grass was crushed by footprints and bodies rolling onto it. We found blood splats of which samples were taken for analysis. We also found two teeth, one of which was broken, the other whole. This denotes that this altercation was very violent, resulting in both parties suffering either minor or serious injury. One of the parties involved in this altercation was found among the deceased. We know this due to the facial injuries and the broken tooth which belongs to the deceased. We assume the other tooth belongs to his assailant.

The teeth were bagged separately to avoid cross-contamination and passed as evidence to the mortuary and then to Detective Cadiston. We took casts of the footprints and noted that one set left in a run and went directionally toward the Black Powder Gun Marquee. There were also a set of smaller prints found and they headed away in a run toward the WC block.

Area Two: In this area, the bodies of the three victims were discovered. The surrounding bushes and grass were found to show signs of a further altercation which resulted in the violent deaths of all three victims, Mrs Sammie, Mr. Walter, and Miss Gloria Larkspere. We could determine the place that each individual body fell by the indentations in the ground and the blood spots left after the penetration of the arrows which were the weapons used to end the lives of all three victims. We could also determine that two of the bodies, those of Mr. Larkspere and Miss Larkspere, were dragged to lie beside Mrs. Larkspere in the attempt to lead the belief that they all died side by side.

We obtained blood samples and the teeth to determine if it is that of a victim or an attacker. We retrieved two stones one from beneath Mrs Larkspere's head the second from within a bush were it had been thrown. These samples will provide DNA and we also took casts of the footprints. We confirmed that the broken tooth came from Mr. Larkspere and assume that the remaining complete tooth belongs to the assailant.

Signed
Sergeant Jooners Forensic Scientist

"All ties in with my own suspicions, Mac. Now, I am pretty sure that Grant was involved in the first of the fights, and as I noted he had sustained facial injuries amongst others. I am certain that once analysed, it will prove to be his missing tooth and that would account for his mouth bleeding when I spoke with him after Kevin's death. I do not believe that he is the killer of Sammie,

Walter, and Gloria. That requires a bit more thought but I still feel very strongly that these killers are at Mandaten or linked to Mandaten somehow. Now we take a short break to freshen up and then we will read Sadie's post-mortem. I expect it will confirm my suspicions." Said Cadiston.

"This will be seven post-mortems, leaving three to go." Said Mac. They took a quick break before the file was laid opened and they began:

The Post-Mortem Result on Mrs. Sadie Mandaten:
Requested by Detective Cadiston
Date of Death Tuesday, 30th September:

Upon the request of Detective Constable Cadiston due to his observation of a small suspicious mark on the left upper arm of the deceased, we began the post-mortem on Mrs. Sadie Mandaten on Thursday, 2nd October. At this point, I would state that we had been advised not to waste time on conducting a full post-mortem by Sergeant Standish as this was a clear case of suicide by drowning. After speaking with Detective Cadiston and understanding his concern that a possible crime had been committed, we decided to ignore the request of Standish and not to miss a possible crime. We decided that we would follow Detective Cadiston's lead and his request and with that, we proceeded to carry out a post-mortem.

The cause of death was by drowning.

The water contained in Mrs. Sadie Mandaten's lungs was tested and was found to be that of the Mandaten lake and the cause of death was deemed to be drowning, however, there was sufficient evidence to perform the full post-mortem that had been duly requested.

In our careful examination of her body, we found that she had bruising on the back of her neck which does not coincide if this had been a suicide. After a deeper analysis on the marks left, they were found to be those made by fingers applying a great deal of pressure to the affected area of her neck. That, in turn, denotes that a person unknown held her head beneath the water. There were also bruising marks to her torso and these could only have been caused by her being carried like deadweight over someone's shoulder and as there were no visible signs of a struggle, we believe that she was already unconscious which aroused our suspicion.

Finding the bruises on the neck and torso, we then looked at the hands, and apart from the effect of a reasonably long period in the water they were normal. We then examined both arms carefully and found on her left upper arm was a small bruise, which had also been observed by Detective Cadiston, that bore no resemblance to Mrs. Sadie Mandaten's other bruising. Upon further investigation of the site, we found that it was caused by the insertion of a very fine hypodermic needle. The entry point of the injection ruled out the possibility of it being self-administrated which again gave cause to investigate further.

Confirming this provided a discrepancy and enough evidence to arouse our suspicions. We then consulted and continued carrying out our full post-mortem examination.

Due to the injection site on the upper left arm, it was then necessary to take blood and tissue samples for testing and analysis. We found that both the blood and the tissue contained an extremely high dose of the drug Ketalar – generic name Ketamine. Note: This is the drug that is used in a hospital to anaesthetize patients who are having an operation and would not be readily available on the open market.

The dose administered was much higher than would be considered a safe dose and would have rendered the recipient, namely Mrs. Sadie Mandaten, into a state of total unconsciousness instantly. It is therefore very evident that in her heavily drugged state, she was in no way capable to stop or fight the effect of her lungs filling with water to give the effect that she had in effect drowned.

We continued to check the body for other marks and found some bruising on her legs that were probably caused when she was pushed over the side of the boat and into the lake. These marks on her body and the damage caused were quite clear to see and would have been caused by handling her dead weight very roughly. There were a few light marks that we believe were caused when Mrs. Sadie Mandaten's body was retrieved and placed back into the boat.

In our full and thorough examination of the body, we also noted that an amount of flesh had been ripped from the upper thigh. This was matched with the sample of flesh received from forensics that had been found on the oar cradle and was responsible for the damage to Mrs. Mandaten's thigh. This evidence shows that Mrs. Sadie Mandaten's death was not a suicide.

Conclusion

We found that Mrs. Sadie Mandaten's lungs were filled with water from the Mandaten lake and in our professional opinion her assailant would have wanted it to look like suicide by drowning. However, when all the other evidence is analysed, a simple case of suicide by drowning is significantly removed. We looked at the possibility of the injection of Ketamine being self-administered to dull the pain that would be experienced in drowning but this was ruled out as the injection site and angle that the needle was inserted into the arm along with the extremely high dosage make it an impossibility. This gave reason to look at Mrs. Sadie Mandaten's death differently and although it was death by drowning, it could not and was not a case of the said Mrs. Sadie Mandaten committing suicide.

As has already been declared the cause of death was undeniably by drowning, with her head held beneath the water, the level the oxygen in her lungs would then be expelled and replaced with water. Our investigation shows that this was not the case and her drowning was forced upon her because of her heavily drugged and sedated state. The heavy dose of Ketamine had rendered her totally incapable of any form of activity almost instantly. It entered her bloodstream, therefore, making it impossible for her to throw herself overboard and of fighting the effect of breathing in water. The bruising on her neck shows that she was being held underwater to make certain that this would happen and our assessment and conclusion of what had taken place is as follows:

When all the evidence is analysed, a simple case of suicide by drowning is significantly removed. We looked at the possibility of the Ketamine being self-administered to dull the pain that would be experienced in drowning but this was ruled out as the injection site and angle that the needle was inserted into the arm with the extremely high dosage make it an impossibility. Also if this had been the case, then the syringe would have been found in the boat by the forensic department. We believe that Mrs. Sadie Mandaten was administered the high dosage of Ketamine whilst she slept in her bed, which accounts for no struggle and the neat injection site. She was then carried to the waiting boat unconscious, hence the bruising to her torso. She was then rowed into the centre of the lake where she was roughly manhandled over the side, hence the flesh that was ripped from her thigh and more bruising to her torso and her legs. Once in the water, her head was held beneath the surface, hence the finger and handprint on her neck, forcing her to take water into her lungs and because she was so highly drugged it made it impossible for her to fight this. The assailant then swam to the shore and returned to their place of residence. It only leaves us to say that Mrs. Sadie Mandaten's death is filled with suspicion and most definitely was not a suicide as Sergeant Standish would have had us believe and it is only due to the diligence and observance of Detective Constable Cadiston that the true cause of death has been found. As already stated, in her heavily drugged state she would be totally incapable of getting from her room to the lake, rowing to the centre, and then putting herself overboard.

Verdict

Mrs. Sadie Mandaten was the victim of a pre-meditated act of murder by a person unknown.

Signed

Mr. Charles Dennasen –- Mrs. Samantha Cadiston

"You already had the thought that this was not a suicide, Cadders. Someone is most certainly cold and callous to continue committing these crimes. I know that I keep repeating myself in saying it but we must get them and see that justice is done." Said Mac.

"Never a truer word, Mac, and we will get them, all of them, whoever they are. I have my suspicions so how are yours coming along?" Asked Cadiston.

"I have Grant and Demmie in the frame ... And to copy your thought, maybe Lizabeth, Tomas, and Kansas. I don't think I suspect Greta or Chad but at this point, can anyone be ruled out?" Asked Mac.

"You are learning, Mac." Said Cadiston.

"I hope so. Now, if any of these family members are the guilty ones that makes them very devious and calculating but what is there to gain from them all killing each other off? I can clearly see a massive case of greed because of the Mandaten's wealth and that is followed closely with their lies, falseness, and jealousy but they are family and hatred should not come into the equation. Where does the theory of a vendetta against the Mandaten family come in? It is all a bit confusing to me, Cadders. Without you, I would still be lost but I know that you will sort it, and if I help in some small way then that will do me a world of good." Said Mac.

"You are contributing, Mac, more than you realise and when I see the information that you and Olito found out about Grant, that will confirm it. Every bit of information that you have both collected will come in use later. That coupled with what I have discovered when we do some follow-up questioning will prove very beneficial. Now my friend, we have more reading as this is connected to Sadie's death."

For the Attention of Detective Cadiston
Report on the Incident at Mandaten Manor
on Tuesday 30th September
From Forensics Friday, 3rd October

Following the finding of the body of Mrs. Sadie Mandaten in the lake at the Mandaten Estate on Tuesday, 30th September, we ignored Sergeant Standish in his instruction not to carry out a forensic investigation. It was my decision at the request of Detective Constable Cadiston that we carried out a full forensic investigation and search of the designated area.

1: The Rowing Boat – Upon inspecting the boat, we found scuff marks on the right side that indicate that a body was pushed roughly over the side. We also removed a piece of flesh from the oar cradle. We knew that Mr. Chadrick Mandaten had pulled the body into the boat so we examined both sides thoroughly and found more marks on the right than on the left side. This was carefully analysed and our findings confirm that the body was pushed over into the lake on the right side. This side contained far more visible scuff marks. More care was taken when the body was retrieved on the left side with fewer marks. As we have already stated, we also found a piece of flesh, which was taken to Charles Dennasen to marry up to the body, on the oar cradle. This confirms the lack of care and rough handling of the body as it was pushed over the right side of the boat.

We have lifted fingerprints from the oars and the boat itself (see enclosed) and these can be married up to those of interested parties to eliminate them from your investigation or be used as evidence to make an arrest. We also found a quantity of the same chalky soil in the boat, especially when some of the loose internal planking was removed (see enclosed). It is thought to be the same as that found in the gun marquee.

2: We examined the Jetty and found no suspicious marks but we did find traces of the same chalky soil that was in the boat.

Samples were taken for examination. After a search around the area, the soil found was completely alien to these surroundings and after checking the area.

NOTE: We strongly believe that these samples are of the same match as those found in the gun marquee on 28th September.

We carried out a thorough search and found no other items out of the ordinary within the bounds of the search area. There was not a great deal of evidence to be found but it is our hope that what has been found will prove to be beneficial.

Signed
Sergeant Jooners Forensic Scientist

"Ok Mac, that is seven post-mortems but eight deaths with Bonnie's child so as it is getting late in the day, we will continue in the morning. We will read the remaining reports of James, Lowell, Demmie, and Chadrick's attack and then you can tell me what you and Olito have found out. Thereafter I will tell you what I have found and then we will examine the case scenarios after which we will have a pretty good idea about each one of these murders and how they were committed. We will then be in a positive position to know what additional evidence we need to collect and for that we will use the team that I have already lined up." Said Cadiston.

"Other evidence and by that I imagine that you mean who made the poison potion for Demmie, just to mention one item." Said Mac.

"And there speaks the man who thought that he would not contribute. See Mac, you are beginning to think like a detective and all the information you have on Grant will be further confirmation of your worth." Said Cadsiton.

"With the help of Olito. I can't see myself ever being as good as you, Cadders, but I will most certainly give it my best shot." Said Mac with a smile.

"As to that, I have no doubt and I am glad and proud to be working alongside you." Said Cadiston.

"And that goes double for me. I just had a thought … There have been eleven deaths and the last one was that of Demmie on 11th October. Strange coincidence or what?" Said Mac.

"Strange it is, Mac. 11 deaths on the 11th and we do not want it to be twelve." Said Cadiston.

"That we do not, it has been a long and informative day so I will say goodnight then, DCI Cadiston and see you in the morning bright-eyed, bushy-tailed and rearing to go." Said Mac.

"That we most certainly will, goodnight Mac." They walked to the car park and with a wave, they went their separate ways. They both had it firmly in their minds that on Tuesday, 21st, it would be 30 days from the first death to the present day. In that time, they had gathered some vital evidence and they would need much more coupled with visual evidence to back it all up. They needed evidence that could not be refuted or twisted by a clever barrister and would stand up in court if they were to gain a secure conviction. They were both eager to return on Tuesday morning to proceed with their investigation and in doing so, they would send out the team of selected officers to seek out and gather the vital visual and verbal evidence required, not discounting their own.

Chapter Thirteen

Building the Case Scenario's

They were both in early on Tuesday morning, before eight a.m., and with coffee at the ready they were ready to continue.

"We were up to James if I remember correctly." Said Mac.

"James it is." Said Cadiston. The file was laid open and with eyes fixed, they read.

The Post-Mortem Result on Mr. James Mandaten:
Requested by DCI Cadiston
Date of Death Monday, 6th October:

Upon the request of DCI Cadiston, we have carried out a full post-mortem on Mr. James Mandaten.

During our full examination of the body, we found that heavy bruising had been sustained around the neck and throat that did not appear to be concurrent with the alleged fall down the open staircase or colliding with the suit of armour. We carried out a further full-body examination and found very few other marks that would have been sustained in such a fall down a staircase. Not satisfied with the validity of this being a simple case of falling, we returned to the neck and throat to evaluate and investigate the bruising further. During our examination of the head, we found a small bleed that denotes that the deceased was struck on the side of the head which is not concurrent with the fall, and this raised concerns. Our further investigation of the head and neck, led us to the concludion that they had been inflicted by a person unknown, asserting pressure to the front and rear of the neck in a stranglehold and by applying pressure at the correct angle, the neck was cleanly broken.

Note: This act would need to be carried out by a person that had knowledge of the human body or had possibly been engaged in some form of unarmed combat training.

Because of the lack of sustainable injuries expected in the alleged fall, it is our professional opinion that Mr. James Mandaten was already dead before falling down the stairs. In other words, he did not fall but was pushed. The body was virtually clean of the injuries that would have been sustained in a fall of this type because the body would be rigid as the person would be making every attempt to stop or break the fall. In most cases of falling down stairs, the back receives the most damage as the faller would most probably slide down on their back but not in this case. In this case, the body was relaxed during the fall and appeared to roll, therefore, eliminating the injuries that would otherwise have been sustained, i.e. broken bones or pelvic injuries that are common in a fall of this magnitude. Due to the lack of such injuries, our suspicions were further aroused as to the validity of this being an accidental fall.

This concludes that the body was limp when it fell which, in effect, protected it from further injury, therefore, leaving it open to suggest that Mr. James Mandaten was already dead before he allegedly fell.

We re-examined the body for any injuries that may have previously been overlooked and during that examination, we found that there was an amount of skin and flesh under the fingernails of the deceased's right hand. Samples were taken for DNA analysis. This denotes that the attacker would have sustained an injury such as deep scratches to the right hand side of their neck and this injury would have bled quite profusely.

The injuries to the body of Mr. James Mandaten were severe bruising around the neck, a few minor abrasions, and a broken fingernail on the right hand, first finger, probably sustained whilst scratching his attacker. With a careful and thorough examination of the deceased and with the lack of the injuries that would be expected with such a fall, we arrived at our conclusion.

Conclusion

The lack of injuries that would have been expected and sustained in this type of fall aroused our suspicions and to that effect, it brings suspicion to the way that Mr. James Mandaten died. First, the blow to his head would have rendered him partially conscious. Second, the bruising on the throat and the rear of the neck denotes that severe pressure had been applied in a choke-hold and with the pressure being exerted in the correct area of the neck and at the correct angle, the neck would have been broken and that is what our investigation found. Mr. James Mandaten died of a broken neck before the alleged fall and in our professional opinion, this was the cause of death and not the fall itself, this was used as a mere cover-up. As we found in our examination, that was the cause of death and we can confirm that this act would have been carried out by a person that knew how this could be achieved. With the visual evidence that the body presented, we conclude that the lack of injuries denote that he was pushed down the stairs.

Verdict

Mr James Mandaten died from a pre-meditated act by an unknown assailant

Signed

Charles Dennasen — Samantha Cadiston

"Now we know that we are dealing with a vicious killer or multiple killers by all these violent acts and the way in which their deaths have occurred. They have tried to be clever in making them all look like an accident. They may have been able to fool Standish but they do not fool us, do they Cadders?" Said Mac.

Cadistton smiled. "Not for one second, Mac. Now, let us see what forensics came up with."

For the Attention of DCI Cadiston
Forensic Report on the site of the Alleged fall of
Master James Mandaten
Tuesday, 7th October

Upon our arrival, we found the deceased lying at the base of a wide, open staircase. There was a suit of armour across the body but by the first visual appearance of the site and the angle that it was laying it did not appear that the armour falling across the body was the result of the deceased striking it. We would look more into this aspect with our further investigation which would confirm this. We inspected the body carefully, noting the position and angle in which it had ended and could deduce from this that it did not look like a conventional fall down a flight of stairs.

We noted that the victim had one tied and one partly untied shoelace. First impressions could lead to the case being instantly closed with a verdict of tripping on an untied shoelace and falling down the stairs with no further investigation to be carried out. However, after examining the shoelace and conversing with DCI Cadiston at the scene, we were not satisfied with this and continued to carry out a full-scale investigation.

We carefully removed the partially untied shoelace and upon a further visual examination of it, we could see clearly that it had not been damaged in any way, which it would have been if it had been trodden on and had been responsible for the victim falling down the stairs. We then carefully removed the tied shoelace and upon examination, these proved to be identical. They were both brand new and undamaged but would be taken to the lab for a full analysis.

We carefully inspected the staircase for signs of damage that would have been caused if the deceased had attempted to stop himself from the alleged fall but there were none. This led to suspicion. There were blood spots on intermittent stairs and samples were taken of these for analysis and it is strongly believed that they will belong to the deceased. We then proceeded to the top of the stairs and found scratches on the floor against the wall which were possibly from a piece of furniture being dragged. There were a number of scuff marks at the top of the stairs and upon close examination, we could find nothing suspicious in them and concluded that these could be from the footwear worn by the family in everyday use.

We looked at the possibility of this being an accident but ruled this out as the evidence presents a case for suspicion as to the validity of it being a simple fall. We re-enacted the incident as closely as possible. If the suit of armour had been struck by the deceased in the alleged fall, the angle in which it lay across the body would have been different. It would have been scattered about the floor. The blow to the deceased's head was not caused by striking the metal suit as it would be on the opposite side which, again, gives rise to suspicion and leads us to the conclusion that the injury had already been sustained.

We carried out a full examination of the incident site and acted out a variety of scenarios after which we can confirm that there was more than adequate visual evidence to place suspicion on this incident and therefore to proceed with a full investigation. In our professional opinion, it is believed that this was not an accident but a pre-planned murder.

Signed
Sergeant Jooners Forensic Scientist

"And there, once again, your suspicions are confirmed, Cadders. You certainly have an eye to find the truth. As if the murders to date were not enough to satisfy their blood lust, they had to also murder young James. All this death seems so senseless ..." He paused and took a deep breath. "The sad thing is, it did not end there because now we need to read Lowell's report's and I would hazard a guess that those reports will also confirm your suspicions." Said Mac.

"It is sad and traumatic, especially for the Mandaten family or what is left of it. As for confirmation of my suspicions ... We will see, Mac, so let us read on." Said Cadiston and they did just that.

The post-mortem report on the death of:
Mr. Lowell Mandaten
On Thursday, 9th October:

Upon our examination of the body of Mr, Lowell Mandaten who was a young, healthy nineteen-year-old, it was evident from the initial viewing that he died from the injuries sustained to his crushed head and chest. At first sight and without further investigation, it would have been easy to assume that this was caused by being trampled by a horse. This was the simple solution but the cause of death, although evident, gave rise to suspicions, therefore, a full post-mortem was instigated at the request of DCI Cadiston. This post-mortem included the checking of the body thoroughly to determine any otherwise unseen injuries that were not caused by being trampled to death.

We found that the chest had received a series of strikes which were mainly concentrated in the center and were struck with such ferocity that the sternum was broken. The evidence shows that this was the initial site of impact before the uneven spread across the whole chest area by a heavyweight which resulted in severe bruising and multiple ribs being broken. The post-mortem proved that the victim Mr. Lowell Mandaten was already dead before the pounding on his chest and the ribs broken which had punctured his lungs and heart and many others had been fractured.

The head was severely crushed completely obliterating the face, making a facial recognition of the deceased an impossibility. This injury was mainly concentrated in the centre of the face, namely the area of the nose, which raised our suspicions further. If he had been stomped on by the said horse, the strikes would not be central but very varied and would have resulted in injuries to either side and not just the facial area as the head would certainly be moved from side to side as the victim attempted to avoid it being struck.

The body was found laying on its back hence the number of injuries to the front of the body, mainly the face and chest. We then turned the body to be certain that there were none on the back. Some of the ribs had penetrated through the body which was what we had suspected would occur with the amount of frontal trauma to the chest area. We then turned our attention to a full examination of the skull. We carried out our examination and discovered an unfamiliar fracture near the base which did not match the other injuries. Upon closer examination of this area of the skull, we found a large splinter of wood embedded into it. For this to occur the strike was extremely hard. After its removal, my assistant telephoned the forensic department to see if they had found a piece of wood such as a club or similar object at the scene. They informed us that they had. They had also found discarded horseshoes and nails which were covered in blood and flesh and had been hidden.

With our suspicions aroused even further, we could not accept the validity of this being a simple case of being trampled to death by a horse. Working with forensics, we took the splinter to their department where it was then married with the piece of bloodstained wood that they had removed from the scene. As suspected, the splinter fitted exactly. There were also a series of holes in the piece of wood that were thought to be nail holes and when the horseshoe, wood and nails were placed together, the holes matched perfectly. With the nails inserted, it was confirmed that it had been assembled for the initial blow to the back of the head which would have rendered the victim unconscious. After examining the blood and tissue on the wood and horseshoe, we found that it matched the victim and after re-enacting the action of striking each blow to the face, we can be certain that this weapon was used to crush the face of the deceased in a frenzied attack and not by the action of the accused horse.

We put the pieces together and as we had already suspected, found that the shoe had been nailed to the wood and was the discarded and hidden weapon used to end the life of Mr. Lowell Mandaten. With this piece of visual evidence on hand, we could deduce that Mr. Lowell Mandaten was struck from behind with the piece of wood, rendering him unconscious, and was struck a minimum of three times with such force that his skull was fractured causing an immediate internal bleed.

Note: Mr. Lowell Mandaten had an unusually thick skull.

From this evidence, we then deduced that he was carried into the empty and previously prepared stall and laid on his back. The horseshoe was then attached to the piece of wood shown to us by forensics and his face and chest were then savagely battered and crushed in the frenzied attack with such force as to replicate it being stomped by a horse. The post-mortem shows that the injuries sustained were prior to the action of being stomped by the accused horse taking place, therefore, ruling out that he had been crushed by the horse attack. We can be certain that the deceased was dead before the forced attack by the accused animal. We can arrive at this by the fact that there were no crush injuries to the back, apart from the base of the skull, and this would most certainly have occurred if he had been conscious when the alleged horse attack was taking place as he would then have rolled both left and right using his arms to protect his body and would have made every attempt to escape the flailing hooves to avoid being crushed.

Because of the density of the central facial injuries, it was a difficult task but we together with the evidence found by the forensics, we concluded that these injuries were not caused by the animal but the weapon that forensics removed from the scene. Again, I want it made categorically clear that if the victim had been conscious he would have moved his head and body in his attempt to avoid being trampled and would have sustained injuries to the side of the head and back but there were none. The face had been completely crushed beyond all visual recognition by direct blows aimed directly to the center.

Conclusion:

Although the cause of death could easily have been due to the head and chest being crushed which resulted in the lungs and heart being punctured by the broken ribs coupled with the brain injury caused, other evidence points away from that and we do not feel that this was a straightforward case of being under a savage attack from the accused animal.

The first attack was a series of blows to the back of the head knocking the victim unconscious and causing a fracture. The splinter of wood embedded in the skull and the amount of dried blood on the rear of the victim's coat confirms this. The victim was then carried into the stall which had already been prepared by the removal of the horses. This information was gained during our liaising with forensics. It has become clear that due to the positioning of the blows, the facial injury was deliberately administered by the weapon found – the piece of wood used firstly as a club then pieced together with the horseshoe – before any other injury occurred and it was this that was the cause of death.

After finding the fracture to the rear of the skull and marrying the splinter of wood that had been removed from the said injury to the weapon, coupled to the nails and horseshoes that were discarded in an attempt to hide them at the incident site, we can conclude that even though the victim's chest was crushed, most of the damage came from the attack with the discarded weapon. The face was most definitely not crushed by the accused animal. We can be certain because of the positioning of each strike aimed directly at the central area around the eyes, nose, and upper jaw, completely obliterating the face. In our full investigation and in our professional opinion, we can be categorically certain that this was not an accident but a brutal attack that led to our verdict. Our investigation gives the time of death as between 23:30 – 00:30 hours.

Verdict:

A cold and callous attack upon Mr. Lowell Mandaten which by the extent of the injuries was filled with rage, can only leave the verdict as a pre-meditated murder by a person unknown.

Signed

Charles Dennasen – Samantha Cadiston

With Mac beside him, Cadiston looked at his opened notebook. "Now that all fits in with my notes and confirms my suspicion this far. Now let's read what forensics have to say and look at the evidence they have given us." With their heads almost together, they began to read again.

Forensic Report on the Stable Block
Following the untimely death of
Master Lowell Mandaten
On the Thursday, 9th of October

Upon our arrival at the incident site, spatters of blood were noticed on a stack of hay bales close to the stable block. We also noticed splatters of blood close to the door of which samples were taken. Upon entry, we first examined the passageway leading to the stall where the victim of the alleged horse attack lay. Before entering, we did a full survey of the area leading toward the body and retrieved any item/article that might have been deemed as evidence.

In our search of the stable stall and surrounding area covered with bloodied straw, we found a broken name bracelet which gave us the identity of the victim that is known as Lowell Mandaten. The face of the victim was so severely damaged that a visual identification of the victim was an impossibility. In the continued search amidst the bloodied straw, we found a nail. At first it was thought to be nothing but as it was blood-stained, we bagged and labelled it. We continued to clear the bloodied straw and found a total of five blood-stained nails which were all bagged. While taking blood samples from the wall, a loose board was discovered. When it had been removed, a single bloodied horseshoe was found hidden behind it. This aroused our suspicions as this was deemed to be an attempt to hide the said horseshoe, this was also bagged. With our suspicions aroused, we looked for any other object and found another bent and bloodied horseshoe wedged in-between the boarding. This was bagged and labelled. It was apparent that this item had been pushed there to hide it from view. We took several blood samples from various areas and these would be sent to the lab for verification. We then examined the victim's body and found that the chest and face had been severely crushed. This made us suspicioous because it appeared that all the blows were directed to the centre. The facial structure was completely crushed and appeared to be folded into the centre which again denotes the ferocity of the attack. The chest had also been severely damaged and although some of the damage caused could be attributed to the animal attack, it is clear from our examination that this was not the only cause of the crushing. The post-mortem will clarify this theory.

We continued with our investigation of the stall while two of the team examined the area of the stable that contained a trap door in the floor that we were told was used as the old contraband store. After a good look down there, we found a piece of wood that was partially covered with soil and contained bloodstains. The wood measured approximately 1m in length and 5 cm in width. It was also noted that there was a splinter missing from the said wood. We found a series of holes that resembled nail holes. When we placed one of the horseshoes onto the said wood, we discovered that the bloodied nails fitted into each one perfectly. We confirmed that this was the weapon used to end the life of the victim.

After the body had been fully examined and removed, we found on the floor beneath it a gold St: Christopher medallion with a broken chain. There was an inscription etched into it which read: To keep you safe as you travel Love Mum and Dad X. We can not determine if this belonged to the victim but this too was bagged. We also found a mobile phone partially hidden in the bloodied straw. The little finger of a latex glove was also bagged.

We now turned our attention to the animal that had been accused of stomping the victim to death. We noticed from the blood splats on the horse's legs and from the state of the deceased that this animal could not possibly have caused so much damage. It is much more plausible that he was already dead before that happened and that the horse was forced into committing the act of stomping to cover up what had already been carried out manually. His face was severely damaged beyond recognition and they will know better during the post-mortem if this is the case. Knowing that we had found discarded and hidden horseshoes, we examined the hooves of the accused animal and found that the front hoves were shoeless. The rear shoes were still present and intact. The front hooves were bloodied but when the bloodied shoes were placed against the accused animal, they were a different size which once again confirmed that this animal is an innocent victim of this heinous crime.

We looked closely at the piece of wood, horseshoes, and nails again and could clearly reconstruct the weapon. We inspected the old contraband store and identified some unexplained scratch marks in the soil. We could find no logical reason for them being there. There were a number of smudged footprints, none were totally eligible. The keen eyes of Jenny spotted a protruding nail that was blood-stained and as this was in the contraband store and not in the stable stall and it was deemed as suspicious. The nail could not be removed but was carefully cut to be visual evidence and provide a blood sample.

We can be reasonably certain that Lowell Mandaten was unconscious when he was placed in the stall and someone bludgeoned his face and chest in their attempt to make it look like it was the horse that had violently stomped and crushed him to death. We took a series of fingerprints from the stable which can be married up to those held on file to eliminate the innocent and possibly aid in the discovery of the killer.

Mac interrupted their reading and said. "Once again this is all pointing to a clever cover-up or rather not so clever because they have left a lot of evidence so definitely not very clever, Cadders."

"As you say, Mac, a clever try at a cover-up. Did you hear Herbert say that a lot of these old Manors were built with secret passageways?" Asked Cadiston.

"That I did. We have to find them and that is on our list of things to do and you have the plans." Said Mac.

"Exactly, we will be looking deeper into the marks in the old contraband store that Jooners' team found, and those at the top of the stairs in the Manor. Now, back to reading as time is pressing." They returned to reading the report.

We liaised with Charles and Samantha in the forensics mortuary who were performing the post-mortem and had removed a splinter from the skull of the victim. When it was inspected, it was not a surprise when it was found to be the missing piece and fitted perfectly into place on the wood found. We then began working together and pieced together the wood, horseshoes, and nails and after they had checked it with the facial injuries, it was deemed to be the weapon used to batter the facial area and chest of the victim. All the blood samples taken were from the victim, apart from the contraband store sample. We can conclude that this was a premeditated callous murder.

We attempted to lift fingerprints from all these objects but due to the amount of blood on them, they were far too smudged. The assailant wore latex feeler gloves so only a partial print was eligible from the finger of the torn glove. By using a computerised program, it may still be possible to match them with a full print from the perpetrator of this heinous crime.

We carefully re-examined the animal accused of this act of violence and again, we are certain that it was forced to commit the act of stomping after the victim was dead. We arrived at this due to the lack of blood splattered on the accused animal's legs. There was none on the foal which also confirms that it was not in the stall when the attack took place. Items of evidence: name bracelet, a gold Saint Christopher with the inscription 'To keep you safe as you travel Love Mum and Dad X', the small finger of a latex glove, and a mobile phone. We hold the weapon used which is the piece of timber and the horseshoes which will be made available when a case is brought to court. Also enclosed are the fingerprints which are very poor quality. If we can assist any further in the investigation, then please call us.

Signed
Sergeant Jooners forensic Scientist

"That killer sounds like a real nasty piece of work to be able to use such intense force to inflict all these horrific injuries. There must have been a real hatred which brings me to remember what you said a while ago was a possible reason behind these murders. A twisted mind coupled with jealousy, greed, falseness, and lies, and a real desire for revenge. It is hard to believe that all this can be found in one family but there it is right in front of us and the family members are getting less. Our suspects are in there somewhere and we must find them." Said Mac.

"We will Mac, we are getting closer as each piece of evidence presents itself. All we need to do is piece it all together and tag it onto the right culprit. I have my suspects to each of the murders but now if I am right, we just need the full evidence to prove it." Said Cadiston.

"All I can say is it could be any one of them or all of them. I wish that I had your mind to deduce the evidence that we have and place it with a suspect so I do not … I will just follow your lead and do what I can to help solve the cases with you, DCI Cadiston." He sat back and smiled.

There was a knock on the door and when it was opened, the desk constable entered with a pot of coffee. "Thought you could do with this." He said and put the tray down. "Going to the hospital this evening?"

"That I am John. I need to keep a close eye on the patient. He has some vital information for us, and thanks for the coffee, most welcome." Said Cadiston.

"Not a problem." John turned and left.

"Well Mac, we are getting there. Slowly, piece by piece, as each one falls into place, we are getting there. We know who murdered Bonnie and her unborn child and her death was caused due to desire, lies, falseness, and jealousy but the sad thing is, it need not have happened. I know that Demmie committed the act of murder but I really blame Grant. He may not have committed the act himself and he may not have known what she was about to do, even so he is just as guilty. They died through his falseness and lies and her mile-wide streak of jealousy. Demmie wanted what she could not have but now she has paid the ultimate price. For each of the other deaths, I have my suspects and now we need to question them all again and find the tinniest missing link. We have fingerprints, shoe sizes, blood, and D.N.A from everyone and once they are all checked against those found at the crime scenes, that may be the missing link we are looking for. Once our team returns with their additional evidence, we will have our killer or killers cornered. We have two more reports to receive and then we will see if my suspicions are correct. Now if they are, my friend, then we are on the way to solve all these cases." Elaborated Cadiston. "The tiniest piece of evidence can prove to be the largest piece of evidence, so to speak." Said Mac.

"You are learning, Mac, that leaves us waiting for Demmie's report and the report on Chad's attack. They should be with us very soon but we have a great deal to be analyzing so let us start to get some case scenarios on the board and that will give us a strong indication of just how the crime was carried out. The additional evidence we will require the team to investigate and collect." Said Cadiston.

"One thing that I strongly believe is that they have slipped up with committing all these crimes so close together and expecting them to be closed as straightforward tragic accidents by Standish. All the clever planning had not included you Cadders. And not forgetting one case of alleged suicide." Said Mac.

"Good thought Mac, and another one is that they were far too complacent in their thinking that would be the case and that is where Standish would play his part but –. I did not say that and you did not hear it." Said Cadiston quickly. "Say what? Sorry, wasn't listening." Said Mac and they both smiled. "To work then, Mac." Said Cadiston. "No time for slacking, Boss." Said Mac. "Start with case one, that of Bonnie and her unborn girl child. We already have the means, namely the syringe and we have the way it was actioned. We also possibly have a motive and that was Demmie's desire, jealousy, and wanting something she could not have. We have the murderer and she has fallen victim to murder also and some would say that is justice. We now need to know if Grant was party to it and if so, bring him to justice. We can put all this information onto the board next to Bonnie. Put a question mark against the photograph of Grant. From this, you can see that a post-mortem on its own is not enough to bring a case against him, it is admissible evidence but it needs to be reinforced by visual evidence. We know for certain that Bonnie and her unborn child were indeed murdered by Demmie and we have the murder weapon that she used, namely the syringe." Said Cadiston.

"An excellent piece of visual evidence." Observed Mac.

"That it is, Mac, and we need other pieces of visual evidence for all the other murders so that we know how it was done. Having matching fingerprints or D.N.A. found at the crime scene or on the weapon used, like that on the syringe which also confirms our murderess was indeed Demmie. To some officers, no names mentioned, that would be an end to the case and it would be closed without further investigation. But not me Mac, as there is an accomplice still out there that we need to find. They are just as guilty of this double act of murder as she is. The syringe that I found is clear evidence but the highly concentrated and tasteless peanut solution that it contained had to be produced by someone who knew what they were doing and that makes them an accomplice to premeditated murder. We need to know who could produce such a solution for her. I have my ideas on this after reading the lab report but let us give Keith a ring and ask him the question." Said Cadiston and dialled the number. and the call was answered after two rings. "Lab, Greg speaking."

"Cadiston here, Greg. I have a question for you and Keith." Said Cadiston. "Ok, fire away and we will do our best to answer it." Said Greg.

"We are going over our cases. Do you remember the syringe that you analysed for me?" Asked Cadiston. "That I do, it had a remarkably high concentration of pure peanut in it and neither of us has seen such a high concentration." Said Greg. "That concentration was used to commit murder, in fact, a double murder. What I would like to know is who would be capable of making such a dose and make it odourless and tasteless?" Asked Cadiston.

"You are referring to Bonnie Mandaten and her unborn child, aren't you, Cadder's? Now that was a real tragedy and very cold and callous to use her allergy syndrome but to answer your question, it can be done but would need someone in a lab with the technical knowhow." Said Greg. "Could you do it in your lab?" Asked Cadiston. "That we could. It would not be that difficult for someone in the know and who knows about chemicals and the structure of food." Said Greg. "Someone in the know you say? What, like a chemist, food technician, pharmacist or someone in the pharmaceutical business perhaps?" Cadiston pressed on. "I would say that is a very strong possibility, probably more like a food technician rather than a pharmacist but they would need the right equipment but a strong possibility." Said Greg. "Thanks Greg, that piece of information is very helpful. If we need to know anything further on the subject, we will give you a call." Said Cadiston. "No problem, Cadders, glad to help." The phone line went dead.

"That is just as I thought and a wide area to cover so we will need some help with that. It is imperative to find out who made the solution for Demmie and that makes her or him an accomplice to double murder. We will need to get a team out there to question every chemist, pharmacist, pharmaceutical firm, and primarily food technicians and that includes hospitals. We must not miss one of them and need to question them all, near and far, until we find the culprit that produced this stuff. For this task, we will call upon PC Howie Julip and he will be accompanied by WPC Nadine Crown. They are both keen to progress into the role of detectives and if anyone can can find out the information, they can. Let us get them out there to begin their search and that will be step one." Said Cadiston.

Howie and Nadine were waiting patiently for the phone to ring and the instant they were called to the office, they were on their way. They were so keen that they almost sprinted and were there within seconds of the call. "Come in Howie, Nadine. I have a task for you both and it is not an easy one. Now, to cut through formality I will call you Howie and Nadine and we are Cadders and Mac. Now, to the task. What I need you to do is to find out who produced the lethal dose of peanut solution used to murder Mrs. Bonnie Mandaten and her unborn girl child. You will need to check all the chemists and question pharmacists, pharmaceutical firms, primarily food technicians and anyone who would have the knowledge to produce such an item and that includes the hospital pharmacists. It is important to keep in mind that no one is beyond suspicion and no one must be left out or ignored. When you have found them, arrest them instantly as an accomplice. Take these photographs, there is one of Demmie who administered the poison and that is Grant, Bonnie's husband." Instructed Cadiston. "Got it, Cadders; To murder a grown-up is horrendous enough but an unborn child, that is the lowest of the low. Leave it with us and we will get straight onto it. We will possibly need to spread our net far and wide and it will take a bit of time as there are many avenues to explore but we will traverse them all. You will not see us again until we have the person responsible in custody." Said Howie and it was seconded by Nadine. "Excellent, I know that I can rely on you both fully but there is just one more thing. You have the photograph but remember that a false name may have been used and it could be a possibility that this person is a family member and to help you there, you will need to know Demmie's maiden name and that I will find out for you now." Cadiston picked up the phone and in three rings, it was answered. "Can you talk, Greta?" Asked Cadiston.

"Yes, there is no one to listen in." Greeta answered. "Do you know Demmie's maiden name?" Cadiston asked. "Yes, it was Brexly and I know that she had a brother but have no idea where he is as they appeared to be distant." Replied Greta. "Thank you, we will see you later when we visit Chad." Said Cadiston. The call was ended. "Brexly so she may have used that name or her brother might be in that line of work." Said Cadiston. "We are on it, Cadders, we have all the information available so leave to Howie and me and we will bring the culprit in for you." The two turned and left. With this information placed onto the pinboard next to the name of Bonnie, he smiled and said. "We are on the way, Mac. That is another string to our bow underway."

"Because I do not completely believe that Grant knew nothing of what was going to happen to Bonnie and although I have not seen it yet with the new evidence that you have collected on him, we must keep our questioning going. Certain things have come out that make my suspicions rise such as when Standish informed him of the cause of death. All he was concerned about was if foul play was suspected –. Why? And when told of the pregnancy, he said that he had no idea and it bears no consequence now that they are both gone. Now, to me that is extremely cold and callous. I believe that he was filling Demmie with lies and falseness and he was grooming and using her to such an extent that he felt that she would do something to get rid of Bonnie and his saying that Bonnie was his and would help him to gain the title was a false facarde, he had guessed that her desire took hold and I believe that she would go as far as to murder for him. I believe that he let her make all the plans but was also instrumental in the planning and made sure that he had covered his own back. When I found the syringe before they had a chance to remove it, he knew that it would lead directly to her. I believe that panic then took over and he was afraid that she would break under questioning and, shall we say, drop him in it. That would then be her word against his and he wanted to avoid any awkward questions. He treated her falsely as he did not really want her and had used her to his own ends and he wanted to get one over on Chad. He was ready to cast her aside because he intended to set up home with Katrine who is his real love. We know all about the venom of a woman who is scorned." Said Cadiston.

"If it is anything like that movie Fatal Attraction then yes, we do. Sends shivers down my spine at the thought." Said Mac.

"As I was saying, I strongly believe that they had planned it together but after she had completed her role, she was of no further use to him. She would not let go so she was on the hit list as well but someone beat him to it. Or was that also pre-planned by him to be rid of her and Chad?" Wondered Cadiston. "So, in effect, whoever did it saved him the job. Unless, as you say, it was already pre-planned by him and then acted upon when the opportunity arrived. He also tried to pin the blame onto poor innocent Chad." Said Mac. "If he killed Demmie we need to discover just how when the evidence says that he was not here when it happened or was he?" "Exactly Mac, now you are really thinking things out. I do not think for one minute that Katrine was mixed up in Bonnie's death, that was due solely to Demmie's twisted mind especially if she also knew that Bonnie was carrying Grant's child. Demmie may have been involved in other incidents but I have not ruled out that Katrine could possibly have been involved in them with Grant to get him the Lordship before he finally got rid of Demmie. I have listened to and watched him very carefully and I think that I have his measure. He is a bully and a mind-twister, he likes to have things his own way and is also a user of people to get what he wants, and he does not like to be challenged, I would not put the act of murder past him to remove an antagonist to his being in control and our evidence tells us that Sadie and Chad have both carried out that task. If he is not guilty of any of these crimes, then there is another one somewhere that he is guilty of my suspicions tell me that." Said Cadiston. "Not a very nice person then. This is just the first case and is going to be a tough nut to crack before we can reach the conclusion and Bonnie with her child can then rest in peace." Said Mac. "Still of the same mind and want to be a full-time detective, Mac and honestly you are thinking like one now my friend?" Asked Cadiston. "I keep saying it, working with you, DCI Cadiston gives me an edge, and yes I do." Said Mac with a smile. "Not promoted yet, Mac, only acting DCI and after this, I will probably be back to plain Detective Constable." Said Cadiston. "After all these cases are solved, that would be a cruel twist of fate so I think it will be made permanent." Said Mac smiling.

"We will see, Mac. With our team out there to find out just who produced the pure peanut that Demmie used, we are another step closer. If someone did it specifically for her then that may let Grant off the hook for Bonnie's murder. Even if we believe that he was involved in it, that will be very hard thing to prove but I feel very strongly that he will be in the frame for another murder. Ok Mac, we have spent quite enough time on that one and we can get no further until we have the other evidence on hand. Now we will move on and tackle Malcolm's scenario and see where that leads us." Said Cadiston eagerly.

"Clear cut case of accidental death in a tragic riding accident is what Standish said in his report. Gees Cadders, why in heaven's name didn't he listen to you? He could not have been more wrong. Makes one wonder how he managed to get so many arrests and convictions under his belt. He should have listened to you and had the forensics examination done, it would have been an immense help and possibly saved lives –." Said Mac.

"We will not even go there and the memory of that is just too painful for me Mac. Sadly, it did not happen, Mac. We will just have to go on what we have. There is something about him that I must find out but the super will be told first and the decision what to do with the findings will be up to him." Said Cadiston.

"Now that sounds very mysterious, one could say rather ominous." Said Mac. Cadiston smiled. "Not really, just something the super needs me to do specifically for him. It is as simple as that, Mac." He made the sign of a zip across his lips. "Mum's the word, then." Said Mac.

"Now, back to business. Did you spot the mistakes that the murderers made?" "Correct me if I am wrong but the position of the body. If it had been left where it fell, or rather was forcibly removed from his horse, rather than being dragged, it would have made it look a bit more like an accident." Said Mac. "Anything else?" Asked Cadiston. "He still had hold of the rein. They should have left the horse standing where he allegedly had been dragged after he had fallen and not cut the rein to release the horse. Better still, leave it where he allegedly fell." Said Mac. "And the piece of masonry?" Asked Cadiston. "Again, it should have been where he allegedly fell. They tried to be too clever in getting the horse to drag him and that is the biggest give away to the crime." Said Mac. "Well done, Mac, you are exactly right that tells me that you have just entered the criminals mind but you would not have made those blunders. They, whoever they are, tried to be far too clever for their own good and slipped up big time." Said Cadiston. "To a trained observant eye like yours but not to some who would bypass it." Said Mac. "Ok Mac, we press forward, you remembered the piece of rein?" Aasked Cadiston. "Yep, it is on the board." Said Mac.

Cadiston opened his desk draw and said. "Here is the rest of it and it has been confirmed by the lab that it was cut so with both pieces together, there is another slice of visual evidence for the board. Now then, while you and Olito were checking on the information required, I visited the museum of building plans and found out that Mandaten Manor has a series of secret passages or escape tunnels built-in." He laid his copies on the desk. "Now, if we start at the beginning when Malcolm arrived at the stable, Herbert told him that Thundist was very unsettled and skittish. Now for the scenario: What if someone, possibly Katrine or Demmie, came to the stable through this passage that incidentally comes out in the contraband hole and then put the frighteners into Thundist so that Herbert would say he was uneasy. He would warn Malcolm but knowing him and how stubborn he was, they knew it would not deter him and he would still go for his early morning ride. Part one of the cover-up. When he arrived at the old ruins near the Devil's Dyke, Grant with either Demmie or Katrine, as I believe that he would use them both one had been in the stable the other up at the dyke, they were already there and surprised him. Now, he was not about to dismount. Someone then dressed as the ghostly Lady Mary Lowell Mandaten spooked Thundist, hence all the messed hoof prints. It may sound strange but when Samantha and me revisited the area to pick up the piece of masonary we both thought that we saw a figure in the fog and it did look ghostly but we have said nothing about it as we did not want to be asked a lot of awkward questions about the ghost." "Undetood Cadders, I would not want that either, in fact are there such things as ghosts that walk the earth." "Who knows Mac, there are those who believe and those who laugh at the thought, anyhow we must press on and not diversify. Now back to the scenario, Grant then took the opportunity to drag him off. With Malcom on the ground, he then knelt on his back to prevent him from getting up and while the other held his head down and whack! Then they lead Thundist forward and placed the piece of masonry to look like he had struck his head on it." "Sounds feasible so far and if not him then who." Said Mac.

"Hmm, we will say him for the scenario, then they cut the rein and one of the female murderessess did whatever to send the horse galloping away in sheer fright again." Cadiston continued. "Sounds about right if it was them. And as I said Cadders, if not them, who else could it be?" Asked Mac. "A good and valied point Mac, I pick on them because they are both good runners and if it was Katrine, she would have her bicycle and could report for duty at seven-thirty so after the deed, they could have headed back to the Manor in a quick time as Grant and Demmie are quite capable of doing this and re-entered through, let me see – Yes, this passage. And if it was Katrine, from the roadway on her bicycle which would not look suspicious. At this time Katrine just turned up for work as usual on Tuesday morning." Said Cadiston.

"All sounds very feasible but what about Demmie asleep in the bath?" Asked Mac. "A good cover story, she would need to cool off after a quick run or moving about in the passage and where better than in the bath?" Cadiston had thought it all through thoroughly. "Perfect alibi, I wish I had your way of thinking, Cadders. Now, whichever one it was Katrine or Demmie that had spooked Thundist in the stable and then hid in the contraband store to make sure it was going to plan? When Malcolm left on an agitated Thundist, she could send Grant a text to let him know that he was on his way and returned to her room. So that means if there is a ghostly costume in the passage, then it is probably Katrine's and not Demmie's. They have been very clever but not quite clever enough and they may have slipped up again. We can confiscate their mobile phones and check the calls and texts made on 23rd of September and check all their DNA. We should get all the phones and samples from the staff members also." Said Mac.

Cadiston smiled and said. "Good thinking, Mac, and that is another task to put on the list. Only one flaw in that theory though, they may have used the estate walkie-talkies or purchased sim-only throw-away phones just for this occasion." Mac went to speak but Cadiston raised his hand to stop him and continued. "I know what you were going to say, where did Chad fit into their plan –. Well, that is simple. If you remember he said that he was suddenly very tired on the Monday evening after drinking his coffee –." "That I do and after going to their room it was not long before he crashed, and now you will tell me why that was." Said Mac. "Simple if you think about it –. Because he had been drugged with a strong sleeping draught in his coffee give to him by Demmie to ensure that he would stay asleep while Demmie did her dastardly deed with Grant." Said Cadiston.

"That is something else, we need to find out where the sleeping drug came from." "Again, good thinking, Mac." Said Cadiston.

"Looks to me like you have cracked it but how do we prove it?" Asked Mac. "That is the hard part. First, we will get all the mobile phones, as you rightly suggested, and have them checked out – including the staff. We will also get all the shoe sizes and that will also include the staff. We will go to the stable and into the house, sorry Manor, and find the passage in question. If I am not mistaken and my suspicion serves me, then we may find a ghostly costume just inside the passage near the exit to the contraband store. If it is not there, then it is hidden somewhere else." Said Cadiston. "And if we have that and Demmie's dress that is already in our possession thanks to Katrine, and the D.N.A. matches then, got you. Gee Cadiston, you are brilliant. But what about up there at Devil's Dyke? What if Demmie was up there and the outfit we find was worn by Katrine?" Asked Mac. "We could be looking for two costumes, Mac. If Katrine is an accomplice then it is her costume is in the contraband store and Demmie's is still up at Devil's Dyke. Her costume has got to be hidden somewhere nearby, all we need to do is find it and if Katrine's shoe size is a four then they will match the small footprints at the Dyke. That means it would have been her up there and Demmie in the stable but that is all supposition at this juncture, Mac. The larger prints were disturbed so we are not able to size them correctly but we will still take the shoe size of all the family and staff as that will have the effect of worrying someone and maybe worrying them enough into making another mistake." Said Cadiston. "And when they do, we will be ready to pounce just like a jumping spider and ensnare them." Said Mac.

"Something like that Mac, we will need to check all the mobile phone records, past and present, as there may be something else that will lead us to the guilty. It is a bit late in the day but if I can get approval, I will get our forensic boys to have a good look up at Devil's Dyke, it is still cordoned off and you never know, they are the experts in searching so they may find something that we could easily miss, even at this late stage. Now we know that Grant was late down to breakfast on Tuesday morning and the reason could be that he had to get back, cool off, and shower as he could not present himself in a hot sweat and that is what delayed him. Demmie just jumped into the bath to cool off and that act provided her alibi. His not sleeping was passed off as the loss of his wife so that is his alibi and that is what we will work on." Said Cadiston.

"He is a cold, callous, and manipulative individual and not a nice person and we need to nail him." Said Mac.

"We will, Mac, as my suspicion is and I am sure that he is guilty of some crime. If we are wrong about them and Malcolm's death, we will need to think quickly about who else it could be." Said Cadiston. "Well, even if it was not them and we have to look for two different culprits, I still feel confident that your scenario repressents the method used." Said Mac. "Hope so but now we will take two WPCs with us to the Manor so that they can collect all the mobile phones and for appearances, all the staff phones also. They can also get the shoe sizes of the family and the staff. The next thing may take a little more time but needs to be done so once they have collected phones and shoe sizes, they can begin by searching through Demmie's stuff for the sleeping drug which could be in tablet or powder form. They will need to be looking in the obvious places and the not so obvious places. If that fails to produce it, their next task is to start asking questions, I think that our Francis Rendham and Olito Paverson will be well capable of handling that for us so we will have their company to the manor visit." Said Cadiston.

"Chemists, pharmacists, even doctors, etc. We need to know who supplied it and to whom. Their help is valuable as it is impossible for us to do everything." Said Mac. "Spot on, we will search out the secret passages ourselves. Now to the piece of rein that he still had in his hand and this is the rein that was being used. If we marry the two together you can see that it was deliberately cut even though the cut is slightly jagged. An attempt was made to make it look like it broke under pressure. We know that Grant has a knife so we will get that from him and if that was used to cut the rein, the lab boys can confirm it. They have already had a good look at this and have confirmed the fact it was cut. Someone who was present at the time did the cutting as they could not force open the dead man's hand without breaking his fingers. Right, we are finished with that." Said

Cadiston. "Evidence that we have and photographs are on the board." Said Mac.

"Now, if you look at that post-mortem –. Not that one, the one on Pedro Santos –. That's it. Now he was found drowned in Devil's Dyke but he had also been struck on the head and had a lump in almost the same place as Malcolm Mandaten. That denotes that he was hit before he was drowned and by looking at the two blows on the different people, I would say by the same person my suspicion tells me that poor Pedro was a practice for striking Malcolm. When his friend, Rafy, was questioned he said that they were walking past Devil's Dyke when a ghostly figure came after them. They were not about to hang about so they ran but Pedro tripped, hit his head and was then taken by the ghost and dragged into the Dyke. I don't think he tripped and hit his head, I think he tripped and was struck after the fall. Now, if the ghost was Katrine, she would not have been strong enough to move his body but Demmie was much stronger and could have managed it. It was also around three months ago on the last family visit. We need to find out if Rafy still works here and if so, re-question him about the incident because I think that we will get a different version of events." Said Cadiston.

"I am beginning to see and understand where your suspicions come from. You just take every little morsel of evidence and piece it all together and that is why you were always top of the class. You look at things that others would just pass by. With you as my tutor I am sure that I can pass the exam." Said Mac bright-eyed.

"When this is done, Mac, we will see ok?" Said Cadiston. "Ok boss." He just smiled. "Guess who investigated the case of the poor, unfortunate Pedro Santos and ignored the post-mortem and then wrote the report?" Said Cadiston sarcastically. "Now that is a hard one you have given me there, now let me think –." Mac joked and had a broad grin on his face. "Could it be –? I would say good old Sergeant Standish. I could see from how it is written and passed off as just another one of his unfortunate accidents with no proper investigation. Makes me wonder just how he did manage to get all his arrests and convictions." Said

Mac. "Just so but we will go one better and solve all these cases properly and possibly a few old ones. Now as I said, we will take WPC's Francis Rendham and Olito Paverson on our next visit to Mandaten and they can deal with phones, shoes, and pills or powders while we find the secret passages." Said Cadiston. "Sounds good to me boss." Said Mac.

"Right, we know what has to be done to solve cases one and two and we must always remember that by solving one case it may lead on to the solving of another if we are dealing with the same killer." Said Cadiston.

"We can but hope." Added Mac.

"Now for Kevin Mandaten and his exploding rifle. I was there when it happened, Mac, and noticed that he was feeling the weight of the rifle and looking a bit baffled. This was the first Black Powder Show of Sunday, 29th of September, and he had not fired it yet. He knew instinctively that there was something wrong so why did he continue before he had examined the weapon further to alleviate and dispel any misgivings that he had? That will always remain a mystery but one thing is certain, he was murdered, the firearms report confirms that. There is no need to read the forensic report as it only contains one valuable piece of evidence, namely the white chalky substance that we found. Some of the same at the Devil's Dyke and when you read another report, you saw that this chalky substance was found yet again." Said Cadiston. "And Grant and Kansas also had some on their clothes. You managed to get a sample from Kansas but missed out on Grant's." Said Mac. "More is the pity. Now, it turns out that it is not actually soil but a form of old white wash used to paint over the walls of the secret passages. Now that we know of them, we can find the ones that were used as they also explain how someone could move about freely without being seen on the security cameras. Look at Kevin's untimely death with a case scenario:

What if Grant, I'm using him as an example, came back to the gun marquee on Saturday evening using this secret passage –." He pointed to the plan of the passages. "Now, security dog patrols were walking the site all night and he would have known their route and timings so it would have been easy to avoid them and even if he was seen, he would probably have been ignored. From that point, we need to ask every one of the guards patrolling the site to check if they saw anyone near the gun marquee and if so then the question is can they identify them. Now back to the case scenario, when in the marquee he gained access to the Kentucky rifle and put in his pre-load, securing it with the disc. Now I have already taken steps to locate the maker of the said disc and have sent WPC's Crowth and Jorde, who are currently investigating, to locate who made it and whom for." Said Cadiston. "I remember those two, they were on my course." Said Mac. "That is why I picked them, now to move on –. Grant then cut the ramrod to size and returned to the Manor via the same passage. On that Sunday, 28th of September, Grant made sure that he was well away from the Black Powder Show when the explosion occurred and had carefully picked his spot. I believe that he was up there in the woods for an illicit liaison with Demmie, not expecting anyone else to be there but Walter was with Sammie and Gloria and threatened to tell Chad what he had seen. Now, because Grant thought that he and Demmie were found out he had a violent fight with him up behind the archery site and that was to be his perfect alibi but he did not get to use it so wanted to cover his tracks and lied to me. Sadly, Walter was murdered on the same day and we will get to that in a minute. He lied to me saying that his cut lip, bleeding mouth, missing tooth, grazed knuckles, and black eye were caused when he tripped on a guy rope in his haste to get to Kevin after hearing the explosion but if this complete tooth matches his then that confirms he was lying." Said Cadiston. "So if I have this right you think that he had the fight with Walter but do not think that he murdered Sammie and her family so who did?" Asked Mac.

"We will get to that later, let us deal with one case at a time." Said Cadiston. "Sorry Boss." Said Mac.

So, we need to locate this passage and follow it back to the Manor to see just where it comes out. We also need to find out who machined that little disc. To that end, the WPC's Janet Crowth and Grace Jorde are on the case. It most certainly was no amateur job. They will be checking out all the quality metal machinists until they find who produced it and have them in custody and then they will find out who they did it for." Said Cadiston. "What would be really good was if we could find some of the chalky stuff or as we now know a form of whitewash in Grant's room but I bet that Katrine cleans in there extra special." Said Mac.

"A safe bet that one, Mac, but nevertheless we will do our search of his room alongside everyone else's. I have a feeling that these passages run a long way and would not be surprised to find that they lead to and from some of the rooms. I saw a chalky residue and cobwebs on Grant's jacket just after young James had his alleged fall." He signed quotation marks with his fingers and continued. "And I believe them to be from a secret passage but then there was the same residue on the sleeve and back of young Kansas and that I did get a sample of. We have the chalky sample but the disc is the only real visual evidence that we have so it is imperative to find its maker and who it was made for. We are making headway so let's press on, Mac. We now know what is needed to help solve cases one, two, and three so on to case four – the multiple murders.

We must look past Grant and Demmie this time so who else would benefit from their deaths? That is the question. Let us look at who is left. There is Lizabeth, Tomas, and their son Kansas – Greta with her son and daughter, Lowell and Jennifer." Mac interrupted. "Hang on a minute, young Lowell is sadly one of the murder victims." "True enough but for the process of elimination we will still include him. At that point in time he was very much alive." Said Cadiston. "Never thought of that, Boss. That is why you are a chief and I am a little Indian." Said Mac. "Only a chief for the moment but you will get there, have no fear, you are well on the way Mac. Now where was I? Ah yes, at that point there was Sadie and James, Chad and Demmie. We know that we have also lost Lowell, as you rightly said, we have also lost

Sadie, James, Demmie, and Chad is in hospital but that does not eliminate them from committing one of the crimes and then falling victim to someone else's vendetta. Currently, all we have left is Lizabeth, Tomas, and their son Kansas. There is Greta and her daughter, Jennifer, and even though presently incapacitated, we still cannot rule out Chad. We need to ask ourselves who should we be ready to rule out." Said Cadiston. "None of them, Cadders! As you said, looks can be deceiving and you must never take things at face value, always look beneath the book's cover." Said Mac. "That is true, Mac, and you are beginning to do just that. Now back to business and first, we will look at Grant. We know that he is cold and callous, and he could have had help from Katrine or paid someone to do it for him. In fact, any of them could have and in that, it applies to them all. Now what would be their motive and what would they stand to gain if the rest of the family were dead? Grant, as the only surviving male heir, would he get the lot, I would think that he would. Lizabeth, she would only get the estate if there were no surviving male heirs and no other siblings to share it with. That in effect places Grant and Jennifer in her way because if there were no other Mandaten blood male kin then the estate would possibly go to Jennifer and that would not suit Lizabeth as the sole remaining eldest Mandaten born blood heir. Tomas would be called Lord Mandaten or would he? What if he was also dead? Lizabeth would revert to her maiden name and then change her son Kansas to that of Mandaten. That would make her Lady Mandaten and she would own the estate but even though she had changed her son's name. That, in effect, would end the Mandaten bloodline because their son is a Kaysten and only partly Mandaten so if Grant were gone that leaves no male heir –." He paused. "Or would it, Mac? I wonder could my suspicion be correct and there is another unknown Mandaten? Think about it, my friend, and you will see that there possibly is another male heir but his anonymity up to recently has saved his life." Cadiston continued. "There you go again with those suspicions." Said Mac. "Just a thought I have, Mac, and it comes from from something Lord Mandaten said."

461

Said Cadiston staring into the distance. His thoughts were racing, piecing together snippets of informmation.

"There it is again, you have been given a snippet and you have hung onto it until it can be used." Said Mac. "You will do no less, Mac, now at some time we will need to visit the maternity wing of the Royal and check their records of births and baby deaths spanning over the last forty-three years and will also be glad to have the family tree of all those concerned here." Said Cadiston. "A question, Boss, do you think that Lizabeth would be capable of murdering her own sister and assisting in the murder of Sammie's whole family as well as the rest of the family just to get her hands on the Mandaten estate?" Asked Mac. "Greed and hatred Mac, it does strange things to people, and from what I have learned, it can lead to murder. There is also the jealousy angle and we know that they were all jealous of each other, so we have Grant, Lizabeth, and young Jennifer as the only three remaining recorded blood Mandatens but I still have the suspicion that there is another undeclared and we are going to find them." Said Cadiston. "Another, do you mean a secret love child?" Asked Mac. "Not exactly that, Mac, but we will get to that aspect later. Now we have all the fingerprints, DNA, and blood from the family so let us spread the net and take it from the staff as well. We will soon discover who attacked young Gloria from that and that will give us the killer or killers of Sammie and Walter as they were all in it together. It may well lead on to the other murders but enough of that for the time being as we have diversified from the case scenario for this triple murder. How I see it is that Grant and Demmie meet up to have, well, you know what but Walter had followed Demmie and appeared on the scene and the fight took place. Then came the explosion and they both ran in opposite directions, Grant to the explosion site and Demmie to the toilet block. Now the real killers had observed the confrontation and calmly approached the three unsuspecting victims. Sammie and Gloria were helping Walter to his feet when the killers took advantage of the situation and struck. Sammie was knocked unconscious, and when dead the stone was place beneath her head, to make it look as though she had fallen onto it. Walter tried to fight in defence of his family but was too weak after his fight with Grant and was quickly overcome, leaving Gloria to fight for her life. She managed to scratch her assailant, probably on the arm, and the D.N.A. from the sample of flesh will tell us who that was. She fought strongly and surprised her assailent with her strength so she was struck with another stone to slow her down, that stone was tossed into a bush and was found by forensics. There were no fingerprints on the arrows which tells me that they wore gloves so all that we have is the flesh sample which will provide the D.N.A. and blood samples that may be the victim's or the assailant's, including Grant." Said Cadiston. Now then Mac, who do we know has scratchers and a damaged arm." "Kansas boss, that boy Kansas." "Exactly, so what do you think of the scenario". "Sounds feasible to me, Cadders, so if that is case seven, should we now do the scenario for Sadie?" Asked Mac.

"Sadie's death which Standish wanted to be signed off as a clear case of suicide." Scoulded Cadiston."But not you, DCI Cadiston." Said Mac.

"Not me Mac, if something does not look right, investigate. That has got to be the golden rule, investigate fully. It is better to have carried out an investigation and if that proves to be nothing then at least you have peace of mind and it is much better than to have no investigation at all. That way, when a later date reveals that it was something that needed further investigation, you have let people and yourself down." Said Cadiston. "Hence a cold case reignited for someone else to cover up your blunder." Said Mac. "Something like that, Mac, now for Sadie's scenario."

"Let me do the scenario this time please, Cadders, and see if I am anywhere near your thinking." Said Mac. "Be my guest, Mac." Said Cadiston."Ok here it goes –. We know that there are a series of secret passages so what if, I will say Grant for example, or one of his accomplices, waited for James to leave his mother's room. When the coast was clear, they went into the room and after checking that she was sound asleep from taking the doctor's prescribed medication, injected her with the heavy dose of Ketalar. Because she was asleep, there was no struggle. How am I doing so far?" Asked Mac. "Keep going –." Said Cadiston. "Once atisfied that she was unconscious, he carried her through the secret passage and put her into the boat, rowed out to the middle and pushed her roughly over the side. Not satisfied with just leaving her there hoping that she would be dead, he held her head under the water to be sure that she drowned. Thereafter, he swam back to the jetty, went back through the passage and into his room. There you have it –." Said Mac. "Not bad, not bad at all so well done, again you entered the mind of the killer." Said Cadiston.

"He would think that he had a perfect alibi as everyone is led to believe that he has a fear of water and cannot swim but after what Olito and me have discovered, that is blown out of the water so to speak." Said Mac.

"Exactly, Mac, and ask yourself another question, if you intended to commit suicide, wouldn't you leave a note to say why? Especially after your husband had just died and you would leave your grieving son alone in the world." Said Cadiston.

"And another thing, would you bother making the bed and making sure that the bedroom was completely clean and tidy? Anyhow, with that much Ketamine in her system she would be spark-out." Added Mac.

"Exactly, just far too precise to my way of thinking. I attended a real suicide with Standish." He shuddered. "I can tell you that it was not pretty. There was no tidying up and by the note that was left, it was a last-minute on-the-spot decision. Not a bit how this has been made to look. My suspicion rose from the moment that I saw her body and the suspicious mark on her arm. I studied it very closely and that on its own was enough evidence for me to question her death. All far too clean and tidy, as though pre-planned and I do not believe that anyone that commits suicide is so precise. We need to check on Grant's, in fact, all the fingerprints and all the shoe sizes, and while we are at it, why not take all the pairs of shoes worn on the show days. They may well have been cleaned but you never know, there may be a tiny piece of mud or something that got missed. Another thing, it may not come amiss to have them from all the staff as well, just for elimination purposes. That will be a job for Francis and Olito. Right, we move on, and again a sad case as this is another Mandaten family wiped out. Just one other thing to know and that is very important in Sadie's case, any idea's?" Asked Cadiston. "Cannot think of anything." Said Mac. "Ketamine, Mac, where did they get it, that is something that is not on the open market?" Cadiston questioned. "I should have thought of that one." Said Mac.

"Never mind, we will need to find out who got it and where from, put that on the board. Then we will have a look at James' scenario and again if we can find the killer or killers responsible for one murder it may well lead to another. I do strongly believe that we are dealing with more than one murderer but all the same, they are linked to achieve the exact same outcome. Different murderers all with one aim and unbeknown to one another, they are achieving each other's goal. I have seen all the victim's bodies and they are not exactly pretty to look at. You saw that for yourself when you were with me and after seeing them you have a better insight into how a murder was committed." Said Cadiston. "True, Cadders. Although the visit was only brief to see the bodies, it is a real eye-opener. Especially Sadie, her body was so bloated and distorted after ingesting so much water. Then there is Lowell's, or what was left of it –. A ghastly sight, and I hope that I never have to see one like that again but if I do, then I will be prepared for the horror of it. Now to James' scenario." Said Mac.

"James and Jennifer ran upstairs to change their footwear for the garden walk. James was ready first and waiting at the top of the stairs and that is when his attacker struck. He must have been hidden and was silent, attacking from the rear. He struck him first and that must have been the first scream that Jennifer heard. As he was partially unconscious, it was made easier to catch James in a strong stranglehold and by asserting pressure in the correct way, snapped his neck. Unfortunately for him and before that happened, James managed to cry out which was muffled but loud enough for Jennifer to hear and that meant he had to act quickly. The attacker then pushed him down the stairs and disappeared quickly before Jennifer could get there. At the bottom of the stairs, time was of the essence so he quickly partially untied one shoelace to make it appear as though he had tripped on the lace. Not satisfied with that, he then pushed the old suit of armour on top of him and again disappeared. The quick disappearing and reappearing to my mind must have been achieved by using the secret passage ..." Cadiston looked on his plan and pointed. "This one from upstairs to the hall below. Now then James was able scratch his attackers neck as he tried to break the strangle hold as the flesh under his fingernails shows, and the moment that we have all the D.N.A. matches we will have our man. The main suspect is Kansas as I did not believe for one minute that he received the scratches on his neck by falling over a rose bush." Said Cadiston. "My thoughts exactly, Cadders, and I have been giving Lowell's death a lot of thought and well, I would not put that past him either." Said Mac. "What makes you think that Mac?" Asked Cadiston.

"His damaged arm and shoulder, the new gash on his hand that is very angry and inflamed and he has already told us lies." Explained Mac. "Good thinking but not enough to make an arrest. As I said, when we have all the D.N.A. and blood samples analysed and when matched to each person, then it will be different and provide the evidence that we need, one other thing, both Grant and Kansas were reluctant to provide the samples." Said Cadiston. "That is murder number ten, Cadders, counting Miss Bonnie's baby, nine post-mortem and forensic reports read, and the case scenarios are done so we know in which direction we are travelling?" Said Mac. "James' report confirms that, just as Kansas said, he was indeed dead before he fell and that may be another slip on his part. If he was the killer, that would explain why he was so adamant about examining the body to ensure death had occurred. Now, I was looking toward Grant for this but I feel that I may have been heading in the wrong direction. He may have been missing from the garden and may have had a chalky residue and cobwebs on his jacket but that does not make him the killer. Two others had disappeared for a short time, namely Lowell and Kansas, and one of them also had the chalky residue on his jacket. I recall seeing that Kansas had some deep scratches on his neck that were bleeding a lot and he told us they were from a rose bush and we know that was a complete fabrication. It would not hurt to see if his D.N.A. matches that found under James's fingernails and check his arms for deep scratches also." Said Cadiston.

"He did say he tripped and fell into a rose bush but when we checked them out, not one was damaged. As a medical student, he would have the knowledge of a human body but would he have had the time to kill James by breaking his neck, then push him down the stairs, then untie his shoelace, then hide in the secret passage, and reappear at the same time as Chad to give him an alibi. There is also the time element from the muffled scream that Jennifer heard and her getting to the top of the stairs and not seeing anyone else until after the event. Did Grant have an ulterior reason and was he there just to check that James was completely dead because he knew and could tell us that it was Kansas that had attacked him. Jennifer was first on the scene and said that she saw no one because whoever it was had already hidden in the secret passage." Mac speculated. "Now you are thinking, Mac. We know that this place is riddled with them as the plan shows and whoever the perpetrator of these murders is, knows them all. I know that Katrine was one of the parties that went to the Museum Archive of Building Plans using the name of a Miss Hurdshaw so that would have been for Grant. The second, not so recognisable, by the name of Grenville that was Tomas and we will discuss that later. Now for Lowell's scenario: He went for a walk to see the barn owls but his killer was waiting for him, and that had to be someone that knew where he would walk. I think that the killer went through the secret passage into the contraband store and then prepared the stall for his act of murder. He hid and waited for Lowell to arrive and was unseen in the dark. The instant that the opportunity presented itself, he acted and struck the unsuspecting Lowell, knocking him unconscious. He was not satisfied with one blow and repeated it to be sure that he would not wake. He then carried him into the stall and committed the act after which he forced Star to trample on his lifeless body. He then returned the same way he came and went calmly to bed after taking a bath to remove the blood that he would have been splattered with. That I think is it in a nutshell. Now, if he got careless, there could be some blood-stained clothes but I doubt it. Our best piece of evidence is the Saint Christopher pendant and the mobile phone, you agree with that Mac?" Cadiston said.

"Every step of the way, now all we have to do is catch him." Said Mac. "I need to make a quick call, then we are off to the hospital to check on Chad." Said Cadiston. "Ok Cadders, while you make the call I will go and fetch the car and wait for you outside." Said Mac. "Ok." With a wave, Mac was on his way. "Hi Charles, can I have a quick word with Samantha please?" Asked Cadiston. "Sam, it's your lovely man." Said Charles. "Hi Ashton, is there a problem?" Asked Samantha. "No, just wanted to let you know that Mac and myself will be visiting the hospital, then back to the office for a late finish. One other thing, I know how busy you are but will ask anyhow, how are the reports coming along for Demmie?" Asked Cadiston. "We have just completed one report and we are working on Demmie's report now and that will be a good read. They will be ready for you soon." Said Samantha. "Ok see you at home, my precious one." Said Cadiston. "See you at home, my lovely man." She said and with a smile, he was gone knowing that soon he would hold the last official reports in his hand and that would hopefully confirm all his suspicions. With all the additional evidence and with Mac at his side, he would be able to challenge the murderers and make the arrests.

At the hospital, Cadiston and Mac met Greta and Jennifer who sat patiently on either side of Chad. They looked at each other and smiled as they could both clearly see the affection that was being lavished on Chad even though they knew that for now, he could not return this affection. They also knew that Greta and Jennifer had both known the sacrifice they would need to make but were fully prepared to make it to enable them to be at his side and give him their full support in the long vigil.

"He is a lucky fellow and fingers crossed it could be a big day for Chad tomorrow if Doctor Mafidsen decides that it is the right time to bring him out of his coma. We need to be there for that but I will find that out before we leave today." Said Cadiston. "That is pretty soon and only ten, no eleven days after his major operation." Said Mac and gave the thumbs up. "Be good if it happens that way." "That it will, an especially big day for our Chad and not forgetting the seriousness of his attack. He is a very lucky fellow. We need to have a serious conversation with him about the incident that put him in here and almost took his life –." At that moment, he was interrupted by Nurse Francis. "You are one hundred percent right, Detective Cadiston, Chad is a very lucky man and if he had not been brought in so rapidly … Well, thank goodness he was and due to that he is still with us. It was touch and go and we almost lost him as he did actually die during the operation." "Now that I did not know." Said Cadiston.

"It was a very long operation that he had to undergo. The truth is that he died twice during the operation but Doctor Mafidsen was determined that he was not going to lose his patient. He fought extremely hard to keep him alive and as you see, he didn't lose him. Now with his recovery imminent, the battle has been won and all the hard work has been worthwhile." Said Nurse Francis. "And all credit to Doctor Mafidsen for that. I had the impression that he was a fighter for his patients." Said Cadiston.

"That he is and that was another reason to place him into the induced coma to keep him stable while he himself fought to recover." Said Nurse Francis.

"And he is well on his way." Said Cadiston. "He most certainly is and much sooner than expected. He is young and strong and has a strong desire to live so has never given up and his fight to live has been very instrumental, as have the visits of Greta and Jennifer which have proved to be a great aid in his recovery.

Now if there is nothing else that you need for the moment –. I will leave you to your visit." Said Nurse Francis as she wanted to return to her duties.

"Thank you, Mac and I have nothing that we need you for and by the look of those two, neither have they." They all smiled as they gazed at Greta and Jennifer and then the nurse turned and was gone. "You have helped him greatly, Greta. I know you say that I am the detective but I do not need to be one to see what I see. I think that the time is right for you to tell him your true feelings, don't you?" He smiled. "My true feelings, whatever do you mean, Detective Cadiston?" She asked. He smiled at Greta. "The true feelings that you have kept hidden Greta because, I believe that you have held back on your true feelings for this chappie for many a year and that was because you were both married and neither of you was prepared to break up a marriage or go against your wedding vows and that, on both your parts, is highly commendable. I am not saying that you did not love your husband or he his wife but you both respected the other enough to hold your true feelings at bay. It is extremely sad how things have turned out due to the events that have taken place so when all this is over, you will have the chance to start over together and have a New Beginning. Good luck to you both, and that includes you, Jennifer, because you will be a part of that union." Said Cadiston with a smile.

"Grandfather said that you had the makings of a good detective Mister Cadiston and I believe that he was right. He said that you had a natural eye and saw things that others would miss. Now, this may not be a crime for you to investigate but you have used your detecting knowledge and have noticed what others have not and although I have kept it to myself, I knew that Mother loved Uncle Chad and that he loved her but, as you said, they were not prepared to break their wedding vows. I may only be ten and I love him as well and if I am completely honest, then he has been more like a father to me and my brother, Lowell –. Jennifer wiped a tear from her eye before continuing. Lowell and myself than our own father ever was."

Cadiston winked at Jennifer who returned her attention to Chad. "You are very grown-up for your age, young lady, and have a good head on your shoulders. Now listen to me Chad, you keep it up and keep improving as we all want to see you back on your feet and that may be sooner than expected. I will leave you with these two lovely ladies that both love you without reservation and see you on Wednesday." The door was opened quietly and just before he left the room, he took one last glance and smiled before closing it softly. "Ah Detective, just the man. I have examined my patient this morning and will leave it for one more day. My decision is that it will be on Wednesday, 22nd of October, that I will start to bring him out of his coma. The procedure will begin at eleven a.m. and I expect that you will be in the waiting room and although unorthodox, I am allowing the two ladies to be with us in the room at his side." Said Doctor Mafidsen.

"I will be there, Doctor Mafidsen, without fail." Said Cadiston. "Then good day, Detective." Doctor Mafidsen turned and disappeared into another room. "That is us done here for today, Mac. Now we head back to the station and continue our work there." Said Cadiston. "I am right with you on that, Boss." Said Mac.

Sitting in the car, Cadiston was in deep thought and began to talk to himself. "That chalky soil was in different locations. This is a major clue because whoever is committing these murders comes to the murder site the same way. Sadie must have been drugged in one place, carried to the boat, rowed into the middle, and then pushed over the side. Hmm, that means whoever it is, knows the lake and is a good swimmer. Big question? How did they get to the lake unseen to put the body into the lake and after that act, where did they return to? Whoever it was must be a good swimmer. Now, I know that Chadrick is and he was the one who swam out to retrieve her body in the cold water, innocent or a possible cover? Malcolm was up at the old ruins and the Devil's Dyke, quite a ride from the stables so how could someone get there and back without detection? They must have known his route and been waiting for him. Chadrick was at the stables at eight a.m. so could he have gotten from Devil's Dyke back there in the time, my suspicion says no not possible for him? The person that tampered with Kevin's gun came to the site via somewhere that has the same chalky soil found at the Dyke and now the jetty −. So that is a major clue to finding where they came from and where they return to. We have read and analyzed the post-mortem, forensic and lab reports of Bonnie and her unborn child, Malcolm, Kevin, Sammie, Walter, Gloria, Sadie, James, and Lowell's all confirming murder. We will have Demmie's reports in our possession soon. Charles and Samantha have done a fabulous job on all these deaths, as have the forensic and lab teams. They must all be congratulated. Now it is up to us to work on their evidence and get our convictions. There is plenty here to be going on and all this information just enhances my suspicions that each one of these people was in fact murdered. Eleven murders and one attempted murder, all in the same family, at the same location and within three weeks and all committed by a person or persons unknown −. At least, presently unknown but I have my suspects in sight, Mac and I will find them." "Talking to yourself again, Cadders?" Asked Mac. "Lots to talk about, Mac, and even more when we get back to the station." Said Cadiston. "Well that will be in approximately ten minutes." Said Mac. "Fine Mac. If the reports are not waiting for us when we get there, we will go through my notebook and get that brought up to date. I have written in it my notes and thoughts on each of these murders and by reading that you will have an even better insight into what has occurred and have my personal thoughts and suspicions into what we are up against." Said Cadiston. "Sounds good to me Cadders, and it sounds like a good read of a detective novel Cadders. I did have one thought." Said Mac. "Only one? So what was it?" Asked Cadiston.

"Well, I was thinking that it is strange that only Kansas remains of the three grandsons and he still has both his parents, alright his father Tomas is a kayston but his mother Lizabeth is Mandaten born so could she be in danger?" "Now, they should not have been there until Thursday but what if he being Kansas arrived earlier and remained hidden until Thursday?" Suggested Mac. "Now that is a good thought, Mac, and worth checking on. You have just given yourself another job." He smiled at him and for the rest of the drive to the station he relaxed, Cadiston made him feel important and a valuable asset to the investigation just as he did with all the officers involved in gathering evidence.

Chapter Fourteen

Grant's Affair Comes to Light

It was now 8.15 a.m. on Tuesday morning, 21st of October, and at Mandaten Manor the family rose as usual. By 8.30 a.m they were all downstairs but all was not calm. In the breakfast room, there was still an air of hostility. Even though they were blaming Chadrick for all the family deaths and were glad to have someone in the frame for the family murderers, there was still a definite uneasiness between them as they eyed each other curiously. They all had their secrets, at least they thought they were secrets but they were just fooling themselves.

The atmosphere was still so hostile that it could be cut with a blunt knife and as the hostilities continued to grow, they were now directed toward Greta. "I do not know what has possessed you, Greta, and for the life of me I cannot comprehend your actions at all. It is quite clear that you are ignoring the effect it has on the family." Said Lizabeth. "And I will add to that, Lizabeth. Why, the very thought of you wanting anything to do with the murderer of our family, including your husband and son, is way beyond comprehension so it must be that you have lost all your senses." Said Tomas.

"She must have, Father. It just amazes me why you and your little brat have not taken up residency at the hospital beside that murderer's bed as you seem to care more about him than your own living family." Said Kansas.

"That is the case and the truth, son, she most certainly does. You spend all day there and most of the night, you must have totally lost all sense of decorum visiting a multiple-murderer like that, it is absolutely disgusting." Spat Tomas.

Greta knew that they were all against her actions and this did not have any effect on her or give her any concerns. She had known that they had not liked her and looked down on her, even before she had married Malcolm. "Well it is my decision,

Lizabeth. You, your husband, and your lying son do not have to like it. In fact, I could not care less if you do not so as far as I am concerned, you can just go and lump it. I loved your brother, Malcolm, and married him because I loved him and did my level best to be a good wife to him and a mother to Lowell and to our daughter, Jennifer." Said Greta.

"And you have, Mother even though father did not always treat you properly." Said Jennifer. "Shut up, Jennifer! There is no need for you to speak. Loved him you say, all you saw was an easy meal ticket, you mean. You were nothing but a children's nanny and managed to worm your way into his affection after losing his wife and now you visit his murderer." Snapped Lizabeth.

"You have no room to talk, Lizabeth. Julian really loved you but that was not enough for you was it? He had no fortune and even though his prospects were good, you could not wait for him to get his qualifications and make his fortune so you ditched him and latched onto Tomas who did. Now that is all gone, even the million pounds that your parents gave him to resurrect his business was wasted needlessly. You are broke, Lizabeth, penniless, and have nothing left. You are hoping that once again the family will bail you out. Julian is now a successful solicitor and you have lost him and seeing his success really annoys you as you missed your chance. And now, from having it all, you have nothing." Said Greta.

"You had best not speak to my mother in that tone, Greta. Besides, your days here at Mandaten are numbered as there will be no room for any more freeloaders and the clock is ticking for you, tick-tock, tick-tock." Said Kansas. "Tick- tock, you are a nasty small-minded little upstart, Kansas, and my mother has spoken the truth and is worth ten of any of you. And so is my Uncle Chadrick. Not one of you has enquired how he is after uncle Tomas struck him over the head with that old knight's hammer. Well just for your information, not that any of you care or are interested, I will tell you anyhow." Jennifer now had tears rolling down her cheeks. "He is not good, not good at all! He is barely clinging to life and that is only by a mere thread. In fact, it is only a machine that keeps him alive. If there is no improvement by tomorrow, which is doubtful, the life support will be turned off." "Turned off, you say? I know that I hit him twice really hard and in the right place while he lay on the floor and if he dies because of it then good riddance to the cold-blooded murderer, that is what I say. Save us taxpayers a lot of good money in him going to trial and keeping him in prison. He is the killer of a lot of our family, that is for sure, and since he has been out of the way, you may have noticed that the killings have stopped so that says everything." Spewed Tomas. Greta had noticed that Tomas said that he had struck Chadrick twice while he was laying on the floor and had told Cadiston that he struck him once whilst standing up. She would relay this to him when she next saw him. Grant, in his drunken stupor with his words slurred, now chipped in. "That isssh for sure, Tooomas. And as far as enquiring about his health goes, not one of us gives a hoot." He shook his head and cleared his throat, then continued but now spoke clearly. "My father is an ill man and has been hanging in there until the killer has been found or these cases are closed as tragic accidents, then he will be ready to make his announcement to nominate the next Lord Mandaten and we have the killer who, thank goodness, is about to die. As I am the only living and remaining male heir, I guess that I will be the one finally to be named the new Lord."

"Think you have it all sown up nice and neat, don't you? Are you not counting your chickens before they are hatched, Uncle Grant? Let's look at it on face value Grant, shall we? It may not be as cut and dried as you may think. Grandfather may decide that you are nothing but a sodden drunk and are not a fit person to carry the title of Lord. With that in mind, he may give the estate lock, stock and barrel to my mother who is a true Mandaten and that will make me the next Lord." Said Kansas.

Grant looked at him and began to laugh. "My, my, my, now you are talking like a silly child, Kansas. Are you discounting your father in that equation of yours? Plus, none of you are Mandaten so that will never happen, not while I live. My boy, I have no intention of dying so that someone else can have what is rightfully mine. The title and all that goes with it will be mine. I have my snubnose 38 protector and will use it and if anyone tries to kill me. Then they will be the ones to die." He laughed before continuing. "There was something that was said and will most definitely happen when I take over and that is there will be no room for any freeloaders so that means Greta and her brat will be gone, for starters. As for the rest of you, well, I may just tolerate having you around as you are the spawn of my sister. As I said, I have my protector here and she is always loaded and close to my chest so anyone that tries to kill me will get blown away." Said Grant smiling. "Your protector, do you mean that gun you have?" said Jennifer. "I most certainly do and if it comes to it, I will use it without hesitation and it will not be the first time. A nice neat snubnose 38 calibre so I am well protected and will be the next Lord Mandaten as I carry the name so step back, Kansas Kaysten, and don't crowd me." Said Grant. Once again, Greta had heard these remarks and told herself that she would inform Cadiston the moment that she saw him. For a few moments, there was silence while they thought what to say but they need not have bothered as the next words came from a voice that they all knew well. "And what makes you think that just because you are the only remaining male heir that you will be the next Lord Mandaten, Grant? There may be another option, one that you have overlooked. Now as for freeloaders, you need to have a good look at yourself in that category as that is all you have been for many a year."

Grant turned sharply with a surprised look on his face. "Father, I did not know that you were there and well, what I said, err ... Well, I meant ..." "Obviously you did not know that I was there, Grant, and you meant every single word that you said. Now all of you get out of my sight apart from you, Greta, and my granddaughter, my little princess, Jennifer, who have both been sitting with our son, Chadrick, with our full blessing. Now all of you get out." They all lingered. "I will not tell you again, go as you all make me sick and a will can very easily be changed." Said Lord Mandaten.

With these words ringing in their ears, they left the room. The moment they had gone, Lord Mandaten turned to Jennifer. "Now what is it you were saying about Chadrick and life support, Jennifer? Is it true that it is to be turned off?" She rested her head on his shoulder and whispered softly directly into his ear. "I will speak out loud so those that are listening will hear in a moment but for you, it is the opposite to what I will say." Said Jennifer. "Understood, a ruse to fool them." Lord Mandaten whispered in reply and at the same time raised his thumb. She raised her head and had tears in her eyes. "There, there, Jennifer, please do not cry." Said Lord Mandaten. She now raised her voice so that all the prying ears would hear. "It is true, Grandfather. The life support will be terminated maybe on Wednesday. If there has not been sufficient improvement in his condition, which is not expected, he is like a ... I do not like to say it ..." Her grandfather took her hand. "Like a lifeless person who is already dead but we have to wait for the final decision by his surgeon. Although he has not said it in so many words, he knows that he is not going to make it and with the machine switched off, Uncle Chadrick will slowly die." To make this sound realistic she began to sob. He tapped his nose to signify that he understood, then raised the volume on his voice. "There, there, Jennifer, my dear girl, it is sad but do not stress yourself if it must be then." He made as though he was wiping his eye so those that pry would be misled. "We will lose another of our family, a most valuable member of our family. Now tell me, Greta, has detective Cadiston been to the hospital?"

"Every single day, he waited there all Saturday night and into Sunday morning to see how his operation went and has been in to see him in this long vigil every single day. I think that I already said that, didn't I?" Said Greta.

"No matter if you did. Just as you and your daughter have." Lord Mandaten shot a glance toward the door where Grant and Lizabeth lingered and raised his voice. "With our full blessing. I told you all to get out of my sight but as you choose to spy and not to obey my instructions, I have this to say to you. Chadrick is no murderer and young Cadiston will prove it even if he is dead. You can be assured he will clear his name."

"Well, all I can say is that with him dead, this Detective Cadiston that you rate so highly will have an extremely hard time to prove anything because all the evidence points to him. He had motive and opportunity for every death and had the gun in his hands after he shot his wife. If Tomas had not hit him hard then he would have murdered the rest of us." Lizabeth snapped. "Well said, Sister, and that is very true. I do not know what evidence he has, if any at all, because there is none that he can find. With Chadrick out of the way, he cannot question him so that will be case closed as we have our murderer and he is dead. Well, almost." Spat Grant.

"Silence, both of you! I will hear no more of this talk and if I were a healthy man, I would be at the hospital with Greta and Jennifer to give my support." Lord Mandaten snapped. "And I would be there by your side, my dear husband, giving you and our son my full support also. Now calm yourself as we do not want you to be rushed to the hospital again, dear. We know in our hearts that our son Chadrick is not a murderer." Said Lady Mandaten.

Grant had a sly grin on his face and spoke with hatred in his voice. "Well Mother, for one thing, he is not your son and no Mandaten blood, not one drop runs through his veins. And I will continue to hate him even after death. Secondly, he is a murderer that is one thing that he certainly is, and still had the smoking gun in his hands. I am your only remaining blood son and he is not, all he is is some adopted stray that no one else wanted and I hate him because he has taken a lot of what I should have had."

"Enough, Grant! I will hear no more of this talk from any of you. You have all had the exact same opportunities as Chadrick and he chose to take them whereas you, Grant, did not. I know all about all of you and even though you may think that you had fooled me with your lies and your falseness, I knew exactly what you were all up to. I will start with you, Tomas. Yes, I know that you are skulking around the corner so you may as well come in

479

and hear me properly." Lord Mandaten began and Tomas crept sheepishly into the room.

"Well, I am here so what do you want to say?" Asked Tomas.

"I gave you a million pounds to start your business, then a further million to top it up but you over-stretched yourself and have no real head for long-term investment and are now on the verge of bankruptcy. It is not all entirely your fault." He glanced toward his daughter. "Lizabeth is partly to blame with her lavish lifestyle and always wanting more. You, like a fool, put yourself into debt to get it for her and give her the sort of lavish lifestyle that you could not really afford on your income. Now you want the Mandaten money to get you out of hock, but you are out of luck, Tomas, you will get nothing, not one single penny.

Kansas, yes you are there also so stop skulking and come in. I know you, boy, and you are not what you would have us believe. You claim to be a medical student but that is an utter lie. You attended for one-year, or rather you were there when you bothered to turn up. We paid a lot of money to the medical college for you and made sure that you had money in your pocket but all you succeeded in doing was to squander it all. You had no real interest in becoming a doctor and thought that you could just live off us or your father's business as your mother did. So like her, you contributed to its downfall and he was far too weak to see it. I see something different in him so is he as weak as you think? Your interest was in fast cars and girls but as the money ran out so did the girls and then your car had to be sold so then you could not swan around and were subdued. Those that you called friends disappeared and you were left on your own. You are so much like your mother in that you are materialistic and money orientated and now the time has come for you have no choice but to work hard to get it.

Now you, Lizabeth, you may be our daughter but you are devious, selfish, materialistic, and never satisfied. With careful planning, you could have had a good life and would have been much better off than most folks are. Greta spoke the truth and Julian would have been far better for you than Tomas but as it turned out, he had a thankful escape. We tried to tell you but you would not listen to us and that was your mistake. You had good people working for you and you treated the workforce with contempt and it was only their hard endeavours that kept the business running smoothly and afloat for so long but you and Tomas were too blind to see it. You were given sound advice by Chadrick but ignored it and continued with your lavishness even though it could not be afforded and like Kansas, the people you called friends have disappeared also. You want the family fortune to pay off the debts and continue with your over-the-top lifestyle. You will not see the fortune so, my dear daughter, you will be not be getting it either. Oh, there will be a small allowance to bring you into reality but that is all. To give you a taste of reality you will need to sell your large eight bedroom house and buy something a bit more modest. The expensive cars will need to go and that means your Jaguar and Bentley. You will only have a conventional family saloon, I have watched you all with your squandering for far too long so now you can taste reality. Do not look so worried, the small house is ready for you to move in and the family car is in the garage. The money that you get when selling all your material goods will give you a start in your new life." Said Lord Mandaten.

"But father I —." Elizabeth started.

"There is no but father, it is done. You will need to get a job and earn your keep from now on. Now take me out of here, Greta, as I have said my piece for the moment and need to rest before continuing so I will not argue the point with them. Let them stew in the truth and as for you, Grant, well, I will deal with you this afternoon." Grant opened his mouth to speak but was silenced by the long hard angry stare. "I will not listen to another word now and will not have another word said against Chadrick, who incidentally even though adopted, has been much more of a son to us than you have ever been Grant. You have always been jealous of him, from a small child because he is a worker and a go-getter. Why, he has more brain in his little finger than you have in your whole body. You would all condemn

481

a man who is at this very moment fighting for his life, purely to cover your own guilt?!" lord Mandaten waved his arm in a forward gesture and Greta began to push the wheelchair from the breakfast room, followed closely by her daughter. In the hallway stood Kansas who jeered at them. "That's it murderer-lovers, you can leave too as we have no desire to be in the same room let alone the same house as either of you or, in fact, anywhere in the world in your company."

At this remark, Jennifer snapped and in a few quick paces, she stood in front of him. She stared at him with a steely glare that no one had seen before. Seconds later came the explosion of a perfectly aimed and very hard slap. He reeled backward with a look of shock on his stinging face but could say nothing. When she spoke, it was with venom in her words. "Be very careful what you say about my mother. I have not got my brother now to stand up and fight for her and soon we will lose Uncle Chadrick but remember this, Cousin, I may be small and only ten years old but I will fight you, in fact, all of you and bring you all down with your lies and falseness. Be warned." Kansas' mouth dropped open, totally lost for words. There were also no comments from the others as they were all struck dumb by this feisty little girl.

Jennifer turned and smiled, then followed her mother and grandparents. Her grandfather looked at her with pride and took hold of her hand. "That is my girl, you make us very proud and if only you were older, then you could have the Mandaten estate in its entirety for you and your mother. Alas you are just that much too young but do not despair, there may be a way." He tapped his nose. "Mum's the word." This statement was overheard, bringing looks of concern but no words were spoken.

At 12:30 p.m the remaining Mandaten family entered the breakfast room for a light lunch. Their parents were already there waiting for them and their father was all fired up and ready to have his say about Grant. They watched the family enter and when he did not come into the room, eyebrows were raised. "No Grant down yet?" Asked Lady Mandaten. "Not yet, Mother, my guess is that he is not looking forward to Grandfather analysing him although I could do that." "Oh! You could, could you Kansas? And just what would you say about me?" Asked Grant as he entered the room. "Afternoon Uncle Grant, I wish you would not creep up like that. Now, what would I say? Hmm, let me think for a moment. Tell you what, let us enjoy our lunch and then I will tell you." Said Kansas.

Grant just grunted and filled his plate. They sat in silence while they ate and because of their inattentiveness, not one of them had noticed that their parents had slipped out of the room and were not with them. "Right Kansas, lunch is done so how would you analyse me and what would you say?" Asked Grant. "I would say that my Uncle Grant is a drunkard and an alcoholic, he is not capable of anything much as he spends more time like a baby on the bottle than off it. Apart from that, he is a very lovely fellow who is kind and considerate to all those around him. He has a helpful tendency and is always there to give his full support no matter what, how is that for you Uncle Grant?" Asked Kansas smugly. "Bloody liar, that is what you are Kansas! A bloody liar because I know that you hate my guts as do the rest of you and I know that every one of you would like to get your hands on the Mandaten money and to do that you would like me out of the way. Dead would suit you all well, you are going to be unlucky there because I have my protector." He moved his body warmer sufficiently for them to see his gun snuggled in its holster. "And I will use it if need be so no more of your lies, Kansas. I like a drink just as the next man but I can just as well live without it, and pretty soon now that is just what I will be doing." Grant's tone had become dark. "You live without it? Ha, that will be the day and for that to happen I will need to see it before I believe it." Lizabeth snarled. "Thank you, my dear sister, thank you. Have you nothing to say darling Greta? No? Well now what a surprise." Said Grant with sarcasm. "Don't speak to her Grant, she is not one of us and is an outsider. She is not in our conversation or in our family anymore. Time you were visiting your murderer, isn't it?" Mocked Lizabeth. "He is not a murderer but all in good time, Lizabeth, all in good time." Said Greta. Do you know something, I have just noticed that granma and grandpops are not down yet, now that is strange". Remarked Kansas.

Greta looked at them and shook her head in disgust. "They were here before the rest of you but had quite sufficient of you all this morning and with that in mind, they have had a nice quiet luncheon in the lounge but do not worry, Grant, they will soon be back and then you will be told the whole truth by your father." Said Greta. "Worry? Me? Why should I worry? I know just what they think of me and it's all their fault that I drink but that is about to end and another thing for you all to take note of, my old life is ending and my new life is about to begin so a New Beginning for me and that will silence you all." Said Grant then paused while he studied their lost looks before continuing, but Greta spoke first. "And that is not with Demmie as some of you may have thought and never was going to be was it Grant because you were only using her to get at Chad. Anyway, now she is dead." Said Greta. "What the hell has she to do with anything, Greta? Plus, it would never have been with her, the devious manipulative cow. Besides, she is dead and Chadrick killed her, now didn't he?" Said Grant. "That is what you say but there is still a question mark over who killed her." Said Greta. "Question mark, my foot Greta. Anyhow we are not talking to you are we Lizabeth?" Replied Grant in a bullish fashion.

"Well quite honestly, you are not worth talking to anyhow and we would rather not talk to any of you either, so there." Said Jennifer and Greta smiled at the fieriness of her daughter. "And that suits me just fine. Come, Jennifer, we will leave them to their own devices and make our way to the hospital, then they can talk about us behind our backs."

"Do not leave just yet, Greta, we would like you to stay and hear what we have to say about Grant." Said Lord Mandaten. "And Jennifer?" Asked Greta. "Absolutely, she is one of the family and deserves to hear everything." Said Lord Mandaten. "Mother, Father, we did not hear you come in." Said Lizabeth. "That is because you were all wrapped up in your own little squabble, Lizabeth." Said Lord Mandaten. "Yes, we were, sorry father, mother, come now sit here with us by the fire. Said Lizabeth smiling. "We will be quite comfortable over here, thank you." Said Lord Mandaten and they all sat down and faced their parents.

"Well, you may as well get it over with. I know that you hate me as you always have so let us be having it." Said Grant. "Hate you, Grant? We have never hated you, that is all in your own poisoned mind. We know that Malcolm and Kevin ganged up on you and told lies about our feelings but then you did the exact same with Malcolm against Kevin, and with Kevin against Malcolm, did you not? That makes it all a bit of tit for tat. They just shrugged it off but you, Grant, you took it all to heart and could not see the truth from the lie. Your devious sisters did not help ease the problem but continued to feed it. You were always so different from Malcolm and Kevin but that made no difference and we loved you all just the same and gave you all the same opportunities to make something of yourselves, away from the estate." Said Lord Mandaten.

"We would have been alright if you had not brought that blasted interloper, Chadrick, into the family. He was the thorn in all our sides, even for the girls, and well we all hated him without exception." Said Grant. "And he knew this of you all and he just returned your hate with love and that really annoyed you, didn't it?" Answered Lord Mandaten.

"Made us feel sick to the stomach and the sooner he dies, the better for us all that are left. That is what they would like to say but cannot or rather will not bring themselves to do it." Grant spat his words out. "Well, Tomas has seen to that for us all, Grant, and you need to thank him for it, he did what you could not brother." Said Lizabeth.

"I will thank him, Lizabeth, when it is confirmed that Chad is dead. Dead and I see his body laid out cold on the mortuary slab." Said Grant. "Well, the instant that we know he is gone then we will ask to see him laid out on the slab as you so delicately put it." Said Lizabeth. "That we will Sister, that we will." Said Grant.

Their father shook his head. "That just about sums you all up in a nutshell, with the exception of Greta and Jennifer. You are a sweet girl and are exactly as we would have liked our own daughters to be but sadly, that was not the case. Somewhere and somehow, we went badly wrong with them because they both turned out to be devious and ruthless but enough about Them. Now with reference to Chadrick and how he came into the family, I will explain to you now. When your mother was rushed to hospital, for some unexplained reason, the midwife did not allow me to experience the birth. I had always been before so that meant it was just your mother and the midwife. I had been there and watched as each of you were born, apart from you, Grant, and I will get to that in a moment. After the birth, we were told that the child was stillborn which we could not understand as up to this time, all the signs had shown that the child was healthy. But the midwife, a nurse Martha Standmore, was quite insistent to this. She had taken the child away the very second that it was born so we never saw it. Your mother was sure that she heard the child cry. We were suspicious and when I was finally allowed to enter the room, your mother told me this and I then questioned this. She went from the delivery room and returned carrying a dead baby, saying that was our child. Meanwhile we heard that in another room a young woman, who had been savagely beaten and was only there because she was with child, sadly died but we were told the child lived and had no other family so would be orphaned. As you can imagine, your mother and I were totally distraught, thinking that we had lost our child. To ease the pain, we told the midwife, this Nurse Standmore, that we would give this child a home. She thought for a moment, then said that we could. It was to be kept quiet as it was against the rules. She then sent a young student nurse, I believe her name was Rachel Huntsmere, to fetch the child that had just been born and whose mother had passed away in childbirth. When she returned, there was a number on the child's wristlet, six if my memory serves me and that is how Chadrick came into our family." Said Lord Mandaten. "That is all very well but all you ever told us was that our own brother had died." Said Grant.

"He was only adopted to give him a good home, was he not?" Asked Lizabeth."Forget that as it is of no interest or anything to do with us now, Lizabeth, so let us get on with running me down, shall we?" Grant said. "Well he is dead now or will be very soon when the plug has been pulled so as you say Grant, it is of no interest to us now and –."remarked Tomas.

"That is enough!" Their father's look was sufficient to silence them. "Now, if you have all quite finished, then we will get back to what we are here for. As we have said, you were always and are completely different to the other boys but we still loved you all without exception, each one in the exact same way. Now then Grant, when you were born after Malcolm, we were very surprised. Neither us nor the doctor that had been caring for your mother knew that twins were due. Your mother had a difficult time but when Malcolm came into the world, we were all very happy. I went with him to the cleaning station where they checked him over to make sure that he was alright and to everyone's delight, he was. With us out of the room, that left your mother alone with the midwife who was cleaning her up. Then came the news of the second child. That was you, Grant, but your mother never had any recollection of giving birth to you. Although she was very tired after giving birth to Malcolm and she knew what to expect but to this day, she has no memory of your actual birth. No one of the medical team had ever heard of this happening before but the midwife was insistent that this was the case and she was alone in the room with your mother so we accepted it as a strange phenomenon. Although we were suspicious and had reservations. Even the doctors that had tended to your mother could not understand this happening. You had a numbered wristlet on and that was twenty-seven and we still have it as we have Chadrick's. Strangely, you were the first of our children to have numbered wristlets. As we watched you grow it was plain to see that you were so different from Malcolm. So much so that it was difficult to believe that you were twins. We looked past this and even though there was this vast difference between you, we still treated you all just the same. There is another big difference between you and your brothers, including Chadrick. They all took their chances and used them well but not you Grant. You wasted every single one of them as you had far more chances than they had. In the end, we had to give up on you and let you ruin your life as you have done. You blamed us for your drinking and that is not so, as you well know. You were lazy but managing reasonably well until you fell in love with the wrong girl. You were warned that she was nothing more than a gold digger but against our advice, you went ahead and secretly married her anyway. The instant she knew that there was no fortune to be had, she ran and that is when you started drinking. She then demanded a divorce with a substantial payoff. That did not happen because a few months after she had made her demands, she was then found murdered in a motel room. She had been shot three times and if you cast your mind back, you were questioned rigorously by the police about her death. You had an alibi for the time that she was killed and that was backed up by the woman that you were supposed to be with. You also used us for that purpose, saying that after she had brought you home drunk, you were still drinking heavily and had to be assisted to your room in a total drunken state. We had to confirm it was so and as far as we know, to this day her killer has never been found. Your story sounded good and was accepted by the police, I did not believe it not for one minute, and I had my reservations but you were free. Then you met dear sweet Bonnie and married her with our full blessing. We watched you together and were appalled at how you treated her abysmally in front of us and goodness knows how you treated her when we were not there to see. You were extremely lucky that she did not leave you and we could see that Bonnie was not a quitter so put up with you until her untimely death. She was not after riches and loved you far too deeply for her own good –." Grant interrupted his father. "Just how much more of this must I take?" "Until I have had my say and not a second before! Now to continue, you were far too blind to see that and we know that she rued the day that she said 'I do' but still stood by you even though she knew that for the past two and half years, possibly longer, you were having an affair behind her back." Said Lord Mandaten.

Grant looked away from his parents as he could not look his father in the eye because he had struck on the truth. "Affair? What affair? There was no affair, she must have made it all up." "I don't think so, Grant, you can lie to yourself and deny it all you want but you cannot lie to us as we know the facts and the truth of the matter. Bonnie had spoken to your sister, Lizabeth, and to Greta about her suspicions and she also spoke with us on the subject for guidance on what action she should take." Lord Mandaten continued. Grant began to look very agitated. "Spoke to you, why would she speak to you"? "We were her family and we were totally abhorrent of your treatment towards this sweet loving girl. She was the best thing that could have happened to you and you threw that all away. We have tried not to detest you and we have always given you love but with all that has happened from your birth to this day, we still find it hard to believe that you are actually our blood son." Lord Mandaten paused while he took a sip of his water and cleared his throat.

"Are you alright, Father?" Asked Greta. "I am fine Greta, thank you." Said Lord Mandaten.

"He is not your father so do not call him that." Snapped Lizabeth. "Enough Lizabeth, Greta is as much a daughter as you are. Now back to you, Grant. It is time for the truth as we have had quite sufficient lies and falseness from you all over the years. We know that the affair you deny began about six months after Chadrick had married Demmie and the affair that you so blatantly deny was with her. So now the truth, Grant, for once in your life speak the truth." Said Lord Mandaten.

Grant looked at his father, then looked away staring out of the window. After a long pause, he returned his eyes to his father and spoke with anger in his voice. "Alright, you want the truth, then truth you shall have. Yes, I did have an affair with Demmie but she threw herself at me and as I hated Chadrick with a passion and shall continue to do so even after death, I saw the opportunity to get one over on him. I didn't want her and used her to get at him but he either knew what was going on and turned a blind eye or had no idea. Yes, it infuriated me as I wanted to have it out with him and to break them up. If I had achieved that, I would have then ditched her but to my delight, I would have got one over on him. She wanted me to divorce Bonnie but to her disappointment, I said that I couldn't not until I was declared the next Lord Mandaten and had claimed my birthright. She said that she would help me and after it had been achieved, we would be married and rule the estate with all its wealth together. She told me that she never loved him and that she hated her life with Chadrick. It was all false and it had all been a lie, and that she only married him to get close to me." Lizabeth added. "And she certainly did that, Brother, by sharing your bed". "Shut up Lizabeth, you bitch, you know nothing about it. You asked for the truth and that is what you are getting. I had a master plan to discredit Malcolm and Kevin and they are both dead so now it is of no interest and before you ask, no, I did not kill them. Lowell and James are both dead and I did not kill them either, I am now the last remaining male heir so it is all mine and you cannot deny me that." Said Grant.

"I cannot deny you that, you say? We will see. Now, what about your first wife, Geraldine, and Bonnie's death? You told the police you had nothing to do with Geraldine's death which I did not believe so did you, Grant? And did you have anything to do with Bonnie's death?" Asked Lord Mandaten. "No, I did not, neither of them. I was questioned about Geraldine for several hours and in the end, as they could not pin it onto me they let me go. I was with a girl when she was killed, then she brought me home and you gave me my alibi because I was drunk and in bed at the time when it happened. I got the idea that Demmie was planning something as she had made several remarks about clearing the way for me with Bonnie but when it happened, I was as surprised as the rest of you. There was nothing that I could do as she was dead and gone and part of my plan went with her. Another thing, before you ask the question –. I knew nothing of her being pregnant until that Standish bloke told us. Demmie was a manipulative, evil woman. She was a liar and full of falseness and what is more, she reminded me of you, Lizabeth, my dear sweet sister. Just like you, she would do anything and stoop to any lengths to get what she wanted. Yes, before you say it, she was a gold digger." Grant paused to take a breather as he knew full well that he was under scrutiny. All the while that he was speaking, his eyes were averted away from his father and this led Lord Mandaten to believe that he was still lying. He knew well enough that a person that is telling a lie could not and would not look directly into the face of the questioner, the eyes do not lie.

"So, are we to believe that she alone connived and planned to murder Bonnie and you are totally innocent. If that is the case, then Cadiston will find that out." Said Lizabeth. "So, dear sister, you also doubt my word. I don't know how you expect that he can point a finger at me or achieve anything that would incriminate me, Lizabeth, as there is no evidence, now is there?" He had a smirk on his face and continued. "There is absolutely nothing to tie me to Demmie's death either as I was not here when she was killed and was brought in by that Macswee bloke when I drove back so there my alibi is a policeman and that cannot be denied, so there is nothing for him to find out." "And that is your belief, is it Grant, well maybe, just maybe you have been a little bit too clever this time?" Answered Lord Mandaten. "My belief, Father? Well, you wanted the truth so yes, that is my belief and how foolish to think that I have been too clever this time, just what are you implying father?" Said Grant in reply. "We shall see son, time will tell, so we will see." Said Lord Mandaten.

"Well, now that Demmie is dead and good riddance as she was becoming a real nuisance wanting me to declare our love. As I said, it was all one-sided as I did not love her and was merely using her to my own ends. So there you have all of it. I got one over on that interloper and now thank goodness they are both out of my life for good and that suits me just fine. Now all this will be mine with my one true love." Said Grant. His father looked at him with a very stern face. "That is not all of it, Grant, now is it? I ask for the whole truth and there is more of the truth to be declared." "More truth, are you never going to be satisfied? I have declared the affair with Demmie so what more is there?" Asked Grant. "The other woman, Grant, your one true love the other woman. That is what there is to declare." Said Lord Mandaten. "What do you know of another woman?" Asked Grant. "Enough Son! Now it is up to you to tell of her, the truth Grant and no more lies as you are very good at them. We know all about it but want to hear it directly from you.This is your chance, Son, to bring it all out into the open. A chance to come clean so for your own sake, take it before that chance also disappears." Said Lord Mandaten.

He looked sheepish now and knew that even though he thought that they had been very careful, everything had somehow been found out and as to this, he did not know how. "Alright, I have no idea how you know all this or how you found out but that does not matter now, so here it is for you all to hear. There is one girl that I admired from a distance for a long while, since I turned fourteen in fact, She was a year younger but as I was under the illusion that she was beneath me and you would not like that, I did not pursue her. I was wrong. She has aristocracy in her ancestry that I have only recently discovered but they fell on hard times and had to sell everything to clear their debts. Her great-great-grandfather was a duke but after the fall of the family, he died. We met again about nine years ago and I had waited a long time to declare my love for her and did so just over a year ago. That love was reiterated and before you say anything about her, she is not a gold digger. She fell for me as I did for her all those years ago and we have been seeing each other on regular occasions before and during my marriage to Bonnie. She is the only girl that is good for me and the only girl that I truly love and have always loved. I shall marry her soon and then my life will really begin yes all of you my New Beginning. You all think that I am an alcoholic, well, maybe I played a good part to fool you all and succeeded. Oh, to be sure I did enjoy a drink or two once but not anymore. All the drinking is just a ploy to keep our secret." Said Grant. "Not a secret that was kept very well, brother dear, as mother and father know all about it." Said Lizabeth. "Why don't you shut up, Lizabeth? You know nothing about nothing, do you?! Well, you ask for the truth now I have told all the truth. I have finally found the girl of my dreams, the girl that I fell in love with when I was fourteen and met again nine years ago but did not declare my love for until just over four years ago and from then we have seen each other regularly." Said Grant.

"And her name is?" Asked Lord Mandaten. "Come now, if you do not know that then you do not know it all, now do you Father?" Said Grant sarcastically.

"Do not be flippant with me, Son. I have given you the chance to tell her name but if you prefer, I shall do so. The name that you try to hide is Katrine and I know of her family's decline." Said Lord Mandaten. "And you employed her as a maid servant." Snarled Grant. "That we did and were glad to do so, we also helped her parents to set up their charity and animal rescue business. It is no shame on her part for her family's misfortune and if you had declared your love for this girl sooner, you would have saved yourself a lot of unwanted troubles and the deaths of two wives and one lover. It is out in the open now and you have the chance of a good future and a New Beginning so let us hope that there are no more **Skeletons** in your closet to be found by detective Cadiston, because he most certainly will find them. For you can be sure that if there are, DCI Cadiston will find them." Repeated Lord Mandaten.

"What are saying, Father? That if I had wanted to be with Katrine all those years ago, you would not have objected?" Asked Grant. "Not at all son, Katrine is a lovely young woman and we would have welcomed her into the family with open arms but sadly, now it may be too late." Said Lord Mandaten. "Too late, how can it be if we love each other and you are accepting her? How can it be too late, better late than never, isn't it?" Asked Grant. "That is the saying but there have been many things that have happened and there are still more revelations to be disclosed as Cadiston investigates all the murders and family deaths that have occurred in the past few weeks. Until there is a closed book, nothing can be settled and return to a normal life. Until that time, Katrine will continue with her position here and after that we shall see what transpires. We shall leave it there. Now I am tired so I will take my rest. Take me to the stairs please, Greta, then you had better be off to the hospital. Alfred can help me up to my room." Said Lord Mandaten and without hesitation, she pushed his wheelchair from the lounge with his wife and grand-daughter in close attendance.

Grant grunted angrily. "Damn them, they have given me years of hell with the wrong women when I could have had just one woman and years of happiness, and that one woman is Katrine. All those wasted years when we could have been to-gether but –."

"For goodness' sake, quit your moaning Grant! It serves ab-solutely no purpose, you must accept some of the blame for your wrong choices although Bonnie was a good one. If you wanted Katrine, then you should have made sure that you got her. As father said, we must wait until Cadiston has finished his inves-tigations and conclusions and then we will know who gets it all and who falls by the wayside. Then we can get on with our lives and have a **NEW BEGINNING**, at least for those of us that are left without fear of being murdered." Said Lizabeth. "And that is what you say, sister dear, we can just get on with our lives without fear of being murdered –. But we will see." Said Grant.

"True brother dear, we will see. As father said time will tell brother dear, time will tell. Now, the day is passing fast and before it is too late as it is already four-thirty in the afternoon, well –. I have something important to do." With those words, she left him standing there wondering what was so important.

It was late on Tuesday afternoon and Mac and Cadiston were reading through the information in his notebook and as it was all written in shorthand Cadiston read it while Mac listened, when the phone rang which was quickly answered. "Cadiston." "Detective, it is Nurse Lynn, could you return to the hospital please, there is an incident and you should be aware of it?" Said the nurse on the phone. "We are on the way, Nurse Lynn." Said Cadiston and the line went dead.

Car Mac and be quick, we must get to the hospital as there has been an incident and let us hope that all is good with Chadrick and there is no mishap." Said Cadiston.

"On the way, Boss." Mac almost sprinted from the office and forty minutes later they were entering the hospital. "Good evening, DCI Cadiston and Sergeant Macswee." Said Nurse Francis. "And good evening to you, Nurse Francis, we got here as quickly as we could as Nurse Lynn's call sounded urgent. How is the patient? Nothing gone wrong has it?" Asked Cadiston concerned for Chad. "Not at all, I can tell you that he is doing extremely well. In fact; much better than expected considering his injuries. Why we called you is there is some information that we think you should know and did not want to disclose it over the phone" Said Nurse Francis. "Good thought so what is this information?" Asked Cadiston. "We had someone else call in late this afternoon at about five p.m. and ask to see Chad but of course she was refused as she had no pass. She said that she was his sister, Lizabeth Mandaten. We told her that he was fading and that he was not going to make it. Nurse Lynn told her that the life support would be turned off tomorrow and with that, she smiled." Said Nurse Francis. "Did she ask to see him again after your refusal?" Asked Cadiston. "She did and was very insistent and said that as his sister she had the right to see him. She was very insistent and after a consultation, we decided to just allow her to look through the door. When she saw all the pipes, tubes, and electrodes she just smiled again and said, 'so it will all be unplugged and turned off tomorrow and he will be –. Well, dead is the only word.'" Then with that, she again smiled and left. Doctor Mafidsen had told us that it was your wish to say that and only to allow Greta and Jennifer to sit in with him. We had been instructed that if anyone else asks about his situation, to tell them that he was going downhill and would not make it. I can say it to you, Detective, I did not like her, not one little bit and she was very happy and pleased that Chad was about to expire. There was something sinister about her that set my teeth on edge." Said Nurse Francis.

Cadiston smiled at this remark. "Good girl, sorry, Nurse Francis." "Do not be sorry, I am forty-two and I like good girl better, it makes me feel young again." Said Nurse Francis and they both smiled. "Can we go in to see him?" Asked Cadiston. "You know the way, Detective. And as usual, he already has his two lady visitors, they arrived at seven a.m. this morning, then went for a break, and returned this afternoon. Nurse Lynn is making some final checks so she is in there also." They made their way to Chad's room and went straight in. As usual, they were greeted as friends not as police officers, "Greta, Jennifer, everything alright?" Asked Cadiston. "Everything is perfect, Detective Cadiston." Said Greta. "Apart from aunt Lizabeth peeping through the window", said Jennifer. "By the way, did you know that Lizabeth came to the hospital late this afternoon detective?" Asked Greta. "Just been told and that is why we are back here now." Said Cadiston. "Do you know why she came here today as she has shown no interest before?" Asked Greta. "To check and make sure that he was not going to make it. When she was told that his life support was about to be turned off, she smiled and smiled even more when she saw all the tubes, pipes and, electrodes attached to him."Said Cadiston. "They did not take our word for it, did they Mother? They had to check for themselves and that is so typical of them. Just between us, all these things are not attached but just stuck on for effect." Said Jennifer. "I did know that, Jennifer, and apart from myself, Mac and you two ladies, no one else apart from the nurses that are caring for him and Doctor Mafidsen knew that. It was, in fact, an idea of his to fool everyone and came up with it when I explained that it needed to look as though he would not make it, just in case the wrong person tried to find a way of getting information about his condition." Said Cadiston."And we have complied fully with that request and now secretly in effect, he will be resurrected when the time is right." Said Nurse Francis. "Life after death." Said Jennifer. "Spot on Jennifer. Now we will leave you three to chat while we speak to Doctor Mafidsen if he is available." Said Cadiston. "He should be in the office. That is unless he has been called away." Said Greta. "Thank you." Said Cadiston and they left. On the way to the office, they were greeted by another nurse that had been caring for Chad.

"Good evening, detectives." Said the nurse. "And a good evening to you, Nurse Summer. We have just paid a visit to our patient." Said Cadiston.

"Thought that you would have, he is getting on very well considering what he has gone through and his two lady visitors, Greta and Jennifer, have done wonders for him. Tomorrow will be a big day as Doctor Mafidsen will begin to bring him out of his induced coma. It will take a few days to be fully effective. One thing to his advantage is that he is strong and has a built-in desire to be well again. We can tell this by the way he reacts in the coma to Greta and Jennifer and that, I believe, is down to you. His two ladies are already there and have been since quite early this morning but then you already know that. I know that Doctor Mafidsen would like a word and he should be in the office so go right in, it will be fine." Said Nurse Summer. "Thanks, Nurse." They did just that and were again greeted as Chad's friends, not as police officers. Mister Doctor Mafidsen return presently he has just been called to check on a young motorcycle accident victim, a van pulled out directely in front of her and the poor girl crashed into the vans side. She lost a leg but thankfully the head injury was not as bad as first thought thanks to an extremely good qyality crash helmet." Said Nurse Chandra who was checking some notes in the office.

"I will fetch you some coffee while you wait. Just take a seat, he will not be long."

They drank their coffee and were beginning to wonder where the surgeon was when Nurse Lynn entered the office. "Would you return to Chad's room, Doctor Mafidsen will see you there." Before they could answer, she had disappeared and within two minutes they were back in Chad's Room.

"Ah Cadiston, you got our message then and good news, I can definitely confirm that Chadrick Mandaten will soon be back with us properly. 'Life after death' I believe is how the young lady described it and that is not far from the truth. He is a very lucky young man as we almost lost him twice during the surgery. Now look at him and we can look forward to his recovery that begins in earnest tomorrow and will be the start of the long recovery road which should remain straight with no detours. What a lucky fellow he is to have such devoted ladies by his side and to be swamped with so much love and devotion, and to have friends like you. You have not missed a day since he was brought in." Said Doctor Mafidsen. As you say, but mainly due to your surgical skills, and for that we extremely thankful and we thank you".Macswee said shaking the doctors hand. "No thanks needed, he was brought in just in time. It was touch and go. As I said, he died twice on the operating table and I was determined that I was not going to lose him and –. Well, here he is. The operation was very successful. Long but worthwhile as he has surprised us all, his recovery is going well and that is due partly to the love and attention that these two lovely ladies have lavished on him." Said Doctor Mafidsen.

"And the excellent nursing care and our thanks to all the nurses that have cared for our Chad." Said Greta. "Truly spoken, Greta, lucky he certainly is and that is partly due to his extra thick skull." Remarked the doctor. "And that fact, is something that I will need to check up on but first things first and that is to get him back on his feet." Said Cadiston. "Just so. And so you, young man –." Doctor Mafidsen now directed his remarks to Chad. "Tomorrow, that is Wednesday, 22nd of October, I will begin to bring you around from the coma and bring you back to all this love that is waiting for you then all the wires pipes and everything else that you have been connected to will be removed fully and those that were for show will just disappear. Now I have other patients to see so until tomorrow. I bid you all a fond farewell." He turned and left. "What a lovely caring consultant he is." Said Jennifer. "One of the very best, Jennifer. So Chad, my friend, he has done his bit for you and now it is your turn. There is a lot of love waiting for you so, my friend, you come back to us and give us 'life after death' as Jennifer put it. That will invite a **NEW BEGINNING** for you all. I can see a good future ahead for you and you certainly do not want to miss out on that. Goodness, it is eight-thirty already and we are running late so I will leave you in the hands of these two lovely ladies and see you tomorrow morning." Cadiston said and with Mac at his side, they left the room. "Hope it all works out for them, Cadders. Just look at them, they make a nice little family unit." Said Mac. "Sometimes a tragedy can bring two people together that should have been together all along and they certainly have had their share of tragedy. You really do have to admire them though, Mac, because even though they both felt the same way about each other, they never once broke their marriage vows even though their respective partners did. Well, Chad's did, I do not know about Greta's. I do believe that they loved their respective partners but not the way they love each other and if you observed the way that Greta looks at Chad, you will know just what I mean." Said Cadiston. "I have seen the look and it warms the heart so yes I do know, you have it with Samantha just as I have it with my Angela. After all this, they really do deserve to be happy together and that will signal a **NEW BEGINNING** for them and the Mandaten family." Said Mac with a smile on his face. "Let us hope that is the case and from tragedy, there is a happy ending, a good 'life after death' and as you said Mac, their **NEW BEGINNING**." Said Cadiston.

"Well, it is almost eight p.m so is it back to the station for us to see if the last post-mortem and forensic reports have turned up?" Said Mac. "I can answer that one now, Mac, something arrived just as we were about to leave to come here." Said Cadiston. "It may be late but I guess it will be the station for us then, Boss, and a degree of very late-night reading for us so best we warn our good ladies." Said Mac. "A good thought, Mac, but a bit too late in the day for that and I do feel that our minds will not be fully operational so best to read the reports when we are both rested and fresh as we do not want to miss anything. For the best part of tomorrow we will be at the hospital. I am keen to read the reports but I am sure that another day will not affect the cases in any way. We will still catch our killers as they are going no-where." Said Cadiston, "Once again, you are right so good thing that you are the DCI and I'm the DS, drop you off at your car then." Said Mac.

"That will do nicely Mac, thanks'." Said Cadiston.

Chapter Fifteen

Life After Death

Now that Grant had nothing to hide about his other women as his affair with Demmie was now out in the open and he had also declared his love for Katrine, he felt that he had nothing more to tell. He felt that he had bested his parents by keeping one secret from them and guessed they knew nothing of this. If they did then his father would have insisted on him telling it. This had left him with three thoughts in his mind: first, to see the end of Chadrick; second, the sooner that Cadiston closed all the cases, the better, and third, to stay alive as he thought that if Chadrick was the killer then he would have needed help and a killer might still be at large. His forth and last thought was that he hoped that Cadiston would not be digging into the past offences of murder as he did not want it all dragged up again. With these thoughts, he knew that he had to stay alert if he was going to survive so taped his gun for security, and felt that his destiny was to secure the Mandaten title and obtain the massed fortune he also had the thought to look at all the past Mandaten bodies in the family crypt to see what pieces of jewellery he could find there to sell.

For Cadiston and Mac there was no quick end, they needed to have all the facts and evidence before an arrest could be actioned, and as the investigation continued, there was still a way to go before the capture of the killer or killers of the Mandaten family. Progress was being made and each day brought the conclusion to all the cases a step closer. Wednesday morning, 22nd of October, saw Cadiston sitting in his office extremely early, contemplating whether to open these final reports or to wait for Mac to arrive with his news. His notebook laid open in front of him but his mind at this time was firmly fixed on Chad and the beginning of his return to the land of the living, 'life after death' he remembered that Jennifer had said and in some respect that is just what it was. He was not aware of how the time was going but by now, Mac had arrived and Cadiston looked up from his notebook to the sound of his footsteps.

"Morning Cadders, you are about bright and early. Turned a bit chilly this morning but will get out fine around midday, typical October day I imagine." Said Mac. "Morning Mac, yep got in early as I needed to finish updating my notebook so got here by six-thirty. So far I have done nothing to it except stare at it and as you can see, the final reports are unopened. I cannot concentrate on them as my main thoughts are at the hospital with Chad. I have given a few thoughts to the last case and I am as far as Demmie Mandaten. I have a suspect in mind for her murder but need the visual evidence to prove it, not forgetting the attack on Chad which ties them together and is all very suspicious. I did not believe the cock and bull story that Lizabeth, Tomas, and their son told us not for one minute. There were cracks in their statements a mile wide and after we have listened to the taped emergency call, it will shed light on that fact. I will be glad when Chad is out of the coma and can talk to us. We haven't read Demmie's post-mortem yet or the forensic reports and they are here." on my desk still unopened and I feel that just for now, they should remain so." Caddiston's finger tapped the envelopes. "We need to be at the hospital by ten-thirty but as I said, I must admit that I cannot concentrate on anything else as all my thoughts are with Chad."

"I know just how you feel, Boss. Like you, I came in with good intentions but my mind is elsewhere. So what shall it be?" Asked Mac.

"We seem to have been here all night, at least that is how it feels. the time now is nine-twenty so what about if we go to the hospital now and wait over a cup or two of coffee, that way we can relax as we will be on-site and ready for the procedure to begin." Said Cadiston. "Sounds good to me and as you are the boss, and I am yours to command, I guess I will go get the car." Cadiston smiled and gave a nod of approval and Mac was gone. Greta and Jennifer were feeling very nervous as they knew that this was going to be a big day for them, the day in which they would see Chadrick return to life. Greta could not help smiling as she remembered her daughter's words, 'life after death.' "Not long now, Jennifer." Said Greta. I can see you are keen to be going, my little princess, by the way you are hovering at the window. A big day ahead for us who care for Chadrick." Lord Mandaten said. "It certainly is, Grandfather, and I will be happy when we know the result." Said Jennifer. Lord Mandaten's fingers went to his lips and the conversation ceased.

"Morning Father, you are up early today." Said Lizabeth. "And is that a problem for you, Lizabeth?" Asked her father. "Not at all, Father. I am just surprised to see you down in the breakfast room without Mother." Answered Lizabeth. "And do you not want to say good morning to Greta and Jennifer?" Asked Lord Mandaten. "If I must, morning both." Lizabeth said snidely.

"And morning to you, Lizabeth. Said Greta but Lizabeth just turned her back and ignored them. "Morning all." Grant said before doing a headcount. "Well, no one got killed in the night as we are all down for breakfast and that proves that Chadrick is or rather was the killer. Now if I am right, his life support gets turned off today so if you do not want him to die alone, isn't it about time that you two were on your way to watch it happen?" Asked Grant. His words angered Jennifer and she snapped back at him. "There is no need for that flippancy, Uncle Grant, uncle Chadrick has been nothing but good to you all through your rotten life even though you treated him abysmally." "You are a silly little child Jennifer and you need to learn a few manners, I hope he rots in hell." Grant shot back. Jennifer was quick with her reply and there was venom in her voice, "Well, if he does which I doubt very much; then you will meet up with him again because that is where you are most certainly going with no reprieve." Greta looked at her daughter, wondering what she would say next while her grandfather smiled at her feistiness. With his hand raised ready to strike, Grant stepped toward Jennifer. "Why you cheeky little –." "Put your hand down, Grant, and step back from my granddaughter. This act just proves that you do not like to hear the truth or have anyone stand up to you and that is also the truth." Said Lord Mandaten sharply. "Father I, ah – Oh! what is the use, I –." Grant turned and left the room. Greta now hugged her daughter. "That was very brave of you." Jennifer knew that Lizabeth was listening so spoke quite loud to be sure that she heard. "He makes me so angry, Mother, and he is so cold but our taxi is here so it is time for us to go and say our farewells to Uncle Chadrick." Her grandfather's wink went unnoticed by Lizabeth, Tomas, and Kansas, They did not worry about Grant as he had already left the room. "I will let you know as soon as we know, Father, Mother." Said Greta.

"Thank you, we will be by the phone waiting for your call, Greta." Said Lord Mandaten. "There she goes again, when will she learn that they are not her parents? Well, she will be out of the way soon and no more problem to us." Snarled Lizabeth. "Whenever it is will not be soon enough for me, Father, I detest them all especially the favourite blue-eyed boy, Lowell, I could kiss the mad horse that stomped him." Said Kansas.

"Patience Son, Lowell and Malcolm are both dead and gone and his wife and remaining child will soon follow them both." Lizabeth smiled and continued. "Banished from ever setting foot on Mandaten lands ever again." "Unless they get killed off by someone before that happens, Mother." Said Kansas. "The killer is about to die thanks to your father, Kansas. Cadiston will then close the cases." Said Lizabeth. "And not a moment too soon." Grant chipped in.

"True Grant, then we can start to live here again properly." Replied Lizabeth.

"Make it soon, Mother." Said Kansas. Grant had returned and momentarily they had forgotten that their parents were in the room. They had spoken quietly but they were still heard. "You take much for granted, Daughter, nothing is settled yet." Said Lord Mandaten. Lizabeth was quick to reply with a hint of reluctance in her voice. "Not a problem, Father, I was just speaking my thoughts." "And I thought you were talking to your son." Said Lord Mandaten.

"Hmm –." She had nothing more to say and with a glance, the three of them left the room and stood by the open front door. They watched until the taxi had disappeared up the long drive and then smiled. "There they go to watch the cold-tainted murderer die" Said Kansas. "Shush, enough now Son! Walls have ears and we can forget all about them now and have a nice quiet day." Said Tomas.

Cadiston and Mac arrived at the hospital and with their car parked, walked slowly toward the café. Picking a table near the window, they sat in silence with their coffee. They did not need to speak as they both had one single thought: Chadrick was about to have 'life after death.' They saw Greta and Jennifer also arrive in plenty of time and as they waved, Mac fetched them to sit quietly with a coffee and soft drink before going to the ward. "This is very nerve-racking." Said Greta. "For us all, Greta." Answered Mac. "Not long now, only twenty minutes to wait." "Detective Cadiston, there is something that I need to tell you. In conversation about Chadrick, Tomas said that he had struck him twice while he lay on the floor and he told you it was only once. In the paddock when Chad was testing his theory, Kansas said that if he had his Uncle Grant's handgun, then he would shoot the mad horse himself. Grant also said that if anyone tried to kill him, it would be them to die as he is not afraid to use his pistol and he has used it before. It may have no bearing but I thought that you should know." Said Greta. "Rightly so Greta, you get that written down Mac?" Asked Cadiston. "I did," Said Mac.

"There is something else. I do not know if it can be arranged but Grant has said that he will not believe that Chadrick is dead until he can see his body laid out cold on the mortuary slab" Continued Greta. "Why, the cold, heartless swine. Sorry Greta, boss but I could not hold back on that." Said Mac. "It is alright DS Macswee, I agree with you but what do you think about Grant's request, Detective Cadiston?" Asked Greta. "I am sure that we can accommodate his request and that act will be a secret weapon in our search to catch a killer. I will speak with his surgeon and I am sure that it can easily be arranged with Charles and Samantha at our mortuary." Said Cadiston.

"There are so few of the family left and I will not ask who you suspect but I will be glad when Chadrick can tell you what he has discovered about Lowell's murder that he thought may help in your investigation. I am certain that it has something to do with the horse that was accused of stomping him and there is some information that he needs to tell you." Said Greta. "We will hear that soon enough but now I think that the time is upon us to get up to the ward." Said Cadiston. They walked slowly together and were greeted at the door by Nurse Francis.

"Greta, you and your daughter may enter the room and as the space is limited, Mr. Cadiston with your associate, would you wait in that room, please. It connects to Chad's and you can observe through the window as the procedure takes its course. Mister Doctor Mafidsen is already in there making his final checks and will be ready to begin the procedure once you ladies and detectives are all settled."

"Good morning ladies and how are you both this morning? I take it Mr. Cadiston is in the other room where he can observe what is happening as it happens?" Asked Doctor Mafidsen. "Yes, we walked up with him and his sergeant and we are both fine, thank you Mister Doctor Mafidsen, very nervous but otherwise fine." Said Greta.

"Understandable my dear, now I am ready and now you are all here, I will begin to bring this lucky young man from the induced coma and I believe it was you Jennifer that said, 'life after death' and in some respects, that is exactly what it is as I nearly lost him twice during the cranial operation. Now, sit back as I require you to be silent as I start the procedure." Said Doctor Mafidsen.

They all sat back and watched as he began to reverse the procedure. Greta and Jennifer were holding hands and both had tears in their eyes while Cadiston and Mac observed through the window. "This is a slow process, not an instant wake-up call like you would have with an alarm clock, and as you probably know your long vigil is not quite over yet, my dears. The procedure is started and now we wait for it to take effect. Some coffee may be the order of the day, Nurse –." Said Doctor Mafidsen. "I will see to it sir". The nurse left and within ten minutes, returned with their drinks. She had not forgotten Cadiston and Mac in the other room.

An hour passed by and to their delight, Chad began to show signs of waking. Every tube and electrode had been removed and now he was breathing in his own right. "Brilliant, keep it up my boy, all is going well and now your course is a nice straight road, do you hear me Chad? I do not want you taking any detours. I will go check on my other patients, then come back in about half an hour. I do not envisage any problems but you have my beeper number nurse if needs be." Said Doctor Mafidsen. The door was slowly opened by the nurse and he was gone. "Would you like to sit beside Chad now and maybe hold his hands?" Asked the nurse. "We would but is that allowed in these circumstances and would we be in the way?" Nurse Francis smiled. "It will be fine, Chad is slowly waking and when he opens his eyes, you will be the first two people that he sees, now what could be better than that for him?" "Nothing, thank you." With Greta and Jennifer holding his hands, they waited. Doctor Mafidsen returned and smiled when he saw them sitting beside him. Greta went to rise but a gentle hand on her shoulder pushed her back down. "You are fine, my dear." He did a few tests, then stepped back and said. "Excellent, excellent, all is going well and on course and he is slowly waking. I prefer not to wake my patient too quickly and Chadrick is right on schedule." He left again. One hour turned to two and to three, each hour bringing Chad closer to 'life after death' and always in close attendance were Greta and Jennifer. His eyelids would often flicker, giving them hope that his eyes were about to open but they were not dismayed when they did not as they knew it would happen in its own time. All day they sat with him, waiting and hoping for the flickering to cease and the eyes to finally open fully. In the next room, Cadiston and Mac were also waiting, just as eager to see Chad wake up. Almost as much as Greta and Jennifer who had been there supporting him from the start of the long vigil and that support was long-term and was never wavering. They had totally ignored any sacrifices they needed to make as their priority was to be at the side of the man that they both loved in this long vigil. And now they were there to see his return and welcome him back after his near-death experience, as Jennifer had said, 'life after death'. Now the wait was almost over and finally his eyes opened, just for a second or two and they were his first sittings since being unconscious. He whispered just loud enough for them to hear. "Greta, Jennifer." He looked directly at them and squeezed their hands, then his eyes closed again but they knew that the recovery was underway.

"You stay here, Mother, and I will let Grandfather know, I will not be long." Jennifer said as she was prepared to leave the room to make her call but the nurse stopped her. "You can ring from here on your mobile now, there is no equipment to be affected so it is quite safe." "Thank you." Said Jennifer. The phone at Mandaten rang and was answered by Alfred. "Can you get Grandfather to the phone, please?" Asked Jennifer. "No need, Miss Jennifer, he is right beside me." Said Alfred. "Jennifer, tell me what is the news?" Asked Lord Mandaten. She made the tone of her voice sound sad. "It is done, Grandfather, and is just as we expected. We are going to stay by his side so that he is not alone." "Alright my dear, I can understand that, we will talk so that you can give us the full details when you are back home." Said Lord Mandaten. The phone went dead. As Lord Mandaten replaced the receiver, he heard the distinctive click of the extension being replaced. "Bring them into the lounge for me please, Alfred, all of them." "Immediately, my Lord." Said Alfred as he turned and ten minutes later, the family had gathered.

"Just one question, who was on the extension phone?" Lord Mandaten asked angrily. Their heads were shaking. "I know that one of you had picked up the extension so there is no need to lie. I ask you again, who was it and I am totally sick of your lies so no more!" There was silence as their heads shook before a voice spoke out. "Me Grandfather, it was me. I should not have done so –." Kansas said while his head was bowed. "So I am sorry."

"Sorry is not good enough, Kansas, you had absolutely no right to listen in. That phone call could have been a private conversation and not for others to hear but it is done. I can guess that the eavesdropper has told you that the life support is turned off –." Said Lord Mandaten.

"Turned off? He may have told them but not me. So, at last, it is done. Now all I want is to see him laid out cold on the mortuary slab." Spat Grant. "Cold-hearted and blunt as usual, brother dear." Said Lizabeth. "Don't 'brother dear' me, Lizabeth, you had no love for him and are just as glad that he is dead if you speak the truth. Now I would bet that you would like to see him on the slab with me beside him." Said Grant. Their father raised his hand and glared at them both with his steely stare. They both fell silent as they had no desire to raise his anger. They looked at each other, not with a look of love but with an ingrown hatred for each other as they both felt that they were within a stone's throw of the family fortune and also knowing that they each stood in the other's way. They felt that it was now within their grasp, knowing that their father would not last much longer as each passing day weakened him further. His demise was only a few days away but he was stronger than they imagined. He began to rub his head then cradled it in his hands. "It is done. Now both of you get out of my sight. In fact, all of you." They did not hesitate. The evening was upon them and it was now seven-twenty. Greta and Jennifer had seen Chad open his eyes on several occasions and each time they were opened, it was a little longer than the previous one. "He is back with us, Mac, we have just witnessed the result of a real 'life after death' experience and it feels good." Said Cadiston. "Thank goodness." Said Mac. "Thank Doctor Mafidsen for his skill and those two visitors of his, they are a real tonic for him along with all the nurses that have cared for him. Now that we know he is going to be alright, I think it is safe for us to go home. We will come back tomorrow afternoon but in the morning we must finish our reading, get my notebook updated, and set our course of action which should have been implemented already. We have been delayed because each time we set out to investigate one murder, there has been another but hopefully, now they have ceased." Said Cadiston.

"Hopefully but the real killer or killers are still out there, so home now then office first thing in the morning, get up to date and then we can take the appropriate action." Said Mac. "Action is right, Mac, we will just take our leave and be away." Said Cadiston and he slowly opened the door to Chad's room and whispered. "I can guess that you will stay all night but as for us, we are away now as there is nothing that we can do. We are just spares as Chad has you both to keep him company. As for what we said earlier, I will get that organised but that is just between us. We have something to do first thing in the morning but will be back tomorrow afternoon without fail and hopefully, Chad will be round further and maybe even able to chat a little. We will most definitely not be putting him under any pressure to answer questions or anything else until we know that he is strong enough. We will bid you all a good night and will see you here tomorrow afternoon."

"I would rather have a word with you now please before you go as I think that you should know what we overheard today." Said Greta. "Alright, just step out of the room and we can talk." Said Cadiston. "It was when they were all talking about Chad, Tomas said that he had hit him twice but before he told you it was once. The second thing, I think that Grant slipped up and you should know that he carries a pistol with him. I think he said that it was called a snubnosed 38 calibre but you will know if there is such a weapon." Said Greta. "Thank you, and well-observed Greta. That small piece of information will be of tremendous help. Now, you get back in there and leave the rest to us." Said Cadiston. She shook his hand then returned to the room. With Mac right behind him, they waved and left a waking Chad with his two ladies.

"Greta has already told us that but no matter, they look extremely happy, Cadders. Their tears have turned to smiles and that warms the heart and is good to see." Said Mac also smiling. "Good indeed, Mac. I would not ask him but there are those that have experienced 'life after death' and have said that there was a bright light and that they could see themselves before they were resuscitated and brought back." Said Cadiston.

"An out-of-body experience I think they call it but like you, I would not want to ask Chad if he had that kind of experience." Answered Mac. "Certainly not. Now let's go home, Mac." Said Cadiston and they walked silently toward the lift. "What Greta just told us about Tomas and the gun that Grant has, she told us that in the coffee shop." Said Mac. "I know Mac but after all the trauma and worry they have experienced, is it any wonder that Greta was a bit forgetful?" Answered Cadiston. "That is why you did not comment on it but quite honestly, I nearly did." Said Mac. "Better to be told twice than not at all but understanding her emotions was why I let it be." Said Cadiston. "And I am learning from you in every aspect, Cadders, so keep teaching." Said Mac and they both smiled. They were soon sitting in the car ready to be on the way home. They sat for a moment in the hospital car park, each lost in their own thoughts of the series of events that had transpired since they first set foot onto the Mandaten Estate. For Cadiston it had been since 23rd September and Mac was steadily catching up on all the details that Cadiston had written and formulated in his notebook. In the time that he had been dealing with the family, he had gained a considerable amount of knowledge about each of their personalities. As he summed them up in his mind, in most cases, he did not like what he had found. Turning to his notebook, he opened the page and began to read.

"Lizabeth: A person that likes the high life, very materialistic, devious, selfish and money-orientated and therefore an expensive commodity. She is riddled with greed and will lie to get what she wants. She was jealous of her sister, Sammie, who appeared to have more than her but would her hatred be enough to bring her to kill her sister? She is very dominant and appears to wear the trousers in that family. She is a very strong-willed person who will stop at nothing to get what she wants. Will only come into the Mandaten fortune if there were no living Mandaten male heirs, otherwise has no claim in her own right.

Tomas: Lizabeth's husband and also riddled with greed. He appears very subservient and under his wife's thumb, at least that is the impression that he likes to give so is that a façade. He takes second place to their son and is controlled by them both, or is he? Would do anything to get her what she wants but would that be as far as to kill for her? There is something suspicious about him and his acting could be lies. He is a Kaysten and has no claim to the Mandaten fortune in his own right. Something suspicious about him.

Kansas: Son of Lizabeth and Tomas, a big-headed and overly confident bossy boy who likes to think that he is better than the rest of the family. Treats his mother well and with respect but dominates his father, or is that another façade and all for show? He has no respect for other members of the family. Treats his father as a second-class citizen and considers himself better than him. He says that he is in med school so has a knowledge of the human body but is also a liar. Would he kill for his mother or father? He is a Kaysten and has no claim to the Mandaten fortune in his own right. Something false about him.

Grant: An alcoholic (or is that an act to throw the scent?) and also filled with greed. He is a liar and extremely lazy and he uses people to get what he wants after which he casts them aside. He is a manipulator and a bully, he likes to have everything his own way, and if he does not then watch out. He does not like to be challenged or told he is wrong. Has a real hatred for Chad, I believe he would stop at nothing to get what he wants. He is the only remaining living male heir to the Mandaten fortune, or is he? Would he commit murder to get it all? Greta: A very gentle and caring young woman, has an inner beauty as well as an outer beauty and has no hatred for anyone, dislike yes, hatred no. It is not within her nature. She is honest and speaks truthfully, there is not a hint of falseness and shows no sign of greed. Has no claim on the Mandaten fortune in her own right – only carries the Mandaten name due to marriage, wife of the late Malcolm Mandaten.

Jennifer: Daughter of Greta and Malcolm and although only ten years old, she has a very sensible head on her shoulders. She is like her mother, gentle and caring but will stand up and show strength if needed. She is truthful and even at her young age, there is no falseness. Has possible claim to the Mandaten fortune in her own right – daughter of Malcolm Mandaten.

Chadrick: Adopted son but has traits of the Mandaten family, especially an unusually thick skull. He is gentle and caring and hates violence of any kind but can and will stand up and fight if the need arises. He would rather walk away to avoid conflict. No sign of greed or falseness. Has no claim to the Mandaten fortune, or has he?"

He had written all these thoughts into his notebook as he knew that to know someone's profile could help when questioning as you would have an idea how they would react. His first case was that of Malcolm Mandaten and he was also looking at the case of Bonnie Mandaten and her unborn child who were callously murdered by Demmie on Monday, 22nd of September. To bring him up to date it culminated in Demmie being murdered and Chad being put into hospital on Saturday, 11th of October, and he hoped that would be the last murder but if his suspicions were correct, that would not be the case. He had to find the killer or killers quickly. He began to mutter softly. "The only person that I can see that stands in Grant's way is young Jennifer and I would not want anything to happen to her so must keep it in mind that she may be in danger." He continued in a normal tone. "You are a very lucky fellow, Chadrick Mandaten. Twice you died but you are still living so I guess you could say that you have experienced 'life after death' just as young Jennifer said. I can see a good and happy life ahead of you with Greta and Jennifer so good luck to you all." His voice now changed from its soft gentle tones into that of anger. "If only Standish had listened to me from the very beginning when I pointed out the way in which Malcolm Mandaten had met his death and the suspicions that I had instead of trying to close the case in an instant before any form of investigation had been carried out. Then there was poor Bonnie with her unborn child and again, if he had acted on my suspicions, then maybe lives would have been saved and the guilty ones would already be behind bars. You had a reason for wanting these cases closed quickly without investigation, Ex-Sergeant Standish, including Lord Mandaten's brother with his family four years ago. So how many others have had the same treatment? Well, I will discover why you wanted them all wrapped up quickly and then let the chief know before anyone else but as for now, Mac, home is calling us."

"I heard nothing else that you said, only that home is calling." Said Mac and Cadiston smiled.

At that moment, there was a tap on his window, making him jump. "Sorry to disturb you but I was just wondering if you were about to leave as I am looking for a parking space. I have had to drive a long way to get here. It is my daughter in the hospital after her motorbike accident and I want to get in to see her. She lost her leg and suffered a head injury but her surgeon; a Doctor Mafidsen has done a marvellous job." Said the man.

"Yes, I know him, he is one of the very best cranial surgeons and I also know the case of your daughter and saw you the other day when you were here. Now, we are on our way home so take this space and I hope that your daughter has a speedy recovery." Said Cadiston. "Sadly, her leg cannot be put back but there are some marvellous advancements in prosthetic limbs so there is nothing to stop her from having a full and active life even so." Said the man. "That is just what we have been told. Let's go home, Mac." Said Cadiston, and the instant that Mac moved the car forward, the space was filled.

Arriving home, his wife was there to greet him. "Hello you lovely man, what a long day you have had." "And hello my precious little woman, it surely was but worth it and I must say that I am glad to be home." Said Cadiston, and they hugged and kissed to complete the welcome. It was basically the same when Mac arrived home. "I found out something else today about Chad, he died twice during the operation but Doctor Mafidsen was determined not to lose him. Young Jennifer called it 'life after death' and Doctor Mafidsen agreed that it was just about right, he is on the recovery road now. Now just one more thing as I don't want to talk shop but must just ask is the post-mortem done for Demmie as it is the last one that we have to read?" Asked Cadiston. "It is almost done and tomorrow we will complete the write-up. The cause of death for Demmie is straightforward, multiple gunshots but we still had to check it anyway. We have already checked the body over briefly and will complete it tomorrow. What I can say is that whoever shot her was at extremely close range. Now, no more shop talk, we will spend a nice quiet evening enjoying each other's company." Said Samantha.

"Sounds good to me. Is there time for a shower before our meal?" Asked Cadiston. "I would say that it will take about ten to fifteen minutes to cook and then it will be ready." Replied Samantha. "Best I hustle then." Said Cadiston and smiled.

At Mandaten Manor, even though there were so few family members left there remained an air of hostility. Just as I thought and no surprise there to see that Greta and her brat of a daughter are still at the hospital. They must have been there all night, they must both be sick in the head wanting to sit beside a dead man". Remarked Grant. "Ug, that is disgusting and so creepy." Said Kansas. "That it is, Son." Replied his father Tomas. "Pity they came back to the Manor at all, it would have been far better still if they had just stayed there. They should have taken a change of clothes with them." Said Lizabeth. "Even bigger pity they do not just pack up and go and never come back. We are almost the family that we want to be, they will only be in the way, they should leave while they still have the chance otherwise they could become victims although the murderer is now dead and they sit with his rotting corpse." Said Tomas. "If that is the case, Tomas, then we will ensure that they go and the sooner the better." Said Lizabeth.

"Well, at least Chadrick is out of the way and –." Started Tomas but Kansas interrupted. "Shush the pair of you, best be quiet now, someone is coming." Lizabeth and Tomas sat in silence looking as though butter would not melt in their mouth while Kansas slipped silently and unseen from the room. "Father, Mother, come sit over here by the fire, it is much warmer. Tea has been ordered and will be here soon." Said Lizabeth smiling. "We heard you three talking so why stop because we are here?"

Asked Lord Mandaten. "Three but there are only the two of us, you must be mistaken father." Said Lizabeth. Kansas, who had snuck out unseen, now returned. "Hello grandparents, that's it, you both go and sit by the nice warm fire. I have just had a walk and it is a bit chilly out now typical November morning with a frost on the ground. Hello Mother, Father you are in the best place by the fire." Lord Mandaten looked around at their false smiles and could feel their caring lies that flowed freely from their mouths. He could almost taste their greed which left his mouth feeling very bitter. "So why did you sneak out as we came in, Kansas? We distinctly heard you talking with your parents." Said Lord Mandaten.

"Me, sneak out? Just as mother said, you must be mistaken Grandfather. I have been in the garden and only just arrived." Said Kansas.

"Do not lie to me, boy, your shoes are dry and I know all your voices well and distinctly heard the three of you talking." Snapped Lord Mandaten. "Calm yourself, Father, you are not well and must be tired as it was only Tomas and myself in here and we were not talking, we sat quietly when you came in." Said Lizabeth. "Maybe quietly when we came in as you have something to hide but all three of you were talking prior to that or are you trying to say that I am going senile?" Asked Lord Mandaten. "Father how could you think such a thing? Why; the very thought chills my bones" Said Lizabeth wping an imaginary tear. "More lies Lizabeth, all lies. I know you all too well and know that you are all just waiting for me to die so that you can get your hands on the estate, it is written all over your lying faces." Said Lord Mandaten.

"Call yourself our father, you have had it in for us for many a year, criticising and telling us how to run our lives. We all know that you always favoured that murderer, well he is gone thank goodness." Spat Grant then he smiled with satifaction.

"Just the sort of statement we have come to expect from you, Grant, maybe you should have heeded our words, then your lives would have been better. Now let me see –." Lord Mandaten glanced around the room and continued. "So I see that those of you that are left are all here hovering and waiting for my demise. Well, so sorry to disappoint you all as I am not going for a while yet. Beats me why some of you left the room only to re-enter behind us, namely you, Kansas, and you, Grant, although you were not included in the conversation with those three, you might as well have stayed." They looked surprised at this remark. "I may be old and to your minds dying but I am no fool and I am most definitely not going senile and still have all my faculties. None of you fool me because I know all your little games and what you are all waiting for. Sorry to disappoint you all but I am not done or ready to go yet, not until I know that Mandaten is in safe hands. To that end, I intend to hang on. I will deal with you first, Grant, your greed explodes from every pore of your body and if you were the next Lord, there would be a sharp downfall and the estate would soon be in ruins and many people's livelihoods gone. You would also steal from the family crypt" Said Lord Mandaten firmly.

"For heaven's sake Father, not all this analysis again. We have already been down that road for you to analyse us, you must have forgotten and –." With a look of steel in his eyes, Lord Mandaten snapped his reply. "Silence, Lizabeth, and listen, I have forgotten nothing from the other day and the fact is that none of you like to hear the truth. I know you so very well, daughter, you with your lavish and very expensive lifestyle, you that live way beyond your means just to look like and to think that you are a cut above the rest. It does not wash, girl, you think that it is the thing to do wearing all your expensive designer clothes and jewellery whilst putting on your false façade! As for throwing fancy parties, well, that all costs a lot of money and that is money that you do not have. All just to impress and look big in the eyes of so-called friends. Friends, indeed they are friends that are onto you and will soon all disappear. You then do something even more lavish in your attempt to keep them and pretend in all the grandeur but you are only fooling yourself as that brings out your falseness. You look down on people who have very little but when it comes to it, they are all better people than you. Now I come to you, Tomas, you are hoping that I will leave the estate to Lizabeth and in so doing you want to bear the name of Lord, it would never happen as you are not a Mandaten but a Kaysten and the Estate name will most definitely will not happen. Do you think I do not know that you are false, and that you cannot continue to give Lizabeth the lavish lifestyle that she craves for and why is that you may ask?" Asked Lord Mandaten. "And you are about to tell me, I expect." Said Tomas wringing his hands and wondering just what this elderly man knew about him so was showing signs of being extremely worried. "Just so Tomas, it is because your business is very close to closing down. I know that your debts spiralled and very soon the bank will foreclose and declare you bankrupt. It is your hope that Lizabeth will get control of the estate and bail you out, well, you can stop hoping as it will never happen. Now to you, Kansas —. Yes you, my boy, you are not left out of this, not in the slightest. All the big talk of you becoming a doctor was just a myth and lies as you had absolutely no intention of seeing it through. Why not? The answer is simple: Because it would involve years of hard work and study and you are far too lazy for that. The money that we sent to pay for your education was gambled and drunk away or spent on a fast car and money-grabbing women. That girl that you were with, now what was her name? Jezebel would have been good as she was using you and when there was no more money, she walked away and that made you very angry. Yes, we know about that. It made you so angry that you wanted to have your revenge on her. Is that why you beat her up so savagely, almost to the point of killing her and putting her for quite a long stay in the hospital with several broken bones combined with deep cuts? Your lies did not fool me one little bit and I know that she was paid off with money that you did not have, paid off to keep quiet and to keep you out of prison. That was a big mistake on her part as she should have let the police prosecute you and let you go to prison and rot, well it may still not be too late for that to happen." "Father, how can you say that about your only remaining loving grandson?" Protested Lizabeth. "Very easily, loving grandson, my foot Lizabeth, he loves himself and because it is the truth. It was our mistake not to stop sending him money sooner. A big mistake but we lived in the hope that he would change but a Leopard does not change its spots and he will get no more. We also know that he attended for one year, at least when he bothered to turn up, and was thrown out of med school before the second year had reached halfway. I will not speak ill of the dead so I will leave them out of this. Now, if Greta were here she would hear me say this to her face. She was a good wife to your brother, Malcolm, and an excellent mother to Lowell even though he was not her blood son." Lord Mandaten paused for a moment to wipe a tear from his eye. "And now, sadly, they are both gone. She never asked for anything. In fact, she was far too good for him and that is a fact. She never complained even though he did not treat her as well as he could have and should have done. He had been told this on many occasions and I am not speaking ill of the dead, before you say anything Grant –." "I was not going to speak, just clearing –." Grant started but he received a long stare from his father. "Well, maybe I was but –." "Another lie just left your lips. All of you here are liars, you just cannot help yourselves. All this caring that you try to lavish on us is filled with falseness and we would need to be blind not to see it. Now, back to Greta who incidentally has been more of a daughter to us than our own and that includes you, Lizabeth." Said Lord Mandaten.

"But Mother, Father, I –." He raised his hand to silence her. "The truth always hits the mark, Lizabeth, and it hurts. That is what you are all getting now, the truth and it is long overdo. You had a taste of it the other day and this is our conclusion and you will hear no more on the subject from this day forward. We had to reinvestigate all of you as Cadiston will be doing but now to continue –. We had four, and it should have been five, grandchildren and now we have only two and one of those is a total waste of space. He is a liar and a cheat, he is a womaniser, a gambler and uses drugs." Kansas looked surprised at this revelation. "Yes Kansas, that is you and the fact is that you are a waste of space. We have heard you talk of freeloaders and you, Daughter, have bred one. You may look, Lizabeth, as you are his mother but Daughter, it is the truth. He is no good and that is down to you. You have mollycoddled him for far too long and at times it has been thrown in your face, especially in one of his temper tantrums, but now he needs to grow up and untie his mother's apron string so that he can stand on his own two feet. There are unpleasant things going on with him and eventually, they will come out. Oh yes Kansas, you may try to skulk and hide in the corner but you are nothing but a small squirt that has no backbone, at least that is what you would have us believe, false because you are much stronger than you display. You put on the act when it suits you and think that we do not know that you are an addicted gambler and have thousands of pounds of debt. You are also a borderline alcoholic and are not opposed to the use of amphetamines. We have seen the jealousy in you of your cousins James and Lowell, who would have made something of themselves, but they have been cruelly taken away from us and that, sadly, just leaves us with you. It is strange that of all the boys it had to be you that is left unharmed, hmm, suspicious. Now to our son, Chadrick —." "Thought he would have come into it somewhere." Interrupted Grant. "And why not, Grant, he is our son and he should be included. Again, it did not go unnoticed, the jealousy that you all had for him, He is a far better son to us than you have ever been Grant." Said Lord Mandaten angrily.

"You mean was Father, as he is now dead." Grant corrected with a smile. "Do not interrupt me, boy! Oh, you may look away with that innocent pout of yours because you know that it is true and of you all, he is the one that I would have named as the next Lord Mandaten." Snarled Lord Mandaten. "As to that, we already knew. He has always been the favourite even though he is not a true son of yours and is not a Mandaten." Said Tomas. "And just how did you know that, Tomas? Ah yes, your favourite trick as a skulker and a sneak hiding in a dark corner and spying on us and during a private conversation, that just about sums you up." Said Lord Mandaten.

"Well, I do not have to stand here and take this abuse, not even from you." Said Tomas. Lord Mandaten wanted to smile but kept control with the stern look on his face. "Feel free to leave our estate and our home any time that you like, Tomas; and never return. There will be nothing here for you and when you go, take your lying, cheating son with you. You may be married to our daughter, whom you married with an ulterior motive that I will soon discover, but there will most definitely be nothing left in the will for you. You all think that we have been hard parents, not so? All we have ever tried to do is to make you all appreciate what you had but all that was abused so now you will have nothing. That will make you forcibly see how the less fortunate are forced to make do. Well, I think that covers it. Now let me see, Grant, Lizabeth, Tomas, and Kansas, you are all here, and sadly all that are left apart from our Greta and Jennifer so that does it. We have managed the Estate for centuries by giving employment to local people we even in the past built our own village for the estate workers to have a good home to live in and yes we did pay them well for all their labours and we treated them all fairly and with their respect that they deserved and as we became richer so they all benefited because without them our welth would not have materialised. Well! I have said sufficient now, unless you have anything to add, my dear?" Lord Mandated directed his gaze to his wife.

"Yes my dear, but only to say how very disappointed we are with all of you. For more years than we care to remember, we have had to stomach all of you with your twisted minds, greed, jealousy, your lies, and your falseness. They have all been a thorn in our sides for far too many years and we should have spoken out much sooner but with each passing year, we lived in the hope that you would wake up to reality and change. Yes, we criticised you for your own good as we have had to watch you all grow into the despicable people that you now are, even our lost family were the same sadly and we would have told them just as we have told you. Although we tried to guide you on the right path, that was not the path that you wanted. We saw how you turned on each other and eventually became undesirable people. Your greed meant that none of you were ever satisfied with what you had even though you were given a far better chance in life than many others. You are no businessman, Tomas, and you would not listen when Chadrick tried to guide you. You lived under a self-imposed illusion, an illusion that you were the best but that was not so. You had a good business but wanted to be too big and that was your downfall, it appeared that it was your plan all along. There are thousands out there who would have gladly traded places with you and been satisfied with what they had and never asked for more but not any of you. It is such a shame that it is the worst of you that remain alive and it makes us sad that we have to say these things but it had to happen. Especially, in the current situation with a murderer slowly killing our family. There is only one child that is the saving grace in our lives, excluding the grandchildren, and he has turned out to be far better than the rest of you put together. I will say no more, shall we leave them to it, my dear?" Said Lady Mandaten.

"Well said, my dear. I feel so much better for getting that weight off my chest. In fact, better than I have felt for some time. Let us leave them to all stew in their own juice. Alfred my boy, we will take tea in the library please as it will taste much better without these –. Well, without them to turn the milk sour." Said Lord Mandaten and they turned and left the family stunned into silence and completely speechless.

Previously, Greta had told Cadiston that Grant would not be happy until he had seen Chadrick laid out cold on the mortuary slab and he, in turn, had explained that the rest of the family should be left thinking that Chad was dead and that he would try to arrange it and it could only happen if Chad was in full agreement. He explained how he would arrange with Charles and Samantha to lay Chad out, so to speak, as though he had passed away. Then Grant would look at him through the viewing window and be satisfied and then at some point, Chad would make a miraculous recovery, 'life after death' is what Jennifer had said. He was not totally coherent but said. "If it will help, then let us do it. There was something that I needed to tell you but for the moment the information evades me but. It will come back Cadiston." "Don't worry about that now, Chad. The priority is to let them all think you are dead. I will get that arranged and very soon. Now, we will leave you with these two lovely ladies as we still have quite a bit of detecting to do and we are now in the month of November, it has taken time but a murder investigation in fact multiple murder investigations take time to complete." Said Cadiston.

"And if my little subterfuge helps I will be waiting here for you to have it implimeted. Well, I am not going anywhere very soon, am I?" That was how their conversation had gone. A few days later and now that time was upon them, Cadiston had liaised and arranged with the hospital and Charles to move Chadrick to the mortuary. Once this move was completed, Greta and Jennifer returned to Mandaten Manor with this information. They had informed Lord and Lady Mandaten of the plan that was about to be put into action before speaking with the remaining family and had Chads parents full support. They prepared themselves and were in tears as they entered the room where the family waited. "You, Lizabeth, went to the hospital and saw Chadrick in his last few hours and now you will have your wish, Grant, he is in the mortuary waiting for you." Said Lord Mandaten. Grant smiled but declined to speak. Greta and Jennifer had been at the hospital a long time and were feeling rather grubby so they turned and went to their room to shower and change.

"Well, that is it then and your visit to the hospital was the 'something important' that you had to do, Lizabeth? You could have told me but anyhow, what did he look like?" Asked Grant. "Like death, he was full of tubes, wires, and things but I was only allowed to peer through the window in the door as I did not have a pass." Said Lizabeth. "No matter, you saw him and now we will take a run to the mortuary just to be sure that he is dead." Greta and Jennifer had showered and changed quickly and had returned to the lounge where the others were talking. "You will need to let them know that you are going." Said Jennifer.

"Silent creeper, Jennifer, we didn't hear you come in, Better make it now, if we must." Said Lizabeth. "What must we do?" Asked Tomas. "You should have been listening, Tomas. We will make the call and be on our way." Said Lizabeth. "It is a bit late in the day now as it is almost six-thirty pm. That means you will need to wait until Thursday morning." Said Greta. "Suits me just fine, how about you, Sis?" Asked Grant. "It will have to suit, will it not?" Lizabeth said sarcastically. Grant shrugged his shoulders. "Suppose so, well he is going nowhere is he so he can wait for us." Greta had given them the number to call so that they could arrange a viewing of Chadrick and at nine a.m., Grant was ringing the mortuary. "Forensic mortuary, Charles Denning speaking." "Chadrick Mandaten's brother, Grant, here. I was given this number to ring as I want to see his dead body." Said Grant. "One moment, please." Said Charles and motioned to Samantha. "Samantha, take over this call, it is them." "Good morning sir, I understand that you would like to arrange a viewing?" Said Samantha. "I would so make it snappy, I want to see him dead and cold on the slab." Said Grant and Samantha thought how abrupt, rude and uncaring that was. "How many family members will there be, sir?" Asked Samantha. "Just two, me and my sister." Said Grant. There was a short delay before Samantha replied. "I have arranged your visit for ten-thirty, if I could have the names, sir?" Said Samantha. "No need for names, we will be there." Said Grant and hung up. "Ten-thirty, Lizabeth." Said Grant.

"What a horrible man, it was all I could do to remain civil." Said Samantha. "Thought you would handle it better than me, I would have lost it with him." Said Charles. "Thanks, Charles." Said Samantha.

Eager to be there, they wasted no time in getting to the mortuary and were instantly taken into the waiting room. Chadrick was then prepared and laid on the slab, "Alright, Chad?" Asked Cadiston. "Alright Cadders, I am dead and ready to go." Said Chad smiling.

"All set, Samantha." She walked slowly to the waiting room and entered. The greeting was blunt and was no more than a grunt. "Hmm –. And about time, we have been here since ten-twenty." She wanted to retaliate but bit back. "Yes, sir, but he is ready now so if you would like to follow me." She said and they walked down the corridor into the viewing room area and were greeted by Cadiston and Mac. "Huh, thought that you two might be here, heavens know why", remarked Grant angrily. "It is to follow procedure." Those were the only words that Mac said. They peered at Chadrick's still form laying on the slab. "Can't we go in there to see him instead of peering at him through this window?" Asked Grant. "Afraid not, sir." Said Mac. "Why not, he is dead?" Asked Grant annoyed. "Cross-contamination, sir," answered Cadiston. "Cross-contamination, what rubbish, he is dead." Snarled Grant.

"Exactly, sir. It is also against procedure as that is a sterile room." Said Cadiston. "Well, we have seen him so when can we have his body to bury?" Asked Grant.

"Not until after the police inquiry has been completed." Answered Samantha Cadiston. "What a load of –. Well, suppose that is down to you, Cadiston. It would have been best if it had all been left to Sergeant Standish, then it would all be over so get a move on, man we are now in November so how long does it take for you to investigate?" Said Grant angrily. Cadiston did not reply but Mac was angry at Grant's attitude and could not remain silent. "Steady down, Grant, there is absolutely no need for that attitude, it will happen all in good time and will take as long as it takes."

"Who are you calling Grant copper it is Mister Mandaten to you?" Snapped Grant in an angry outburst. "It is your name and that means it must be you." Mac had a look of steel. "Hmm." Grant said nothing more. "If you follow me, I will show you out." Said Samantha.

"Well, we have seen him, Lizabeth, and just as I wanted, laid out dead and cold on the mortuary slab." Said Grant.

"Have you nothing to say, Mrs. Kaysten?" Asked Cadiston. "No need, my brother has said it all." Said Lizebeth and they followed Samantha out, wasting no time in driving away from the place where they thought Chadrick would lie until his body was released and he was buried. "Grant is a very nasty person, Ashton. I just do not know how I kept my emotions in check. He is so uncouth but strangely, I found that the sister was a bit demure and for siblings they are so different." Remarked Samantha.

"Tell me about it, Samantha. I saw that from the first meeting. Well, we had better get Chad back to the hospital now that they are gone." Said Cadiston. "Already in hand, the transport was parked at the back, out of sight, and is almost ready to leave." Replied Samantha. "Ok, we will follow it just to make sure he gets back safely and thanks' for that. And thank Charles for us please." Said Cadiston. "That I can do, see you at home, my lovely man." Said Samantha.

"You have it, my precious little woman." Cadiston blew her a kiss, then turned and followed Mac to the car.

At the hospital, they checked that Chad was alright and they were pleased to see that he was sitting up in his bed enjoying a nice cup of tea. Greta and Jennifer had made their way there unobserved and were sitting beside him. As Mac had said, they looked like a perfect happy family group. "Well just look at you –. My, you do look well for a dead man, Chad." Said Cadiston smiling. Chad smiled back. "Well thank you, Cadders. I feel it, still a bit woozy but Doctor Mafidsen tells me it is quite natural after such a long sleep. Now, I cannot remember much about our little subterfuge so did it work?" Asked Chad. "You made the perfect corpse and it is safe to say that it worked. Now, you just rest and get well quickly, we will leave you with these two lovely ladies as we have quite a bit of detecting to do." Said Cadiston. "I want to remember what I need to tell you but it eludes me. I will remember soon as my memory is slowly returning and will be waiting here for you. I am not going anywhere very soon, am I?" Said Chad. Cadiston smiled and waved as they left the room.

Cadiston took the lead and made his way toward the reception. "Hang on, Cadders, the car park is the other way." Said Mac. "True, no time like the present so we will do some investigating.

I would like to have a look at the hospital maternity records for infant births and mortalities. I have a strong suspicion and a theory and if I am correct, the answer is somewhere in that book." Said Cadiston. "You lead the way and I will follow so let's do it, it is on our list anyhow." Said Mac. After checking with the receptionist, who made a quick call, they found their way to the record storage department. The door was open and when they walked in, they were greeted by Damson and Frank who were painstakingly transferring all the paper records onto the computer. "Come in detectives. Now, tell us what year or years you would like to look at and the month of that year." "A long shot but forty-three years ago and thirty years ago. I do not know the exact month." Said Cadiston. "Let me think, where they would be –. Uhm –." Said Frank.

"Fifty-four and sixty-seven." Said Damson. "That was quick, Damson. Shall I fetch them or will you?" Asked Frank. "It's ok Frank, I will go." She walked away down the long line of files and books to search out the records. Thirty minutes had passed before she returned pushing a trolley that contained a mountain of record books. "These are the years that you asked for, Detective. Now, if we had the months, it would make finding the entries that much easier." Said Damson. "A thought Cadders, what about asking Greta? She would probably know." Said Mac.

"Good detective thinking DS, fancy a walk back to ask her while I make a start on January?" Asked Cadiston. "Already on the way." Said Mac.Cadiston sat at the desk and began to look carefully at each entry from the first day of January 1954. His finger carefully followed the names down the page and would not stop until he had found the name Mandaten. "Damson, sorry to disturb you but I just had a thought. Are there separate books or records for the births and infant mortalities for the private maternity ward?" Asked Cadiston. "No, they are all entered within those record books and without the day and month, it will be a very long and heavy trawl through every page." Replied Damson. "You are right there, I have been at it for thirty minutes already and have only covered two pages so far. Mac will be back soon, and then it should be easier to find the entries that we are searching for." Said Cadiston. The instant he went back to his search and right on cue, Mac entered the room.

"Got them Boss" He shouted with excitement. "Malcolm and Grant are 26th April and Chadrick is 16th May so now that we have the dates, hopefully our search will be made easier."

Damson had heard him and walked over to them "Which year is April?"

"That is Malcolm and Grant Mandaten and the birth date was 26th April 1954." Said Mac. She started to search through the record books and ten minutes later she said. "There you are, Detective, April 1954, the 15th to the 30th. That should make what you are looking for easier to find. The other date was 16th May and if I remember correctly, that was thirty years ago so that would be 1967." She again searched through the record books and handed the book to Mac. "There you are, all the entries from 16th to 31st May 1967. I hope that makes it easier for you to find the entries that you are looking for." She said.

"It most certainly will, thank you for your help, Damson. Now, don't let us stop you from getting on with your work, and hopefully we will not need to disturb you again." Said Cadiston.

"Well, detective I am not far away." She smiled at them, then returned to her computer, and seconds later they could hear her typing away. Mac stood for a few seconds watching Damson as her fingers flashed around the keyboard. "She is quick on the keypad Cadders, makes me look like a one-finger wonder." Said Mac. "Me too. Now the records and we will see if my theory is correct." Said Cadiston. "What are we actually looking for then?" Asked Mac. "The first entry we need to find is the correct date, then we check all the entries very carefully to see if they have been altered or defaced in any way. We are primarily looking for the name of Mandaten and any alterations." Explained Cadiston. "Now that makes sense to me so got it in one." Said Mac. The first book was opened and the date of 26/04/54 was found. Cadiston then produced a magnifying glass from his pocket and studied the entry for Lady Florence

Mary Mandaten and did not appear surprised at what he was seeing. "There it is, Mac. To Lady Florence Mary Mandaten at 8.35 a.m., a son, Malcolm, Fitzgerald, Morten delivered by Nurse Midwife Standmore, a son and just as I suspected, not twins. Then added to it as if an after-thought and in a different handwriting, which is very small and squashed in so that it fits the page, a second child at 8.40 a.m., a son, Grant. Now the investigation really begins. We need to check every entry for this day as there is something amiss and the answer is in here, all we need to do is to find it." Said Cadiston. With Cadiston's magnifier at hand, they scoured every entry but it was Mac's keen eye that spotted a discrepancy. "There, have a look at that entry boss. You will see it more clearly with your magnifying glass. One has been scratched out and another written over the top of it." "Well spotted and it does look suspicious." Said Cadiston and he examined it thoroughly with his magnifier. "Now I would like to know what was scratched out before the visible entry was written over it, and that is a job for Jooners and our forensics lab. What has been written over it is to Emily Cartridge at 8.39 a.m., a stillborn son, delivered by Nurse Midwife Standmore. Her again and on the same day and nearly at the same time so how could she be in two places at the same time? This book will need to go to the forensic lab, they will be able to identify what was scratched out and that could be the answer that we want. We will need to find Emily and ask her about the birth. It would do no harm to investigate this Midwife Standmore either." Said Cadiston. "You have your suspicions again, boss, and again, you can see what I am missing." Said Mac.

"It all seems very strange and listening to things that are said can lead to a major discovery. You have heard it said that Grant is nothing like his brother Malcolm, in fact, not like a Mandaten at all. Also at the birth, no one was expecting twins. Well, I think that Lady Mandaten gave birth to one son, namely Malcolm, and not twins. Emily Cartridge gave birth to Grant but she was told that her child was stillborn. It is her child that was the one given to Lady Mandaten, alleging that she had twins. We need to trace Emily and ask questions about the birth of her son and her answer may help to confirm my suspicions." Said Cadiston.

"Your suspicions again, you think that Grant is really the child of Emily Cartridge and is not a Mandaten. Wow, if his Lordship knew that then his own suspicions would be confirmed and that would mean that Grant would not be in the running to be the next Lord. What if Grant already knows and if he does, how would he react to it?" Mac pondered. "I would think quite violently and possibly murderously. Now, let us look at Chad's birth as I believe that is shrouded in mystery also." Said Cadiston. "And you get that from what has been said and your observations." Confirmed Mac. "That is right, so it pays to listen when people are talking, just like Greta did, and then you can pick up all sorts of titbits and that may come in useful. Especially Chad's characteristic of the thick Mandaten skull. Always remember to write them down." Said Cadiston.

"I think that I have the idea that Chadrick is actually a Mandaten child, at least I believe that is in line with your suspicion." Said Mac.

"Well done DS, now we need to find the entry." Said Cadiston. The book was opened then the pages were slowly turned until the entry was found.

"I have it, there it is, to Lady Florence Mary Mandaten at 10.28 p.m., a son and again, an attempt to scratch the entry out but I can just make out a C and that looks like a k and it is written over with the word stillborn. Guess who was the midwife?" Asked Cadiston. "Standmore again?" Asked Mac and Cadiston nodded. "So another book to the forensic lab −." Concluded Mac.

"Correct but we will look for other births on the same day and about that time that have also been altered." Said Cadiston. Again, they scoured the pages until another scratched entry was found.

"To Caterina Dovetson at 10.29 p.m. and again, scratched out and written over. This reads a stillborn son and the midwife was Standmore again." Said Cadiston. "She certainly was busy but this time she had a student nurse with her, a Rachel Huntsmere. We will need to find her and ask questions about that day." Said Cadiston. "So boss, what is your theory on this one or can I have a go to analyse it?" Asked Mac. "Be my guest, DS Macswee." Said Cadiston.

"Right here it goes –. I think that Caterina gave birth to the stillborn son that was shown to Lady Mandaten after her own healthy son, namely Chadrick, hence the C and k that are not completely obliterated, was taken quickly away. Then by some twist of fate, he is given back to Lady Mandaten when she adopted him. That in effect, means the Mandatens had adopted their own child and we know this by his thick skull and a D.N.A. test will confirm his identity. Oh my god! That means that Chadrick is a blood Mandaten and the only remaining male heir to everything. Do you think Grant knows?" Asked Mac. "Looks that way, Mac, hence the reason to keep his recovery a secret." Said cadiston.

"It's been thirty years so do you think that the nurse who was there will remember this one incident amongst all the other births that she must have attended? In fact, Emily and Caterina, the two mothers also." Said Mac. "The memory is a marvellous thing, Mac. People sometimes have a clear memory of an incident that they would rather forget or an incident that they always cling on to but whatever it is, you can be sure that it is stuck there so in answer to your question, yes I do think that they will all re-member." Said Cadiston. "Best we get onto it then, Boss." Said Mac and Cadiston looked at his watch. "Three-fifteen so still enough time." said Cadiston and searched the numbers on his mobile phone. With the touch of a button, the number was ring-ing. "Detective Inspector Richard Folkes." "Hi Richard, Cadders here, need to ask a favour." "Ask away then." Said Richard into the phone.

"I need the addresses for four ladies: Emily Cartridge, Caterina Dovetson, Rachel Huntsmere and I have not got the Christian name of the fourth, the surname is Standmore. Can you look them up or locate them for me please?" Asked Cadiston. "Standmore, thought you were going to say Standish for a second. All part of your investigation I guess. Could be easy, could be hard so give me a little time and I will see what I can come up with. I will get back to you a.s.a.p." Said Richard. "Cheers Richard." The phone went silent. "Now we sit and wait or better still, Cadders, we find out if that midwife, Standmore, and the student nurse, Rachel Huntsmere, still work here." Suggested Mac.

"You are thinking like a detective, Mac." Raised Cadiston. "That comes with from being with you boss, upstairs then to staff records." Said Mac. As they were about to leave, Cadiston turned to Damson and Frank. "I think that we have all we need but we will require to take these two record books to be checked over. They will be returned when we have retrieved the further information that we will need. Many thanks to you both and now we will leave you in peace to do your work." Said Cadiston. A hand was raised in a wave and they left.

Back in the reception area, they approached the desk. "Sally, a question for you. The staff records, where would they be found?" Asked Cadiston."I know that you are policemen but the only person who could authorise for you to view them would be the hospital manager. Can you tell me who you need to know about? I may be able to answer your query and I know that will bypass the correct procedure but it will also save you some valuable time. Now, you have been to see the records of births and infant mortalities so is it a midwife you need to trace?" Asked Sally. "Sorry, Sally, cannot tell you that and procedure must be followed." Replied Cadiston.

"I understand, I will call Mr. Bartholamew for you." She made her call and then reported. "Mr. Bartholamew will see you in ten minutes." "Thanks for that, Sally, we will wait over there." Cadiston pointed as he spoke. They watched as a middle-aged lady dressed in a smart fawn skirt, cream blouse, and matching fawn jacket approached the reception desk. Sally pointed to Cadiston and Mac and she approached. "Good afternoon detectives, my name is Helen. Now, if you like to follow me and I will take to the Office." They both stood and followed silently. It was only a short distance and they were soon entering the outer office. The door to the inner office was open, and sitting behind the desk was an elderly man dressed in a suit and tie. "Good afternoon gentlemen and how can we at the Royal be of assistance to our police force?" He asked. "We need to look at some staff records concerning your midwives. If you can organise that for us it would be much appreciated." Said Cadiston. "I appreciate that you have a job to do, Detective, and if you follow my secretary into the other office, she will find the record that you seek. However, I cannot allow them to be removed and it is all strictly confidential." Said Mr. Bartholamew. "Absolutely, we only need two names." Said Cadiston.

"If you could tell me those names, it may save you a lot of time. Again, in the strictest confidence, whatever is said in here stays within these walls. With the names, my secretary can withdraw the files that you require to look at." Said Mr. Bartholamew. Cadiston thought hard for a moment before answering. "Nurse Midwife Standmore and Student midwife nurse Rachel Huntsmere." Mister Bartholomew looked toward his secretary and five minutes later, she returned with two files. "There you are, Detective, and I will stress again that they cannot leave this office." Said Helen. "There is no need to remove them as we will get all the information we need to know here and now." Cadiston replied. The files were opened and they both looked at them. "Interesting, Midwife Standmore is retired and is aged 94. Write her address down, DS Macswee." The file was passed to Helen and the second one was opened. "Now, that is also interesting DS. Rachel left in 1969 and if my maths is correct that makes her 50 now. Got the address?" Asked Cadiston.

"Got it sir. Strange that, now my suspicion rises –. Only two years after –." Cadiston's glance stopped him from saying anything further. The file was passed back. "Thank you, Helen. Now then, these two record books we do need to take away as there is some investigating to do within them. They will be returned when we have finished." Said Cadiston as he stood and with Mac following, they left the office before the hospital manager had a chance to object. "What now, Boss?" Asked Mac. "It is now 4 p.m. so we will make our way to call on Rachel Huntsmere for starters." Answered Cadiston. "The nurse, she may have some answers for us."

Forty-five minutes later, they were standing on her doorstep. Mac pushed the doorbell and a few minutes passed before the door opened. They were then eyed up and down by a smartly dressed lady. "Can neither of you read my sign? I do not buy anything at the door and I do not want double glazing or a conservatory. If you read, it states No Cold Callers and if you are anything to do with –" Cadiston produced his warrant card. "Not one of them, I am DCI Cadiston, this is Detective Sergeant Macswee. Before we proceed further and as we may possibly have the wrong person, will you answer just one question for us please? Are you Rachel Huntsmere, ex-nurse from the Royal?" Asked Cadiston. Her glance went from Cadiston to Mac, travelling back and forth for a few seconds. "Police you are and that Rachel Huntsmere is me so I guess that you had better come in off the step and ask your questions." She said.

Rachel led them into the lounge where they all sat down. "I think that I know why you are here. It has been a long time comming, thirty years in fact I would say but ask your question, Detective." Said Rachel. "Before I do that, enlighten us please, why do you think that we have called on you to ask questions, especially after it has been a long time, thirty years in fact?" Asked Cadiston. She looked very sheepish and said. "It is to do with a baby incident that took place in 1967." "You have an excellent memory, Mrs. Huntsmere. Now, will you cast your mind back thirty years and tell us all that you can remember about that event." "I told her that it would come out eventually and now it has. I should not have gone along with it but after her threat, I did and now must face the consequences." Said Rachel wiping her eyes. "We will get to what it was in a moment but firstly, what was the threat and why did you go along with it?" Asked Cadiston. "She told me that her family had a long memory and a trail of revenge that went back centuries and if I knew what was good for me, I would do exactly as I was told. I was very frightened. She also said that if I did not comply, it would not be just me that would suffer but my future family would also suffer their wrath and there would be no escape." Explained Rachel. "And that would be Midwife Nurse Standmore?" Asked Cadiston. "You know of her then?" Asked Rachel. "We do. Now, tell us the full story of what happened thirty years ago." Said Cadiston. "It was 16th May 1967 and I have spent the past thirty years looking over my shoulder, expecting this day to come. I remember it well as it is etched in my brain and haunts me like a bad nightmare. Lady Mandaten had a difficult delivery but had given birth to a beautiful healthy little boy and had already told me that his name was going to be Chadrick and that was being written in the book. The instant the child was born, Standmore immediately removed it and replaced it with Caterina Dovetson's child that had been stillborn. The poor young woman had been badly beaten and lost her child then on the way to the hospital in November 1967 she was involved in a tragic motor traffic accident and sadly died with the rest of her family so that played into Standmore's hands as she could question the birth of her child earlier. She told me to take the healthy child to the orphan's ward and label it as Caterina's and leave it there. I questioned this act but she said it was part of her family's centuries-old and ongoing revenge on the Mandatens for what they did to her family back in the days of the English civil war. She said her family name was Standlyhope then but would say no more. I said that was silly as that took place in sixteen-hundred and whatever. It was then that she scowled at me and issued her threat. I had no option but to go along with it." Said Rachel and began to cry. "We are not blaming you, Rachel, so please do not distress yourself. All we have to do is arrive at the truth, correct a thirty-year wrong, and bring the guilty forward to be punished. You are not one of the guilty, Rachel, but an innocent bystander drawn into the revenge trail, you my dear are a witness for the prosecution so please continue –." Said Cadiston.

A few moments later, she had calmed herself sufficiently to continue. "When I returned to Lady Mandaten, she was terribly distressed and cradling the dead child, as was her husband, both believing that she had lost their child. Standmore told them she could fix it as there were a lot of newborn babies that had no parents. She told them that she could get them one without all the red tape of adoption and in their distressed state, they agreed. She then told me to fetch child six for them, which I did but –." She paused and smiled. "Unbeknown to her, I placed the wristlet number six onto the wrist of Lord and Lady Mandaten's own child so, in effect, I corrected a wrong. She checked the wristlet and with a sly grin, she handed the child over. Two days later, they left the hospital taking their own child with them. She again issued the threat, telling me to keep quiet or else. Two years later, I was close to breaking and I could not live the lie any longer. My nursing was over, I left and now work in an office." Said Rachel. "Now let me get this straight, from what you have just said there were no official adoption papers, is that correct?" Asked Cadiston. "It is correct and there are none. There was one other thing that she said and that was that this was the second child that is not Mandaten. It was their plan to wipe them all out. She had placed a second child with them, saying it was a twin." "Grant." Cadiston and Mac said in unison. "But I had nothing to do with that. Where does that leave me now, Detective Cadiston, will I go to prison?" Rachel asked. "You have been a great help and have confirmed my suspicions so just carry on as you normally would. Stick to your same routine and please relax. You have given all the information to us that I had suspected so we will leave you in peace and will contact you again at some point in the future to read and sign your statement once it has been typed up, ok and you will not be going to prison Rachel?" Said Cadiston. "Are you saying that I will not be prosecuted for my part in the wrong doing?" Asked Rachel. "Not at all, my dear woman. You have done nothing wrong and have absolutely nothing to worry about." Said Cadiston. "You righted a wrong, Rachel, and that is highly commendable." Said Cadiston in reply. "Ok, I will wait to hear from you in due course." Replied Rachel as they all stood and walked to the door. "We will be in touch and thank you." Said Cadiston.

They heard the door close behind them as they walked to the car, Mac could not suppress himself. "You are right again,

Cadders. You amaze me how you do it, all of it just as you had suspected. The Mandatens have been bringing up their own son for the past thirty years. Well, that confirms Chad is a true blood Mandaten and the DNA confirmation will seal it, Rachel may have been under Standmore's threat but she found a way around it so well done to her. I don't know how you do it but once again, your suspicions are spot on. (Mac repeated.) Now I see where the centuries worth of revenge trail comes in and the desire to wipe out the Mandaten family name. So now we know that Grant is not Mandaten and Chad is so do we check out –." He flipped the pages in his notebook. "Emily Cartridge?" Asked Mac. "Well done Rachel indeed, Mac. As you say, Chad is a true blood Mandaten and the final D.N.A. will close that circle. Now, as for Grant –. That is a different story but as –." At that moment, his phone rang. "Speak to me, Richard." Said Cadiston into the phone. "Got that information you wanted. Caterina Dovetson is sadly deceased, she was killed in a car crash with all her family back in October 1967 they were on the way to the hospital after she had been badly beaten, as you needed to know about her I pulled the file and it was investigated by Standish, so was case closed and other prosecution took place as they were hit by another vehicle. Emily Cartridge lives at 26 Jonquel Close, Numbenton. That is a little village about thirty minutes away on the B1130. Then Rachel Huntsmere –." "We found her address from a hospital file already and Standmore's also but not Emily so thanks, Richard. I owe you two now." Said Cadiston. "No problem and who is counting? Glad to be of help and maybe I will need your help at some time in the future as I am bogged down with these robberies." Said Richard. "And you will have it." Said Cadiston and again, the phone went silent. "Fancy a run out to Numbenton, Mac?" He asked. "Thought you would never ask." Said Mac smiling, and they both chuckled as they made their way to the car.

Thirty-five minutes later, they were ringing the doorbell of number 26 Jonquel Close. "Yes, what do you want?" Said a young man abruptly. With their warrant cards on display, they introduced themselves. "DCI Cadiston." "Detective Sergeant Macswee." Said Mac. "Ma! Ma, best you get here bloody quick, it's a couple of blasted coppers at the door." The boy stepped back, making way for a smartly dressed lady in her late sixties. "Police?" Again they held up their warrant cards and she continued. "Yes, how can we help you? And please forgive my son for being so rude and abrupt." "Not a problem. First question is to be sure that we are speaking to the correct person, are you the Emily Cartridge that gave birth to a child, a boy some 43 years ago at the Royal hospital maternity ward?" Asked Cadiston. "Yes, that would be me and to this day, my husband and I still wonder what happened to our child. We both heard him cry but he was taken away by the midwife, saying that he was stillborn, dead at birth but we have always thought different, a mother knows those things." She said.

"Thank you and we appreciate just how painful it must be for you to talk about it but we have reason to believe that your son lives." Said Cadiston. "He lives? I knew it! Gerald, get here quick." Within a few seconds, her husband was at her side. "He lives! Our son lives and no matter what he has turned out like or what he has done, we want him back. He has a brother who you just met and if he is anything like him, then he will have similar nasty characteristics." Emily was squealing with delight. "At this point, we cannot be a hundred percent certain but if you could provide us with a D.N.A. sample, then we will be able to compare them. It will take a few days to complete the investigation but at least there will be a firm answer at the end of it." Said Cadiston. "Well best you come in and do whatever you need to do. We have waited for an answer for 43 years, my dear, so another few days will not matter. We will provide the D.N.A. and leave it to you and your sergeant, DCI Cadiston." Said Emily. "DS Macswee, D.N.A. kit." Said Cadiston but Mac was already at the car and moments later, returned. "Quick of the mark, Mac, well done!" Mac took his samples, and when they were secured, Gerald said. "I will show you out." As they left, Mac turned and said. "We will be in touch, Mr. Cartridge, you can rest assured of that." They heard the door close behind them and were quickly in their car. The engine was started and they were heading for the station. "That is another day gone, Boss. What is on the agenda for Friday morning? Now let me see, Bonnie and child died on Monday, 22nd September, so from then to now is fifty days because now it is November the 8th and good progress is being made, just a shame it could not have been done quicker." Observed Mac.

"Progress yes Mac but what we need are arrests. There are so many loose ends to be tied up that to arrest one will pre-warn another and we do not want that. We want them all; Mac. Now Friday we will keep Grant happy for a while thinking that Chad is dead and if he is guilty of the crime, then we will lull him into a false sense of security" Said Cadiston. "Then we spring it on him with Chad's 'life after death' and boy-oh-boy, I do not want miss the expression on his face when Chad walks in" Said Mac. "And you will be right there by my side when it happens but first job on Friday morning will be to pay a visit to ex-midwife, Standmore, and see what she comes up with." Said Cadiston. "Sounds good to me, Boss, so where shall we meet?" Asked Mac. "Here at the station will be ok." Said Cadiston. "Night then." Said Mac. "Night Mac." Said Cadiston and they went their separate ways.

Thursday evening passed quietly at Mandaten Manor with most of its occupants feeling very smug but beneath the surface, there was an eruption waiting to happen. Friday morning the 9th of November at breakfast, Greta and Jennifer had to put up with the sibling's sly remarks but the second their taxi arrived, they left to looks of surprise from Lizabeth and Grant. "Now where do you think they are off to this early in the day? Surely they are not going to the mortuary to sit with him –." Said Lizabeth.

"Gross but who gives a stuff, Lizabeth, at least they are out of our hair." Said Grant. "For a while they are but the trouble is that they will be back unless we can somehow manipulate things to be rid of them." Said Lizabeth.

"Don't know how we can, Sister. For the moment, we will just have to sit back and let it ride its course." Said Grant. "True but they will eventually be gone and then –. Well, never mind that." Said Lizabeth. Grant looked sideways at that last remark by his sister, wondering what she had meant. He placed his hand onto the gun that nestled in its holster beneath his shirt. Friday morning, 9th of November saw Cadiston waiting in the office and surprisingly, Mac was late. To fill time, Cadiston was reading through his notebook again. He looked up to the sound of the door opening and was surprised to see that Mac had only just turned up but when he arrived, he was very apologetic. "Morning Boss, I am so sorry to be this late. It took longer than I thought but I think you will like what I have. I am so sorry to be late without telling you first but I had a hunch and acted on it." "Morning Mac and apology accepted. You say you are late in and I haven't been watching the clock so what time is it?" Asked Cadiston. "Almost ten. I had too much going through my head last night and couldn't sleep very well so I decided to check my hunch and suspicion out and got a result." Said Mac at such a speed it was hard to follow. "A hunch you say, ok tell me what it was that you checked on –." Said Cadiston.

"In training, we had a case to look at that was never solved. It was a shooting and it bugged me all night. It just rattled around in my brain. The victim was named Granchister and as I kept thinking about it, it suddenly came to me and I remembered the other name. Should have come to me a lot sooner as it is one that we know very well and that is Mandaten and it is to do with Grant. He really bugs me, Cadders, although he may be directly innocent of Bonnie's death –. I just know that he is guilty of something, it is written all over his face. I read my notebook and could not get what Greta told us out of my head and that was that Grant has a handgun so I went to records and did some digging. Every time we see him, my skin crawls. He acts very sheepishly which gives the impression that he is hiding something. However, I first went to records to check it out, and after a search the file was found. You probably know that Bonnie was his second wife but what I found out is that his first wife had the maiden name of Granchister and was found murdered.

In fact, shot three times in a motel room. Grant was questioned but had a perfect alibi confirmed by the woman he was supposed to be with at that time and surprisingly, his parents. According to his statement, he was out with this girl, a Jonnett Muskaday, and after visiting two restaurants she took him home and said that he was drunk. He continued to drink until he was put to bed. When questioned, his parents had to confirm that he was with this girl who brought him home supposedly drunk and they had to put him to bed. According to the time element, he was in bed drunk when the shooting occurred and that, in effect, gave him a double alibi. I got to thinking seriously, he has a handgun and she was shot, there are secret passages in the manor that he knows about and after everything else that Olito and me found out about him I got suspicious." Said Mac. "That is excellent work, DS Macswee! To follow that up, we need to find and re-question her and you have saved me the job as you have already got records to find the file for us. Is there any visual evidence?" Asked Cadiston. "Already thought of that. While I was down in records and after pulling the case file, we checked for any visual evidence linked to the case. Now that was a moment and, lo and behold, here it is −." He held the bag containing three lead slugs. "What is more, we have the bullets that she was shot with and our firearms said that they were probably 38 calibre. It is a long shot but he has a handgun at home and if I am correct, that is against the law. I also thought that if we find the gun and it is his then firearms ballistics can match the bullets and then we have found her killer, some five years after her murder. So Boss, what do you think?" Asked Mac.

Cadiston smiled. "What do I think, Mac? Excellent work and all carried out on your own initiative. I told you I would make a detective of you! Now think back to the hospital and what Greta told us." Said Cadiston.

"It may sound strange but being with you seems to give me an edge. The piece of information she gave us −. Grant has a pistol and it is snubnose 38 caliber. His first wife was murdered with a 38. He used that girl, Jonnett Muskaday, to give him an alibi but we have been told so many lies that could turn out to be another one. To follow that up, we need to find her and put her under some strong questioning. Now Boss, what were you doing before I rudely interrupted?" Asked Mac. "I was going through my notebook and bringing it up to date. I have recorded all the Mandaten incidents that I have attended and was reading it through to see if there was a piece of evidence there that would help to catch us a killer or killers." Said Cadiston. "Well, I am here now so we can go through it together or continue with the visit to Mrs. Standmore, if that is alright with you." Said Mac. "The book is going nowhere Mac but if she got wind of our visit to the hospital she will go into hiding to avoid the questions that we have, so the Standmore visit it is. Without delay, we need to start checking on the location of our Jonnett Muskaday. I will ask Richard if he can do that for us." Said Cadiston. "Well, Boss, from this latest piece of information I feel that we may be close to closing an unexpected cold case, that of Geraldine Mandaten Granchister but to get the gun from him for our firearms to check it out is something else and carries a major risk. Now, I will fetch the car while you see Richard and then we are off to visit Mrs. Standmore." Said Mac.

"Good detective work Mac, let's go." Said Cadiston. Mac needed no second telling and disappeared to return a few minutes later. "The car is ready, Cadders, so to Standmore's now unless you have changed your mind and you have another plan?" Said Mac.

"We still have a mountain to climb and I haven't heard all the information that you and Olito collected on Grant apart from what you have just told me. We will stick to the original visit to Standmore first and let us see where that path leads." Said Cadiston. The gear was selected and after a forty-minute drive, they were walking up the path and wringing the doorbell. A young woman, who looked very familiar to Cadiston, answered the door. "Good morning, could we speak to Mrs. Martha Standmore please?" Asked Cadiston.

Chapter Sixteen

The Investigation Takes Shape

"That would be my grandmother so what do you want of her and I am not buying anything –." Said the young lady. Their warrant cards were shown and with the introductions made, Cadiston begun. "We are not selling but are seeking the Mrs. Martha Standmore who was a midwife at the Royal back in the fifties onward and you are too young to be her." "Like I said, that would have been my grandmother but –." She paused and smiled before continuing. "You are a bit late to speak with her as she passed away two days ago, what did you want her for?" "And is your grandfather still alive?" Asked Cadiston. "No. He passed four years ago. What did you want Grandmother for?" She asked again. "And is your mother at home?" Asked Cadiston.

"No, it is Friday morning and she is not my mother but my mother-in-law and she is at work. Anyhow, what is with all these questions?" She was starting to get annoyed. Mac now got a question in. "Your mother-in-law is at work, right, and that I believe is at the Royal in the operating theatre?" Her smile now disappeared and was replaced with a worried frown. "Yes, but what does that have to do with anything? How did you know that and what of it? You still haven't answered my question." She now sounded upset. "So, you are married to the grandson of Martha Standmore and his name is?" Asked Cadiston. "Who the hell is it there bothering us, Heather? Just get rid of whoever it is quick and get back in here as we have work to do to complete the next plan to be rid of them all!" Said a male voice from inside. "Hush up you fool, it is the police and I have repeatedly told you it has nothing to do with me and that I want no part of it!" Said Heather. "Police? Stupid woman, why the hell didn't you say so?" Said the man. "Just did." Said Heather.

Cadiston raised his voice so that the man inside could hear him clearly. "We would like to ask you a few questions, sir. We can do it here or at the station, it is entirely up to you."

They heard the back door slam shut and without thinking, Mac ran to the rear of the house and arrived just in time to see two men and a boy jump into a car and drive straight at him. Luckily for him, he had quick reflexes and he was able to avoid being struck, making them think they had gotten a clean getaway. They were wrong. Mac's mind was as sharp as a razor and even though he had almost been run down, he still managed to get the registration number written down. When he returned to the front, Cadiston saw his dishevelled state. "Are you alright, Mac?" "Fine thanks, the swine tried to run me down and almost succeeded but I still got their registration number. I will contact traffic and when the reg is circulated, they will not get very far. There were two men and a young boy in the car. The question is, why did they run?" Said Mac and got out his phone.

"That is a good question, Mac." Cadiston looked hard at the young woman in front of him, then it clicked. "Now I recognise you, of course, you and your son were at the Black Powder Gun Show held at the Manor and after all the talk about how your husband had died just a few days before and you attended it in his memory, Those were all lies. Your husband is still alive and has just attempted to evade us by running my sergeant down. I recall that you left just prior to the explosion as if you knew what was about to happen."

She turned and tried to slam the door shut but Mac's foot was in it and as she tried to run, she tripped and fell. Cadiston was there in a flash and as he picked her up from the floor, he cuffed and cautioned her.

"Mrs. Heather Standmore, I am arresting you under suspicion of being an accessory in a plot to commit murder. You do not need to say anything but anything that you do say will be taken down and used as evidence." Said Cadiston. She grinned as though she could not care less and said one word. "Knickers." And then she laughed. After she was placed in the car, they secured the property and made a phone call. Moments later, a team of forensic officers were in attendance. Mac had acted quickly and with the registration number, make and model of the car circulated, the vehicle chase was on. Back at the station, Cadiston and Mac took their prisoner to the interview room.

"For the purpose of the recording, the time is 11:25 a.m and present are DCI Cadiston, Detective Sergeant Macswee and ..." Cadiston pointed to the mic and she grinned then said. "Gloria Standmore and I have nothing to say."

"The person that called out to you said Heather. Now which is it, Heather or Gloria?" Asked Cadiston. "I get called both, it depends who is talking to me." She said. "As you have stated Gloria on the interview tape, that is the name we shall use. Also present is WPC Rendham. Now Gloria, tell us who was in the house with you?" Asked Cadiston. She sat quietly staring at the celling and then said. "I have nothing to say." "That is entirely up to you but you should understand that you are in serious trouble and it will not help your defence if you withhold information that later becomes known. Now shall we start again? Where do you work, Gloria?" Said Cadiston. "I suppose you will find the answers to your questions even if I don't tell you as you are detectives." She said. "You can be sure of that." Replied Cadiston.

"Alright then, I have nothing to lose and I do not want to be accused of a crime that I did not commit. I have told them repeatedly that I wanted no part of their scheme but they drew my son and myself in. You ask where I work, at the hospital. I am a nurse there." She said. "You told us that your mother-in-law works there. So you also work at the hospital? In which department do you work?" Asked Cadiston. "I am an anaesthetist's assistant but what has that to do with anything?" She asked. "We will ask the questions and all you have to do is answer them. Now, who were the two men and the young boy in the house with you?" Continued Cadiston. "My brother-in-law, my husband, and my son." She answered. "And their names?" Asked Cadiston. "All of them are Mister Standmore, of course." She said. "First names, please?" Cadiston looked at her. "Suppose there is no harm in telling you as you will find out anyhow. Tomas, Bernard, and Roger." She said looking at her hands.

"And Tomas also uses another name doesn't he Gloria?" Asked Cadiston.

"Does he?" She asked. "You know that he does so what is that name?" Pressed Cadiston. "You are the detectives, you tell me." She said smugly.

"It will not help your case if you try to get smart with us, we know a lot more than you may think we do. That is how we turned up on your doorstep?" Said Mac. She looked at him and smiled. "I talk to the chief, not the little Indian."

Mac sat back. "Talk to me then, Gloria." Said Cadiston. "Alright DCI Cadiston. Yes Cadiston, Harry mentioned you. Ok, now you tell me a name and I will say if it is right, then I will not be telling, will I only confirming it and that is not grassing someone up is it?" She said. "Kaysten and Grenville." Cadiston said. She looked surprised at hearing thiese names and nodded in recognition.

"I need to hear you say the answer for the taped record of this interview." Said Cadiston. "Yes, he used the name Grenville." Said Gloria. "Next name, Kaysten?" Cadiston looked at her. "You really are a detective Cadiston. There is something about you −. Before you say anything for the tape, yes he is currently using the name Kaysten and married Lizabeth Mandaten as part of their plan to get on the inside, that suit you?" Said Gloria. "And that plan involves a centuries-old trail of revenge and the total annihilation of the Mandaten family?" Asked Cadiston. "Wow, you are a clever detective, Cadiston. I want it known that I quite categorically wanted no part of that and told them repeatedly to keep my son and myself out of their family vendetta. The Mandatens have been very good to my family so we have had no hand in anything that has happened." Said Gloria."And your family name was Mulbatern which is why you wanted no part, isn't it?" Asked Cadiston. "Harry was right about you, you have some sort of inbuilt sixth sense." She said.

"Alright Gloria, we are almost done, for the time being. Just before you go, was Tomas one of those that ran from the house, and was it to avoid detection?" Asked Cadiston. "Yes." Answered Gloria. "Working as an anaesthetist's assistant and with your mother-in-law also in the operating theatre, you must have access to certain drugs like Ketamine. Why did you supply this to your brother-in-law?" Asked Cadiston. "I did not supply it to him but to my sister." She said. "And that was Katrine who works at Mandaten Manor." Cadiston said. "I must say that you already appear to have all the answers. Gee Cadiston, you are something else." She said. "Never mind me, Gloria, just continue with your answers please." Said Cadiston. "I did not take it, it was my mother-in-law that took it and gave it to me for her and Katrine said it was for a sick animal." Said Gloria. "And you believed her?" Remarked Mac. "You know that it was not used for that purpose but to commit a murder and that makes you an accessory." Said Cadiston. "No, no, no! That cannot be right, she reassured me that it was for a sick animal to put it out of it's misery for our parents. She told me later that they had put the animal out of its pain and she would bring the rest back to me tomorrow. I am not an accessory to anything. I gave her the Ketamine, that much is true but don't know anything about it being used in a murder. I was a fool to give her the drug, I know that but she assured me it was for a sick animal and it was used there. Our parents run an animal shelter and charity shop." Said Gloria.

Cadiston and Mac looked at each other as they both recognised the mention of this.

She then continued. "I wanted no part in their plotting as I have nothing against the Mandaten family and neither do any of my family. We all owe them a lot of gratitude but they forced me to go to the show and gave my son his speech to make. We could not get away from carrying it out as we were being watched and they had threatened to destroy the animal rescue farm and kill my parents if I didn't do it. As you noticed, we left before the explosion, that is all I know." "Do you know, Gloria, I am almost inclined to believe you." Remarked Mac. "Now tell us, what is your mother-in-law's full name?" Asked Cadiston. "Mrs. Margery Standmore." Said Gloria. "You know what to do now,

DS Macswee." Said Cadiston. "Already in mind, Boss." Said Mac and left the interview room. The interview was temporally suspended. Ten minutes later, he was sitting beside Cadiston again. "In hand and two officers are on their way." Said Mac, and the tape was turned back on. "Have you ever made a tasteless peanut solution?" Asked Cadiston. "Too technical for me, I would not have the know-how. Besides, why would I want or need such a thing?" Asked Gloria. "What is your sister's name, the one you gave the Ketamine to?" Asked Cadiston. "I reckon that you already know the answer to that as you are the detective. I am giving nothing away. It is Katrine, my sister's name is Katrine and you have already told me that." She replied. "Just wanted it confirmed by you and it is as I suspected. Now it may surprise you to hear that we know your family history." Said Cadiston. Gloria looked astonished. "We know that your family members are descendants of the Duke of Trevane who fell on hard times and lost all the family fortune, basically leaving them as paupers. The family was known and friends of the Mandatens and it is them that helped to set your parents up in their charity for animals. This we already know and that is why you owe them a great deal. Now, what is the relationship between you and the ex-Sergeant Standish?" Asked Cadiston.

Gloria looked surprised at first, then sheepish and looked away from them. "He is an uncle of theirs and I did not like him from the moment that I first met him. I was meant to be out to enable them to talk in private but I returned home early and was forced to hide so they did not know that I was there. From what I overheard them say, it was that they would commit the murders and he would then close all the cases quickly as tragic accidents, just as he had done with Baron Lasseroie Mandaten and his family." She said. With that, Cadiston terminated the interview.

"That will be all for now and thank you. We shall continue this interview later but the information that you have given us will be a great help and sufficient to continue our investigation. Until we have evidence to the contrary –. I am sorry but we are holding you as an accessory to murder as you supplied the drug

Ketamine. What you have told us will help your case. The time is now 14:15 p.m. and the interview with Mrs. Gloria Standmore is suspended." Said Cadiston and the tape was switched off.

"It will help your case if you are truthful and tell us correctly the answers to our questions. Although you gave the drug to your sister, if you are innocent of a major crime, it will most definitely be to your advantage to cooperate with us. We are holding you as an accessory. Although if you are telling the truth, an unknowing one. Sergeant and WPC Rendham, would you take the prisoner to the holding cells please?" Requested Cadiston. "Right away, sir." Said WPC Rendham.

Fifteen minutes later, Mac was back in the interview room. "All secure, Francis has gone to fetch Gloria some tea. Now what do you make of that then, Cadders? Was it what you suspected?" Asked Mac. "Not completely Mac, there were a few twists that came to light but near enough. Tomas Kaysten is an alias and her brother-in-law and that means that he is born a Standmore which I believe to be a variation of Standish. The family name before was Standlyhope before the vendetta began and it is my belief that they changed the name to hide the identity of what remained of the family. He is also using the false name of Grenville when it suits him. I did know that he was false but did not know that he is a full-blood Standmore. I had my suspicions about his validity so there is one link. Katrine is Gloria's sister, that is two links but –." "There is that but again." Said Mac and Cadiston continued. "My suspicions tell me that they are not involved directly in any of the murders, they have been inadvertently drawn in unknowingly. Her association with Grant, however, tells me that he could be involved in the murder of Sadie and she had supplied the drug Ketamine. I suspected Tomas of some dastardly deed but not Katrine. But remember what I told you a while ago?" Asked Cadiston. "Looks can be deceiving." Said Mac. "Exactly, I had her taped as an accomplice but there may be more to that young woman than meets the eye. With that in mind, it throws a new light on Sadie's and Demmie's murder and also on Chad's attack. Now let's get back to the office, then you can give me the information that you and Olito collected about Grant. From all accounts, you and Olito had a busy time." Said Cadiston. They continued to talk as they made their way from the interview room.

"You could say that, Cadders. It took us a fair way but hopefully, I have all the answers that you wanted and some of your suspicions confirmed." Said Mac.

"Ok, we have our drinks so take a seat and let's have it. Sit here and spill, Mac." Said Cadiston.

"Firstly, I must say that it was a good idea to send Olito with me and I must admit that she was a big help. Although we did not expect any success, we started with the local swimming pools and fitness clubs. No joy there so found a list of private tutors in our area but none of them had tutored him. They were very helpful and gave us some more names and places to try and so it went on. Anyhow to cut a long story short, we eventually ended up ninety-four miles away in a small out-of-the-way village that Olito found called Twiterhampton, apparently named after a rare bird was seen by a lot of twitches' in the late eighteen-hundreds. But back to the subject and I think we have what you want. We went first to see a Mister Frewser and when he saw the photograph of Grant, he was instantly recognised him but not as Grant Mandaten but as a Mr. Grant Gutheroads. He had, as you suspected, used a different name to hide his identity. He had been taking swimming lessons with a Miss Samosat a retired Olympic champion and she will be prepared to stand up in court and testify to it that Grant Gutheroads is Grant Mandaten and she will swear to his identity. He had running lessons with Mister Frewser and by the end of his training, he could run a half marathon at a pace of 6.24 minutes a mile and much quicker over a shorter distance. He would also be prepared to testify that the photograph is that of Mr. Gutheroads who we know is really Grant Mandaten. That is very fast running and Miss Samosat said that to swim a mile was like a walk in the park for Grant. One more thing, he paid for everything by cash so there are no card transactions to be traced for their payments but we were not going to give up there. Olito came up with the idea that he had to stay somewhere local and with that in mind, we did a bit of investigating. Because he used cash in all his transactions, we also had a word with his bank and that is what caused the delay in getting back but that is not of interest now. By the look on your face, I see a question coming from you, possibly how did I know which bank he was with?" Cadiston just nodded so Mac Continued. "Answer is Barclay's as I was able to see the banks insignia because I saw his debit card sticking just far enough out of his wallet that lay on the table in the lounge. I knew it was his because when he saw me looking at it, he picked it up rather quickly and put it into his pocket." "Well spotted, Mac, and that is detective in you coming out, excellent work!" Said Cadiston.

"Again, that comes from being with you. Anyhow, the bank was reluctant at first and I think that I would probably have given up but after Olito had explained that it was in connection with and an extremely important aspect of a case, and that we could get a court injunction which could even see the bank closed for a day while we investigated, he succumbed to the pressure. Without giving away any personal information, the manager agreed to give us a list of all his transactions. He had withdrawn a substantial amount of seven hundred pounds which would cover the cost of his two fees but not his accommodation. That is where he slipped up, and again, down to Olito who found out that he was staying at the Foxborough Hotel. He used his card to pay the bill which was quite substantial on several different occasions and what is more, he was never there alone. He had the most expensive suite in the hotel and without fail, he was always accompanied by a very attractive young lady who he said was his wife. We knew for a fact that it was not, it was not Demmie either. They heard him call her Christina and they gave us a description of her and that is as follows, she had lovely auburn hair –."

Cadiston raised his hand and interrupted. "Hazel eyes, lovely figure and a complexion as smooth as silk?" "What are you a mind reader or a fly on the wall?" Asked Mac. "Neither Mac but we have seen and spoken to this young lady and I have come across her again while you were on your travels. We first set eyes on her at Mandaten Manor. While you were searching for this information about Grant, I was not idle. I found out that she had paid a visit to the Museum Archive of Building Plans using the name Hurdshaw. Tomas was also there and used the name of Grenville. Suspicions rise, Mac. Why were they there finding out about the secret passageways?" Asked Cadiston.

"Easy access to and from the crime scenes." Said Mac. "Exactly Mac but if they are working together, why did it need them both to check out the secret passages as they are brother and sister-in-law?" Said Cadiston. "Crosswires or maybe to lay a false trail so if one was caught the other would get away undetected?" Offered Mac. "Could be and a good thought but I think that Katrine was finding out for Grant and that had nothing to do with Tomas but to give them free and secret communication with each other and another reason for Grant that I believe Katrine was not aware of." Said Cadiston. "Ah, shall we say a link for bedtime," "very possible Mac." Answered Cadiston. "Now please continue with your investigation knowledge." Said Cadiston. "There you have it, Cadders, Grant is an excellent swimmer and runner and that puts him in the frame for Malcolm and Sadie as a possible murderer." Said Mac.

"Good work Mac and I believe his accomplice is –." He pointed at Mac. "You know her name, Mac, think on it and tell me." Asked Cadiston. "I know her name you say? Hmm, not Demmie –. Thinking Cadders, thinking, ah of course, he told me her name because she was his alibi when Chad was attacked and Demmie was murdered, didn't he? It has to be Katrine but in the Foxborough hotel, he always called her Christina." Said Mac. "Got it in one." Replied Cadiston.

"To be fare, I cannot take all the credit as this was a joint venture and it was Olito that discovered that there was another hotel, the Wilborough not as high class as the Foxborough where he always took Katrine. That one was where he used to take Demmie and in both cases, they were booked in as Mr. and Mrs. G B Mandaten so again, a possible slip up because he left a trail. We know it is them at the Wilborough as it was confirmed with the photographs you gave me of him and her. There again he slipped up because he always paid with his bank card so although he used an alias for his running and swimming to cover his activity and lay a false trail, he used his own name for the hotels." Said Mac. "Excellent work so congratulations to you both! I do believe that he used Demmie for his own ends to get one over on Chad. That much of his story I do believe but she had served her purpose and he was ready to cast her aside because she had completed her task. She was not prepared to let that happen and was probably putting pressure on him to get a divorce so, I think that he would have killed her to keep her quiet because he feared that after rejection she would disclose what he had been up to. Maybe the little green monster took hold and that someone beat him to it or on the other hand, was that his pre-planned?" Suggested Cadiston.

"You mean that Katrine could have murdered Demmie?" Asked Mac. "A strong possibility Mac, jealousy can have strong effects and be a major factor. Remember, you must never judge a book by its cover. Now all we need is the solid evidence to be absolutely sure that we arrest the right person for the crime that they committed. We must be sure who murdered Kevin, Sadie, Sammie, Walter, Gloria, James, Lowell, Demmie, and Malcolm. Not singly but with help but something tells me it is not Katrine but, – she is not out of the running yet." Said Cadiston.

"That is quite a list and if Katrine did shoot Demmie then, as with all the others, blood, fingerprints, and D.N.A. will give us the answers. We will soon have all the matches made and with other evidence, we will have them." Said Mac smiling.

"Just as we would have had Demmie, Mac, if she had not been murdered. As I have always said, we are dealing with more than one killer. I think that they all wanted the same outcome and, unknowingly, have been working together and it is not all over yet, not until they are all dead that is those who stand in the way. We have a list of suspects: Tomas, Kansas, Lizabeth, Grant, Greta, Katrine and Chad for at this point in our investigation, no one can be deemed innocent. We are moving forward, Mac, and will soon have enough real visual evidence to make our arrests." Said Cadiston.

"Not quite finished with the information yet, Boss. After finding out about Grant's first wife, I did some more digging and after a series of phone calls and a visit, I found out that Grant belongs to a backstreet pistol club by the name of Gutheroads. It is a legal one and is licensed but keeps its identity a secret. The only way in is by recommendation. He used to be a regular and was one of the best marksmen but he has not been for some time. In fact, since shortly after his first wife was found shot dead. We delved further and the gun that he used and owned at the club was a snubnosed 38 calibre. It should remain there, secured under lock and key, and guess what, he took it away." Said Mac.

"Excellent work Mac, and you did all that on your own back again and following your own hunch, that is the detective in you Mac." praised Cadiston. "I keep telling you, Cadders, it is being with you. It somehow just seems to give me that additional edge." Replied Mac. "Well whatever it is, it is a job well done and everything that you and Olito have found out is all that we can follow up on. We are gathering more and more information and evidence and coupled with my own suspicions we are making real headway and when our teams return we will have a lot more evidence and once it has all been collated we can move in and make our arrests Mac. Now when it comes to the gun, the question is has he got it hidden or does he carry it with him? We can be certain that he still has it because of what Greta told us but to prove that he murdered his first wife, we need it to confirm that the slugs removed from her body came from that weapon. Now back to the present and with the case scenario compiled, they can be coordinated with the evidence that we have gained this far. We have a pretty good idea of what their motive is, in fact, a compilation of motives. Forensics have given us some real evidence, the means, and how it was done which matches our suspicions. So Mac, we are well on our way and can begin to move in and begin to put a bit of pressure on. I have said we are dealing with more than one murderer and they will all have their own agenda to archive their aim and, unbeknown to any of them, they are actually working together until one succumbs to the other so that is what we are up against and to that end, we have a fight on our hands." Stated Cadiston.

"So, you found out that it was Tomas who used the name Grenville and Katrine who used the name Hurdshaw. Why would either of them need to know all about the secret passages if it were not to access and retreat from the murder scene unobserved? Then there is Grant who used the false name of Gutheroads to do his training and so the plot thickens and with each piece of evidence it gets deeper, Cadders. As you said, we are not dealing with one or two killers here but multiple ones it would seem I agree with your thought that they are not actually working together but unknowingly are helping each other to achieve their aims. We have an excellent example of that with the peanut solution and very soon now we will know who that was." Said Mac. "That is a fact, Mac, but there may be another reason for Katrine and Grant wanting to know the location of the secret passages and I have a thought on that." Said Cadiston. "Another reason?" Asked Mac. "Yes but not a sinister one, we said it before my friend, it is to visit each other unobserved and spend the night in the same bed, but Grant would need to be certain that Demmie would not put in an apperance." Said Cadiston. "Of course, Katrine to Grant's bedroom and vice versa hence the white and cobwebs on his jacket." Said Mac. "Got it, Mac. One thing is a bit strange −. That after all these years of living in the Manor, they have only recently found out about all the secret passageways. Any ideas on that, Mac?" Asked Cadiston. "Maybe because before Grant and Katrine only required to know access to each other, but now as part of the master plan to end the Mandaten line." Suggested Mac. "You could be right and that is my thought. Now, they will all have their own motives and agenda to obtain what they desire and as I have said before, they are founded in greed, jealousy, hatred of each other, twisted minds, falseness, and lies. We have now seen and witnessed that first hand, we have the link to the past and that brings an age-old desire for revenge into the equation and after our first arrest today, that seems to be coming to fruition. Background checks on all the suspects, Mac, and that is everyone with one exception that of the Lord and Lady of the Manor." Said Cadiston.

"As to that aspect, we have Richard Foxhall and Hatie Morset in the archive of ancestry compiling a complete family tree on all the subjects whose names are linked to the murders." Informed Mac. "And that one is down to you. However you look at these deaths, every single one of them has been clearly orchestrated to look like an accident and one was made to look like a suicide but we are onto them. We have secured an excellent piece of evidence. We now have eleven murders on our hands to be solved. The one good thing is that they all happened in the same location, all at Mandaten Manor, and that is where we will find most of our evidence and our killers. Still want to be a detective, Mac?" Cadiston asked once more.

"Working alongside you, with you as my boss, DCI Cadiston? No question about it and even more than ever now." Replied Mac.

"So now we start our full investigation in more depth. We have already started with case number one: Mrs. Bonnie Mandaten, the wife of Grant and her unborn little girl child. I have a feeling and a strong suspicion that when one murder is solved, except Bonnie and her unborn child, it will lead on to another being solved and so on. After today's arrest, I feel even stronger that it will happen. We need to get busy, Mac, if we are going to solve these cases and as there are so few left in the Mandaten family, stop any more deaths." Said Cadiston. "Some of the other guys that I spoke with said that they had worked with Standish in the past and he could be very bullish and never listen to any other comment but had a one-track mind and he would close a case on his own first impression. He had a lot of arrests and they believe that some of those convicted were under his false evidence just to get a conviction. Most of them were minor crimes so short sentences, never the less, his victim has a tainted record. They also said that he should have listened to you more. He may have been the senior but he was supposed to be helping you become a fully-fledged detective. It seems that instead of that he was hampering you and still going his own way with his own agenda just to get a quick case closure." Said Mac.

"Never mind all that now Mac, he is not with us any longer and I have a free hand to investigate as I see fit. Be assured that if you have a comment to make, I will listen. Now, my friend, we can go and investigate properly. With all this added information, my suspicions have escalated. We have a major task on our hands and will need the additional support to collect other evidence which is on course." Said Cadiston.

"You are the boss but what if we run through the people that are helping with the investigation and are currently out there searching for the required information and evidence. It is now 16:30 and I guess a visit to the hospital will be on the cards so half an hour on this? What do you think, a quick run through the agenda?" Asked Mac. "That sounds good to me Mac, and will confirm that we are going to leave a stone unturned, so lead on." Said Cadiston. "We will soon be on our way to the hospital so we had better begin to get the board up to date and line up the requirements for gathering our evidence. I have my notebook as you have got yours –. Mind you, yours carries much more detail than mine and it will be yours that is read out in court so shall we start a new one detailing all the investigation scheduling and who is on them?" Asked Mac.

"Good idea, that will keep things separate yet together." Was Cadiston's reply so a new book was produced and opened.

Case One: Mrs. Bonnie Mandaten and her unborn little girl child
Visual Evidence – Syringe (contents confirmed as concentrated peanut)
Post-mortem – Forensic and Lab reports received and read.

Murdered by Demmie Mandaten – Proven beyond all doubt.

Further evidence required:
Find the maker of the peanut solution that was used to inject into Bonnie Mandaten's desert and arrest them to be held under

suspicion of being an accomplice to murder. Get the name of the person it was produced for.

On the case – PC Howie Julip – WPC Nadine Crown

Check out all chemists and pharmacies – pharmacists – main concentration on food company's technicians, etc. Also inclusive of hospital pharmaceutical staff.

Confirm Grant's solicitor for divorce papers, name Woods – Gray and Stebbings. Further questioning for Grant on the death of his wife and unborn child.

(Re Question him about the death of his first wife)

Case Two: Mr. Malcolm Mandaten
Post-mortem – received and read.
Visual Evidence – Cut reins – Chalky sample – Footprint casts

"I will just give Jooners a call." Said Cadiston and dialled the number.

"Forensics."

"Jooners, Cadders here. I want to ask you a big, very big favour." Said Cadiston. "Ask away then, DCI Cadiston." Said Jooners. "It is a big ask and may prove to be fruitless but I must try. If you can, even though it is a bit late after the event, would you send a team up to the Manor and have a good search around the old Manor ruins and Devil's Dyke? I am sure that there is a piece of vital evidence hiding up there somewhere. The area is still cordoned off so can that be done?" Asked Cadiston.

"Wondered when you would get around to ask me that one. I am one step ahead of you and have already sent a couple of the team up there to give it the once over, only in their case a thorough going over. There are four of the team up there. That is the best I can do, good enough?" Asked Jooners. "Good enough, thanks Jooners!" Said Cadiston. "No problem." He replied and the phone line went dead.

(1) Get the area around the old Manor ruins and Devil's Dyke searched – scheduled for Friday, 24th October, by forensics.

(2) Get all mobile phones and check calls, texts etc – made on Tuesday, 23rd September

Get all shoe sizes

Search Demmie and Chad's room for sleeping pills or powder – if found follow up with finding out who supplied it to Demmie, could be a possible accomplice?

On the case – (1) Team from forensics – Friday, 24th October

(2) WPC Francis Rendham – WPC Olito Paverson

Locate secret passage from Manor to stables

On the case – Cadiston and Macswee

Case Three: Mr. Kevin Mandaten
Received and read – Post-Mortem – Forensic – Lab – Firearms reports
Evidence – Exploded weapon – Chalky sample – Small Round Disc

(1) Investigate and locate the maker of the small round disc that was used to block the barrel and hold the overload of black powder in Kentucky Rifle

Get name of person it was made for. Arrest the maker as a possible accomplice

(1) On the case: Detective Janet Crowth – Detective Jake Soams

They have the disc to show when they check out all precision machinists, companies and private – arrest makers as a possible accessory for further questioning. Find out who it was made for.

(2) Check out security firm to identify if any member of their night patrol saw anyone near the gun marquee late Saturday night/ early Sunday morning 27th/28th September, if yes who? (Check all their log books and remember they could be an accessory)

(2) On the case – Detective Connie Smethdale – WPC Grace Jorde

(3) Locate secret passage from Manor to the wood

(3) On the case – Cadiston and Macswee

Case Four: Mrs. Sammie – Mr Walter – Miss Gloria Larkspere
Received and read post-mortem – Forensic and Lab reports
Visual Evidence – Murder Weapons (Arrows) Broken teeth
Check DNA from under Gloria's fingernail against DNA on file
Check everyone for signs of scratch marks
Check blood samples taken at scene against samples on file
Check men for signs of fighting (already suspect Grant lied about his injuries)
On the case – Cadiston and Macswee

Case Five: Mrs. Sadie Mandaten:
Received and read – Post-Mortem – Forensic and Lab reports
Evidence – Chalky sample – Blood and tissue samples containing Ketamine

Note: We have now discovered the source of the drug Ketamine and who supplied the said drug and the recipient of the said drug.
DONE (Arrested Gloria Standmore)
Question all those who had access to the drug to determine if any of them provided it and to who – Arrest and hold on suspicion of being an accessory.
DONE – One arrest made, need to arrest the mother, Margery Standmore, as she provided the drug (In hand)
Check out the fingerprints removed from the oars and the boat against those held on file
On the case – Cadiston and Macswee

Case Six: Mr. James Mandaten
Evidence – None visible – Undamaged shoelaces
Received and read Post-Mortem and Forensic reports

Check D.N.A. found under his nails against that are held on file. Locate secret passage at top of stairs and re-enact possibility of breaking James' neck, pushing him downstairs and then make his escape through the secret passage to re-emerge at the bottom of staircase where he then untied the shoelace and disappeared from scene before being seen and then to reappear after Jennifer's screams.

On the case – Cadiston and Macswee

Case Seven Mr. Lowell Mandaten
Post-Mortem – Forensic/Lab reports received and read
Evidence – Broken Name Bracelet – Gold Saint Christopher
(To keep you safe as you travel – Love Mum and Dad X) –
Weapon – mobile phone

On the Case – WPC Amelia Stroud – PC Steven Arkens

Check out all Jewellers to trace where the Saint Christopher was purchased and by whom?

"That just leaves us with Demmie and Chad's reports but as soon as I have downed this coffee, we must be off to the hospital. Hopefully Chad is awake fully and not still hazy today. We will still need to take it steady as we do not want to put him backward." Said Cadiston.

"He is an important witness in these cases especially in who attacked him and murdered his wife so yes, I agree and would not like to do that." Said Mac.

"That is all up to date and the action taken. When the teams return with their findings then we will have real evidence and a few suspects to question. Now, a visit to Chad and then, armed with as much information as possible, we are back to Mandaten on Monday morning, 12th of November, 50 days after the first tragedy or rather murder." Said Cadiston. "Just a few days past a month and a half. In that time we have moved forward quite a bit." Said Mac. "Quite a bit but not enough, now the hospital." Said Cadiston. "Ok Boss, I will bring the car to the front." Said Mac. "Thanks, Mac. Be with you in two minutes, just need to pay a visit." Said Cadiston. With their cups emptied, they left, Cadiston going one way and with a smile on his face Mac went the other, happy to be working with him.

At the hospital, they again found Greta and Jennifer sitting with Chad and the only difference now was that he was sitting up in his bed and was able to carry out a conversation with them. Seeing his surgeon Cadiston asked, "How is he doing?" "Very well, very well indeed and his little excursion to your mortuary did not affect him at all in fact it made him smile. In a month, that will be December or maybe a little bit longer, he will be back with us fully but he will still need quite a bit of convalescence. 'Life after death' Cadiston, that is what the young lady said, 'life after death'. That is exactly what it was and from what I have experienced from watching those young ladies with him, I feel very strongly that he will receive all the required aftercare that he needs. Now I must get on." Wth a wave he was gone.

"You are looking exceptionally good, Chad, and making steady progress so, my friend, you keep it up." Said Cadiston. "Cadiston, I am glad you are here as I have remembered what it was that I needed to tell you. It may sound daft to someone that does not know the horse but Star spoke to me and I assessed from her actions that Lowell's killer was probably Kansas. I noticed that he was favouring his right arm and shoulder the morning after Lowell died and he also had a deep gash on his hand. He tried to palm it off as being cut using a wet shave but if that was the case, it would have a smooth clean edge but this was jagged. He said the problem with his arm was that he had laid awkwardly in bed." Remembered Chad as his memory was returning fully. "Good evidence, Chad. Now don't think about that anymore, you just rest and get fully recovered as there will be another major role for you to play before this is over: an act of 'life after death'." Said Cadiston. "Bring it on, Detective. I want the killer of my family put away for keeps infact they should be executed for their crimes." Answered Chad. "The killers of your family, they will be Chad, they most certainly will be. Now, there is something I need to ask you if you are up to it." Said Cadiston. "Ask away, my friend we have no secrets here." He replied smiling at Greta and Jennifer as he spoke. "When did you last see your mobile phone Chad? I only ask because it was found in the same stable stall as Lowell. What I need to know is can you explain how it got there?" Asked Cadiston. "So that is where it went, the crafty little blighter is trying to incriminate me in Lowells death. I left it on the sideboard on Wednesday evening and on Thursday it could not be found. My guess is that whoever killed Lowell took my phone and planted it there to incriminate me. My guess is Kansas." Said Chad. "I can confirm that as Jennifer and myself helped him to look for it on Friday as he needed it for you to contact him after he phoned the station to give you his information." Said Greta. "And I was not there and that is the pity." He glanced at Mac. "That confirms my suspicion and now we are closing in but I can say no more than that. We will leave you with your two beautiful ladies and see you next week." Said Cadiston and with a wave, they were gone. Back at the station, they looked at the envelopes lying on the desk. "Now we will see if it agrees with your suspicions." Said Mac. "That we will, Mac. We have read my notebook and now we will read the post-mortem report on Demmie, followed by the forensic report and then we will see how close they match each other." Said Cadiston. "And I can guess your suspicions as I am beginning to understand your thinking. All these cases are murder but I think there was another reason for wanting a post-mortem on Demmie." Cadiston smiled at Mac as he opened the first envelope and produced the post-mortem report and the first file was then opened.

Post-Mortem Report
On
Mrs. Demmie Mandaten
Died Saturday 11th October

Although the cause of death was known as the victim had been shot at close range with a double-barrel blast from a shotgun and as there was cause for further suspicion, DCI Cadiston requested that we perfom a post-mortem to itemise any other evidence.

The blast had struck the deceased in the chest and caused severe damage. The top half of the body was virtually separated from the lower half. The damage caused was extensive and because the shooter was standing extremely close to the victim, because of the way that shotgun cartridges are made the internal organs were found to contain a high quantity of small lead pellets. Both lungs had been completely shredded by the blast and the heart appeared to have exploded, there was a small quatity of lead pellets from the shotgun blast in the liver and kidneys and because of the closeness and the way in which a shotgun cartridge spreads, a quantity had passed through the body and were embedded in the wall. (This was learnt with our liaising with the forensics team.) The body was in a real mangled state but we persevered with our investigation and found that Mrs. Mandaten was two months and five days pregnant. Because of the closeness of the shotgun blast and the way that the body was torn and ripped apart by the lead pellets, it is not possible to itemize every single injury that her body sustained and therefore, cannot say whether there were other injuries received apart from those received by the shotgun blast.

We carried out a full body survey on the remains and can confirm that the distance that the deceased was shot from would be three and no more than four feet. Because of the proximity of the shotgun and almost within reaching distance of the shooter, the victim would have been in a state of fear and this was found in the chemical analysis of the victim's body. Due to the severity of the injuries, the deceased would have died instantly. Being faced with a person holding a loaded shotgun pointed at them at such a close distance, the victim was probably in a state of fear and anguish just before the trigger was pulled.

Conclusion
Without finding evidence to the contrary and from the evidence received from the forensic department and once collated with the post-mortem evidence, along with the state of the victim's body, we can confirm that Mrs. Mandaten died from the double blast from a shotgun. During the examination, it was also found that the deceased was two months and five days pregnant that therefore makes this is a double murder.

Verdict

Mrs. Demmie Mandaten died a violent death which can only be called murder in the first degree by a person unkwnown

Signed

Charles Dennasen – Samantha Cadiston

"Is that what you suspected, Cadders?" Asked Mac.

"I had that thought, Mac. Mybe her being pregnant was another reason to be rid of her just as she wanted to be rid of Bonnie, nasty sight to see though – a complete blood bath. Now for the forensic report on the room which may shed some light on it. After that we need to hear the emergency call recording because I think, no I know, that it will be different to what we were told in the interviews." Said Cadiston.

"I agree, if someone is unconscious, how could they fire a gun? By magic? I think not." The report was laid open and they read on.

Forensic Report on the Bedroom Named the Lowell Suite
Location Mandaten Manor
Friday, 10th October
The Scene of a Shooting

"On our arrival, we proceeded directly to the Lowell Suite bedroom, the scene of the shooting. Upon entry, we found two victims. The first was lying unconscious near the door, the other against the wall near the bathroom. The second victim had been shot in the chest and was pronounced dead at the Scene. The other person, allegedly the shooter, had been struck over the head and was bleeding from the wound received. Under the instruction of DCI Cadiston, he was immediately removed and taken to the Royal Hospital for treatment for the severe head injury.

We examined the victim and could asses that she had been shot at extremely close range with the shotgun that lay on the floor and after we had measured and logged the position of the deceased victim, she was also removed. At the request of DCI Cadiston, she was taken to the forensic mortuary for further post-mortem investigation.

With the bodies removed, we were able to re-enact the scene of the shooting and our investigation shows that it is not at all possible for the alleged shooter to have shot the deceased from the position that he was found lying unconscious on the floor. By the examination of bloodied footsteps leading away from the deceased, we strongly believe that there was a third party involved in the shooting.

We knew that the alleged shooter had been struck hard and the weapon used was an old medieval knight's hammer which contained blood and hair residue. This was bagged and removed for forensic evidence. From my initial examination, I could asses that he had been struck on the top and at the base of his skull which had resulted in a serious fracture and resulted in a lot of blood being lost. First attending officers Constable's Jake Monahue and Ivan Strow were asked if the gun was still in his hands when they first surveyed the scene. They confirmed that they left everything just as it was. With the preliminary investigation being satisfactorily completed, we then entered the room to carry out our extensive survey of the murder scene. We discovered that the alleged shooter was still holding the gun. This was very suspicious especially after receiving what could be a killer blow from the said hammer. We were suspicious as there were a number of cartridges scattered all around him and to our way of thinking, if you were going on a shooting rampage the cartridges would be secured either in a pocket or in a cartridge belt. (The cartridges were collected and bagged to be checked for fingerprints.)

We checked the position that the alleged shooter would have been standing to take his shot and hit the victim with enough force to carry her through the air and collide at her resting place against the wall. If he had his back to the door and then shot both barrels into the victim, the distance would be excessive. He then reloaded, two more shots were fired but they went into the ceiling. This does not fit. Why shoot into the ceiling unless you want to frighten someone but according to a witness statement at the time of the second shot, the alleged shooter was lying unconscious.

First impression without looking too close for evidence would be deemed first-degree murder and that is what this case is but not by the person named as the alleged shooter. The first thing that discounts this is the positioning of his body. If he had stood with his back to the door so that the person that knocked him unconscious could strike down onto his head, he would approach from behind. Secondly, he would need to be above him to strike the top of his head. From the wound that the alleged shooter received, he was hit hard but not just once. My guess is that he was struck again while he was on the floor, partly unconscious. I set up a re-enactment and after being struck the first time on the top of the head, to achieve this, the striker would need to be above him. He fell so the first blow was made by someone that was higher, possibly standing on the chair that was just behind the door. The victim would have entered and seeing her husband on the floor, would have run to the bathroom to fetch a towel to press on the head wound. The shooter would have confronted her and shot her. The striker (Tomas) would then have entered, forcing the shooter to hide in the wardrobe as he would then have struck the partly conscious alleged shooter, that we believe is the second victim, twice at the base of the skull. The striker would then have attempted to put the gun into the alleged shooter's hands but fired it accidentally before running downstairs to take over the emergency call. I noticed that the blow was aimed at the exact same spot that killed Malcolm Mandaten. I was curious as to why there was no forensics called to this case so went to the mortuary and Charles accommodated in letting me see the body. When I saw that this victim had been struck in the exact same place, I started thinking that maybe it was the same the killer of Malcolm Mandaten. We are in possession of the names of all the parties concerned. They were used in the full re-enactment scenario:

Chadrick Mandaten goes into the bedroom and his assailant is waiting for him. He or she strikes him hard on the top of his head and he falls to the ground. Before anyother action can be taken upon his body, his wife comes upstairs and enters the room. Seeing her husband lying on the floor and bleeding from a blow to his head, she immediately runs to the bathroom to fetch a towel but as she leaves, she is confronted by the real shooter who shoots Demmie. The shooter needs to hide as the door is slowly opening so the first place available is the wardrobe. (We know this as bloodied footprints were found inside.) Tomas Kaysten sees Demmie shot to pieces and Chadrick lying on the floor and he then strikes him twice with the old knight's hammer that is already lying on the floor. He attempts to place the gun into Chadrick's hands but it fires so he runs downstairs and takes over the emergency call his wife made. The real shooter emerges from the hiding place and also tries to place the gun in Chad's hands but again, it fires and the shot goes under the bed but the empty gun is in Chad's hand so the real shooter now disappears. We re-enacted a series of scenarios to ascertain what took place in the Lowell Suite and in our opinion, the re-enacted scenario portrays exactly how this first-degree murder happened as this is how all the evidence presents itself. If Chadrick Mandaten dies from his injuries, namely the blows to his head, it could be deemed as a double murder.

Signed
Sergeant Jooners Fornesic Scientist

"I remember reading your report after you had translated from your shorthand and it is just as you have detailed it in your notebook, Cadders. How did you know that Demmie was pregnant? You certainly have a good eye to spot things and we have got food for thought. We know that Malcolm Mandaten was murdered by being struck on the base of his skull and now Chad has been struck in the exact same place. I think that Jooners has a good point and correct me if I am wrong but they could be one in the same person and that points away from Grant and to Tomas." Said Mac.

"You are right with that analogy and although we only used Grant as to formulate our scenario, I had him in the frame for Malcolm as the evidence and knowledge that we have pointed to him as a possible perpetrator of the crime. Now it looks like I need to think again. As for knowing that Demmie was pregnant, purely by her mannerism and she was also gaining a little bit of weight since my first meeting with her. Also by something said when I was interviewing Lizabeth after the shooting." Said Cadiston. "Well spotted and remembered, I would have missed that. If it now looks like it was Tomas that murdered Malcolm, the question is who was there to help him? I remember that Kansas has an unusually small shoe size and there were small prints up at Devil's Dyke so I am thinking that Kansas was up there with him. But then who would be in the stable to scare Thundist? Do you think that Lizabeth would do that?" Asked Mac.

"Maybe but what you just said about small shoe size –. I know that you were not there but at the scene where Sammie's family was murdered, there were also small footprints. I think we need to get the D.N.A. sample for Kansas and the victims tested quickly for a match. I know that these things take time and we need the answers as soon as possible because I am thinking that he is involved in at least four of the murders. I am certain that if we look at his arms we will find the scratches left by Gloria and those on his neck were by James as he attempted to break free of the strangle hold. When Amelia and Steven return with information on the Gold Saint Christopher, I strongly believe that it belongs to Kansas so there is positive evidence to place him in the stable when Lowell died. It must have been him that planted Chad's mobile phone to incriminate him but slipped up with losing his Saint Christopher Medallion." Said Cadiston.

"Now, if I am getting this right, we need a positive identification from the D.N.A. and blood samples and the additional visual information from the team that is searching for it. Then we question and make our arrest?" Asked Mac.

"Spot on Mac, with all that evidence we can move in and carry out our questioning of the suspect. With the evidence on hand, there is no way that they can wriggle out of the fact that they are guilty of the crime." Said Cadiston.

"We nearly have them, Cadders." Said Mac. Before he could answer, the phone began to ring and was quickly answered. "DCI Cadiston's office, DS Macswee speaking." "Hi Mac, can you put Cadders on please." Said DI Richard Folkes on the other end. "Richard for you, Cadders." Said Mac. "Hi Richard, have you some news on the whereabouts of Jonnett Muscaday?" Asked Cadiston. "I have and sorry it has taken so long but it is not all good. It has been quite a task to locate her but finally, I succeeded. I had to get on to the boys at the met and they have been in touch with the French Police and they have tracked her down for us." Said Richard.

"What you are telling me, Richard, that she is found but now lives in France?" Asked Cadiston. "That is exactly it but all is not lost. I have explained the reason for wanting to speak with her and the French Police are going to arrest her and send her back to us. It is being arranged as we speak so she will be with us on Tuesday, is that ok?" Asked Richard. "Brilliant job, Richard. That is another one that I owe you, I will keep it in mind and repay it soon, many thanks." Said Cadiston. "Glad to be of help and may need to keep you to that as the case I am on has me stumped." The phone was hung up.

"That is brilliant, we are closing in on Kansas and Grant but we still have to find the accomplices." Said Mac. "I don't think they will be too far for us to look but now I would like to hear the emergency call recording from the 11th when Demmie was shot and Chad attacked. It will be interesting to see just how it ties in with what they told us." Said Cadiston. They left the office and asked John at the desk to ring the call center and tell them the reason for their visit. The car burst into life and they were on the way. Mac was a steady driver and knew the way well and he wasted no time in getting them to the call center to hear the recording.

"Hi Cadders, Mac, come in. We got your message and have the recording ready for you to hear." Said Julie from the front desk."Nice one Julie, thanks." They settled down to listen.

Operator: "Emergency, which service do you require?"

Lizabeth: "We need the police and be quick."

"Pick up on that, Mac?" Asked Cadiston.

"Her voice sounds very calm."Replied Mac.

O: "Police, how can we help?"

L: "Oh my God, we are in danger. You need to hurry to Mandaten Manor, I fear for all our lives. It's Chadrick and he has gone completely mad and was threatening to kill his wife and we have just heard two shots fired. He said he had killed before and this would be easy, hurry please, hurry."

"Once again Mac, notice anything?" Asked Cadiston.

"Voice has changed from calm to make it sound like she is in a real panic."

O: "A car has been dispatched, madam, now try to remain calm and tell me your name please."

L: "Lizabeth Manda –, No, Kaysten."

"Nearly called herself Mandaten, pre-empting that do you think?" Mac asked Cadiston.

"Could be, Mac." He replied and they continued to listen.

O: "Lizabeth, it is important for you to remain calm. Now tell me, can you see him, and are you under immediate threat?"

L: "Stay calm you say, with a mad gunman on the loose? But in answer to your question, I cannot see him. He is in their bedroom and – (sound of two gunshots) My goodness, that was gunshots again. I believe he has done it, what should we do?"

"Voice change again, Mac." Said Cadiston.

571

"For someone that thinks they are under threat, she sounds almost calm again." Said Mac.

Kansas has taken over the call, they never told us that.

"Now what is that noise?" Asked Cadiston.

"I can answer that, Cadders, that would be Tomas running down the stairs. For a few seconds, there is silence and I thought the mouthpiece was being blocked. If you keep listening, it is about thirty seconds then Tomas was on the phone." Said Mac.

O: "Lizabeth, Lizabeth can you hear me?"

"You are speaking Julie but there is not an answer until the phone is passed to Tomas. Strange, it is as though they need to converse to get their story straight." Said Cadiston.

"That thought had crossed my mind." Said Mac.

O: "Lizabeth, can you hear me?"

L: "Yes, but my husband wants to speak with you."

"There it is again, so calm." Said Cadiston.

Tomas: "Hello operator?"

O: "Hello sir, tell me, can you vacate the building easily and safely?"

T: "Yes, we can, he is still upstairs shall we get out? Oh, by the way, this is Tomas Kaysten speaking. Oh yes, we are not in any immediate danger now as I have just had to hit Chadrick hard over the head but sadly not before he had shot and killed his wife. He shot at her twice and she is in a hell of a mess. From what little I could see it looks like she has been shot in the chest. I do believe that he may have been coming to kill us all but I have stopped him."

"Good grief, Cadders, he sounds as cool as a cucumber. Sorry, just an expression but if their situation was one of being in danger, he would not be so calm. At least I would not think he would.

He said they could get out, then as if an after-thought, he said he had hit him." Said Mac.

"Doesn't sound right, Mac." Agreed Cadiston.

O: "You have stopped him, Tomas, how did you manage that?"

T: "I had no choice but to hit him in self-defence, you understand? It was the only way to save my wife, my son, and the rest of the family. I don't know but he may have been the one that was killing the family so please hurry and get here. We are safe now and he is knocked unconscious but get here quickly."

O: "The car will be there directly.

(Sound of two more shots fired)

T: "Shots, two more shots."

O: "I thought that you told me he was knocked unconscious, Tomas, but if you think there is a threat then leave the premises. The car is on route and will be there in a short while, sir. If you can, keep an eye on him but stay safe."

T: "Stay safe you say, that I intend to do but that was two more shots fired!"

O: "I heard you say that you had rendered him unconscious, sir, just stay away from him and if he starts to come down the stairs, vacate the premises."

T: "That we will, and I think the police are here now."

"Correct me if I am wrong, Julie, but is that how you would expect this sort of emergency call to sound?" Asked Mac.

"Not at all Mac, there were too many variances in the tone of their voices. One second they were calm, then frightened, then calm again. When Tomas was on the phone, by the tone in his voice, you would think that he was taking a walk in the park with not a bit of panic until the final two shots. That makes six in total but spread quite widely apart. Now listen to this recording of a previous shooting incident, then you can compare them."Said Julie and pressed the play button. The recording started and they listened intently.

"Now what do you think? Plenty of room for suspicion on my part so over to you, Cadders" Said Mac.

"I think that confirms their falseness and you have summed it up very well Julie, sounded strange and not the whole truth. Let's just have a read on my notes about that shooting." Cadiston said and turned the pages of his notebook to read and form their analysis:

"Now then, who was it that made the initial 999 emergency call?" They continued reading the statements from the interview that day.

Cadiston: "Did you see the gun in his hands?"

Kansas: "Well, err, not exactly but I did hear it click."

C: "Kansas thank you, then you came running down, Tomas?"

T: "I did, I had to hit him to stop him from doing any more killing. He said that he had killed before and it would be easy. Now for the rest of you, he had already shot his wife and reloaded so I was protecting my family."

C: "You struck him hard then with a loaded gun in his hands?"

T: "Just as hard as I could, Detective."

C: "And how many times did you strike him?"

T: "Only once, that was sufficient. He fell straight away and did not get up." Cadiston: "And what weapon did you use, sir?"

Tomas: "An old knight's hammer but you already know that. Anyhow, after I had clobbered him what else could I do? So I just dropped it on the floor and ran straight down the stairs. I came downstairs and took over the phone call to the police from my wife and told them what had happened."

C: "And that call will have been recorded, is there anything else that you can tell me?"

T: "Not a thing, Detective, but I think this shows who the killer of our family is. He is not one of us, just an adopted unwanted child who has been sponging off us for many years."

C: "One more question sir, did you actually see the gun in his hands?"

T: "Oh yes I saw it alright and just before I clobbered him, he was turning so I hit him hard."

C: "Thank you. Now to you, Miss Jennifer, can you shed any light on what has happened?"

J: "None at all really, I was in the garden with mother and when we came back in, Aunt Lizabeth and Kansas were talking then uncle Tomas came running down but I ..."

C: "Go on Miss, you were about to say something else and do not worry, if it helps with this incident and is the truth then that is all we ask for."

J: "The truth, yes the truth. Well, Mother and I walked beneath their window and did not hear any of the shouting and arguing or anything else until the gunshots."

C: "And how many were there?"

J: "Two very close together, then there was a space of maybe four or five minutes before the next two."

T: "That must have been while he reloaded." (sheepish glance between Tomas, Lizabeth and Kansas).

Mac: "Yes, thank you, sir. We will ask you questions in a moment."

C: "Yes, thank you, Tomas, but if you do not mind speaking when spoken to and I will ask the questions. So, you were downstairs all the time? Thank you, Jennifer. Is there any other little thing that may help?"

J: "You said you wanted the truth. Well, Aunt Lizabeth has lied. We could see her sitting in that chair while we walked, they were all talking and then Kansas and Uncle Tomas went upstairs."

T: "Silly child, you were not in here so how could you tell where –."

C: "That will do Lizabeth, you will get a chance to answer in a moment. Is there anything further that you would like to add?"

J: "As I was saying, Aunt Lizabeth was in that chair when we went for our walk and still in it when we came back in and wearing the same clothes. We can see it clearly from the path and you can confirm that, Detective Cadiston, by looking for yourself."

C: "Thank you, Jennifer, we will. Now Miss Greta, where were you?"

G: "Walking with my daughter, then here in the lounge and like her, I heard nothing until the gunshots. I agree with her, I cannot believe this of Chadrick he is a very gentle man. To be honest, I have never heard him raise his voice in anger. Although he has sometimes been pushed beyond many people's limits, he always remained calm. Like my daughter, I could see Lizabeth and it is exactly as she said so why lie, Lizabeth?"

T: "You two must be completely blind then, we were all upstairs until we came down and he was found with the gun still hot and smoking in his hands and my wife has no reason to lie so —"

C: "That will do, thank you, sir. It does, well, that is of no concern.

Mac and Grant enter.

C: "Grant, I just need to know your whereabouts for the past hour."

G: "I have been out and only just driven back. Your constable here nabbed me before I had even turned the engine off."

C: "And there is someone that can collaborate your story?"

G: "There is but I will not say here in front of them. I have already told your constable and I am sure you do not need to hear it again."

I took Mac to one side and he whispered in my ear. "Was with a young lady and she works here."

C: "You have her name?"

M: "I do."

C: "Thank you, Grant, and you have some white residue on your coat. (he brushed it off straight away.)

C: That will be all for now. All of you, please stay in this room as I may need to speak to you further. Mac, with me. We will go and have a word with Jooners." We then went upstairs and ran through a variety of scenarios with forensics. They finished reading what Cadiston has written in detail —

"And there it is, as you can clearly see, there are several lies in there if I am not mistaken, Cadders. Why did Lizabeth lie about being upstairs changing her clothes if she stayed down? It makes no sense. All the lies to cover up the truth and makes me think that they were all in it together." Said Mac.

"You have it right, Mac, a complete fabrication of the actual events and why lie to cover the truth? They all have something to hide and we are getting close to finding out just what that is. Thank's Julie, that is very helpful, we have all that we need so will be away and head back to the station." Said Cadiston. With their farewells completed and with a wave, they left. On the way they chattered.

"Remember what Greta told us?" Asked Cadiston.

"If you are referring to what Tomas told us, yes. You have it documented that he struck only once but when he was talking about Chad, Greta heard him say twice so straight away a lie. Also, why lie about being upstairs to change yet still wear the same clothes? Apart from Tomas and would he have had time to change a bloodied shirt for a clean one after striking Chad?" Asked Mac.

"You noticed Tomas had a very clean ironed shirt on so as you say, had he made a quick change after striking Chad because he was blood splatted. Explains the delay in him taking over the phone." Said Cadiston.

"Never thought of that, just took it that he had changed while he was up there with his family which we now know, thanks to truthful Jennifer, was a complete lie. As you said, he probably did a quick change after his attack on Chad as that is what I now think he did." Said Mac.

"Mac, you are thinking again. I agree with that entirely but now we are at the station so let's see if any members of our team are back yet." Said Cadiston.

"If they are, we will have more evidence and possibly a few prisoners after they have made their arrests." Said Mac.

"And we will soon hopefully know the answer to that." Cadiston looked around. "I can't see any of their cars so a bit longer to wait." With the car parked, they made their way to the office.

Chapter Seventeen

The Evidence Mounts

"Any messages or anyone come back while we were away, John?" Asked Cadiston. "Not a thing, Cadders, on both fronts. All very quiet for a change." Said John at the front desk. "Thank's John, I'll be in the office." With a wave, he was gone. In the office, they both stood deep in thought while staring at their incident boards.

"Well Mac, we have all the post-mortem, forensic, lab, fire-arms –. In fact, all the reports. We have the D.N.A. and blood samples that are being checked as we are speaking. It will not surprise me to find that we have more than one match with the murder sites. We have a small quantity of visual evidence with more to come from our away teams so I think we should go home now and enjoy the weekend. On Monday morning, 15th of November which is exactly 55 days since Bonnie and her un-born girl child were murdered by Demmie, we should be able to make our move." Said Cadiston. "And the saddest thing is that they both died needlessly and died through Demmie's de-sire for Grant and we know that he did not want her but was using her for his own ends." Replied Mac angrily. "You have that right, Mac. And it does make one angry although she has paid the ultimate price for her misgivings and some would say that is justice. Now to get back on track, we will visit Mandaten Manor and carry out a lot more questioning on Monday 15th of November but this time, we will include every murder. We need to put some pressure on them now, Mac, and we start that from Monday, I would like these cases to be concluded and our arrests made before Christmas and with the return of their true son that will be a great Christmas present for the Mandatens Mac. Another thing and before we go to the Manor, will we start to re-investigate Lord Mandaten's brother's death. That should not take us too long as we have the file and the addresses of witnesses that were never questioned so I think that someone slipped up there by not deleting them just in case there was a follow-up." Said Cadiston.

"If you are referring to who I think you are, no name mentioned, then I think that he was a bit complacent thinking that it was all signed and sealed and no one would want to question or reopen it. As to that, he did not count on you, acting DCI Cadiston." Said Mac. "Well, we have done just that, Mac, and together we will make a start to investigate it first thing on Monday. Now home and we can enjoy a weekend with our wives because I have a very strong feeling that from Monday, 15th of November we will not be getting another day off until all these cases are satisfactorily closed." Said Cadiston. "My thoughts exactly so good night, Cadders, see you Monday and an early start, me thinks." Replied Mac.

"8 a.m. will do, night Mac." Said Cadiston and they went their separate ways.

From the moment that they had been asked to trace all the family trees connected to the Mandaten family, plus the family tree of Standish, Standmore, and Brexly there was little time to rest in the department of Ancestral Records. Richard and Hattie were extremely busy researching and compiling the required family trees for Cadiston from every available source. They were reaching a few stumbling blocks as to where to find the relevant information. This fact was leading to increased pressure on them and was proving to be a hard task. They knew the importance of this information which gave them the will to persevere. The Mandaten family had proven to be no problem but when they began to investigate the other families that came into the scenario, things became a little more involved. They were searching through the electoral rolls, parish records, births, marriages, historic records and everywhere that they could think of to find the required information.

Surprisingly, the Mandaten family tree had survived from pre the time that they first set foot on the shores of England with William the Conquerer in 1066 which culminated in the battle of Hastings when Harold was defeated. After the defeat and when all had calmed, the first Baron was endowed with lands to befit his station as a loyal subject, and thus came the birth of the Mandaten Estate, and the family tree was kept current right up to the present day. They had remained loyal to the crown through the centuries that followed and slowly, their wealth was accumulated. During the English Civil war from 1642 to 1651, this came under threat and when it was discovered that the parliamentary forces were winning the day, Lord Lowell Gaston Francoise Mandaten changed sides and joined the parliamentarians thus protecting their fortune. For the remaining years of the civil war, the family became informers of other Royal supporters. As Richard and Hattie compiled the records, they discovered the family that was the most persecuted by them was the family of Standlyhope. They had been given the name of Standish and Standmore to work with and had a long and hard task tracing it from present to past but through hours of research and dedication to the job at hand, their endeavours were finally rewarded. They discovered that the name Standlyhope disappeared from all records after 1651 and two new names appeared: that of Standish and Standmore. They had also discovered that they were one in the same family and hoped that the changing of their name would ensure the continuation of their family line and that at some point in the future, their true family name could be resurrected and once again the name of Standlyhope would be seen. They now worked to bring the family trees to life and had worked it down to the last remaining family members that still lived:

Tomas Standmore Bernard Standmore Albert Standmore
Wife Wife
Gloria Mulbatern Margery Toits
Son Son
Roger Standmore Bernard Standmore

In their long search, they had discovered that the name of Standmore appeared in records around 1651 and the name Standish did not appear until 1658. Both names are derived from the family name of Standlyhope.

Alfred Standish – Son – Harry Standish
Wife Wife
Frieda Crows Angela Morteson
Son Daughter
Charles Standish. Harriet Standish
Wife (Deceased)
Josie Cluwnes
Daughter
Sheila Standish

"As with Standmore, the name Standish is a derivative of the family name Standlyhope and both families are connected and are one and the same. We had to dig deep and from the information that we have been able to collate, I am and sure that you are also of the opinion that the two remaining Stanlyhope brothers, Richard and Geffory, took on the two names. Richard taking the name of Standmore and Geffory the name of Standish in the hope that at least one would survive the parliamentary purge to be rid of royalists but both brothers managed to survive hence the two separate names for the same family." Said Hattie. "Couldn't agree more with that analogy, Hattie, the next one is easy to trace as it is almost there." Just as Richard had said, the Mandaten family tree was already written so to formulate the derivatives was an easier task and all they were required to do was to complete the last segment bringing it up to date:

The family tree of Greta was carried out ending in:
    Greta only daughter of Samuel and Dorothy Finnley. (Second wife of Malcolm Mandaten) Daughter Jennifer son Lowel from previous marrige

The family tree of Bonnie was completed ending in:
    Bonnie Malderhay only daughter of Henry and Francis Malderhay. (Second wife of Grant Mandaten)

The family tree of Walter was carried out and ended in:

Walter Larkspere only son of Stephen and Malinder Larkspere

Wife – Sammie Mandaten – Daughter – Gloria Larkspere (All deceased.)

The family tree of Sadie was carried out and ended in:

Sadie Joitisson daughter of Franklin and Henrietta Joitisson (Wife of Kevin Mandaten)

Daniel Joitisson son of Franklin and Henrietta Joitisson (deceased 1969)

"Wow, what a task we have had, Hattie." Said Richard.

"You can say that again, Richard, and it is not quite finished yet although I am not sure where this person fits in." Said Hattie.

"We have been on this for a while and we have even gone the extra mile for Detective Cadiston by working on Sunday, now you tell me that we are not quite finished so who haven't we traced?" Asked Richard.

"Adam asked for the family of a Demmie Brexly to be traced." Replied Hattie.

"Well, it is two-fifteen already, we had better get to it as I would like him to have this information tomorrow. We were told it was urgent for their case." Said Richard.

"Best we do not delay then." Said Hattie as their computers whirred to life. Any paper records that they held were worked through.

"Six-twenty, Richard, how are we doing?" Asked Hattie.

"I think that we are almost there, just need to recheck this last piece. Thankfully it is not a massively long tree to search for and I think that will do it." He replied.

They had worked long and hard on discovering all the information and formulating the required family trees and were about to complete the final one. With the tree complete, it ended in:

Henry Brexly – Wife – Amanda Faversum

Daughter Son

Demmie Brexly Edward Brexly

Seven p.m. and I have had it, how about you?" Asked Richard.

"Totally Richard, now let us go home as I think that our families will have forgotten what we look like." Said Hattie. "Not worried about the family, Hattie, it's the dog. If she has forgotten who I am, I could get savaged." Said Richard.

"Knowing your dog, Richard, the only savaging you will get from her is with a wet tongue." They both laughed. With their scrolls secured and ready to take to Cadiston on Monday morning and relieved knowing that their work was done, they made their way home.

On Monday morning, at 8.01 a.m., Richard made a call to the station to check if Cadiston was in and was relieved when he was told that he was. "Tell him that Richard and Hattie from the Ancestral Records are on the way and should be with him in no more than twenty minutes. He will know what it is about." Said Richard. "That I will, sir." Replied John, then the phone was hung up. "Looks like we need to delay for a while, Mac. Richard and Hattie are on their way to see us." Said Cadiston.

"They must have completed the family trees that we asked for. They have had a long job but if it produces what we want then all worthwhile." Said Mac.

"Go wait at the front desk for them, then you can bring them straight to the office." Said Cadiston. "Already on the Way, Boss." Mac said as he left the office. Five minutes later, he was on his way back followed by the two visitors with their information. "Hattie, Richard, come right in and welcome to our humble abode. Now please take a seat and before we start, can we fetch you a coffee?" Asked Cadiston. "That would be good, I missed mine this morning leaving home so early." Replied Hattie. Mac needed no asking and was already on his way. He did not delay and was promptly back as he was eager to see what they had found out in formulating each family tree for them. With coffee poured and ready to drink, their first scroll was unrolled and laid in a cleared place on the desk. As they looked at the tree, Cadiston noticed a missing name. "The Mandaten tree looks fine apart from one person is missing." "Not according to the records so who do you think is missing from the family tree?" Asked Hattie. "Chadrick Mandaten." Richard looked at Hattie and they both looked puzzled. "Chadrick Mandaten, you say, but we have gone through a multitude of records on the Mandaten family and there is no mention of –." "Hang on a second, Richard, let me trace this back, I have it written in my notebook. Hmm, there it is a stillborn child a son to be named Chadrick but that was thirty years ago." Said Hattie. "We know that Hattie but well remembered and from what we have already discovered, you may well need to alter that entry. We will tell you more on that when it is finally confirmed." Said Cadiston. Happy with the information, the next scroll was laid onto the table.

"I am looking at Demmie Brexly and you have found that she has a living brother named Edward, that could be very relevant. I had better contact Howie and Nadine as that may well help them in finding out their information." Mac picked up the phone and dialled their number.

"PC Howie Julip." "Howie, Macswee here. We have some information that may help in your search. We have just found out that Demmie has a living brother named Edward Brexly and he may be the one that you need to find." Said Mac. "Thanks for that Mac, it may well be advantaged because so far we have drawn blanks. We are in Highhayten now and about to pay a visit to a food manufacturing company named Hertfords Fine Foods and if he works here, our search could be over and we could have our man. Best not delay, Mac, as we have been watching as the workforce entered the site and as they are all in now. We do not want to spook anyone and give them time to do a runner, we had better get in there now." Said Howie. "Understood Howie, good luck and hope you find him." Said Mac and hung up. "Good work, Mac. Now back to Demmie as there is no record of Chadrick apart from thirty years ago when he was supposed to be stillborn. He was married to her but there are no marriage lines to find." Said Cadiston.

"To be honest, Detective, as she is not registered in any record as being married and Chadrick is not shown to be alive, we did not look at marriage lines for her." Said Hattie. "Not a problem, now the next one." Said Cadiston and they went through the recorded family tree for Standish and Standmore and were satisfied with the information gained there. "You have no more scrolls and there should be another family tree, there is another person missing, one Tomas Kaysten." Said Cadiston. "Now in trying to find Tomas Kaysten, we came upon a major stumbling block. The only record that was quite easy to find was the marriage between him and Lizabeth Mandaten but that was only because he is mentioned in her family tree. Apart from that, he appears to be a non-existent person. We have searched and searched every single available record from John O Grote to Lands' End and cannot find any records of the family Kaysten or that name anywhere. We even tried abroad and had help from our international counterparts but there is absolutely nothing to show that he exists at all apart from his marriage to Lizabeth Mandaten. We thought that this was very strange. We worked until 7 p.m. Sunday evening trying to find him but the family name of Kaysten does not exist and he, as far as records go, is a none existing person." Said Richard. "You have done exceptionally well, the pair of you, and we cannot thank you enough for all your hard work. Now to put your minds at ease, we can answer why the family name Kaysten cannot be found and that is because Tomas invented it to hide his real name and that is Standmore. We thought that he may have left a false trail attached to the name but as you say, there is nothing." Said Cadiston. "We thought that it had to be something like that but what about Chadrick?" Asked Hattie.

"At birth, he was born a healthy baby but was taken away and the stillborn child substituted. They were then offered another child but the student nurse, for reasons we cannot divulge, brought him back to the Mandatens and gave them their own child to raise." Explained Cadiston. "So that is why we will need to alter the family tree." Said Hattie. "Exactly but do not do anything until we have wrapped everything up and got hold of our concrete proof." Said Cadiston.

"Understood, now if you are happy with what we have brought you, we will leave you to get on with your police work as we are certain that you have a great deal to do." Said Hattie. "You do not know the half." Replied Mac. "As Mac said and yes, we have plenty to do. Once again, thank you both for all your efforts." Said Cadiston. "Glad to have been of help, Detective." They stood and left, leaving Cadiston and Mac to analyse the information they had brought them. "That is done so now we can begin to re −. Or rather begin to investigate Baron Laseroie Mandaten's tragic death." Said Cadiston. "I will bring the car around but can I just ask Richard a favour please." Said Mac mysteriously and he left. At that moment, Cadiston's phone rang.

"Cadiston." "PC Whimsdale from traffic here, we located the vehicle that was reported to traffic and sadly, after a high-speed chase, the vehicle crashed. There were two occupants in the vehicle and were both were taken to the Royal Hospital. The only survivor was a Bernard Standmore and he is in surgery now. The other was his son, Roger Standmore. Sadly, he died at the scene because he was not wearing a seat belt. There is a police guard stationed at his room. That is if he survives the surgery and he will be handcuffed to his bed." Said PC Whimsdale. "Good work PC Whimsdale. As soon as he is able to talk, we will need to interview him at the hospital. That is if he survives." Said Cadiston. "Understood." Said Whimsdale and the line went dead. "That is another one caught but sadly, the youngster died in the crash." Said Cadiston.

"A bitter blow for his mother that is, very sad, especially when she told us that she wanted nothing to do with their vendetta." Said Mac. As he returned to the office to check on the phone call. "You are right Mac, they are responsible for her son's death, and with that in mind I expect that she may well want to talk and tell us more. Before we do anything else, we should inform her of her son's death. May be bad timing but then ask her a few questions." Said Cadiston. "I saw Olito in the outer office, I will get her to bring Gloria from the holding cell up to the interview room." Before Cadiston could answer, he was gone. In the interview room, Cadiston waited and was wondering what revelations may be exposed from the grieving mother of Roger. She would blame her husband for the death of their son but he also knew that in a state of grief, he may get absolutely nothing from her. His wait was over as they entered and his question was about to be answered. "Come in, Gloria, and sit down please." Said Cadiston.

"Thought you had done with me for today." Said Gloria. He made sure that she was comfortable, then broke the sad news. "Gloria, it is with a sad heart and with deep regret that I need to inform you that during a high-speed car chase, your husband crashed the car that he and your son were travelling in. There is no easy way to tell you this, your husband Bernard is in hospital receiving treatment for his injuries and may not survive but sadly, your son, Roger, died at the scene of the crash." Gloria said nothing. She just sat there stunned. "Are you alright? Can we get you anything? A cup of tea or coffee perhaps?" Asked Cadiston. "Everyone thinks a cup of tea will be the answer but, that will not bring my son back, will it Cadiston? Damn him, damn him to hell! To hell, he should have died and –." She wiped her eyes. "Sorry, I mean it should have been him that died and not my Roger, he should be the one to live. Dam them all, dam the complete family of Standlyhope to hell they are all responsible for my lovely Roger's death. I told him repeatedly not to involve us in their vendetta as we had nothing against the Mandaten family, only gratitude. You may have said it before that they want to wipe the whole family out because of something that happened way back in the 1650s and I told them it was silly. They said that they would carry their family grudge and seek their revenge until there was not a single Mandaten left. Now their vendetta has claimed my son who is innocent of everything and should not even have been at home but at school. Things have not been good between Bernard and myself for a while and I was preparing to leave him. Damn them all, Detective! Damn them all and their stupid vendetta." She wiped the tears from her eyes again then sat bolt upright, Roger was the only good thing to come from my marriage, my parents warned me that Bernard was no good, but I was young and foolish and fell for his lies. "Alright, I reckon that you would like to ask me a few questions. Well, ask away Detective because now I have a reason for seeking revenge on them and that is the unwarranted and unneeded death of my son." Said Gloria with anger in her eyes and voice.

Cadiston thought to himself that Gloria was a hard woman but striking while the iron whilst hot might lead to information flowing. "Are you sure that you are up to this, Gloria?" Asked Cadiston. "Do it now, Detective, do it now while my anger is high and before I calm down." She replied. The tape was switched on and introductions spoken. "Tell us all that you know about an incident four years ago when the Baron Lasseroie Mandaten's vehicle was run off the road." Cadiston said calmly. "That is exactly what it was, Detective, and they thought that they had got away with it. The car was run off the road by Tomas and Bernard and the car that they used is still in the scrap yard, an old Land Rover. I guess that you will find paint from the car they ran off the road on it." Said Gloria. "The scrap yard's name?" Asked Cadiston.

"Just A Load Of Metal and it is out on the Numberton village road." She said.

"DS Macswee." Said Cadiston. "On it, DCI Cadiston." Mac left the interview room to get a team to investigate it. "Is there anything else that you can tell us?" Asked Cadiston. "Not really, just the car and gun thing." She replied.

"Do you know who tampered with the gun?" Asked Cadiston. "Tomas did, he somehow managed to get hold of it and brought it here. He and my husband took it to a friend of theirs that is a machinist, I think his name was Crichie but that is probably a nickname and the only one that I heard them mention." She said. "Do you know where we can locate this Critchie?" "His workshop is in Lothan road Amptil, detective Cadiston". "Alright Gloria, now would you be prepared to turn state's evidence and assist us in putting these murderers in prison away from decent people?" Asked Cadiston. "You mean stand up in court and swear to what they have done?" She asked. "Something like that and if we can prove that you had nothing to do with any of the incidents, you will not face any serious charges. You may face a lesser charge of withholding information and perverting the course of justice but saying that you have turned state's evidence and a witness for the prosecution, you may get away with a suspended sentence, and we will have a good word to say on your behalf." Said Cadiston. "I hate them, Detective! I should have listened to my parents, especially my mother, who did not want me to marry him. I hate them even more now that they have as good as murdered my son. He died because of them." She started sobbing uncontrollably. It took her a while to calm down and then she said with a cold stare. "So yes, I will do as you ask and will achieve great satisfaction in doing so." Gloria replied with a smile.

"Good, and we will do all that we can to help you. Olito, will you take Gloria back to the holding cell please and see that she has all that she needs in the way of food and beverages please?" Asked Cadiston. "With pleasure sir, come along, Gloria." Said Olito. Gloria stood up and gave a half-smile before saying. "Cadiston, you get them for me and lock them up and throw away the key." She turned and left the room. The interview tape was turned off.

"Team on the way to the scrap yard, Boss. That will be a major piece of evidence to get the vehicle that they used but will we still need the witness interviews?" Asked Mac. "That we will, Mac. We are now going to pay them a visit and get the witness statements. The eye witness addresses are here and as long as they have not moved, it should be easy to find them." Said Cadiston. "Need a piece of luck then." Said Mac. "It helps Mac, it certainly helps." replied Cadiston.

"While I was at it, I gave Janet and Grace a call and gave them the name Crichie and his address as the machinist of the small disc." Said Mac. "Well done, Mac. And again, you were thinking without being told." Said Cadiston. "Still down to you, Cadders, you give me that edge to enable me to think." Said Mac. The car was fired up and they had soon arrived at the first eye witness's address, Hewsten's Farm. They found their way up the long drift and into the yard and were then greeted by a middle-aged stout lady. "And what can we do for you men? Don't usually get smartly dressed ones here on the farm in a smart car, usually lorries." Remarked Mrs Hewsten. "Good morning." Cadiston glanced at the clock on the wall. "Or rather afternoon, I am DCI Cadiston this is DS Macswee and we would like a word with –." He flipped through his notebook. "Mr John Hewsten please and I am guessing that he is not your Husband?" She smiled at Cadiston, "That would be my son, out ploughing but I will give him a call on the radio for you." Said the lady. The radio crackled as she called. "John, are you hearing me boy? Two bobbies here want a word, hope you haven't been a naughty boy and have got into trouble with the law." She said into the radio. "Hear you ma, just finished this field so be there in ten." Replied the voice and the radio fell silent. "Have some tea detectives and a nice piece of our farmhouse fruit cake while you wait. Come on in the kitchen, and don't mind the dog, he is a big softie. Wouldn't make a guard dog. I think he has lost his bark, all we get from him is gentle woof." She said. They followed her into the kitchen and sat at the old kitchen table. The tea was soon poured, then the cake sliced and just as they were enjoying it, John walked in. "Wow, Mother, entertaining two police officers, whatever next and what would pop think bless him?" He then laughed. "Joking aside, how can I help you, detectives, and by the way pop passed away last year, so Ma me and borther Jimbo run the farm now?"

"We understand that you witnessed a road trafic incident four years ago." Said Cadiston. "Wondered when I would be interviewed for that, you boys in blue certainly took your time." Said John. "There is a reason for that, sir, and I am not at liberty to divulge it. Now, what can you remember about that incident?" Asked Cadiston. "Everything and in detail. I was ploughing the dyke field and saw a blue Jaguar coming very steadily toward the bridge. As it slowed down, this Land Rover raced up beside it and forced it off the road. It crashed through the railings down the bank and into the dyke upside down. The passenger of the Rover got out had a look, then got back in and they left. I could see that they were laughing. I raced to the site in the tractor and jumped into the water and tried to get the occupants out but the doors were all jammed solid and nothing would move. I got back to my tractor and grabbed the sledgehammer. Got back in the dyke and went underwater then smashed the windscreen. By this time, two other cars had pulled up and the drivers were up to their necks in the dyke with me. Well, we managed to free the five people and get them out onto the bank and tried resuscitation but alas they had all died, drowned. Horrible way for them to go, their bodies were bloated and not a nice thing to see but we gritted our teeth and got on with what was needed. The other two had arrived after the event and didn't see the incident first hand but could see what had happened so did what they could. The Land Rover disappeared down the Numberton Road but I can tell you that there were two men in it. I would even now recognize the one that got out. That was no accident, Detective, but a deliberate running off the road; it was murder." Said John. "Thank you, sir, and you would be prepared to stand up in court and say exactly what you have told us and that I have written down?" Asked Cadiston. "Should have done that at least three years ago but you know why it didn't happen so yep, you bet I will. We are tenant farmers here and the farm belongs to Lord Mandaten, it was his brothers farm and it was his family that were murdered in the dyke. Have you spoken to Hue and his wife, Veronique, yet? They were out walking their dog and poor old Hue got hit by the Land Rover as it sped away. Damn swine broke poor old Hue's leg. I got to him first and from what he told me, he got a good look at the driver. They live in the first house just over the bridge and I know for a fact that it really shook them up." Added John. "Thank you for that, John, and they are our next port of call. We will be in touch." They returned to their car and drove slowly back down the drift to their next address. "Well what about that ma? Nice couple of coppers ma, much better than that first one standish that was his name, so I wonder why he did not carry on with the investigation and now these two young officers have taken it over years down the line." Said John. "They certainly were, Son. That DCI is quite a hunk but don't tell your father I said that, he would turn in his grave son." They both laughed.

The door was opened before Cadiston and Mac had a chance to knock.

"Was waiting for you, Detective. Mrs. Hewsten just rang and told us you were on the way. Now come in and take a seat, then you can ask your questions." Said Hue. Once seated, they began. "What do you remember about the incident that happened four years ago when the blue Jaguar was run off the road?" Asked Cadiston. "Nearly took us as well that mad, crazy driver in the Land Rover did, deliberately ran the Jag off the road then tried to run us down. I pushed the wife out of the way and got a broken leg when he hit me. John tried so hard to get the people out of the car but they were all drowned. Then he noticed me, first one to do that." Said Hue. "I believe that you got a good look at the driver?" Asked Cadiston. "As close as we are and before you ask, the answer is yes, I would recognise him in a crowd, his face is etched in my brain." Said Hue. "Now, if you would agree, we will set up an identity parade. Then perhaps you will have a look and identify the driver for us and possibly his passenger?" Asked Cadiston.

"Be glad to, Detective, glad to. Those poor people that died in that car were murdered without a doubt and those responsible must be put away. The whole of Lord Mandatens family gone murdered, he owned these properties you know as part of his estate, his broter another Lord Mandaten owns it all now. These places were built for the farm workers, and although I am retired the good Lord allows us to live our days out in this our home. Well, if there is nothing else, our afternoon program is about to start on the TV and don't want to miss the start." Said Hue. "Not a problem, sir, we will be in touch." They heard the door close behind them. "What a lovely polite old couple." Said Mac. "That they are, Mac, and as well as the Mandaten family needing justice so do they, let's head to the scrapyard and see what our boys have found there." Said Cadiston. There were two men in handcuffs talking to a police officer while others were involved in the search for the Land Rover. They had been there for thirty-eight minutes when a shout went up. "Over here, chaps! Looks like this is what we are looking for." They all made their way to where the officer was waiting and sure enough, there it sat hidden under a taupe.

"Get a truck in here and take this to the compound," said Cadiston "No touching it lads, could be valuable evidence there," said the sergeant in charge, "Well said sergeant, then forensics can go over it with a fine-tooth comb. Even without that, I can see blue paint still clearly visible on this left side." Said Cadiston. "Thanks to Standish, they thought they had got away with it so never bothered to clean it off. How do we get to make a match on the Jaguar as we don't have that to match the damage and the colour?" Asked Mac. "Already thought of that, Mac. I had a read of the report, and the Jaguar was recovered by AM Motor recovery so with a bit of luck, they may still have the Jag in their yard." Said Cadiston. "Next port of call then?" Asked Mac. "You have it, Mac. Leave you boys to tidy up here. The yard is closed from now until further notice and those two can be held as possible accessories until we have finished questioning them." Said Cadiston.

"You got it, DCI Cadiston." Said Sergeant Jake stone. "Over to you then, Jake." Said Cadiston. They were quickly back in the car and making their way to the recovery yard. "Afternoon gents, and what can we do for you?" Asked the man at the desk.Cadiston and Mac presented their warrant cards and with the introductions over, Morris stepped backward in surprise. "Police hey, whatever it is, we didn't do it." He then laughed nervously. "Only joking, so how can we help?" Morris asked. "Just a long shot but four years ago, you retrieved a blue Jaguar from the dyke near the bridge on the Old Rectory Road –." Said Cadiston. "Four years ago, blue Jaguar you say –. Need a bit of help there, Al, get your butt out here now. He has a better memory than me." A stocky man appeared. "Yep, what do want me for?" "Can you remember a recovery of a blue Jaguar four years ago?" Asked Morris.

"Let me think for a second or two –. Four year ago –That would be the recovery from the dyke where that Baron some-one or other died. Five of them in the car all died at the scene, him, his wife, and three kids, a girl and two boys. Drowned, horrible way to go. Yep, I remember it, blue Jaguar and still up there at the back of the yard. Never been taken away for anal-ysis by you boys so still there." Said Al. "Can we have a look at it?" Asked Cadiston.

"Right this way, gents." They walked briskly behind Al and once uncovered they were soon staring at the blue Jaguar. "Lot of damage to the driver's side, DCI Cadiston, and even four years on, looks like green paint and that could be a match with the Rover." Said Mac. "Looks that way, DS Macswee. Al, can you take this vehicle to the police compound for us?" Asked Cadiston.

"Wondered why it didn't go there in the first place. That de-tective bloke told us to bring it here and would be in touch but never heard another word." Said Al.

"The detective bloke, can you remember his name?" Asked Cadiston.

"Think man think, Tandsher no, Frandiash no, it was some-thing like that. Got it, Standish, that's the name, Standish. Didn't like him too abrupt and said this was nothing more than a tragic driving accident, said the baron must have been travelling to fast and lost control of the car, and that was that." Said Al.

"Thanks'for that, now I can check on his report. Now, the Jaguar?" Asked Cadiston. "Doing nothing right now so can do it straight away. That suit you detective?" Asked Al. "Absolutely, we will meet you there." They returned to their car and left. "Am recovery. Al and Morris makes sense", remarked Mac.

"Now that was a real stroke of luck, Boss, what say you?" Added Mac after a short pause. "Definitely Mac, so now we have both the vehicles and when they are in the compound together, Jooners and his team can get to work on them." Said Cadiston. They knew that they would have a wait but wanted to be there to see the vehicles delivered. Cadiston phoned Jooners to inform him of what they had found and that he would be required to carry out a full forensic analysis on both vehicles and he hoped that after four years, the evidence would still be there. The wait for the delivery was not very long, in fact, much quicker than expected. The first to arrive was the forensic teams low loader carrying the Land Rover, and fifteen minutes later the Jaguar was there. With both vehicles present, Jooners was informed and the team from forensics began their investigation.

"No point in you two hanging about, Cadders, this will take some time. We will give you a call as soon as we have the information that you want and anything else that we have found." Said Jooners."Ok Jooners, thanks." They got back into their car. "It is all falling into place Mac, slowly but surely falling into place. We will soon have them." Said Cadiston. "And I want Grant in cuffs, Cadders. It looks as though he may not have committed the Mandaten murders but from what has been found out about him, I am convinced that he was the one that murdered his first wife. He thinks that he has a solid alibi but we know better and when we have re-questioned Jonnett Muskaday and gotten the real whole truth from her, I think that his alibi will be proven false. If it is alright with you, I would like to be the one to caution and cuff him?" Said Mac. "Be my guest, Mac. After a lot more questioning with him, I think that he will break. With the false testimony of Jonnett disrupted which equates to more lies being told, you can have the pleasure of cuffing him and reading him his rights while I stand back and watch." Said Cadiston. Thanks' for that, it will give me great pleasure to wipe the smugness off his face. So Cadders, what do we do now? It is a quarter to five." Said Mac."Back to the office, do a quick recap on today's events, then home. Tuesday 16th we should have Miss Muskaday to interview and that will put a spanner in Grant's alibi for the night his first wife was murdered." Said Cadiston.

"You know something, Cadders, I feel really sorry for Gloria Standmore. I have watched her very closely and I know that you cannot always judge by looks but I strongly believe that she is innocent of a major crime and only passed the drug on with the belief that it was for a sick animal. It is true that she took it and she was going to return what had not been used but that was her only mistake. As for withholding evidence, I strongly believe that she was under a threat of violence from the Standlyhope clan to keep her silent. I think we should try and help her if we can. I think it is a case of getting in with the wrong people and as to that, she was ready to get away from them." Said Mac. "I agree with you, Mac, but we have to see it through and let the courts decide how to deal with her. We will do all that we can to help her. Her family have had a lot to contend with over the years." Said Cadiston.

"From riches to rags you mean?" Said Mac. "Something like that but with the help of the Mandatens, they have picked themselves up. She has suffered big time through the Standlyhopes with the loss of her son and we will see what can be done. Police work is not all about making arrests and getting convictions, as you are finding out. A degree of compassion comes into the equation and that does you credit. You are learning, Mac, learning how to read a person and decipher the truth from the lie."

"I have a good teacher, Cadders, so keep teaching." Mac said and smiled. Back in the office, they looked at the day's events and itemised them all in detail. "We have Gloria's testimony, and we have statements from John Hewsten, Hue and Veronique Hurst who were eye witnesses to Baron Lasseroie Mandaten's car being run off the road. We have had a major piece of luck and recovered the two vehicles involved, namely the blue Jaguar of Baron Mandaten and the green Land Rover of Bernard and Tomas Standmore. We have a link to good old ex-Sergeant Standish from that incident and we have evidence collected by Richard and Hattie, is there anything else, Mac?" Asked Cadiston. "I think you have got it all covered. Jooners and his team are investigating the two vehicles and Jonnett Muskaday will be with us tomorrow but that is for Tuesday. We have given Howie and Nadine the name of Edward Brexly, Demmie's brother, and are waiting to hear back from Janet and Grace about the name of Crichie. I think that sums up the day's events." Mac hesitated. "Just one thing bothers me though. We will have Tomas and Bernard for pushing the Jaguar off the road but how will we have them for the murder of Lord Mandaten's brother with all his family? A good solicitor will push for that to be dangerous driving or driving without due care and attention and label it as manslaughter and not murder." Said Mac. "That one is a bit more difficult and will require some thinking to charge them with their murder. They will most definitely face the charges of driving without due care and attention, and forcing another vehicle off the road and add to that with the intent to kill, leaving the scene of an incident, dangerous driving, and a hit and run charge but we will need the legal team to find a way to charge them with murder and make it stick otherwise they may get off with it being the lesser charge of manslaughter." Said Cadiston. "We have them but do not have them, if you know what I mean." Said Mac sadly. "I see exactly what you mean, Mac. It worries you as it does me that unless we can find a secure charge with the evidence to back it, they may walk free." Said Cadiston. "We cannot allow that to happen, Cadders, no way can we allow that." Said Mac. "We will not Mac, the legal team will see to that. Any loophole will be plugged so a clever solicitor cannot wriggle through it." Said Cadiston. "Best we get them thinking on it then starting with Tuesday morning." Said Mac. "Had that in mind, Mac. As you already know, there have been guilty parties that have managed to wriggle free of a major charge and get away with a lesser one and I do not want these to have the chance to do that." Said Cadiston. "You mean not guilty of murder but guilty of manslaughter?" Asked Mac. "Exactly, now there is nothing more that we can do today so home now, then we will be ready to interview Jonnett Muskaday in the morning –." Before he had finished, the phone rang. "Bit late in the day for a phone call, hope it is not another tragedy at Mandaten." Said Mac as he picked up the receiver. "DS Macswee."

"Sergeant Davidson here from the met, is DCI Cadiston there?" "He is, did you need to speak with him personally or can I take a message as I am his detective sergeant." Said Mac. "Of course, should have recognised the name Macswee and a detective sergeant now. How are you Mac and how is the detective training going, or have you finished that must have being a detective sergeant? I would say yes." Said Davidson. "Davidson, of course, Buck. Well, blow me down, good to hear you. I am fine and working with Cadders as his sergeant but enough of the chit chat. What do you need him to know?" Asked Mac. "Just tell him that Jonnett Muskaday is in our custody and will be with you by 10:30 a.m. Tuesday morning." Said Davidson.

"Brilliant, we will be looking forward to speaking with that young lady and if there is time, catch up with you. Thanks Sergeant Davidson and see you in the morning." The line went silent. "That was good old Bucanon Davidson or Buck for short. He is a sergeant with the met now and will be here in the morning at 10:30 with Jonnett." Said Mac.

"Haven't seen him for a while. He left here and transferred to the met to take his chance of the promotion and his move has been worthwhile so good for him. Be good to see him again. Now I am satisfied with today's events and what we have discovered so, my friend, home for us as we have many more busy days ahead." Said Cadiston.

"And if they all go as well as they have done today then we will soon be making some serious arrests." Added Mac. "And that cannot be soon enough. Now it's 6.38 p.m. Mac, so home for us before we start on something else." Said Cadiston. "No more to be said then so night, Cadders, see you in the morning." Said Mac. "Night Mac." Mac left and Cadiston took a lingering look at their incident board, and shuddered when he gazed upon the photographs of Kevin and Lowel, then whispered. "Get that up to date in the morning. Then Jonnett Muskaday, we will see what you have to say for yourself and find out under questioning if the alibi that you supplied Grant was a false one, something tells me that it was and he is responsible for destroying your life now." He turned and walked from the office closing the door behind him.

Chapter Eighteen

The Final Pieces of Evidence

Cadiston and Mac spent a very restless night and with their sleep being disrupted. They could not settle to sleep soundly and the sleep they did have was in stages. They were both very aware that their investigations were nearing an end and arrests were imminent. After that would be the court case followed by the guilty being placed in prison and that would be a very satisfactory conclusion and final closure. They were also aware that if everything was not correct to the letter, for example how they had collected evidence, how statements were obtained, and if they had badgered the person that was under arrest then a clever solicitor would use that to obtain an acquittal or to secure a lesser charge and this they wanted to avoid at all costs. Their investigation had gone well to date and they both knew that they were on the home straight and as Jonas had said to Cadiston a while ago, 'Dot the i, cross the t, with a full stop at the end'.

Tuesday the 16th of November, and Mandaten Manor was feeling the November morning chill but not all due to the weather. It was 4 degrees outside but as the remaining family arrived in the breakfast room, an eerie silence chilled the air below zero. Even though there were so few remaining, these few still eyed each other with suspicion. The time was 09:15 and their parents now made an appearance.

"Morning Mother, Father, I have ordered fresh tea and coffee and if you would like a freshly cooked breakfast then I will order it for you now." Said Lizabeth. "No thank you, Lizabeth, we took our breakfast in our room. Her father looked around the room. "Greta and Jennifer not here?" He asked. "No Father, they are not. A taxi picked them up as usual at 9 a.m. and I cannot for the life of me imagine where they are going every morning and always at the same time. Very strange and peculiar that is, it has been that way since that murdering, sorry, I mean since my brother, Chadrick, died so I cannot imagine what they are up to." Said Lizabeth. "Well Mother, they cannot be sitting with him now not unless they are sitting with a corpse and that would be very morbid but then I would not put that past them." Said Kansas snidely.

"You changing your tune, Lizabeth, calling him your brother?" Asked Grant. "Well, like it or not, that is what he is or was just as you are Grant, brother dear." Said Lizabeth. He sent a look of hatred toward his sister. "I have told you before, don't call me 'brother dear', Lizabeth you know how I hate it. Or –. Do you do it just to annoy me?" Grant replied angrily. She smiled at him. "Not at all, Grant, not at all. I was just wondering, Father, DCI Cadiston has not been here for a while. Do you think that he has closed all the cases now that Chadrick is dead? Well, he was the murderer so maybe we will be left alone now?" Asked Lizabeth in a demure voice. Lord Mandaten glanced at Lizabeth with a look of steel then gently shook his head. "Why Daughter, do you want them all to be closed quickly? Have you something to hide, something you would rather he did not find out?"

"Not at all, Father, I want to or rather need to know if it was Chadrick that has murdered the family if it was then we can rest easy without fear of being murdered." Answered Lizabeth. You just stated that he was the murderer as though proven." Retorted her father. "I should have said it looks like it was and if it was then we have nothing more to worry about and can get on with our lives. But if he did not then the killer or killers are still out there then we still have plenty to worry about." Said Lizabeth. "How silly of you, Lizabeth. Of course he did it, his wife at least, and the gun was still in his hands." Added Grant quickly. "And you saw that did you, Grant?" Said Lady Mandaten.

"You don't catch me with that one, Mother, I was not here remember and came in after the shooting, remember? That detective bloke Macswee brought me from my car the moment that I pulled up." Said Grant smugly.

"Well, as we were not here, either we could not comment on that." Said Lady Mandaten. "Maybe you were not but they certainly were, they can confirm that I was not here until after the shooting and so can that detective, the one that is with Cadiston, what is his name –, wow I just said it a second ago –. Macswee, that is it, Macswee. So I am in the clear and have a solid alibi backed up by a policeman no less." Said Grant. Lord Mandaten looked at Grant remembering that a few years ago after his first wife was murdered, he had also come up with an alibi for that occasion. She had been shot to death and sadly they were part of his alibi. "Yes Grant, well to get back to Lizabeth's question, no, I do not think for one minute that Cadiston has just closed all the cases. I do not believe that Chadrick is guilty of any of the murders and I believe that Cadiston is extremely busy with his investigations and when he is ready, we will have another visit from him. Until then we wait." Said Lord Mandaten.

"But what if Chadrick was not the killer, Father, what then?" Asked Lizabeth tearfully. "Well, if he was not, sister dear, which I doubt then I have my protector tucked up close to my chest. No one had better come after me." Said Grant smugly. "Yes, Grant, and we do not need to be constantly reminded of that. Now Tomas and I have an appointment with the bank at 11 a.m. so we need to be getting ready. I guess that I asked a question that cannot be answered so forget that I asked, come Tomas." He stood, promptly following her upstairs to their room.

As neither could sleep very well, both Cadiston and Macswee had arrived at the station early but had not been idle and brought their incident board up to date and as they stared at it, the phone rang. "Cadiston."

"Morning Cadders, Jerimiah here and sorry to disturb you but there is something that has been bugging me." Said Jeremiah. "And what might that be, Jerimiah?" Asked Cadiston. "It may be nothing but well it has bugged me so thought I had best tell you. It was on the day that Chad was attacked and Demmie shot. He thought that no one would see it, well I did. I saw Grant's car parked and almost hidden up near the old ruins. He had tried to cover it but as the sun shone through the trees it reflected off the screen causing a flash of light. I was curious so went to look and there was his car. Like I said; it may be nothing but thought it strange it was parked up there and that you should know." Said Jeremiah. "Could tie in with a thought and suspicion that I have so thanks for that, Jerimiah, but keep it to yourself." replied Cadiston. "Will do and if it helps glad to have told you, bye." the line went dead. "Interesting bit of information, Mac." Said Cadiston and just then the phone rang again. "Cadiston." Cadiston answered again.

"WPC Janet Crowth here, just letting you know that we have found the maker of the disc, his name, Crichie real name, Trevor Crichon. He has confirmed that he is a friend of Bernard and Tomas Standmore and it was him that made the disc for Tomas. He tried to run and after knocking me over he tried the same trick on Grace but she was more than a match for him and had him cuffed before he knew it. We are both fine and have no injuries to report and are on the way in with him. It will take us about a half hour to get there. It may be nothing but I was suspicious when I saw a brand new mountain bike partly cut-up." Said Janet. "Good work, both of you. Bring him in and see you in half hour you say, that will be 10:15. We have an interview at around 10:30 so take him directly to a holding cell and we will get to him when we have questioned our other witness." Said Cadiston. "Will do, see you in about an hour after our interview." the phone line went silent.

"That is good work, with him in irons we will have our witness to give us the evidence to arrest Tomas for the murder of Kevin. And if Jonnett spills the beans and tells the truth then she will be our witness to arrest Grant for the murder of his first wife, Geraldine Mandaten nee' Granchister. We have or rather you have, with a small input from me, solved the murders of Bonnie and her unborn girl child by Demmie. And now the testimony of Trevor Crichton will be enough verbal evidence to arrest Tomas for the murder of Kevin. That's three of the eleven murders solved, Bonnie and her unborn child and Kevin so that is three down and eight to go. Slowly, we are gathering the required evidence and soon we will have them all. Now, who is left? Malcolm, Sadie, Sammie, Walter, Gloria, James, Lowell, and Demmie plus the attack on Chad. That is a good –. No, hang on I need to go back to school, there is a miscount. Let me just re-cap – Hmm, err silly me, that is where it is. I have not counted Grant's first wife in the 'almost solved' and did not include Lord Mandaten's brother, Lasseroie, and his family either in the 'under investigation'. Best that I try that again. We had a total of eleven recent murders, then two re-opened cases, bringing the total up to –." Mac tapped on his fingers as he counted and continued. "Seventeen murders and one attempted murder to investigate altogether. We have enough or will have enough evidence to arrest the culprits of them all eventually. For starters, we now have the evidence to solve nine and for those, we can arrest Tomas, Grant, Bernard, and Demmie who is deceased. That leaves eight and one attempted murder to solve so still a way to go."

"Bet you are not so glad you joined me now." Said Cadiston. "You must be kidding, Cadders, this is what it is all about, and working beside you I love it so bring it on, my friend." Said Mac. The phone rang and was instantly picked up by Macswee.

"There is a Sergeant Davidson at the front desk with a prisoner for you." Said John on the other end. "Thanks, John, be right there," The receiver was replaced. Without delay Mac made his way to the front desk to collect their prisoner and potential witness. Come through Buck, sorry, Sergeant Davidson. DCI Cadiston is waiting for you in the office." Said Mac. On the way, he caught the attention of Olito and Francis. "WPCs Rendham and Paverson, would you escort this prisoner, Miss Jonnett Muskaday, to interview room two please? Would you fetch her something to drink and get her settled and we will be with you shortly." Said Mac. "With pleasure, Sergeant Macswee." They took charge of Jonnett while Mac took Buck to see Cadiston. After their handshake, greeting, and a smile or two, they chatted.

"You don't look any different, and how is life in the met?" Asked Cadiston.

"Not a bed of roses that is for sure but glad that I made the move." Said Buck.

"It certainly paid off for you." Said Cadiston. The conversation flowed between them. "And you both have been promoted?" Asked Buck. "Only temporary promotions, just while we investigate these Mandaten cases." Said Cadiston.

"Well now, you have your prisoner and I need to get back so must be going as it is a long drive. It was good to see you again and catch up with the pair of you but now must go." With more handshakes, he left. They watched him go then Cadiston and Mac went to interview room two.

Before entering, they looked through the window and could see that the WPCs had provided a drink and a few biscuits for the prisoner who was looking agitated. "Let's do it, Mac." The door opened and as the WPCs went to leave, Cadiston stopped them. "Best you both stay for this interview please." They stood by the wall. "Get two chairs and we will wait to begin until you are back." They opened the door and left. While they waited for their return, they sat in silence and could see that their prisoner was beginning to get fidgity and guessed that she was nervous. They were not prepared to break the silence, at least not just yet.

"Delay, delay, I am sick of this and I haven't got a clue why I should have been arrested and brought all the way back to England from France. I have done nothing wrong and have been living there for the past three and a half years so I ask you what is this all about?" Asked Jonnett with a hint of anger in her voice. "When our WPCs are back, we will begin." Replied Mac, then as if to order, the door opened. Once seated, the interview tape was switched on and with all the introductions made the interview began.

"Now, you ask why you had been arrested and brought here and you say that you have no idea why?" Asked Cadiston. "Correct, so now perhaps you will enlighten me so that I can get out of here and get back home to life in France?" She snapped.

"Impatient to return to France are you, Jonnett? it is alright to call you that? Is it or have you any objections?" Asked Mac. "Jonnett is just fine. Now, stop messing around and hesitating and get down to why I am here so that we can get this over with and

I can be taken back home." She said. "You were given no idea of the reason when you were arrested?" Asked Cadiston. "None at all. I was only told I was required for questioning. Now for goodness' sake, get on with it." Jonnett said angrily. "All we are looking for is the truth, Jonnett. Not a pack of lies but the truth, do you understand?" Asked Mac. "Understand, of course I understand but I still do not know what you want the truth about." Said Jonnett. "We are giving you ample opportunity to remember, Jonnett. Now, as you are still in ignorance of why you are here please look at this photograph and tell us if you know this woman. For the record, we are showing a photograph to the prisoner. Have a good, long look at it before you give your answer." Said Cadiston. She stared hard and began to shuffle in her seat. "Never seen her before. Besides, that is a picture of a dead woman." Said Jonnett. "Look again please, Jonnett, and remember we want the truth, not a lie but the truth. Look again, very carefully." She looked sheepishly at Cadiston and he continued. "The photograph, Jonnett, and tell me if you recognise her." "Well, maybe a bit but not too sure if it is her as she is dead so not a good likeness." She said as she wrung her hands, then crossed her arms. "The truth, Jonnett, you recognize her, don't you?" Asked Cadiston.

"Alright, yes I do, it is Geraldine Granchister – Mandaten and this photograph tells me that she is dead but what has that got to do with me? I did not kill her." Said Jonnett. "I understand that you know her husband, Grant Mandaten?" Said Cadiston. She looked at the wall and again looked very sheepish. "So what if I do know him? No law against that, is there?" She said defensively. "No law against that, Jonnett, but there is a law against providing a false alibi in order to pervert the course of justice." Said Cadiston. Jonnett's face coloured and her arms were held tightly against her body. "W-w-what do you mean false alibi? I have not given a false alibi." She stammered. Mac looked at her then shook his head before speaking. "Tutt, tutt, come now, Jonnett. We know it all so tell us the truth now and that will help your case. We have your original statement and that is a complete fabrication of the true events of that evening, now isn't it? We are giving you the chance to remember so just think for a moment before you speak again as it will not help you at all to continue lying. You said that you had no idea why you were arrested but I would have thought that was now obvious. We have evidence and know that you are lying, Jonnett, so there is no reason to continue with the charade. The truth, now that is all we require, nothing but the truth. This is your chance, Jonnett, so before you utter another word, think extremely carefully." "As Detective Macswee just said, think carefully before you speak. We know that you lied four years ago. The law has a long arm that is why you are here now so think very carefully. We have the false statement that you made four years ago so now it is time to correct that wrong. The sooner that you tell us the truth, the sooner you will stand a chance of leaving here. Plus, that young woman, Geraldine Mandaten, can finally rest in peace once her murderer has been arrested and punished for his crime." Said Cadiston.

"Well it was not me, I did not kill her." Said Jonnett as she sat back in her seat in silence. Her eyes moved from side to side looking first at Cadiston and then at Macswee. Back and forth her eyes travelled and then she broke down in tears. A box of tissues was placed on the interview table. After she had dried her eyes she turned to Cadiston. "I do not care about what happens to him but what will happen to me?" She asked. "Tell us the whole truth now and be a witness for the prosecution and we will do everything that we can but the outcome of that will be down to the judge." Replied Cadiston. "So what charge would I face if I tell you the truth now?" She asked. "Withholding evidence, providing a false statement and alibi plus perverting the course of justice." Said Mac. "That is quite a list, what a fool I was." Said Jonnett still crying. "Better that than an accessory to murder." Added Mac.

Her voice now had panic in it as she spoke. "Murder, not me! I saw Geraldine in the motel. She told me to get out so was alive and cursing him for treating her false and telling her lies about his wealth and his cheating with other women especially one named Demmie. The wealth was all that she wanted him for, he had promised her the high life. The truth was that he had no money of his own and only had a small allowance from the estate and knowing that, she left him. He waved a gun at her and I thought that it was just a toy gun made of plastic and she laughed at him saying, 'Oh, look at the big man with the small cock trying to look big but even the gun is small. This angered him and he slapped her hard knocking her down, then we left. I had nothing to do with any murder and all he wanted me to do was give him an alibi and that is all I did. I took him home in a taxi and left him there under the pretence that he was drunk. I thought that he should be on the stage as he was putting up such a good act of being just that." Mac then asked his question. "And where did he leave his car parked so that he could return to it later?" "You know of that –." Said Jonnett in surprise. Mac nodded, "We are detectives, Jonnett, and you can be sure that the truth will eventually come out and we already know more than you may think about that evening." "He had it parked behind some bushes on the private road into the Manor and had it hidden well out of sight." She continued. "And is that where the taxi picked you up?" Asked Mac.

"Yes, he had already arranged for the pick-up and gave the driver fifty pounds and told him if he knew what was good for him then he would forget about this, this little trip." She said. Cadiston now took over the questioning. "You knew what he planned to do then, you knew that he planned to kill his wife?"

"No, no, no! I did not know that he wanted to kill her, not for certain. I thought that it was all talk. You must have come across the saying 'oh I could kill you' and they are just words. All he told me was that he wanted to scare her as she had done the dirty on him and he wanted her to pay for her betrayal." Said a frightened Jonnett. Mac now asked another question. "You saw his handgun?" "Yes, but I thought it was just a toy gun and he would use that to scare her." She said. "So how much did he pay you and do not lie about how much as we can easily find that out. It will help you to tell us instead of us searching the bank to find that piece of information." Said Mac. "He paid me £35,000 just to take him home in a taxi and say that we had been out and that he was drunk." She said. Mac continued with another question. "So where did you go on this date so that would enforce the false alibi, the Mari Gras?"

"You really are detectives, aren't you? Not like those others who must have been just playing at it. You have certainly completed your homework knowing the restaurant that we went to and if I had been more vigorously questioned four years ago then I don't think that I could have lied. I was not asked any of this before and that is why it worked for him. He had taken me to the Manor so that the family could see me with him. Then after the row with his wife, we went to the Mari Gras. Thereafter we went to the Old Rectory Restaurant and had another meal, although we did not eat it all, and two bottles of wine. When no one was looking he cleverly poured it into the plant pot that was next to our table. We were asked to leave because he was getting rowdy, and left there with him making out that he was drunk and once away from there, the taxi took us to the Manor where I left him. Then it took me home. The whole truth is that after meeting the family, he had driven us to where the car was to be hidden, then we walked to the main road and were picked up in the taxi that was there waiting for us. The driver then took us to the restaurants, then back to the Manor, then me back to my flat. Two days later, he turned up with a case that had the money in it and a one-way flight to France where he had a house and told me I could live in it and look after him when he visited. There were no visits so that was the last time that I saw him. That is where I have been for the past three, almost four years and have a good job and a good life with my Frankie that is the name I call him." She said. "You said he was having an affair with a young woman named Demmie, what happened to her?" Asked Mac.

"She ended up marrying into the family, I think his name was Chadrick as she was already engaged to him but that did not worry Grant. I had guessed that he was not the type of man that I would want to spend the rest of my life with but he knew of something in my past and if it was broadcast then I would lose my job with the company that I worked for in England who also had an operation in France. I told them I had a place in France and after that, I was transferred to the French office. He had me in the palm of his hand and I had to go along with what he said and that is the whole truth." She said. "And the secret he held over you that was for soliciting, you served a six-month prison sentence and that was followed with a two-year probation period." Said Mac. "You really are a detective and have done your homework. I served my time and have been clean since and got the job with this company. It will not be declared, will it? Please tell me that will not be against me, will it? I have a good life and job in France and if I lose it then I do not know what I will do –." She began to sob. "I will do all that you ask and stand up in court and tell the truth. When I saw in the paper that Geraldine had been shot dead it was only then I realised what I had done. I immediately knew that it was him and regretted giving him the alibi and panicked. I have been living in fear every day waiting for a clever detective to search out the truth and for this to happen."

Cadiston looked at Jonnett and could understand her motive even though it was wrong. "Now, you have stated that you will be prepared to stand up in court and repeat all of this and be a witness for the prosecution?" "Yes, if I had known that he was planning to murder his wife and the gun was not a toy then I would have gone to the police and I would not have gone along with it but I thought just to give an alibi there was nothing wrong in that. It was wrong and now it has gotten me into serious trouble." Said Jonnett. "Help us and we will help you. Thank you, Jonnett. The time is now 13:39 and the interview is suspended." The tape was turned off.

"Would you take Jonnett back to the holding cell please and see that she gets some lunch?" Asked Cadiston. "We will, DCI Cadiston." Olito and Francis escorted her to the cell and when a meal had been brought, the door was locked. They rejoined Cadiston and Macswee, then they all returned to the central office. When they arrived, Janet and Grace were waiting for them. "The prisoner, a Trevor Crichon nickname of Crichie, is in a holding cell for you."

"Excellent, now have you two girls had lunch?" Asked Cadiston. "Not yet." They said in unison. "Right, you be away for that and we will interview Crichie when you return." Said Cadiston. "Wait for us and we will come with you." Said Francis before turning to Cadiston and Mac and asking. "Before we go, did you really know all that information, Cadders? And what about you, Mac?" Mac smiled and answered, "I did a bit of homework on Jonnett just to know her better. They smiled and looked at each other. "Not all of it but I guessed that it had to be something like that. So did a bit of playing it by ear." Replied Cadiston.

"I am baffled, taking him back to the Manor is clear but how would he leave the Manor without being seen?" Asked Olito.

Mac looked at Cadiston and he signaled for him to answer. "Easy Olito, he used the secret passage from the Manor to the woods, then over the wall and into his car. He drove to the motel, leaving his car close enough to get to quickly, then back to the hiding place and then returned the same way."

"And how would he retrieve his car?" Asked Francis.

"One of two ways, he either got Demmie to drive him in her car or took a taxi under the pretense that he was going to collect it from the restaurant."

"You two really are good." Said Olito. "I keep saying it but being with Cadders gives me an edge." Said Mac with a smile. "Well whatever it is, you are getting the answers and the evidence that is required and if we help in some small way then we are happy with that." Said Francis. Cadiston now answered. "As to that, you both are a great help and well done Olito on your trip out with Mac, you are not finished yet. We will be paying them a visit tomorrow for some serious questioning, beginning with Grant. After that to make our arrest so while we are there, I need you to search the Lowell Suite for the sleeping pills or powder that Demmie used to put Chadrick out."

"Not a problem, now if it is alright with you then we will be off to lunch with Janet and Grace." Said Olito. "You go and enjoy." The four WPCs left.

"If I have this right, Cadders, it looks as though Grant knew of the secret passage from the Manor to the woods three years ago but strange that he did not know of the others hence Katrina had to find that out for him." Said Mac.

"At that point, Mac, he did not need them all. Now lunch sounds good to me but must admit that I am not that hungry." Said Cadiston.

"Nor me so maybe just a sandwich and a biscuit washed down with a coffee." Replied Mac. "I will go get them." Said Cadiston. "Not a job for the boss." Answered Mac smiling and he was gone before Cadiston could answer.

While Mac was away, more information came in. Jooners had sent the report and what had been found at the Devil's Dyke search plus what they had found in the Standmore house search. He had worked on the vehicles quickly with his team and his report was also there for that. Howie and Nadine had arrested Demmie's brother, Edward, and were on their way back and would arrive later this afternoon. Amelia and Steven had the required information on the Saint Christopher Medallion and were also on their way back. Lastly, Peter and Jenny had retrieved their information from the security guards that had been on duty patrolling the Black Powder Gun Show site and they were prepared to be witnesses. From having some information and evidence, they were suddenly being swamped with it. Now all they required was the completion of the D.N.A. and blood tests from the Samples that were taken and those found at the incident sites to confirm if there was a match to the suspects.

When Mac returned, he was quite excited to hear of the information that had been gained and he did not try to hide it. "If I did not know better, Mac, I would think that you were a cat that had got the cream or a child that had just found their favourite toy that had been misplaced." Said Cadiston with a smile. "Sorry, Cadders, but it is rather exciting to know that we are on the home straight. Well, for me it is anyhow. It will all help to close the cases satisfactorily." Said Mac. "True enough but let's get these sandwiches eaten and then we will interview Trevor Crichton otherwise known as Crichie with Janet and Grace." Said Cadiston. Mac gave the thumbs up and took another bite from his sandwich. The moment that the WPCs returned, they made their way to the interview room and with the prisoner sitting in front of them, Cadiston activated the interview tape.

"The time is now 15:05 on Tuesday the 16th of November and this is a recording of the interview between DCI Cadiston, Detective Sergeant Macswee, and Trevor Crichton nickname Crichie. Present also are the arresting officers WPCs Janet Crowth and Grace Jorde. Firstly, what name do you wish to be called by during the interview?" Asked Cadiston. "Everyone calls me Crichie so that will do. Before you go any further and ask questions I wish to formally apologise to these young ladies for my unwarranted behavior, it was totally unnecessary. I fully understand if you want to charge me with the assault of a police officer and will go quietly." Said Crichie.

"We will get to that in a moment but first we need to know about this small disc and for the tape, I am showing the disc to the prisoner. Am I to understand that you made this for Tomas Kaysten?" Asked Cadiston. "Yes, I made it alright but not for Tomas Kaysten. Don't know any Kaystens. It was for Tomas Standmore and I must say, it was not a straightforward or easy task. I had made five before I got number six to fit exactly but I was curious what it was needed for. I don't know much about guns but thought it a strange piece to be connected to a gun. That Kentucky Rifle was a beautiful weapon and the replication was first class and when I ask Tomas what that disc was for, he said that it was part of a safety thing to stop it from being overloaded. I asked him if he wanted me to place it in the barrel for him, then he got angry and snapped a bit and said. 'Definitely not that would not achieve what it is for, all you had to do was make it and that you have done'. He then paid me and went and that is all I can tell you." Said Crichie. "Why did you take on the job?" Asked Cadiston. "He and Bernard have been friends of mine for about 30 years, from school days. I did it as a favour, plus I needed the money as there are not that many people that require a quality precision machinist. I was glad of the work and they did pay me handsomely to do the job. £3000 and they told me to keep quiet about it but when your two ladies asked about the disc, I guessed that there was something not quite right and guessed that there must be something amiss and I panicked. Sorry ladies, I hope I did not hurt either of you." Said Crichie.

"Not at all Crichie, no damage done." Said Grace. "As to that I am glad. I hated myself for trying to fight you and you got the better of me anyhow but still sorry." Said Crichie. "Sorry for the attack on them or sorry that they caught you?" Asked Mac. "I was not aware of breaking any law so definitely because of my attack, Detective." Said Crichie. "Now Crichie, you made the disc and were told that it was needed to stop the weapon from being overloaded?" Asked Cadiston. "That is spot on, Detective. I can guess that something is not right but I am at a bit of a loss. Surely there is no crime in doing a piece of precision machining, is there?" Asked Crichie. "None at all, Crichie, but in this case it is. It was used to commit the crime of murder." Said Cadiston. "Murder! Now just you hang on, Detective, I know nothing about a murder. All I did was to make the disc and that was it. Thinking about it now, which I did not do at the time, it was strange that they paid me to keep quiet about it, another £15000 and that was on top of the £3000 to do the job. To make the disc and the rest not to talk about it and what he said about not achieving what it is for –. Now that makes sense. Still a bit baffled though just how could that little disc be used in a murder?" Asked Crichie. "Put a heavy load of black powder in the gun, then secure it at the bottom of the barrel with the disc that you had made. When the weapon was fired, it exploded." Said Cadiston. "Gees Detective, if I had known that was the idea and what it would do then I would not have made it for them. You know something although we had been friends since school days, I had not seen either of them for a couple of years or so then suddenly in the last six months they couldn't see me often enough. It all makes sense to me now. Gees Detective, I am so sorry to have made that dammed thing. I know that it is an old cliché but I can't turn the clock back or take it back and if I had known then what I know now, I would not have made it. No way, so who was it that got killed?" Asked Crichie. "Kevin Mandaten." Said Cadiston. "Mandaten, yep I saw something in the paper about that. His gun exploded but didn't connect it. If I had then I would have come to you boys in blue straight away. I made it right enough but in all innocence Detective. I had no part in no murder or plot and that, Detective, is God's truth." Said Crichie. "As to that, I believe you Crichie. Now tell us about the mountain bike." Said Cadiston. "Saw your WPC looking at that. Kansas brought it in to me on Tuesday morning that would be 23rd October and if I remember correctly the day after Malcolm Mandaten fell off his horse and died, he told me to cut it up and melt it down. I started but had my work cut out making that dammed disc." Said Crichie. "That will be all for now, thank you. You will be pleased to know that we will not be holding you but stay in the area as you will be required as a witness when it goes to court." Said Cadiston. "That I will do gladly, Detective. Gees, with friends like them that use you like they have done to me to make them something to commit a murder and could have gotten me in some serious trouble, who needs enemies? I am a God-fearing man, Detective, and they did a bad thing, a very bad thing. I will be glad to help you put them away for a very long time and as for friendship, they can kiss that goodbye." Said Crichie. "We will be in touch, we are done for now and you can go but stay in the area and thank you." Said Cadiston. "Be my pleasure to put them away, Detective. I hate crime of any kind but murder? That is something else and totally unacceptable." Said Crichie. The tape was turned off and Grace held the door open.

"Oh, just before I go, what about the assault on your WPCs?" Asked Crichie. "Help us and we will forget that if our WPCs agree." They smiled at him. "No damage done. On this occasion, if you discount my laddered tights and what has transpired with your evidence, we will say that there will be no assault charge." Said Grace. "That is a weight off my mind, thank you. I will be only too glad to buy you a new pair. Thanks ladies, thanks a million." He turned and left.

"Ok let us bring Edward Brexly into the interview room now and get him sorted." Said Cadiston. "Howie and Nadine arrested him so shall I get them in?" Asked Mac. "Please, Mac. They can bring him from the holding cell." Said Cadiston. Mac was enjoying this and almost sprinted away to fetch the two officers to attend the interview of their prisoner. The moment that they were all settled, Cadiston switched the recorder on and after all the introductions had been made, the questioning began. "Firstly, may we call you Edward?" Asked Cadiston. "You can call me whatever you like deective but not late for a meal." Said Edward. "That attitude will not help your case, Edward, as you could be in serious trouble." Mac said angrily. "Who gives a shit anyhow? I know why you have arrested me! Well, I am caught and there is absolutely no sense in trying to bluff it out. I told Demmie it was a bad idea of hers and that we would eventually get caught but she had this strong desire thing about that Grant Mandaten fellow who she wanted to marry. She had this desire for him years ago, even before she married that Chadrick but would not listen to me as she was determined to make sure that he was named the next Lord Mandaten. She told me that he would not divorce his wife and she wanted a way to be rid of her and it was up to her to do something about it. She said that there was a foolproof way and she knew how it could be done and made to look like an accident using her nut allergy. But she had not reckoned on a clever detective like you, Cadiston. She told me that this Bonnie had an allergy complaint and had to steer clear of anything with nuts. She told me that if I helped her then there would be a lot of money in it for me when she was his wife and Grant was the Lord. She asked me to make her a tasteless, odourless, highly concentrated peanut solution and like a fool, the thought of all that money to get me out of my gambling debt went to my head and I made it for her. That is all I did Detective, just made the stuff for her and had absolutely no part in her plan to get rid of Grant's wife. When I knew what she wanted it for, I should not have made it for her but all that money would free me. I guess it is right and as I told her, I would be classed as an accomplice and guilty of murder by association or something like that and it is a fact that I am ashamed of it. I feel really bad that I helped her to commit a murder as that is what it was but then you already know that, don't you?" Said Edward. "We do. Now, was Grant any part of the plan?" Asked Cadiston. "Grant? Good grief no, he wasn't connected to it in any way. This was all Demmie's twisted mind and her desire for him. Totally her own idea, the stupid girl, and she was two months pregnant with his child and was not going to be cast aside. Will I be able to speak with my sister and tell her just what I think of her? She has gotten me involved in her murder plot and now I will be doing time all because of her desire for Grant and her –. Well, whatever it was dosen't matter now, I am cooked." Said Edward. "You knew that your sister was pregnant but did you also know that Grant's wife, Bonnie, was also pregnant?" Asked Cadiston.

"His wife pregnant? No, I did not know that. Oh my good Lord, that makes it a double murder, she killed an unborn child. She is my sister but that is despicable, she deserves to go down for that alone." Said Edward. "Exactly." Said Cadiston. "Can I see her and speak with her to give a piece of my mind for getting me mixed up in all this?" Edward asked again. "You do not know about your sister then, Edward?" Asked Cadiston. "Know about her, know what?" Asked Edward. "Your sister, Demmie, was also murdered on Saturday, 11th October." Said Cadiston. "Demmie is dead? Well, that is not a surprise. Grant get fed up with her, did he?" Asked Edward bitterly. "What do you mean by that remark?" Asked Cadiston. "She told me that he could be very awkward and stubborn. He could at times be very violent if he did not get his own way and she knew just how to handle him and that was by using her body. She was my sister but I must admit that she was a stunning beauty and as to what she did with him, well, I did not want to know the details. So, she is dead and now I am going to prison for providing her with the means to commit a double murder –. I guess that is called justice. She is dead but what about Chadrick, her husband? She had a plan to be rid of him as well." Said Edward. "We cannot comment on that." Said Cadiston.

"Understood. Lock me up, Detective, I deserve it and I plead guilty as charged. I will not fight in any way as I am guilty and there you have it." Said Edward. "Edward Brexly, I am arresting you as an accomplice to the murder of Bonnie Mandaten and her unborn child. You do not need to say anything but anything you do say will be taken down and used as evidence, if you do not say something now that you later rely on in court it may harm your defence." Said Cadiston. After the caution had benn completed, Edward stood up before speaking. "I plead guilty, Detective, quite openly with no pressure, there I have said it so lock me up and throw away the key." Said Edward.

"Take the prisoner down, PC Julip." Said Cadiston. "Yes, Sergeant." They all stood and left. "The time is now 17:40 and the interview with Edward Brexly is ended." Said Cadiston.

"Well he came clean easily and that was a surprise." Said Mac. "It happens sometimes, Mac. He knew what he had done and in his own way, he regretted it so relented and I do believe that he really is sorry for helping her especially when he leaned that Bonnie was also pregnant. Done here for now so back to the office for us." Said Cadiston. They walked in silence but as they entered, Peter and Jenny were waiting for them. After passing on their piece of information from the security company with a written detailed statement from the officer, they left. After a few seconds of silence Mac spoke. "So now we know that Demmie acted on her own and Grant had no part in his wife's murder. No real surprise there but she did it with the help of her brother who made her the peanut solution and who has confessed quite openly without a question being asked. It is all on the tape so that is Bonnie and child's case solved."

"We have not got Grant for Bonnie's murder but we certainly have him without a doubt for the murder of his first wife.

Geraldine after Jonnett's statement reversal. We do need his handgun for forensic analysis. Anytime now we will have all the D.N.A. and blood results so we will have the guilty parties for all the Mandaten murders within our grasp. I have my suspicions about Sadie but the results will confirm or deny who murdered her. She stood up to one person and he did not like it, and as we have just heard he could be violent if he did not get all his own way. I think he murdered Sadie to get even for her standing up to him and also for revenge on Chadrick for defending her. We are not done yet, Mac, and I think that we can go to Mandaten Manor and carry out some serious interviews. We now have quite enough evidence to make an arrest. In fact, maybe more than one and hold them for murder. Especially Grant for the murder of his wife, Geraldine. That will be a good time to resurrect Chadrick, if he is up to it. But first, we will see what Amelia and Steven have found out about the Saint Christopher found under Lowell's body. They are on the way back with their evidence but that will wait until the morning. We know who the mobile phone belongs to that was found in the stable and I am sure that was planted to try and incriminate him so there you have it." Said Cadiston. "Bit late today, it is gone six so in the morning Wednesday the 17th of November 57 days after the first murder at Mandaten we will pay the manor a visit, or do you want to get there now?" Asked Mac. "Morning will do, Mac. By then we may have all the remaining pieces of evidence to arrest the lot of them." Cadiston said hopefully. "Sounds good to me, Boss, so if it is alright with you, I will be off home?" Asked Mac. "Not a problem, my friend." Said Cadiston. "Night then, Cadders, see in the morning." Said Mac. "Night Mac." He turned and left the office. With Mac on his way home, Cadiston sat quietly looking at the envelopes and the packages on the desk. He knew that they were from forensics and the lab and would contain vital information. The pen that he held was tapping on his notebook as he pondered what to do but his curiosity got the better of him.

"Should wait for Mac really but he can read it in the morning." He said to himself he then opened the first one. This was from the team that had searched Devil's Dyke and with that came two small parcels. As he read the report which told him that after a lengthy search and investigation of the area where Malcolm's body was found, they had not been able to find any evidence around Devil's Dyke and that being the case they were going to concentrate on the old Manor ruins. He visualized the four forensic officers as they carried out their search of the whole area and he was confident that they would find some evidence that was now contained in the report that he held. He closed his eyes and was there with the team as they began to search –. He envisioned the search for any form of hidden evidence being carried out in the ruins. Sharon took an interest in a dead Oak tree that once would have stood majestically on the driveway that lead to the front door. As she examined it, she had noticed that there was a discoloration in the bark and at first paid it no attention as the tree was long dead. She had always been fascinated by trees and she hated to see one in distress and as this was a very old oak, it saddened her even more. She whispered softly as though talking to it. "It is so sad how you have been burnt. Now I would think that you could tell us a tale or two but just look at you now, you poor old thing." She felt like crying as she looked at the old oak tree. Footsteps made her turn and she was joined by Julian who knew of her love for trees. "Sad to see such a majestic tree in that state, Sharon, and I know how it distresses you." Said Julian. "That it does, Julian." She looked closer at the trunk and realized that a section of the bark was a slightly different colour and not attached as it should be. She touched it and found that it was very loose. Her first thought was that it was due to the state of the tree and anybody else would have ignored this and passed it by but not Sharon. She was a highly trained forensics officer, and anything out of the ordinary made her suspicious. Her curiosity made her investigate it further and when she saw that it could be easily removed, her curiosity grew. With the bark removed, Sharon found that there had been a hole bored into the trunk, and pushed into the hole was a package which she carefully removed. After finding this evidence, they then rejoined their team members to assist them in completing the search of the old Manor ruins. They were amazed at how much ivy had grown over this old building but again it was Sharon that spotted a variation in the coloration of the ivy leaves. "Over here boys, I may have found something." She said. With the four officers gathered together, the ivy was carefully removed they could then see that the block of masonry beneath it had been moved. When it was lifted, they found another bag that contained heavily bloodied clothes hidden beneath it. "Well spotted Sharon, best we get these findings back to the lab for testing, blood type and DNA". Stated Julian the team leader. That is two bags containing clothes and a set of tyre prints which we have a plaster cast of boss." Replied James. "This just proves that DCI Cadiston has been right all along", stated Sharon. "Well I know for certain that he will be pleased with all this evidence, especially after it has been tested fully. Right team we can say that we are done here so let us get this stuff back to the lab and start working on it to extract the hidden evidence", said Julian.

They wasted no time and returned to the lab to investigate the hidden packages and carry out a full examination and analysis of the contents. They were carefully unwrapped under clinical conditions to avoid any form of accidental contamination which would then invalidate anything that they found on them. The greatest of care was taken in every way as they were opened. With the contents on full display, they were then examined. They consisted of a ghostly skull mask accompanied by a long grey wig and a tattered dress. They all knew of the story of the Devil's Dyke being haunted to which they guessed that this was the costume to dress up in like the ghost of the Lady Mary Lowell Mandaten to put some authenticity into the tale. They had raised D.N.A. and blood samples from these items and had to their delight, been able to raise a secure match with those held on file.

Cadiston had read the report and seen the evidence now came his thoughts. "Now that is very interesting. So you were the one that dressed up as the ghost and that explains how Rafy saw the ghost drag poor Pedro Santos into the Dyke and it would have taken more than one person for Malcolm's murder so there must have been another person up there with you –. I am positive that I know who it was after other evidence that has come to light. Now, how many of these deaths can be attributed to you and the question remains as to who helped you in the stable but we will soon discover that." He mumbled to himself.

He was satisfied with the findings at Devil's Dyke and they had served to strengthen his suspicions. He then returned to reading the report. The second bag had contained the bloodied clothes. They had been analysed and the blood on them was matched to Demmie but interestingly they had found D.N.A. on them and that matched –. "Now that is a surprise although not completely. So you are the one that murdered Demmie and did the first attack on Chadrick. We have you and there will be no way for you to wriggle out of it. If this other piece of evidence is a match then we know how it was accomplished. Good work from your team, Jooners and I must congratulate them in person." He then opened the second envelope and read it. This one was the report on the forensic search of the Standmore house. In their thorough search of the premises, they had moved furniture and had found an area of carpet that was not tacked down and looked as though it was constantly being lifted because of the crease that was clearly visible. When the carpet was rolled back, they then discovered loose floorboards, and when they had been lifted the team had found detailed plans of each of the intended Mandaten deaths to wipe out the complete Mandaten bloodline. The Standmore family had thought that they had been well hidden but Jooners and his forensic team were expert searches and they missed nothing, not even the smallest detail. The murder plan had been drawn up with military precision and went from Malcolm to Lizabeth but did not include Sadie, Bonnie, Demmie, or Chadrick as they were considered as no real threat to gaining the Mandaten fortune or continuing the family name. If they were in the way then they too would be dealt with.

"I guess that you sadly got in the way, Walter and Gloria." Cadiston mumbled. The name that was on the hit list that had surprised him was that of Lizabeth and with that, he knew that the danger was not yet over even though they could now arrest the suspects that the evidence pointed to. The person that he was most concerned about was Jennifer as she was a true-blood Mandaten and was on the list. With this newly found evidence, he knew that Chadrick was in no way the killer of any of the family even though his mobile phone had been found in the stable after Lowell had been brutally murdered. He also knew that if he were there, he would stand up and fight to defend Jennifer. However, so soon after he had undergone major surgery and in his weakened state, he would not be strong enough to fight at this time. He returned his attention to the plan and read how it detailed just how they would carry each murder out and make them look like tragic accidents and how they would be covered up. They also included when they would activate the plan. That was where his separate investigation gave him the name he wanted and how it was connected to each case. He now understood implicitly and had the evidence and information he needed. To allow for errors, there was also a second plan to be implemented if the first one failed or the opportunity did not arise and that too was followed by a contingency plan to be used if all else had failed. He read on and saw that they had guessed that Malcolm would at some point take an early morning ride as this was his usual routine and who would be waiting for him but there was no mention of the stable or frightening the big black stallion. "Now that is a mystery. Was someone acting on their own initiative in the hope that he would be thrown and die in the fall? A search of the contraband tunnel from the Manor would probably solve that." Cadiston mumbled to himself. Lowell would at some time take a night walk to see the barn owls so that was a case of waiting for the opportunity to present itself and if he was accompanied, then whoever was with him would be dealt with.

"Just as well Jennifer had not gone with him on that fateful evening." Cadiston thought. He read on and there, detailed, was how he would be killed and who would carry out that task. James was detailed to be killed as and when the opportunity arose and again who would carry it out. He was not surprised at what he was reading and most of it fell in line with his own suspicions. It was now 19:34 and he wondered whether to leave the next one for Wednesday morning or open it now. He did not need to think very long and opened it. This was the report on the two vehicles and again he was not surprised at what the forensic team had found. The paint matched and drugs were itemized, every bit of information that was contained in these forensic reports were acting to strengthen his own long-term suspicions.

He had come this far so he opened the last envelope. This was the forensic report on the boat used in the murder of Sadie. They had matched the D.N.A., blood, and fingerprints with those held on file and he was not surprised to finally know for certain the murderer of Sadie Mandaten. There were also matches of D.N.A. from the flesh found under the fingernails of James and Gloria and again, there was no major surprises for him about who had committed the crime. He had worked tirelessly on all these cases and had followed his intuition and suspicions every step of the way. He had been thwarted by Standish and his attempts that had been made to silence him but he had finally come to the end of his patience and had spoken up. He had only one regret and that was that he had not spoken up sooner. If he had, then his thought was that lives would have probably been saved. That was over and done with and now he had been free to investigate. In his hand, he held more than enough evidence to question and to arrest all or either of them. They were not all suspects of each crime as his suspicions had pointed him to believe that there was more than one killer. He also had the evidence which confirmed his suspicion on Standish and his quick case closure which confirmed his involvement to take to his chief. He glanced at his watch and as it was getting very late, he just briefed over the other evidence that had been supplied, namely from the arrests made by WPCs Crowth and Jorde, namely Trevor Crichton or nickname Crichie, and PC Julip with WPC Crown, namely Edward Brexly. Of those prisoners, one was in the holding cell and the other was released. He looked at the information from PC Roland

and WPC Borrows and was satisfied although on this evidence his suspicion had been partly wrong. He shrugged his shoulders. "Can't be right all the time but almost is better than nothing at all. Just need to see Amelia and Steven in the morning and will find out then what had delayed their return. Hmm, good, very good. That should be all the evidence collated. Now, it is nearly eight so best I get off home and get what rest I can as there is a very busy day ahead for us tomorrow. Another busy day would have been correct. Come on, Cadders, you cannot stay here all night talking to yourself so get off home to that lovely wife of yours and your unborn child, now." He slapped his wrist, smiled and went to his car.

Chapter Nineteen

The Truth is Out

Wednesday morning the 17th of November 57days after the first murder at Mandaten, and the family was once again assembled in the breakfast room.

"Well now would you look at this, we are still all here. Even you, Greta, with your cheeky little brat. Once again, no one was murdered in their sleep last night." Mocked Grant. "Not something to treat lightly, Grant. If it turns out that Chadrick was not the murderer, which I strongly believe he was not, then the real murderer is still out there and we are still in danger." Replied Greta sharply. "I am beginning to believe it too, Greta." Said Lizabeth shyly. "Are you, Lizabeth? Really?" Asked Greta. "Yes, really." Said Lizabeth.

"Well, there is a turn up but I have no fear of being murdered. Not me, Greta, and no one can get me for anything as I have my solid alibi's and my protector." Snarled Grant. "Get you for anything, what do you mean?" Asked Greta with curiosity. "Mean? Nothing. Besides, isn't it strange you are still here, you are normally away to wherever it is you go and no taxi today –." Said Grant mockingly. Greta replied quickly, "Not today, Grant." "Not today, what is so what is different about today?" Questioned Grant. "That is for me to know." Said Greta firmly. "Secretive are we, Greta? Well, I don't give a tinker's cuss for you or why you go on your early morning trips or why you are staying now." Said Grant in his devil may care attitude. "Would you tell us where you go please, Greta? I believe that I was wrong about many things and we are only worried about you." Said Lizabeth. Jennifer now stepped in. "Worried about us? More lies from you, Aunt Lizabeth, you could not care less where we go or where we are just as long as it does not interfere with you and the false life that you lead. I call you aunt but I am much better off without you."

"Enough Jennifer, you are nothing but a child and should show some respect for my mother." Said Kansas. "That is right, a child should respect her elders." Added Tomas.

Jennifer was on fire and was not about to hold back. Her voice summed up her anger and like a firecracker, she exploded. "Respect you say, Kansas? And you uncle Tomas –. Well, where was the respect, sympathy, and consideration for us when my father was murdered? And where was the respect, sympathy, and consideration when my brother was murdered? Yes, they were both brutally murdered. You all make me sick with your falseness and lies! All any of you care about is yourselves and that is a fact. I may only be ten years old, well nearly eleven, but even I can see through your facard of falseness and lies." They all stared at Jennifer amazed at her fieriness. "Well said, Jennifer, and I completely agree with you. You are a very sensible young lady and ahead of your age in your thinking." They all turned toward the door to see their parents standing there. "Good morning mother, good morning father". Said Lizabeth sheepishly. "Not a very good morning outside, rather on the cold side, there is a frost on the ground and I believe we can expect some snow later in the day, but I have a feeling that it is about to get much warmer and better inside." Said Lord Mandaten with a smile. "A strange thing for you to say, Father, so whatever do you mean?" Enquired Lizabeth. "For the answer to that, you will just have to wait, Daughter of mine." Said Lord Mandaten still smiling. "I don't know, this all looks like a mystery unfolding. First, Greta and Jennifer have not gone out this morning, now you say that things will get much warmer and better inside –. It all sounds rather ominous to me." Said Lizabeth. "And what if it does, Lizabeth? Who the hell cares we are free at last?" Said Grant in a nonchalant voice.

"We do, Grant, we care and want to see this episode in our lives come to an end and hopefully that will be very soon, I have been stupid and have a lot of ground to make up and a lot of mistakes to correct." Said Lizabeth. "Question to ask, is that Detective Cadiston turning up unanounced again today? It has been a while since we saw him." Said Tomas. "Who knows, Tomas, who knows. We will all just have to wait and see what the day brings forth." Said Lord Mandaten.

"Oh for goodness' sake Father, just tell us what it is that you know and put us out of our misery!" Said Lizabeth. "Put you out of your misery, Lizabeth? We have had years of misery trying to bring you all up and guiding you on the right path but try as we might, we failed and now look at yourselves." Said Lady Mandaten. "Look at ourselves, mother?" Asked Lizabeth. "Yes, sit back and take a good look at yourselves. Unfortunately, you are the only one that is left of the blood Mandaten family, and each one of you and means you Tomas and Kansas but, – excluding Greta and Jennifer, are filled with so much greed and are so full of lies that you cannot tell a lie from the truth and your falseness just overflows. We wanted you to grow up and be good people but sadly you are not." Lady Mandaten shook her head and continued. "Not one of you." There was a moment's silence and then Lizabeth began to cry but this time the tears that she shed were real. "But Mother, I –. Yes Mother, you are right and what Father said when he did his analysis was also right. I have become obsessed with what I could not have and what was just out of reach. I plagued Tomas for all the best things like £1500 for a dinner set when one that cost around £60 would serve the same purpose. You are right, both of you, in what you have said to us and I am truly sorry for letting you down. Can you find it in your hearts to forgive me for all my years of wrong doing? I promise that from now on I will change and become the person that you always wanted me to be." "It will take time, Daughter, but, the forgiveness will come if you are true to your word" Said Lady Mandaten. "I will be, Mother. Greta, dear sweet Greta, who never did any harm, I owe you an enormous apology also. I have been so jealous of you and a real bitch since you married my brother and you were a good wife to him and a good mother to Lowell even though he was not your blood son. I will try to make it up to you as even through my cruelty toward you, you only returned love. I truly am sorry, Greta, and if you can find it in your heart to forgive me, – I will do my level best to undo all the wrongs that I have bestowed upon you. Now you, Jennifer,yes I owe you an enormous apology also you are a dear sweet child and you also spoke the truth. I have not been the best aunt to you, have I? But that will now change, please, please, both of you, forgive me for all the hurt that I passed out to you and let us make a new start." Said Lizabeth with real tears and a real softness in her voice. "Or better still, a, *NEW BEGINNING* Aunt Lizabeth. That is if you mean what you are saying?" Said Jennifer. "I promise that my words are true." Said Lizabeth. "I said some hurtful things to you and –." Lizabeth placed a finger to Jennifer's lips. "You need to say nothing more, Jennifer, what you said was the complete truth and it was nothing more than I deserved." Said Lizabeth. "Well this is all very well and good for you, Sister, but leave me out of it. I have done nothing wrong and have nothing to apologise for. I am out of here before all this lovie cuddly stuff makes me throw up." Said Grant in a very bullish manor.

"There is no need for that kind of talk, Son, and if your sister can finally see the errors of her ways, although it has taken a while, why can you not see yours?" Said Lord Mandaten. "Because I have none, that is why. I have been a model son and you have always put me down and favoured Chadrick over me well he is dead and I am here so now you can treat me better father, so if there is any fault then it is all yours, not mine." Said Grant snobbishly.

Lizabeth now saw red at Grant's outburst and attack of their parents so took her chance and fired a full salvo back at her brother. "That will do, Grant! Mother and Father have always done the very best for us all, you included. Maybe even more for you but it has taken the words of a child to finally bring me to my senses. I know that I was too blind to see it until now and it has taken all this tragedy to make me finally see the errors of my ways. If you are too pig-headed and stubborn to see your mistake's then I disown you as a brother and wish that Chadrick were here so that I could apologise to him. You have never really looked like

628

a Mandaten, Grant, and not a bit like a twin to Malcolm so do you know what I think? I think that you were swapped at birth and you are not my brother at all. And I have a real brother out there just waiting to be found. You had just as many if not more chances than the rest of us because our parents would not give up on you, Well, maybe they should have." "Shut your mouth, Lizabeth, or I will be forced to shut it for you for good!" Said Grant coldly.

"Over my dead body, Grant." He turned to face the speaker. "And that could very easily be arranged, Tomas, so be very careful what you say. I have –. Well, no matter what I have. You make me sick and –. Ah to hell with all of you!" He turned and left the room.

"Now there goes someone who is full of guilt, hatred, and jealousy and I am ashamed that for 33 years of his 43 years I have had to call him brother. No more, I have done with him. I will atone for the errors of the past years and try very hard to make it all up to you, every one of you, starting with you, Greta. I would deem it a great privilege if you would be my sister and Jennifer, I would like to treat you as if you were my daughter and if only I had not been so evil to Chad." Said Lizabeth. "And we will all help you, Aunt Lizabeth." Said Jennifer. Lizabeth smiled at Jennifer. "Bless you, my child, and thank you." Said Lizabeth. "Gees Mother, are you saying that I will be forced to call her sister? I –." Shouted Kansas. "Best for now, Son." She warned. He looked toward his father who winked at him.

"Best for now then, welcome to the family, Sister Jennifer." Said Kansas. Jennifer just looked at him, knowing that his action was false and knowing what she did, she felt very uneasy but could say nothing. She was hoping that Cadiston would soon be able to arrest him and it seemed like an age had passed by since her brother's murder.

At 08:00, Cadiston and Mac walked into the office and a few minutes later they were joined by WPC Amelia Stroud and PC Steven Arkens. "Morning Cadders, Mac. What a trip we have had, travelled quite a few miles to check out the Saint Christopher but we finally got the right place. We had a major problem when the darn car broke down on our way Back. With the repair done, we drove through the night and only got back twenty minutes ago but we have what you needed to know in this envelope." Said Amelia.

"Good work, both of you." He opened the envelope and removed the document it contained. "A copy of the receipt for the Saint Christopher and it details the inscription and who it was sold to and we have the medal as well. Brilliant work, both of you. Now you must both be tired after that long drive so go home and get some very welcome sleep. Well done and thank you." Said Cadiston. "Thank you, Cadders for trusting us with such an important aspect of the case. We are glad we could help." They turned and walked slowly away.

"All falling into place so that is it, Mac, the final pieces of evidence. It has taken a while to collect it all but now we can safely say that the truth is out. Bring the car around and we will be away to Mandaten Manor to ask some questions and see what answers we get. After that, we can make at least one arrest today and hopefully more –. We will see. While you fetch the car for us, I will get Olito and Francis who will accompany us." Said Cadiston.

"Who is first on the list, Boss?" Asked Mac. "I was going to tackle Grant first but Chad is undergoing tests today so will not be able to make his appearance. I will leave him until Friday the 19th of November. Today we go in for Kansas, we have him connected to at least four of the murders so by all accounts, he is a vicious and dangerous person to be dealing with and the sooner he is locked away, the better." Said Cadiston.

"I will go get the car." Said Mac. Cadiston had no time to answer him as he spoke on the run.

At 09:30 the car pulled up in front of Mandaten Manor. They saw a single face peer at them through the window, then they retreated hastily. Grant swallowed his drink then blurted out in a way that sounded almost like a panic. "Dam, I must have talked them up, the police are here now, that Cadiston and his sidekick Macswee with two police women, so best behave while they are here", he said.

"Come in, Detectives, I saw you coming down the drive so waited to open the door for you. The family is still in the breakfast room. If you would like to follow me." Said Alfred. The walk was brisk and as they entered some of those present just stared at them. "DCI Cadiston, and DS Macswee, and two WPCs to see you, my Lord." Said Alfred. "Thank you, that will be all, Alfred. Now then Detective Cadiston, to what do we owe the pleasure of your visit today? And with DS Macswee and if I remember correctly, WPCs Rendham and Paverson?" Said Lord Mandaten. "A very good memory, my Lord. Our visit today will involve a search of some rooms and then we will require to conduct some interviews. If I can ask you all to stay in this room until you are called, that would be appreciated." Said Cadiston. "You look where you need to Detective. Turn this old Manor upside down if need be, and don't worry about them, they will all stay put and you can use the study for your interviews." Said Lord Mandaten. "Thank you, that will be fine, my Lord." Said Cadiston. As they left to start their search, Grant stood up. "Sit down, Grant, you are going nowhere." Said his father in a very dominant fashion. "They don't command me in my own home, or tell me what I can and can't do or stop me from doing anything so if I want to leave, then I will." Said Grant. "Step outside that door, my boy, and they will arrest you for disobeying their instructions." Said Lord Mandaten. "Arrest me? Can they do that?" Asked Grant shocked. "Step outside that door and you will find out." Said Lord Mandaten. Grant hesitated. "Huh." Then he sat down.

Cadiston had sent Olito and Francis to search for the sleeping pills or powders while he and Mac had made their way up the staircase and were now inspecting the panelling close to where the scratch marks were on the floor. "Here, Cadders, I think this could be it." Said Mac. "Looks that way, Mac, so give it a try." Said Cadiston. Mac had been checking very carefully for anything suspicious and had found a spile that was not sitting quite securely. He removed it, then pulled the piece of trim away that was hiding a leaver beneath it. He smiled and slid the leaver down and sure enough, the panel opened. "Well done, Mac, now we need to re-enact James' incident but first have a look inside to see where it opens." Said Cadiston. "Got it." Said Mac.

"Now, I will stand here just as James would have done, then action." Said Cadiston. Mac slid the panel open and as he did it, Cadiston turned to investigate the noise. He then made the action of hitting him with a weapon on the side of his head, followed by the stranglehold. Leaving Cadiston, Mac closed the panel and ran down the steps to re-emerge at the bottom first. Cadiston was lying on the floor so he untied the shoe lace and disappeared.

"Right time for the action, Mac?" Asked Cadiston. "From start to finish and for Jennifer to arrive, four and a half minutes in total." Answered Mac. "That is how it was done then. We have all the evidence DNA and blood, so we have him for that one." Said Cadiston. "And for Lowell, Malcolm, and Gloria because we also have the evidence and he cannot refute that." Said Mac.

"True Mac, one thing to do before we question Kansas. I want to look in Sadie's room and Grant's room as I have a suspicion that they may be linked." Said Cadiston. "I get your thinking, Cadders, so lead on." Said Mac. They went first into Sadie's room and their search began. Twenty minutes of searching resulted in Cadiston's suspicion being confirmed when they found the connecting passage. "Runs straight through from Sadie to Grant. Now, if he had drugged her, he would have then carried her to the boat and the rest we know. I believe that there may be another passage that goes into the Lowell Suite so keep looking, Mac." Said Cadiston. "Here Boss, from Grant's room behind the paneling into Sadie's, then through into the Lowell and guess what?" Asked Mac. "It goes through the wardrobe." Guessed Cadiston.

"You are just too good at this, Boss, but exactly right. Just had a thought –. Hmm, I am beginning to think that it was him that clobbered Chad and shot Demmie." Said Mac. "Evidence looks that way, why else would his car be parked at the old Manor? Plus we have his fingerprints taken from the shotgun cartridges so he was a little bit careless there and the bloodied clothes. Well done, Mac. Now let us get into the study and start the questioning. We will start with Kansas and he may be a tough cookie but I think that under some strong questioning and the irrefutable evidence, he will break. We will not pressure him and listen to what he has to say first, then turn up the volume." Said Cadiston. "Right with you there and the little ghostly surprise for him, acted out by francis, Cadders." Said Mac. "I will head for the study while you go and fetch him." Said Cadiston. "Be my pleasure. Said Mac. Cadiston headed for the study and Macswee to the breakfast room.

"Ah Sergeant, did you find what you were looking for?" Asked Lord Mandaten. "We did, my Lord, and now we would like to begin our interviews today. Purely to be able to tie up all the loose ends." Said Mac. "And that is understood." Said Lord Mandaten. "Let me see –. (He flipped the pages of his notebook.) Ah yes, first we would like to have a chat with you Kansas." Said Mac. Lizabeth dropped her cup, Tomas stumbled backward ending up in a chair and Kansas just stood with his mouth wide open. "Me why me when there are others". "Luck of the draw, this way please, Kansas." Said Mac.

"Nothing to say, Grant?" Asked Lizabeth. "They want to talk with Kansas so why should I have anything to say?" Answered Grant.

"I just wondered, Brother, as you usually do. You normally have plenty to say." He did not reply to his sister but turned his stare to the ground. "Wait, what do you want my son for, Detective? He has already been questioned and he has done nothing wrong." Said Lizabeth. He could sense their anxiety and knew that he could not show any form of anger. He told himself to be like Cadders and speak calmly. "No need to worry madam. As I said, Mrs. Kaysten, we just want to have a little chat with him first just to clear up a few details, then we can end all this and close the cases. Do not worry because we will get to you all eventually." Said Mac calmly.

"What if I do not come with you? I have told you everything I could and know nothing else so there should be no more that you need to ask." Said Kansas. Mac remained calm. "Just come with me now please, Kansas, and don't make things difficult. You should have no objection to answering a few more questions and if you want to make it difficult we could do this down the station." "I don't see why I should be the first, why not Grant or her?" He pointed at Greta. "We will be speaking to everyone in due course. Now, if you make it difficult to speak with you here then we will have no choice but to take you to the station for questioning." Said Mac.

Lizabeth looked at her son and said gently. "Go with the detective, Kansas, it is better to speak with them here and now." Kansas looked at his mother, then turned to follow Macswee. Tomas went to follow but Mac stared directly into his eyes which made him stop dead in his tracks. "Not you, Tomas, just Kansas. You just wait here until we come for you." Said Mac. He turned and with Kansas by his side, walked briskly to the study. "I do not like it, Lizabeth, I do not like it at all. Why would they want to speak to him?" Said Tomas nervously. "I have no idea, Tomas, we will know when they have finished speaking to him. We will just have to stay here and wait." Said Lizabeth.

"You look very worried and are agitated, Tomas. Now, why should you be if Kansas has nothing to hide? Or is there somehing to hide or is there something to find?" Asked Lord Mandaten. "You may be the Lord of the Manor but I do not like your implication." Said Tomas. "What implication is that, Tomas? All detective Cadiston and his sergeant want is a little chat so what harm can there be in that?" Asked Lord Mandaten.

"They may try to pin something on him to get a conviction, we all know that it was Chadrick who killed the family and they have the evidence to prove it was him. His mobile phone was found in the stable next to the body and that is the one they should investigate, not my son." Snapped Tomas. "How did you know about the mobile phone being found, Tomas? We certainly did not. As far as we know, when an item of evidence is found the police do not broadcast its finding, so it has not been broadcast about for everyone to hear." Said Lord Mandaten."Well, err –." Tomas went silent.

"If I know anything then it is that if a piece of evidence is found, the police would not disclose it so answer my husband, Tomas, how do you know?" Asked Lady Mandaten. He looked even more worried and his face was drained of all its colour, he was as white as a sheet. "Well someone must have said it. No wait, he could not find his phone on Thursday and we helped to look for it, that must be it. I will say nothing more to you." "Alright Tomas, we will find out soon enough what Cadiston has discovered." Said Lord Mandaten. With that, Tomas sat down but he had a very anxious and had a worried look upon his face. "In you go, Kansas, there is a chair all ready for you so please sit down." Said Mac. The interview tape was turned on. "The time is 09:59 and this is a recording of the interview between DCI Cadiston, Detective Sergeant Macswee and Kansas Kaysten." Said Cadiston. With the introductions made, "So Cadiston, all official then and being recorded so what do you want me for? I can tell you nothing more than I already have. Besides, we all know that Chadrick is or rather was the killer especially my poor cousin Lowel he had dropped his mobile phone in the stable and tried to make out he had misplaced it and had us looking for it." Said Kansas smugly. *Just what I suspected he would say*.

"And you can prove that, can you Kansas?" Asked Cadiston. "Well I saw him with the gun just before he shot Demmie and if Father had not stopped him, we would all be dead." Replied Kansas. "Not what I have written down here but we will get to that in a moment. Now, we just need to ask you a few questions about the other incidents to clear things up, is that alright?" Asked Cadiston.

"Other incidents, ok Cadiston, no harm there, so ask away." Said Kansas.

"And you will answer truthfully, will you Kansas? This is the time for the truth so no lies or fabrications." Mac said. "Macswee, isn't it? Well, I have no need to lie and I guess that you will both be asking questions so Cadiston, ask away." Said Kansas. "We will start with Tuesday, 7ᵗʰ October, the day that your cousin James died. Now, can you tell us all that you remember about that incident?" Asked Cadiston. "Easy, I was in the garden when I heard Jennifer screaming so I rushed in but tripped and fell into a flower pot and got scratched by the rose. I came in and James was on the floor. I checked him over but his neck was broken and clearly, he was dead." Said Kansas.

"And that is what you are saying and claiming to be the truth?" Asked Cadiston. "Well, yes of course it is, Cadiston, it is the truth and you cannot prove it otherwise." Said Kansas. "Alright, let us look at Thursday, 9ᵗʰ October, just two days later, the day that your cousin, Lowell, died. What do you remember about that day?" Asked Cadiston. "Everyone had gone to bed apart from Grant and he was drunk. Lowell went for his usual walk and asked if anyone would go with him, no one did. He went out and I went to bed and that is it. The next morning he was found dead, stomped by the mad horse and you saw him." Said Kansas with a half smile. "And that is your slant on what happened?" Asked Cadiston. "Don't quite follow that, Detective, he was found in the stable stomped and trampled to death by that mad horse. Chadrick had something to do with it, then you turned up and the rest you know." Said Kansas. "You think that Chadrick had a hand in Lowell's death, do you?" Asked Cadiston. "Stands to reason as the evidence shows." Said Kansas. "What evidence would that be?" Asked Cadiston. "Whatever you found, Detective." He said snidely. "Hmm, evidence –. So have you any idea how Chadrick's mobile phone came to be in the stable as no one was informed that it had been found?" Asked Cadiston. "Well, there you are then. If you think Lowell was murdered by someone and not the horse then you have the evidence left by the killer just as I said." Said Kansas. "And 23ʳᵈ September, what do you remember about Malcolm?" Asked Cadiston.

"Malcolm, I was in bed and he was up at Devil's Dyke so if you are thinking I had a hand in his death, you are barking up the wrong tree." Said Kansas.

"Interesting that you mention a tree." Said Cadiston. Kansas looked surprised at this answer. "Again, I don't follow you." "Sir, I don't want to be a scare monger but I just saw a shadowy figure going past the window that looked like –. No, I must be seeing things, must be the mention of Devil's Dyke." Said Mac."Hang on, Sergeant, I heard something out in the hall. Better turn this off before we investigate." Said Cadiston. The tape was switched off.

"The family should all be in the breakfast room so best we go and look. Stay here, Kansas, we are not finished with you yet." Mac slowly opened the door to be greeted by a ghostly figure. "I saw you, Kansas, I saw you and you will fall to me at Devil's Dyke or in your bed but I will have you for mine." The figure slowly disappeared behind the prepared secret panel. The air cleared and when they looked at Kansas, he was hiding and quivering in the corner.

"No, no, she is not real. There is no ghost of the Lady Mary Lowell Mandaten, this is some trick. There is no such thing as ghosts, it was m –. No, it is in my mind, she is not real." Stammered Kansas. "Well we saw her as clearly as you did, Kansas, and that means she must be real or are you saying that someone dressed up?" Asked Cadiston. "Tell you what, Sergeant, she put the frighteners into me, come to think of it when Samantha and me paid a vist up at dyke we saw a shadowy figure disappear into the old manor ruins and now I believe in ghosts." Said Cadiston. "Well she looked real enough for me Boss", added Mac. "No, not so, there is no ghost. It is all a trick and you don't catch me with that one." Said Kansas. "Alright now, settle down and we will continue." The tape was switched on. "Now then, we were about to discuss Malcolm's incident." Just then, there was a knock on the door and when it opened, in walked Olito carrying the costume. "What the duce? Where did you get that, Cadiston?" Asked Kansas sheepishly. "It was retrieved from where you hid it, Kansas, in the dead oak tree near the old Manor ruins so no more lies. We know that you were up at Devil's Dyke when your Uncle Malcolm was murdered." Said Cadiston. The next question came from Mac. "The truth now, Kansas, and no more lies. Now tell us what day you arrived."

"Thursday, 26th September." Said Kansas. "Try again, Kansas." Said Cadiston. "Why?" Asked Kansas. "We know that you arrived on Monday 22nd and booked into the Chesingter Hotel near the rail station. We also know that you rode your cycle, a yellow and blue mountain bike, from there to the Manor and then hid in the contraband store. We also know how you first frightened Thundist in this costume." Cadiston picked it up and shook it in front of him. "You then rode your cycle up the roadway to be at the Dyke before Malcolm arrived." Kansas grinned. "All supposition and conjecture, you have nothing." "Wrong, we have plenty. Now, no more lies, Kansas. We have the costume that you used lying there in front of you with your D.N.A. retrieved from it, we also have your cycle." Said Cadiston. "That is a lie, Detective, you are trying to trick me. The cycle is –." "Go on, Kansas, why stop there, you were saying the cycle Is what?" Said Cadiston. "You are trying to catch me out and it will not work, you can prove nothing." Said Kansas.

"Do not let your lies fool you or the lies that you have been told. Now there is a man by the name of Trevor Crichton, Crichie for short to you?" Said Cadiston. "Crichton, nothing." Spat Kansas. "We have the evidence that you thought that the cycle would not be found as you were under the impression that Crichie had cut it up into tiny little pieces and melted it down but it was seen and retrieved before it happened. No sense in lying, Kansas, as we have him in custody and he has told us everything." Said Mac as he looked him straight in the eyes. "Damn him! I told Father that we should have watched him do it." Said Kansas. Cadiston looked at Mac then at Kansas. He knew that they had him and wanted to smile but he kept himself in check.

"Take a minute, Kansas, then we will start over from the beginning and this time, we will have the truth with no more lies as we have all the evidence and we know that you were involved in five of the family deaths, we have DNA, Blood and fingerprints and a cast of your shoes size four." Said Cadiston. Kansas turned white and began to sniffle. "As my DCI has said, we have all the evidence, Kansas. So there is no sense in continuing with the lies, it is time for the truth." Said Mac. They watched him shrink into his chair. He then blew his nose and wiped his eyes. "What possible evidence could you have? A silly Halloween costume that someone planted? We were careful and Harry had us covered so there is nothing!" "D.N.A. blood sample, shoe size." Said Cadiston. "Shoe size?" Asked Kansas. "We have impressions of the footware and size of the shoe and they match a pair of yours." Said Cadiston. "All right, damn you, Cadiston. You are too clever by half. Uncle Harry was right, said you could be the stumbling block, he said he would have it covered as long as he could silence you. Go on then, ask away, I am ready." Said Kansas.

"We will start again from James and no more lies as we know exactly how you did it and have the evidence to prove it so the truth, Kansas." Said Cadiston. "You think that you are so damn clever, Cadiston, so what do you say is your proof?" Said Kansas. "Blood, D.N.A., the scratches on your neck that you lied about, the skin sample under James' fingernails, there is also the white chalky sample taken from your jacket and that matches that of the walls of the secret passages. It is useless to lie anymore, Kansas, so for once in your life, do yourself a service and tell us the truth." Said Cadiston. "Ok so I did kill James, the spoilt brat that he was. I waited for him at the top of the stairs behind the secret panel, hit him with the old knight's hammer, then broke his neck and pushed him down the stairs." He looked at them both waiting for a response but got none. "I ran down the steps and out at the bottom but Jennifer was on her way by then so just tugged the shoelace and pushed the suit of armour over. I hid until Chadrick and Greta were there and then reappeared, that suit you, Detective?" Asked Kansas. "Just as we had analysed it. Now, we will move on to Lowell and that was particularly brutal." Said Cadiston. "I had nothing to do with that, it was Chad and his mobile phone proves that." Said Kansas. "So how do you explain your Saint Christopher being under his body? For the record, I am showing the Saint Christopher necklace plus a sample of your blood was found at the scene on a rusty nail and that explains the deep jagged gash to your hand. There is also your damaged shoulder and we have your D.N.A. that was found in the stall where he was murdered. That is how and, there were items found in the contraband store and we know of all the secret passageways. We know that it was your father using a false name that found out about them, we also know your true birth name and your heritage." Said Cadiston. "Damn you, Cadiston. You got in the way, we had to hurry and complete the plan before Uncle Harry retired so we had to rush. The plan was carefully worked out and would have worked. Uncle Harry should have dealt with all the cases, then we would have been home and dry. Damn you for interfering. As for Lowell, he deserved to die. He stood in our way and I did him good and proper. I went through the secret passage to the stable and came out in the contraband store. I waited for him to get near the barn, then I walloped him, carried him into the stall that I had prepared ready and battered him. Well, you saw the result so −." He had a smirk on his face. "You know that I did a good job of it." "Yes, we saw him and that was a particularly savage attack." Remarked Mac. "I hated him, I hate them all for what they did to our ancestors!" Said Kansas. "A centuries old revenge trail to wipe them all out, did you know that your father was going to kill your mother the moment that she had been endowed with the Mandaten estate so how do you feel about that?" Asked Cadiston. "How did you know that detail?" Asked Kansas. "We know and that is sufficient. Now answer the question, then we will move on to Malcolm." Said Cadiston. "She is a Mandaten and has Mandaten blood and she had to go. I have had to stomach her fussing over me for all my life and make out that she had all my love but inside, I cringed and would have been glad to see her gone." Said Kansas. "So that means that your whole life has been a lie from the moment you were old enough to understand and were brian washed by your father. It was from that hatred that you have been made into a savage cold-blooded murderer to seek revenge." Said Cadiston. "Not made, I loved it. I started with animals by bashing their heads in, then moved up to people. I started when I was fourteen and have done for five apart from the Mandatens and it was heavenly to watch and see the victim squirm as I battered them. Gloria and Walter should have stayed clear as we only wanted Sammie but when the chance came, we did for them all. I pushed the arrows in, it was all so easy." Said Kansas. "We will get to the arrows in a moment but did you know that you, Kansas, were also on the list to be murdered?" Asked Cadiston. He sat silent for a few minutes. "Me, why me? I have killed four Mandatens and assisted in one for them so why me?" Asked Kansas.

Mac shook his head in disbelief. "They lied to you and had you brainwashed, the simple answer is because you have Mandaten blood from your mother."

"The bastards, my own father would see me killed after all I have done for the Standlyhopes? I thought they were my family, kill me the bastards!" Yelled Kansas. "They used you, Kansas, and you fell for their falseness and lies but now we will return to the murders and your Uncle Malcolm." Said Cadiston.

"I have no reason to hold back now, do I? They were going to murder me. Well, I will nail them all first and you already know what had transpired. You had it all worked out from the beginning, Cadiston. As I said, you are just far too damn clever and could run rings around Harry. Well again, I used the contraband store and with that garb on –." He pointed to the ghost costume. "I put the frighteners into Thundist, then jumped on the cycle and raced up to the Dyke where my father was already waiting to meet me. He pulled Malcolm from his horse and knelt on his back while I held his head still then whack! And the rest you know." Said Kansas. "And your Aunt Sammie's family?" Asked Cadiston. "Might as well tell you. Father saw Demmie going into the prohibited area so he called me and we followed her, taking care not to be spotted. She met up with Grant, thinking that they were out of sight and without drawing a picture they were, well, at it shall we say. We were very well hidden and saw Walter with Sammie and Gloria who had also followed her so kept an eye on them. Walter shouted at Grant and Demmie and then the two of them had a massive fight, Grant was the easy winner, leaving Walter almost unconscious and was boasting about his prowess. When the explosion was heard, he then ran off. Sammie and Gloria went to help Walter and when Demmie ran past our hiding place, that is when we took our chance. As we approached, Gloria cried and asked us to help. We helped alright. I picked up a large stone and lumped Sammie over the head. She went down like a ton of bricks. Gloria then turned on me but she was easy to get the better of to quieten her I picked up another stone and hit her with it but she was stronger than I Envigaged and we had quite a struggle, that was when she scratched my arm. As it was close to the archery, we got hold of some arrows and the rest you know. Father saw to Walter and I saw to Sammie and Gloria and if it had not been for you and your damn persistence, we would have gotten away with it. I had nothing to do with Kevin or Sadie and Chadrick did for Demmie." Said Kansas. "You took part in one murder, that of your Uncle Malcolm, and committed on your own admission four more, that of your Aunt Sammie and Cousin Gloria, followed by your cousins James and Lowell." Cadiston shook his head and continued. "The names of your earlier victims please?" "John Crow in May '94, Peter Palmer in September '94, Carol Smolet in April '95 after I had made it with her, Andrea Barns in August '96, and April Moores in December '97 and made with them also before I silenced them." Said Kansas. "Kansas Standmore, using the name of Kaysten, I am arresting you for the murders by your own admission of John Crow, Peter Palmer, Carol Smolet, Andrea Barns, and April Moores. You are also charged with the murder of Sammie and Gloria Larkspere, and James and Lowell Mandaten. You are also charged with being an accessory in the murder of Malcolm Mandaten, you do not need to say anything now but anything you do say will be taken down and may be used as evidence, do you understand the charge?" Asked Cadiston after he had completed the caution. "You are too clever by half, Cadiston. You have me bang to rights and I can tell you that my loving father, now there is a joke, killed Malcolm with my help,

Walter and Kevin on his own." Said Kansas."One final question, was your mother involved at all?" Asked Cadiston. "Her? You must be joking. The sooner she was got rid of the better." Said Kanssas. "Hold your hands out, Kansas." Said Cadiston. As Mac went to place the cuffs onto his wrists, he smiled. He had other ideas and attempted to make his escape by pushing him over. He was down the hall and had the front door open in a flash. Seconds later, he was out in the open. He started to run, thinking that he had made his escape and as he started to run up the long drive toward the open gate he suddenly felt arms wrapped around his legs just like a rugby tackle and found himself lying on his face with his hands behind him and his hands cuffed. He had not allowed for the quick action of WPC Francis Rendham.

"Damn, I forgot about you, you bloody police woman." Cadiston and Mac had given chase and were standing beside her. "Well done, WPC Rendham, but are you alright?" She then brushed herself down and replied. "I am fine thanks. It is nothing more than a scratch and a ladder in my tights." They all smiled. "Good work, WPC Rendham." With the prisoner secured, they returned to the study. "The time is 12:42 and the interview is ended. For the record, the prisoner tried to escape after being cautioned but has been recaptured and will shortly be en route to the station." Cadiston said and the tape was switched off. While Cadiston made a call to arrange for their prisoner to be picked up, they sat silently.

"What is taking them so long with Kansas?" Asked Tomas. "You ask a question that cannot be answered so just wait like the rest of us." Answered Grant. At that time, Lizabeth was looking out of the window and screamed out when she saw Kansas running up the drive and was then promptly body tackled by the WPC. "What are they doing to Kansas? Why is he in handcuffs after being knocked onto the ground?" She ran from the room and followed them toward the study. She began to push the two officers but Francis and Olito kept Lizabeth away from the room.

"Get out of my way, that is my son in there and I demand to know what is going on!" Shouted Lizabeth. "Calm yourself please madam, you will be told in due course. Now, please return to the breakfast room and wait until you are called for." Said Olito. Between the two of them, they ushered Lizbeth back to the remaining family. "They won't let me see my son, Father, tell them to let me. I must see and speak with him to know what is going on and why they have him in handcuffs, they will tell me nothing." Wailed Lizbeth. "Calm yourself, Daughter, they have their reasons and I am sure that you will be told eventually. Now, sit down, stay quiet, and wait." Said Lord Mandaten.

"Yes, you are right Father, I apologise to you, WPCs Paverson and Rendham, it will achieve nothing to scream and shout at you, now will it? I must sit and wait until the the detectives are ready to tell me." Reluctantly, she did as her father had told her. This was a new and improved daughter, one that did not argue.

Twenty-four minutes after Cadiston had made the call, the prisoner transport van arrived and with Kansas on board, they left. "Wow, after all that excitement we can tell you that we have found the sleeping powders, Demmie had hidden in the mattress, by making a small cut in the stitching, and from the label we can be certain they were prescribed officially by a doctor Jessop," Olito informed Cadiston. "Pre-planned for that occasion then. She really was a devious woman. Now then, we have arrested Kansas for multiple murders and we now know that he is nothing more than a cold-blooded killer. He is on his way to the lock-up so now we will have words with his father, Mister Tomas Kaysten or rather Tomas Standmore." Said Cadiston. "I will go get him." Said Mac. "Tomas Kaysten, I don't see him so where is he?" Asked Mac. "He said that he needed the rest room." Answered Lord Mandaten.

"Thank you my lord." Said Mac and walked down the hall and waited outside the door. Five minutes passed and he had not appeared so he listened at the door. He could not hear any noise from inside. "Strange." He tried the door. There was no resistance and it opened easily but the restroom was empty. Mac ran back to the study as quickly as he could while calling. "DCI Cadiston, we have a runner, Tomas is gone." "Gone and is there no sign of him?" Asked Cadiston."Not a sign, made out that he needed the restroom and has done a runner after he saw his son under arrest." Said Mac. "Start a search, DS Macswee, he has to be on the premises somewhere." Said Cadiston.

"Sir, just a thought, if he was going to the restroom there is the secret passage across the hall that goes upstairs and toward the stables, coming out in the contraband store." Said Mac."Worth a try, Mac. Ladies, check all the rooms upstairs and downstairs, followed by outside. He may try to grab a car so watch them and retrieve all the car keys that are hanging up. Mac and I will check out the stables and other buildings." The search was on. "I think he came this way as the panel is not properly closed." Said Mac. They followed the passage and came out in the contraband store moved into the stable block. They heard a horse gallop away and ran to the door only to see Tomas galloping across the meadow. "What do we do now, Boss?" Asked Mac. "Problem, Detective?" Asked Jeremiah. "Could be Jeremiah, Tomas is trying to escape and is on a horse going through the meadow. We cannot give chase in our car and although we can set up a roadblock, just where would it be positioned as we have no idea where he will come out.", While Cadiston had been speaking Jerimiah had saddled another horse and was mounted and ready to ride. "Leave it to me, I will get him for you." He said and with that, he tapped the flanks of Thundist and the stallion galloped forward, the chase was on. "What in heavens name is all the commotion, Detective?" Asked Herbert.

"A prisoner is trying to escape us and has taken a horse but your son has taken up the chase on the big black and is after him." Said Cadiston. Herbert had a quick look in the stable and was smiling when he returned. "Have no fear, Detective Cadiston, Jeremiah will catch him for you. I take it he is on Thundist and your prisoner is on Hietim so fear not, he cannot outrun him, not even with a good head start. Hietim is a twenty-year old and Thundist just five so in my book, there is no contest. You go back to the Manor, Detectives, and carry on with what you were doing. Do not worry, we will bring your prisoner to you."

Said Herbert. "Thanks Herbert, we will be in the study." Said Cadiston with a grin. With that, they returned to continue with the questioning. In the study, the four officers talked about the event that had just taken place and after what Herbert had said, they were confident that Tomas would be brought to them. "Olito, Francis, would you fetch Lizabeth please." Asked Mac. "Right away, Mac." Said Francis. They disappeared down the long hall and were back with Lizabeth within fifteen minutes.

"Mrs Kaysten for you, DCI Cadiston." Said Olito. "Come in, Lizabeth, and please sit down, will you WPCs stay also please." Said Cadiston. After she was comfortable, Cadiston continued. "Now, it does not take a genius to know that you are wondering what is going on. I could not tell you before as it may have put you in even greater danger than you were already in." "Danger, me in danger? Whatever do you mean, Detective? Me in danger but from who?" Asked Lizabeth. "This is not easy for me to tell you but it must be said. We have discovered that it was your son, Kansas, that murdered his cousins James, Lowell, Gloria, and his aunt, your sister, Sammie. He was also involved in the murder of your brother, Malcolm, making a total of five murders." Lizabeth began to cry. "Take a minute, then I will continue."

"I will be alright, Detective Cadiston, just tell me everything please, hold nothing back however painful it is for me. I must know the truth. Chadrick was being blamed for all those deaths and they even planted false evidence like his mobile phone and now I know how Tomas knew about it. From what you have just said, Greta was right all along and Chadrick is innocent so who was it that attacked him and murdered Demmie? Was it my son and husband?" Asked Lizabeth. "As to that, I cannot comment but to continue, your son is responsible for five of the eleven deaths here at Mandaten and he has also confessed to five more that he committed from 1994 to 1997. I am sorry to be the bearer of bad tidings and if you are prepared for this, your husband is responsible for three murders, your brothers Malcolm and Kevin and brother-in-law-Walter." Said Cadiston.

"Who did they kill? Murder, all while pretending that all was well with me, Detective Cadiston, tell me again please?" Asked Lizabeth in shock.

"Kansas murdered your nephews, James and Lowell, your niece, Gloria, and your sister, Sammie. He also took part in the murder of your brother, Malcolm, and confessed to five more murders. Your husband was responsible for the deaths of your brothers Malcolm and Kevin and your brother-in-law, Walter." Said Cadiston.

"Now, if I have this right my son is a vicious multiple murderer. Oh my Lord, what have I raised? It must be my fault, I have tried to give him everything but in retrospect probably far too much. My husband has murdered multiple times and both of them committed murder within our family, I know where my son is but where is my husband now?" Asked Lizabeth.

"First let us get one thing straight, it is no fault of yours that your son became a multiple murderer, it is in his birth name and he was groomed, lied to, brainwashed, and falsely led by that family." Said Cadiston.

"Birth name, Kaysten, what can be attached to that?" Asked Lizabeth.

"The name of Kaysten is a fictitious name and it was made up and used by your husband. His real name is … Before I tell you that, what do you know of the family name Standlyhope?" Asked Cadiston.

"Not very much at all, they were a family of royalists and were wiped out by the parliamentary forces in the English Civil War. I think that our ancestors changed sides and became parliamentarians and then informed on them and that is how they were all found." Said Lizabeth.

"Not quite all, there were two Standlyhope brothers that managed to escape and changed their names, one to Standmore the other to Standish." Said Lizabeth.

"Now both those names I do know, that midwife at the Royal was Standmore and that other was that detective, a Sergeant Standish but where do they come into anything?" She asked. "The brothers swore to avenge their family however long it took and return their birth name so that, once again, the name of Standlyhope would be seen. They wanted your family, in fact, the complete Mandaten bloodline wiped out and they have been the target for their revenge from way back in the late seventeenth century. Apart from your father, you, Jennifer, and one other that shall be disclosed soon, they have almost succeeded." Said Cadiston. She thought for a moment. "You said one other bears our name and you did not mention Grant so is he not one of us? I said as much a short while ago when I suspected it as he is so different but who is the other one?" Enquired Lizabeth. "Sorry, I cannot disclose that to you yet but it will all be revealed in due course. Your son is being held on a charge of multiple murders and your husband is currently trying to evade capture." Disclosed Cadiston. "I am married to a murderer of my family, I think I am going to be sick." She swallowed hard and breathed deeply. Mac stepped forward to assist her. "Thank you but I will be alright, Detective. You said that I was in danger but not who from?" Asked Lizabeth. "It is your alleged husband and son." Said Cadiston. "My husband and my son, oh my, they could have killed me at any chosen moment." Said Lizabeth. "Not quite any chosen moment. They could not take that step until you were the only remaining true blood Mandaten and had secured the Mandaten estate. Then you were to have met with an unfortunate accident. It does not end there, the plan was then to rename the estate and it would then carry the name of Standlyhope. What is more, they intended to murder Kansas also." Said Cadiston.

"Kansas? But he has killed for them so why?" Asked Lizabeth. "He carries Mandaten blood and with him gone, the Mandaten bloodline would be totally erased." Said Cadiston.

"I know he has part Mandaten blood but to kill him would be killing half of one of their own. You really are a detective, Cadiston. My father always said that you would unravel everything in time but how do you know so much about the Standlyhope and Mandaten families?" Asked Lizabeth. "By reading history books and the local history of the area in which I work. Very good backup help and support and following my own suspicions. It makes no difference how much a criminal may try to hide their crime, there is always a link and evidence to be found somewhere. It may take a while to discover and to find it requires a deal of perseverance to seek it out." Replied Cadiston. "And you have certainly persevered. Now I know that my brother, Chadrick, is totally innocent of all the family murders that throws suspicion on his guilt for the death of his wife." She began to cry so Mac passed her his clean handkerchief. "I am so sorry but at that time I detested him. I am sorry I lied in my statement. If only he were here now, I would then have the opportunity and could apologise to him for all the years of hate that I have shown toward him but now it is too late as he is gone. I am so ashamed of myself for all my past behavior, for my life of lies and falseness but I have now come to my senses thanks to the words of a child, far too late. If I have this right, the danger to me has passed with Kansas already arrested and Tomas soon to be under arrest. Will Jennifer be safe now also?" Asked Lizabeth. "That is correct." Said Cadiston. "What is the truth about Grant's wife Bonnie, can you tell me now; did he kill her?" Asked Lizabeth.

"I can tell you the result of that investigation now. Bonnie and her unborn little girl child were cold-bloodedly murdered by Demmie with the help of her brother who produced a highly concentrated peanut solution for her to inject into Bonnie's food. As you know, she has been murdered and he is in police custody." Said Cadiston. "You have worked hard and tirelessly on all these murders and if it had been down to the other detective, that Standish, then they would all have been closed as tragic accidents and the murderers would be walking free. Oh my, I too would be dead and the lovely child Jennifer also murdered as they would not care about her being a child would they. My father murdered, oh my, the thought and knowing all this is mind shattering. My Father is a very wise man and it was he that asked you to investigate and no matter how painful it was or who it was, to catch the murderers and that you have done. I will not want to have the name of Standmore so I will get it changed back to my birth name of Mandaten. If Grant has the estate then good luck to him, he is not a nice person but I expect that you have found that out. But without you saying, it he is not a Mandaten. I will just have to try to get along with him and whoever his new love is. One more thing, was I ever a suspect?" Asked Lizabeth. Cadiston smiled. "Everyone was a suspect, Lizabeth, until we delved deeper and the evidence began to show. After that, not at all. You were to be another victim. Now as far as changing your name, there will be no need as you are not officially married to Tomas." Said Cadiston. "Not married? But –. All these years –." Said Lizabeth.

"The marriage was a farce. Sorry but you are a single lady. All records have been checked and there are no official marriage lines as the person that conducted the ceremony was not an ordained reverend but his brother Bernard. You were all duped and led falsely and it was all documented by them and we have their documented plan, this was all a part of their masterplan to get into the family." Said Cadiston. "I am a single woman, not married to a murderer and that is a major relief although it makes me sick to know that I shared my bed with a murderer. The sad thing is that I have given him twenty years of my life. Now shall I inform my parents of all these revelations or will you?" Asked Lizabeth who now had a smile of relief on her face.

"That is down to us, Lizabeth, you must say nothing to anyone about our conversation as there are other crimes to close. If you are alright, then we will now have a chat with your parents." Said Cadiston. "But you have not spoken to Grant or Greta yet and what about young Jennifer? Another thing, you have not mentioned my sister-in-law, Sadie." Said Lizabeth. "All in good time, please keep what has been said here to yourself, do not speak about anyone of what you have been told. Especially not to Grant and Greta as we have not interviewed them yet. I am sure that non of us want them knowing any information as that may be detrimental. Now, I think that is enough for today so now a word with your parents, WPC Paverson will you escourt Miss Mandaten back to the lounge and request the company of her parents please." Said Cadiston. "Shall I ask them to come down to the study?" Asked Olito. "That will not be necessary, we will speak to them where they are sitting, thank you." Said Cadiston. They all stood and together they walked to the breakfast room. "If it is alright, a word with you, Lord Mandaten, and with your good lady but without the remaining family present as we have not interviewed them as yet, Lizabeth can stay," Said Cadiston. "You heard the detective, please leave now and no evesdropping or spying. Alfred, take them far enough away and stay with them until they are called and any that disobey can be arrested." Said Lord Mandaten. "WPC Paverson will you with WPC Rendham escourt the family to another room please and keep them there, any that try to leave will be arrested. "Yes sir, that we will", replied Olito. Lord Mandaten looked at Alfred and gave him a nod, "Alfred". "Right away, my Lord. This way please." The family obeyed without hesitation. Cadiston winked at Greta as she passed him as she was in on his plan. With the family gone, Cadiston then explained all that had transpired in the interview and questioning of Kansas and why Tomas had run to attempt avoidance of his imminent arrest. He even told them that Jerimiah was giving chase across the open fields on Thundist and they would return to the stables and wait for his return, hopefully with Tomas. Lord Mandaten smiled at this and said. "Good man, I knew that I had you right and had not underestimated your talents." They said their farewells and went immediately back to the stables to wait for the return of Jeremiah.

It had been an hour since the chase began and they were getting a bit worried that Tomas had eveded Jerimiah and that would mean a nationwide search would need to be implemented. "Taking a while, Boss." Said Mac. As they chattered, Herbert saw two horses and one rider coming across the field. "There you are, Detective, that's my boy and just like the renowned Royal Canadian Mounted Police, he has got your man tied across the saddle." Said Herbert. "It must have been one hell of a chase and reminds me of the old wild west and the chase by the lawman to catch the outlaw. One big difference, there was no shootout thank goodness." Said Mac. "Just as well, DS Macswee, we do not want a lot of gunplay. Innocent people can easily be in the line of fire." Said Cadiston. They watched as the two horse's approached and when they arrived at the stables, Cadiston saw that Tomas had been well bound and was tied across the saddle he could see that he was a bit battered and bruised but Jerimiah looked unmarked. "There he is, Detective Cadiston, just like a Canadian Mountie I got your man. Sorry that I had to ruff him up and he is only a little bit damaged. I wanted to get him for you as we owe a lot to Lord Mandaten and if he had a hand in the murders –. Well, I got him. It was quite a chase and he was not going to stop so I had to literately jump on him to knock him off the horse." Said Jeremiah. "What like in the westerns, Son?" Asked Herbet. "Just like that, Pops. Anyhow, he put a bit of a fight but as you can see, I have him for you. Said Jeremiah.

"Thanks' Jeremiah but I would not have wanted you to place yourself in any kind of danger." Said Cadiston. "No danger for me, Cadiston, but as for the prisoner, plenty." Replied Jeremiah. "Thanks again Jerimiah, you have done us a great service." Said Cadiston."Always ready to help the law and if he had anything to do with the family murders then I am only too glad to catch him for you." Said Jeremiah. They placed him into their car and with a wave, they drove away.

Back at the station, Tomas was taken to a holding cell and after receiving a bit of medical attention for his cuts and bruises, he was given a meal. "Almost seven, Cadders, so do we question Tomas tonight or leave him to stew over night, I would leave him until Thursday morning?" Asked MAc.

"He is not going anywhere so we will let him stew in the cell for tonight, in the morning will do for him. I also have planned for tomorrow the 18th to check up on Chad and see if he will be well and strong enough for us to implement our little ruse for Grant on Friday the 19th November if not it will need to be delayed until he he is fit and well enough." Said Cadiston. "You mean Chad's 'life after death'? Now, that sounds good to me and as you are the boss, I am not going to contest it." Said Mac and laughed. Cadiston wanted to laugh with him but kept a serious look on his face. "Go home slave and be back here at 08:00 hours sharp and by the way –." He smiled. "Don't forget to bow on your way out." Said Cadiston. "Yes, oh Lord and Master." Said Mac as he complied and they both burst out laughing.

"It is a tough road and I would not want to travel it with anyone else but you, I am glad to be with you, Cadders, so see you in the morning." Said Mac. "Night Mac and by the way, it is good to have you at my side and I would not want anyone else either." They waved and went their separate ways.

It was now Thursday, 18th of November 58 days since the first death of Bonnie and her unborn child that would not be forgotten at Mandaten Manor, and the breakfast room would see fewer family members but now there was a better atmosphere. There was a touch of warmness instead of icy cold. "Good morning sister Greta and did you rest well?" Enquired Lizabeth. "I did, thank you Lizabeth, and what of yourself?" Replied Greta. "I must admit that it felt a bit strange at first but then I told myself that I had been sharing my bed with a murderer and he had plans to murder me so after that I slept very well." Said Lizabeth. "Tomas was going to murder you?" Asked Greta. "Yes he –." Lizabeth put her hand to her mouth, then continued. "Oh dear, Detective Cadiston ask me not to tell anyone. In his investigations he found that out that fact and that means he actually saved my life and I cannot thank him enough. Say nothing to anyone else please and I should not have told you." "We are the first down so your secret, if it can be called that, is safe with me. Why Lizabeth why would he want to murder you, the mother of his son?" Asked Greta. "Well you may ask, Greta –. Ah, there is Jennifer now, we had better not say anything more on the subject. Good morning, and how are this morning my dear sweet Jennifer?" Asked Lizabeth. "I am good, thank you Aunt Lizabeth, but what were you saying to Mother? I thought that I heard your husband was planning to murder you?" Asked Jennifer. "Yes, that is true, my child, but maybe not for your ears to hear." "I can hear it and will understand everything you say." Said Jennifer.

"I was asked not to tell anyone but alright then. It must remain our secret until after the investigations are complete. Cadiston found out that it was Kansas that had committed a lot of the murders, including your brother, Lowell.Tomas had this plan to kill all the family and then when I was the only Mandaten left alive, as I strongly believe although have no proof that Grant is not a true born Mandaten, then I would inherit the estate, and the moment that it was all secured, I was to meet with an accident. Detective Cadiston has the plan that he was to use to make it look like an accident and by finding that out, he saved my life." Whispered Lizabeth.

"Oh dear, does that mean that mother would be –. And that means me too –. We would have been murdered?" Asked Jennifer. "You, my dear child yes as you are true blood Mandaten but not your mother as she is not Mandaten blood, not unless she had got in the way of their evil plan but thanks to Detective Cadiston, we are all saved." Said Lizabeth quietly.

"That sounds like I was to be murdered if I knew too much, as well as the rest of you. I guess that he has saved us all, at least those that are left." Said Greta. They heard footsteps on the stairs so quickly changed the topic of conversation. "Well that detective was here a long while yesterday and he took my son Kansas away I wonder why that was, and then my husband was taken away also but I do not know why but, he will inform me in due course when he is ready. He has proved his worth and father had him right and was correct in requesting that he be allowed to investigate every killing. (Lizabeth turned toward the door.) Morning, Grant." Said Lizabeth smiling.

"Morning, now what are you all gabbling on about that detective? Well, it proves that father was right in his assessment of Cadiston and he is not so dumb but a very clever detective after all. I told him I had nothing to do with Bonnie's death when he was asking. Well, now he knows that for sure, it was all down to Demmie, the devious cow and Chadrick saw to her." Said Grant. "Not at all dumb, Grant, he is a brilliant detective and has managed to solve all the cases in just 58 days after the day that your Bonnie and little girl child were murdered on the 22nd of October." Said Lizabeth quietly.

"Whoopee for him, so they are all solved, are they Lizabeth? And it was your son and husband that did it all I guess as they have been arrested. I guess that means we had it wrong about Chad, apart from his wife." Answered Grant with a hint of nonchalant attitude in his voice and facial expression. "I think so. Anyhow, we must wait for him to finalize everything. I think it was Tomas that killed Demmie because after they had arrested Kansas, he panicked and tried to run but they caught him. He is locked up. I expect that Cadiston will be back later today to tell us the rest." Said Lizabeth. "And he will probably need to speak with me as he has not interviewed me yet and he has not spoken with you, has he Grant?" Added Greta. "ME, hmm –. Got nothing more to tell him, Greta, he has his murderers and that is an end to it. Chadrick was not guilty of their murders after all but he shot his wife, as to that, there can be no doubt and he still had the gun in his hands after Tomas hit him. I don't think Tomas did it, Chad did well it was not me and I have an alibi as I was not here and that detective saw me return after I had been out so a police alibi no less for me." Said Grant smiling. "Maybe, I don't know but we will find out when Cadiston returns to tell us and interviews you and me." Said Greta. "What about her"? Grant asked and pointed. "By her you mean my daughter, Jennifer. Well, he may want to talk with her as well as us. He likes everything to be tidy so, maybe he is not quite finished yet, he likes to tie up all the loose ends before his final closure." Said Greta. "Hmm –." Was all that Grant replied. While they spoke, their parents sat quietly listening. Grant looked toward them, then walked to the breakfast bar and filled his plate.

"Morning Mac." Said Cadiston. "Morning Cadders, just checked on the prisoners and they all have been given some breakfast so after Tomas has eaten, should I bring him up to the interview room?" Asked Mac. "Let us grab a coffee first, by then he should be ready and chomping at the bit. While you fetch him, I will get the interview room ready, fresh tape, pen, and paper and anything else that we may need in the way of evidence. I will also have a WPC present." Said Cadiston. "I will get us a coffee and ask one of them to attend." Said Mac. While Mac was away from the office, the phone rang. "Any news for me, Cadiston? You know what I mean." Asked the superintendent. "Yes sir, I have all the information that you require documented in a file sir, on the matter that we discussed and much more than I anticipated. I am about to hold a questioning session with one of the murderers of the Mandaten family and will come up to see you when that is completed." Replied Cadiston. "Good show Cadiston, knew that I could rely on you." Was the reply and the phone was hung up. "Your private thing with the chief?" Asked Mac. "Yes, and you know nothing about it." Said Cadiston. "As to that, I don't know anything so there you have it." Said Mac. "Good, drink this then let us get Tomas into the interview room. After that I have to speak to the chief and then we will go to the hospital to check on Chad. Mac, a question for you, how did you know about Kansas being here on Monday and the cycle being how Kansas got from the stable to the Dyke so quickly after putting a scare into the horse?" Asked Cadiston. "Remember after the girls had found him and when we followed up his interview and saw Crichie in his workshop –." "Yes, remember it well." Replied Cadiston. "Well, I remembered what Grace and Janet said about spotting pieces of what looked like a fairly new cycle and remembered what you had said that if it was Grant and Katrine then she probably used a cycle to travel the distance in such a quick time. I followed up my suspicion that he was here before Thursday and checked out the nearest hotel to the station. With that in mind, I played a hunch and he had checked into the hotel on Monday but slipped up by using his own name, Kansas Standmore." Said Mac. "And a very good hunch, that worked perfectly, well done Mac and excellent detecting" Said Cadiston. "I am always saying that you pick up a snippet of information then store it until required so I just copied you and did the same. Replied Mac. "And a good snippet to remember, Mac, so again, well done, now shall we?" Said Cadiston.

While Mac went to bring the prisoner up, Cadiston prepared the room and sat quietly waiting for them to arrive. It took twenty minutes before they were settled and ready to begin the interview. The interview tape was switched on and with the introductions made, they began. "Now then Tomas, tell us why you tried to escape." Said Cadiston. "Never mind that, I want to bring a charge of assault and grievous bodily harm against Jeremiah Stott." Said Tomas. "You can forget about that, he was shall I say deputised to seek out and arrest you by whatever means were deemed necessary, he used the appropriate amount of force required to apprehend a fleeing suspect of a murder charge and actioned a citizen's arrest with my full approval. Now with that out of the way, Tomas Standmore using the false name of Kaysten, I am arresting you for the murders of Malcolm Mandaten, Kevin Mandaten, and Walter Larkspere, you do not need say anything but anything you do say will be taken down, and may be used as evidence. If you do not say something now that you later rely on in court it may harm your defence, (then with the caution fully completed.) Do you understand the charge?" Asked Cadiston. "Fully and if you think that you can pin anything on me then go right ahead and try, you stinking copper! You have nothing on any of us because, we were –." He went silent. "You were saying?" Asked Cadiston. "Nothing to you, copper." Said Tomas. "A bad attitude will not help you at all, Tomas." Replied Mac. "Shall we begin with Kevin Mandaten, why did you want him dead, Tomas?" Asked Cadiston.

"No comment." Replied Tomas. "Why did you tamper with his Kentucky rifle and before you answer, think very carefully as we have the evidence. I am showing the accused the small round disc used to hold the overload of black powder charge in the barrel." Said Cadiston. "Don't know why you are showing me that piece of metal, I know nothing of that disc; Cadiston." Said Tomas. "Think very carefully, Tomas, and remember that you are under caution, and we have a witness statement that tells us differently." Said Mac.

He stared at him with hate in his eyes then turned his stare to Cadiston. "Critchie." He whispered. "Would you like to reconsider and answer the question again, Tomas? Only this time answer with the truth." Asked Cadiston. "Witness statement you say." Tomas thought for a moment. "Only one it could be –. Why the little sneak Critchie. Damn him! I bet it was him that told you, damn bible pumping moron. We should have eliminated him instead of paying him to keep quiet, he always was too damn honest for his own good, he would not steal the sweets from the shop when Bernard and me helped ourselves. Ok Cadiston, you are a clever bastard, you and your cohort Macswee, just would not leave well alone. Harry warned us about you. I had him make a disc so what of it? You can't prove it was in that gun of Kevin's it was made for." Said Tomas. "Maybe not alone I couldn't but our forensic and firearms ballistics teams are experts in piecing things together and the powder burns on the disc match the exact same black powder used in the barrel of Kevin's gun so there is the proof. Even though it was burned, it still had your fingerprint on it and with our new forensic science we can discover a lot of things that in the past remained hidden, and a statement from the security guard that saw you enter the gun marquee on the evening of Saturday, 28th September." Said Cadiston. "Damn it, knew I should have worn gloves. Bloody security guard, he was paid well to keep his trap shut so can't even trust them. Damn you, Cadiston, you should have left it all to Harry then it would have all been sound. Damn you, all of you know far too much." Said Tomas angrily. "A lot more than you realize, now the truth Tomas." Said Cadiston. "You want the truth? Seems to me that you already know it but here it goes –. Right, so I tampered with the gun and blew his head off. Some of my ancestors were beheaded thanks to the Mandatens so I don't call that murder, I call that justice." Said Tomas. "And we call it murder." Replied Mac.

"Damn you as well Macswee, or whatever your name is, damn you all! We had it all planned and worked out until you poked your nose in it. Harry should have silenced you. So I killed Kevin and I guess that my son has told you the rest, the little squealer! Suppose he told you that I bashed Malcolm's brains in and stabbed Walter while Kansas killed Gloria and Sammie, so there it is. Damn you, Cadiston, you are just far too good a detective but I want it made clear that I did not kill Sadie or Demmie, those three, yes, I admit that but not those two. Kansas killed James, Lowell, Sammie, and Gloria and helped me with Malcolm but even though I confess to these three, I did not kill Sadie and Demmie and that is the truth. I hit Chadrick twice while he lay on the floor but someone else had got to him first and before you ask the answer is, yes, I wanted to kill him as he had some incriminating evidence on my son and that is it. We all lied when you spoke to us, even Lizabeth, she is such a blind fool and could see nothing. She thought Kansas loved her, she could not have been more wrong. Ha, he told me she made his skin crawl, he hated her and just played along." Said Tomas.

"You have admitted that you are guilty of the murders of Malcolm and Kevin Mandaten, also Walter Larkspere. Are there any other incidents that we need to take into consideration?" Asked Cadiston.

"Other incidents?" Asked Tomas. "Other incidents, Tomas, and now is the time to declare them." Enquired Mac. His eyes again flicked between Mac and Cadiston. "You two know something, don't you, dam you both for your investigating, you know something else about us?" Asked Tomas. "Would you like a small hint to jog your memory?" Asked Mac. "No need Macswee, I know what you are on and that was four years ago and brother Harry had it all settled tragic car accident." Said Tomas. "Well, we have unsettled it so do you want to tell us the truth now?" Asked Mac. "Blue Jaguar, we ran it off the road into a dyke and it landed upside down, and before the occupants could be gotten out, which we hoped for, they all drowned. Five more of them Mandatens gone and good riddance. When I said we I meant Bernard and me. Well, you have got me but not him as he gave you the slip. We even eliminated those that were still in France, wiped out the rest of them there, six more Mandatens out of the way." Said Tomas. "And you wanted to kill them all, making it a cold-blooded, pre-planned act?" Asked Cadiston. "No other way, is there?" Replied Tomas. "Not to commit murder." Said Cadiston.

"Yeah right, if we had not done it then we would have all them Mandatens left alive and we did not want that. If Harry had got his act together and stopped you, Cadiston, we would have gotten away with it all and killed the lot of them." Said Tomas angrily.

"You admit that it was you and Bernard who ran Baron Mandaten off the road and we know that Bernard was driving. As far as Bernard goes, I can tell you that he is in hospital after crashing the car that he was driving." Said Cadiston."Is he dead and what of the boy, Roger?" Asked Tomas. "You have been charged with multiple murder and have openly admitted your guilt, you are entitled to a solicitor and if you do not have one, then one will be appointed for you, do you understand?" Asked Caditson.

"Just get on with it." Said Tomas. "The time is 11:43 and the interview is ended." The tape was turned off. "Take him down, DS Macswee, while I have a word with the chief and then meet me in the office." Said Cadiston.

"You be away, I will get this one locked up." Replied Mac.

"Morning JJ, the chief needed to see me as I have some information for him." Said Cadiston as he walked into the office. "He is waiting for you so go straight in." Said JJ. "Ah Cadiston, take a seat and tell me all that you have discovered about Harry Standish." Said the superintendent. "I will keep to the point, sir, as the whole story is quite lengthy and is all detailed in my written report which I have here for you." He passed the file to his chief. "I have discovered that he is a descendant of a family called Standlyhope and this name goes back to pre-sixteen hundred. There is another name linked to his, that of Standmore, and they are one in the same family and have carried a centuries-long revenge vendetta against the Mandaten family because of what happened during the English Civil War. The aim was to wipe out the Mandaten family completely, leaving not a single blood tie to the family name. It was also planned to murder the son of Tomas Standmore and his alleged wife Lizabeth Mandaten but that is all in the file, sir, and explained in detail. With the family dead, they would then take all their wealth and the estate and then return the ancestral name to the records and then re-name it Standlyhope estate. They did all the killing and Harry Standish being in the police force was to investigate the cases and close them all as tragic accidents, therefore, allowing the murders to be hidden. That, sir, is why he wanted to keep me quiet and stop me from carrying out any form of investigation. The only crime that he committed, sir, was to falsify, camouflage, and floss over the truth so he was covering up murders and in effect perverting the course of justice. All the information is in this file, sir, and as I said all, very carefully documented. There are also pieces of information on the interview tapes. I hope that answers the question of his misgivings and why he wanted to close the cases quickly, especially the Mandaten ones." Said Cadiston. "Excellent piece of detecting, Cadiston, now how are the murder cases progressing?" Asked the chief. "To move on sir, we have made arrests for most of the Mandaten murders and we have all the accused in the holding cells. We have very strong evidence and have self admissions as to their guilt and again, their confessions are on the recorded interviews sir. They refused to have a solicitor present at the time of the interviews so every care was taken to be correct sir. They now have access to their solicitors and now sir we need a preliminary hearing for it to go trial by judge and jury" Replied Cadiston.

"So what murders have been solved?" Asked the chief.

"The murders of Bonnie Mandaten and her unborn little girl child and the unborn child must not be forgotten sir, Malcolm, Kevin, James and Lowell Mandaten, the murders of Sammie, Walter and Gloria Larkspere and their murderers are in custody." Said Cadiston. "That is nine murders, Cadiston, are you telling me that there are more guilty parties still at large?" Asked the chief. "Just two deaths and one vicious attack, sir, and we will be dealing with that possibly on Friday but, that depends on a major witness being fit and well enough sir otherwise it must be delayed until they are ready sir, but the guilty party is going nowhere sir and is under suveilance. As for the case of Baron Lasseroie Mandaten and his family which equates to five murders covered up by Standish and again, that is documented in the file. We have witness statements, we have the vehicles involved and the perpetrators of the crime in custody. One is in the cells, the other under police guard in hospital after the car that he was trying to escape in crashed, he is not expected to survive sir. We have a written detailed plan as to the Mandaten murders and it was done with military precision detailing every aspect so real solid evidence, sir. There are also the blood and D.N.A. samples and fingerprints and we also have other items of visual evidence. Tomas Standmore, using the false name of Kaysten, has also declared that they were responsible for six Mandaten deaths in France and that being the case, we should notify the French police who are or would be investing those deaths." Said Cadiston. "Well Cadiston my boy –." "Sorry sir, not quite finished, sir. Kansas Kaysten or rather Standmore had confessed to five murders that he committed in 1994, 1995, 1996, and 1997 all covered up by Standish. Sir, I feel that the files on these cases should be drawn from the files and where an innocent person is falsely imprisoned due to Standish's false connived evidence, they must be released, sir." Said Cadiston. "And rightly so. You have proved that my intuition about you was correct so very well done, you have not let me down. Now go and finish the job, acting DCI Cadiston and I will inform the French police and have those case files brought to me." Said the chief. "One other case came to light during our investigation, sir, and it was acting Detective Sergeant Macswee who found the information to that crime." Said Cadiston.

"Well then, why are you still here, go and complete your arrests." Said the chief. "That I will gladly do, sir." He left the office.

"Go alright with the chief?" Asked Mac. "It did Mac, now we need to get arrest warrants for Alfred and Frieda Standish, for Charles, Josie, Harriet and Sheila Standish –. In fact, the complete Standish and Standmore families as they all played their part in the murder plot. We have in custody all that remains of the Standmore family but they are all from one family and that is the family of Standlyhope." Said Cadiston.

"Should we interview Margery Standmore now? All we can get her on is stealing the Ketamine drug as her name was not on the plan of the murders." Said Mac. "We can put her away for that theft and for perverting the course of justice so let us see what she has to say for herself." While Francis and Olito fetched the prisoner from the cells, Mac and Cadiston went to the interview room. "Sitting comfortably, Margery?" Asked Cadiston. "Yes, thank you but you will get nothing from me." She said and as she eyed them both. "You may as well give up now." She added. "We will see." Said Cadiston and the interview tape was turned on. "The time is 14:10 and this is a recording of the interview between DCI Cadiston, Detective Sergeant Macswee and Margery Standmore. Present are WPCs Rendham and Paverson. Why did you steal the Ketamine Margery?" Asked Cadiston. "You are the detective, you tell me." Said Margery. "You gave it to your daughter-in-law, Gloria, for her sister, Katrine, to ease the suffering of a sick animal but it was also used to commit a murder." Said Cadiston. "Murder, I don't know of any murder using that drug, it was genuinely for a sick animal. They did not have any drug on their death list or plan b –." She stopped talking and put her hand to her mouth, realising what she had just said. "You know of the death list then so tell us about that and there is no need to lie as we have that list and the detailed plan." Said Cadiston. "Impossible, it was too well hidden." Said Margery. "Nothing is too well hidden for our forensic officers. They know all the little tricks and secret hiding places." Said Cadiston. "Harry said that he had to keep a close eye on you, Cadiston, you are too clever by half. He said it is as though you have this voice in your head and an invisible helper on your shoulder to guide you." Said Margery. "In that case, you had better tell us everything. We hold all the information and visual evidence so there is no point in continuing to lie." Said Cadiston. She thought for a moment. "I told them that it was high time that they stopped their trail of revenge and that there would be a very clever detective one day that would investigate and work it all out and then they would all get caught. They thought that they were so clever, especially with Harry to cover their tracks, but they had not reckoned on you, Cadiston. I will tell you everything but I had nothing to do with any killing and that is the truth. My only crime was not to report it and for that I am sorry." Margery then went on to tell the whole story of how the plan had been drawn up and how Kansas had been with his father all along and had to pretend not to get on with him. She described how he acted falsely toward his mother and had said that he hated her. Once she began there was no stopping her tongue-wagging, she even detailed the running off the road of the Baron Lasseroie. She spoke for almost an hour and everything that she said was confirmed with the evidence that they held. "And that is all I know, Detective. I have told you everything about their centuries-long trail of revenge and the desire to get the Mandaten fortune so there is no more to tell. I am sorry that they used the Ketamine to kill someone that was not the intention. You probably know –. Well, of course you know that Gloria's parents run an animal shelter and that was what the drug was for and no other purpose. You probably know as well that her sister, Katrine, works at the Manor." Said Margery. "We know a lot of things, Margery, and most of what you have told us we did already know but we appreciate your truthfulness. Margery Standmore, I am arresting on the charge of perverting the course of justice and for the theft of a drug that was used to commit a murder, you do not need to say anything but anything you do say will be taken down and may be used as evidence. If you do not say something now that you later rely in court it may harm your defence. (When the caution had been completed.) Do you understand?" Asked Cadiston. She just nodded her head and wiped a tear from her eye. "You need to answer for the tape." Said Mac. "I understand." She said. "You are entitled to a solicitor and if you do not have one then one will be appointed for you, do you understand?" Asked Cadiston.

"I do." Said Margery. "The time is 15:53 and the interview is ceased." Said Cadiston and the tape was turned off. "WPC Rendham and Paverson, take the prisoner down please." "Right away sir." Said Francis.

With the prisoner on the way to a cell, Cadiston and Mac returned to the office. "We have them, Cadders, every one of them guilty as charged. We have all the guilty parties in custody apart from one main character but we will get to him soon, in the meantime we have warrants for the arrests of their remaining families. You have cracked it, Cadders, and if you had not been stopped earlier by Standish then it is my thought that a lot of these deaths would have been avoided. It is a pity that he cannot be arrested as an accessory to murder or at least for perverting the course of justice. Wat do you say to that?" Asked Mac. "Not my place to say anything, Mac, and best left well alone by us. If anything is to be done then it is out of our hands and we will not speak of it again." Said Cadiston. "Copy that Boss, mum's the word." Said Mac. "Ok my friend, it is 16:12 so we will pay a visit to the hospital to check on Chad and then we can see about implementing our final plan for his return, his 'life after death' appearance." Said Cadiston.

"I will fetch the car around." He turned and walked briskly away. At the hospital, they went straight up to his room and were greeted with smiles from Greta, Jennifer, and Chad himself.

"I understand that the truth is finally out, Cadiston, and that is down to you. Greta has filled me in on the arrests that have taken place and it confirms my suspicion that Lowell was murdred by Kansas. It is hard to believe that one so young could be so vicious so who else did he murder?" Asked Chad.

"Apart from Lowell, he murdered James, Gloria, and Sammie and assisted in the murder of Malcolm. He also admitted five previous murders." Said Cadiston. "My God, he really was a little thug then and if he had not been stopped who knows what kind of a killing spree he would have gone on. Thank goodness that you have put an end to his reign of terror. Greta tells me that his father is also under arrest for a series of the family murders and was also going to murder Lizabeth and Jennifer." Said Chad. Cadiston looked at Greta. "We were so excied that the killings have ceased and the murderers ar in custody, sorry it just came out." Said Greta. "No harm done just as long as Grant has not been told as we are not finished with him." Said Cadiston. "Definitely not." Said Greta. "That is right. Tomas was the one that tampered with Kevin's rifle so in effect murdered him along with Walter and Malcolm. He also admitted to six murders in France. Bonnie and her unborn girl child were murdered by your late wife and that makes her a double murderess. Grant was not involved but her brother was." Said Cadiston.

"Brother, Demmie had a brother? She told me that she was an only child, that just shows what a liar she was. So it was Demmie who murdered Bonnie and her unborn little girl child but why? What would she hope to gain?"Asked Chad. "She hoped to gain Grant who she had a strong desire for and had been seeing him for two and a half years and in turn when he gained the Lord title, they would have all the wealth. Sad thing is that he did not want her in that way. You probably know that they had been seeing each other for quite a while and I don't think you need a picture drawn. She had a strong desire for him and had treated you falsely before and for most of your married life. Sorry if it is painful for you to find that out." Said Cadiston. "On the contrary, Cadiston. Greta has filled me in on all the details and they were welcome to each other. Now, you have said who Kansas and Tomas have murdered along with Demmie but not who murdered Demmie and Sadie?" Said Chad. "That is where you play a part if you are up to it." Said Cadiston. "You bet I am, well my brain said I am but the doc says another week at least before I can excert any sort of activity." Said Chad. "Okay, we will need to wait for another week before we implement the plan to bring you home my friend, we cannot go against doctors orders. "Cadiston then explained the plan to him and the part that he would play.

"Simple but effective, roll on Friday and that will now be the 26th of November with the docs permission. I will be looking forward to it." Said Chad. "You rest up now with these two lovely ladies and we will see you at Mandaten Manor on the morning of the 26th when you will experience your life after death as Jennifer put it, and that will be the final murderer brought to justice and the family will then be told the truth of your birth."

Said Cadiston. With a wave they left leaving them wondering. "What did he mean by the truth about my birth Greta, do you know?" Asked Chad. "I have no idea Chad." Said Greta. "

A mystery until he discloses it then. In a weeks time" Said Chad.

"Back to the office boss?" Asked Mac. "Let me see, it is 17:40 so I think the cars and home. A week Tomorrow, Mac, we arrest our final suspect in the murders of the Mandaten family but before we do that we must have a word with Katrine about the Ketamine. Talking to Gloria and her mother-in-law there was an element of truth in why the drug was stolen so on the way back, we will call into the animal shelter and have a word with their parents and that should clear any querry up about Grant." Said Cadiston. "I know where it is, take about forty minutes to get there." Said Mac. "Drive on then, my good man." Said Cadiston. Mac smiled then the engine roared into life and they were on their way.

"Mr. Mulbatern?" Asked Cadiston. "Yes, but the centre is closed so if you wanted anything you will need to return in the morning." Warrant cards were shown. "DCI Cadiston and DS Macswee. We just need to clarify something." "You had best come in then and I will just fetch my wife, she is feeding the animals." He turned and walked slowly away. "Shame what befell this family, he seems like a nice man." Said Mac. "Detectives, this is my wife Clair. Now, how can we help you? We have done nothing wrong here at the centre, have we? Oh please no, there is nothing wrong with our daughters, is there?" He asked as his wife was gripping his arm tightly and looked frightened. "Not at all, sir, so please do not be alarmed. All we need to confirm is did your daughter, Katrine, supply you with a drug, namely Ketamine?" Asked Cadiston. "Yes, she did, it was to help to put a sick animal out of its pain. We used what was needed and gave the rest back to her. She will not get into trouble, will she or her sister Heather?" Asked Mrs. Mulbatern.

"And that would be Gloria, sometimes called Heather?" Asked Cadiston.

"Yes, but she did not take the drug from the hospital. Her mother-in-law, Margery, got it for her and we did not use it all so Katrine was going to give the rest back to them." Said Mr. Mulbatern. "What is this about, Detective? Our girls are good girls and would not knowingly do anything wrong and definitely not break the law. Oh, Frederick, it must be to do with Heather's horrible husband, Bernard, or that horrible family." Said Mrs. Mulbatern.

"Never did like those Standmores. There is something evil and fishy about that family, Detective." Said Mr. Mulbatern. "No need to worry yourself on that score, Lady Mulbatern. ("Oh! my I have not been called that in a long while detective.") Both your daughters are fine and are not in any real trouble. In fact, they are helping us with our enquiries. Now, you have answered our query and we are quite satisfied with the information that you have given us." Said Cadiston. "We do know it to be the truth so thank you, Lord, Lady Mulbatern." Said Mac smiling. "As my wife said we have not been called that for a long time detective." "We know all about your family history sir, madam, and your daughters are just fine and we will ensure that Katrine does not make a serious mistake, but nothing for you to concern yourselves with," added Cadiston with a smile. "But why did you need to know about the ketamine, have we done something against the law? Will we get into trouble?" Asked Mrs. Mulbatern. "Not at all Mrs. Mulbatern, not at all. You have just confirmed what we had been told earlier and as you are aware, all information received needs to be verified so it must be followed up and confirmed. You need have no further concerns, all I will say is that next time, call the vet." Said Mac. "True, but, –. It is a matter of cost detective". "We thank you for your time and we should not need to bother you again." Said Cadiston. They turned and walked back to their car. "Now they are a nice couple and doing a good job in looking after the animals that have been less fortunate. Hang on, Cadders, back in a minute." Said Mac. "If you are going to do what I think you are, take this as well." Said Cadiston and he gave him sixty pounds. Mac was out of the car and in a few quick strides, was knocking on the door. "No need to worry, Mr. Mulbatern, I just wanted to give you this small donation from us both." He handed him one hundred and twenty pounds. "That is most generous, thank you both." Said Mr. Mulbatern. "You are welcome, and we are sorry about your family misfortunes but for now, good night and keep up the good work." Said Mac. He returned to the car with a broad smile on his face.

"A noble gesture Mac, worthy of a Lord and Lady now shall we go home."

Chapter Twenty

Cadiston Triumphs

Friday, the 19th of November, and Cadiston and Macswee were in the office, "Okay boss, we must delay on the final arrest so what is on the agenda for today." "First we will clear the incidents board of the closed cases, but ensure that all the visual evidence and photographs are clearly labled and stored ready for the trials. We will leave the evidence and photographs of Sadie and Demmie on the board until we have closure". "Right boss, you know something even though we have been looking at Sadie and Demmies photographs for a while they still make my stomack churn, poor Sadie's bloated body and Demmie's in such a mess." "None of the photographs will be pleasant for the jury to see Mac but they will". Now with that task completed we will away to Mandaten and have a word with Nᴅᴡᴜ̨ᴅɪ

Friday morning the 19th of November had arrived without fanfare and Mandaten Manor was feeling the chill of a frosty morning with a light dusting of snow on the ground. In the breakfast room, there were smiles and sighs of relief. A new warmth had entered the remaining family and the years of bitterness, lies, and falseness had been finally been put behind them. Even Grant appeared to be a different person as he greeted the family with smiles. There were so few of the family left now and after the initial chat, they selected their breakfast in silence. It was Grant that again broke into the peaceful silence.

"Well that is that then, it is all over and no detectives here today, and at last, the murderers are in prison and the rest of us are free. Now Father, with us all here, is it not time to say who will be the next Lord Mandaten. Well it stands to reason that as I am the only one left standing it must be me?" Said Grant hungrily. "Are you in that much of a hurry, Grant? The murderers may have been taken into custody but they have not been tried in a court of law and found guilty as charged and had sentence passed on them so, Grant, and that being the case son it is not over yet." Said Lord Mandaten. "Come now, that is a mere detail surely, Father. Cadiston, as you said he would, has sorted the truth from the lies so in my book, it is a long-drawn conclusion and as I am the only remaining male heir, we can now get on with our lives. **'A NEW BEGINNING'** I believe Jennifer said to Lizabeth." Said Grant. "You are a fool, Grant, if you think that it is all over. Until we hear it from Cadiston officially, I will hold the thought that it is not completely over." Said Lord Mandadnten. "Well that is as it may be but it does not alter the fact that you have to nominate the next Lord and as I am the only living male heir, well, it must go to me." Said Grant. "Maybe Grant but we will wait a little bit longer until we have heard it officially from Cadiston that apart from the trials it is all over." Said Lord Mandaten. "He was here on Wednesday doing his interviews and made his arrests so there is nothing more to be settled." Said Grant. "Not so Grant. He has not spoken to Greta, Jennifer or you so there are still some, shall we say loose ends to be tied up and I believe it was Jonas that said dot the I and cross the t with a full stop at the end then it is complete Grant and not before so we need a little more patience don't we." Said Lord Mandaten smiling. "Loose ends be buggered, Father, this is all a delaying tactic because you do not want to make me Lord and in the end, Father, you will have no choice." Said Grant angrily, his father looked at him but the new Lizabeth answered first. "Patience Grant, patience is a virtue. We have changed and are now going to live as better people and you should adapt and follow our example. Everything comes to those who wait, I am waiting for the final closure and if it is to be you, then I will be looking over your shoulder to make sure that you carry on running the estate as Mother and Father have and as they intend it to continue. I will not allow you to ruin it, brother dear, and do not dare to speak to Father in that tone. You have quickly changed from being pleasant to your usual bitter self in a matter of minutes but then that is no surprise."

"I have told you many times not to call me 'brother dear' Lizabeth and it is all right for you to say, Lizabeth, as you are not in line to get the estate and do not forget that it was your blasted husband and basted son that murdered our family." Said Grant. "As to that, I need no reminding, thank you You will not know but I was also on their death list along and this dear sweet child." She put her arm around Jennifer and gave an affectionate squeeze. "Now thanks to the brilliant Detective Cadiston we are safe and as Father said, not in so many words, it is not over until it is over, dot the I and cross the t and a full stop at the end." Said Lizabeth smiling. "A fine sentiment, Sister, but I want to know where I stand." Said Grant. "On your two feet Uncle Grant", replied Jennifer who was still in her feisty mode. "Shut that mouth of yours little girl, you have not got Unle Chad to protect you now so be very careful what you say." "Oh my, Brother, you do exasperate me and I am here and will protect Jennifer from harm." Then she turned away from him but her face was red with anger at Grant.

The week from the 19th to the 26th of November passed slowly for Grant as he was eager to secure the title of Lord. He had returned to his usual grumpy self but Greta, Jennifer and Lizabeth were not dismayed by this. Greta knew more than Lizabeth but had kept the secret along with Jennifer well.

With breakfast over Lizabeth stood near the window and could hear the birds chirping even on a cold frosty morning and looked out of the window but it was not the birds that she was looking at but a car pulling up. She stayed silent but, watched as the occupants stepped from the vehicle and then, spoke, "Well Grant you must have talked them up it has been over a week but they had their reasons for the delay." "Talked who up Lizabeth, stop talking in a riddle". Snapped Grant. "Not a riddle Grant, because here are the detectives again. raising her hand to her mouth, she then gasped. The family looked at her and could clearly see the colour drain from her cheeks. "I am not seeing this, he is not real, not seeing this at all. I saw him lying there and he was dead but if it is him and not an illusion then I am glad." She stammered in shock and almost collapsed. "What are you going on about, Lizabeth, not seeing what and who is dead?" Asked Grant.

Lizabeth laughed, "You will find that out soon enough, Grant." He looked from the window but could see nothing apart from the parked car. "Who got out of the car, Lizabeth? Was it that detective and his cohorts?" Asked Grant. "Wait and you will see, they are now coming in." Said Lizabeth. They heard the footsteps as they approached and waited to see who would enter the room. "Lot of fuss over the police coming in, it is only Cadiston and his cohort Macswee and with them WPCs paying us another visit so let us hope he will tell us that it is all over and the cases are solved." Said Grant. With Mac at his side, Cadiston stood in the doorway for a moment, looking at the faces that stared back before speaking. "Good morning Lord and Lady Mandaten, are you prepared for this revelation and an early Christmas present from us to you?" "Good morning detective Cadiston, the answer is yes, we are prepared, it could not come soon enough." Said Lord Mandaten in reply with his wife beside him they prepared themselves.

"Then without delay, I would like to introduce to you, your only surviving true blood son, –. So without delay I introduce to you your son Chadrick Mandaten, and in the words of young Jennifer, he has risen to 'life after death'." Said Cadiston. The room was silent as he stepped out from behind Cadiston and Mac and walked into the room. "What is this game, he is dead, we saw him laid on the mortuary slab." Said Grant bitterly. "Afraid not Grant, I am quite alive and thank you for caring so much and not visiting me in the hospital after you tried to kill me." Said Chad. "Tried to kill you, I would not have tried but succeeded. This is some sort of police trick, the real Chadrick is dead you are just a look-alike. We saw him laid out on the mortuary slab, didn't we Lizabeth? You are not real but a kind of mirage. I hit you so hard, then Tomas finished you off for me." Said Grant. Mac picked up on that remark as did Cadiston and as he went to step forward but Cadiston held him back and whispered. "Not yet Mac." He stepped back acknowledging his DCI.

"I assure you that I am real, Grant. Here, touch my arm and you will see that I am flesh and blood and very much alive no thanks to you. Yes Grant, alive and walking which is more than Demmie can say. It was all very hazy for a while but then it all came back to me. I saw you briefly from the corner of my eye just seconds before you struck the first blow. You did not kill me when you struck and as I lay on the floor, Demmie came past and you followed her to the bathroom and when she left it you shot her. You probably hoped that Tomas had finished the job for you when he hit me again but not so. He failed but now I have a metal plate in my head thanks to him. I am living proof of that and all due to the skill of Doctor Mafidsen." Said Chad. Grant just stared at him remaining silent while his brain tried to take this revelation in. "So I am to believe that you are not dead and what is all this garb that you are spouting, Cadiston? You are trying to say that he is a blood born Mandaten? Another trick, there is no way he is that, this is a sick trick on your part. He is not a true blood Mandaten, he is adopted." Spat Grant. "Not so Grant, and sorry to disappoint you but we have all the documented proof and a witness statement verifying his birth plus a perfect D.N.A. match. Also, other Mandaten family characteristics. We also have the proof that Chadrick was taken away at birth and substituted with a stillborn child to fool Lord and Lady Mandaten." Said Cadiston. "You mean my parents." "As to that we will explain in a minute now back to the truth. As part of a centuries-old trail of revenge to eliminate the Mandaten family name, the midwife a nurse, Martha Standmore, took Chadrick away the instant that he was born and as I have said, replaced him with the stillborn child of Caterina Dovetson who had sadly died with her family in a multiple car crash. The nurse Standmore said that she could get another child, a newborn whose mother had died and she had no other family to take the child. As you know, my Lord, you agreed but the student nurse, a Rachel Huntsmere, did not like what had been done to you but had been threatened so was forced to go along with it. Unbeknown to Standmore, Rachel returned Chadrick to you and so Lord, Lady Mandaten, for thirty years you have been bringing up and looking after your own son." Said Cadiston. Lizabeth now burst into tears. "I have a real brother, I actually have a real live brother and his name is Chadrick and I love him." She walked over to him and gave him a kiss on each cheek then a hug. "My brother, Chadrick, can you, will you forgive me for all the harshness and bitchiness that I have bestowed on you? I truly am sorry for all the hurt that I have caused you and as young Jennifer said, we have the chance for a **'NEW BEGINNING'**, as a very bright Jennifer said, all of us together. I know you think it strange behaviour on my part and I have finally seen the error of my ways and it has taken all this tragedy and the words of a child namely Jennifer to make me come to my senses. So! What do you say, brother, shall we have a **'NEW BEGINNING'** together my dear lost and returned brother?" Asked Lizabeth. "After that revelation, Lizabeth, I can only say yes and if I had a drink then I would raise my glass and drink to that. Yes Lizabeth, we will put the past behind us and happily look forward to a **'NEW BEGINNING'**." Said Chad with a smile and a hug for Lizabeth. "You have said about him so what of me then, Cadiston? Where do I come into your analysis?" Asked Grant bitterly. "You, Grant, are not a Mandaten and never were the twin of Malcolm hence the reason that you are so different. Your birth mother is Emily Cartridge and she was also told that she had a stillborn son and we now know that she had given birth to you and Midwife Standmore had taken you from her and made out that you and Malcolm were twins. We again have documented proof of this, they had been altered but the birth records have been gone over very thoroughly by our forensic lab and there is another secure confirmation and that is your D.N.A. so Grant, you are not a Mandaten but a Cartridge." Said Cadiston. The colour drained from his cheeks and he went silent while he pondered over all the information that he had just been given, information that he did not like.

He turned his back on them while his hand went beneath his shirt and when his hand came into the open, it held a gun. "Well, if my name is Cartridge, here is one for you, Chadrick." Mac was quick to respond and lunged forward. As he grappled with Grant, the gun was fired. Mac fell to his knees holding his right shoulder, the blood from the wound oozing between his fingers. Grant aimed the weapon at Chad again but now Olito stood in front of him, Grant screamed at her "Get out of the way you –." "Do not say it Grant screamed Lizabeth. He fell silent but continually squeezed the trigger only to hear the solid click of the hammer as it fell on the empty chambers. "Damn!" He shouted as he continued squeezing the trigger hoping that it would fire but to his dismay, the hammer still fell on empty chambers. Grant was not about to give up and he knew that although the shooting of Mac was an accident, and with the WPC standing in front of Chadrick if the gun had fired and she had been killed then it would not be deemed as an accident but would be labeled as attempted murder. He had wanted to shoot Chadrick but had failed and in his instant rage, he threw the gun at him but it struck Olito, then he made a grab for a sword from the many on display sending them clattering to the ground. Now armed, he thought that he would have the advantage but Chadrick, even in his weakened state, had also taken up a sword.

Cadiston with his two WPCs were attending to Mac and trying to stop the bleeding and in doing this they ignored Grant. "Now you will get yours! Damn you, Cadiston, why didn't you leave it well alone? First you, then him." Said Grant. With the sword raised, he lunged at Cadiston. Chad had taken up the challenge and had blocked the blow. "So, at last, we cross real swords." Said Grant. "Bring it on, Grant!" As the swords clashed, the ring of steel on steel rang out. The sound of grating steel made them turn and then with the flashing blades, they were powerless to help. The sound of the grating steel on steel filled the large hallway as the two swords clashed like they did in battle. It was clear to see that Chadrick had the upper hand. The fighting was fierce but luckily, no blood had been drawn as these two antagonists battled ferociously. One to take a life, the other to save a life. There was no holding back in the ensuing confrontation but these weapons being used were old and blunt and each strike that Grant received did not cut but stung all the same. He was again losing his fight against Chad which made him even

676

more bitter toward him but a battle with these weapons could not last. Although they looked good for display purposes, they could not stand the stress of a vicious battle and as Grant intensified his fight to win this confrontation and striking with such ferocity eventually, both blades broke, leaving them holding the hilt. Grant threw the broken weapon at Chad and in avoiding the flying metal, he lost his balance and fell. Now with no weapon in his hands and before he had the chance to obtain another, Cadiston took his opportunity to launch his own attack. The two wrestled and grappled with the odd punch being thrown by Grant but Cadiston moved quickly so they made no connection. Grant was the larger of the two men and of the opinion that he was stronger, and that he would win and make his escape. He was utterly surprised when after seven minutes of their fight, he was secured in Cadiston's handcuffs. If Grant had known that Cadiston had been trained in unarmed combat, he would have avoided a fight with him. With the fighting over, it was time to deal with the injured and Lord Mandaten's first concern was for his lost and found son, Chadrick "Are you alright, Son?" "I am fine Father, do not worry about me, it is my friend Adam Macswee that needs the hospital." Said Chad. "The very moment that the pistol fired, we knew that someone would have been shot. When we saw Macswee fall and the blood flowing it was confirmed. We Instantly rang the emergency services for an ambulance and one should be here in a few minutes." Said Bradinham the old butler who had come through to see the return of the lost and found son of Lord and Lady Mandaten. Greta was tending to Mac and had a large compression bandage, brought in by Alfred, on his wound putting direct pressure onto its front and rear which was helping to stem the blood flow. Lizabeth was also helping, and between them they were making him comfortable. Francis and Olito had taken charge of the cuffed Grant and Cadiston was back at Mac's side. "That was either a very brave thing or a very foolish one, DS Macswee, and you undoubtedly saved Chadrick from being shot." Said Cadiston proudly. "Well put it this way, there was no time to think and I could not stand by and watch

Chad get shot, not after all that he has been through and especially not after his 'life after death' experience but do not worry about me, Cadders." Even in pain, Mac smiled. "I am big and tough, I can take it." Even in this situation, he could still joke. They all chuckled with him, even Lord and Lady Mandaten. "Your hand please, DS Adam Macswee, thank you, thank you for your bravery and for saving my son's life and bringing him back to me." Said Lord Mandaten. Mac smiled. "All in a day's work, my lord." Replied Mac and although in pain he could still raise a smile. The ambulance had arrived a few minutes earlier and Mac was being attended to and refused to sit in the chair and be wheeled out. He walked to the waiting vehicle with Olito and Francis on either side of him. "Gee, Olito you stood in front of Chad and if that gun had fired you could have been badly wounded or killed, like me brave or foolish." "Are we not charged with protecting the citizens our public DS Macswee." "That we are WPC Paverson, very brave of you and it will be documented." With Mac on board, the ambulance and comfortable and although not in the rules Cadiston insisted on Olito travelling with him to be checked over for any injury after being struck by the flying gun thrown at Chad. They drove up the long drive and to the hospital for him to receive the full treatment that he needed and for Olito to be checked over as the gun had struck her in the head and it was bleeding.

"Well Cadiston, you have kept your word and have solved all the family murders but what of my brother Laseroie?" Asked Lord Mandaten.

"Solved my Lord, both the perpetrators of your brother's family's murder are being held pending their trial, in fact one is in hospital after a car chase and has died from his injuries sir. Now, sir, not wishing to be rude but we must get Grant to the station where we can interview him fully." Said Cadiston.

"You be away, my boy, and I, no, we cannot thank you enough for returning our son to us." Said Lord Mandaten. "My pleasure, sir." Said Cadiston. With his WPC and the prisoner, they left. "I have the gun bagged, sir, should we get it directly to firearms, ballistics when we are back at the station?" Asked Francis. "Please, Francis, and tell the boys that if it is possible, I would like a quick result. When we get to the station, I will give you the bullets to take with the gun as I need them to check if that is the gun they came from." Said Cadiston."Got it, check slugs against that gun, do it as soon as we are back." Said Francis. "Gosh I cannot get over the way Olito placed herself unselfishly and risking her own life between the gunman and Chad Cadders, a very brave act if I may say Cadders." "Extemely brave Francis and Olito's action will be documented along with Macs in my report of the incident". Replied Cadiston.

"When that is done, you will go back to the Manor and ask Katrine what happened to the rest of the Ketamine that her parents gave her and that she was going to return. Take Amelia with you" Said Cadiston. "Will do and I will bring you her answer as soon as we are back." Said Francis. "Probably be in the interview room so bring the answer there." Said Cadiston in reply.

Back at the station, Cadiston gave Francis the bullets and she took them straight to the firearms department for analysis. Then Francis and Amelia returned to the Manor. Cadiston went immediately to the interview room and when it had been set up, Grant was brought in. "Remove the handcuffs please, PC Julip. Now take a seat, Grant." Said Cadiston sternly. "No Macswee with you, then, should have been you shot not him? Think you are so clever, don't you Cadiston? Well, all you have me for is resisting arrest and accidental wounding that Macswee and that was an accident. If he had not grabbed my hand and grappled with me, it would not have happened and that means it was his fault." Said Grant. "We will get to the charges against you in a moment but first we will get your integration recorded officially." Said Cadiston. The tape was turned on and the introductions made but Grant sat silently. "Speak your name please." Said Cadiston. "No harm in that, Grant Mandaten, or I suppose that I should say Cartridge now thanks to all your snooping. I know the routine and the introductions are over. I have done all this before so what do you need to ask me? Now, I have already given my alibi at the time of the shooting of Demmie and that deective Macswee is my alibi so there should be nothing else." Said Grant smugly. "And what other shooting would that be?" Asked Cadiston. "What do mean what other shooting? There is only one, Demmie of course." Said Grant. "Alright, we will start with her, how long were you having the affair with Demmie?" Asked Cadiston."Gees Cadiston, we have already been over this ground a million times and I told you then and will tell you now I was not having an affair with her." He said angrily. "What was it then if not an affair, just an occasional fling?" Asked Cadiston. "Alright if you must persist in raking it up again, Detective, and as you have nothing else on me, you know when an attractive woman makes advances on you because she wants you, well –." He said it so casually. "I have no need to paint you a picture. We got together a few times but that was it." Said Grant. "Before you told us that she had given you comfort, as you put it, after your wife had died on the way back from the hospital so how many times did it take place, sir?" Asked Cadiston. "Alright, two and a half years maybe but it was her pestering me. She wanted it to be more than I did but would not take no for an answer. When she asked me to divorce Bonnie I said no. She said that she did not love Chad and only married him to get into the family and get closer to me. She said it was me that was her true love and she hated her life with him and felt like she was living the life of a pauper. She craved for the high life and the riches that would go with being the Lady of the Manor but not with him, with me as the Lord. She was a bit overpowering and I had already found the one that I intend to be my wife after I had divorced Bonnie and it was not her." Said Grant. "Just when did your liaison with Demmie start?" Asked Cadiston.

"Already told you, a couple of years ago." Said Grant. "We have it on good authority that it actually started before Chadrick and Demmie were married." Said Cadiston. Grant sat silent staring at him. His eyes were like a blank canvas with no emotion, then he couged before speaking. "Damn you, Cadiston, you know way too much for your own good." "Now back to

Demmie, you wanted to be rid of her so is that why you killed her Did you have knowledge that like your wife, she was two months pregnant with your child and why did you lie about her before? You have told so many lies and now is the time to come clean and tell the truth from the start and belay any of my suspicions." Said Cadiston.

"I had nothing to do with Bonnie or Malcolm's deaths and there is no way that you can pin either of them onto me. Besides, you have the family murderers locked up. I had no idea about the child that either of them had in their belly, anyway why should I want them dead?" Asked Grant. "Bonnie to be rid of her and Demmie to silence her because she knew too much and also to be rid of her." Said Cadiston. "You have it all wrong, Detective." Said Grant. "I do, well I do not think so, Grant. The Monday evening that your wife died, why was Chad suddenly so sleepy?" Asked Cadiston. "Well, you are not so clever after all if you do not know that." Said Grant. "We have the sleeping drug that she used to drug him." Said WPC Nadine Crown who was standing in for WPC Francis Rendham. He glared at her. "Clever bitch, cleverer than I thought then for a woman." Said Grant. "She spent the Monday night in your bed, didn't she? And for an alibi, ahe made out to have fallen asleep in the bath." Said Cadiston. "You know that so why bother to ask me. We spent the night together so that proves that I did not kill Malcolm so there is no way you can pin that onto me. Got you there Cadiston, and it was all her own idea to kill Bonnie, not mine. I would have divorced her when the time was right and not when being told to. After the announcement and the next Lord Mandaten declared, being me of course, then I was going to get a divorce and had already seen my solicitor who has the papers drawn up, ready for me to sign. I already told you that so now you can check on it. My solicitor is Woods, Gray and Stemmings." Said Grant. "And that we already have confirmed, we know that you did not murder your wife, Bonnie. That I know to be true and you should not have lied to me about your fling with Demmie. As for your affair or not as the case may be with her, again, you should not have played false and lied to her as it is directly linked to the murder of your wife and her murder."Said Cadiston. "Not my fault, she was a nut job." Said Grant.

Cadiston looked at him in disgust at his use of words. "Now, from your second wife to your first wife, Geraldine Granchister." Said Cadiston. He looked surprised at this being brought up. "What about her? I have been cleared of her murder and have a solid alibi. I –." He suddenly went silent as though he had something to hide.

"You have a false alibi, Grant, that we know so now what about you telling us the truth about Geraldine's death." Said Cadiston.

"I was out with another woman and drunk, we had a meal at the Mari Gras, then to another place as I was still hungry, ("The Rectory Restaurant".) then she took me home. Even my parents were my alibi and if you can prove it false then good luck with that." Said Grant. "You went to the Mari Gras followed by the Rectory Restaurant. Yes, we know who you were out with and your parents did not know that you were faking being drunk as you put up quite a show." Said Cadiston. He looked surprised at Cadiston saying he knew the woman that he had been out with and his faking being drunk.

"Alright clever clogs, if you know so much, you tell me how a drunk man can commit the crime. You tell me how I can be out in a restaurant with a woman and then drunk in bed and commit murder if you are so clever. Ha, I got you there haven't I Cadiston? Because you have no answer to that." Cadiston remained calm as he answered, "I will give you another chance to tell the truth, Grant. The truth about how you murdered your first wife." Said Cadiston. "I did not kill her, Cadiston, and I have been exonerated from that crime and you cannot prove otherwise so I have nothing to tell. Got you Cadiston, you will not get me on a murder charge especially one that I have been cleared of, and, you know nothing." Said Grant smugly.

"Alright Grant as you refuse to tell me the truth, it leaves it to me to tell you how you did it. You picked up a girl by the name of Jonnett Muskaday." Grant suddenly sat bolt upright at the mention of that name. "You had some background information about her past that she was putting behind her and living a clean life when you picked her up. You threatened to tell her boss if she did not play along with you. You took her to the Manor to allow the family to see her, then went to visit your wife and frighten her, then you went to two different restaurants and caused a scene at them both so that you would be well noticed and remembered as part of the false alibi. You had several bottles of wine but did not drink them but poured them into the plant pots. You had driven your car to the private road where you hid it and had already called a taxi to take you out and return to the Manor on the pretext that you were drunk. How am I doing so far, Grant? Hitting the truth? Please feel free to take over any time you like." He sat silent. "No? Then I will continue. You were put to bed, then crept from your room via the secret passage and returned to your car. You drove to her motel and shot her three times, returning to leave your car hidden and then back unseen to your room. The next day, you called a taxi under the pretext of going back to the restaurant to collect your car, thus securing what you thought was a perfect alibi. How do you answer that, Grant?" Asked Cadiston. "You made that all up, Cadiston, my alibi was checked out and the coppers could not fault it. Fool of a detective, you won't trap me like that." His voice was filled with anger but Cadiston's remained calm. "I am not trying to trap you, Grant, just source the truth from your own lips. I know that you are innocent of Bonnie and her unborn little girl child's murder directly and it was your lies, falseness, and deceit with Demmie that was the cause so indirectly you took part in it. I know that you are innocent of Malcolm, Kevin, James, Lowell, Sammie, Gloria, and Walter's murders but then we have the murders and one attack that you are guilty of, so the truth now Grant, there is Sadie, Demmie, and Geraldine plus the attack on Chad so is it not the time for you to start telling the truth, and stop lying Grant?" Asked Cadiston. With his injury bandaged, his arm in a sling, and a nurse in attendance, Mac returned to the station and requested entry to the interview room. He then sat beside

Cadiston and after his introduction, the interview continued. Grant was staring at them with hate in his eyes. "You cannot prove I killed any of them, I was way too careful and had solid alibis even you Macswee." Said Grant.

"Not quite careful enough, Grant. We have your blood, and D.N.A. that matches samples taken at the scene of the crimes. We also have your fingerprints amongst other evidence. We have all that is necessary to solve any of the cases of murder in the first degree committed by you. You can lie all you want but be assured that the truth will come out eventually and we are giving you the time required to do just that, Grant. Now, as for shooting me, that will come later but now the truth about the murder of Geraldine, Sadie, and Demmie and the attack on Chad and remember we have got the evidence –." Said Mac.

He glared at Mac and snarled like a wild beast then spat at them. "The prisoner just spat at DCI Cadiston and DS Macswee."

"That's it get it all down properly, you damn bastard coppers! Father was right about you, damn good, just too dam good; Alright, I killed the first bitch just as you said and it was a good plan and if you had not been so damned smart and left it well alone instead of digging up the past, I would have gotten away with it. Tell me how you know about Jonnett's false alibi?" Asked Grant.

"We had her traced and that is all you need to know. Now, your attack on Chad and the murder of Demmie." Said Cadiston. He smiled at them. "I want to see just how clever you damned detectives are, you tell me how I did it when I was not there, got you this time clever clogs. Your detective saw me drive up so he is my alibi." Snarled Grant. "You drove your car up the drive to make it appear that you were going out but you parked it up by the old Manor Ruins and hid it under the ivy. You then re-entered the Manor via the secret passage and took up your position to wait for Chad who you knew would at some time come up to his room. You stood on a chair behind the door and when he came in, you struck with the old nights war hammer, but –. you heard someone on the stairs and listened. You recognized the footsteps as Demmie. You retreated through the panel and took

Chad's shotgun that you had already removed from the cabinet to which you all had keys, filled your pockets with cartridges, and re-entered the room in time to see Demmie coming from the bathroom. She backed away and you shot her at close-range, getting sprayed with her blood. You then heard Tomas and hid in the wardrobe until he was gone, you heard two more blasts from the gun when Tomas messed up his attempt to put the gun into Chads hands. You returned to the scene and again tried to put the gun into Chad's hands but it fired again. You left via the secret passage and went back to your car where you changed your clothes, leaving the bloodied ones beneath a piece of fallen masonry. You then drove back down the drive to be confronted by my DS Macswee." Said Cadiston.

"Damn you, Cadiston, you must be some sort of psychic. That is two analyses you have done and both are spot-on. Gees man, with you on the force criminals better look out but what is the evidence that you have?" Asked Grant. "We have the bloodied clothes that you discarded up at the Old Manor ruins plus D.N.A., fingerprints and casts of the tyre prints that match your car perfectly right down to the small piece that was cut from the near side rear tyre." Said Cadiston. "Got me bang to rights then, Cadiston, you are a clever bastard, you have done what others failed to do. Now, I reckon that you want to know about Sadie and that will be my hattrick so to speak. If she had not rattled me and gotten Chad to stand up for her, making me look small, the bitch, then I would have left her alone. You are so clever so go on you tell me just how I did for her." Said Grant. Before he could answer, there was a knock on the door. The pause button was activated and the door opened.

"John has got the information that you wanted from firearms, DCI Cadiston." Said PC Arkens he is in the reception waiting for you. "Thanks, a job well done." There was a second knock at the door and WPC Amelia Crown entered the room. She passed Cadiston an envelope, is WPC Rendham alright", asked Cadiston, a bit shaken afer her initial experience at the Manor sir and needed to use the small room sir otherwise fine.

He opened the envelope and read the report. "Just as I thought, Katrine was going to return the Ketamine that had not been used but you stole it from her room while she was at work and used that to drug Sadie." Said Cadiston. "Ok, just how Cadiston?" Asked Grant. "You waited until her son and niece had left her room, then checked that she was asleep. Satisfied that she was, you injected a lethal dose of Ketamine in her left arm. You made sure that it had taken effect before taking her through the secret passage to the lake to drown." Said Cadiston. "A good theory but flawed because I have a fear of water after almost drownding in that lake." "Yes Grant we knew that could not swim then and you were saved by Chad". Replied Cadiston. "Not so now though is it Grant. You see, my DS with a WPC, did some checking up on you, and at one time true, you could not swim but not now, you had lessons with a Miss Samosat." Said Cadiston. "You are just too good at this detecting lark Cadiston but how do you do it?" Asked Grant. "I follow my grandfathers lead and put myself in the head of the criminal." Cadiston replied with a smile.

"Well you certainly got into my head and you have got me so now I guess comes the caution and arrest." Said Grant. "May I, sir?" Asked Mac standing up. "Be my guest DS Macswee." Said Cadiston. "Grant Cartridge, known as Grant Mandaten, I am arresting you for the murders of Geraldine Mandaten, Sadie and Demmie Mandaten and for the attempted murder of Chadrick Mandaten. You do not have to say anything but it may harm your defence if you do not mention when questioned, something you may later rely on in court but anything you do say will be written down and may be used as evidence, do you understand?" With the caution fulfilled Mac sat down again.

"I am not stupid, of course I do Macswee." Said Grant. You refused to have a solicitor present at the time of the interview, and I now inform you that you are entitled to have a solicitor and if you do not have one then one will be appointed for you, do you understand?" Mac asked Grant. "I have mine so will use him. Now, lock me up as that is what you want to do." Said Grant. "The time is 17:58 and the interview is ended, take the prisoner down please PC Arkens." Said Cadiston and the tape was turned off. With him gone, Mac stood but now stumbled. This worried Cadiston, "Mac, you need to get back to your hospital bed." Said Cadiston.

"I guess so, as I am feeling a bit weak but I needed to arrest him and now I have done that so with –." He then came over faint and with assistance was returned to the transport and on to the hospital. Waiting in his office was John from the firearms ballistics. "Been waiting for you, Cadders, and was that Mac being escorted out? Thought he was in hospital after being shot." Said John. "I told him that he could be the one to arrest Grant and he was not about to let it go." Said Cadiston.

"And I guess that he has. Now, Francis told us of the urgency about this 38 so we rushed it through for you. It will please you to know that the result is a perfect match. Those three slugs came from that gun, there is no doubt so you have the weapon and you have your shooter. Anything else you need, just call on us." Said John. "Thanks John." With a wave he was gone.

"That's it then, the murders are all solved. Standish is in the hands of the chief and that is good. I will go and pick Samantha up, then to the hospital to see how Mac and Olito are." He closed his office door and 45 minutes later they were sitting beside Mac's bed. "What a hero you are, Mac. You put yourself through more pain coming to the station." Said Cadiston. "I rode the pain Cadders, you said I could arrest Grant and I was not about to let it pass me by." Said Mac. "And we have confirmation that his gun was the one that was used to kill Geraldine his first wife, so we have it for that also but, now you just rest up and recover my friend. We are all proud of you Mac and especially you Angela." Remarked Cadiston. "Well, he was my hero even before this but he was just doing his job, the job that he loves especially working alongside you, Ashton, all I hear is Cadders did this and Cadders suspicion proved to be correct." Replied Angela. "Well, even so, he saved a life with his quick action and he will be rewarded for that so there you have it. Did they say how long you would need to be kept in Mac?" Asked Cadiston.

"Just overnight to make sure there are no complications so with my arm in a sling, I will be in on Monday morning." Said Mac. "You, my friend, will be having a few days off to recuperate and do not worry, you will be there for the court cases and the final closure." Said Cadiston.

"You did it, Cadders, you solved all the cases and have all the guilty parties locked up. You have witnesses and evidence so there is no way that any of them can wriggle free. There are those that are not as guilty, for example Gloria, we must help her to get her life back on track." Said Mac. "True but get it right, Mac, we did it together. You, me and a few others in our team, it was a joint enterprise. Now, you rest and get that arm working. Sam and I will call at your house to see you when you are home. Until then, rest and get well you little hero." Said Cadiston. "Get away with you, Cadders." They had been there for an hour and as he had his wife there with him, We are going to check on Olito they kept her in also after that gun struck her on the head, she may have a small fracture, with a handshake they smiled and left. They visited Olito who was sitting up her bed and comfortable with her head bandaged, "Tell me Olito what did they say." "A small frcture but nothing very serious and I will be out after a few days bed rest and kept under observation". "Well you little heroine, you rest up and get well, we will vist you again Olito". "How is Mac doing." "Just fine, a clean wound the bullet went straight through and did no severe damage just ripped the skin, he will be fine. No you take care and do as you are told by the nurses and doctors Miss Paverson." With a wave they left her smiling. "Weekend to ourselves, Samantha. Then Monday 29th I will go and tell the Mandatens all the developments." Said Cadiston. "Sounds good to me." Said Samantha.

On Monday, 29th November, at 10:30 a.m., Cadiston arrived at Mandaten Manor. As usual, he was greeted at the door by Alfred and taken to the lounge where the family was waiting to see him.

"Come in, young man, and before anything else tell us how is that young Detective Macswee and that extremely brave young WPC Paverson doing." Said Lord Mandaten. "Both, very well, my Lord and they will be home in a few days for convalescence." Answered Cadiston.

"Excellent, now what other news have you to tell us?" Asked Lord Mandaten. "As you know, we have discovered the identity of the murderers of your family and they are all being held pending their trial dates being set and their appearance in court. They will have access to a solicitor but we have very strong evidence on each case and that includes DNA, blood, and tissue samples, a cast of tyre tracks, and clothes amongst other items. You will be glad to know that after questioning, they have all confessed as the evidence stacked against them was irrefutable but that does not mean they will stand up and plead guilty in court, they may still try to get off. There are some that are not as guilty and will be dealt with accordingly. Now we must wait for the trials and their convictions. We also solved the case of your brother, Baron Laseroie Mandaten and his family. There were two involved, one is under lock and key the other died in hospital after a car chase. They have also confessed to six other Mandaten murders in France and that information has been forwarded on to the French police. We also solved the case of Grant's first wife, Geraldine, and her death." Said Cadiston. "Can you tell us who killed who?" Asked Lord Mandaten.

"As there are trials pending, no. In fact, I have already told you more than I should and all I will say is that between them, they murdered all your family but will murder no more and it is a shame that we do not still have capital punishment. Now, if there is nothing else, I will take my leave of you." Said Cadiston. Chad and Greta stood holding hands with Jennifer in close attendance. "We have one piece of news for you, Cadiston. Our son, Chadrick who will become the next Lord Mandaten, and Greta and Chad are to be married in the spring next year and Jennifer is to be their bridesmaid." Said Lord Mandaten. Cadiston smiled. "I knew that was going to happen, I just did not know when." Jennifer gave a little chuckle. "You really are a good detective, you saw it all along, didn't you? And kept it to yourself, they did not fool you, not for one minute did they?" She smiled again. "You really are a clever detective, Mr. Cadiston." Said Jennifer smiling. "He certainly is, Jennifer. Now then, we would like you and DS Macswee to attend the wedding as our guests, would you be able to do that?" Asked Greta."

Names are Ashton Cadiston and Macswee is Adam. I can speak for Mac as well as myself and in answer to your kind invitation, Greta, we would be delighted and hounoured to attend and to wish you both well in your *NEW BEGINNING*. Just let us know the time, date and place." They shook hands and he left.

With the Mandaten investigations over and the dates for the trials to be set, Cadiston now needed to finalize and collate all the evidence that was to be used for each individual murder. He also was required to charge and caution Grant for the murder of his first wife Geraldine Mandaten, nee Granchister. This would involve him for a while as he would have to ensure that there were no loopholes to be slipped through, for that, he would speak with the legal department. After the trials had reached their conclusion, he could then sit back and wait for his next case to land on his desk. As he worked on his evidence, he had a thought. If Standish had not been so lapse and involved, then none of this would have been necessary but when it came down to it, he was glad to have been challenged and thankful that he had Mac to help along the way, not to mention all the other help. "Well, best get back to it." He mumbled to himself.

He had the wedding between Chadrick and Greta to look forward to and this would be a bit of light relief after the completion of the Mandaten trials. Before his next case both he and Mac would know what positions they would hold. He thought that he would return to Detective Constable and Mac would finish his training and after retaking the final exam, he to would be a detective constable. But that would be then. As for now, there was paperwork to finish and a wedding to look forward to. What was more, both he and Mac would be there to signal in the Mandaten family's *NEW BEGINNING*.

Coming soon

Follow Cadiston on his next case

Obsession.

Ein HERZ FÜR AUTOREN A HEART FOR AUTHORS À L'ÉCOUTE DES AUTEURS MIA ΚΑΡΔΙΑ ΓΙΑ ΣΥΓ
JÄHTA FÖR FÖRFATTARE UN CORAZÓN POR LOS AUTORES YAZARLARIMIZA GÖNÜL VERELIM S
UN CUORE PER AUTORI ET HJERTE FOR FORFATTERE EEN HART VOOR SCHRIJVERS TEMOS OS AU
ZÕINKÉRT SERCE DLA AUTORÓW EIN HERZ FÜR AUTOREN A HEART FOR AUTHORS À L'ÉCO
UNAÇÃO BCEЙ ДУШОЙ К АВТОРАМ ETT HJÄRTA FÖR FÖRFATTARE À LA ESCUCHA DE LOS AUT
AUTEURS MIA ΚΑΡΔΙΑ ΓΙΑ ΣΥΓΓΡΑΦΕΙΣ UN CUORE PER AUTORI ET HJERTE FOR FORFATTERE EE
LARIMIZA GÖNÜL VERELIM S ZÕINKÉRT SERCE DLA AUTORÓW EIN HERZ F
VOOR SCHRIJVERS TEMOS OS AUTORES UNAÇÃO BCEЙ ДУШОЙ К АВТОРАМ ETT HJÄRTA F

The author

Colin Oakes was born in Norfolk on 16 May 1945
and has had a varied career covering catering
as a trainee chef, leading on to management.
He attended Norwich City College to gain
qualifications in catering and sage bookkeeping.
He also spent time as a building labourer and in a
meat processing factory ending his working life as
a self employed gardener/handyman.
Colin lives with his partner Janet and together they
have 2 daughters, 1 son and four grandchildren
living in England and Tasmania.
Having made up stories for his daughter, Colin
housed the dream of one day being able to write
novels for all to enjoy one day. Now in retirement,
he has the time to do just that. His main interests
in writing are crime and fantasy. Colin's dream
is that as an author it will allow a wide variety of
people in various age groups to enjoy his stories.

Printed in Great Britain
by Amazon

32144405R00391